# STONE CRADLE

## LOUISE DOUGHTY

POCKET
BOOKS

LONDON • SYDNEY • NEW YORK • TORONTO

First published in Great Britain by Simon & Schuster UK Ltd, 2006
First published by Pocket Books, 2007
An imprint of Simon & Schuster UK Ltd
A CBS COMPANY

1 3 5 7 9 10 8 6 4 2

Simon & Schuster UK Ltd
Africa House
64–78 Kingsway
London WC2B 6AH

www.simonsays.co.uk

Simon & Schuster Australia
Sydney

A CIP catalogue record for this book is
available from the British Library

ISBN-13: 978-0-7434-4039-4
ISBN-10: 0-7434-4039-0

Typeset by M Rules
Printed and bound in Great Britain by
Cox & Wyman Ltd, Reading, Berks

# ACKNOWLEDGEMENTS

Thank you to Sharon Floate and all at the Romany & Travellers' Family History Society. Many of the RTFHS's publications were extremely useful, those by Robert Dawson in particular. Thanks also to Gordon and Margaret Boswell of the Romany Museum, Spalding. Thanks to the Banff Centre in Alberta, Canada (again) and to Jerome Weatherald (again). Thanks in particular to Thomas Acton, Jill Dawson, Jane Hodges and Jacqui Lofthouse for support and advice, to Suzanne Baboneau and Rochelle Venables, and to my agent Antony Harwood. I am indebted to Kevin Smullin Brown for the title and Toby the Sapient Pig for the poem.

The characters in this novel are invented but many of the incidents that occur are drawn from the memories and recollections of real-life sources, some of whom prefer to remain anonymous. My debt to them is immeasurable. *Paracrow tutis, my Petulengros, all Petulengros and jinimengro pals everywhere.*

The few words of Rummanus, or English Romanes, that I use in this book are drawn from a variety of personal and written sources. Where these did not agree, I favoured the personal as I interpreted it, thus any inaccuracies are entirely my responsibility. The only word which readers need to understand is *gorjer*, a pejorative for non-Romanies.

*For Nathalie and Anna*

# CONTENTS

*If foky ken jins bute,*
*Má sal at lende;*
*For sore mush jins chomany*
*That tute kek jins.*

Whatever ignorance men may show,
From none disdainful turn;
For every one doth something know
Which you have yet to learn.

traditional rhyme
from *Romano Lavo-Lil*
by George Borrow

# PROLOGUE

## Peterborough – 1949

An autumn funeral, orange and black: it is November. Sunlight strikes the gas tower behind Wellington Street and makes the huge, corroded cylinder glow as if on fire. The iron walkway wrapped about it stands out in sharp relief, a stairway leading nowhere but around. Purgatory has come to Peterborough.

Lijah Smith, about to bury his mother, stares at the gas tower as the undertakers bring the small coffin from the house. He is standing on the pavement, next to the hearse, chewing tobacco and enjoying the twitching of the neighbours' curtains. Only Mrs Martin from number sixty-three has come out onto the pavement to stare honestly. Her husband worked at the Horse Repository before the war and Lijah knows them both. He nods to her. She nods back. He sees she has put on her best shoes and guesses by the way she is standing that they discomfort her.

There are four pallbearers but Lijah's mother is so tiny and light that one of them could have managed the coffin crossways in his arms. Two of the four place their end of the coffin onto the hearse, then step back to allow the others to slide it home. They turn their backs on Lijah and gather for a whispered conversation. Lijah guesses that the man in charge has decided he doesn't need them all.

Something changes hands between the men and two of them turn and bow, then stride off down the road. The chief undertaker steps forward and holds open the door for Lijah to climb into the rear seat of the hearse. Lijah turns and lifts the lid of his mother's dustbin, spits his tobacco into it and replaces the lid. He settles his cap on his head and shakes out the cuffs of his shirt. Before he gets in, he leans sideways on one foot. The coffin inside the hearse provides a surface so that he is able to see himself mirrored in the long window. He checks to see if the oiled kiss-curl that he plasters to his forehead each morning is still in place. He licks a finger and adjusts the curve of the curl, then turns back to the open door in time to see the two undertakers exchange a look.

'Righto, gentlemen,' Lijah says with pride, and steps into the hearse. For what he knows will be the first and last time in his life, he watches as a man – bought and paid for – bows and closes a car door after him.

It seems a shame to waste any of the plump black seating, so Lijah sits dead centre and leans back with his arms resting across the top of the banquette. As the hearse pulls away, he moves forward and taps on the sliding window. The undertaker in the passenger seat opens it. Lijah shuffles forward further and says, 'We are going up Eastfield, aren't we? We're not taking the back route?'

'Not unless you wish, sir.'

'Eastfield, right enough.'

'Of course, sir.'

The man has only just slid the window back into position when Lijah taps again.

'Yes, sir?' The man's voice has become exaggeratedly respectful.

'Nice and slow, like.'

'Of course, sir.'

'No, I mean, even slower than usual.'

'Yes, sir.' The man slides the window back and Lijah sees him mutter to the driver. Lijah had glue-ear for two years as a boy and has never lost his talent for lip reading. The man is saying, 'Bloody Norah, any slower, we'll be going backwards.'

Lijah sits back with a smile of satisfaction. They pass the Corporation Depot and turn into the main road.

The service is brief. Lijah is the sole mourner. Soon, they are outside again in the cold sunshine. The ochre-coloured tiles on the houses opposite the church look soft and textured in the light – two crows sit on a chimney pot. It is an autumn funeral, orange and black.

The hearse turns slowly into Eastfield Cemetery and proceeds along a wide path. Lijah knows this cemetery well. They are returning to the plot where his wife Rose was buried twenty years ago. The grave has been re-opened and Lijah is going to put his mother on top of his wife.

A new plot on the far side of the cemetery would have cost twelve pounds. Opening up an old one can be done for eight. The car was three pounds six shillings, counting petrol. Lijah offered to bring his own, but they weren't having it.

The vicar is no longer with them, which suits Lijah fine. His mother would not have wanted all that ashes to ashes nonsense. Lijah watches as the two undertakers slide the coffin out of the car and place it on top of the sheeting laid ready on the ground beside the open grave. You motored, Dei, Lijah says to himself, feeling a tickle of emotion inside him for the first time. You motored all the way up Eastfield Road, nice and slow, just like I promised you.

He steps up to the grave and looks down into it. He peers, trying to see what might be seeable after twenty years: the ant-riddled wood of the coffin lid? Rose's skull staring up at him, soil-filled sockets for eyes? The very image of death: he half fears and half desires it, for then he will be able to say to himself that he has seen it, and it is nothing.

All he sees is earth: dark earth. They mun't dig right down when they open it up again, he thinks. Well, I suppose that's just as well. Poor Rose. It was a very different funeral for her. No motor for his Rosie – they still used the horse-drawn bier twenty years ago, the crowd trailing behind on foot, led by Lijah and their three daughters sobbing fulsomely, and Dan all stiff and silent – but no Bartholomew, just a big hole in the air where Bartholomew should have been.

He broke his mother's heart that boy, Lijah thinks to himself. *What was left of it, that is.* Lijah scratches his right ear.

He realises that the undertakers and the gravedigger are waiting for him, so he gives the nod and the men lift the coffin up on the sheet and lower it down into the grave. They stand back with their heads bowed.

Lijah is suddenly angered by their solemnity. Have they not realised that this is a job to be done, without their foolish sentiment? He waves an arm to indicate they can go, for all he cares. He and the gravedigger can finish the job. He steps back onto the path and lifts a hand to his waistcoat pocket, fishing out his tobacco.

The head undertaker approaches tentatively and says, 'Would sir like to call in at the office later, to conclude arrangements?' Lijah still owes them six pounds.

'I'll settle here and now, thanks very much. Your job's done, young fella.' He unbuttons his jacket and waistcoat so that he can reach his second waistcoat, the one underneath, where he keeps his wallet.

The undertaker is clearly relieved. 'Oh, very good, sir . . . Cigarette?' He reaches into his trouser pocket and withdraws a packet of Capstan.

Lijah smiles. 'Right you are, then.'

When the undertaker has taken Lijah's money and lit his cigarette, he lights one for himself, nods towards the grave and says, 'Don't normally get mother and daughter buried in the same grave. Spouses, sometimes.'

'They weren't,' says Lijah. 'It's my wife in there, and it's *my* mother is going in on top.'

The undertaker raises his eyebrows. 'Close, were they?'

'In a manner of speaking.'

There is a short pause, then the caretaker murmurs, 'Can't say I'd like my mother-in-law on top of me.'

Lijah takes a sideways glance at the man and thinks, I daresay she'd not be too keen on it neither.

The undertaker nods across the cemetery. 'Still, nice day for it. You were lucky with a bit of sunshine.'

'Aye, I was that.'

Pleasantries concluded, the two men shake hands. The undertakers climb into the hearse and reverse with some alacrity. As they pull away, they give Lijah a wave.

Lijah is suddenly tired. He sits down on the edge of the path to watch the gravedigger fill in the grave. The gravedigger is an old fella – perhaps even the same one who shovelled the earth on top of Rosie twenty years ago. Is it really so long since she died? A picture comes into his head, unbidden: the children traipsing up the stairs, one by one, to say their goodbyes to their mother – the looks on their faces as they came down. It was a painful death. Stomach cancer. *Of the many things they blame me for, I'm surely not to blame for that.*

No stomach cancer for his mum. She had stayed tough as old boots until her nineties. Then she had dropped dead without warning in the street, on her way back from the tobacconists. She had outlived her daughter-in-law by two decades.

*Were they close?* Lijah's features lift in a grimace at the thought.

His mother and his wife had hated each other for nigh-on thirty years.

The gravedigger pauses to withdraw a handkerchief from his pocket and wipe his face. Then he resumes. The earth is soft, his task noiseless.

Lijah stares across the cemetery. I'll be here one day. Well at least there'll be no room for me in there with those two, thank God. They'll have to dig another hole. Came into the world in a graveyard; leave it in one. In between has been just passing time.

Beyond the grave there is a row of silver birches, their white trunks scarred with black, leaves mostly fallen. The oaks are still shedding slowly, unwilling to acknowledge the coming winter. The grave on the right of Rosie's is a beautiful piece of black marble. *Bet that cost a bob or two.* A scattering of orange leaves lies over it, looking just right.

The sun disappears. The cemetery is cold.

*Dei, in my deari Duvvel's tan. Eh, mandi? The kitchema, that's all I'm good for, Dei. You always said as much. Ne ken, never has been.* Lijah sniffs loudly and wipes his eyes with the back of his hand. The gravedigger glances up, then bends back to his work.

The gravestones that stretch to the left are all carved of stone. Peculiar how many are in the shape of books, Lijah thinks: open books – must have been fashionable once – all open in the middle. That's wrong for a start. They should be at the final page. The stone adjacent to Rosie's grave has a husband and wife in it. He can just make out the carved lettering. *Resting*, it says at the top, then underneath the names and dates. *Reunited*, it says at the bottom.

*Resting. Reunited.* There's a laugh.

An autumn funeral – right somehow. I'd like to go in the autumn, he thinks. He rises and brushes the seat of his trousers. The grass is damp. Lijah checks his watch. Time to raise a glass to his mother's memory at The Ghost Pig. He remembers what Rosie said she said to her, that time she turned up to live with them in

Cambridge. *You've married my son, and you'll sup sorrow by the spoonful 'til the day you die.*

Lijah tips the gravedigger and strides down the path. Over the nearby fence, he can see they are building another housing estate, across Newark Hill. New houses are springing up like crocuses these days. Peterborough is blooming. It will be one vast suburb, soon. Behind the bar at the pub, they have an unopened bottle of single malt. She was worth a large one, was his mother. Clementina. Lemmy. Lem.

# PART 1

1875–1895

# Clementina

# CHAPTER 1

Elijah Smith was born in the graveyard of the church at Werrington, a village in the Soke of Peterborough. I can tell you this for certain, as I am his mother and so was there at the time.

It was a wild winter, dordy, yes. I've never forgot how bad it was. Me and my mother and father were staying in this cottage, for a bit, in the corner of the graveyard. Well, I call it a cottage – it was but one room with a little range and a dirt floor and an alcove for firewood, which was where I slept.

When my pains started, my mother wasn't there. She had gone to the Markestede and wasn't expected back 'til late – it was Wednesday and Werrington was the carrier-cart's last drop-off on a Wednesday. I had no idea when the baby might be due, being only a young 'un and not knowing much about those things. So there was no question as to my mother not going to market that day. It could've been another two months for all I knew.

At first I thought maybe I'd had too much fried bread at teatime. I had a wild hunger on me when I was carrying and would eat until I couldn't sit down any more. So there I was in the cottage, wiping down the little range, with my father sitting in the far corner, snoozing 'neath the lantern. It was dark outside. I'd been feeling peculiar ever since we'd ate and was swaying a little as I worked the cloth, rocking back and forth on my feet, which seemed to help. I didn't feel tired, though, not at all. I felt as though I could scrub that range 'til I could see my face in it.

I had just finished the surround of the hot-plate when it came, out of nowhere. It was as if the pain inside me had been like a few pebbles in the bottom of a washing bucket, swooshing around in lots of water, then suddenly all the pebbles gathered up into a rock which punched the side of the bucket, the inside of me, that is, and suddenly I knew there was a rock inside me and it was dragging down, down, on its way out.

There was no time to finish my cleaning. I dropped the cloth into the bucket next to the range and grabbed my shawl from the chair behind me. Thank God Dadus was asleep. I made it outside before I disgraced myself. I dropped on all fours and cried out.

I knew I had to get round the back, out of sight, in case my Dadus woke and came to look for me. I had a few minutes to crawl on all fours before it came again, *aieeee* . . . Luckily, it was windy and my Dadus was a sound sleeper. A few more yards. By the third time, I was only just behind the cottage but beyond caring who might hear or see me. The ground was damp, so I crawled to a flat gravestone and crouched down low over it, on all fours, gripping its sides. The pain came again, *uurrrr* . . . This time, a different sound. I was bellowing like a cow and pushing, inside. Then it eased.

In the short space it gave me before the next wave, I turned on my side and pulled my skirts up. I wasn't frightened. I wasn't anything but strong. I still remember that. The feeling of the pain goes away – nature's way of trying to fool you into doing it again – but

I have never forgot how determined I was. Every bit of me was up for doing one thing. My baby was coming.

He was trouble from the beginning, was Lijah. I know how people like to say how it was growing up without a father but he had fathers right enough, had them coming out his ears by the time I'd finished with him. No, he was a right bugger from the start.

We were not cottage-dwellers by nature at that time, oh no. When I fell pregnant with Lijah, we were living in our wagon on the green, alongside the others. There were four families altogether. There was my cousins, and some other Smiths they knew, and the Greys with the husband as fat as a pig who took the bed-box all to himself and made his wife sleep on the grass outside with her eight young 'uns. We weren't keen on them, the Greys, but Redeemus Grey was good at finding work and so we'd found it advantageous to stay with them. There's something ironic.

The villagers hadn't bothered us much, so we were quite surprised when the Constabulary came over. They took their hats off, all polite like, and said there'd been a vote or something at the Council and we had to go, and that's when my Dadus kicked up a bit of a fuss, pointing at me and my belly.

Eventually, the vicar showed up and said there was a cottage at the bottom of his cemetery we could have, just the one room like. Of course, what Dadus was most worried about was our *vardo*, but after a bit of talk, the vicar said, 'What if we say your wagon may be parked safely behind the vicarage?' There was even a field for the horse.

So for all the trouble that belly got me into, it got me and Dei and Dadus moved into a cottage in a graveyard.

The others went off, which was just as well. Things had been difficult since I'd started showing. Even before then, everyone knew certain things, and no one was saying anything, and in a little camp like ours there was no getting away from the badness of that.

I've seen girls in my kind of trouble put out to walk the highway on their own, but my mother and father stuck by me. Dadus was mad as a bear when Dei first told him, mind you, and called me every name under the sun. But I was his daughter, and he was damned if any other so-and-so was going to call me names as well. So they made it clear, without saying anything to anyone. Yes, their daughter was going to have a baby and, no, there was no husband within a hundred mile, but that was our problem and nobody else's and anyone who didn't like it could take it up with my Dadus.

My Dadus was like that, soft and hard at the same time. I think it's called being a good man.

I know rightly what you're wondering. It's what everyone wonders in a story like mine. *What was the fella what done it?* Who was Lijah's father? Well, you might ask . . .

When you have a babby yourself, you look at your own mother and father in a different light. My Dei was a small woman, even smaller than me, and I remember staring at her as I was nursing Lijah one day and thinking, I can't believe she did what I did – four times, in total. There was a boy who died firstly, then a girl who was an idiot and they had to give her to the asylum, then me, then another little boy who died when I was small. Four times my Dei did what I did on that gravestone, and only one child to show for it.

My Dei, she was the kind of woman who kept all her suffering locked up inside herself. I never heard her complain once about anything. She had very fine wrists, delicately boned they were, and well-kept hands like a lady. She used to keep a little brass tub with oil in it, which she perfumed with lavender and rubbed into her hands at night before she went to sleep. She took such good care of her hands you might think she was a fine lady or something, instead of a Travelling woman who worked from dawn to dusk her whole life: beautiful hands, but as strong as you like.

I lay on that gravestone after Lijah was born, with him tucked inside my blouse for warmth and the mess that came with him all around me – and I knew that for all the hardness of our stone cradle, all I had to do was wait until my Dei got to me and everything would be all right, and it was.

Four times, my Dei did it, and I knew she carried the ghosts of her three lost babies around with her always, like shadows inside, but she never mentioned them.

After Lijah I knew in my bones that whatever fell upon me in the years to come, I'd never be doing it again. Taken from the outside, then taken from the inside – that was enough for me. I wanted life to be nicer than that.


The vicar must have said something in his church when Lijah was born as for a short while his parishioners left meat pies on our doorstep. I can tell you that was the first time such a thing had ever happened to us, then or since. Dordy, it was a bitter winter. I stayed inside nursing my new babby and it was like the world outside had stopped and gone cold and dark because there was no point in it being otherwise until my Lijah was ready to step into it.

But after a while, the pies had stopped coming and we ran out of coal. We had all felt such a wild happiness, the first few weeks. Then the realness of Lijah being with us and no pies and no coal sank in and the tiredness which I hadn't minded 'til then started to get a bit much and I thought how I had never been inside anywhere as much as I was then. It's a bad time to have a baby, that time of year. Isn't natural. All else calves in the spring.

One morning, Dei said, 'It's Sunday, now Father why don't you take me out on that horse round the villages? We need coal for that babby.'

Dadus replied, 'It's a mean winter, Mother, no one'll give us so much as cup of water even it being a Sunday.'

And Dei said, 'We'll take the babby then they'll have to.'

I loved listening to them talking about my baby like that, arguing about what was best for him. I loved the fact that they loved him like I did, that he was parcelled up with love.

I did think my Dadus was right, though, so I said, 'No, Dei, it's too cold outside.'

'Give him a good feed,' she said, 'And I'll wrap him tight and he'll sleep the whole way round.'

I didn't like the thought of my Lijah going door-to-door so tiny but he'd been up half the night and I knew she was right about him sleeping if I gave him a bellyful. And I must admit I did think that I could crawl under the blankets and sleep a bit myself as I was still *mocadi*, you know, Unclean, and Dei wasn't letting me cook or tidy or anything.

'You stay wrapped up and we'll be back before you know it,' said Dei.

As soon as they were gone, I settled down on my straw mattress all ready to sleep the whole morning, thinking how, in fact, it was a lovely thing to have a few hours to myself for the first time since Lijah was born. I was going to sleep like a log, I told myself.

I should've known.

I couldn't get comfortable. I was so used to Lijah next to me, it seemed strange to be able to move around on the mattress how I liked. Then I started to think of Lijah and wonder if he was all right and think how maybe I shouldn't have let Dei take him after all and that was a mistake. There was no sleeping then. And even though I'd given him a big feed from both sides before they left, I felt full of milk for him straightaway, and sore, and one side of me seemed a bit hot and hard and Dei had said if you ever get hot and hard you've got to feed him until it's clear otherwise you get a fever. I started to sweat just thinking of it, and I leaked a little which made my blouse damp and I knew I'd never get to sleep then.

I started to imagine all sorts of things happening to Lijah. I thought of Dadus being careless and cantering and Dei falling from the horse. I thought of some *gorjer* housewife taking a stick to them and not realising there was a newborn babby in my Dei's arms. What if he needed a feed while they were out? *Be quiet, you fool, you fed 'im right enough. He'll sleep the whole way round the Soke*. I rolled over and pulled the eider round my ears, closing my eyes.

We'd had dogs set on us often enough. My son would make a tasty morsel for some old rangy hound.

Soon I was up and out of bed and wrapping a shawl around my shoulders. I knew I couldn't tarry in the cottage. I would go mad with it.

Well, it was far too cold to wander round the village like a bed-lamite. So even though it wasn't wise, there was really only one place I could go.

It was back in the summer that I had first got into the habit of sneaking into the church services. I can't really say why I started doing it, except I was troubled in my head at that time, for obvious reasons, and it made me feel a bit better. Even before we got given the cottage, we had had some dealings with the vicar who had been good to us. He was a handsome man, tall and straight, white-haired he was, and a kind of peace came over me when I sat there. I suppose it was the only time when I was not with someone else or running errands or some such. It was the only time I could sit and think about things. It is not really done to just sit and think when you're a Traveller, especially a *biti chai* like me. Thinking doesn't get a fire built, nor catch a rabbit to stick on top of it.

I hadn't been inside the church since Lijah was born, so I felt a little strange as I crossed the cemetery, even though I could hear the service was well under way and knew how to get in without being spotted. I never used the main entrance – the iron door-latch clanged up and down like anything – but there was a little side door that pushed open right easy, so I could sneak down the side and sit at the back, where nobody could see me. From that position, I could watch the *gorjers* being holy.

I crept to my place, at the end of an empty pew, tucked away behind a pillar. Nobody paid any mind to me. They were all on their feet singing away and a right racket they were making.

> *Oh, the blood of Jesus,*
> *Oh, the blood of Jesus,*
> *Oh, the blood of Jesus*
> *Cleanses white as snow.*

> *Oh, the blood of Jesus,*
> *Oh, the blood of Jesus,*
> *Oh, the blood of Jesus,*
> *Yes, it cleanses white as snow.*

I closed my eyes and listened, and I thought how the hymns always seemed to be on about blood, and it made me think of the blood when Lijah was born and how it seemed clean blood in spite of all the other muck because this beautiful, new thing was coming through the middle of it. And I felt sad, all of a sudden, about how beautiful and new Lijah was, and me being so dirty and sinful, there in the church, and how he deserved a better mother than me. *The mud, the coin, the buckle pressed against my cheek.* And I found myself wishing things could be different for him, and perhaps he would have been better off if I'd left him on the vicar's doorstep, for what had he got to look forward to with the life we led? It must have been the lack of sleep made me think like that, for I'm not usually the type to fall to thinking on myself.

The vicar had started his sermon. I listened with my eyes closed, letting the words float about me. When I felt a bit better I opened them and sat up. It was a small church. I couldn't see the pulpit but I could hear him all right. He had a lovely voice, did that vicar. I've long forgot his name but I've remembered his voice: deep and soft, like he was going to be good to you.

'And so, good members of this parish,' he was saying, 'we must never forget that in our own lands we too have a heathen tribe among us . . .' It was something like that. 'Long may we dwell upon the vile hordes that afflict the Holy Land. For it is easier, is it not, to look at our neighbour's garden and see the weeds and bitter fruit therein than to contemplate our own dandelions?'

*He's got a lovely voice but he doesn't half talk a load of blether,* I thought to myself, giving a huge yawn and leaning against the pillar. The villagers were restless, too. I could hear them shuffling, up at the front. From where I sat, I could make out the Freemans. I could not see Thomas among them. I felt a sudden yearning for the life of a maiden, the life I had had before Lijah had befallen me, and left me a woman who would always be a mother of a bastard child whatever else happened. Thomas Freeman would sooner spit at me in the street than smile at me now, I thought. How smug his family would feel; how right in their judgement of me.

'And so I come to the matter in hand . . .' the vicar continued. How warm his voice is, I thought, and closed my eyes, '. . . our very own degraded heathens. I speak, of course, of the road-side Arabs, the *gipsies.*'

My eyes snapped open.

'As you will all know, I consider myself something of an expert on this unfortunate race, as we have in our very own churchyard here our own examples, among whom an innocent child has been born. As I was saying last week . . .'

Later, I decided that it was that particular phrase that hurt me more than anything. *As I was saying last week . . .* It was not just bad luck for me to have wandered in there that morning and hear him talk of us in such a way, oh no. He did it all the time.

'. . . it is the fate of these unfortunate children which most nearly concerns me, and the charitable trust I advise. Are we really prepared to cast them into the yawning jaws of hell?' And here, his voice rang like a bell. 'No, my good Christian fellows!' At this point, he must have leaned forward or pointed his finger or something, for there was a hush in the church that told me people were actually listening to him. I held my breath. I would have to wait until the next hymn before I crept out, for what should I do if anyone noticed me here?

His voice went back to normal. 'And so I come to the purpose of today's collection. You all know well, my friends, my abiding interest in the education of our youth. Before too long, I can report, I will be travelling to the Great Halls of Westminster to give evidence on the necessity of compulsion when it comes to the children of rogues and vagabonds. A truly evangelical mission to raise the monies necessary! As our good Lord himself said when he came upon . . .'

He was back to the Lord, but I did not need to hear any more. *As I was saying last week* . . . How long had he been making these plans? He was probably eyeing up my fat belly before Lijah even popped out of it. All the stories Dei and Dadus had told me about *gorjers* stealing our children – I'd always thought it was something grown-ups said just to frighten children into being good. *As I was saying last week* . . . How long had we got?

I was sweating. It happened when my dugs were full of milk. The back of my neck prickled with it, then felt cold. I was dizzy and leaned against the stone pillar, turning my face to it to cool it. Where had my mother and father taken Lijah? When would they be back? I wanted to be back inside the cottage, but my legs felt weak and I did not trust myself to stand. If I tried to leave now, and fell down, then I would be discovered. My only hope was to wait until they were singing like a bunch of crows and slip out the way

I had come. I wanted my son. I wanted to hold him and hold him and whisper to him that no matter how bad things got for us I would never, never give him over to the *gorjers*.

Dei said that by the time they got back to the cottage I was raving like a lunatic. I had our things all packed and bundled up. They'd only just got in the door when I was sobbing how the vicar was going to come and steal our babby and make him live with a *gorjer* family and go to school and be turned into a little *gorjer* boy. And that's how come we took to the road again, in the middle of the winter, all unprepared and with no proper plan in mind. We upped and left that very morning and I have never since ceased to blame myself for what happened as a consequence.

Lijah knew nothing of what was going on, of course. My innocent son was but a few weeks old.

Yes, well, like I said, he was trouble from the start.

# CHAPTER 2

If there is one thing I have always been afraid of, it is being shut away. I am so afraid of it that thinking of it makes me go almost mad. And then I fall to reasoning how that's what madness is. It is like you're shutting *yourself* up, inside yourself, and the more frightened you get the madder you get and the madder you get the more afeared you are. And there is something round and round about this that makes me want to put my hands over my ears and shut my eyes – to shut myself away from the thought of being shut away. And then I see all too easy how a person could fall to screaming for no reason. It is like all the bad things in your life start spinning round and round you until they are like a wall you can't see past, and then you are finished, *oh dordy*, you are finished right enough. Not to think on't, is the only way.

My Lijah, when he was an old man and me even older and still around to see it, was fond of trapping wasps in jam jars and tapping the jar and shouting *garn wi'd yer*! and laughing and would never understand why it upset me so. We were living together then, in our little house in Peterborough, him an old widower, and me an even older widow. I could never sleep unless the door was propped open. I used a conch shell that I made shiny with shoe polish. And Lijah always said how it was all those years of Travelling made me not like closed doors and I never told him it was more than that.

I have thought on my fear of being shut away and happened across two reasons for it. (Living for as long as I have gives you the time to come up with the reasons for almost anything.) One is the thing that happened when we took to the road that winter. We would never have done such a foolish thing were it not for my ravings after I heard the vicar's sermon, and I have cursed for ever since that I had the bad luck to go into the church that day and listen when I was not quite of my right mind anyway, being a nursing girl and therefore sorry in the head. It was losing my wits that Sunday in Werrington that led to the awful thing that happened as we crossed the Fens, the thing that took Dei from us.

The other reason is, I met a madman once, a real one, and the meeting of him left such an impression on me that it is the thing I remember mostly from my childhood.

I am not sure how old I was, seven or eight or nine, thereabouts. The years of things are difficult for me to recall as I had no reading or writing and do not know even the year in which I was born.

Anyroad, when I was nobbut a little *chai*, Dadus sent me across the fields one day to see if I could find the tents where my cousins were camped. We were stopped at a big camp at Stibbington and were expecting them to join us, when we were all going down to Corby for the Onion Fair. After a day or two and they had not come, a cattle drover passed by that Dadus was friendly with and he told him there were bender tents over at Yarwell.

'Lemmy,' my Dadus says to me, 'Go over the fields and see if it's your cousins, and if it's not, asks them whereabouts they've been and if they've news of them.' He was thinking we might have to put the word out we had gone to Corby. The folk we were stopped with wouldn't tarry.

So I set off across the fields and I was happy as a little lark because it had got me out of butter.

We had the use of a milch cow at that time, a fine roan-coloured one, as I remember, and Dei was making butter that day. It took sixteen buckets of water for each churning and guess who had to fetch them sixteen buckets from the village well?

I was halfway there when I realised I had the carrot in my apron pocket. This was unfortunate.

We had finished off the carrots last night, when we had had dumplings and a bit of warmed-up gravy. As she dished up, Dei had passed me a piece of carrot and said, 'Put that in your pocket and keep it safe, it's for the butter.' You got a much better yellow with a bit of carrot added. I had forgotten all about it in my haste to get off and now I did not know what to do. Dei would be wanting that piece of carrot for the churning. I stopped and looked behind me. I had gone so far it was a bit late to turn back.

I was stood in the middle of the field. It was one of those fields that had a rise to it, as if the earth was breathing. I was right on the top of the rise and could see in all directions: the dip and lift of the world around me, distant trees looking grey and green and smoky and not a soul in sight. Before me, the ridges and furrows of the fallow earth tumbled and clambered. If I stopped still, then rocked on my heels, it looked as if the field was moving. It was a warm day, but with a breeze, a lovely day for walking to try and find your cousins. I looked up at the sky, closing my eyes to squint at the sun, as if there might be answers up there and something should happen to tell me whether to go on or go back.

I usually find that if you ask the sky to tell you something, it answers back, sharpish.

I had just dropped my gaze from the sky when I saw it. In the near distance, something was moving against the hedge. At first, I thought my sight was maybe a little squinty on account of the sun, so I closed my eyes and opened them again. I was right, something was moving to and fro in the hedge no more than thirty yards ahead of me.

At this I began to feel a little afraid, as I could tell it was an animal of some sort, yet it was too large for a dog, too small for a cow and too nimble for a sheep.

A terrible thought came to me. What if it was *Bafedo Bawlo*, the Ghost Pig? (That is the thing I am most afeared of next to being locked up and will tell you about some other time.)

Whatever it was, it was moving restlessly from side to side along the hedge, as if it was looking for something in the undergrowth. I thought maybe I should just turn and run but whatever it was must be able to see me plain as I was standing right there in the centre of an empty field and I reckoned most animals could probably catch me in a chase. I did not want to approach it, neither, so I took a middle course and started to walk to the corner of the field that was to its right. This way I was a-signalling that I was no threat to it but was not afraid of it neither.

Then a heart-stopping thing happened. It started to lollop alongside the hedge so that it would catch up with me at the corner. I stopped dead in my tracks and looked around but there was no help for miles around and I knew I must find out what this thing was. So I walked calmly, keeping my eyes on it, until after a few paces it became the shape of a man.

I say a man: it was as much beast as man. It was on all fours, but crouching on its haunches and using its knuckles to walk itself along. It was dressed in a shabby shirt and trousers of the same colour, which should have warned me of something. It had no shoes upon its feet and there was soil in its beard and on its hat. It was nothing but a tramp, a poor, filthy mumper come on hard times, and I did my best to take pity on it as I approached while wanting nothing to do with it if I could.

It was clear that the mumper was determined to speak with me, but then as I neared him he crouched down and flopped both arms over his head and shoulders, as if to protect himself from a beating. I stopped and stared at him. He raised his head suddenly, and I saw his face.

He was an old man. His eyes were big and watery – the lines on his face dark grooves. He had a few days' growth of beard that was grey. It was the face of someone in great pain.

We stared at each other for a while, then he threw his head back and gave a short bark of a laugh. This startled me and I went to continue on but he held out his hand and said pleadingly, 'No, child, child, stay a minute.'

I stopped and we stared at each other again. 'Pray, child, tell me,' he said, 'are you a member of the sooty crew?'

Who's he calling sooty? I thought indignantly. Has he looked in a puddle lately?

'I mean, are you part of the lawless clan? I think you have that look about you, and I cannot tell you what joy that is for me. Are you a child of Tyso, perhaps? You resemble him somewhat. Is he hereabouts?'

At this I began to wonder if he could be a *Romani chal*, but I could not believe that one of us could ever sink to such a state of degradation. I knew not what to do.

'I must be on my way, sir, I am expected,' I said gently, giving a little bob of a curtsey, Lord knows why.

He pointed across the field and said with pride, ''Twas in yonder brook I came across a sizeable gudgeon.' There was no brook anywhere nearby that I could see.

It was at this point I had the misfortune to notice that his trousers were unbuttoned. I gave a start, for I had never seen such a thing on a grown man. A sizeable gudgeon indeed. I was now becoming fearful again because my mother had always told me three things about mad people: they feel neither heat nor cold; they undress themselves at any moment; and they do not realise you are a person at all because they are mad and do not even know what people are.

I realised that the man in front of me was truly mad and so might do anything. He seemed to have forgotten my presence, for he was staring at the earth and muttering, 'Ah, the marshy fen . . . the marshy fen . . .' Then he fell to saying, 'Marshy, marshy, *marshy* . . .' as if there was something in the sound of the word that upset him.

There was nothing for it, I bobbed another curtsey, turned on my heel and began walking back the way I had come.

I only realised he was following me as he was almost upon me. I heard his breath close behind and turned on him. He had been running but at once dropped on all floors and bowed his head again.

'You can't come home with me, sir,' I said firmly, although my heart was knocking in my chest. 'My mother and father would not like it.' *Dei, I've come back with the carrot, oh, and I found a lunatic in a field and I've brought him back with me, too.* I had a sudden image of the lunatic spinning and bumping inside the butter churn.

Then he did something most alarming. He grabbed my hand. He kept his head bowed, though, and said, 'I am knocked up and foot foundered, Mary. I have walked from Essex. If you do not take me in, I will surely die.'

Well, he's not one of us, just a common vagrant, I thought, but I can't leave him in the field. I'll have to take him back to Dei and Dadus.

'Come back with me to the place where we are stopped,' I said, trying to sound as high and mighty as was possible. 'And you can speak to my father.'

I could think of nothing else to do. I could hardly turn up at my cousin's tents with a lunatic in tow.

He was good as gold after that, following behind me at a respect-ful distance, not speaking, only humming to himself now and then.

You should have seen the look on Dei's face when she saw me walking back towards the camp, my very own lunatic following close behind.

Later that day, the men held a meeting. There was a big clunch pit on the edge of the camp and they would walk around it to the far side and sit behind the bushes, so that they had their privateness from the rest of the camp. I did something I had never dared to do in my whole life before, or since. I followed my Dadus, at a safe dis-tance, mind, then peeled off and went down into and up the other side of the pit, so's I could hide behind the bushes and listen to what they said.

It was a wicked thing to do, as I was naught but a girl, and I knew'd if I was caught listening to the men talking the talk I would be beaten to blazes. But I was passionate about the lunatic then, in the same way that my cousin Elias was passionate about the mon-grel puppy he had bought off the farmer the week before. The lunatic was a *gorjer*, that much was certain, but he was my *gorjer*. I think I had somehow got the idea that I could feed him bread soaked in milk, like Elias did his puppy, and bring him back to health. I think it was due to me not having had any little brothers or sisters and not having enough things to look after. There were plenty of babies in our camp – we were in a big camp then – but there were lots of young girls as well and I only got jobs like clean-ing and butter churning and I think I thought I was big enough for more than that.

The meeting was a great disappointment, as they rambled on about men's stuff – the horses and the metal-working – and I could-n't for the life of me think why it was always such a big secret when they went off to talk for it's not as if the rest of us would be interested anyway.

Then it came to my lunatic. My Dadus said how he thought it might be useful to have the mumper around for a bit, as he could be put to work fetching and carrying and how we could leave him when we moved on to Corby. And one of the other men said how my Dadus would have to be responsible and Dadus agreed and that was the end of it.

And before they had finished talking I slithered back down into the clunch pit and scrambled up the other side and got my clothes all chalky but I didn't care as I ran back to our camp across the fields because I couldn't wait to see my lunatic.

And so it was, the very next day, I had him carrying sixteen buckets of water to and from the well, while I walked behind him. And he was as quiet and biddable as a lamb, and the other girls crowded round me asking me how I had tamed him so quick and I could see in their eyes that they were right jealous and wanted to go out in the fields and get their own lunatic.

I was only a *biti chai*, otherwise I would have realised that some-one in the village would have seen him going to and from the well with me and said something to someone else.

That evening, I took my lunatic a plate of potatoes and a cup of buttermilk. He was sitting on the edge of the camp, cross-legged, seeming to understand how he mustn't go too close to anyone's *vardo* or interfere with anything. I carried the tin plate over, heaped with potatoes and onions all fried up nice and brown, and a spoon to go with and the cup in the other hand, and he looked up at me with shining eyes as he took it all from me.

I sat down next to him, at a little distance, and watched him feast. He ate and drank with great purpose, like a man who could not think of anything else until it was done.

When he had finished, he put his plate on the grass and looked up at the sky. It was a warm evening. The last of the sun was on his face. He belched, then stared at me. His look made me uncomfort-able, so I turned away. When I glanced back at him, he was staring at our camp. The women were all cooking, and smoke rose from the fires and drifted around, hazing everything: evening light, golden. It suddenly came to me, all at once, how good my life was, for I was seeing it through his eyes.

My lunatic gave a sigh. 'I wish I could die, here and now,' he said, his voice quite level and normal. 'For I think there can be no contentment greater than this, the open sky. What is it about potatoes cooked under the sky, do you think? Can it be the summer air gets into them?'

'My mother used a bit of the fresh butter,' I said.

'Ah . . .' he said.

I was enjoying this small, normal conversation, and was thinking about asking him some questions about his life and how he came to be a lunatic. Then, suddenly, he started smacking the side of his head with the flat of his hand, as if there was something in the other ear he was trying to dislodge. 'Gone! Gone! Gone!' he groaned. I felt a rush of disappointment, for I had persuaded myself that with enough fresh air and potatoes, he might be brought sane, then I would have the pleasure of telling people I had cured a madman once. But I saw my own folly at once.

He muttered into the ground, as if he had forgotten me. Then he lifted his head and glared at me. 'That blackguard Taylor! I'd like to take a stick and knock his hat off!' His shook his fist at me, and I rose without a word and ran back to the safety of the camp, leaving his empty plate and spoon on the ground.

The men came two days later. They entered the camp as *gorjers* do, marching around like they own the earth and can go anywhere whenever they like. As they strode up to our *vardo*, the men and boys gathered round, at a discreet distance but watching carefully, in case they had come for one of us. My Dadus raised his hand in a signal that it was naught to bother about, for he knew why they'd come right enough.

The lunatic was sitting cross-legged by our *vardo*, and my Dadus pointed him out. I thought the men would go and speak to him, but they said not a word. They went over and grabbed him, one arm each, and hauled him to his feet, then dragged him across the camp, to the edge of the common. I ran after them, and Dei and Dadus followed behind.

The lunatic had begun to struggle and whimper like a baby. It wasn't mad crying out, it was moaning in fear. It was horrible how not-mad it was. As they reached the edge of the common, he broke one arm free and began to flail it about. At this, the men lost their tempers and pushed him face down in the dirt. One sat astride the lunatic's back and pulled his arms behind him. He cried out in pain, his face pressed to the dirt. The other had a bit of rope and he began to wind it round the lunatic's wrists to bind them, cursing as he did.

I tugged at Dadus's sleeve and he understood me right enough. 'I think you may be gentle with the old fella,' he said to the men, 'he was ill when my daughter found him and has not fully recovered. He told her he had walked from Essex.'

One of the men gave an unpleasant, disbelieving sound. 'Essex, my arse. He's escaped from Northampton General Lunatic Asylum.' He stood and hauled my lunatic to his feet. 'Come on, John,' he said, 'that's the last you'll be bothering folk for a while.' His tone was not unkind, more casual, which somehow upset me all the more.

I followed to the start of the lane. Parked by the verge was a small wagon with a flat roof. It was so tiny that the whole of the back of it was the door, and they lifted my lunatic up and into it and it was then he began to cry. They slammed the door shut behind him and bolted it and there was a small barred window in the back and he stared at me through it.

The look he gave me as they pulled the wagon away will stay with me until the day I die.

My Dadus came and rested his hand on my shoulder. 'It's what they do with folks that lose their wits,' he said gently. 'They are chained up and beaten like dogs and the more they howl the more witless they are thought to be.' He shook his head and then turned back to the camp.

I realised I was crying too and wiped my face with the back of my sleeve. My mother came and gave me a gentle cuff about the head. 'Here,' she said, and thrust a handkerchief at me to wipe my face. 'That's how it begins,' she said, 'You lose your dignity and next thing, you're sliding down into the mud.'

I knew she didn't really mean it, that wiping your face on your sleeve was the beginning of losing yourself and going mad, but I took the point all the same. It didn't matter what happened to you, how much you were hurt by the world, you must never break down in front of others and let them see, because once you lost your dignity other people thought they owned you. They thought they could push you into a tiny wagon no bigger than a dog kennel and you had no right to mind. I've never forgotten that, although I know that my lunatic had probably forgotten me by the time his little wagon had turned the corner at the bottom of the lane.

When we left Werrington, that winter when Lijah was just a new babby, we headed straight off Whittlesey way. I felt bad because I knew Dei had liked the cottage in the cemetery, liked being able to cook and clean more easily for a while. Dadus had never been happy there, mind you, and was glad of an excuse to get out. There were ghosts in the ground, he said. Evil spirits.

We took it slow, a few miles a day, as we'd not used the *vardo* for a while. We were as far as Prior's Fen when Dadus stopped and said there was a problem with the back axle so we all had to get down. The wind blew down the road and Dei and me huddled round tiny Elijah. Then it began to rain, that freezing, stinging rain which feels as though someone is sticking needles in your face.

Dadus told us to go and shelter beneath the oak by the crossroads for we couldn't go further until he'd moved everything about in the *vardo*. The weight inside needed shifting, he said. So Dei and me hurried off down the road and the rain came down and down and by the time we got to the oak we were both soaked through and my feet were wet and slipping in their clogs.

We huddled down against the trunk of the oak. It was rough against our backs but the rain made the earth smell warm and at least we were sheltered which was more than Dadus was bending over the *vardo*'s back axle. Dei was shivering, and I felt worried for her, for I knew she was thinking how we could have all been back in the cottage. It would be dark soon, then we'd have to pull the *vardo* onto a verge, which is the thing most likely to get you in trouble with the gavvers.

I said, 'Should we go back to Eye Green, d'you think, Dei?'

Dei said, 'I'm not keen on the folk at Eye.'

After a while, a farmer rode past on his horse, leather cape over his shoulders. He slowed as he passed by, looked down at us huddled beneath the tree, and spat at our feet. Then he trotted on.

It was near dark by the time Dadus trotted up to us and still raining. 'I've fixed it up enough so's we can make it to that row of oaks,' he said, 'but Dei will have to walk.'

'I'll walk,' I said.

'Don't be foolish now,' said Dei, as she struggled to her feet.

In the end, we all walked, all but Lijah of course, who lay swaddled in a basket inside the *vardo*, and as I put him in I thought how wonderful to be a little babby and to be wrapped up warm all the time and have nothing to think of. Dadus led the horse, which was starting to shiver, and Dei and I guided the *vardo* by pushing either side, but it was all we could do to get it round the corner and in the dark we could hardly see the lay-by and we were all soaked to the bone. Dei and I went in first and lit the lantern and took our wet things off and stowed them, then hung the curtain for Dadus. He wasn't speaking when he finally came in, he was that soaked and cold. And we were all hungry and there was nothing but Dei gave me a last bit of bread and said a nursing girl had to have something inside her. And I must say as Lijah woke and cried to be fed I felt right sorry for myself, for I felt as though everything was wrong but I didn't know yet how much wronger it was going to be.

We were low on oil, so we shut the lantern as soon as I'd finished feeding His Lordship. There was nothing for it but to bed down and wait until the morning. Dei took down the curtain and hung up our wet things so that the warmth of us would help to dry them in the night. I went to sleep on the floor of the *vardo*, with Lijah next to me, hearing the clatter of the rain on the roof, which is a sound that has always helped me go to sleep. But there was also the not-so-nice tap-tapping of the drips from our wet clothes that smacked and busted against the polished floorboards, right close to my head. And these two sounds didn't get along, for all they were both water, and they argued in my head until I went to sleep.

Lijah woke me at first light, and I fed him. I could tell from the movement of him that he'd dirtied his swaddling things and I had better change him. Dadus and Dei were still unmoving on the bed-box, so I levered myself up gently, with Lijah in the crook of my arm. The box where I kept his clean cloths was in the cabinet beneath where they slept, and it was hard to lift it out one-handed without disturbing them. When I opened the door to go outside, the cold, white light flooded the *vardo*'s shuttered darkness and I stepped out as quickly and carefully as I could, pulling it to behind me.

The rain had stopped during the night and, although it was chilly, the air was light, and there was that nice feeling you get when a horrible night has ended – like, whatever's going to happen today'll be better than yesterday, for certain. The grass was soaking, so I sat on the step and laid Lijah across my knees and unwrapped his swaddling and cleaned him as best and quickly as I could. His little barrel body went blue with the cold and his arms and legs were flung wide and flailing against it. Then I wrapped him up again, hoisted him and tied him to me with my shawl.

I stood holding his dirty things, wondering what to do. I could just go back inside and stow them, but I didn't know when Dei and me would next have the opportunity to boil some water and wash them out. There are some parts of Travelling with a babby that are not right easy. So's I thought to myself, I'll take a walk down the lane and see if there's a stream nearby.

I had my heavy shawl on, but even so I went quickly. Lijah was awake, and looked up at me with those black eyes of his, as if he was wondering what I had just put him through and what I would do to him next. I talked to him as I walked. 'You've nobbut yourself to blame, *amaro chavo*. *Akai, adoi, atchin tan or duva in the biti drom in a brishenesky cheerus*, you've to be wiped . . .' He gave a squirm, and screwed up his face, as if he wanted to cry but couldn't quite decide if it was worth the effort. '*Kushti tikner mush* . . .' I soothed him.

We'd been down this way before and I had a memory of a ditch with a stream beyond the crossroads. The Fens is like that. You get water almost anywhere. I found it right enough, no more than a trickle, but enough to unfold the swaddlings and lay them flat on the stones beneath the water, weighted down. Dei said how she'd seen babies die of not having their swaddlings changed enough, of how the skin got reddened until it swelled and cracked and the babies got a fever. She thought it dreadful some mothers didn't realise that – although I have to say my Dei was hard on other mothers as only a woman who has lost three children can be.

I can still remember squatting by that stream, Lijah strapped to my chest, looking up at me with his eyes wide, while I watched the clear water run over the yellow staining of the swaddling clothes. I can remember thinking how it was good to have a mother who told you what was what. How would I have managed Lijah without her there to tell me?

It was the last time I was happy and ignorant like that. Happy, despite the cold. Clear water running. My baby on my chest, dark eyed and knowing everything.

As I was walking back to the lay-by, I saw them, standing by the *vardo*. There was two of them, one of them holding their horses' harnesses, the other a-banging on the side of our wagon. 'Dei! Dadus!' I shouted in warning. The men heard me and looked round.

I began to run towards them, but I couldn't go so fast with Lijah strapped to me and the wet swaddling in the crook of one arm. While I was still some yards away, Dadus came down the step, pulling his braces over his shirt. The men turned to him.

I reached them as they were showing Dadus a piece of paper. As I ran up, Dadus glanced at me and said, all cross-sounding. 'Lem, go inside.'

'Is it all right, Dadus?' I whispered.

'Go inside,' he said.

Inside our *vardo*, Dei was pulling on her outer things. Her face was set.

'Dei, it's the gavvers . . .' I said. 'What do they want?'

'Same thing they always want,' said Dei, and I could hear in her voice that, though she was trying to sound casual, she didn't feel that way at all.

'Pack stuff up,' she said, and together we began to roll blankets and stow the eider. Having Lijah strapped to me made me slow and clumsy but he had gone back to sleep and I didn't want to shift him.

The door opened, and Dadus came in. He stood there for a minute, looking at us.

'They want my hawking licence,' he said.

I looked at him, and at Dei, and I knew in that minute that we all had the same stricken look on our faces. Dadus had let his licence run out before Christmas. *Joseph Smith, Hawker of licensed goods, Knives, Kettles and Sundry Kitchenware*. It cost two pound to renew it, and he said he'd get another when he'd been to the wholesalers at Whittlesey as there was no point 'til then. But *Licensed Hawker* is what he called himself, and the gavvers wanted the proof.

'Show them the old one,' said Dei. She lifted the lid to the high chest.

'I'll ask them if you can stay here, at least,' he said, and went out again.

I looked at Dei. At least?

Turned out it was more trouble than it was worth, apprehending us. I heard one say it to the other, as they hitched our *vardo* to the horse. They had to send for a cart from Eye for us and all our things, on account of the back axle. Then they took us to Whittlesey and we spent the night in the *vardo* in the yard and they fed us quite well with a sort of stew. In the morning, they said we were going down to Ramsey but they wouldn't say why. Well, they weren't going to bother with the *vardo* all that way, so they put us in a huge wagon with a load of others.

I don't think I understood even then how bad it was, on account of how Dei and Dadus kept saying to me I wasn't to worry. I should have realised, they said it so often, that worry was exactly what I should have done. But looking back on it, even though I had a baby, I was still something of a child. Dadus told me he had been *apprehended* four or five times and nothing had ever come of it. Quite cheerily, he said it.

The others in the big wagon were mostly loose women and tramps from round about, so we wouldn't lower ourselves to speak to them. We went the back route, across Glass Moor, and they stopped at another village and picked up a Travelling family like us. We rokkered to them right enough and they said something about how there'd been a load of trouble down at Pondersbridge and across the Fens on account of it being such a bad winter, and how the gavvers were going around picking up Travelling people all abouts. They said how they had been part of a big camp, and their horses were all tethered in the next field and a whole gang of local men had come and untied the horses and flapped umbrellas at them to frighten them away. And some of them had run away on foot but they hadn't as they had old folk with them who were poorly.

We were in Ramsey a week, kept all together in a lock-up, a filthy, low place. I don't care to describe it. I suppose it was then I began to realise this might be bad. There wasn't a proper court-house, so the magistrate held our hearing in the local pub one morning, in the top room. It's all a bit strange to me now. A woman came and said how a *gipsy* had come to her door and she'd turned her away, and later her chickens had gone poorly and started stag-gering about, then another pair had come and offered to buy them off her cheap. I was only half listening. Then she said the second two was a young 'un and an old 'un and they had a baby with them, and she pointed at me and Dei. I wanted to laugh out loud, it was that foolish. I had never seen the woman in my life.

The magistrates called her the *prosecutrix*. When she went to the back of the room, she stood next to a big fella, and I saw he was the farmer that had spat at us as we sheltered underneath the oak tree.

There were so many other people in the room saying things that I lost track. I just held my Lijah. But I could feel Dei and Dadus either side of me getting stiffer on the bench in a way that meant they were upset. Then we were all standing, and the magistrate in the middle, a white-haired fella, was saying, 'One week hard labour followed by five years in a reformatory,' and Dadus was stepping forward with his hat clutched in his hands and tears were running down his face and he was talking about Lijah and saying how I was still a nursing mother and so young and all – and it was only then I realised they were talking about me. I looked at Dei, and she was crying too, with her eyes closed and lips a-flutter, which meant she was praying.

We all sat down again, and the white-haired fella goes into a huddle with the others.

There is a way to get through being told something terrible, and that is not to believe it until it is proved to be true. At least, I thought so's at the time, although I have since changed my mind and am more into plain speaking.

I think we were let out the room for a bit. I can't rightly remember. I know that, some time that day, the lady who ran the public house came up to me with some bread and cheese and said I was nobbut a child myself and had not a scrap of flesh on me and if I was to look after that babby I needed feeding up. I gave some to Dei and Dadus but they wouldn't take it.

We were back in the room then. It had a lot of windows and a low ceiling. They probably had wedding parties and such when it wasn't for the magistrates. The white-haired fella said how he had been moved by what my Dadus had said and the fact as how Dadus had been a licensed hawker and had not been in trouble before spoke something. But he could not let people like us think it was all right to go around poisoning people's chickens just whenever we felt like it. But he was mindful of how to take an infant from a nursing mother was not right. As such, I was getting a fine. Our *vardo* and things would be sold to pay for it if we did not have no money. But he had to make an example of all miscreants and because of that Dei would get four weeks' hard labour, not two, and I understood she was doing my hard labour for me and I started to cry but Dei and Dadus were quite calm by then because I wasn't going to the reformatory neither. Dadus got a fine for not being licensed.

All I understood was that I wasn't going to be put away and Lijah would not be taken from me. I didn't really understand about

Dei. She was being sent to the House of Correction in Huntingdon, they said. Dadus and I would have to stay in Ramsey to sort out our fines.

When we got outside, it was cold and sunny. There was the same wagon waiting. Dei went forward and I went to go with her, but Dadus put his hand on my arm and said, 'No, Lem, you and me are staying. It's just Mother is going.' And I stood holding Lijah and staring at her as she climbed up. There were windows in the wagons, and I waited for her face to appear at one, but it didn't, which was perhaps for the best.

'When we've sorted out the fines we'll go down to Huntingdon and find somewhere to stop until she gets out,' Dad said.

*Hard labour*, our Dei? 'They won't make her lift rocks or anything, will they?' I asked Dadus but he wouldn't reply.

# CHAPTER 3

Cannon balls. It wasn't rocks, we found out, it was cannon balls.

We were lucky, and managed to get the fine paid up in a fort-night. Dadus found some local Lees who helped us out a bit, and we stopped with them while we came to an arrangement. They paid our fine and then kept our *vardo*, which was a beautiful bow-top, while we set off on the horse for Huntingdon. They would keep the *vardo* for us until we returned with Dei and paid them back. We were that relieved, as to have sold it outright would have been the end of us.

We had a little money left over after we'd paid the fine, so when we got to Huntingdon, we tried to get a room at an inn called The Sun. I could tell the inn was called The Sun, as I could see the sign swinging in the wind and the bright yellow sun a-painted on it, with pointy rays. There was sleet falling, at the time.

They turned us away, even though we could see there were no horses in their stable, but the woman came out after us and said there was another place at the bottom of St Peter's Hill that took what she called *all sorts*. It was worth us trying, she said, on account of it being close to the House of Correction. She didn't like to think of the baby having nowhere to lay its head what with the sleet coming down an' all. We thanked her right enough.

The other place had a sign that was a dog raised on its hind legs snarling at a bone that was flying past in the beak of a big black bird. The downstairs bar was dark and crowded and there was a terrible noise of shouting coming from upstairs, and the young man who spoke to us said there were eight to a room but only six in one of them so we could have that. At this, Dadus told some story of how Lijah was awake all night and the young man would get complaints in the morning and wasn't there a shed or something out back, next to the stables? He looked at us a bit funny but of course we could have told him that we would rather stop by the horses than with a bunch of stinking, drunken *gorjers* any day. We didn't like paying for it when there were any number of stables in the town we could have slept in for free if we'd left the sneaking in until dark, but considering the position we was in we could not risk getting into trouble. Dei would be depending on us.

As it turned out, there was a shed with a hayrick behind the stables which was as cosy as anything and we saw to the horse first and then the young man gave us some blankets and a talking-to about not lighting a fire, as if we were stupid. Dad went off and came back with the good news of having found a baker's shop where they would give us bread each day if he was there two hours before dawn to help unload the furnaces. And this piece of luck was so large that I felt almost cheerful as we settled down at the bottom of the hayrick and ate fresh rolls, and talked about how the next day we would queue at the prison with the other relatives and send a parcel of rolls in to Dei. We talked about how pleased she'd be to get them.

*

The next day, after Dadus had done his shift at the baker's, we set off for the prison.

There was a right old crew queuing at the gate of the House of Correction. You've never seen such a bunch in your lives. There was the bony women with their bony children waiting to see the Debtors, and the loose women with their faces painted and even some gentlefolk, standing to one side, who were let in first, of course. Dadus said how he heard one say his brother was in there for *sedition*.

'What's that?' I asked quietly.

'Talking about not liking high-up folk,' Dadus replied.

I had never been near such a place before, and it felt strange to see the whole world there, and to think that such calamity could happen to anyone. It made me feel a bit better, I suppose, like even high-up folk had their bad luck sometimes. Maybe that was one of the reasons why I stayed hopeful, even then; why I was not on my knees in fear.

After a while, we were let into a yard. It was rutted and muddy but the mud was frozen so at least we weren't ankle deep. Some of the people who were waiting were squatted against the wall but it was so cold I had to keep moving, up and down, bouncing Lijah on my arm. One of the loose women came over and started pulling faces at my Lijah over my shoulder, to play with him. I was for putting up with it, but then she lifted a finger to touch his cheek with her long scratchy nail. I turned away, for I would not have my child touched by such a woman. She cursed me under her breath and went back to squat against the wall.

I cradled Lijah's head with my hand, and kissed him, and whispered to him, 'Well, at least we're out of the wind now, aren't we *chavo*?'

We waited and waited and Lijah began to cry on account of wanting feeding. I didn't want to leave Dadus but I couldn't feed Lijah in the yard with all the hungry eyes that would stare at me.

Eventually, he'd had my knuckle to chew and all the dandle I could manage and I said to Dadus, 'Dadus, I'll have to go off and feed him,' and he said, 'Right you are, Lemmy.'

So I left Dadus in the yard and slipped out the door past the others still waiting in the wind and went and found a lane and a fence with a gap. It was freezing, but for all that it was nice to be out of that yard for a few minutes. It was just me and Lijah, and the good feeling of making him completely happy, his little mouth a-pulling at me, and his fist a-clenching 'round my finger. *Biti*. Little. It was all I could think, looking down at him. You are so *biti*. I let the shawl around his head drop back so's I could stroke his fine baby hair while he fed.

I winded him, then he was asleep on my shoulder for a bit, and I think I must've dozed a bit myself with my back against the wooden fence, for I started awake and the light felt different, so I sorted myself out then hurried back to the yard.

There was no sign of Dadus, and it was only by asking that I found out he had gone in. I thought the warder might not let me past but he took pity on me and I found Dadus was still queuing but in a stone corridor now.

Came our turn, right enough, and we went into a room with a faraway ceiling, where the windows were so high up too you couldn't see out of them even if you stood on a table and jumped. There was a man with a big book behind a desk and when we told him who we were there to see he frowned, still looking down at the book. He asked us to repeat the name. Without saying anything, he got up, slammed the book shut and left the room by another door.

Dadus and I glanced at one another.

Eventually he came back and said we're to go away again, but that we're to come back the next day, only not to join the big queue in the yard but to go to a side door. After that he wouldn't say nothing, only opened his book again and made it clear he wanted us to tell the next one to come in.

'What d'you think's happened to Dei?' I asked Dadus, as we walked away from the prison, and I knew he thought it bad for he snarled, 'Leave it, Lemmy,' then strode off down the dirt road that led to our lodgings, leaving me to hurry after, clutching Lijah to me.

I tried not to think on't, but that night I lay awake, and heard by the silence next to me that Dadus was awake too, there on the straw. In the gloom, I could see the shape of his broad back. He was turned away from me, and I felt frightened then, frightened of everything.

The next morning, soon as Dadus was back from the baker's, we went back to the House of Correction and found the side door and rang the bell, and at the little tinkle of it my Lijah jerked his head.

The warder who opened the door to us was a cheery sort of fella. He had a beard that ran from one ear, down to the chin, then up to the next ear, just on the edge of the face like, with no moustache, so's it looked like his beard was a strap that was holding the rest of his hair atop his head. He took us down a narrow corridor and into a little room that was the warders' room. One wall of it was shelved and on the shelves was jars of beer. In the other corner was a barrel, with two other warders sat either side.

The two other warders were reading a newspaper and looked up at us, unfriendly like. Normally, I would've stared back, but I dropped my gaze, as I knew how important it was that we were on good terms with them so that we could find out what had happened to Dei.

Dadus was staring at the jars, and said to the bearded one, 'D'you not lay your jars on the side, on account of the sediment?' I realised he was being friendly too, for the same reason.

'The shelves are not deep enough,' the warder replied.

'That's a fine load of beer, anyroad,' Dadus said, 'You fellas must have a fine time in here,' and the seated men's faces cracked into smiles.

The one with the beard explained how's they were allowed to brew the beer that got sold to the prisoners, and how it was only the most trustworthy of them did such a thing. He made it sound like an honour, but one of the seated ones gave the game away by saying, 'We wouldn't be able to keep our rent up, otherwise, not on what the County give us, you know. You'd be amazed if we told you how little it was.' Later, Dadus explained to me how the men were paid very bad and that was accounting for how they were often the lowest sort and behaved in an evil way towards the prisoners sometimes, but I still don't think it makes it right.

Then, the two seated fellas stood up and put on their top hats and buttoned their jackets as to leave, and the bearded one said, 'Bateman, should I get the nurse to take these two down?' and the other said, 'She'll not be allowed to leave the sickroom, you'd best do it yourself, but not just yet as she'll still be attending to them.'

Third one said, 'Best leave it 'til she's done.' And two of them went out.

At the mention of a nurse, I saw Dadus go pale and I felt myself start to sweat and I took the liberty of sitting down where one of the other wardens had been sitting – luckily the bearded fella didn't seem to mind.

'Can you tell me what has happened to my wife?' Dadus asked the question as casual as if he was asking the hour of day.

Bearded fella looks surprised. 'Did they not say?'

Dadus shakes his head.

I was glad I was sitting down then, for what the fella said was so horrible I think my knees would have given had I been standing.

There had been an accident. Both her legs were broken. It happened on the tread-wheel, the second week she was here. The first week of hard labour was always shot drill, the fella said. There was never enough room for all the hard labourers on the tread-wheel, so everyone got put on shot drill for a bit when they first arrived.

'What is shot drill?' my Dadus asked, and I could hardly believe how he could keep his voice so steady.

So the bearded fella told us and afterwards I wished he hadn't.

Shot drill was where you took a cannon ball from a pile in the yard, stacked up against a wall, and you carried it over to make another pile, and it was a pyramid, and there had to be ninety-one cannon balls in each pyramid. And if there weren't you did it again.

I imagined my tiny, little Dei counting as she staggered across the yard in the bitter cold, '*Axis . . . nevis . . . tay . . . enin . . .*' I imagined her counting to stop herself from thinking of the pain of it.

I thought of how she must have been relieved when they told her a place was found for her on the tread-wheel.

It was on account of the water, the warder told us, that the accident had happened. He didn't agree with the use of water on tread-wheels. He had been a warder up at Kirkdale where they had the biggest tread-wheel in the country and they used it to grind wheat and some others used theirs for weaving. But ours is used to turn water, he said, and that makes the steps a-slippery and accidents are not uncommon, I'm afraid.

It was only later that I thought, I never asked him what the turning of water was for. I had these strange thoughts of rivers and streams being turned over and over, in the way you might air an eider, but for no good reason – and my Dei having been crippled on account of this turning of water for no good reason. And that, of course, was even worse than her being crippled for the milling of wheat.

I think he must have realised what bad news this was for us, because he said then, 'I'll just leave you for a minute and go and see if the nurse will have you,' and went outside.

Dadus came and sat next to me and we couldn't even look at each other. He put his hands over his face, and I knew he was struggling with himself for my sake. And I felt our lives fall away from us, like water through my fingers, for whatever happened after this we would never be the same as before.

After a while, one of the ones with a top hat came back in. He took six of the beer jars down from the shelves, one by one, and stacked them by the door.

Dadus said to him, lightly like, 'So how do accidents happen on the tread-wheel, then?'

'Folk slip, go under,' was all his reply, then he started saying how we shouldn't believe everything the first fella had said on account of him having once been a felon himself and that was how he thought himself an expert on the tread-wheel. He claimed to have been a warder elsewhere but it was well known that he had served three months for bastardy up at Kirkdale and only got out when he had paid the four pound fine to the workhouse for the upkeep of the child.

This took my mind off our current anxiety, for a bit, as it astounded me to think that a man could go to prison for the getting of a child and I couldn't help thinking how much I would have given all the gold in the world to have taken my Dei off that tread-wheel and put there a certain man who shall remain nameless.

Top-hat fella went out again, with two of the jars of beer, and we sat some more for what seemed like a long while. Lijah was asleep the whole time. Eventually, Dadus got up and went over to the small, square window in the wall next to the shelves of jars. He stared out of it for a while, and the light on his face showed me how old he was, and I thought, *he looks an age older than he did this morning*.

The bearded fella never came back. A different one, one we hadn't met before, came in and took us to the door of the sick-room, and I knew'd we were getting near it still some feet away from the stench that came from the open door. We knew the stink of sewerage right enough, but this was something different, something deep and coloured. 'What is that smell?' I whispered to Dadus, as I tucked Lijah tighter into my shoulder.

The warder accompanying us heard me and leaned towards me staying sternly, 'It is the stink of corruption, young lady, and let that be a lesson to you.'

As we reached the door, he said, more normal like, 'Gangrene. We've a few cases at the moment.'

The room was another high-ceilinged one but the windows were smaller and didn't admit much in the way of light. There were about a dozen beds in there, made of boards. I looked quickly down one row. The two women in it nearest to me were both sitting up and knitting. They both had triangles of cloth over their noses, held around their ears with bits of ribbon. The rest of their faces was red and pockmarked and Dadus told me later they had an evil *gorjer* disease that was eating off their faces bit by bit.

It was a soft sighing sound made me look the other way, and it was then I saw Dei. She was flat on her back, with her legs slightly raised. She was turned towards us – her face was pale and her gaze misty with pain. She lifted a hand.

A nurse in a grey uniform got in front of us as we went to her. 'I can allow you a few minutes only,' she said, 'and then we have to lock this room as I must attend elsewhere.' She turned away and left us to it.

Dadus reached out to Dei and took her raised hand. I went around the other side, turning Lijah towards her so she could see his sleeping face. Her head was bare and her hair white at the temples. Her skin was as grey as the nurse's uniform and seemed to hang on her face like it was too loose for the bones beneath. I could not believe the change in her. She was an old woman, suddenly, and I felt this thick load of panic inside but I did not want her to see it, so I smiled. She smiled, and tried to speak, but it was clear the pain was too great, so we talked to her and told her how we'd quit our fines and had found lodgings nearby until they let her out. I bent and put Lijah down on the boards, next to her, and she managed to turn her head a little and look at him.

After a short while, the nurse came over and fussed us out. It broke my heart to be leaving Dei there but we made sure she knew we would be back just as soon as they'd let us.

As the nurse locked the door behind her, Dadus said, 'Whereabouts in the town can we purchase laudanum for her?' and the nurse told him the name of the chemist's, and said how we was not to worry about her being sent back to the cells but as soon as she could sit she would have to quit her sentence with light labour, like the others. She saw what we thought of this by the looks on our faces and said that in most other prisons a hard labourer with broken legs would have been tossed back in the cells to take their chances with the rest. It was only on account of Huntingdon being so progressive that there was any such thing as a room for the sick and injured.

All the way back to our lodgings, my father said nothing, but his fists were clenched and he strode at such speed that I ran to keep up.

We got Dei back when her time was done. She hadn't had to do the light labour after all, on account of being in too much pain to sit. Dadus used the last of our money to hire a cart so that we could get Dei back up to Ramsey and get our *vardo* back from the Lees. It was a big problem how we'd get the wherewithal to pay them back, and to keep buying laudanum for Dei, but all I could think of was how once we got Dei back then it would all be sorted. I realised how, though she had always been the quietest one of all of us, she had always done the most and held it all together.

We took Dei on the cart across the bridge. There was a big common on the other side of the river where some of our Travelling folk camped sometimes and Dadus was thinking how we might be able to stop with them for a few days while we worked out whether Dei could make it up to Ramsey.

It was the coldest day of all. We piled blankets on Dei but she was shivering and sweating in turn. Dadus had talked a pie out of the baker, to give to Dei, to celebrate the getting-of-her-back. She took a nibble at the crust then said she couldn't manage the rest, and this worried me more than anything for after four weeks of gaol fare she should've fall'd on it.

As we crossed the bridge, with Dei on the cart and Dadus leading the horse and me carrying Lijah, I looked down. The river had frozen over. The *gorjers* were out skating. I could see a group of women just past the arch, about six of them. They were skating in a circle, slowly, with their hands tucked into fur muffs and their long coats flying out behind them. One of them slipped and wheeled her arms and then fell, and they all burst out laughing.

I looked back as we left the river behind, at the dark figures skating on the grey ice, flying around like big birds, as free as you please.


The Travellers on the common took us in. They were a small group and it turned out they were related to the others we had been in the wagon with on our way across the Fens. They were eager for news of them, and we were sorry as our trial had been before theirs so we knew not what their sentences had been. But Dadus promised he would find out when we got back to Ramsey, and get word down to them.

They were mostly Smiths, and Greys, but none of the Greys were related to Redeemus Grey and his lot that we'd been with in Werrington, although of course they knew of them. There was a cousin of Dei's, from the Kent Marsh Smiths, and when she saw the state Dei was in she fell to a-wailing and a-weeping and swore to us she would nurse Dei like her own daughter, and though I was grateful I couldn't help feeling that what Dei needed most was quietness, and me. They weren't well-off folk, otherwise they would never have been stuck on the common with the weather so bad, but they were better off than us and took us in.

Dei died four days later. I was with her, holding her hand. Dadus had gone out with some of the other Smith men. The other women had taken over the caring of Lijah and I just had him for feeds. I sat next to Dei the whole time, in the bender tent the folk had, with an extra layer they built over to try and help. It was bitter cold, but she didn't seem to notice. I stroked her fine-boned hand and I talked to her softly of what trouble Lijah was going to give me and how she'd better get well soon as I'd be needing help of her. At that, she gave a small smile, though she was long past speaking by then.

When she was gone, I couldn't bear her cousin, a-weeping and a-wailing. I felt like she was trying to take my grief, for who was she, after all? It was an uncharitable thought. I would have cried myself, I think, but for the wailing cousin. She made my face stony, for I wanted to be different from her to show her how much less my Dei was to her than me. You wouldn't think such things should matter at a time like that, but they do.

I let the cousin's wailing tell Dadus what had happened. He would have heard it as he came back towards the camp. I hope he let himself stop for a minute and take a breath, a deep breath, as it would have been the last breath he took before he knew for certain that our Dei was gone.

We burned her, that very night. We put her on the cart, with her few things, her shawl and her sewing things, and took her to the far side of the common and laid her down and piled wood on her.

Dadus and me stood by and we were getting through it, just watching the flames alongside the others gathered round who were our new family now. Then, all at once, there was a loud bang, and an orange flame shot skywards, and the branches we had piled on collapsed inwards. A shower of sparks flew up into the night air, and it was like Dei was escaping into the black sky. And Dadus next to me fell on his knees and bent over with both arms across his stomach as if he was going to be sick. He opened his mouth wide, and there was an awful, long moment when no noise came, but then he let out his howl, and it filled the sky. I dropped to my knees as well and put my arm around his shoulders, and tears were running down my face; but I realised I was frightened by Dadus collapsing down more than wanting to comfort him. I thought, after this he will be broke, just like Dei's legs were broke, and I will have to take care of him just like I do Lijah, and I already saw me making the decision about getting the cart back to the farrier and how we would pay back the Lees up at Ramsey and the whole future was falling on me, and I was foreseeing it – and I had never really thought on Travellers who tell the *gorjers* they see such things, but I saw my life there, going up in flames.

And then I could not forgive myself for thinking of myself and not of Dei.

Dadus stayed to see the fire out, but I could not, and, as it died down, I took my leave and said I would go back to the camp for Lijah. I was wept out and spent by then, and was full of air and nothingness, and this hollow feeling hurt so much inside that I had my hands pressed to my chest as I crossed the common in the dark. And so it was I came to the camp where some of the women were seated round a fire and the Marsh cousin took one look at me and handed me a bundle and I was in that much of a state it took me a moment or two to realise she was handing me my son.

I took him, and I thought how he seemed heavier since Dei had died. He was quiet for once, and I put his arm around my neck, and I felt myself begin to weep, and I did not want to frighten him so's I tried to do it quietly but he must have felt my body shake, for he did something he had never done before. He clutched at me. He was so little, he was only just able to move his arms and do such a thing. But as I held him, he held me back, and it was the sweetest feeling I had ever had. And I loved the weight of him, my son. And I thought how my Dei must have held me like this once, and how these things continued, and how my Lijah was now all to me, *all*, and as long as there was breath in my body, nothing nor nobody would ever take him from me, and if I close my eyes I can still see the loud orange flames against the blue-black sky and the shower of sparks and hear my Dadus howling and feel my soft, heavy son in my arms, even now.

# CHAPTER 4

The time has come to talk of Lijah grow'd, for that is the marrow and fatness of my story.

I sometimes think on't, that Lijah is my story. Until you have a child, you believe the story is yourself, for your small mind cannot stretch beyond that, and why should it? You have no other way of thinking. It is when you have a babby that you realise the world goes on and on, and you are not the story any more, you are just a small part of someone else's story. A bit like us going round the sun 'stead of the other way round. I had my son, and then I went around him, and when he was not there it was dark – and I'm not saying we don't all need a bit of night-time too, for we do, but there was no daybreak until I knew where my Lijah was and what he was about.

When he was small, I thought it might stop when he was grow'd, but if anything my feelings for him grow'd as well. It was because he had naught else but me, so I had to be enough to make up for that, and I reckon it became a habit I could not stop.

No girl would ever have been good enough for my Lijah. I'm not so stupid as to think that. But of all the lasses in the Fens, the flat old Fens where you can see as far as you like and know the world is big enough for anything, he had to pick *her*, the *grasni*, all clouds of gingery hair and great huge cheeks and hips and all bigness and softness like an eider you could lose yourself in. Oh, I'm not saying I couldn't see the attraction.

The thing is, about redheaded people, they smell a bit high.

We went fruit picking every summer when Lijah was a boy. The travelling was all a-slowing down by then, for they had made a new law, the *gorjers*, that said we should not camp on the commons no more and this made it very hard as we were not allowed to stop on roadsides or farmers' lands neither. The only way we could stop anywhere when we needed to was by breaking the law – and as we were breaking the law we only did it for a short bit before moving on to break the law somewhere else. So their new law meant we had to break the law a lot more often than what we had before.

The only time the farmers wanted us was when it was a harvest, of course, and then we had fine times for it was like the old days with folk showing up from all over. That and the horse fairs was the only times it was like it was.

It was by the cherry orchards of a farmer named Childer that the part of my life as it was ended. I was married by then, to Adolphus Lee, and then widowed within half a year of Lijah being married himself, but I am getting ahead of myself and getting things in not-the-right-order again, so I will go back awhile.

Dadus and I made out all right for some years after we lost Dei but I can't say as I remember it as a good time. Dadus hawked his kitchen goods but without the talent he had had for it before, for Dei had been behind him, suggesting all the time. And I remember things being hard, going from place to place. And our only joy in all this time was Lijah.

We even went so far as to try and settle once, on Lijah's account. We found a site over at Paston, where a large group of Lees had managed to buy a bit of land off a farmer, Lord knows how. So they were making their own little kingdom, these Lees, and they were a bit high and mighty with it but we thought we'd give it a go on account of trying to get some schooling for Lijah. I had never forgiven the vicar at Werrington for killing my mother, but I had come to the conclusion that if Lijah was going to get ahead in life when he was grow'd then a bit of *heducation*, as Dadus called it, was maybe no bad thing.

We asked around a bit and found what looked like the perfect place for him. I didn't know a right lot about schools, having never set foot in one in my life, but I was rather taken by this big old building in the middle of a field, with a church attached, just a couple of miles from the site. It was organised by nuns and I had to go and speak to them first. They were like big crows – big crows who had starch for breakfast every morning. I liked the look of them. *They'll put 'im right*, I thought.

First morning, I had him up nice and early and into the clothes I'd pressed the night before. He wasn't going to let me down, I told him, or he'd catch it from me, good and proper. He was small for his age, was Lijah, with black hair and heavy brows. He often had a fierce look, for he was not the sort of child who was inclined to smile unless he knew there was something in it for him. I saw the way that people looked at him sometimes, wary like, as if he was a terrier, and I always wanted to say to them, *but you should see him when he's sleepy, when he clamps his arm around my neck like a vice and won't leave go, and I have to lie beside him until he's sound asleep and if I try and move too early he cries out and pulls me closer.*

I knew nobody else saw what I saw in my Lijah, the small boy who cried out, so I worked hard to make him look as sweet as possible that morning, so that the nuns might find him appealing and not be hard on him. I brushed and oiled his hair, and for good measure I took a comb and gave him a kiss-curl in the middle of his forehead. I do swear it was the first time in his life that boy had looked angelic.

Before we left, I gave him a sugar sandwich wrapped in brown paper for his dinner, and a lovely little *lolli pobble*, a red apple, which I'd polished to a shine. The apple was for break time, I told him, and he was to go into a quiet corner to eat it. He wasn't to show it to none of the other children he'd be associating with. They were only the children of the local peasants round here and they'd probably never seen such a lovely little apple and would have it off 'im soon as look at it. I was proud of that red apple, as you can probably tell, which was my undoing as it turned out.

Anyroad, we walked over there at a brisk pace, him holding my hand and trotting to keep up, and I was that keen not to be late that we were early and had to hang around and he kept getting the apple out and looking at it and I said put it in your pocket and leave it there. Eventually, one of the nuns came to open the place up, a tall woman with a long nose, not one of the ones I'd met. She looked down the length of the nose at us and smiled. 'My, we are punctual,' she said, and I didn't much like the tone in which she said it, to be frank.

Lijah was looking at the ground, so I poked him on the shoulder and he lifted his head and said, 'Morning, Miss.'

'Sister!' I hissed at him.

'Morning, Sister.'

She gave another of those smiles, and I still didn't like it.

Before I turned to go, I bent down to him and said, 'You show me up today young man and I'll tan your hide so hard you won't sit down for a week. And don't let nobody touch that apple.'

He turned without a word.

*

I got the full story later, of course. They always like to make sure you get the full story, don't they? What I think happened, more or less, was this.

My Lijah gets into the classroom and to start off with he behaves himself right enough, even though he hasn't a clue what's going on. He knows enough to watch the other children and to copy them, and the lesson begins, and there's a nun at the thing on the wall they call a Black Board and she's writing on it with chalk and they all have their slates and chalks and they're copying her. And maybe the other children aren't quite as common as I thought as I'd stood behind a bush and watched them arrive after Lijah had gone in: the girls all had pressed pinnies and aprons and the boys had cleaned shoes and oiled hair, although none of them had a kiss-curl as smart as my Lijah's.

What I heard is something like this. While one nun is writing on the Black Board, another nun is walking up and down between the rows of desks to keep an eye on the children. Maybe she's flexing a ruler, just to make sure they knows what's what. She gets to the point where she's passing Lijah, and she stops and she sees a bulge in his pocket. 'Elijah Smith!' she says, and heads lift. 'What is that in your pocket?'

'It's my apple, Sister,' Lijah says.

The nun sticks out her hand. 'No food allowed in the classroom, boy, you should know that.'

At this point, I reckon my Lijah is faced with what you might call a bit of a dilemma. And the dilemma is this: what is he more scared of, the ruler in the nun's hand, or the leather strap that I keep in the *vardo* which I take out each morning and hang from a nail in the porch? Well, there's no contest, the strap wins hands down.

'I'm not to give the apple to nobody, Sister.'

At this, the nun might've got nasty, of course, but some of them looked quite nice so she might have just as easily been understanding and kind being as it was my Lijah's first day and he was only a poor, ignorant *gipsy* boy. 'It's all right, Elijah,' she might have said. 'You can give the apple to me, and I will keep it nice and safe for you and give it back to you at break time.'

Well, my Lijah wouldn't have been fooled by that. Oh no, the kindness would have tipped him off. This nun wants that apple for herself, he would have thought. She's heard tell of how red and shiny it is, how it is hard as a conker and will burst with juice as soon as you bite into it. The very thought of it is making her mouth water. She's feeling peckish. She's thinking, if I've got to walk up and down this class half the morning flexing this ruler, I reckon I need a little something to keep me going.

He always went a little red himself when he was angry, did Lijah. 'You can't have my apple, Sister.'

At this, the kindness would have disappeared, I reckon. The nun would have held her hand out and lifted the ruler. Meanwhile, the other children would be staring open-mouthed – little slugs would never have seen such defiance.

Well, at some point, my Lijah decides to bolt for it. The nuns told me he did it of his own accord but I reckon one of them tried to grab him because suddenly he's up and running rings round them. They chase him round and round the classroom and when one of them nearly catches hold of him, he leaps up on a desk and the next thing he's leaping from desk to desk over the heads of all the other children who are squeaking like mice and cowering and the nuns are shouting for help and it all ends up with Lijah standing on the nun's table in front of the Black Board where she has foolishly left a pile of spare slates and he picks up the slates and as a nun rushes towards him he spins it at her and, BANG! Right on the forehead! Down goes the nun.

And he doesn't stop there because by now he's enjoying himself so spin goes slate after slate, in all different directions. The other children duck so they won't get beheaded and crash go the slates through the big, long windows that look out of the field. (This bit I know is true as I saw the windows for myself when the nuns took me on a tour of the damage Lijah did, and the postman stopped us to say how he'd never been so surprised in all his life when he came up the lane and saw slates come crashing through them windows and flying towards him.)

Eventually, Lijah runs out of ammunition and the last remaining nun is closing in on him, so he jumps down from the table and belts for it, but he sees the postman in the drive so he swerves and runs to the church. The side door is open and somehow he gets in the tower and bolts the door behind him and he's up those stone steps quick as a squirrel and he finds the bell-pull and by then he's probably shouting, 'Dei! Dei!' having quite forgotten the leather strap and thinking only of how he's saved his apple so far and wants me to come and get him before the mad *gorjers* do him in.

So he does the only sensible thing he can think of doing. He grabs one of the bell-pulls, and swings on it.

Now, those bells had not been used in living memory, I got told, so the tolling which rang out across the fields and the surrounding district would only mean one thing to the dozy inhabitants: imminent Napoleonic invasion.

By the time I got there, the whole village was out.

There was nothing for it. I stood at the bottom of that tower, and I lifted my finger to my Lijah, who stared down at the vast crowd beneath. I rokkered to him straight, in Rummanus like, as I wasn't going to have the whole village understanding me. Roughly translated, it meant, *if you don't come down right this minute, I'll kill you.*

That was the start and the finish of Lijah's *heducation.* Aye, the kiss-curl was the only good thing came out of that *hexperiment.*

We moved on from Paston after that. For a while, we were over in Northamptonshire. I made baskets for a shopkeeper and taught Lijah how to wet and weave and he was talented at it, as I knew he would be. I taught him his coins as well, and all the other things he needed to know to do business in the world, and I reckon by the time he was ten or twelve he knew enough from me and Dadus for a good enough life and never mind the nuns. Those smart children in their pinnies and shirts might be able to write on Black Boards but could they coax milk out of a goat what didn't want to give it? No, I don't reckon they could.

There were many times he didn't get fed proper, of course, and he stayed a small fella. As a consequence, he developed the habit of looking after himself, so's he wouldn't get picked on. That's the thing about camp life. You have to let the *chavos* go off being hectic when there isn't a job to keep them busy, and then they fall to arguing and before you know it you've another mother standing outside your *vardo* rolling her sleeves up and calling you out. My Lijah learned to look after himself pretty sharpish, on account of him being small and also on account of being got at sometimes.

I suppose it's when boys are nearly men that they feel they have to start really getting at each other, for without knowing they are already strutting about like cocks in the farmyard in preparation for the competing they've to do later in life. We were back on the Fens when Lijah reached that age, on another big site with a whole load of Smiths and Herons and Lees.

'Dei,' he said to me one afternoon, thoughtful like. We was sitting next to each other on upturned boxes, by the fire. It was one of those times when there was no money for tea, so he was burning some old bread on a spike, then I was going to scrape the burnt off, into the water I was cooking. I laugh to think we had to do that, now, but it wasn't bad if you got it right.

He didn't normally talk to me thoughtful like, so I knew there was a question coming. I looked at him. There was light shining on his hair, which was soft and shiny, and I thought how hard it must be for a boy his age: a boy no longer, nor not yet a man. What a strange, in-between creature that is. What was he? He must've wondered that, and I couldn't help him, of course, having been a girl at that age myself.

Not for the first time, I felt a small ache inside, seeing him sitting there. It was his shoulders. He had bony shoulders that made him look fragile, like a bird, and I wanted to just hold him when I looked at his shoulders and keep the whole small, tough-little body of him wrapped up inside myself, all safe.

'Yes, Chicken . . .' I said.

'Dei . . .' He scratched his head, then held the toast up, turning the spike round to see it was done enough both sides. 'Was my Dadus a *gorjer*?'

Looking back, it was something amazing he'd not asked before.

'Why are you asking that, Chicken?'

He decided the bread was blackened right enough and went to pull it off the spike, but it was too hot and burned his fingers. He gasped with annoyance, shook his hand in the air, then put the fingers in his mouth.

That kept him quiet for a moment or two. Long enough.

'I had a fight with Zephyrus and his brothers . . .' he said.

'I know, I heard about it.' There isn't a thing can be done in a group of Travellers but the whole camp doesn't get to hear about it.

'Well it was 'cause they were a-calling me a half 'n' half.'

I knew'd that too, but it saddened me to hear him say it, for I could not bear he was getting into fights on my account.

I leaned forward to him, so's he knew I was serious. 'You listen to me, Lijah Smith,' I said. 'You are going to be as much a *Romani chal* as any *chavo* in this camp, in the whole district, in fact. Don't you let nobody ever tell you you're a half 'n' half. No one in the world has the right to call you that, for it ain't true.'

He paid attention to the toast, but I could tell he was pleased. I thought perhaps that was the end of our little talk but then he caught me out by saying, 'So who was my Dadus, then?'

'Your Dadus . . .' I said, as I took the cooled-off toast from him and picked up a blunt knife to scrape it into the saucepan, 'Well, you might ask . . .' I could see from the corner of my eye that he was watching me carefully.

*Tshk, tshk, tshk* went the knife against the toast and the tiny black crumbs fell into the water. 'Your Dadus was a Romany King, that's why we had to keep the love between us a big secret, as the whole of his kingdom would have fall'd apart if word of it had ever got out.'

I glanced at him. His eyes were big as teacups and dark as down-a-well. 'He had a *kingdom* . . .' he said.

'Aye, Chicken, he did. He came from the Kingdom of Russia, where the Russians live. He was just King of the Romany bit of it, mind, and as well as being a King he owned a thousand horses, and it was part of his job to bring the horses to this country and sell them, and that's how come he passed through Werrington one day, with the horses, and that's how come you were got. And he made me promise on my life never to tell a soul, for he was bound to go back to the Kingdom of Russia and marry some cold princess that he did not love, but he said he would remember me for ever.'

'And did he know you had a babby by him?'

I thought I could detect a note of not-quite-believing in his voice. *Tshk, tshk, tshk* went the knife against the toast.

'He did not, my poor child,' I said sombrely, 'for I had no way of getting word to him, nor will we ever have, for he is on the other side of the world being the King of Russia, but I know he thinks on us from time to time, when it's all snowy there, as we talked of the fine son we might have together one day. And I think in his heart he knows that son is out there somewhere and longs for him, for the cold princess will have got him nothing but girls.'

I had taken the crumbs from the toast and it was enough. There was only a crust left but I handed it to Lijah and said, 'Chew on't, if you like.'

He took the toast. 'So, are we rich then?' he said thoughtfully.

'Aye,' I said, stirring the tea we had made together. 'In our hearts, *amoro chavo*, you and me is richer than this whole camp put together.'

It was that very next day that I first set eyes on Adolphus Lee. I was with a group of the older women, and we had been out dukkering, which was mostly older women's business but as I am small and dark they let me along. I was what the *gorjers* expected, I suppose. I didn't like it much as it was a daft business and I wouldn't do it if there was anything else going. I'm not saying I couldn't see things when I looked at a person. Especially the young women. It was the young married women who wanted their fortunes told most as they were the ones most hungry to know if there was still something to look forward to. I looked at some of them and saw their whole lives before them. But I never told them what I saw. That would be demeaning to what I was able to do. I told them what they wanted to hear, which was quite a different thing altogether.

So me and the old 'uns was walking back through the camp when we passed a new group just joined up, and there was a big fella standing by a tin tub atop a tree stump. He was washing himself, passing the cloth up his forearms, and splashing water over himself. He was big in a not-handsome sort of way, to my eye, as if he had grow'd a bit wrong, clumsy-like. But a big fella is a useful thing in our sort of life and so we all gave him the eye as we passed, which is a thing none of us would have dared on our own, but as we were all together and the others were all old and well past the age of meaning it, it was sort of jesting with him.

And he seemed to take it in good part, for he looked up at us, a little bit smiling but only a bit, and straightened himself, flexing his arms as if to show off, and we all obliged him by giggling like girls. And then his gaze fell upon me.

He was not to know, at the time, that I already had a child who was a strapping lad, for I always looked younger than I was at that time, and I suppose I wasn't quite worn'd out with it yet.

And I stared right back at him, a thing I would never have done were I not with the old 'uns.

The way it went in those days, you saw someone you liked the look of and you did a bit of asking round. But it was up to the boy to go a-asking – wasn't seemly for the girl to do it. Anyway, I wasn't a girl no more and Adolphus wasn't hardly a boy, neither. I found out later that his family had been on at him to find a girl for years.

Anyroad, for all I thought my life was sorted at that time, I couldn't help myself from wondering about the big fella I see'd washing himself, and each evening when Dadus came back we would sit together and I would wait for him to broach the subject with me, for it would be my Dadus anyone spoke to first. But nothing happened, so I thought no more on't, and I didn't see the big fella again for a while, although I happened to walk past the spot where the new lot were pulled up perhaps one or two times more than was strictly necessary.

I found out, though, as you can always find out eventually as long as you are sly about it. His name was Adolphus Lee, of the Derbyshire Lees, who were well thought of as wagon makers. And they had settled for a bit so's Adolphus could finish his own *vardo* for he was right set on that before he took a wife. It was not really usual for a man from a family like that to make his own, but rumour had it he was so proud he would not accept help from even his own cousins. And proud he must have been, for it was something of a mystery as to why he was not wed yet. No one good enough for him, they said, which made him something of a challenge. As a result, every marriageable girl in the camp was finding an excuse to wander past and take a look at the fine catch who insisted on doing his own sawing and planing.

It takes a long time to build a *vardo* on your own, I thought, and most girls round here don't have the patience to hang around that long, for they're too scared of losing a chance elsewhere. Young people nowadays like things settled quick, to allow themselves more time for repenting, I s'pose.

But the other part of me knew it was foolish to even think on Adolphus Lee. They were quite a grand family, those Derbyshire Lees, and we may have been a grand family once too but now we were shrunken and what were we but a broke old man and a small boy and soiled goods between?

It was because I had no hopes in that direction made me bold. I was interested in Adolphus Lee and his *vardo* and felt I could show an interest without anyone thinking on't too much. And so it was, one spring morning, I found myself going past the edge of the camp where he was a-building.

The frame was already in place – he'd had help with that of course – but now he was on the smaller jobs and working alone. I had taken my Dadus along with me, although he was under the impression that he had taken me along with him. Lijah was off somewhere, being hectic.

Adolphus Lee looked up as we approached, nodded to Dadus, then bent his head back to his work. We stood and watched and it seemed he understood that we didn't want him to stop. But after a while, he did, pushed his hat up from his forehead and said to my Dadus, 'I'll be starting on the porch floor tomorrow, I reckon.'

My Dadus says, 'It's the sealing of it is the thing. Folk forget how a porch floor gets the rain when it slants in and they go rotten something easy.'

Adolphus nodded.

They carried on a bit more like this, then Dadus said, 'Well, we'll not keep you from your work, young man.'

'Aye.' He nodded. 'Good day to you.'

We turned, but not before he took the trouble to look at me and give me my own nod, separate from my Dadus's. And that was when I first got the idea I could have him if I wanted him.

This thought threw me somewhat, for up until then I thought I knew'd the whole shape and colour of my life to come. I wanted no husband, nor any more children, and had seen myself getting old and Dadus dying and it being just me and Lijah and him grow'd and taking care of us. But Dadus was slowing down fast now, and it was coming to me that we might be losing him sooner rather than later, and I had to start thinking on what would happen to me and Lijah then. And here was Adolphus Lee, in front of me, and I still didn't want no husband or children but I found myself a-thinking as we walked back to the camp, *I hope he's planning rails for the shelving*. It's the kind of thing a man forgets until a woman points it out to him, for ornaments and china need a rail to keep them in place, in case you ever have to move off sharpish and don't have time to stow them all.

And so it was that me and Dadus and sometimes Lijah got in the habit of visiting Adolphus Lee as he worked, once in a while, to see how the *vardo* was taking shape. And sometimes, when we got there, there would be young girls there with their brothers or fathers a-giggling and offering him tea, but I never saw him nod to one of them the way he nodded to me that first time we went.

And the fact that I had no hope of him helped me be cool, and not a-giggling like the other girls, and often I had Lijah round my feet anyhow. Adolphus was right good with Lijah. It was Lijah helped him plane the roof ribs out of ash. I was standing by them and heard him tell Lijah how the best flooring you could get was sailcloth like they used in sailing ships, and how you could paint it your own way with oil paints but that it was right expensive and a lot of work. Then, without looking up at me, he added, 'But then anything worth the having of is a lot of work, Lijah, I 'spect you know that now. I wouldn't value anything that came easy.'

That night, I could not sleep for thinking of Adolphus Lee.

Then, I did not go there for a while, because of the unfortunate thing that happened.

I was on an errand to find dandelion roots. There was a long hedgerow ran along the camp that was thick with them, but they had mostly been picked, so one day, early evening, I found myself walking a long way along it and thinking how it was nice to be a bit away from the camp for a while. So I decided to go a bit further. And then I came across them.

I saw her face but not his, as he was atop her and had his back to me. I recognised them as a man and wife from our camp. I don't think she saw me as she had her eyes closed and was holding his hair in her two fists. Her head was thrown back, her bare knees raised either side of him. *The mud, the dirt of it* . . . Horrible noises, they were making, both of them, like animals. And I turned and fled back to the camp full of disgust trying to shake the sight and sound of it from my head. And that night I could not sleep again for thinking, *that is what he will expect of you, you fool. That's what being married is*.

The next day, Lijah comes a-running up and says, 'Shall we go and see Mr Lee's wagon, Dei?' and I replied, 'You go if you like. I'm going to be too busy for a while.'

I knew this would be repeated, and I knew he'd get the message right enough.

I thought I would see no more of Adolphus Lee, and was getting used to the idea, when he turned up at our *vardo* about a fortnight later to speak to my father. He was walking into the village, he said, and was going to buy some pitch for the porch floor, which was finished, and which sort did he think he should get?

Well, he was making himself pretty obvious, but I was resolved by then.

It didn't help when Dadus said. 'Go to the blacksmith at the end of the village, not the first one, he's a *bafedo mush*. I've done business with the other and he's *kushti*. Take our Lemmy, he'll remember her.'

To this day, I'll never know if my Dadus knew what he was doing. He was getting on a bit by then, but even a man who's going a bit strange in his head knows what he's doing when he tells another man it's all right to walk his daughter down the lane.

Well, we had to take Lijah with us, otherwise there would have been an almighty scandal, but of course we were only just beyond the camp when Lijah ran on ahead and had soon disappeared round several corners, and there was a mighty silence between us then as it was the first time we had been alone together.

Eventually, we talked a bit about the *vardo*, and he said, 'Of course, you'll see when you come next, as I've done quite a lot since you last came by.' That was a bit pointed, and led to a little more silence between us.

I thought to myself as we walked, I must be honest with this man, for he deserves a pretty young girl who will be a full wife to him and give him a dozen children. There is score of them at least back in that camp who would be happy to do it. I knew that I could not allow him to have any hopes of me, but in truth it broke my heart, for I knew then he would leave off thinking of me and it had been a nice feeling, the past few weeks; to be a-walking round thinking on someone else who was maybe thinking on me. There were plenty of girls waiting for him. Word had got round the camp about our visits to him and I'd seen the way they looked at me and thought me fortunate to have his attentions when I already had another man's child like a millstone around my neck. But it was not fair on the man to lead him a dance, so as we walked along that lane, I said to him, casual like, 'I do feel right sorry for Delilah with those sixteen children round her neck and it makes me more than ever certain that one of them is enough for me.' I was talking of a Heron woman we both knew of who was in the habit of having twins and had three sets of them as well as a load of others. She was something famous in that camp, for not only had she had so many, they had all stayed alive.

There was yet more silence between us for a few paces after that, and in that silence I thought I could hear the heavy tread of his boots on the path a little heavier, for you know how it is when a quietness gives one sound a certain weight.

I knew he would not speak, for I could sense he was a little flummoxed. So, I continued. 'Not that I am saying I do not love my Lijah, he is everything to me, for all the trouble that he causes. He is all the man I shall ever be in need of.' All I needed from Adolphus was one sign or word to say that he had understood me, but he refused to be provoked.

I saw there was nothing for it but plain speaking, for I could not conclude this walk until I was certain I had released him from any obligation to me. He would be on my conscience else. 'Which is why I have always thought it best not to marry.'

At this, as if to prevent further declarations, he burst out, 'But a child is not the same as a husband, Clementina!'

I kept looking straight ahead as we walked, for I knew he would be bright red in the face and be trying not to be, and I thought of how my Lijah always goes red at certain times as well, and I ached inside at the thought of losing Adolphus Lee and all the goodness inside him. He could be Lijah's father, I thought. Why should he not be? *And what when he asks of you what a husband always asks of his wife?*

'Aye, you be right there,' I said bitterly. 'A husband asks for a certain thing a child would not, and a child grows up and leaves you and stops asking but a husband is always there and always asking.' I could not have been more plain if I had stopped in the middle of the path, taken up a stick and drawn a picture in the dirt.

Again a silence between us and again the tramping of his boots. Even the birds seemed to have stopped singing in honour of the business being decided between Clementina Smith and Adolphus Lee.

'What if you were to have a husband who never asked?'

There was no silence then, for I could not hold back from letting out a little, scornful yelp. 'No such man exists upon this earth. Any girl will tell you that.'

And at that Adolphus Lee stopped dead in the path. And I had to stop too, a few paces on, but I could not bring myself to turn and look at him, for I was allowing love for him to creep into my heart and it was hurting me. It was hurting like the pain you get in your side when you have been running too fast, and I even pressed one hand against my ribcage to prevent it, breathing hard. I did not want him to see my face. He would guess at it.

He spoke to my back. 'He does, Clementina.' Then his voice became a whisper. 'I swear, he does.'

It was too much for me. I could not stand that happiness was being offered to me, for I was so used to the lack of it. Without looking back, I gathered my skirts and ran off, calling out for Lijah.

That evening, the folk in the next *vardo* called us over as they had some boiled bacon. Way it was back then, all us Smiths tended to pull up together, as if we were our own a-little-bit-separate camp. We was close to the Herons but not so much to the Lees and the Boswells as to be honest I think they thought not-so-much of us. Sabina Smith had said would I do the leeks to go-with, and of course I said yes, so I had a pile of leek rings in a great skillet, the green mixed in with the white, all soft and slippery with butter, and I took them over, and everyone was in a right good mood. Things had not been so good lately but here we all were with some boiled bacon and leeks and fried bread to go with, and soon the men were full as anything and the children were running round.

This was the best bit of life back then, when the men and children were happy and fed, and you got to sit down and light a clay pipe with the other women knowing that just for a few moments nobody expected you to do anything.

Sabina Smith and myself were quite close at that time and we had shared a pipe of an evening often enough. She piled up the tin plates and gave them to her three girls to take down to the stream and settled herself down on a tree stump with her skirts spread around her.

I squatted next to her, poking the fire with a stick.

Sabina nodded after her girls. 'Jeppy's a woman now, just this morning.'

All at once, I felt I could not bear Sabina, or her Jeppy, and I thought how I would like to take the hot stick and poke it in her ear.

'Aye?' I said.

'When it happened to me, my mother gave me a slap, and when I said why did you hit me she said, you're a woman now and you've got to get used to what a woman's life is like.'

Sabina was like this, always wanting to talk about what it was like being a woman.

She must've expected me to join in with some such story but I wasn't in the mood to talk about things like that and I thought why is it some people need to be a-talking all the time, and what is it with us folk? Here's Sabina telling me her secrets, and Jeppy's into the bargain, and she's telling me like no one else is listening, but she knows that anything said will be known by all the women in the camp tomorrow, as that's the way it is.

I suddenly felt how I was not-liking our sort of life so much. Do *gorjer* women do this, I thought? Probably not, as they have a wall and some air and then another wall between them. And I fell to thinking how there might be times when it was nice to have walls to shut out other people.

I had not often thought like this before and it was strange I should think such thoughts that evening, with boiled bacon inside me. The men happy and fiddling, dinner done – this was usually the best of it. And I felt sad thinking how nothing was right for me at that moment. All I wanted was to be away from it all, and Sabina and her gossiping. I wanted to be on my own.

It was a bad thing in our life, to want to be on your own, for we had only got along by helping each other – and fighting each other as well, if the moment came. But to want to be away from other people, well that was thought of as something not right. And I thought wistful-like of Adolphus and how often he was working alone on his *vardo*.

And it came to me. The *vardo* was an excuse. He could have married years ago – many a man does before he has his own wagon. He hadn't married because he didn't want to be married, no more than I did.

Sabina's sister Evadina joined us and that got me off the hook a bit. She had pickled some nasturtiums but I hadn't had them with the bacon as I like them best in a sauce.

It rained overnight. The next day, I gathered my skirts in both hands and picked my way clear of the puddles and walked to the far side of the camp, right through it rather than round it, so as many people as liked could see which way I was going.

Adolphus Lee had pulled the covers from his *vardo* and hung them from a bit of rope strung between two trees. He had a fire lit. He glanced at me as I approached but I couldn't tell if his look meant anything.

'Did the damp get in, then?' I asked him, nodding at the covers.

'No, they held.'

As he said it, one of the ropes loosed from where he had tied it and one of the covers slipped with a sighing noise to the ground. Together, we went over and lifted it, one side each.

'This one's dry already,' I said. 'We might as well fold it.'

We held a side each, arms wide, and walked together.

When it was folded, Adolphus turned to the *vardo* and said, 'I've to decide on the windows.'

'I like sash,' I said.

I saw him hesitate. Sash windows are a wee bit heavier than

other sorts and every ounce counts when you're going uphill. He was the kind of man to weigh such a thing.

He looked at me. 'Sash it is, then,' he said.

And things between us were agreed.


We had twelve years together, myself and Adolphus Lee. He was as good as a father to Lijah, as good as my Dadus had been before he came along.

Dadus passed away during that time, and I don't know how I would've managed that without Adolphus or what would have become of me and Lijah. Dadus had been a broken fella ever since we lost Dei but it still hurt me terrible when he went. I think perhaps I am not so good at the letting-go of people.

I let go of my Adolphus easiest of all. I think the truth was, he always loved me more than I loved him, and that gave me a nice safe feeling, and he bequeathed that to me after he was gone. He clutched his chest one evening and went to bed early.

But I am getting things out of order. I said yes to Adolphus Lee, and in the twelve years we were together he never gave me cause to regret it. Twelve years – how many nights is that? He kept his promise for every one. We never talked about it. You didn't talk about things back then. Nowadays, people go on about it all the time, as if it's the only thing that matters. That side of life is over-thought-of, in my opinion. People talk as if it is all, and it is not.

# CHAPTER 5

Let me tell you a small story about dead people. Us Travelling folk do not like to talk about them much. Some people think that a dead person cannot help but think ill of the living and that is how a ghost is always evil. Some think it is bad luck even to say someone's name once they're dead. But I have not altogether agreed with that. I like to think on the dead.

There would be many of our type who would never have taken up the vicar's offer of the cottage in the graveyard at Werrington. There would be many who would rather have slept in a bed of nettles. But I am thinking that it is one thing to be prejudiced against the dead for a good reason, a-Travelling, and another when you are settled and a dead person is not such a problem. Let the *gorjers* have their *mulladipovs*, with their holes in the ground full of ghosts, good and bad. Is that any worse than to be a soul a-wandering all the time?

You can tell I am a little unusual for my type and of course I did end up in a house by the Corporation Depot, but let me tell you there are plenty of worse places to end.

Lijah was born at a time when little children died often. Rich or poor, Traveller or *gorjer*, made no difference. If there was sickness in a village it could come a-knocking any time. Of course, it stood a better chance of getting in if you were poor.

That whole time I was carrying Lijah and we were living in the cottage in the graveyard, we would see them, the secret burials. They always happened at night. We would hear the creak of the cemetery gate, the turning of the handcart wheels on the gravel path. We would go to the door to watch. Past our cottage they would come, the vicar leading, praying as he came. Behind him would be a poor family, sobbing and sobbing, pushing the handcart with a little dead child wrapped in cloth and lying on it.

They were the worst off of the parish, folk who could not afford a plot or a gravestone of their own. They must have begged the vicar to put their little one in Holy Ground and he had found a way to do it. Him and his sexton together, they opened up a grave, in the dark, and put the little child on top and closed it up again. They opened up the graves in no particular order, as far as I could see, whoever they belonged to. They just worked their way along the rows.

After the first time we saw it happen, the vicar came over to us afterwards and gave us a coin not to say a word to anyone. We took the coin, of course, but it upset my Dadus. When they were gone and we were back inside, he said, didn't they realise that if they kept opening up the ground then the *mullas*, the ghosts, would be getting up and walking abroad? He thought it wasn't good for me to see it in my condition. My unborn child would be cursed.

But the next time we heard the creak of the gate and the turn of the wheels on the gravel, we still went to the door to watch, peering in the dark. I know it sounds peculiar, but I found something comforting in it. I thought it was good that these poor little children should not be put in the cold earth by themselves but should rest in the arms of someone, even if it was a stranger. And maybe it was nice for the folk already in their graves, lying there alone for all eternity, to be joined by a little girl or boy who would keep them company. I thought it a nice thing.

I can't rightly think what it was made me think of that story. I was about to start telling you of her.

We were picking sour cherries. It was fine work. It was a huge estate we were on, owned by a farmer who went by the name of Childer. He always used Travellers to pick his cherries so we saw the same folk year in year out and whole families would go out together. You would go and take your basket from the shed with a strap to put over and then when it was filled you would go and get it weighed. Some people would complain about the cherry picking, about what hot work it was and how the strap across your shoulders would chafe and your hip would ache once the basket started getting full. But I liked it. I liked the freshness of it. I liked the staining of the fingers and the testing of a fruit, a small tug to see if it was ripe enough. Even the darkest ones were not ready sometimes and resisted, and I liked the way that everyone knew to leave a not-ready fruit undamaged so that in a day or two someone else would get the benefit of it.

And, of course, there was no danger that sour cherries would get eaten up the way sometimes happened with apples or strawberries. It would be a man and a half ate more than a fistful of sour cherries. The most I ever managed was one, at dawn. The picking started at first light and a single sour cherry would always wake me up. You could eat a box of lemons easier.

Sour cherries. That is how came she came into our lives.

Rose Childer. She was the farmer's stepdaughter. I found out she was only a stepdaughter later on, of course. At the time, all we knew'd is that every Friday evening the farmer's daughter came around the wagons collecting the rent. She did it then as we had all just been paid. She had a leather bag slung over her shoulder, and everyone knew this big farmer's girl as she had bright red hair like a cloud about her head. She tied it back in a velvet ribbon, but it was that soft, frizzing sort of hair that would not stay tied and floated round her.

We was all right nice to her, of course. We knew'd which side our bread was buttered. She would come along of a summer evening and go from *vardo* to *vardo* and it was always the women who would deal with her, straightening from their fires and wiping their hands on their aprons. 'Why it's young Miss Rose . . .' they would say with great, beamy smiles. 'Will you stop and have a cup of tea with us?'

Mostly she would say, 'Thank you kindly, but no, I must get round,' or some such, but once in a while someone would persuade her to stop and then out would come the china teacup which would only be given to a *gorjer* guest and the children would come and stand around with fingers in their mouths. Once, I even saw her pull a Boswell boy onto her lap and tickle him until he ran off. And most of the other women fell for it right enough and said, 'That farmer's daughter is decent enough for a *gorjer* girl.' As if they were forgetting we were all so nice to her because we wanted to stay the right side of Childer.

The men would always make themselves scarce, of course. No man who ever stared at a *gorjer* girl would find himself forgiven by his wife, so they took their hungry looks off elsewhere and it was us women dealt with young Miss Rose. She wasn't so young, in fact. She must have been past twenty and should have been long wed, in my opinion. She wore white blouses with lots of pleats in them that blossomed round her. Her skirts were wide too. The ribbons in her hair were always smart looking but she had great big open boots, farm girl's boots, fit for striding round a *gipsy* camp.

I have always had dainty little feet myself and whenever I could

I made a show of them in pointy lace-ups, even if the weather was not quite fit for it.

My Lijah was gifted at many things but fruit picking was not one of them. He was magical with the horses, mind, and made a tidy living out of the buying and fixing and selling of them when he was older. And he could fashion anything out of wood or metal. He had not been with Adolphus and myself for the first part of the summer as he had been down at Stow. Then he joined us back up at the Fens and set to making pegs and cutting boards. He had an idea to carve patterns around the edges of the boards as he said it was a thing a *gorjer* housewife used several times a day in her kitchen and a nice-looking one would fly out of a hawker's basket. I said to him it was no use if he was going to be a pack-man that summer as they would be too heavy to carry in any number. And he said how he was a planning on getting hold of a knife-grinding barrow and would build a special basket on the side to keep the boards in and would sell the boards when he'd sharpened the knives. I could tell he was pleased with the poetry in this.

Anyroad, it was because of his plans to sell the cutting boards that he was by the *vardo* that evening. He had come back with some blocks of wood a little earlier and set them down by the step. I had taken the horse from him and said I would rub it down. We had a nice little bay at that time, quiet and cobbish, with a fine amount of feather. I was fond of it. We called him Kit.

I had taken Kit over to the shade beneath the trees for tethering, watered him and stroked his nose. I liked to feel the bone beneath. I was walking back towards the *vardo* with the bucket, when I heard voices.

As I came around the front, they fell silent. She was standing in front of him, looking down. The sun was behind her. He was looking up, and he had a look on his face that I had never seen before. He was holding a knife in one hand and a block of wood in the other.

I waited for them both to start at the sight of me, but instead, the farmer's daughter looked at me calmly, gave a half-smile, then reached into her leather bag and got out her pencil and notebook.

Lijah went back to his carving.

I gave her the money and finished with the bucket and did a few other things and then I came and tended the fire. Miss Rose moved on to the next *vardo*. Lijah was intent on his cutting board.

I took an iron and turned the logs. 'You might've turned this before,' I said. 'We'll need it high if we're to eat before nightfall.'

He did not look at me, just carried on, which was a thing he commonly did as a boy and young man and it always made me mad as anything.

'That's if you can bring yourself to think of anything as ordinary as supper.' I said, rising.

After we'd ate that evening, Adolphus said how he was going to lie down a bit. He'd been doing that a lot lately, feeling slow and poorly of an evening. His bigness had turned to fatness and he often looked bad around the stomach, as if the insides of him was bursting to get out and his skin was tight with it. I was a little worried about him, for to my mind he was not yet old enough to be getting slow and pained in that way.

Lijah rose as well and said, 'I'm off to take Kit into town, Dei.'

Well, that was like a red rag to a bull. I knew'd what he was up to. All the young lads had taken to it recently, visiting the public houses in the town a few miles off where they weren't known and coming back all hours even when most of them had to be up before sunrise. Lijah was the worst of it, for a hawker keeps his own hours. I could not stand the thought that he liked a drink from time to time. Neither my Dadus or my Adolphus ever drank and I knew'd not how it had begun, this habit of his.

'That horse has done enough work for one day and you've enough to keep you busy round here,' I said sharply.

He turned and snarled, 'Leave it, Dei!' before snatching his coat and hat from the peg and striding off.

I was ashamed that he should talk to me like that in front of Adolphus.

Adolphus did his best. 'Shall I go after him?' he asked, knowing what I would say.

'You're not well,' I snapped, and turned away, and then felt bad that I had been unpleasant to Adolphus only on account of Lijah being unpleasant to me.

I heard him come back later. He was bumping around beneath the *vardo*, where he always slept in summer. It was black as black outside, so I knew'd it was late. Once, he had come back so lathered he had forgot to tether Kit but that horse never wandered off. It had more sense than the lot of us. I turned beneath the eider, enough to make the *vardo*'s boards creak so Lijah below would hear me and know I was awake. Next to me, Adolphus was breathing softly.

In the morning, at first light, I was woked up by Lijah whistling to himself. By the time I had got down from the wagon, he had blow'd on the embers of the fire and got it flaring up and was heating the kettle. He grinned at me and clapped his hands together. 'I reckon you'd like a cup of tea before you're off to strip another of those cherry trees, wouldn't you, Dei?'

Perhaps he isn't such a bad lad after all, I thought to myself.

He stayed cheerful all the rest of that month. And though he went off to town drinking a lot he was never sore and silent in the mornings like he had been before. He made a whole pile of cutting boards and they were stacking up but he said he had a few other things to be getting on with before he hired the knife-grinding barrow. We started to talk about where we should move on to once the harvest was done. In years before, we had stuck around that site for a while and just earned the rent by other means, but some of us weren't so sure that Childer would be on for letting us do that again, so the talk was all of whether we could persuade him round or not.

That was how come Delender Lee said to me one day by the stream, in front of a whole bunch of other women, 'Course, Clementina, what we need is for your Lijah to put in a good word for us in high places and we'll all be fine, won't we?'

I looked at her. One of the other women muttered, 'Low places, more like . . .' and there was a whole load of smirking and looking down went on.

That was the worst of it. If they had all burst out laughing out loud I could have laughed too and pretended I knew all about it. But the fact that they looked down and just glanced at each other meant not only did they know, they knew that I didn't.

I gathered up my wet things and threw them into the tub even though I was only halfway through. I picked up the tub and left without a word. I suppose I should have just ignored it but I couldn't carry on washing clothes with them after that. I felt their gazes on my back, and their exchanged looks as I climbed back up the rise to walk back to the camp, and as I crossed the field I had to bite my lip to stop my eyes watering with shame.

I knew I had to tackle Lijah. For what sort of mother would I have been if I had just ignored it and let him make himself a laughing stock? I must do it right away, I thought, before I lose my nerve.

I dumped the tub down behind the *vardo* and found him where I knew'd he'd be, a-sitting on the step. Afterwards I thought, he knew before I spoke to him what it was about on account of how he didn't greet me. He had probably been expecting it.

I stood over him for a moment, but he did not look up. Instead, he continued cutting at a new block, and I stupidly watched the pile of shavings grow between his feet, all the while waiting for him to give me my cue. And all the while I felt my blood boiling up as I thought of how the whole camp knew more about my son than I did. There he sat on that step, the person who'd been everything to me these last twenty years, even though it killed my Dei and kept us moving and gave me more trouble than a dozen other children could have done. And I had poured everything into him. Everything he was; his neat shirts that I stitched, his fancy waistcoat – the kiss-curl on his forehead. It was all me. I thought I would burst with it, with him not realising.

Eventually, he knew'd I would stand there all day unless he spoke first. Do you know what he said?

'Say your piece, Dei.'

That was it. He didn't even look up. *Get it over with, makes no difference to me.*

So I let him have it straight. 'I don't know what you think there is to be so not-worried about,' I said, and I was surprised at how calm my voice sounded. 'It may not bother you to have the whole camp talking about us behind our backs but it bothers me and I think you might do a bit of respecting of that. You've always gone your own way. You've always done whatever you've wanted to do without so much as a thought for me or Adolphus. I suppose I should've got used to it after all this time . . .' He stopped shaving the block, although he still did not look up.

'Dei . . .' he said, but I was under way by then.

'Ever since you was a boy you've done exactly as you please with never one thought for what folk might say. You've larked about and disrespected, never mind the drinking you've been doing recently. But in all my born years, with everything that's happened to us, I never, *never* thought that you would sink so low as to be seen mooning over a *gorjer* girl. I would have thought you'd have more pride than that.'

That stung him. He looked up then. His eyes narrowed. 'You can talk, can't you?'

I gasped out loud. 'Don't you dare bring that up. That's years ago. I've told you, you ain't no half 'n' half, whatever they say, don't you dare say that to me.' He must have seen the fierce look on my face for he dropped his gaze again. There was a silence between us. *He's slipping away from me*, I thought, full of misery, *my only child*.

Then he said, 'I likes the way her hair looks in the sun, Dei.'

That was it? For that, he was prepared to tear everything apart, to leave me and lose his work and be always looked down upon by all the people around us and have his children sniggered at? *Rose*. A farmer's daughter, with her cloud of hair and her broad hips and shoulders and that great body of hers that said, look how large and soft I am – and what more did any man want? And suddenly I thought of my poor, tiny little Dei, as small as a bird, who was broke so easily on the tread-wheel all those years ago, snapped like a twig, and I thought that big, soft Rose looks at me and she thinks I'm like a little bird as well, but I've got news for her. I'm tougher than my Dei was. I won't break nearly so easy.

*I likes the way her hair looks in the sun.*

It doesn't matter how much you love a child. It counts for nothing, not when he gets grow'd, and sees a girl's hair in the sun.


I was sore after our argument, right enough, but we had argued plenty before and the thing about me and Lijah is we fought like anything but then we cleared the air and the next day we just got on with it. Adolphus always found that hard to understand. He would hear us a-shouting at each other and off he would go on some errand or other, shaking his head. Then he would come back and Lijah and I would be chatting all peaceable, and he would shake his head again. I think he felt a bit left out, in truth, for he and I never shared a cross word in the whole twelve years we were together.

Lijah had gone off somewhere after we spoke and was not back before we went to bed but I didn't think on't and the next day I got up at first light as usual and stepped down. I took the clods off the fire and blew on it, and smoked it up into life. I put the tripod over and hung the kettle, which I had filled the night before, and only then did I turn around to stir Lijah.

The ground was damp with dew. The early morning air had that fine freshness that summer mornings have, when you know it will be hot later so you don't mind the little chill of it. Just breathing that air was like quenching a thirst. A thrush was hopping in the grass. As I turned it took fright, fled.

Lijah wasn't there.

That was it. I knew it. He'd gone for good. His blanket roll was gone too, and his pack that he normally put his head on and I didn't need to go round to the back to know his box of small tools and his blocks would be gone too.

I drew breath, great large gulps of that fresh, dew-laden air. Then I clamped my hand over my mouth to stop myself from crying out.


It was three months before I got word of them. They had married in Cambridge, in a church. Apparently, she had said how if she was giving up her family and everything then the least he could do was wed her proper, so they did it just like a pair of *gorjers* with a vicar and everything.

I only heard all this because once they were settled in Cambridge, Lijah got to know the local hostelries, of course, and a man he drank with there was a Heron, a nephew of Manabel Heron, who was married to a fella in our camp. It wasn't Lijah sent word to me or anything. I found out just like anyone might find out when word gets round about what so-and-so is up to, and of course the whole of our camp was agog with the news that Lijah Smith had run off with the farmer's daughter. They were talking about that one for months. Yes, you can imagine how much I enjoyed walking around the camp after word of that got out.

Tale was, after Rose Childer's father had found out she was consorting with *gipsies*, he horse-whipped her and locked her in her room, but she got out and shinnied down the drainpipe and came to Lijah in the night. I can't rightly credit it, as I can't see her shinnying down anything myself but that was how the story went. In the morning, her father and her brothers went after them on horseback but they couldn't find them, which was a good thing for my Lijah.

I don't know how long after that they was married. But this nephew of Manabel's said Lijah told him that none of her family showed up, even though she sent word of the where and the when, hoping they might forgive her as she was getting properly wed in a church an' all. Not one of them showed, but the church bells was rang as they came out, and later we found out her father had paid for them to be rung, though he would not show his face.

No one sent word to me, of the where, and the when. No one asked for my forgiveness. Perhaps they thought there was no need.

Anyroad, about ten years later, Rose said to me how it would've been better if one of those church bells had fallen off and killed her stone dead, such a life she had with Lijah.

It was later that same summer that I lost my Adolphus. And by the time it had happened I had sort of thought it was coming soon on account of how he was getting short of breath all the time and had pains in his chest a lot.

There was nothing I could do for him when he was poorly, but there was something I could do once he was gone. No one was ever going to pull that fine *vardo* of ours but him. I had promised him that much, and it went up in smoke with him. I could've sold it for a pretty penny, and nobody would have held it against me on account of how I was left with no one and would have to be looked after by the camp and have people pretending they respected me when they pitied me, in fact. But it had to go with him, his *vardo*.

He had planed and painted every inch himself. Even the sailcloth flooring with the swirls that meant something to us alone but no one else could ever read them. Unusual it was, with its sash windows. I saw a few men shake their heads with sorrow as they piled the branches on.

I had been into town the day before and gone to the dressmakers, and do you know what? I had to buy a child's mourning dress. They said they had nothing small enough for me and it would have to be made to order and of course there was no time for that so I bought a child's dress and did a few adjustments. It had pleats down the front. At the neck, I wore a broach, and Manabel Heron said to me that when I walked back in the camp they thought a fine lady had come to visit.

I bought some pointy lace-up boots, as well, but I did not wear those in the camp as I did not want to ruin them. They were for my journey. Those, and the new carpet-bag I bought for my things, the buying of them took most of what I had kept by.

I had nothing after that: no son, no husband, no *vardo* to live in and no way of living in it even if I had. When I burned Adolphus I burned up my whole life until that moment, all the miles I'd Travelled and everything that went with it. Lijah had taken Kit with him when he went. I had given my china to Manabel and sold my few bits of jewellery to buy my dress and boots and bag. There was only just enough left over to pay someone to take me down to Cambridge.

# PART 2

## 1877–1901

# Rose

# CHAPTER 6

My name is Rose Smith and I was born on Paradise Street, in East Cambridge. I wasn't a Smith when I was born, of course. I was Rose Blumson. My mother was Emmeline Blumson, laundry maid, and my father was nowhere in sight.

I became a Smith when I married my husband, Elijah Smith, who I met when he came fruit picking at the orchards that belonged to my stepfather. That was later, of course.

East Cambridge. The Garden of Eden, they called it. Lots of those streets south of Maids Causeway had their own allotments back then, and the grocers and fruiterers had shops and warehouses nearby. Fruit 'n' veg was big in that district. The traders round there supplied the colleges and all the posh folk. That was how that area got its name.

The houses on Paradise Street didn't have anything fancy out back like allotments, just a yard and a privvy. Paradise was south of Fitzroy Street, one of the new terraces that they built not long before I was born, on account of all the railway workers coming to town. The houses were neat enough but they hadn't got the roads or pavements sorted out and when I was a baby my mother had to take me to lodgings on Prospect Row, on account of the flooding and the sewerage problem. Great lumps of it would float down the road, apparently. We had a spell on Adam and Eve Street, then back to Paradise.

My mother called me Rose because I was born in the Garden of Eden. She might as well have called me Carrot, or Swede, to be perfectly honest, but as a child I liked to tell myself that I was born beautiful and perfect, like a flower in a garden. My mother was a simple woman, loving but simple. She was sixteen years old when she had me, and unwed. It's a common enough story – so common, in fact, that I was inclined to embroider it when I was little. She was a college laundry maid and I used to have lots of fancy thoughts about how my father was probably a lord or something. The young gentlemen at the colleges thought nothing of getting a handful of bastards along with their learning, after all. There's plenty a child runs along the poor, narrow backstreets of East Cambridge with blue blood in its veins. Perhaps my father had a great mind to go with his great fortune, I used to think, and I would one day come across him on Jesus Lane with a book in his hand and a frown upon his brow. I imagined him as a noble young man, with a head of fair curls. Maybe, one day, he would be out punting on the Cam and I would fall in from the bank and he would rescue me, and after one look at my face he would embrace me as his own dear child. I would never have to turn a mangle handle again.

I nagged my mother terribly to know who my father was and my ideas were so fancy that I daresay she thought she had better disabuse me as soon as I was old enough to believe her. When I was about six or seven, she took me by the hand and marched me round the corner to Fitzroy Street, where there was a whole load of big shops – a fishmonger's, and the shellfish shop, and a grocer's by the name of Rawson's. The Rawsons were a significant family round our way, owning quite a few places and renting out allotments in return for produce.

We stood across the road, my mother and I, holding hands. It was a busy morning and there was a lot of pony and cart traffic going to and fro but we could see Rawson's well enough. Boxes were stacked up high upon the slope outside. They had just had in a load of new cabbages, the pretty ones with dark, crumply leaves, and they had been arranged nicely in the boxes so they blossomed out, as if begging you to buy them. Apples gleamed in piles on the other side. I can still picture it. It was riches to me, then.

Through the window I could see Mr Rawson, a large fella with a belly to match, a drooping moustache and no hair on his head. He was patting butter on a slab. One of his sons was helping out behind the counter, holding a fold of blue paper and flipping it over to make a bag.

'That's your father. So, are you happy now?' my mother said.

'What, the young fella?' I said, a little confused, as he was married not the week before and we had all gone out onto the street to see him bring his wife back on the cart belonging to the Orchard Tavern pulled by two beautiful greys.

'No,' she said, 'not him, the old fella. Mr George Rawson. He got me with you and hasn't spoken to me since, nor will he ever. And if you were to go in there right now and call him Dad, he'd chase you out of his shop with a big stick. But I reckon most folk round here know it, and you should know it too.'

Well, this was something large to squeeze into my small head. George Rawson, my father? But he was big and fat, with four grown-up sons, and his wife still living. And they all had houses in the streets round ours and we must pass one or other of them in the street every day, although we had no need to go in their shop as there was a little fruiterers just at the end of Paradise owned by a man called Empers.

When you're that age you just accept what you're told, and although in truth I was mightily disappointed that my father was not a lord with a noble brain, I can't remember feeling much about it except just an oddness in my stomach if I saw one of the Rawson family around.

You could say that fruit and vegetables played an overly significant part in my early days. Apples, potatoes, cherries and the like. That was how I ended up with a stepfather.

When I was ten years old, my mother stopped being a laundry maid and got a job helping out at the shop at the end of our road. It was owned by our neighbours, Lilly and Samuel Empers, who became like my aunt and uncle. After she went to work for them, my mother and Lilly Empers got as thick as thieves.

Lilly had worked the shop-front all her life but she was some-what older than my mother and had an inflammation of the spine that meant she could not stand for long. So, when their shop expanded and business increased, they asked my mother to give up her laundering and help them out. One of their regular suppliers was a farmer named Childer, who had his farm up near Cottenham, on Smythey Fen. River Farm, it was called, on account of the closeness of the Old West, part of the Great Ouse. Muddy river, the Ouse.

Farmer Childer must have come into the shop when I was there, as I helped out often enough, every day after school, but I don't recall being introduced to him. I can't help feeling that if I'd only seen him, I might have also seen through him, in the way that chil-dren can. I might have been able to warn my mother not to marry him. But perhaps that is no more than wishful fancy on my part.

In truth, what can a ten-year-old girl do with her life? What power has she? None, I soon discovered. You are no more than chaff.

No, I do not remember meeting Farmer Childer in the shop, nor do I recall being told when he first took an interest in my mother. The first I knew of it was when my mother went away for one night and I stayed with Aunt Lilly, and Aunt Lilly said when my mother returned, she might have some news for me.

She had news all right. She was married. I had a father. He was a Fenman, an important farmer, she said, and we were going to live together on his farm. Oh, and I had a set of new brothers into the bargain.

She told me this in the shop, as I sat on the stool, eating the sugar twist she had brought back for me as a gift. Her eyes were shining as she knelt before me and looked up at me, hopefully.

'Rose,' she said, 'Guess what I had for breakfast this morning?'

I sucked on the twist, staring down at her.

'Toast and chocolate.'

Later that day, I overheard a conversation between my mother and Aunt Lilly. Aunt Lilly was saying, 'Are you sure you want to take her? Are you sure he doesn't mind?'

'Lilly, no, I said, didn't I?'

'Well I just wanted to say again, just so's you knew.'

They were in the back of the shop. I was behind the counter, stacking the weights in the right order next to the scales. We were due to close soon. There was a thick curtain across the doorway that led through to the back: not thick enough, mind. They were trying not to be heard, but only in that half-hearted way that adults do when they think a child won't understand anyway.

'Part of why I'm doing this is to get her out of East Cambridge.'

'It's not that bad.'

'It is, Lilly, and you know it. At least there's no soap works on the Fens. You know my Rose's chest has always been bad.'

'Well, it was good enough for you, wasn't it?' I could tell by Aunt Lilly's voice she getting stiff and upright in the way she sometimes did.

My mother lowered her voice. 'It wasn't, Lilly, you know it wasn't. I was near taken for the Spinning House. And my Rose, who knows but she might end up like I did.'

'Emmeline!'

'Well, I'm sorry but it's true. Facts is facts. I don't want Rose being like me when she's grown. I want to see her a proper married missus, with a husband to look after her.'

I remember the day we left East Cambridge. That I do remember. A young man came to fetch us on a cart, and my mother said he was one of my new brothers, Horace. I took one look at Horace and gathered he was none too happy about the arrangement either but my mother seemed oblivious to any of it, loading up our few things and cheeping like a canary.

The neighbours gathered round. People who had scarcely been on nodding terms with us helped my mother with her trunk and hugged her and wished her luck.

Mrs Chadwell from number eleven came up to me and bent to give me an embrace. 'Now, Rose,' she whispered in my ear. 'This is your mother's big chance in life so you be a good girl and don't go messing it up. You're very lucky that a man like that is prepared to take you on, all things considered.' I understood her right enough. Funny, but I never felt like a bastard until my mother married.

Farmer Childer was a deal older than my mother. He had three sons. The first was the grown-up Horace whose coldness had a very simple history, I soon discovered. His mother had died in childbirth and he had known nothing but his father as a boy. The next two were William and Henry, by the farmer's second wife, Agnes. She had died of the Fen ague not six months before the farmer met my mother.

At least William and Henry had been raised by a mother. William was a soft, pale thing, who wore his grief like a child who is playing ghosties wears a bed-sheet. It covered the whole of him. Henry was a terror, for ever neglecting his farm duties and running off. They were both older than me and had finished their schooling and worked all their daylight hours on the farm. Three sons meant no hired help for Farmer Childer, except when a harvest was due in. But he still needed a wife for keeping house and book-reckoning.

The fact that Farmer Childer had got through two wives already was a disadvantage when it came to finding himself another in the immediate locality – and he needed another in a hurry. Being an unsociable sort of man, I don't think Farmer Childer came across women in his daily business. And anyway, his needs were quite specific. Jobs around the farm were already allocated. He didn't want a woman who was going to march in and run things her own way. No, he needed a woman like my mother who knew her place and would roll up her sleeves and work like a beetle from dawn 'til dusk. He wanted a woman who would be nice and grateful. And she was, my poor mother, oh she was, even though the cup of chocolate she had tasted on her wedding morning was the only one that ever passed her lips in the whole of her brief married life.

It is hard for me to go into what happened next, for my mother's death was as sudden and unexpected to me as her marriage had been. We had been living on the farm for less than two years. They had not been happy ones. Horace, the eldest son, was as mean as his father and did his best to make our lives a misery from the start. My mother worked in the kitchen all hours, when she wasn't looking after chickens or the vegetable patch or the goats, and seeing as she was a thin young woman who had not been raised for farm life she acquitted herself very creditably, I think.

I wish I could say it was the work that wore her out but I know it was more than that. It was disappointment. She must have been wondering, the whole of my childhood, what it would be like to have a husband, and I suppose she had gilded her imaginings somewhat, considering how hard it was without one. Then she got one, and he was the kind of man whose sole comment at the supper table was, 'Mrs Childer, I believe I have noted before how a stew must be well salted, have I not?' with an air of such disdain you would have thought he was addressing the lowliest of serving girls.

*Mrs Childer*. I hated that he called her that. She had a name but he never used it, not in front of me, anyway. He probably called all his wives *Mrs Childer*, to save him the trouble of learning a new name when one died on him. He killed my mother, did Farmer Childer, as sure as if he cut her throat with his own razor.

It was a damp, cold March. She had had a cough and a fever for a week, and was losing her food both ends, although he did not know that bit of course as it was me that tended to her.

One evening, he came and stood at the door to her room while I was mixing beeswax and tar for a poultice. I was doing it in a small metal dish held above a candle. The smell was deep and warm and the yellowy beeswax was goldening amidst the tar. Tiny bubbles surfaced as I stirred.

I was not frightened at that time, for what child can imagine that their mother is about to leave them for ever?

Farmer Childer – Father, as I had been told to call him – stood at the door and said, 'Mrs Childer, must I get help from Cottenham tomorrow? The vegetable patch wants attending and if we need help in the morning then I must send Horace now, I think.' He could have told me to do it, of course, or one of the boys. He was making a point. She had been ill quite long enough, in his opinion.

And she replied, in her weak, chirrupy voice, 'Oh no, Mr Childer, there is no need of that. Another night and I shall be right as anything.'

After he had gone, I brought the poultice dish over to her and said crossly, 'What did you say that for, Mum? You know you need more rest.'

She did not reply, but lowered the sheet and unbuttoned her nightgown so that I could spread the poultice on her chest.

I blew across the top of the dish. It is a tricky thing to apply a beeswax poultice. It must be cool enough not to scald a person but not so cold as to thicken before it is spread.

She closed her eyes. I spread it on her with the wooden spatula, then laid brown paper over the top so she could button her night-dress over it.

'This will do the trick, I'm sure,' she said.

I sat by her for a while, holding her hand. I thought perhaps she was falling asleep. Then, without opening her eyes, she said, 'Why do you never speak when Mr Childer is in the room? I don't think I've ever heard you speak when he is nearby.'

I was twelve. I did not know how to answer. Now, I know the reason. I know it was because I hated him for looking down on my mother, for accepting her gratitude as his due – for looking at her and seeing no more than his third wife, when she was everything to me.

And I hated her a little bit too, sometimes, because I could not understand why she seemed to think so little of herself. Girls of twelve can't understand that of their mothers. They only learn that women should think little of themselves when they are older.

My mother fell asleep shortly, and I watched her face in the candlelight and saw how much older and more lined it seemed – and still I did not have the sense to be afraid.

She got up the next morning, of course. The poultice hadn't made the slightest bit of difference and her thin body shook with the coughing as I helped her dress. She went out in the cold and damp and weeded the vegetable patch. That afternoon, she took to her bed again and two days later it was obvious even to my stepfather that a doctor must be sent for and he came and gave her pills and they made no difference either.

She was in bed another three days before she went.

And that's how come I ended up living on a farm far from where I grew up, with a stepfather I hated and stepbrothers who hated me. Well, two of them hated me: Horace because he hated everybody, and the youngest, Henry, because my mother had replaced his. The middle one, William was kind enough. When he saw how grief stricken I was, I think it eased his own sorrow a little. He gave me a handkerchief at her funeral. The next day I laundered it, and when I returned it to him, pressed and folded, he said he would like me to keep it as a sign of how sorry he was.

Farmer Childer did not marry again after my mother's death. I would like to be charitable and say he could not bring himself to – but I think the truth was, he didn't need to. I was twelve, old enough to take over the cooking and cleaning and the hens and the vegetable patch. What did he need another wife for, after all, with an almost-grown stepdaughter in the house?

# CHAPTER 7

The Travellers came every year. Funny now to think Elijah and I might have passed each other on the way to the water pump when we were children and not known each other.

I don't remember first seeing them or thinking them strange – on the contrary. It was a little bit of the outside world coming to our farm. Suddenly, there was noise in the fields, and other children my own age, although I was not allowed to play with them, of course.

I finished my schooling the year my mother died. There was too much for me to do on the farm for my stepfather to allow me to continue. One of my duties was to go collecting the rent from the wagons, at the summer and autumn harvests. They rented the field from us, whether they were working our harvest or not, and sometimes some of them stayed on after harvest was done. There was often other work locally, which suited them and suited us as we rotated their campsite each year so the fallow fields brought in a little income, which was always welcome.

I was thirteen the first time I went rent collecting, and I can still remember how important it made me feel, with my little notebook in my hand and big leather satchel slung across my chest. The children of the camp would stop and stare at me as I passed and I did not mind the hostility in their gazes for their mothers were most polite to me and treated me like a little queen. The only time I felt bad was once when I was leaving the camp and a boy halfway up a tree called down to me. He was pulling faces at me. Come to think of it, it was probably Elijah.

One day, when I was about fourteen, a piglet got out of our pen behind the farmhouse. It was my fault. I had been pouring feed in the trough and was leaning over and my leg had nudged the gate, which was not properly latched. Out shot the little so-and-so, like a bullet. I saw it happen and would have had him but as I turned I slipped on some damp straw and ended up on my knees in the yard while the piglet disappeared behind the cart shed. I knew there was no time to be lost, so I jumped to my feet, pulled the pig-sty gate firmly closed and ran after, scattering hens like nobody's business as I ran.

As I rounded the cart shed, I saw the piglet scoot across the field. I scrambled over the fence and headed after him but I reckon that piglet was bewitched as it ran pell-mell across the field, into the next and across it too, and straight into the Traveller camp. It disappeared in there and I stopped and burst into tears. I knew how much trouble I would be in if I could not find it and for all I knew it had been kidnapped already and would be roasted that very night if I did not save it.

One of the men was striding out of the camp on his way somewhere. He saw me wiping my face with my apron and asked me what was up. When I told him he said, not to worry, he would find the piglet for me, and off he went back into the camp.

While I waited for him, two girls around my age came past.

They were both carrying babies, and I smiled at the babies. They stopped and came over and gave me the babies to hold. I didn't know if they were boy babies or girl babies but they were such sweet, swaddled dumplings that I forgot about the piglet for a bit. One started to cry, and I jiggled it up and down a bit. The girls laughed at me when they saw I didn't know how to hold it properly but they weren't unkind about it. They showed me how to put the baby in the crook of my neck and let it nestle there and were astonished when I said it was the first time I had done it. When I told them I was only fourteen they declared it was time I got a move on and had some of my own.

After they left, I hung around a bit more, but the afternoon was getting late. I gave up on the man who said he would find my piglet and went back to the farmhouse with my head down, hoping that at least nobody would notice the piglet was missing that day and I might have time to go looking for it the following morning.

My stepfather was waiting for me in the kitchen. Where had I been? he wanted to know. I told him I had been collecting worms for the chickens. Where were the worms? He wanted to know that too. I burst into tears, such a poor liar was I. He gave me three strokes on my arm for lying to him and six strokes for losing a piglet; then another six for wasting time talking to *gipos* and another three to remind me never to do it again. Each stroke was weighed and measured. He never beat me in a temper, I'll say that for him.

I went outside afterwards, to cry and find a dock leaf to rub on my sore arm. William came over and said the piglet was safe and sound. The man had found it while I was talking to the girls and, thinking I would have returned to the farmhouse by then, had brought it back directly, swaddled in a blanket and tucked under his arm. Father had given him a shilling for his trouble.

I took care not to befriend any of the Traveller children after that, although I looked out for the girls my age and their babies and was pleased each year when they came back. The children grew, and more babies were added, and depending on which field they were camped in and the direction of the wind, I could sometimes lean out of my window in the evening and hear the shouts and cries from the camp, the playing and running around.

*Was* Elijah the boy who sneered at me from the tree? I have sometimes wondered. It doesn't seem important now.


Elijah Smith was firmly on the ground the first time I remember setting eyes on him. It was several summers later. We were both full grown.

It was a pleasant evening, warm and sunny. We had had a lot of rain that month but that day had been fine and things were drying out nicely. We were midway through a goodly cherry harvest and the camp was large that year. I enjoyed my Friday evening walks over there – as I approached, the smells would float toward me: wood smoke, the cooking of onions and potatoes, tobacco from their pipes.

As I neared that evening, I saw that a new wagon had pulled up on the edge of the camp, an elaborate green and gold one with gilt porch lamps. I pulled my notebook and pencil from my satchel and turned to the last page, to make a note of it. I saw that a young man was sitting on the step, and had time to think it unusual that I was about to speak to him, as it was normally the wives I dealt with.

I stopped in front of him.

He looked up at me.

The sun was full on his face, which was wrinkled for a youngish man – weather beaten, I suppose. His eyes had a look in them, both childish and knowing. His teeth were crooked. He looked like a friendly dog, sitting there, a dog looking for someone to adore. He was dressed in a leather waistcoat with fancy buttons, I remember noticing that, and on his head he had a brown felt hat. Just showing beneath the brim of the hat was an oiled kiss-curl that curved across his forehead. There was something in the vanity of that kiss-curl that pleased me, for I lived with four men who never looked in a mirror from one week to the next. He was working at a piece of wood with a knife and, as I glanced down at it, I noticed how clean his hands were. I looked at his face again and saw he was smiling at me.

We did not speak.

We smiled at each other.

What was strange was that it was just as if we were having a conversation, all the things that were said with our smiles. We held each other's gazes for so long that there could be no mistaking our smiles for mere politeness. I felt a feeling I had never felt before, as if the solid core of me had melted away and inside there was nothing but air. I was eighteen years old and a great lummox of a girl by then, but I felt suddenly as if I was light enough to float up in the sky, if I wanted, to rise above the field and the wagons and the farm and the muddy old Ouse and everything that kept me tethered to the Fens.

Then I noticed a tiny, dark-skinned woman who was standing next to the wagon. Her hair was drawn back into a headscarf and her apron reached almost to the ground, making her seem quite doll-like, although the expression on her face was not at all the friendly, open gaze of a child's toy. Quite the contrary. Her brow was furrowed and her mouth tightly pursed. She stared at me with pin-prick eyes. She reached into her apron pocket and drew out a small cloth purse, then stepped forward and handed me some coins.

I took them and opened my hand.

She said, sharply, 'You'll find it is the exact amount.'

I did not like the insolence of her tone and made a point of continuing to stare at the coins as if I was counting them, although I had seen at once that the money was indeed correct.

The young man sitting on the step watched the two of us.

I put the money away, opened my notebook and ticked next to where I had written: *Green and gold wagon, gilt porch lamps*. Rent was due by the wagon, as we never knew who or how many stayed in each one from one night to the next. I would always write little descriptions of each wagon in my notebook so's I knew who had paid up, although sometimes when I arrived they would have been moved around, to confuse me, I think, in the hope I would not bother to count up and maybe miss one. I have a good memory for colours and patterns, however, and I don't believe I was ever fooled.

I hesitated for a moment. I wanted to speak, to assert myself somehow, but I could think of nothing to say. I nodded, without really looking at either of them, and turned away.

As I walked off towards the other wagons, I was dying to look round to see if he was watching me go but knew I must not, for fear of the humiliation if he wasn't.

On my way back to the farmhouse, I fiddled with my hair ribbon and inwardly bemoaned the unruliness of my dry locks. George Rawson the greengrocer might not have given me his name or any acknowledgement, but he must have had red hair somewhere in his family as I had inherited my horrid frizz from somewhere. My mother's hair was sleek and dark. I cursed the father I had never known, that day, and wondered a little desperately whether, if I oiled my hair every night between now and the following Friday, I might be able to fashion proper ringlets.

When I got back, I pulled my notebook and money-bag out of my satchel immediately and sat down at the kitchen table. Horace was at the other end, slumped back in his chair and drinking tea. Father must be out, I thought, otherwise Horace wouldn't be drinking tea when he should be checking the irrigation ditches.

As I took out my pencil and turned the pages of my notebook, I thought of how thirsty I was. I promised myself a drink of water as soon as I had added the first column. Horace would have gone by then, hopefully.

William came and stood in the doorway with his boots still on and said, 'Rose, have you seen Henry? He said he'd help me with the sow. He said he'd be back by now.' We had a bad sow at that time. She bit when you tried to pen her.

Before I could reply, Horace snarled at William, 'She's just this minute come in and she's got to add up before Father gets back.'

William left without a word.

I glanced at Horace, surprised. He had never shown concern about me finishing my duties before now, not if he wanted something to eat or a collar starching. Everything had to be done straightaway for Horace. I looked after William, frowning slightly, and wondered whether to go and help him with the sow myself, for I knew he was afraid of her and I was not. Sows are like dogs, only more so. They can smell fear.

When I looked back, I saw that Horace was leaning forward on his elbows and staring at me. He was a bulky man, like his father, dark haired and red faced, with lumpen features. There was no kindness in him, not a drop – that much I knew after eight years on the farm.

'Have you ever given thought . . .' he said, as if we had been in the middle of a conversation when William had interrupted us, '. . . as to what might happen when Father passes on?'

It was such an extraordinary remark that I made no reply.

He rose, swaying slightly, to his feet. I wondered if he had been drinking. He walked casually round to my end of the table. He stood next to me, and looked down at me.

'No?' he said. He was standing very close to me. I was aware of the strain on his belt buckle. He was on the last hole of the belt and the leather was giving. His stomach moved in and out a little with each breath and for some reason he seemed to be breathing hard.

He smelled of turned earth and dried sweat, of River Farm and the brown Great Ouse.

He put a hand on my shoulder and leaned his weight on me. He lowered his face to mine and murmured, 'Perhaps it is time that you did.' He squeezed my shoulder once, hard, then turned and strode outside.

I returned to my column of figures but as I looked up and down I was unable to add one digit to the next, for too many other things were adding up inside my head: my stepfather's age; the way Horace was more and more in charge these days; the growing antagonism between him and William. When I put these thoughts together, the sum total was large and unpleasant.

I had always assumed I would leave the farm one day, when I was fully of age. It was not my home, after all, and never had been. I was little more than a servant. I had not thought of what I would do or where I would go to, but I had never once seen myself slaving away and growing old there.

Now I saw that, in the absence of my making any firm plans for my future, plans were being made by others, on my behalf.

Friday evenings were my favourite part of the week. I saved my sewing until then, which meant a whole evening sitting down. Once I had cleared away the supper table, I would go up to the linen cupboard outside my room and take down the mending that had piled up since the previous Friday. There was always a great deal of it, as farm working men collect a fair amount of wear and tear on their things. I should have really done a little of it every evening but I liked to save it all up. It would not have been acceptable for me to sit down for two or three hours at a stretch for any other reason, but even my stepfather knew that sewing had to be done.

The summer evenings were best of all, for I did not have to do it by candlelight. I would take my favourite seat in the kitchen, by the open door, and sew until dusk fell and I was forced to move inside. Lately, William had taken to joining me with a book. His father asked him once what he was reading and he said, 'An analysis of Fen drainage patterns, Father,' although I do believe I once caught him reading a novel.

That evening, William was seated next to me with his book, and Horace and his father were in the kitchen with their pipes. Henry was in disgrace for his absence earlier in the day and so had been given the entire list of evening duties to perform on his own, which would take him until well after dark. The dog, Eddy we called him, was asleep on the step. I was sitting right by the open door and was weaving a length of cotton in and out of a tear by a shoulder seam on one of Henry's shirts. He did the least work but damaged his clothing most greatly, which was a thing I never fathomed.

Horace was brooding and silent, but that was more or less as normal.

When he had finished his pipe, Father rose. 'I shall retire early,' he said, to the room in general.

I put down my sewing. Father liked to take a cup of hot milk up to bed with him.

He lifted a hand, 'No milk for me tonight. I am still bloated from supper.'

He was rising at three in the morning to go to visit another farmer at Chatteris Fen who had a disc harrow for sale. Believe it or not, Farmer Childer was still using a bush harrow in those days, so unwilling was he to pay hard cash for anything. The stubble we had, he should have invested in a disc harrow years before.

'Shall I leave bread out or pack a breakfast for you, Father?' I asked.

'Pack it,' he said. 'I won't eat before I set off.'

After he had gone upstairs, Horace, who had been staring gloomily ahead, looked at me and said. 'You can make *me* some hot milk. I'd like some honey in it.'

I had just picked up my needle. 'I'll finish this seam if you don't mind, Horace.' I was tired and irritated by his strange behaviour and I suppose some of my annoyance must have showed in my voice. My thread had ended and I was raising the garment to bite it off the needle, otherwise I might have seen him rise and come towards me.

I looked up as he reached me. He raised one hand and struck me with the flat of it, soundly, across my face.

The room blurred and blackened. He did not knock me off my chair, not quite, but my head reeled as I righted myself.

William had jumped to his feet and let his book drop to the floor.

Horace was standing before me, panting, as if he had surprised himself by his action as much as he had surprised me. Then he looked round. I followed his gaze and saw my stepfather standing at the bottom of the stairs, staring at us. I don't believe there was ever any other occasion when I was grateful for his appearance.

We all waited for him to speak. He did not move, his gaze flicking from me to Horace, then back again. After a pause he said, 'I have changed my mind. You may leave my breakfast out.'

He turned and went back upstairs.

We all remained motionless for a moment, listening to the creak of the stairs beneath Father's heavy tread. Then I was unable to prevent myself exhaling in shock.

Horace was still standing in front of me, looking pleased with himself. His look said, *See, I am in charge now. Now do you understand?*

I put down the sewing on the windowsill and rose from my seat, my legs trembling slightly. William was still standing next to us. I could not look at him. I turned and walked across the kitchen to the larder, where there was a full churn of milk.

Had I been thinking straight that evening, as I lay in bed turning the events of the day over in my mind, then I could have written the rest of my life story right there and then. Horace's slap had sealed my fate. But all I could do was stare at the blackness of the air above me, where I knew the ceiling was, and wonder if the roof was still up there, in the dark, for I no longer felt certain of anything.

It rained heavily overnight, as it had done most nights that month. Sun and rain: what every farmer wants. The next morning, I rose at dawn as usual, my head full of thoughts and clouded-feeling. I tiptoed downstairs. My stepfather had already left. I had put his breakfast out the night before – bread and a piece of cold mutton on his pewter plate in the larder, covered with a dampened cloth to prevent the bread from drying overnight. I checked to see if he had eaten it but he had not. I lowered the cloth gently, as if I had been peeping at a corpse. *I must be careful how I tread now*, I thought.

I was keen to be out of the house by the time the others rose. In winter, there are the fireplaces to be cleaned and laid first thing but without that to hold me up, I was able to slip out with my wicker basket, to go and look for eggs. The brothers often went out and did an hour or two around the farm before returning for breakfast, so I reckoned if I timed it right I would be able to avoid Horace until mid-morning.

Once the eggs were collected and the goat had been milked, I was a little stuck. I knew I should really return to the farmhouse and get on with my chores there but I could not bear it just yet, so I racked my brains for an excuse to go over to the Travellers' camp. It came to me quick enough. I owed Mrs Boswell four shillings. I had not had the right change on me when I saw her the night before and had said I would knock it off the following week's rent. She had seemed happy enough with the arrangement but, I thought, I could always pretend I was passing that way this morning and thought I would drop by. Perhaps I would go past the green and gold wagon on my way. I wondered how early the smiling young man liked to rise.

I grimaced as I set off, thinking that in my haste to put the eggs and goat's milk in the larder, find four shillings and get out of the farmhouse, I had not even brushed my hair – my wretched hair. As I walked, I pinched my cheeks to bring some colour to them.

The field they used as the campsite got muddy very quickly, as you may imagine, for the soil was already broken up so well that even in summer a light rain could make it boggy in an hour or two. When I walked over from the farmhouse, I always tucked my skirt into my waistband to stop it getting dirty, but that hitched it rather high and showed an unseemly amount of petticoat. As soon as I was near enough that anyone might see me, I would pull the folds of my skirt out from the waistband and hold it up, but not too much, as I picked my way towards the wagons.

It was still early but as I approached I saw the camp was up. Some of the older women were tending fires, as usual. I supposed the younger women and the men had already gone over to the orchards for the day. I wondered whether William would remember to check that the Orchard Manager had showed up. We had a man come from Rampton to weigh and grade the fruit but he drank and was unreliable. It was William's job to go over each morning and make sure he was there.

The green and gold wagon was shuttered and no one was about. I felt both disappointed and relieved. I wanted to see the young man again but did not feel at my best that morning.

A little separate from the camp was a group of five caravans that all belonged to the same family, a large group with many children, always nicely dressed. I gathered that they were perhaps a leading family in some way by the way I saw the other Travellers speak to them. The woman in charge was large and fair skinned. She always plaited her hair with ribbon and wore long earrings and many bangles. When I first visited her, I could not stop myself from staring beyond her into her wagon, for you have never seen so much fine china and engraved glass as was in their home. I could not imagine how even a pair of geldings could pull their wagon with all the grandeur it contained. How she managed to keep it all, and herself and her children, so smart and tidy with a life on the road is a thing I have never been able to fathom.

The family was down in my book as Boswell. Most of the others on the site called themselves Smith or Price, although I had learned that names were a somewhat fluid concept in the encampment and I never set much store by what they told me. I liked Mrs Boswell, and realised as I approached her wagon that I was hoping she would be there and the others not around. She usually offered me a cup of tea, although it had taken me a couple of visits before I got over my shyness enough to accept it. She offered it as though she meant it, as though she was truly concerned that I might need one. She would never take a cup with me but sit and watch me with great care while I sipped my own. She liked to ask me questions, showing a great interest in the life of the farmhouse and in the domestic habits of our family. She seemed to think there was something strange about the way we lived. For instance, I once told her about how one of my morning tasks was to go from room to room and empty everybody's washing bowl. She looked most shocked and said, 'You mean you take the men's washing water that they have put their hands in and just tip it outside the back door?'

'I usually water the parsley with it,' I replied.

She explained to me that each member of her family had their own washing bowl, which was never used for any other purpose. Everyone disposed of their own water with the utmost care, for it was like getting rid of a little part of yourself, and to allow someone else to just tip it away was like scattering your secrets. When she told me this, she was most hesitant. I had to encourage her with looks. 'And the idea that you should put your dirty water on something that might be *eaten* . . .' Her voice had become a whisper and she was unable to finish the sentence, as if we were discussing something too foul for words.

That morning, I found myself hoping hard she would offer me tea, so we could have one of our little chats. I would talk to her about almost anything, I thought, as long as I could sit down for a while and not go back to the farmhouse.

She was there all right, boiling water and chiding one of her children, but I saw as I approached that she was busy and would not be inclined to indulge my unexpected visit.

I stopped in front of her, feeling foolish. 'Mrs Boswell,' I said, reaching into my apron pocket, 'I was passing and thought I should return your change to you. I am sorry I did not have it on me last night.'

She looked a little puzzled and said, 'You did not need to come this way for that. Friday would have been fine to settle up, Miss Rose.' We had agreed as much the night before.

I wondered if there was an implied insult in my returning the money early, as if I thought she might be in need of it. 'I was passing,' I repeated, which was a silly thing to say when the encampment was stuck out in the field and not on the way to anywhere.

I handed her the money, then said hopefully, 'Well, I won't keep you . . .'

She did not take the hint. She dropped the coins into her apron pocket and looked back at her child.

I was sorry I had come. I turned to go.

She said, 'Miss Rose.'

I turned back. She was regarding me in a kindly fashion. 'You need a porte-jupe, do you, Miss Rose. The bottom of your skirt is muddy. Are you telling me a fine young lady such as yourself does not have a whole drawer of them?'

I had not the faintest idea what she was talking about.

'A porte-jupe, a skirt grip.' She glanced down at her own skirts, that were held elegantly in place by a series of grips attached to long ribbons which hung from her waistband, lifting her skirt slightly at pretty intervals so it was clear of the mud. The front ones were invisible beneath her long apron.

Well, of course I knew what a skirt grip was, although I had never heard it called by such a fancy name.

I knew it was overly familiar of her to comment on my dress but I was in need of sympathy that morning and could not help myself from saying, 'I live with four farm-working men, Mrs Boswell.' She knew my mother had passed on. 'I am afraid the feminine aspects of life are not really catered for in our household.' At this, and with current events to the front of my mind, I felt tears come to my eyes and I bit my lip.

She turned away without comment. I felt rebuked and trudged slowly back to the farmhouse, awash with self-pity.

Horace, William and Henry returned to the farmhouse mid-morning for their breakfast. I had made eggs with dill and parsley, a favourite of theirs. I served it in silence, allowing myself a moment of grim satisfaction at the thought of how – according to Mrs Boswell's philosophy – I was giving them herbs coated in their own filth.

They didn't talk between themselves and none of them spoke to me. The four of us didn't even look each other. I realised that, despite the strange events of the previous evening, our day would continue as normal – silent, weighted with routine, and I felt as though my life was like a huge eiderdown smothering me, as if I could hardly breathe or move.

They left. I stacked their plates at the table. As I was walking to the scullery holding them, I stopped in the middle of the room and just stood there for a minute, looking at nothing, just breathing. I closed my eyes.

The following day was a Sunday. We did not even attend church in that household, so removed were we from the outside world. Cows still had to be milked and vegetables dug, earth turned, sows and piglets fed. With a harvest in progress the men were busy all day and my own duties trebled. I forked over the stinking straw in the pig's pen with renewed vigour that morning, turning and turning the damp, blackened straw, staring at our vicious sow with hatred. She made no move to nip me. My misery had made me invincible.

Monday came, and Tuesday – the week progressed, and I realised that the only thing keeping me on my feet was the thought of Friday teatime, when I would go to the Traveller camp and collect the rent. I needed his smile. I needed it more than bread or salt. I dreamed of his smile all day long. I thought of it so often I felt I was wearing out the image in my head and it was becoming bled of colour, faded.

It was only as I walked towards the camp on Friday afternoon that it occurred to me that I was, perhaps ... deluded. I had not exchanged so much as one word with the young man with the crinkly eyes. A smile, a look – small stuff to hold on to. Was I going mad, in my unhappiness, to wonder if he had been thinking of me that week, as I had been thinking of him? Foolish girl, I chided myself, as I strode over. He probably looks at a hundred girls a day – you've seen yourself how that camp is full of slim, pretty things with plaited hair. What makes you think he'll have thought of you, a big hulking farm girl with red frizz on your head? That hair alone is an embarrassment.

My attempts to fashion ringlets had come to naught and I had tied my hair up with my usual velvet ribbon, but it was a windy summer's day and already strands were escaping and sticking to my face.

As soon as I see him, I'll know, I thought, as I approached his wagon. I'll know, from the look on his face, whether he feels the same as me.

There was no one by the green and gold wagon. The door and shutters were firmly fastened. I glanced about but could not see him. Disappointment washed over me like cold, dirty water. If his smile had meant something, then he would have been there the following week, surely, to see me again.

I hovered around longer than was decent and soon noticed a group of three women at the neighbouring wagon, staring at me. Was I imagining it, or were they laughing at my expense?

I went over. One of them I recognised. She gave me her rent and then some extra, nodding at the green and gold wagon. 'This is from them. They've gone to Long Stanton.'

Long Stanton. Never had Long Stanton sounded so far away. I took the money and turned.

The last wagon I visited was that of Mrs Boswell. She gave me the rent and watched me tick my book, then handed me a small parcel, wrapped carefully in brown paper and tied with ribbon. 'This is for you, Miss Rose,' she said, 'to be opened in the privacy of your own room.'

I looked at it, then back at her. She had already turned away.

When I got back to the house, I was burning to run up to my bedroom and open the parcel. Could it be a message or a gift from him? But why would he leave it with the Boswells? I knew I had to do the books immediately and take the reckoning to my stepfather, then get on with making supper. Then there was an evening of silent sewing to endure.

It was not until bedtime that I was in my own little room with the door locked behind me. I took the small parcel from my pocket and held it up to the candle on my windowsill, to regard it properly in the soft, yellow light.

I could hardly bear to open it. When it was opened, I would know what was inside and was bound to be disappointed. A gift. I bit my lip as I looked at it, for I was realising that, since my mother had died, nobody had given me a gift. Not one. Birthdays were not acknowledged in our house, and even Christmas was marked only by a dinner of goose, cooked and served by me, as all the farm duties still had to be done and Father did not believe in excessive celebration. I think one year I had an orange from William.

Eventually, I slipped off the narrow blue ribbon and unfolded the brown paper.

Inside my little parcel was a brooch of some cheapish metal in the shape of a sunflower, with a boxed clasp, and a long, fine chain attached. At the other end of the chain was a slender grip, fastened by a clasp, which you slipped along its length. It was a tawdry thing, somewhat worn and old-fashioned, but practical, and it brought a lump to my throat. Even if it was Mrs Boswell's own and not bought, she had folded it and wrapped it and tied it with ribbon. She had told me to open it in my room because it was a woman's thing, a thing a man could not know about or understand. I sat holding the skirt grip beneath the candlelight and wept for my mother and for all the things she might have said or given to me as I became a woman myself, if she had been given the chance. I wept for her as I had never wept before.

It was that night, in the dead darkness before dawn, when I was sound asleep and wallowing in dreams, that Elijah Smith threw little sticks against my windowpane.

The sticks themselves did not awaken me – I only knew what he'd thrown when I found some of them on the windowsill. I was woken by the barking of the dog, Eddie, in the yard. By the time I got to the window and raised it, Eddie's racket had frighted him off. I was just in time to see Elijah leap the fence – no more than a glimpse in the moonlight, but enough to recognise him by.

I watched the shape of him be swallowed by the darkness. So I was not deluded, after all.

# CHAPTER 8

It wasn't much of a wedding – I have to own that now, although at the time I was so cheerful that we had pulled it off that what was missing hardly mattered. I told Elijah I wanted it done properly in St Matthew's Church, so we had to wait for the banns to be read. We went to church for each of those Sundays, and my heart sang as the vicar announced our names for the whole wide world to hear – oh, I wanted every man, woman and child in the country to know I was to be wed.

Elijah proposed to me exactly three weeks after he threw sticks at my window. We were lying on the bank behind the Traveller encampment. It was the fifth time we had managed to be alone together.

It was early evening. The sky had already lost its goldenness and was taking on the purplish, slightly sickly hues of dusk. It was making me sad. I dreaded having to return to the farmhouse and was telling him so. By then, he knew everything about my stepfather and brothers, about the strange behaviour of Horace.

'Sometimes I think I will go mad if I spend one more night there,' I was sighing.

'Come away with me, then.'

I looked at him. He was lying on his back with his hands behind his head, chewing on a piece of long grass and looking at the sky.

There had been no pause before he said it, and it was lightly said. You might have thought he was suggesting, *How about a cup of tea?* I sat up and looked down at his face, searching for some sign of the weight behind his words, but his eyes were shut and the rest of his face remained closed too. After staring at him for a moment or two, I was none the wiser.

When I did not answer him, he opened his eyes, looked up at me squintingly, and repeated the suggestion. 'Come *away* with me, and when you're mine, there won't be a man in this world but me has a right to lay a finger on you.' He put one hand on my sleeve. 'You'll be my Rosie, for good. And that will be it, my girl.'

Within a space no longer than a few tickings of a clock, I moved from thinking, *how absurd* to thinking, *yes*.

How could I possibly run away with Elijah Smith and just leave everything?

Well, what, precisely, would I be leaving? I had very few possessions and no money, my stepfather had seen to that. The only thing I valued was a gold chain my mother left me which I wore round my neck day and night, so that was easy enough to take along with me. I only had that because she had given it to me herself when she became ill. She must have known by then I would get nothing from the farmer. That and the skirt grip Mrs Boswell had given me were the only possessions I valued in the whole wide world.

The farmer. My stepfather. I thought of his fury when my departure was discovered, and that of the dreaded Horace. And then I thought – and I must confess this gave me no little pleasure – of how affronted my stepfather would be to have a Travelling man for a son-in-law, of how he would have to lie about it to his Alderman friends and always wonder if his lies would be discovered. We might not mix much with the local people but that didn't mean we wouldn't be worth gossiping about. *Have you heard about what the Childer girl has gone and done? She's run off with a Gypsy!* Oh my, how it would wound him and Horace to have that whispered. That wouldn't do much for their marriage prospects.

I looked at Elijah. He was a handsome man, with his crooked teeth and smile that made me dizzy. I thought about him all day long. If I saw him talking to somebody else, man or woman, I felt ill because he was attending to them, not me. We had kissed three times and each time it was like drowning. When he had his mouth on mine, I forgot the rest of the whole world. I forgot I needed air to breathe. *Put your hands on me*, I wanted to say. He had been quite polite so far. He had held my head, and stroked my face, that was all.

I had never been touched tenderly by a man before and it was as though I had discovered some extraordinary secret. I burned with it, in places where I had not realised it was possible to burn.

I loved him, but I knew nothing of him, really. He might abandon me, for all I knew.

'I'll not give myself to you until we're legally wed, you know that, don't you?' I said boldly to him, and he replied with a broad grin, for he knew that meant I was going to agree.

'I know that, girl.'

'But where shall we go to?' I already had a feeling that the practicalities of this matter would be down to me.

'Let's go to a town,' he said, 'for I've had enough of fields and mud for the time being.'

'We can go to Cambridge,' I replied. 'I have an old friend of my mother's there and we can stay with her while we find our own little house.'

He frowned and stroked his chin. 'A house? So you're going to make a proper *gorjer* of me, are yer?' Then he smiled again. 'You had better make me some fancy clothes if I'm going up in the world, my girl.'

'I can sew well enough.'

He stood. 'Better go and pack your things then, girl.'

I must confess I felt a little dissatisfied as I crept back to the house, for in truth I had always imagined that when a man proposed to me it would be with great protestations of love; but I already knew that Elijah was not a man for great protestations of any sort, and that was something I would just have to get used to.

I may not have had the romantic side of a proposal but I had something just as good – the excitement of running off. I hugged it to me. I was going to pack my things and run off in the dead of night and my stepfather and stepbrothers who thought they owned me were going to wake in the morning and find I had slipped from their grasp.

I should have left them a vicious little note, something about how they would have to boil their own milk from now on – but in truth I was too afraid to do it, and reckoned the empty bed they would discover in the morning would speak for itself.

Our arrival in Paradise Street must have caused a small stir, I think; given folk something to talk about. There had been no means of warning Aunt Lilly we were about to show up on her doorstep, and I had not had any contact with her for years. We just showed up one afternoon. Standing on her doorstep, waiting for her to answer the door, was almost more frightening than running away from River Farm in the dark, wondering what on earth I would do if Elijah and his horse were not waiting for me at the end of the lane.

The door opened, and there was Aunt Lilly, scarcely changed from when I had last seen her eight years previous – apart from the fact that she had taken to dying her hair orange. A look of puzzlement, then curiosity, crossed her face. Then her hand went to her mouth and she gave a cry of recognition. She stared at my cloth bag, and Elijah standing beside me, then she shook her head and pulled a face both tragical and comic, lips pressed together and mouth wide, like a duck. I couldn't work out if she was pleased or not.

She stepped back from the door, turned her head slightly and called out, 'Samuel, Samuel, come here directly.'

Samuel Empers came to the front door slowly. He had aged much more than Lilly.

Lilly turned back to me. 'It's Emmeline's girl. Our Rose,' she said, as if I might be the one in need of reminding who I was. She opened her arms.

They gave us tea and we discussed where Elijah might lodge. She had a nephew over at Old Gas Lane who owed her a favour or two – and there was a small stables and yard behind his place where we could put the horse and Elijah would be handy to care for it. We told her Elijah was a horse-dealer and general trader, and she knew well enough what that meant. I saw her looking a little askance at him but thought, ah well, she'll get used to the idea.

Elijah didn't say much during this first encounter. It was strange to see him quiet and unsure of himself. He did not know whether to sit or stand and clutched his cup of tea like someone drowning. He kept glancing over at Samuel Empers, as if he thought the man of the household might help him out, but Samuel Empers was always entirely ruled by his wife so Elijah had no assistance from that quarter. When it was decided that Samuel should walk him over to Gas Lane, Elijah leaped to his feet in gratitude and gave me no more than a nod before he was out of the door.

We all retired as soon as Samuel returned from safely stowing Elijah. It was agreed that I was to sleep in their bed, with Aunt Lilly, and poor Samuel deposit himself on the settee downstairs. There was nowhere else in those little houses. I had gone out of my way to ensure they knew Elijah and I would not be a burden to them – we would wed as soon as we could, and find our own little house to rent. Exactly how we were going to support ourselves was a matter we did not discuss.

The only awkwardness came as Lilly and I were in the bedroom, preparing for sleep. We had performed our ablutions. I was sitting up in bed, beneath the quilt, and Lilly was wrapping papers around locks of her orange hair, one by one, and pinning them to her skull.

We were talking of my mother.

'And where is she buried?' Aunt Lilly asked, as she licked her comb and pulled it gently through a section of hair.

'Cottenham,' I replied. I hesitated. 'It was a small funeral. Just the family.'

Aunt Lilly stopped what she was doing and looked at me. 'I only heard of your mother's death from another farmer. Mr Cooper at Chatteris Fen Farm.' She looked down at her lap. 'He was bringing in radishes that year, although I think he's now moved over to sugar beet.'

'Mr Childer did not write to you?' I had always wondered why I had never heard from Aunt Lilly after my mother died.

Her face grew grave. 'He did not, my dear. I wrote to him, however, after my conversation with Mr Cooper. I offered to have you. We should have – well, Samuel and I not having our own.'

I stared at her.

She lifted her arms to apply another paper to her hair, then let them drop. 'Perhaps I was clumsy in my letter – I am not good with words. He stopped supplying us after that.'

We lay next to each other in the darkness, Aunt Lilly and I, but for a long time after she began to snore, I could not sleep. I was turning over in my mind my stepfather's wickedness. Of course he did not want to send me back to East Cambridge. He did not want to lose an unpaid servant. No wonder he stopped supplying Aunt Lilly. He wanted nothing more to do with her.

After I knew this, I began to regret my cowardice in having run off from River Farm without giving my stepfather a piece of my mind. I wanted to hurt him back for all the hurt he had caused me. I should have liked to have written him a letter in which I told him exactly what I thought of him, but in truth, I was still too afraid of him to do it – I was not fully of age, after all. What if he came after me and tried to take me back to the farm?

After a week or so in Paradise Street, I thought more calmly and realised that if he and Horace were going to try and get me back they would have done it by now. No, he had washed his hands of me, probably assumed I had lain beneath a hedge with Elijah and become a *gipo* on the spot. The more I thought about it, the more wounded I felt that they were not even bothering to enquire after me. I bet he's already forbidden his sons to mention my name, I thought bitterly, as if I never existed.

So I wrote to William instead. William was the only person I regretted leaving behind at River Farm. I knew he would find it hard without me. Without a woman to bully, the men in that house would turn upon the weakest among them. And pride came into it, a little. I wanted William to know that I wasn't sleeping in a gutter somewhere, that I was going to be a decent married woman. I didn't want him to think badly of me, and I suppose if I'm honest I was hoping the information would leak out to the rest of the family, then, whatever else they thought of me, there was at least one bad thing they would not be able to think.

So, soon as we had a date fixed for the wedding, I wrote to William, telling him the where and the when. I said he was welcome to come and give me away if he liked, as I regarded him as my nearest male relation. I don't know whether he ever got the letter safely – perhaps my stepfather intercepted it – but either way he never showed up at the church. Elijah and I were married in front of Aunt Lilly and her Samuel, and two new friends of Elijah's. More of them later.

At least the sun came out, as bright and cheery as a blessing from the whole wide world, as if to make up for the fact that Elijah and I had not a single relative between us to see us intertwine our lives. As we walked out of the gloom of St Matthew's Church, it was as if the whole street was bathed in light. We all stopped on the steps and beamed at each other.

We were doing the whole thing on the cheap, of course. We had to borrow for the marriage licence, which was a lot more than either of us had expected and there was no chance of a gold ring or anything like that – we used a cheap dress ring of Lilly's – but honestly I didn't care. It was in a church and it was legal, just like my mother would have wanted for me.

Then, as we made our first move down the steps, the church bells began to ring. We all looked up at the blue sky, amazed, as if the peals were coming from heaven itself. Lilly cried out, 'Now, isn't that lovely!'

I hadn't expected any extras like that. I turned to Elijah and said, all happy about it, 'Where did you get the money for them to ring the bells? I didn't know I was getting that!'

If he had had any sense, he would have just smiled and got the credit but instead he shrugged and said, 'I didn't know they would be rung.' I could see he was as surprised as me.

'Aunt Lilly?'

'Don't be daft!' she laughed.

We all stood around for a minute, smiling and listening. When the peals stopped, Lilly said to Samuel, 'Sam, go on in and ask the vicar. Ask him who paid for the church bells to be rung.' She was nodding at Elijah. I think she still thought he had done it but wouldn't own up to it.

Samuel caught up with us as we were walking down the road. We were all off to the Old Norfolk for a celebration of wine and little cakes. 'A gentleman who wishes not to be named,' he said, as he drew alongside us, tapping the side of his nose.

*William*, I thought to myself, for there was no chance my step-father would ever do such a thing. And even though I was happy as anything to have my handsome new husband by my side, I felt a tiny twist of pain inside me, like a stitch but only momentary, at the thought of William's sad, pale face, and what would become of him now I had left.

It's funny how you can make yourself joyful when you put your mind to it. My wedding was nothing like I had fantasised about when I was a girl. I had always seen myself in a gown with a long train. I had always thought I would have months to plan it, to make favours and embroider my underthings with bluebirds. And somehow, Lord knows why, I had always pictured the church full to the rafters. But even though I had married with not a single relative to witness it, in a brown wool dress and a bonnet rented from the pawnbrokers, I was happy, yes happy, as we strode along Gas Lane and up past the Victoria Soap and Candle Works. We were a tiny party – and me hardly a beauty after all – but I was young and strong and smiling, and I paraded in front, arm in arm with Elijah, holding a posy. And people came to their doorsteps to smile back at us because everybody loves a wedding, however meagre.

I had made my own decision to run away from my stepfather and make a new life with Elijah Smith, and, for the first time in my life, I had done something for myself instead of being done to. It was a grand feeling. It was a blue-sky day, and cloudless. My feet hurt in my borrowed shoes but I didn't care. I was a properly married lady and the church bells had rung as I came out into the sun.

I won't pretend that first year was all plain sailing. I sometimes find myself thinking that everything was fine and dandy between me and Elijah before she showed up but I know that is no more than a comforting falsehood and it does me no credit to rely on it. No, there were many things about Elijah that would have been difficult however it had gone between us.

I had no illusions about our lives together, how difficult it would be for us to support ourselves. Some might have thought me mad to leave a well-off farm and go back to the town – for whatever else was wrong in that sad house, there was always enough food on the table. I ate meat every week I lived there. I was a strong girl, as a result, and would have happily rolled my sleeves up and got work but as I was soon to be a married woman that was going to be difficult.

And the minute I *was* a married woman, I started wanting things in a way I never had before. On the farm, where I had scarcely owned the clothes I stood up in, it had never occurred to me to desire objects – well, I never came across any objects I desired. But once I was back in Paradise Street, in a city full of shops, well, I couldn't help noticing that other people had things that I hadn't.

Somewhere to live, for a start – and things to put in the somewhere. Even before we had our own little parlour, I started dreaming of a proper hair couch to put in it – forty shillings it would be, I said to Elijah, but if we settled for cloth it would only be twenty-five. A marble-top washstand for the corner of our bedroom – now that was my idea of luxury, to have a grand thing like that that was not even on display for visitors, but just for me and him. That was my idea of wealth, that was, to be able to afford something like that.

Oh, I did want a marble-top washstand. I think I thought my whole life would be complete if I had one of those. When I told Elijah, he rubbed his chin.

I couldn't quite work out exactly what it was my new husband did for a living. Sometimes he had a bit of money on him and sometimes nothing at all. Either way, he had a confidence about him that reassured me we would get by somehow. He had told me he dealt in horses sometimes and that he did some hawking. He was certainly very good at fixing things and could turn on the charm all right when he needed to.

There was one small incident, not long after we arrived in Paradise Street, which tells you all you need to know about Elijah. We were having a light supper with Lilly and Samuel, and they had gone to some effort for us even though it was a small meal, putting out the best tablecloth and cutlery and all. Lilly had dished up in the kitchen and brought the plates into the parlour laden. As she entered, she said, 'Sit down, the lot of you, let's eat while it's hot. I can't abide a cold supper.'

We sat and she put plates down before Elijah and myself – corned beef fritters and cabbage in gravy. I saw Elijah frown, lift his hands to the edge of the table, and move it a little.

'You've got a wobbly table leg, here, Mr Empers,' he said to Samuel.

Samuel was unperturbed. 'I have that, young man. I'll get around to fixing it one of these days.'

Lilly had gone back into the kitchen to get the other two plates and overheard this as she returned. 'I wish you would, Samuel. I've been on at you about it long enough.'

Elijah jumped to his feet. 'I'll sort this out soon enough!' he declared, clapping his hands together and rubbing them, and blow me if he didn't lean forward and whisk the plates from under our noses. Off came the cutlery. Off came the candlestick. Away went the best tablecloth while Lilly and Samuel sat there staring at him. And he upended the table and fixed it there and then.

It was done in a trice, but all the same I could tell Lilly was none too impressed. She had a point. A cold fritter is not nice, after all.

When he had finished, Elijah righted the table in one swift movement and stood back with a flourish, looking at us all for applause.

Lilly rose stiffly and went to retrieve our supper.

Elijah looked at me, a little baffled. Had he not done a nice thing, for our friends who had been so good to us? Where was his congratulations?

That was Elijah.

I spent my wedding night, and every night for the next month, sharing a bed with Aunt Lilly, while Elijah went back to Gas Lane. Finally, in July, we were able to get the rental together and find our own house. We were lucky to get one in that area at all as East Cambridge had got mightily crowded in the eight years I'd been out on the farm. An old lady living at number twenty-two, just three doors down from Lilly and Samuel, passed away. The rental of the property should have passed back to the Corporation but the old lady's daughter was still officially on the books even though she'd moved in with a friend on Norfolk Street. The daughter was a friend of Aunt Lilly's and Aunt Lilly had had quite enough of me sleeping in her bed and her husband on the settee. She put a bit of pressure on, and number twenty-two was sub-let to us, furniture and all.

So Lijah and I had been married a month before we got our own bed. When we first closed the door of number twenty-two on everyone, the day we moved in, we stood and grinned at each other for a moment, before Elijah chased me shrieking up the stairs. We were so pleased with ourselves that what happened next was a bit noisy, if you get my drift.

*

It wasn't the first time we had lain together, mind. We couldn't wait that long. No, the first time was a few days after we were wed, at the Midsummer Fair.

The fair had come every June when I was girl and my mother and I would always go together – so there was no chance of me missing it my first summer back in the Garden of Eden. I pleaded with Elijah to take me but in a way that made it quite clear I would go with Lilly and Samuel if he didn't.

So one bright afternoon, we dressed up as much as we could and set off down Maids Causeway, along with most of East Cambridge.

It was a fine thing to be promenading with my new husband. We passed lots of folk who remembered me from my childhood – I daresay word had got around – and so many stopped to congratulate us that we felt quite the swells by the time we reached Midsummer Common.

Not far past the first displays there was a man in an apron doing a hog-roast: two hog-roasts, in fact, as one was turning on a spit and another was laid out on a carving table with an onion in its mouth and its legs pulled diagonal, as if it was running. The hog-roast man was sharpening his knives, about to commence the carve-up, and a queue had already formed.

I turned my head away, not wanting to take too close a look, for I was hungry already and the sign said a serving of hog-roast was two and six for gentlemen and a shilling for ladies. I glanced sideways at Elijah as we walked on, hoping he might ask me if I'd like some, but he was looking carefully ahead, and I gathered by that we could not afford it. I gave a small sigh, and looked around for some amusement that was cheap.

Luckily for us, there were plenty of amusements where it was nothing at all to stand and spectate. There was Catch-a-Pig, where the men all paid tuppence to chase a piglet around and if they caught it and slung it over their shoulder they could keep it. I didn't think a great deal of this, as I could remember being beaten for failing to catch one once, so it didn't seem all that amusing to me, and besides it was obvious the piglet had been greased with soap so nobody could get it. But we stood and watched for a while and pretty soon some fella fell in the mud and Elijah started roaring with laughter and I joined in and before we knew it the whole crowd was off. The young men started queuing up for the next go and I do think Elijah would have joined them if I had not prevented him.

What would a Midsummer Fair, or any fair for that matter, be without pigs?

Just past the apple-bobbing, I saw a large sign: TOBY, THE SAPIENT PIG.

Elijah didn't seem keen on taking a look. He frowned, as if there was something sinister in it, but I dragged him by the arm and we stood behind the first row watching and moving our heads from side to side to peer between the others.

Toby the Sapient Pig was a large white with black patches and one black ear. He was held in a sty with clean golden straw, around which had been strewn a number of volumes: *The Plays of William Shakespeare*, I spotted, and some foreign-sounding names I did not recognise from my small amount of schooling.

Toby stood amidst these, ignoring the crowd. A man stood next to him, in a cape and top hat, beaming proudly as if he was presenting his newborn child for our delectation. 'Ask me anything you like, ladies and gentleman!' he declared. 'Shortly I will allow you to question the Sapient Toby – as you can see, he is currently having a short repast.' The pig was eating a book.

'What's he eating?' a man called out from the crowd. The manner in which the question was asked did not ring of true curiosity, in my opinion.

'Plutarch,' responded the man in the cape. 'He is fond of the Ancients.'

'How was he discovered?' called another.

'Well, his first master . . .' the man began, and then began spilling some nonsense about how he had been sold as a piglet to a schoolmaster who had taught him all he knew.

Pretty soon the crowd grew restless and the man clearly decided it would be politic to let the pig show what he could do. At this point, he withdrew a pack of playing cards and there followed some game, which involved putting them down on the straw and letting the pig choose one with his trotter and some young woman in the audience affecting amazement and shouting, 'The very one I was thinking of!'

Meanwhile, a young boy went among us with a cap. I saw Elijah toss something in and was surprised he was contributing as he had a rather sour look on his face. 'Come on, Rosie,' he muttered, 'let's be off.'

We were turning away, when the man in the cape called out, 'Now, you look like a highly intelligent young miss, if I might say so.'

I glanced about. A woman next to me hissed, 'He means you!'

The people in front of us parted and I was ushered forward. I looked back at Elijah but he had crossed his arms with a mildly amused but still sour look on his face.

'Young lady! Young lady! You of the lustrous locks. My Toby has eyes to read but can also appreciate human beauty. Do please honour me by showing yourself to him . . .'

I hope he doesn't think I'm climbing in that sty, I thought. But no, he merely wanted me to stand in front of it while he scattered some pieces of card with letters painted on them in front of the pig. The pig snuffled in front of some of them and the man bent to the straw, picking up R, O, S and E.

He held them up, fanning them for the crowd to see. 'And what is your name, fair one?' he asked me with a small bow.

'Rose!' I said, looking round at the crowd, hoping that they would see by my genuine amazement that I was not in on the act.

A few people at the front clapped and I blushed as if they were applauding me rather than the pig. I looked for Elijah but could not see him.

The man thanked me and handed me a small posy and a piece of paper which had on it a poem that he said had been written by the pig himself.

I found Elijah when I worked my way out of the crowd. He was standing a few feet off, looking grumpy.

'How did you do it?' I asked him gaily.

'Do what?'

'Tell him my name.'

'I didn't do any such thing . . .'

'Elijah,' I said, 'you were in on the joke, weren't you? Don't tease me now. Look I got a poem and a flower for my trouble.'

I planted a kiss on his cheek – but he really did look quite annoyed.

'I tell you I didn't.' He brushed me off.

We stood in awkward silence for a moment. Then, all at once, his face brightened. He nodded. 'Be right back, Rosie. Just seen a fella I know.' And off he went.

So I was left holding my paper flower and my poem written by the pig.

I stood around for a bit, then I read the poem.

> *Of the crowds who the Sapient Toby have seen*
> *Not one of them all disappointed have been;*
> *But all to their friends have been proud to repeat*
> *That a Visit to Toby indeed is a Treat.*

TSP

Elijah is a queer one, I thought. He must have told the man my name and got me the flower and the poem so why did he not take credit for it?

I was still standing close to the crowd that was watching Toby, so I heard the boy with the cap shouting, 'Oi! Which of you mean bastards put a button in my cap?'

I decided to take a wander around, figuring that Elijah would be able to find me when he chose as long as I did not stray too far. It was sixpence to go inside the tent of the Menagerie and see the Elephant Ridden by a Valorous Maiden and of course I had no money on me – so the Steam Powered Rides were out of the question as well. I watched the Eel Dipping, for a bit, which was quite droll. Next to the eels was A Three Legged Cat in a cage but I thought that was horrible and didn't look. The novelty of hanging around on my own was beginning to wear off and I began to feel annoyed with Elijah. Why could he not have taken me along with him to see the man he knew? I was hungry.

By the time he returned, I was ready to be sharp with him, but before I could say a word, he lifted up one fist and shook it in the air. It made a rattling sound. I could tell he was pleased with himself.

'What's that?' I said.

He dropped whatever rattled into his pocket. Then, he showed me that both his hands were empty. Next, he clapped them together, shook his sleeves, then lifted one hand from the other to reveal a palm full of coins; some pennies, thre'penny and sixpenny bits – even some florins.

'Elijah!' I cried. 'Where did you get that from?'

He tapped the size of his nose. 'Never let it be said I don't know how to show my Rosie a good time . . .' He linked his arm with mine and turned me. 'Now, where was that hog-roast man?'

The hog was roasted so well his skin was as orange as Aunt Lilly's hair and hard and crispy as a sugar stick. As the butcher sliced into it, you could see the white fat slithering beneath its shell and

# CHAPTER 9

I like to think that was the night my first child was conceived – my son, Daniel. I could be wrong about that, of course, as Elijah made sure we had one or two other opportunities before we moved into number twenty-two. I do so like the idea that my Daniel came into being inside me on that night, when Elijah held me in his arms beneath the stars. I suppose it could have just as easily have been the next time, when we did it awkwardly and sweatily, standing up in the stable behind Gas Lane, with Elijah's horse snorting and breathing next to us. I got my back bruised against the wooden wall.

My Daniel. How should I begin to describe that child? My first, my plumpest . . . the only one who never gave me a moment's worry. I think if any mother is honest they will admit they love the first in a way they cannot love the others, especially if that first is a boy. The first one cracks you open. With the first, your whole life goes topsy-turvy and nothing is ever the same again – for it is the first that turns you from an ordinary mortal into a mother. It is a coronation you never forget.

He was born in Paradise Street, the following March.

But before that, she arrived.

Elijah had not said much about his mother before we ran away together, nor after, for that matter. I knew he lived in his wagon with an older woman and man who I assumed were his mother and father. It was only when I started to talk about my mother dying, and how I never knew my real father, that he told me the story he had learned from his mother as a boy, about his father being the King of Russia. When I laughed, I saw I had offended him. He didn't think it funny at all.

I did think it a little odd that he didn't want to talk of his mother at all, or his life on the camp. I asked him once, in Paradise Street, was there no one he wanted from his old life at his wedding? He scratched his head and pulled a face. 'Well, it's not really the done thing where I come from,' was all he said. But surely he wanted his own mother? 'Well, I'm not sure she'll be all that pleased to be perfectly honest with you, Rosie . . .'

'Why not?' I asked, but I couldn't get a straight answer out of him. I didn't press him. To be honest, I liked the idea that we had jointly discarded our old lives.

He had a good way of silencing my curiosity in those early days. Upward, he would look, then down. 'Well, you might ask,' he would say, with a mock frown. Later, I was to find this phrase of his infuriating, but in the first few weeks of knowing him, it only added to his air of mystery and, anyhow, he often followed it with a kiss.

Those kisses – full of everything. He would hold my face, quite firmly, hands either side of my head, and pause for a moment, looking at me, long enough to let me know that I was his now, that he would not release me for the world. Then his face would move towards mine and I would close my eyes without even meaning to. And then it came . . . the meeting and the parting of the lips, his mouth first hard on mine, then soft, the grazing of our tongues together and the feel of his hands holding my face. The surrender of it . . . to be held firmly and kissed softly – is there any more a girl can ask for? They were hypnosis, those early kisses.

Why should I be curious about his mother?

I had been out to see Lilly. Her inflammation of the spine was bad and she had been in bed for a few days. It was past Christmas and I was too obviously with child to be out and about in the wider world, so visiting her was a nice excuse to get out of the house. The air was icy but I scarcely felt it – so huge was I my shawl could hardly cover me. I was like a great balloon as I floated down Paradise Street. People would jump into the street when they saw me coming, as if they were afraid that bumping against me might detach my moorings and send me sailing skywards.

I had left Elijah snoozing at home. He often snoozed after dinner if he had to be out late. I didn't like it much, but he brought money home with him so I could hardly complain. New horses would appear in the Gas Lane stables now and then – then disappear a few days later, but he never got rid of the horse we rode to Cambridge on. He said every man had to have one horse that was special.

He wouldn't let me near the horses once he knew I was carrying. He said it was bad luck. I didn't mind. By then, I was used to the fact that he was superstitious.

Lilly loved my pregnancy. It was the nearest she would ever get to having one herself, she said, so she wanted all the details, even the private stuff like how often I needed the privvy and how I craved potato. That afternoon, we'd had a long chat and it was getting gloomy by the time I ambled down Paradise Street. I expected that Elijah would have gone out, but when I opened the door he was standing in our little sitting room, and in front of him was a small, dark woman, in an old-fashioned mourning dress with a brooch at the neck. She looked a little comical, in fact, as she also had pointy, lace-up boots on her feet and a large hat with a drooping ostrich feather. Round her neck was a fox fur which, to my mind, looked as if it had been taken from the rest of the fox by an amateur, not necessarily a two-legged one. As I entered, she drew herself up to her full height, which was still a great deal shorter than me.

I looked at Elijah. He exhaled, then dropped himself down into his armchair. 'Well, Rosie, looks like we've got company.' He stared ahead.

The woman drew in her breath. She glanced me up and down, then picked up an old leather bag from the floor, lifted her skirts and turned to our staircase. I watched her ascend. What was this strange woman doing, going up our stairs?

Then I saw a huge carpet-bag on the floor. The penny dropped.

I rushed over to Elijah. 'Elijah!' I hissed, bending a little so she should not hear me, 'that's not your mother?'

'Who else might it be, my love?' he said calmly.

'Elijah!' I said. 'What were you doing sitting yourself down? Haven't you been looking after her? Why didn't you fetch me at once from Lilly's?'

'She's only just this minute arrived,' Elijah replied irritably, waving a hand.

'Well have you offered her some tea?' I could not believe how ill mannered he was being, to his own mother.

'She's not in the mood for tea. She's had some bad news.'

'What news?'

'Her husband died. She'll be with us for a bit, all right? Now leave it be, Rosie.'

He was often gruff when he was upset, Lijah, but I had not fully learned that yet. Later I knew not to press him on anything that he might be feeling something about. 'But, here? She's staying here? Shouldn't we have a talk about it?'

'There'll be plenty of time for all that,' he huffed, rising from the chair. 'Mark my words.'

He strode over to the door and took his jacket and hat from the peg on the back.

'You're not going out?' I cried in dismay.

'Oh yes, I am.' He went to the mirror by the bottom of the stairs to check his hat was on straight.

I was bewildered. 'What am I to do with her?' I asked.

'Well I daresay you'll have plenty to talk about, you two women.'

I tried firmness. 'Elijah Smith, you cannot go out on one of your appointments when your mother has just arrived after not seeing you for months, and her husband dead, and, you can't . . .'

'I'm not off on an appointment,' he said, 'I'm off to The Bleeding Heart.'

'Elijah . . .'

'Oh stop beefing, woman. I'll be back later.' And he left.

We had a small settee that we had bought on the never-never not long after we'd moved in. I sank down onto it and knew I was about to cry. I wept often when I was carrying. I was bewildered by Lijah's behaviour. How could he be so rude to his own mother? It shocked me, that he was capable of treating someone like that. It was a side of him I'd not seen before. And what would I say to her? I would have to make some excuse for him. I could hardly say he had gone down the pub.

I was still sitting there in some disarray when I heard a light tread on the stair. Elijah's mother was making her way down, slowly. The stairs came straight into the sitting room so I was able to observe the last few steps of her descent. Her little booted feet were pressed sideways against each stair. She was holding up her skirts with one hand and clutching the rail tightly with the other, as if she had never used stairs before.

She stood before me. She had removed her hat and the fox fur and I could now take a close look at her old-fashioned mourning dress, which had pleats down the front and puff sleeves with lace, like on a child's dress. I was about to rise and offer her a cup of tea but something in her strange look kept me pinned to the settee. She was staring at me as if she was trying to see beyond my face, to what was inside, my secret thoughts.

Then she said, 'Ee's gone down the pub, I s'pose.' She had a thick Fenland accent.

Had she been eavesdropping on us? I am ashamed to say that more tears sprung to my eyes as I nodded. I felt humiliated, all of a sudden, as if it was my fault Elijah was off down The Bleeding Heart, as if she was judging me for being unable to keep my husband in the house.

Her eyes narrowed, became two pin-pricks, and I suddenly remembered the hostile stare she had given me the very first time I had seen Elijah sitting on the step of their wagon.

'You've married my son,' she said evenly, 'and you'll sup sorrow by the spoonful 'til the day you die.'

She went back up the stairs.

It was not what you'd call a good start, I suppose.

What was extraordinary to me was that the next day, Elijah and his mother behaved as if there had been nothing odd in either her sudden appearance or his reaction to it – as if it was quite normal for people to drop in and out of each other's lives with hardly a word.

She had not reappeared the previous evening and eventually I went to bed alone, presuming she would look after herself in the tiny box room next to ours. She had closed the door and, after her pronouncement, I was far too timid to knock on it to enquire if she needed anything.

Elijah returned some time in the night. He had been drinking ale, which always made him snore. I was finding it difficult to sleep, so lay awake most of the night, heaving myself from one side to the next every now and then when my position became uncomfortable. I finally dropped off not long before dawn, and within minutes was awoken by the sound of creaking on the stairs. I started awake – each of my pregnancies gave me wild nightmares and I frightened easily. My first reaction was to shake Elijah and tell him there was an intruder in the house, but then I remembered his mother. What on earth was she doing up at that hour?

In the morning, I left Elijah where he was, pulled my shawl over my nightdress and clambered carefully down the stairs. I slipped on Elijah's boots over my bed socks and let myself out the back door, shuffling down the path to the privvy. The night-soil man had been, thank God. He didn't always do his duty, and the smell out the backs of the houses if he missed our street was quite unbearable. I let myself into the privvy.

As I came out, I let the wooden door swing shut behind me. A blackbird was sitting on the bare twig of a nearby bush. The banging of the door made it take flight. I shuddered with cold and turned to shuffle back up the path – and then I got a right old fright.

Elijah's mother was squatting on her heels by our small vegetable patch. She was smoking a thin clay pipe and staring at me, puffing on the pipe by pursing and unpursing her lips in short, sharp movements but otherwise as motionless as a garden ornament.

I saw myself through her eyes – a huge woman in a nightie with wild red hair, her bed socks round her fat ankles and her husband's unlaced boots on her feet. I hurried back inside.

When the kettle was on the stove, I went back upstairs and dressed noisily, to wake Elijah. I was damned if I was breakfasting alone with his sprite of a mother.

It started that first day. After breakfast, the silence broken only by a casual remark about the weather or a horse, she got to her feet and picked up our dirty plates. I had only just sat down after serving us all, but I jumped to my feet instantly. 'Do sit down . . .' I hesitated over what to call her. I didn't know her name. 'Mother, please. I can do that.' At the word *mother*, I thought I saw her and Elijah exchange a glance.

Either way, she ignored me, taking the plates over to the sink and placing them in. Then she turned and cleared away our cups, including mine, which still had some tea in it.

'Had enough, Lijah?' she said.

'Yes, thank you,' he replied meekly. He stood.

'Right then,' she replied, as she began to unbutton her sleeves. 'You'd better be off, then, and let me and your wife here get on with our chores.'

I stared at him.

'Right you are,' he said, and turned away without meeting my gaze.

'I'll wash these things,' Elijah's mother said. 'Now, this is your bowl for dishes, isn't it?'

'It's my bowl for everything,' I said. We lived in a house scarcely wider than the wagon she was used to. Did she think I had a scullery or washroom?

She stared at me. 'You've buckets I can take outside when I do the laundry, I hope.'

*The* laundry?

'Yes, Mother, we have buckets, but you'll not be wanting to wring cloths outside in this weather.'

She drew breath, blew it out slowly through pursed lips, shook her head and turned back to the sink.

If it hadn't been for Lilly, I am not sure how I would have got through those first few weeks. Elijah's mother was the most peculiar person I had ever met. Her ways were beyond me. Each afternoon, I would escape to Lilly's bedside and tell her of the latest antic. 'And yesterday, she served up some potatoes and she had not put any cabbage in gravy on my plate and it took me all my courage to say something to her and do you know what she said?'

'Go on . . .'

'She snapped at me, *it's bad luck for a woman in your condition to eat anything green*. And that was it! I'm not allowed to eat cabbage in my own house.' I'd never liked cabbage much anyway, but that wasn't the point.

Lilly would be agog. Like any invalid, she was bored and it was rare entertainment for her, my stories of Elijah's mother.

'You'll never guess what now . . .' I said one afternoon as I dropped my bulk down onto the edge of Lilly's bed. The bedsprings squeaked in protest. It was nearly March and I felt in my bones that my baby would be coming soon.

'What?' Lilly said, as she took the plate of fried potatoes I had brought over for her. I had put another plate on top of it, to keep it warm.

'This is a great one, this is. Last night, we was all talking. Lijah was at home for once and we were seated at the table. I rose up to get a cup of water and my back twinged, as it does, and I gave a gasp. Well, Lijah's mother jumps to her feet and orders Lijah out of the room. He's about to go when I tell them both to sit down for heaven's sake as it's only my back, and Lijah's mother starts questioning me. Do I feel peculiar in any way? Have I had a sudden urge to scrub the floor or anything? No, I say firmly, my baby's not coming but I think it's only a day or two if they want to know the truth. When Lijah leaves the room, his mother says to me, all confidential, that she's sure it's soon too as my bump has dropped down lower, but I shouldn't really say such things in front of my husband as it was indecent to mention women's matters. Honestly, all I'd said was the baby was coming soon. It wasn't as if I went into any detail.' Lilly was forking fried potato into her mouth while she listened. A small piece had dropped onto her bed shawl. 'Anyway, that's not the end of it. This morning, I get up. She's up before me as usual. She always is, no matter what time I rise. Sometimes I think she gets up in the middle of the night and goes out for her smoke just to make sure she beats me to it. Anyway, she's downstairs this morning, and what is she doing?'

Lilly paused, fork halfway to her mouth.

'She is draping scarves over the mirrors.'

'What?'

'This is her latest. I'm not allowed to look at myself now.'

'Why not?'

'She said the baby might come any minute, and I might walk past a mirror holding the baby on my shoulder and the baby might look into the mirror and lose its soul into it, or something. Oh, God knows, Lilly, the woman is completely batty and Elijah never says a word to her and what am I supposed to do?'

'That big mirror that you've got over the settee, the one with the painted frame that looks like gilt?'

'It's covered with a black shawl with orange flowers on it, frame and all.'

Lilly frowned at the trials I was undergoing. 'You can always bring that mirror round here, if you like.'

There was one aspect of having Elijah's mother around which I have to confess was useful, apart from the work she did about the house. Elijah cut down on his drinking a bit.

It hadn't really bothered me that much at first. Well, most men like a drink or two, don't they? And growing up in East Cambridge I would have thought it a bit odd to have ended up with a man who didn't partake once in a while. I was even fond of the occasional cup of cider myself sometimes, when we first moved into our house, and as the evenings drew in we would sometimes sit down together and share a jug and I would read aloud to him from *Ally Sloper's Half Holiday*. He loved Ally Sloper. Most Frequently

Kicked Out Man in Europe. 'Only 'cos they've not met me yet!' Elijah used to say, slapping his knee.

Then, as my pregnancy drew on, I realised I couldn't really drink more than a cup without it making me feel sick and dizzy, but I still sat with him and read aloud. I remember those evenings fondly. And the baby hadn't put me off intimacy with him, not at all.

But as I got fatter and more awkward, and more tired, Elijah started going out more and more and by the time his mother showed up in our lives it was already causing a bit of strain between us. But something became clear to me within a few days of her arriving – he was a deal more afraid of her than he was of me.

Then, one evening, just after the mirrors were covered up by Elijah's mother, Elijah and I had an unpleasant argument.

It was a Sunday night. He had been out drinking the night before. At teatime, I asked him for the rent money, which was due every Sunday. He hadn't got it.

Now, this had happened before, and Aunt Lilly's friend that had the rental on the house had been very good about it, I might say. We had never fallen more than a week or two behind before Elijah got hold of it somehow, but even so it embarrassed me mightily as it was a friend of Lilly's we were holding it back from, not some horrible Corporation man. I wouldn't have given two hoots about being late on the rent to one of them.

Eventually, the knock came at the door and I went to it and there stood Lilly's friend, Miss Riley, and I said how sorry I was and how next week there'd be double, and she looked a little crestfallen, but then leaned in and said, 'Don't you worry, my dear, you've got quite enough on your plate as it is.' She glanced behind me, to where Elijah's mother was standing in the room.

I went back inside and said, 'Well I hope you're happy, Elijah. That's Miss Riley's week ruined. She buys her groceries with the rental from this place, you know.'

'I thought you said she lived with a friend,' said Elijah's mother, although I had not been addressing her.

'She does,' I replied, 'but that is hardly the point, Mother. We owe her that money fair and square and she's been good to us.'

'And made a pretty penny out of it. I can't believe what you pay her to live in this box.'

Oh, a box, was it? A box that was good enough for her, for weeks on end, and with no word whatsoever on how long she might be with us. I could not be rude to her but my blood was beginning to boil. So I turned on Elijah. 'I do think you might consider my feelings,' I said to him. 'You go off doing as you please but I deal with the womenfolk in this street and by tomorrow lunchtime everyone is going to know how we are taking advantage of Miss Riley.'

'Well, she should hold her tongue, then,' Elijah snarled. 'What right has she got to be telling everyone our business?'

She wouldn't, of course. She would tell Lilly, and Lilly would tell everyone else. He had a point, but that was not the point.

I've never been much good at arguing. It upsets me too easy. I say whatever comes into my head and make myself look foolish. 'They are friends of mine,' I said tremulously, 'and . . . and . . .'

I looked from one to the other and saw how they were united against me. And I saw, moreover, that they would always be united against me in any sort of argument; that as soon as I disagreed with one, the other would be with them, and I would never win. I knew I would cry if I was not careful, so I left the room.

As I clambered up the stairs, I heard Lijah's mother say, quite distinctly and with no effort to avoid me hearing, 'How do you stand it . . .'

Lijah came up to bed later. I pretended to be asleep but he put his arm around me from behind.

'Don't bother yourself so, Rosie . . .' he said in a low voice. 'You know I'll get the money together by next week. I always do. You get in such a lather. Loads of folk are late with the rent, my chicken.'

'You're forgetting something,' I muttered bad temperedly. 'I used to go rent collecting myself, remember? It isn't as easy as you think. And if someone doesn't give you what they owe you it's dreadful because you never know if you'll get it or not and you never know if they're going to give you no end of trouble.'

He let go of me and lay on his back. 'You get in too much of a worry about such stuff. You'll feel better later.' He meant, *when the baby's come.*

Oh no, I thought. I'm going to be much worse then. For surely, once we had a baby to worry about, being behind with the rent would be ten times as bad? And anyway, I had had quite enough of how anything wrong with me got put down to the fact I was carrying.

I lay on my back next to him for a moment, but I couldn't do it for long. It didn't feel right. I rolled over on my side again, but towards him this time.

'What did she mean, *how do you stand it*?'

'What?'

'What did your mother mean?'

'She ain't used to houses, that's all. It's a bit cooped up for her here.'

Is that what she meant? I wondered to myself as, unusually for me, I began to fall asleep.

The next morning was a Monday and I got up early after sleeping quite well and checked and stoked the range. When it was firing up nicely, I left the door open so the air could help the flames along and I went out to the privvy. The garden was empty. As I came back into the house, I listened for Lijah's mother moving about. All was quiet upstairs, so I knew that she was still asleep. I took a deep breath. How nice it was to have the house to myself for a few minutes.

The fire in the range was burning up, so I closed the door and started making Elijah's bacon and onion roll. I always rose extra early on a Monday morning and did it fresh, then we all had some. The rest of the week, his mother and I had bread while Elijah had a slice of the roll cold with his mug of tea. He always sliced it exactly so that there was enough to get him through to the following Sunday.

I chopped the bacon and onions and set them on to fry, then I began rolling out the suet. It was then that the words I had heard the night before came back to me. *How do you stand it?*

She wasn't talking about the house. What did Elijah think I was, some kind of fool?

*How do you stand it?*

Me, she meant. How do you stand *her?* And suddenly it came to me, the malice in those words. She was clever, that one. She knew better than to say outright, *your wife is awful*, for that would get Elijah's back up, and he might tell her to mind her own business. No, she was smarter than that.

*How do you stand it?* They were words to make him think how wonderful he was for putting up with me. The thought that I was something to be put up with would sneak in behind that other thought, but be planted in his head all the same.

It was a mean trick, to hide her dislike of me behind her love for Elijah. Mothers can do that – take any unkind thing they feel for another person and justify it to themselves by their love for their child. They can resent and resent, and twist their resentment into something noble. I've done it myself. When I coveted Mrs Herne's new hat in which she paraded up and down the street at Christmas, I thought to myself, *imagine her spending that on a new hat for herself when her child goes about in his dad's old shoes with newspaper stuffed into the toes. I'd never buy a hat like that when my child wanted for some-*

*thing.* So I went back into the house in a high dudgeon, congratulating myself on what a wonderful mother I was going to be to my yet-unborn baby, so much a better mother than Annie Herne. And it was only later when I calmed down that I admitted to myself that from what I'd seen of her she wasn't a bad mother at all and loved her little boy dearly. It was just that I wanted her hat.

*How do you put up with it? My poor lamb, my dear Lijah, when you deserve so much better than the wife you've got and here am I, your mother, to tell you so and to love you so much more and so much better than your wife will ever be able to.*

Hatred: a small word, but one that holds so many different feelings all tightly packaged up into two short, hard syllables. Envy and meanness and resentment and plain old misery – a whole load of stuff, but spin them all together and what do you come up with? Let's be plain speaking and call it by its name: hatred.

So, I thought, she hates me. I cried, of course. Bitter tears of self-pity ran down my cheeks and dropped freely from my face onto where the suet lay in a helpless lump on the rolling board. I had to stand still for a moment while I gathered myself, then wipe my face with my sleeve as my hands were sticky and I didn't want to reach inside my apron pocket for my handkerchief. Fortunately, Elijah liked his suet rolls well salted. I heaved a breath.

*Well, Mrs Smith,* I thought as I bent back to my task and pressed down on the rolling pin, *or whatever your name may be.* The suet bulged like flesh beneath my efforts. It was sticking, so I reached for the open bag of flour. *Well, what you have forgotten is that I am going to be a mother too, and your equal, and if hatred is what you want to bring into this house, then you shall have it back as large as you like.*

All my fierce thinking and kneading of the suet had distracted me and I had let the bacon and onions get too brown. I rescued them from the hot-plate and took the pan to the board, scattering them on top of the suet. Then I drizzled the cooking fat over the top and began rolling the whole thing up. It was then that it happened – a feeling inside me, like something tearing. Water rushed down my leg. I stared at the puddle on the floor. I took a deep breath, and stepped backwards. Then panic overcame me.

I hobbled quickly to the bottom of the stairs, and shouted up, in a voice high and hollow, '*Mother*!'

# CHAPTER 10

And then came Daniel.

We got rid of Elijah double quick, of course. Clementina went for Mrs Dawson. Lilly got wind of it and rose from her sickbed to come over and Mrs Dawson brought her two nieces along as they were in training. Our tiny house was suddenly full of women – although I registered them all only dimly as I was pretty far gone by then.

Afterwards, I held him, my Daniel, upstairs in our bedroom, while the others busied themselves. One of the nieces brought in strong tea with lots of sugar and toast dripping in lard, and I ate and drank with one hand as I couldn't bear to put my baby down. I thought I would never put him down, ever, in my whole life.

Daniel. I stared at his shiny little cheeks, the smear of blood on one of his eyebrows, the slick of dark hair on his head. His eyes were clamped tight shut, like he was saying to us, *I've got a lot to get used to so you're all going to have to give me a bit of time.* 'It was you in there,' I whispered to him. 'All that time, I was walking around and I didn't know who was inside me. And all along it was you.'

When I had finished my tea and toast, the niece came back with a hairbrush and began to brush my hair firmly. 'Aunty says you're to tell me where to find a clean nightgown to put on you. We've to get you tidy, so we can let your husband come in.'

Husband . . .? Oh, yes, I thought, Elijah. I carried on gazing down at Daniel while I let Mrs Walton's niece pull at my hair. *I suppose I had better show you to your father, hadn't I, my little one?*

When I had been got ready, they all left me alone. Daniel still had his eyes clamped tight shut and I was still looking down at him, when I became aware of a shape in the doorway. I didn't lift my head, but whispered, 'Come in quietly, Elijah. He's asleep.'


I was the Queen of Paradise Street, for a while. No boys had been born on our street for some time, so he and I were fussed over something rotten. The stuff we got given – Mrs Herne bought a green lace bonnet from Peaks. It was the oddest thing you'd ever seen in your life, with a little tuft on top, like he was a pixie, but I could tell it cost a fortune. Mrs Walton made us rhubarb crumble twice a week for weeks on end – said I had to keep my strength up – and I'd quite liked rhubarb up 'til then but, after a while, the very smell made me feel ill and to this day if I smell rhubarb I come over a bit poorly. Every child in the street came round and begged to be allowed to take Daniel out in his pram. We belonged to everybody. I had never been so important, or cosseted. It was the best time of my life.


Then, one night, I was awoken. I had no idea what time it was, but I stirred to see my husband standing on my side of the bed. He had been out all day and evening and I had gone to bed early.

'Move over, Rosie,' he said, his voice slurry and affectionate.

Daniel was on my other side.

'I can't,' I said sleepily, 'the baby's . . .'

'Move the baby then!' His tone had changed completely. I sat up on my elbows.

I knew what he wanted, of course, and I didn't think it unreasonable as it had been several months and it was a side of our lives that had been quite important to us before. It came to me that I hadn't paid Elijah any attention at all since Daniel had been born. More than one woman in our street had whispered to me that I mustn't forget my husband's needs if I didn't want him to stray.

My head was in a fog. I had fed Daniel not an hour before and had been in one of those deep, drugged sleeps you get after feeding, but I roused myself and picked Daniel up. We didn't have a Moses basket for him yet; that was the one thing we hadn't been given. Elijah had said he would weave one and I was still waiting for it. I didn't want to put Daniel on the floor, so I opened the top drawer of the chest of drawers in the corner and laid him gently down among my underthings. He didn't stir.

I got back into bed, lay on my back and hitched up my nightie.

It wasn't that I didn't like it. It just felt wrong. When he touched me, I couldn't escape the thought that he was stealing something that belonged to Daniel. He was gentle enough, on account of it being my first time since, but I was still a bit out of sorts down there and could hardly feel him. He managed it, but I didn't get the feeling he enjoyed it all that much either.

Afterwards, he drew away from me and sat up. I rolled over and eased myself to the other side of the bed.

He came round his side after a moment or two, undressed himself properly, and got in. I picked Daniel up from the chest of drawers and put him back between us, and could not prevent myself from giving a satisfied sigh as I snuggled down next to him. Bless him for not stirring that whole time.

Maybe Elijah heard my sigh and understood it. Maybe he realised that, for the time being, he was something to be endured.

After a short silence between us, he said awkwardly, 'How's the little fella been today, then?'

'All right,' I said, drifting back towards sleep. My last thought was, well, at least you can't get pregnant when you're feeding a baby already.

Turned out, I was quite wrong about that.

Mehitable was born just before Christmas that year. Mehitable Smith. She was early; a tiny, scrawny thing, with folds of dark skin and a head of jet-black hair. She slipped out easy as anything but was a nightmare to feed – completely different from my Daniel. She was that restless on the breast, as if it made her uncomfortable in some way. She would toss and turn her head – while staying clamped on to me, mind – and kick her thin, little legs. It hurt me in a way that feeding Daniel never had. She was colicky as well. That was a trial. I thought it was only boys got the colic but I was soon put right about that.

Just after teatime it would start, the screaming, and it would go on for hours and hours, and the only thing that kept her quiet was feeding and that only worked for as long as she was actually doing it.

I thought it would never stop, the screaming. I couldn't think what I had done to produce such an unhappy baby. It drove us all near demented.

Well, I say all. What I mean is me and Mother and the poor, unfortunate neighbours at numbers twenty and twenty-four. Elijah was never there. Things were not going too well between me and him.

Elijah's mother had been gone for the whole of the summer – where to, I do not know – but she had taken off somewhere doing whatever it is her sort do in the summer. I wish I could say Elijah and I were happier with her gone but we weren't. He was twitchy and bad tempered the whole time she was away, and once I snapped at him, 'Oh for heaven's sake, why didn't you go off with your mother?' He gave me a look so dark it made me frightened.

Come the weather turning colder, she was back. Daniel was glad to see her. She spoiled him rotten. It was quite nice to have her around the first few days, helping out, and I thought maybe it will be all right this time. Then, she started. Why was Elijah out so much and coming home with so little lovah to show for it? *Lovah*? You know, cash. *Don't ask me, Mother, he's your son. I haven't a clue what he gets up to in the evening.* Was Daniel maybe getting a bit squinty? Had I been taking him out in the wind too much? Didn't I know it was bad for a baby's eyes? *Mother, Daniel's fine. He's the healthiest baby in the whole of Cambridge.* Was that Empers woman still getting poorly and taking to her bed? Her poor husband. *Actually, Mother, Lilly nearly died in July. Samuel was beside himself.*

I didn't say any of these things, and perhaps that was my mistake. I thought to myself, just let it all wash over, you know what she's like. So all the things I would have liked to have said to her piled up inside me, month after month. I would lie awake at night – bigly pregnant and unable to sleep, yet again – and I would rehearse in my head my smart retorts to all her snide remarks.

Of course, what I really wanted to say was, if you don't like it round here, Mother, then why don't you *jef*? Oh, I'd picked up a bit of their cant, right enough, even though they usually only talked it to each other when I was out of the room. I wasn't near as daft as they thought.

Then Mehitable came along, and everything went downhill from there.

I think, in my head, I thought I would be spoiled again when I had another baby. It was so short a time since Daniel I could still remember how everyone came around and how even Elijah would hold him and sing songs and tell me I was a clever Rosie to have produced such a handsome boy. What I didn't know was that, with baby number two, everybody just assumes you've done it once, you know the ropes, and what's the point of making a fuss of you? Which in my case was something of a disaster, as I needed far more help than I had ever done with Daniel.

Two weeks after she was born, I left them both with Elijah's mother and said I was going to walk to the street and back, just for a breath of fresh air, and to see the candles lit up in people's windows. It was nearly Christmas and I hadn't been out of the house in a fortnight. It was almost dark. I had just got to the end of the road and was turning to come back when I saw Mr Winfield pass on the other side of the street, on his way to his evening shift at the brewery, probably.

He raised a hand to me. 'Evening, Mrs Smith. Hoping for a Christmas baby, I expect?'

He went on his way and I waddled home with my spirits so low. All right, it was dark, and I was still huge and had a shawl on and he couldn't tell I'd had my baby already – but with Daniel the whole street knew the minute he was born. They almost hung bunting out the windows. With Mehitable, a lot of folk didn't even notice, let alone care, and that's the truth.

Then the colic started. They knew I'd had the baby then. Ha, that told them. Mehitable Smith made her presence felt loud and clear, then.

I should probably explain something about the children's names. It was not my doing. Turned out Elijah's mother had pretty firm ideas about that, like she did about everything else.

When Daniel was about four weeks old, she put him on her shoulder one day and said she was taking him out for a bit. I hated the way she used to tie him to her with a shawl – we had a perfectly good pram that we'd borrowed from the Field family, but she never used it. I had had a rough night feeding him, however, so I said okay. Elijah was out, as usual, so I thought I could get a bit of rest.

Little did I know what she had in mind. A couple of hours later, she's back, and she's telling me about how she thought it was going to rain on the way home but it didn't, then she adds, as relaxed about it as you like, 'Oh, by the way. I got him registered. I called him Adolphus.'

I stared at her in disbelief. I was sat on the settee, and she was standing picking bits of fluff off her hat. '*What?*'

'Adolphus. You was saying last night we've got to get him registered, it's the law, so I thought I might as well do it while I was out. There wasn't any queuing up or anything. I took him in and said I've come to get the baby registered. And they said, what's his name?'

From her tone of voice, I gathered that this question had surprised her.

'So I said Adolphus. Adolphus Smith.'

'*Adolphus!*'

She looked at me irritably. 'Yes, that's what I said, weren't it? Adolphus.'

For once, I could not restrain myself. 'What sort of name is that? For heaven's sake, Mother! How could you do that? What kind of name is that?'

She stopped picking fluff off her hat and her eyes narrowed. 'It's a perfectly good name, a very respectable name.'

'We've been calling him Daniel for weeks!'

'I know that,' she said crossly, 'what difference does that make? It doesn't matter what name you tell the registration folk, does it? You could tell them his name is Lemon Thyme. It's got nothing to do with anything, does it?'

Exasperated and shaking her head, she went into the kitchen.

When Mehitable was born, I stared down at her, but nothing came into my head. In truth, I had been convinced it was another boy. I'd been carrying low, exactly the same way as I was with Daniel. I was planning in my head how I would register this one myself and his name, in life and on paper, would be something nice and normal like Frederick or William or George.

I didn't have a single girl's name in my head. I suppose I should have named her after my own mother, but my mother always hated her name.

'What's your Christian name?' I asked Elijah's mother, as she busied herself at the foot of my bed, gathering the soiled sheets.

'Clementina,' she said without looking up. 'But most folk calls me Lem.'

Oh well, that's out, I thought.

I glanced back down at my poor, scrawny little girl. I wish I could say I felt overwhelmed with love and protectiveness, how I had with Daniel, but I felt nothing much – just a strange, dull emptiness inside.

Elijah's mother came and stood by the side of my bed and looked down at her too. There was a long silence as we stared at her, as if all three of us were, quite calmly, contemplating the difficulties that lay ahead.

'Mehitable,' Clementina said simply.

I turned my head away. 'All right.'

It upsets me to think about the next few years in Paradise Street. What came later was hard, but those years were hardest because they had started off so well, me and Elijah happy together and me full of what a good wife and mother I would be; and I was, to start off with, I swear I was.

It is hard, when a child is sick on you. It is hard not to blame your-self and then to blame the child, for you cannot bear the thought that if you'd done something different it would have been all right. That doctor that we got, eventually, I felt like he was blaming me. You never stop being wrong when you're a mother, I soon discovered.

Elijah started disappearing, for days on end sometimes. Daniel took it stoically enough, but Mehitable would cry and whine for her father something rotten. I remember one day, Mehitable had been crying and moaning all day. Elijah had been gone a couple of nights and we'd run out of everything. I had borrowed and borrowed from everyone in the street, and we had a reputation now, and even Lilly was getting fed up with it. I didn't even want to show my face outside that day, so ashamed was I, so Mehitable and I were cooped up together. Clementina was off somewhere. Daniel was old enough to go to school in the mornings.

At dinnertime, Daniel came trotting home. He came and found me in the kitchen. He must have only been five or six but he was the little man of the house, no doubt about that. In he came, crackling away. It was the vests I made him, out of brown paper. I had tried newspaper but the print came off on him and made him filthy, so crackly brown paper it was. That's how cold it was outside.

He had already been into our little parlour, the only room with a fire lit, where Mehitable was lying on the settee clutching a blanket and staring at the walls.

'Me and Mehitable need something hot to eat, Mam,' he said firmly, as he came in the kitchen.

I said, as gentle as I could, 'There a piece of bread each I've saved. It's a bit stale but it'll be okay, we can toast it. I've got a slice of brawn for you to share but there's nothing hot.' Brawn was the cheapest thing the butcher had that was edible. Elijah sometimes ate whips, but you can't feed children on cow's tails.

'Why don't we warm it up in the fire?' Daniel suggested.

I wasn't thinking straight. I said. 'All right. Use the spike.'

He took the toasting spike, found the slice of brawn in the cold box in the pantry and brought it in. Then he took it into the parlour room. I heard him say, 'Here you are, Billy. We're going to have hot brawn on toast.'

She always smiled for Daniel, did Mehitable. He was like a god to her.

There was a moment's silence, then a wail of despair from Mehitable. *In Lord's name what now?* I thought and went into the sitting room.

Daniel was sitting on his heels before the fire, holding the empty spike and looking disconsolate. Mehitable was sat next to him, her mouth open, howling.

'Sorry, Mam,' said Daniel.

The slice of brawn was in the fire. When Daniel had held the spike in the flames, the fat had melted straightaway, of course, and the brawn had fallen off among the coals. It was all I had for them. There was nothing else but stale bread in the house.

'Never mind, Daniel,' I said, thinking of how stupid it was of me to have let him do it. Mehitable was still screeching. You would've thought it was her on the end of the spike.

'Oh for God's sake, Billy, shut that wailing, will you?' I couldn't help myself from snapping at her. Daniel had been trying his best.

We all three of us looked into the fire, and I thought, *marrying Elijah Smith was the biggest mistake of my life.*

Later that afternoon, Clementina came home. Somehow she had got the wherewithal to buy us some giblets, so's we could make a broth. She was more helpful that way than her no-good son; I'll give her that.

I was feeling low, as low as low could be, but as she came in, I forced myself to rise from my chair and take the packet from her. A little blood was leaking at one corner. I unwrapped the giblets and put them in the colander, rinsing them under the tap. I left them to drain while I washed my hands and put the kettle on.

And then she started in on me. Were the children over at Mrs Herne's house, yet again?

Yes they were, I replied. Mrs Herne had three boys now and Daniel loved playing with them – he liked doing boy's games that he couldn't do with Mehitable.

Did I know that Mrs Herne felt so sorry for our two that she fed them?

I had always suspected as much as they didn't nag me for tea when they came home – I had been pretending to myself that I didn't know.

I let her rattle on at me while I tipped the giblets on to the chopping board. The butcher had already trimmed the crop, so I didn't have to worry about that. I took the short knife and cut the top off the heart. There was a small well of dark red blood inside, which I cleaned beneath the tap.

How did I know what Mrs Herne was feeding my children? Clementina went on . . .

I turned the liver. It was fresh and shiny, the colours shimmering on its surface. Behind me, Clementina had stopped going on about Mrs Herne. There was a moment's blissful silence. *Oh please just leave the room*, I prayed to myself, *please just go away and leave me in peace.*

Then she said, calmly and purposefully, 'Don't forget to cut out the bile.'

I slammed down the kitchen knife, leaned on my knuckles on the counter top and took a deep breath. 'Yes, thank you, Mother,' I said between gritted teeth. 'I think I know how to trim giblets by now . . .'

I still had my back to her, otherwise she might have seen the look on my face and realise she shouldn't push me further.

'Oh we are Miss La-di-da this afternoon,' she remarked casually. 'Well, it's a good job I know how to buy them, isn't it?'

I still had my back to her and managed to keep my voice light. 'You wouldn't need to be going down to Neave's for giblets if that son of yours brought a bit of money home once in a while.'

I knew that would needle her, criticism of her sainted boy.

'Lijah's been very busy lately.'

'Aye, yes, and he's been keeping the landlord of The Bleeding

Heart busy and all, all that pulling of pints he's been doing for Elijah. Rushed off his feet.'

I turned to face her. She had sat down at the table. She looked at me steadily. 'Bit full of airs and graces today, aren't we?'

'If it's airs and graces to want my children fed, instead of relying on other people's charity, then yes I am. My mother raised me all on her own and she never had to do that.'

At the mention of my mother, she made a *humphing* noise. 'Yes, well, I daresay your mother found ways to get the wherewithal to feed you, didn't she?'

I stared at her. She stared back. The kettle on the hot-plate began to whistle and I turned and removed it. I realised I was shaking. We were rushing headlong into something, this woman and I, and I knew something unpleasant was about to happen. I felt sick, and the palms of my hands were sweating, but I could not stop myself. Without either of us meaning to, we had crossed a line.

'What's that supposed to mean?' I asked, quite calmly, as I turned back to her.

She pulled one of her faces, turning down the corners of her mouth. 'Well, let's just say *I* knew who my father was.'

I was so astonished that she should raise this that I stared at her in disbelief, and when I spoke my voice was unsteady. 'It may be true,' I faltered, 'that I was born illegitimate, but as I understand it so was Elijah.'

'That's none of your business!' she snapped back, and closed her mouth firmly, glaring at me.

'It is my business when you start making unfair remarks about my mother and casting judgement on me,' I replied. 'Do you think it is easy to be a fatherless child? I assure you it is not. Indeed, it was one of the first topics of conversation between Elijah and I, that we had this in common.' I saw from her face that this remark hit home, that she did not like the thought that Elijah and I had something in common and that we had discussed it between ourselves, especially something that affected her so closely. And then I added something I had not intended to add, but in truth my head was spinning with her rudeness and I was a little too flush with having got one over on her. 'Although it is true that our stories differ in one respect, mine and Elijah's. *My* mother never lied to me.'

Her mouth had opened again, but only a little, to form a small, round 'o'. Her eyes were tiny and black as raisins. I knew that I had cut her to the quick. I should have had the sense not to press home my advantage, but all the small slights I had received since she had come to us were boiling up in me, and I could not prevent myself. How dare she sit there casting slurs on my mother, and me not able to say a word against her son who had all but deserted his family?

'And as far as I gather, you continue to lie to him. The King of Russia! Do you think you're the only one who told him stories? The rumours he's heard, and to this day he does not know who his father is, and have you never stopped to think what that might be like for him? He has children of his own now and still he does not know . . .' I was speaking fast, my words running away from me, spilling from me.

She raised one hand sharply and held it up flat, to silence me. I stopped, breathing hard, awaiting her response. But instead of speaking, she levered herself up from the chair slowly, pressing her knuckles against the tabletop to raise herself, as if she was infirm. She turned to leave the room.

I could not stand that she would answer me with silence. It was not right, not when I was making a fair point and had bested her in argument. 'I am talking of Elijah's feelings,' I insisted, my voice high and hollow with fury.

She had her back to me by then, and lifted her hand, again flat, then patted the air with it, as if to push away some invisible force that was pressing in on her. With the other hand, she reached out and grasped at the rail of the range, to steady herself. Then she walked slowly to the door.

I allowed her to reach the bottom of the stairs, then stepped after. Still she did not turn.

As she mounted the stairs, leaning on the banister, I called up after her, wildly, 'He's not stupid, you know! He's got a good enough idea! His father was a baker's boy by the name of Freeman, that's what he got told, although *you* may never have owned up to it! A baker's boy who fancied a bit of *gipsy* skirt, was he? I s'pose it was in a ditch somewhere . . . or . . . or maybe . . .' I had nearly used up all my strength, '. . . beneath a *hedge!*'

At that, she stopped on the stairs, bent almost double, but did not speak or turn. Then she continued up.

I stood at the bottom of the stairs, shaking. I felt such a sense of triumph and anger that I was almost alight with it. I burned.

Then, almost immediately, a feeling of wretchedness and shame washed over me. My knees almost gave. I thought of how, with these small houses, all the neighbours up and down the street had just heard me shout out how Elijah was got – and how they would all look at Clementina and me next time we went out of doors . . .

I turned and went back into the kitchen and put the kettle back on the hot-plate, not because I wanted to boil the water but because I had to do something ordinary. And my chest was heaving up and down, and, sure enough, the tears came. I thought of how, for the first time since her arrival, Clementina and I had argued openly, and how I had wounded her, how I had won. And I knew that the feeling should have given me great satisfaction but in truth it did not.

Clementina stayed in her room for the rest of that day. When the children arrived back from Mrs Herne's, the three of us ate our giblet soup together. Hungry as I was, I could not finish my bowl. It had no taste. Later, I put the children down, head to toe in my bed as Clementina had still not emerged from her room and there was not so much as a single sound coming from it. I found myself tiptoeing down the stairs afterwards.

I tidied and cleaned, swiftly and quietly, listening all the while for her door to creak open and wondering what on earth I could say to her when she emerged. I prayed that Elijah would come home that evening, so that I would not be alone with her, but he did not, and I retired to bed at my usual hour, pushing the children over gently as I climbed in, so as not to waken them.

Elijah had still not returned by the following morning, which was not unusual at that time. Daniel went off to school and Lilly came over and said would Mehitable like to come and sit in her shop and help her count the pennies? Lilly often had her in her shop in the mornings, out of pity, I suppose. Usually I couldn't wait to get rid of Mehitable so that I could get on with my chores undisturbed, but that morning I said, 'I am not sure, Lilly, Mehitable seems a bit chesty. Maybe she should stay at home.'

Well, of course Mehitable piped up, 'No, I'm not, Mum, I'm not chesty at all,' and gave a clear cough to prove it. Children always like to make liars of you, don't they? Mehitable loved going to Lilly's as there was usually a small treat in it for her if she was good.

Lilly gave me a straight look.

I sighed and said, 'All right then, but no spoiling her. She's gets spoiled quite enough as it is.'

So it happened that I was alone when Clementina finally emerged from her room. I had been laundering bed linen and it was flapping nicely on the line. It was warm and breezy outside and the sheets would dry quickly. I had just sat down for a minute, and was resolving that, whatever I said when she came down, I would not apologise. Or maybe I would apologise but make it quite clear that she had pushed me to it. Or perhaps I would just wait to see what she said, then take my cue from her.

As I was thinking this, I heard her step on the stairs. The back of my neck prickled with anxiety at the sound. I rose to face her. She came into the kitchen and said, 'Those sheets should be ironed while they've still got a bit of dampness in them. If you heat up the iron, I'll do it.'

Instead of all the speeches I had prepared in my head, I found myself saying. 'The stove is stoked. The iron'll heat in a minute.'

'Best go and fold them, then,' she said, and turned towards the back door.

I put the iron flat on the hot-plate and followed her out, meek as a lamb. While we folded the sheets, we talked quite normally of how the sky was darkening already and it was a good job I'd done them early and not waited until the afternoon. I could not believe how normal we were being, and even started to question in my own head whether the events of the previous day had really happened at all.

What is she thinking? I thought to myself as we took the folded sheets inside. Is she in inner turmoil, like me? She shows no sign of it. She was acting quite ordinary – much more ordinary, in fact, than she ordinarily did.

When we got back inside, she said, 'I'll do this. You get on, if you like.'

So I left her to it and went about my other tasks, a little humbled, I have to say, a little washed out and empty – and enormously relieved.

It's amazing we lasted as long as we did in that house. We staggered on for another year – and amidst all our difficulties another baby came, Bartholomew. He was small like Mehitable but healthy, thank God.

Then came the night when there was a knock at the door. Elijah was out, of course, so his mother answered. I was upstairs feeding the new baby but looked out the top floor window as the men left. They stalked off down Paradise Street in the dark, three big bulky fellas, and Elijah's mother ran after them and pleaded with them, and I thought, *that's it*. We've borrowed from friends and neighbours until we can't hold our heads up any more. We're weeks behind with the rent. And now he's brought the bailiffs down upon us.

A few days later, Elijah's mother sat me down and explained, quite gently, that the men were debt collectors and if we didn't leave that very night, they would be back tomorrow, take everything we owned and put us out on the street, in front of everybody. Elijah was going to come to the house after dark that night, to help us get away.

'Where's he been?' I said, dully, trying to summon the strength to be angry – but in truth the fight had long gone out of me by then.

'Sorting things out,' was all she would say. 'He's found somewhere we can all go. Friends of his.'

He had not come home to discuss it with me, needless to say. He and his mother had it all arranged. She knew more about the parlous state we were in than I did. Me, his wife, I counted for nothing. He had not even had the courage to come home himself and explain to me that his boozing and gambling had lost us our home.

'I'll go and pack,' I said. As I mounted the stairs, to parcel up what had not already been sold or pawned, I thought to myself, and to think I once craved a marble-top washstand from Peak's.

We crept out before dawn, skulking down Paradise Street like stray dogs who'd been starved and beaten. Elijah and Clementina both had heavy bundles and I had the bedding, which was lighter, but I was bent double all the same, bent double with shame. I could not believe my life had come to this. I prayed and prayed as we slid down the street that nobody we knew would be up and looking out of a window. I was finished in East Cambridge. I would never be able to come back after this.

As we reached the corner of Adam and Eve Street, Mehitable, who was just in front of me, tripped over a beer bottle left out on a step. It clattered and rolled with a jingly-jangly sound that echoed down the empty street. I gave her a sharp kick on the leg and hissed, *'Be careful, you clot.'*

Daniel was carrying Bartholomew and I heard him turn and mewl. *'Hurry up . . .'* I hissed, to all of them.

I did not begin to feel easier until we were well out of the Garden of Eden, past the narrow streets where I was born.

We were heading for the edge of town, to Stourbridge Common. Elijah said the friends who would help us out lived near there. Probably one of his drinking pals in some tumbledown cottage, I thought with foreboding.

But no. It was worse than that, much worse.

When he said *near* Stourbridge Common, what he actually meant was *on* it. I did not realise precisely where we were headed until we were walking up Garlic Row, past the Oyster House and on to the open grassland of the common.

There, ahead of us, were the dark shapes of tents and wagons just visible in the breaking dawn.

I stopped where I was, in the middle of the common, and put down the bundle of bedding. 'Oh Elijah,' I breathed, and my voice caught in my throat. 'Oh no.'

He turned, looked at me and scratched his head. The children stopped too, baffled.

Elijah grimaced, as if he was about to speak, but his mother cut in. 'Beggars can't be choosers,' she snapped. 'If we spend this night with something over our heads, even be it a bender tent, you should think yourself lucky.'

I glared at her. 'You may be used to this, Mother, but I am not,' I said sharply.

She glared back in response, but Elijah stepped in. 'Shut it you two, will you?'

Mehitable burst into tears.

'What's *wrong* with you?' I asked.

She shook her head, and sobbed. Clementina stepped forward and bent her head to the child, then lifted it and said, 'She's thirsty.'

'Well, we'll be there soon,' said Elijah. 'Come on, then.'

I picked up the bedding. I had no choice.

Elijah had given me the impression that he knew the folk we were visiting, but as we approached the first row of tents, I could see him stiffen and glance around, as if sizing the place up. Clementina strode ahead a little. Elijah dropped back to me and said, 'Keep your mouth shut to start off with, all right, Rosie?'

'What do you mean?' I said.

'Just keep it closed, all right?'

We walked forward in a line, and as we did so, a young woman emerged from the nearest tent. She saw us, and stared at us. Her skin was dark, even darker than Clementina's, and her cheeks were hollows, her hair black and straggly. She was wearing a huge man's shirt which came down to her knees but her legs and feet were bare. *What on earth have we come to?* I thought, shocked by the state of her and wanting nothing more than to snatch the children and run for it.

As we passed her, the young woman turned and shouted across the still quiet camp. I did not understand the words she used. They were full of *ushing* sounds.

Immediately, other figures emerged from other tents, in various states of undress, and came over to us quickly across the grass: men, women and children in a swarm. Within a moment or two, we were surrounded by a crowd that pressed in on us unsmilingly and prevented us from moving further into the camp. I looked from face to face, but still nobody spoke a word. I put my arms around Daniel and Mehitable and pulled them in close to me. Daniel was still holding Bartholomew. Mehitable clung to my legs. Still the people pressed forward, not smiling or speaking. We were effectively trapped. Lijah was separated from me a little and I looked to him for help but he just glared at me, and I understood from his glare that I must not speak.

Mehitable said, 'Mother . . .' in a whining, frightened voice and I took my arm from around her shoulders and clamped my hand over her mouth.

One boy was insolently close to me. He reached out a dark, dirty hand and plucked at the fabric of my sleeve. I shook the sleeve free, but he just pressed in closer and continued plucking. I felt someone else, behind me, tug at my skirt, and resolved that if Elijah did not intervene soon to save us I would shout out, whatever he had told me.

Just at the point when I thought I might suffocate with all this unwanted attention, a man emerged from the light-grey gloom and strode quickly towards us. He stopped a few feet away and the crowd fell back. He was looking at Elijah.

He was a tall man, barrel chested. He was wearing a shirt that was unbuttoned, despite the cold, and I could see that he was strongly built. He had a huge moustache that draped over his upper lip and hung down either side. He stared at Elijah very directly but ignored the rest of us.

Then Elijah started to speak, and I looked at him in amazement, for though I had heard him and Clementina use the odd peculiar word together, I had never heard anything like this – a proper language.

There were a few exchanges between Elijah and the man with a moustache, the crowd listening intently all the while. Then all at once, the man broke into a smile. At this, the crowd all smiled too, and the atmosphere changed completely – the people around us loosened, fell apart. Some returned to their tents or wagons – others began chatting among themselves. A couple of women came forward and gestured that we should walk with them.

As we were led towards the centre of the wagons, I realised that Clementina was not with us. Looking around, I saw her, heading off to another part of the camp, chatting in a lively fashion to a woman about the same age as herself. A young boy walking beside them was carrying her bag. It was the last we saw of Clementina for a couple of days.

I did my best to fit in, I really did. I'm not one for moaning when there's no point in it, and after my initial shock and a short period when I felt very gloomy, I saw that I had better get used to the idea of being a . . . a what? Lijah had told me, a long time ago, never to use *that word* in front of him. *Gipsy* was an insult, he told me – bad language. It was only *gorjers* who used the word *gipsy*. Travellers is what they called themselves and Travellers is what they were. Romanies. The People. I can't say as I really understood the difference myself at the time, but I understood well enough how the word *gipsy* got used as an insult. I'd heard the way my stepfather used it in the kitchen at the farmyard. 'Have those damn *gipsies* all paid up, Rose?' Or sometimes, 'Take a good look round the camp when you go down, Rose, and see if any of those *bloody gipos* have lifted my sharp spade. I can't find it anywhere,' when I knew for a fact that Henry had left the sharp spade in the yard.

I thought the Travelling folk who came to the harvest were a bit queer in their ways and I was a little scared of them, but they were always nice to me and the fact that my stepfather hated them was a pretty strong recommendation as far as I was concerned. And I did fall for one of them, after all.

Sometimes, when Elijah and I fought, he would try and use it against me, being a Travelling man. 'You've no idea, woman, when you've lived the life I've had . . .'

'Don't you use that as an excuse, Elijah. I wasn't exactly born with a silver spoon in my mouth, you know.'

I wouldn't have Elijah trying to make me feel bad on account of what a hard life he'd had – and I never blamed his bad behaviour on his being a Traveller. Elijah was Elijah, and if he'd been born a lord he'd have been exactly the same.

So what I'm saying is the problem with the Stourbridge Common lot was not on account of them being Travellers. It was on account of the fact that I wasn't, and they made sure I knew it.

I think the problem was I expected they would be like Mrs Boswell, who had always been so nice and kind to me back at River Farm. She would have explained things to me and I would have understood the life much quicker then. Mrs Boswell was a lady, whatever she called herself, and she always made me feel like a fine lady too. She respected me, and I respected her back. There was no one in the Stourbridge Common lot who was like her, I saw that the very next day.

The man who had spoken to Elijah when we arrived was a Cambridgeshire Smith, and I gathered some weeks later that he and Elijah had decided they were distant relations in some way. Bartley, his name was, or Bartle or something like that. Bartley Smith's wife was called Morselina, although I was never invited to be on first-name terms with her. She was a thin, suspicious-looking woman, and I knew as soon as I set eyes on her that she had decided not to like me.

I went over to their caravan the very first morning, with Elijah. We had gone to bed for a couple of hours after we first arrived, in a tent which someone else had been sleeping in that night, for the blankets were all mussed and the ground warm. Me and the children were so tired we thought nothing of it.

At full light, Lijah nudged me awake and, whispering that we should leave the children to carry on sleeping, told me to brush myself down and come with him.

I didn't want to leave the children. They had only that night left their home and all they knew behind. What if one of them woke and was afraid? Lijah told me not to be stupid. If the children woke up, they would be looked after by whoever was nearest to them; that was the way it worked in a camp.

*It's not the way I work,* I thought to myself as I brushed myself down and tried to make myself presentable.

It was a chilly morning and my bones ached. I had a terrible thirst and was dying for a cup of tea. How will I ever get through this day? I thought to myself as we made our way across the damp grass to the Smiths' wagon.

The whole family was up already and a fire lit. Bartley Smith and two other men were seated on upturned boxes. An elderly woman, older than Clementina, was squatting on the grass beside them. Morselina Smith was pouring tea into the row of tin mugs that sat on a tray on another upturned box.

Bartley Smith rose and greeted Elijah. He ignored me, and I should have taken the hint. Instead, I did what I would have done had we just arrived as guests at a house in Paradise Street. I sat myself down, and waited to be offered a cup of tea.

Morselina Smith straightened herself from pouring the tea and stared at me. I stared right back. She lifted the tray up and I half lifted a hand, expecting that I would be offered tea first, but she gave tea out to all the men, including Elijah, and then the old woman. There was no cup left for me, and I was left sitting like a fool with my empty hands in my lap, while they all drank noisily and nodded their appreciation.

I could have wept with disappointment. I had been up half the night and left my home with nothing but what I could carry. Was it too much to expect a little kindness from these people?

Elijah was glaring at me but I could not work out why.

Then he and the other men began to talk to each other in their strange language. I thought it most rude of them when they knew I could not understand.

So I had to sit there, in the damp and chill, with my shawl wrapped around me, while the men ignored me and drank their tea, and I could feel my cheeks growing pink with humiliation. Elijah had never behaved this rudely toward me in company before, whatever rows we may have had in private.

All this time, the old woman had been staring up at me keenly. Eventually, she rose from where she squatted and spoke to the men. Whatever she was saying, I knew it concerned me as she nodded in my direction when she spoke. The men took notice of *her*, all right. In fact, they all grinned from ear to ear. I gathered she had made some joke at my expense.

She came over to me, and grasped my upper arm. She was bent quite double with age and scarcely taller than I was seated. She had no teeth at all. She gestured some way distant.

I could not understand her, but rose anyway and looked pleadingly at Elijah, who suddenly became interested in the interior of his tin mug. I understood that he had completely deserted me, and I was to be left to sink or swim with these people on my own.

The old woman led me round the back of the caravan and across the grass to where a large group was gathered. As we neared, I saw it was all women and children, including Morselina Smith, who stood in the centre while several young girls were busy around the fire. She stared at me in an unfriendly manner as we approached and spoke to the other women, two of whom laughed openly.

'Where I come from,' I said firmly, my voice high, 'it is considered unkind to laugh at guests.' It was a stupid thing to say, but I could think of no better, and it certainly quietened them for a minute. Morselina Smith spoke to one of the young girls, who turned and came towards me with the largest tin mug I have ever seen, enamelled bright red and painted with a flower design. In it steamed hot, dark and, as I discovered to my bliss, heavily sweetened tea. I took the cup from the girl, carefully as the mug was so hot it was necessary to hold it precariously by both handle and rim. I looked down at her. She had a round, sweet face, and heavy black eyebrows. She smiled at me, warmly, and I was so grateful for her kindness that had I not been holding the tea I think I would have fallen on my knees and hugged and kissed her in front of everybody.

I sometimes wonder, did we get it the wrong way round? When Elijah and I first ran off together, it never occurred to me but to go to Paradise Street, to get back to where I had been happy before and where, I assumed, Elijah would be happy too. I've sometimes wondered, every now and then, whether we got it all wrong. Perhaps I should have just joined the Travellers at River Farm and gone off with them somewhere and let Mrs Boswell help me find my feet. I was still young and in love with Elijah then, and maybe I would have thrown myself into it a bit more. As it was, by the time we became Travellers, I had three children to look after, and I was worn out and my heart was heavy with the humiliation of our debts back in our settled lives.

Maybe it wouldn't have made any difference, anyway.

I didn't let Elijah near me the whole time we were Travellers. I told him I wasn't having any babies born beneath a hedge.

Morselina Smith never liked me. I had made a grave mistake in sitting and expecting her to serve me tea, that first morning. I realised that pretty quick.

Clementina said to me, when I saw her a couple of days later, 'I hear you've still got your la-di-da ways, then?' She had a grim but gratified smile on her face.

Somehow, I felt able to stand up to her then. 'Yes and I'm sure it gave you no end of pleasure to hear about that, didn't it, Mother?'

She looked at me, surprised I had spoken back at her. Then, unexpectedly, she smiled. 'You're learning, *rawnie*,' she said, nodding approvingly. 'You're learning.'

I was indeed. It was time to stand up for myself more often, from now on. Facts is facts, as my mother would have said. Like it or not, for the time being, I was a Traveller.

# PART 3

1895–1914

# Clementina

# CHAPTER 11

We were on Stourbridge Common for the whole of the winter, waiting for springtime when the weather would be good enough for us to take to the highway on our own. It wasn't a bad winter, as winters go, but still not exactly the best time to be getting used to life on a Traveller camp.

It was hard on the children, and harder still on Rose. Morselina Smith took against Rose so bad that I found myself obliged to stick up for her and put the word around that anyone who had a problem with the *rawnie* had better come and see me. Well, she was mother to my grandchildren, after all. There was one incident I couldn't prevent, however, as I was off the site at the time. One of Morselina's gang, a thin woman, a Cooper, had a go at Rose one morning, over Mehitable tripping up a pail of milk or something – I never got the details. Anyhow, it ended with this Cooper woman squaring up to Rose and Rose, to her credit, squaring up back – and although she got a black eye for it, she got the respect for standing up to her and was quite thick with the Coopers after that.

Morselina Smith was another matter, mind. Morselina Smith always called Rose a stinking *gorjer* and a *grasni* and one hundred other names behind our backs – and my grandchildren were naught but filthy half 'n' halfs. Now, where have I heard that before, I thought? I had to tread a bit careful with that lot myself as although I was an Old One and due some respect I had been living in bricks that five year past and there was some who weren't shy of reminding me of it. Five years. Had I really been away from my old life, on and off, for five whole years? I'd never been good at the marking of time. If it wasn't for my grandchildren being born, I'm not sure I'd have noticed that the years were moving at all. To me, it seemed like last week or the one before when I had packed my old carpet-bag after Adolphus passed away, and set off for Cambridge.

It weren't easy to find Paradise Street, that first day. Manibel Heron's son had taken me down to Cambridge on his cart, letting me off in what he said was the area. He wanted to stay until I found the right house but I sent him off sharpish. I weren't sure what sort of state my Lijah would be in when I found him and I didn't want the Heron boy talking when he got back to the camp.

I asked around a good deal before it was pointed out to me: a long, narrow street, full of little houses all packed together. Children were running up and down playing with balls and skittles but it was a bit parky for the women to be standing around so I had a chance to take a good look. It was a poor neighbourhood. Boxes, those houses were, squat little things all tight against each other with no air in between. Just looking down that street made me come over all poorly.

I had been told a certain house, so stood across the street from it for a few minutes, looking to see if anyone came in or out. Nobody did, and I couldn't stand there all day as the children were staring at me something funny when they ran past. Probably aren't used to finery like I've got on, I thought to myself, glaring back at them.

After a while, I caught a glimpse of a woman passing an upstairs window. She glanced out briefly and I could see she was wearing a nightie and had bright orange hair – some old trollop still a-bed of an afternoon. That can't possibly be where my Lijah is living, I thought. I went into the tobacconists at the far end of the road and he told me which house and I knocked on the door and who should open it but my Lijah.

Well, we've never been the kind to fall into each other's arms. I'm not one for all that sentiment-type nonsense and so Elijah hasn't never been neither.

He looked down at me. 'Hello, Dei,' he said, nodding, and stepped back to let me in.

The door opened straight onto a little parlour. There was a settee and an armchair that didn't match. Above the fireplace was a large mirror with a wooden frame that had been painted golden, quite badly. It was not hanging completely straight and there was the brown speckling of mirror spoiling in one bottom corner. Such poor workmanship made me wince. I wondered what had become of my Lijah that he could put up with such an object in his home. He left our fine *vardo* for this? I thought to myself.

Perhaps a little of what I thought showed on my face, for when I looked at Lijah I can't say he seemed particularly overjoyed to see me.

'So, this is what you've been up to then,' I said, glancing round.

He was never one to beat about the bush, my Lijah. 'I'm wed now, Dei,' he said.

'Aye, so I heard . . .' I replied. No matter how old a man gets, he is still a boy when he faces his mother. I was quite gentle as I added, '. . . and I'm a widow now, son.'

He stared at me, then fell to scratching his ear, which was always his gesture when he felt bad about something. 'I'm right sorry to hear that,' he said eventually.

Then the door opened, and in it swept.

I took in right away that she was expecting. It shouldn't have shocked me but for some reason it still did.

We stood there for a moment, all three of us. Lijah had a slightly panic-stricken look in his eyes. I knew if there was any awkwardness about to happen, he would bolt. Maybe I had best leave them to it, I thought, so he could explain to her how things were. I picked up the skirts of my dress and headed up the stairs. At the top, there was a small wooden landing and a door left and right. I pushed at the door on the left and saw a bed with a green eider. So that was where they slept. In the other room, there was a wooden rail with things on and some crates. So, this is where I'll be stopping, I said to myself.

I had left my carpet-bag downstairs for Lijah to bring up. There was nothing for me to do but sit on one of the crates and wonder if they were laid end to end whether they would take a straw mattress. And I decided they would, right enough.

There was a little square window with no shutter, so I went and looked out of it. It looked out over the back – their tiny garden with a small shed for the doing of private things and, beyond, a narrow dirt alleyway. It was all so small out there it was like the houses that backed onto theirs were pushing in and I thought I shall never be able to breathe with others living so close. How do they stand it?

Below me must've been the sitting room, for I could hear raised voices coming up through the floorboards. I say raised but I mean lowered, for though it was clear they were having fierce words about something, they were whispering to each other. I would have been able to hear every word otherwise.

I tried not to hear but waited for Lijah to bring up my things.

His voice grew into a murmur, sometimes a growl. Hers stayed steady, and then rose.

Then, all at once, there was the slam of the back door.

I went to the window. Lijah had come out into the garden in a hurry, his jacket unbuttoned and his hat askew. He didn't even open the back gate but placed one hand atop the wall and jumped over it, then strode off down the back alley. *Now why has she made him go and do that?* I thought vexedly. He hasn't even brought my things up. I sat back down on the crate.

Downstairs, all was silent.

Well, I couldn't stay there all day and I was feeling I would like nothing more than a cup of tea and a bit of something to go with it after my journey. I was thinking maybe I should go and help her put the supper on, just to show how I wasn't there to take advantage or anything. Most women in her condition would be glad of a bit of help around the house, I thought, and I may be a small body but I've worked from dawn 'til dusk with my bony little fingers ever since I could walk and I'm not here to be waited on.

So there was nothing for it but to go downstairs and straighten things out with her.

I stood, and brushed down my skirt, and I thought how I was prepared to put my best foot forward here, to get off on the right footing like, and she'd be a right fool if she didn't realise it. Plain speaking was the thing. I came down the stairs slowly, clutching on to the rail, as I weren't used to them. And I was also feeling how I didn't want to startle her as I wasn't right sure what sort of state she would be in and when someone's going to have a baby you have to not-shock them, after all.

She was sank down on the settee but raised her head as I came down the stairs. Dordy, you've never seen such a sight. Her face was all red and puffy and tear streaked. She was clutching the edge of her petticoat in her hands. She let it fall but I do believe she had been wiping her eyes with it. Her hair was all hanging loose from where she had pinned it with fluffy feathers of it sticking up here and there and a strand across her face. She looked like she'd been dragged through a hedge backwards. Daft hayputh, I thought, feeling right sorry for her. She'll never keep him if she lets herself go.

She looked so fat and soft with her great big belly. She was not so much a-sitting on the settee as spread all over it.

She looked at me, all miserable like. 'He's gone down the pub, if you want to know,' she said, and I thought I saw something defiant in the set of her mouth.

Oh, of course he's gone down the pub, I thought to myself. What else is a man to do when his wife cries all over him? She's been married this year – has she not yet realised that much? And she married my Lijah to boot, who has always been trouble and always will be. What did she think she saw when he looked up at her from the step of our *vardo*? A halo floating over his head? A choir of winged angels a-singing in the background?

My husband, my Adolphus, was dead and I had nothing. And here she was with her husband and a baby coming and her little house – and me to help her out into the bargain. And she was crying because he was off down the pub? She had better get to grips with how things are, I thought. It won't do any good if she fools herself longer. I know my Lijah and I know he's only going to get worse in that way, not better, and his drinking is something she's going to have to live with. She'll have me and her babies for company, and when Lijah chooses to come and shine on us that's all well and good, but any girl who thinks her man will be the whole of her has got a nasty shock coming. She had better know now, so's she can get used to the idea and make the best of what she's got.

'You've married my son,' I said, as gentle as I could. 'He's not a bad type, but there are things about him you won't change, ever, and you'd better get used to it, or you'll sup sorrow by the spoon-ful 'til the day you die.'

She stared at me.

I spied my carpet-bag in the corner, so I went and picked it up. She did not move to help me. I turned and climbed the difficult stairs. I saw I would be sorting out the little box room all by myself.

*

I hated that house. How I stayed there as long as I did I will never know. I felt it was my duty, really, what with the babies coming thick and fast and Lijah's wife having no one to help her out but me. If she'd had her own mother around it wouldn't have been so bad, I suppose.

It took a bit of getting used to, her high-handed ways, and I kept saying to myself how's you can't expect a woman who's carrying to be in any way normal and I must make allowances. But nothing I did was good enough for her. If I washed dishes and put them away I would catch her moving them around from cupboard to cupboard afterwards. If I folded clothes, she refolded them. And I never had a word of thanks.

Where I come from, a woman of my age got looked after by her daughter-in-law, not the other way around.

And I knew she talked about me to the orange-haired trollop. I was horrified to discover they were friends, for it made me wonder what sort of background our young Miss Rose had come from, before she moved out to the farm. She'd enough airs and graces then, all right. I began to wonder if maybe her mother had been a woman of loose morals or some such and thought, I'd better keep a close eye on what goes on in this house.

When my first grandchild was born, my Adolphus Daniel, the midwife-woman who had helped him out gave him firstly to my daughter-in-law, as was right and proper. Then a few minutes later, Rose needed to sit up. And what did she do with her new babby? She handed him over, not to me or the midwife-woman, but to the orange-haired trollop, who was waiting in a chair by the bed. All I could do was stand in the corner of the room and watch. I was his flesh and blood, that little boy – and she gives him to some lazy tart who lives up the road. That was how she thanked me for everything I'd done.

I got acquainted with the boy in my own good time. He was as good as gold, that *bobum*. I couldn't believe how good he was when

I remembered what a perisher my Lijah had been as a boy. She didn't know she was born.

I blessed him, that boy, as soon as I got the chance. I waited 'til one night, when they were sound asleep and I heard him stir and I crept into their room and lifted him up. And I took him down to the garden, and I showed him the stars. It should have been done by his mother when he was but a few days old – but I was his Romany mother, I suppose, mother to the Traveller bit of him, and I held him up to the stars and I asked for breath and long life and good fortune for him and an unusual breeze blew and I knew he would be blessed all right. I lowered him, and sat, and put him on my knee. Lovely thick eyebrows, Daniel had, even when he was a baby.

The boy, the warm breeze, all asleep around me – it was as good as when I had my Lijah. Better, in fact. You can love them straight and simple when they're yours but not yours. I sang to him softly and my heart was so joyful it was like bells ringing. Oh, it was the greatest feeling I'd had in years.

There was much I didn't care for in daughter-in-law, as you may have gathered by now, but if there was one thing she was good at it was producing grandchildren. Aye, the babbies came thick and fast, those early years. They fair popped out of her.

Daniel may have been an easy little thing – but the next one was a different matter. Mehitable, dordy, she was a madam.

She came early, did Mehitable – slithered out, all thin and slimy. I took one look at her and knew some dark days lay ahead. It began almost as soon as she was born – the screaming. It was something chronic. I did not blame my daughter-in-law for not loving that child, oh no, for I could see how difficult it was to love a child that unhappy. There is, after all, only one thing we ask of our Little Ones – that they outlive us, and that they be happy with it. That is all our hopes and dreams, all wrapped up into one request. If some stranger came along and started making your child miserable, day in, day out, would you not hate them with all the passion in your heart? Yes, you would – and even when it's your child is making *itself* miserable, you can't helping hating it for doing it to itself, while still loving it at the same time. And that sets up a new kind of torment, inside. I watched my daughter-in-law hating and loving that sickly babby – and I was not surprised that often she would thrust her at me and say, 'Mother, you do something with her, she don't want me.'

I would take Mehitable off for a walk or out into the garden and she would maybe quieten down for a little bit. I suppose it must have seemed unfair to my daughter-in-law that I could calm her child but I couldn't really – she was just an unhappy baby, and that was that. The only difference was, I wasn't all tight about her being unhappy, like her mother was. I could accept Mehitable's unhappiness and think of it as part of her, not take it personal like. I loved her at one remove, without blaming myself for everything that was wrong with her.

Whatever I did, it never lasted long. And there were times when even my comforts had no effect. Mehitable's moaning was ghostly, sometimes. It was like she was not a human thing at all, and it could go on for hours and hours. I did everything I could for her. I sang the old songs to her, about the moon and the sun. I placed charms under the padding in her Moses basket. Nothing worked. She was beyond me, or anyone. It was like there was a devil in her. I even started to wonder if I should take her out into the country and find one of our people who could really help. I don't think my daughter-in-law would have minded, she was that desperate. I think we all went a little mad at that time – no wonder Lijah stayed out drinking so much. So would we all, if we'd had the choice.

She was an odd-looking thing, Mehitable. Dark eyes, straight dark hair. She put on hardly any weight as an infant and when you bathed her you could see her ribs sticking out funny, her chest heaving in and out as she bawled. (She hated being bathed as much as she hated anything.) Then when she was grow'd a bit to the age when she should've been walking, all she could do was haul herself up on the furniture and move along it, clutching on for dear life. Her legs were bent funny, bow-legged but more so. She'll never stop a pig in a passage, I used to think.

My daughter-in-law went on something awful to Lijah about getting a doctor for her but proper *gorjer* doctors cost a fortune. Oh, I ached to take that child out into the fields to lead a proper life.

When she got bigger, she could still hardly walk. She would stagger along, holding on to the furniture, her chest all puffed up and heaving, with her dark hair and dark eyes staring – it was like having our own baby blackbird. Our cripple. Our Mehitable.

The money was saved for a doctor, eventually. He came one afternoon and looked at her and stared at us like we'd done it to her on purpose. Rickets, it was called. It was on account of not getting the right food and we had to get liver inside her or her bones would set wrong and she would never be right even when she was grow'd. She would need braces on her legs anyway. I said to him, did that account for how she had always cried as a baby and he said, yes, it hurt their bones to have rickets.

After he had gone, my daughter-in-law and I were sitting in the little parlour. We had got Daniel to carry Mehitable outside. My daughter-in-law had her hand over her mouth, which I had learned was a sign she was not right happy.

'Well,' I said, 'when Lijah gets back we'd best tell him to be off down the butcher's with whatever he's got, find some way to feed that child up.'

My daughter-in-law stood up, looked at me with thunder in her eyes and said, 'Don't you mention Elijah's name to me. I don't even want to hear his name *spoken*.' Then off she went upstairs and slammed her bedroom door and would not come down the whole day and night.

When Lijah got back that evening, I told him about the doctor's visit, and he frowned. 'Well, there's lots of children don't eat proper,' he said after a while, 'but it don't make them bow-legged.'

'It's more than that, if you ask me,' I said. 'It's how she's cooped up here all day long. Because she can't walk proper she never goes anywhere, just lies around being sickly and miserable. I know your wife's got a house to run but she's got to get that child out and about more. You've got to make a little cart or something so's I can take her with me when I goes shopping. Just think of all the air going stale in this house. If she was out in a field, she'd grow strong enough, you'd see.'

He turned away without speaking, that habit of his.

'Nobody never had rickets when you was a boy,' I added.

'Oh yes, that's right, Mother,' he said, in a nasty-sounding voice, turning back to me. 'Nobody *never* got poorly, did they, and we *hall* had a right good time with enough to *heat* and nothing to do but sit round a campfire singing songs to *heach* other?'

I was shocked that he could be so ironical with me. 'What has got into you, Elijah Smith?' I asked. I knew what had got into him of course: the strong, black stuff, Audit Ale – evil, it was. They served it down the pubs on a Friday when everyone had just got paid and my Lijah drank it whether he'd been paid for anything or not.

He muttered something but I couldn't hear him properly. I let it go.


That house, that house. It was like the graves in the cemetery at Werrington. It was like we was dead people all packed up into little boxes. Night after night I would startle awake and lie in the dark thinking maybe I was dead and crammed into a box all on my own and I was going to lie there, underground, for all eternity. I would feel hot and clammy at the same time, and my breath so raggedy it would make my throat ache. When I got like that, the only thing that would calm me would be to go down to the garden: to sit in the night air and light my pipe and feel the cool smoke in my throat. I would look back at the house and think, how do they stand it?

Mehitable got to walk when she was older, and she only had to have a brace on one leg, which seeing as we had to borrow for it was a good thing. Things got a bit better for her, after that, and she was even able to hobble around after the other children in the street, in a fashion. I've seen some children be right horrible to cripples, but no one never said a thing to Mehitable. She was such a peculiar little thing. When she turned her smile on, it was like the sun after a storm, on account of it being so rare.

No, the other kids never bothered her. Maybe it was because their parents told them not to pick on the poor crippled girl from what was now the poorest family in the street – or maybe it was because they knew her big brother Dan would thump them if they tried. Mehitable being a cripple brought out the worst in my daughter-in-law and the best in my grandson. For Daniel learned from when he was very young that it was his job to care and look after a small thing what could not look after herself – and I think that kind of lesson gets stuck in you when you learn it young enough, for Daniel was the kind of boy who spent his whole life looking after other people and never thinking not once of himself.

Next was Bartholomew. Along he came, Barty-boy, and he was half his brother and half his sister: small and dark, but healthy with it. The third child – just the next thing, really. He had the good luck to be ignored a bit more often than the other two and it never seemed to harm him. Things went a bit bad for us, after he was born. It was probably a good thing he weren't paid much attention to, as I don't think it would have been the sort of attention he'd've liked.

Yes, things got bad all round, for a bit. After her third baby, my daughter-in-law went down with the melancholia. Sometimes, she wouldn't even leave the house. She started saying how all the neighbours hated us because we brought the down the tone of the street, which was naught but foolishness as that street was about as low as you could get before any of us set foot in it. Once, when Rose was crying about how hard her life was I pressed her and she owned up to having borrowed money from the Empers and how she couldn't face them as she couldn't pay it back. Well, that explains a lot, I thought – those askance looks I get from time to time. Lilly Empers was the key to that street. Cross her and you were finished.

The mirror went, with its ugly golden frame. Lijah's one suit that she had laboured over to make him, with a sewing machine she had rented for a shilling a week – that went, but only to the pawnbrokers. She managed to get it out so Lijah could wear it to get each of the children christened.

A dark time it was. I would have disappeared myself if it weren't for the grandchildren. Lijah was off as much as he could get away with – which didn't mean he brought any more *lovah* into the house, and the less he earned the more he drank, as far as I could tell. The money situation got a bit desperate. I took to a little dukkering, on the quiet like, without telling Lijah or his wife, and that brought in a few pennies from neighbours who were sworn to secrecy with the reasoning that if rumours of my extraordinary powers got out, there would be queues that stretched as far as the common. But there was days when there was no food in that house and things between Lijah and Rose got pretty chronic.

Then came the incident that really put the lid on it.

It was September. Time for the farmers to get their corn in, if they haven't already. But not where we was living.

\*

Lijah was out. He'd been out all evening, on one of his benders, no doubt. Sometimes he didn't come home at all but went and slept in the Gas Lane stable with Kit the Second, which was the best thing, often enough.

It was late. The children were asleep upstairs. Daniel slept across the foot of his parents' bed and Mehitable and I slept toe-to-tail on my straw mattress. The new babby was in a Moses basket on top of the chest of drawers in Rose and Lijah's room. That house was far too small now there were three Little Ones as well as three of us.

Barty-boy was restless that night and my daughter-in-law had just gone up to see to him. I was cleaning, wiping all the surfaces in their little parlour with a damp cloth as we'd had a bit of autumn sunshine earlier in the day and I'd thought they looked a bit dusty. It was dark, though, and I couldn't really see what I was doing by lamplight. I had just about had enough and was thinking of going up myself.

There came a knock at the door.

I knew straightaway that it was not a good knock. A good knock is light, a little apologetic, even. Someone who means you well is worried that they might be disturbing you, and they communicate that with a light tap-tapping, with little breaks in between – merry tapping, like a dance.

This was three knocks, more bangs than knocks, in fact. They were done with a closed fist.

I went quickly to the door, the cloth still in my hand.

Three men stood on the doorstep. The light was dim but I could see them quite clearly. One, the biggest one, had mounted the step and the other two were pressed in behind him. They were rough-looking types, around my age, working men with flat caps on their heads and leather waistcoats beneath their jackets.

The one in front said to me, 'We want to speak with Smith.'

I knew I had to think quickly. Lijah might be back any minute. I took care to look each one of them in the face, long enough so's he knew I would remember him another time.

'My son is away on business,' I said, eventually.

What the first one said next was shocking. I don't like to repeat his actual words. 'You *eff*ing pikey,' he said, his face contorted. 'I want your son out here now or I'll come in and get 'im.'

One of the others put a hand on his arm. 'Bert,' he said, 'there's no need to be rough with the lady. He might not be here.'

'Don't be daft,' Bert replied, shaking his arm free. 'He's here, all right.'

I stood back. 'Come in, gentlemen, if you don't believe me. You are welcome to search the house. I just ask that you don't disturb the children what are sleeping upstairs.' Such an invitation would have been understood as a clear refusal where I come from. No *Romani chal* would ever enter another's *vardo* uninvited, however strong his grievance.

The first one stepped up – but the second held him back.

'He's not here, Bert.'

I waited for a minute. It seemed at first that 'Bert', whoever he was, was persuaded and they might leave. Then he shook his head, and pushed past me. The others followed him in.

'May I ask . . .' I began, but I was interrupted by a sound from above. Bartholomew had started to cry and Rose was moving around her bedroom. Her door opened and she called down. For once in her life, she said the right thing. 'So he's back, is he?'

The men glanced at each other. Bartholomew's crying rose in pitch.

'My daughter-in-law has retired for the night and will not be decently dressed,' I said, 'but I am perfectly prepared to call her down if you wish, gentlemen.' Then, for good measure I added, 'She has probably finished feeding the baby by now.'

I went to the bottom of the stairs and called up, 'There are three men here to see Elijah.'

Rose came to the landing, holding Bartholomew on her shoulder. 'Oh Lord,' she said, 'what's he gone and done now?'

I turned back to speak to the men but they had already left, leaving the door open. I went after them, closing the door behind me as I went. They had hurried off down the street and I was forced to run after them in the dark. When I caught up with them, they turned. I could see that Bert was still angry, not in control of himself, so I addressed my question to him. He was most likely to give me an answer, however indelicately put.

'Excuse me, but you must tell me. What has my son done? Is it money? Does he owe you money?'

One of the others replied. 'He does not, missus. It's a deal worse than that.'

*Worse*? 'Why have you come looking for him, then?'

The third, the one who had not spoken yet, answered me. He had a piping voice and dry, gingery hair, like my daughter-in-law's. 'He beat up our father. He punched him good and hard, even though he did nothing to him. He set upon him outside The Bleeding Heart. There's witnesses.'

'I am sorry, gentlemen,' I said firmly. 'But you must be mistaken. My son would do many things but he would never set upon an old man, never in his life. Why, that would be a wicked thing.' I knew for a fact my Lijah had never had a fight with any man but was his equal.

They could see my opinion was not feigned and I reckon that must have softened them a little, for they glanced at each other.

'Is your son Elijah Smith, the *gipsy* what deals in horses at Gas Lane?' said the second.

'Aye, he is, but he's not capable of . . .'

'Well, I tell you he is,' insisted Bert, angry again. 'There were three or four folks witnessed it. It was one of his own friends pulled him off.'

'What happened?'

The one with the piping voice said, 'Our Dad was drinking in The Bleeding Heart. He's an old fella and doesn't have his shop any more. Anyway, he gets chatting to the *gipsy*. The next thing, the *gipsy* flew at him and dragged him outside and started hitting him.'

I could not believe this story. What could an old man have said that was so insulting to Lijah?

'He must've been provoked.'

'He was not, missus. The others followed them out and broke it up. I asked Fred what happened, and Fred said he'd asked the *gipsy* what was up, and the *gipsy* pointed at my father lying on the ground and said, his name, that's what's up.'

'What is his name?'

'George Rawson. He's our father.'

The name meant nothing to me. I was bewildered. All I could think about was how I could stop these three men from tracking down my Lijah and beating him to a pulp. They must've been to Gas Lane already, so that meant he wasn't there. With any luck, he would have taken himself off somewhere for a few days.

'Gentlemen,' I said, 'I am most distressed to hear this story. I promise you, when my son reappears, I will send him to you at once with his explanation.'

'I bet!' Bert spat viciously onto the pavement.

The second one pulled at his jacket. 'Come on, Herbert, there's no point in being bad to the missus. It wasn't her beat up Dad.'

As Bert was pulled away by his brothers, he called back over his shoulder to me, 'You make sure your son knows I'm looking for him, missus. Rawson's my name an' all . . .' He jabbed a finger at his brothers, each in turn. '. . . and his, and his. You make sure he knows!'

We had been talking quietly enough up 'til then, but at that shout, one or two folk came to their doorsteps to see what was going on. Another black mark against us.

*

It was four days before I had any sign of Lijah. I knew he would go to Gas Lane sooner or later, to make sure the horse was all right. I had been feeding Kit myself and walking him round the yard so's he didn't get stale. I left my mark in chalk on the stable wall and drew a picture of a box and a line through it, so's he knew not to come home.

When I went back the next day, Lijah's mark was beside mine.

Two days later, when I went, Lijah himself emerged from behind a straw bale. He looked terrible – a week's stubble on his cheek, his face grey. I'd never seen him look so bad.

'Have you been eating?' I asked him.

He shook his head. 'Nor drinking, neither,' he said grimly.

'Well that's one good thing,' I huffed, and went to tend to Kit.

Lijah sat down and watched me. 'So, they've been to the house, then?' he said, philosophically.

'Aye,' I rubbed Kit down ferociously. 'This horse needs some proper exercise.'

'Does Rose know?'

'She does not, but she's frantic wondering where on earth you are.'

'I didn't mean to hurt the old fella that bad. I just wanted to learn him, that's all.'

I stopped rubbing down Kit. 'How bad did you hurt him, Lijah?'

'Bad enough. He'll be all right.'

'His sons seem to think it was bad enough, and there's three of them and they're big fellas.'

'I know. I know them. I seen them in there.'

'If you was going to have a fight, then why did you pick a family like that, for heaven's sake?' He did not answer me. I turned to face him. 'Them sort of *gorjers*, they don't fight clean, you should know that by now. You can't box one of them fair and square like another *Romani chal*. They don't work like that.'

He had closed his eyes and leaned back against the stable wall. 'I know that, Dei, don't go on . . .'

'Then what were you thinking of?'

'It was men's business, Dei.'

'Don't give me that. It's my business now you've brought those men to our house. They stepped inside, Lijah. They came over the threshold, into our home. If any man had offered me that insult on the Fens, my Adolphus would have dealt with him fast enough.'

He jumped to his feet. 'That was what I *was* doing! Give me credit for once, will you, Dei? You bloody women never give me any credit, do you?'

I was facing him. 'Are you going to tell me or not?'

He sat down again. 'Only if.'

'What?'

'Swear you won't never tell Rose.'

Well, that was easy enough. There were a whole lot of things I was never going to tell her anyway so I didn't see how one more made a difference either way.

'Course I won't.'

'Swear.'

'I swear it now get on and tell me, will you?'

Lijah looked at the floor and mumbled. 'He paid for the church bells to be rung.'

'Who did?'

'Rose's dad. Her real dad. Old Man Rawson. He told me. He boasted about it. He boasted about how her mother was, well, *little tart*, was the words he used, if you must know. And how he'd paid for the church bells to be rung when Rose and I was wed. When he knew who I was, that's what he said.'

I stared at him.

'I'd been nodding to this old fella in the pub for upwards of a year. Never knew'd who he was 'til the other night. Then we got chatting and he worked out who I was, and off he went. It was like he was boasting about how he'd bought us our wedding, as if he was some rich fella and we were nothing and he could buy us any time he liked. He never gave nothing to Rose in her whole life, not even his name. He'd had a few, like, must've done. And he laughed like he thought I should be laughing too and called her mother a good little tart and asked if her daughter had taken after her and that's when I hit him.'

I sat down next to him. What was I going to do with my son?

I still had straw in my hands from wiping down Kit. I let it fall. 'We've got to leave, you know,' I said, brushing some small strands from my sleeve. 'As soon as they get wind of you back in Paradise Street, they'll be back. I know their sort. They don't give up.'

'I know that, Dei.'

I gestured towards Kit the Second. 'How much do you think you'll get for that horse?'

He rubbed his chin. 'Not sure. I won't be able to sell it round here. I might on the other side of the city. It's not a bad horse.'

'Well, you'd better do it tonight. Leave word for me here tomorrow. I'll start working out what we can take with us.'

I stood. I felt better, now there was stuff to do. It was always the same, moving on. Whatever reason you had to do it for, there was a rightness about it, so whatever sadness you felt there was a goodness inside too.

'What about Rose?' he said.

'I've told her they were debt collectors,' I said. 'We're that behind with the rent. She's had enough. She'll go.'

I leaned against Kit the Second and put the palm of my hand on his nose, by way of saying goodbye.

# CHAPTER 12

We stopped on Stourbridge Common for the whole of that winter, but as soon as the weather got good enough the following spring, we took off on our own with a cart and a bender tent. Lijah scraped together the wherewithal for a grinding barrow and him and me would go round a village while Rose went door-to-door with the children. Lijah sharpened knives and I dukkered or sold stuff out of a basket. I liked doing that, flattering the housewives while we stood together on the doorstep and watched Lijah at work. I liked seeing the sparks fly off the knives as he worked at them and hearing the *shk-shk* sound of the blade against the spinning-stone. Each sound meant a few more pennies. Each turn of that stone took us a few more inches away from going hungry.

People weren't always bad to us, neither. In one village, we met a vicar on the High Street who crossed the road to speak to us. I am always wary of vicars, with good reason, you might say, but this one had spotted me and said he was having a Meat Tea for Old Folks that afternoon and would I like to go along?

Well, it was a right laugh. I ate 'til I was stuffed. Then we sat back, all us Old Folks, and the vicar showed us Lanternslides of Foreign Parts. As I left, he blessed me, and gave me a packet of tea, which he pressed into my hands with many kind words about how *Members of Your Race*, as he put it, were always welcome in his church. I decided I quite liked vicars, after that. I began to see the point of them.

The children grew. Daniel was a fine boy – Bartholomew a mischief. Mehitable . . . she stayed a singular child.

She was my only granddaughter, at that time, so I made sure to teach her a little of what I knew. I taught her how to curtsey so her calliper showed and she looked brave for trying. I taught her how to hold a lady's palm and trace the lines on it with the very tip of her finger. 'You must touch a lady softer than she's ever been touched before,' I said to her. 'You must hold the hand firmly, but touch softly. That way, a person feels protected, cared for, coaxed. You must never hurry it, my chicken. Hold a person's hand properly and they'll pay you the going rate, whatever you claim to see lying ahead of them. For a moment, they have been concentrated on – and that's what they are paying you for. They are paying you for being curious about them.'

I never met a happy *gorjer* who believed in all that nonsense.

And what lay ahead for us? Well, it has never been my way to look towards the future. That sort of thinking is brooding. Brooding leads to badness. When you have a cooking pot to fill, then you have to be doing, not thinking. So, if you had said to me at that time, where do you think you all might be in a couple of years hence? I would've shrugged. Same way I shrugged when Lijah and I was harguing one day and he said, you've got to realise such and such, Dei, it's the twentieth century now, you know. I can't say as I'd noticed that the century we had slipped into was a great deal different from the last.

What I am trying to say is, I didn't know whether or not we was going to carry on living on the road – we were at that time, and that was it. But I did know that it was hard and that after a while I was not altogether happy about it. At first, it had been good to be back where we belonged. But after while, I found myself thinking sometimes that a solid ceiling above you is quite pleasant when the rain is that sharp rain like pointy needles.

In truth, it was just like always. I wasn't at all sure where I belonged.

It's horrible, that feeling, the knowing-you-are-different. That knowledge – that there is a wrongness or a badness or a not-fitting-in-ness that is inside and around you the whole time. In Paradise Street, it was easy. I was an outsider because I was one of the People, a Romany woman and proud of it. But now I was back among others of my kind and it turned out it was not so simple at all. There was still something not quite right with me – something lost, or taken. *You can be pushed in the mud any time, you know.* That little voice spoke to me, all too often. It had never gone away.

I think I knew, as a result, that this being back on the road was not a permanent thing, that it was only a matter of time.

We joined back up with the Smiths and the Coopers come the wintertimes. You can't really manage on your own when the weather is bad, not when you have Young 'Uns. You need to be with others who can help you through the dark and cold and wetness of it. We all came off the road in a big group, from November through to March. There wasn't much work in the district, though.

That year, it was just after the first frosts and the parsnips were in and there was a misunderstanding with the landowner and he told us we had to *ife* by the end of the week. Well, that would have been all right but it had been raining solid for a month and we weren't ready for it. The landowner wouldn't listen to reason, though, and sent the gavvers in – so off we all set with things not stowed properly and it pouring with rain and our cart going, humpitty-humpitty down the rutted lane on account of one of the wheels being askew.

We had only got a mile down the road when Lijah pulled up and said we had better all walk otherwise we might lose an axle. Then him and Rose had words about the children having to walk in the rain. I must admit, they did look like a trio of poor mites as they stood there, all sorry and wet while their mother and father shouted at each other and the rain pelted down.

Mehitable had grown into a tall, lanky girl, still skinny as any-thing and still with a calliper and a bad limp, still the unluckiest mite of all. She'd had a cold that week – she was prone to them on account of her weak chest, and was constantly sniffing and blow-ing into her hanky. The nose was going bright red with it, and the skin round it cracking. When Lijah and Rose had finished holler-ing at each other, the boys went over and helped their father with the cart, so Mehitable was left standing on her own beneath the tree with the water dripping on her from above, and she did look like the most miserable little sparrow.

When the men had finished their men-jobs with the wheel, I said to Lijah, 'Let Billy ride up with you. She's poorly. The boys can push and I'll lead the horse.'

He looked at Mehitable, with her shoulders all hunched up and said, 'Rose can lead the horse. You stay on that side and shout if we veer off that verge.' Then he helped Mehitable up onto the cart.

We set off again, slowly. The other carts and the *vardos* had gone on ahead. They had long since disappeared round the bend but we knew where they were headed.

If we didn't catch up soon, someone would head back to find us and I did find myself thinking that if it was the Coopers I might get offered a lift in their *vardo*. *I'm getting a bit old for this traipsing in the rain*, I thought to myself, a bit grumpy like. I've been doing it since I was a *biti chai* and I'm ready to sit down in front of a fire and not have to spend the evening cleaning mud off everything I own.

Thinking of all the times I'd walked down a lane in the rain, it came to me: the time just after Lijah was born, when we set off in bad weather, just like this, and my mother got taken from us and killed. I have always done my best not to think of that time. But the rain came down – and it came to me how my mother and I had sheltered beneath a tree, like Mehitable had done just then, and how the farmer had come by and spat at us for no reason. And a feeling of dread and gloom came over me and I found myself raising my face and looking around to make sure we were all together and no one was coming after us. There was Lijah, on the cart, huddled down with a blanket over his head to keep the worst of the wet off, the reins drawn tightly in. Mehitable was sat on the edge of the cart sideways, facing out with her legs dangling over – Lijah said he wanted her on that side for balance. She was holding on with just one hand as the other was clutching her shawl round her head. The hand she was holding on with was white with the cold, the knuckles raw.

Rose was at the front, leading the horse and stumbling in the mud. At the back, the two boys were one at each corner, ready to push when needed. Daniel was a big, strong lad, by then. Barty was only a little thing but wiry like my Lijah. Above us, the sky was gathered tight and grey, the clouds all packed in. The rain pelted and the branches of the trees bent and shook above us. The brown mud gave beneath my feet with each step I took. It was as if time had slowed right down, as if we had been making our way down this wretched, sodden lane for all eternity.

Then, time became even slower.

I saw it all happen, just before it happened. A picture came into my head, but I was so slow in my thoughts I was powerless to do anything about it.

We was trudging. The wheel beside me was turning slowly, with an ancient, creaky sound. The rain came down. All was slippery. *Folk slip, go under*, I thought, and shook my head to push the thought away: the lane, the rain – the sight of two gavvers banging on the side of our *vardo* as I came back from the stream and the hollow feeling inside as I ran towards them, baby Lijah clutched on my chest. There was an almighty cracking sound from the other side of the cart and Rose's head whipped round. Lijah looked that way too, then leaned to one side. The boys at the back called out.

'Dadus!' cried Bartholomew.

'It's going, Dad!' shouted Daniel.

'Push!' bellowed Lijah back at them, over his shoulder, and cracked the whip over the horse. Rose shouted something else, above their shouts, her hand up. I was looking toward her and only saw sideways – Mehitable's arm, wheeling up in the air. Then she tumbled, just dropping down from the cart, like a blackbird swooping for something on the ground. The cart lurched forward. There was a cry in my throat that could not find release. Instead, it came from Mehitable, as if my fear found voice in her, as the wheel of the cart pushed her down into the mud.

Then, too late, came the panic, the busyness of trying to do something. Lijah jumped down from the cart. Rose ran around from the front, pushing Lijah out of her way to get to her daughter. I was nearest and there first, already calm enough to think, the ground was soft and gave, that will have saved her.

She had struck her head as well, somehow, but it can't have been that bad as she was screaming fit to burst, and Rose was beside her, holding her on her lap and screaming too. They were both of them covered in mud. And I heard myself saying, babbling, 'It was my fault. It was my fault, Lijah.' And he gave me a glance as if to say, *last thing we need right now is you going daft.*

He sent Daniel off to run ahead and find the others. Barty helped us lift Mehitable out of the mud and onto the verge, in the shelter of a bush. And we all wept and the rain came down and I was on my knees in the mud with my hand pressed against my chest thinking, *but it was my fault. I made it happen by thinking of my Dei and the rain and the tread-wheel. Bad things follow me.*

As if she had not had enough pain already. As if she hadn't already had her fill. I think that is how come Mehitable wanted to leave us. She knew how unfair it was that such an accident should happen to her, of all people. She couldn't take any more.

The Cooper lads came back with Daniel and we got Mehitable onto a cart. Rose and Daniel went with her into the next town, where they found her a doctor. They brought her back later that day, one foot a huge ball of bandage. It was broken in different places, Rose said, but the leg was saved by the calliper. It was that iron thing what had tormented her all her life, what stopped the rest of the leg from being mashed. She had a poultice on her forehead, too, but the doctor had said the head wasn't serious.

But then, when she was laid up, a fever set in, and we all of us knew how serious that was. We couldn't find any infection in the foot and we burned leaves in a dish but still the fever worsened. It all came back to me, as horribly clear as if it was the day before – it was just the same; taking Dei to Huntingdon Common when we got her out of the House of Correction; her pain and fever; her slipping away, just slipping from me like something I had been clumsy and dropped out of sheer carelessness.

I started preparing in my mind for losing my only granddaughter.

*

We stayed in the clearing for a fortnight. There was the Coopers with us, and some Kentish Scamps they were related to who stayed behind as well and were right good to us, taking charge of the mending of our cart.

We had been there three nights and Mehitable's fever was at its height. Lijah and I were sat outside the bender tent, smoking. Rose was inside with Mehitable.

Lijah and I had not spoken much since the accident.

After a moment or two, he said quietly, 'Why did you say it was your fault, Dei, when Billy fell off the cart?'

How can you explain that sort of thing to a son when he is grow'd? Grow'd he may be, but he's still your boy and you want to protect him from realness.

'I saw it about to happen,' I said. 'I had a bad feeling and got a picture in my head. I should've shouted.'

He looked at the cigarette he was smoking, one of his own rolled-up things with a few shreds of 'baccy and lot of dried leaves. 'It weren't your fault, Dei,' he said, with a long sigh. 'It were mine. I was too busy looking at the other side and thinking about how it was going down. That's how come I made the horse go forward.' Of course, it was all our stupid faults for letting her sit on the edge of the cart in the first place.

*Ghosts*, I thought. I felt the ghost of my own Dei, broke on the tread-wheel. I felt it as strongly as if she was squatting on the damp grass beside us. I knew she'd long forgiven me for my part in her death – but she didn't want to let go, neither. She was lonely. *You can't have Mehitable*, I whispered to her, in my heart. *Not yet. We've need of her.*

The ghosts of dead children are the worst sort, of course, the most evil, that is, for they are the ones who went wrongly, before their time. They are the ones who haunt the living with the most fierceness. I would walk through a whole field of adult demons in the dark before I crossed the path of one ghost-child in broad daylight.

I knew that if Mehitable died she would haunt us, and it would not be nice.

'Lijah,' I said, 'I've been thinking.'

'Aye,' he said, still staring at his roll-up, not bothering to relight it.

'Let's settle for a bit,' I said. 'For the children's sake. They've schooling to catch up on. They've missed a good few years what with one thing and another. And Billy's never really been strong enough for all this. Let's go to that village, the one where the old mush offered you that dyke work. The boys could do some too.'

Lijah was quiet. 'Well you weren't too keen on house-dwelling, as I remember,' he replied eventually.

There wasn't much I could say to that. 'Rose would be pleased,' I said, after a while.

'Sutton,' he said. 'It was called Sutton. I wasn't keen on that mush, he was only paying by the chain. It was handy for Ely, though.'

Daniel approached us, over the clearing. He was holding an enamelled dish in his hands. 'Ida Scamp brewed us a basin for Billy,' he said, as he came near. There was a cloth over it, to keep the vapours in. I tossed my head to indicate he should take it straight in, before it lost its goodness. He bent into the tent.

Lijah and I were silent while Daniel was in there, just smoking and waiting for him to come back out.

He emerged, after a while. Lijah and I both looked at him. His face was downcast, which meant she was no better.

'Take that dish back,' I said.

Mehitable is going to die, I thought. She is going to die and haunt us for all eternity.

You do not get to keep a person when they are a ghost. You only get to keep what was bad of them, what you and they resent. A ghost is not made up of nice memories – it is made up of all the horrible things that have happened to a person, all the things you want to forget.

I had not thought of it in years, but as Elijah and I squatted on the grass outside that tent where Mehitable lay trying to die, the story of the Ghost Pig came into my mind.

It happened not far from a village called Kennyhill, on Mildenhall Fen, east of Ely. As a result, I will never go east of Ely again in all my born puff.

I say Mildenhall but actually the place we was stopped near was more on Burnt Fen.

Burnt Fen was an evil place. It looked like it sounded. The black peat earth was hard work and of course it was our men hired to dig it. They said after dark you got spirits coming out of the earth and it wasn't safe to walk abroad, although my Dadus said that was a load of foolishness. There were gases in the earth that came out when you did the digging.

Maybe that accounts for how the Ghost Pig appeared to us that one black night. We were all pretty spooked, even before then. It's when you're spooked that the Evil Ones know they can come and get you. There is something in your mind that lets them in.

There were fifty or so of us in that camp. It was before the time of the big camp which we joined later – it was only Smiths and I was so little that I can hardly remember it, so I think I was probably only just big enough to join in the work with the other children. All us children, and some of the mothers, was employed at stone picking on this big estate, the same one that the men were digging peat for. Stone picking was filthy work, and poorly paid. We only did it when there was no other work to be had. We would form a line across the bottom of a fallow field, first thing in the morning when the cold still shuddered our bones. As the grey light of dawn revealed the black earth to us, we would move forward, taking care not to break the line, either bending or on our hands and knees. The soil had to be looked at and felt through, so's we could pick out any stones and the field could be dug over without breaking the ploughs or harrows. Any stones we found, we dropped into the cloth bags we had tied round our necks.

It was horrible work, especially when it had been wet. We would move so slowly – you wouldn't believe how long it would take to get across a field. It had to be done with great care for the landowner's man came and inspected the field afterwards and if he bent and picked up so much as a pebble we would none of us get paid until we'd done the field again. I remember pushing my hands into the muddy earth and hating the way it blackened my fingernails. To get them clean again, you had to soak them in frozen stream water until you thought you'd scream with pain. I can remember how it was a relief when you filled the bag round your neck with stones because although it hurt your neck, at least it was an excuse to stand up and walk back to the edge of the field to empty your bag, and that was lovely for your back. You couldn't take too long about it, mind, as the whole line had to stop until you got back to your place. I can remember most is how my knees used to go bright red with the cold. Later, they would crack, and my Dei would have to rub oil in them.

I hated that work, as you can probably tell. We hated the work, and the landowner hated us. I'm not sure what sort of farmer he was as he wasn't a regular sort with crops and cows. We couldn't rightly work out what he grow'd. He was a wealthy man, that much was certain, and it seemed a bit like he was playing at being a farmer as his house was not a low farmhouse but a tall thing with fancy drapings at the windows, and he was always dressed up to the nines himself and riding fine mares, not proper farm horses.

He had a pig, and the pig was his pride and joy. My Dadus was one of the men picked to go and get our wages as he had a way of dealing with *gorjers*. He said this landowner had been quite pleasant one day and taken them outside and shown us his prize sow in a spotless pen. There were ribbons pinned to the gate of the fen. She had won lots of prizes, apparently. She was huge.

But relations between us and the landowner went bad not long after that. The men finished their digging after a week or so and they asked if they could be put on to helping with the stone picking. The quicker all our jobs were finished, the quicker we could move on and get other work. Well, the landowner refused. Women and children got paid less, of course, and it was cheaper for him to have us finish the job than let the men help. This meant we had the choice of stopping on Burnt Fen with the men not getting paid for anything, or moving on and losing what little us children would earn.

After news of this got back, there was some discussion of whether the men sent to talk to the landowner had handled it right. One of the men had the bright idea of sending a couple of children up to the big house, to explain the problem politely. The smallest, sweetest boys were chosen, and dressed up nice, and were sent off with smiles as they looked like little angels.

The landowner set his dogs on them. One of them got bit.

I have never seen such dark looks as there were on the men that night, and the darkest of all was on the face of the man who'd had the idea in the first place.

Well, I don't know all the details, of course, but I suppose what happened was that some of the men decided that the boys being bit on purpose could not go unanswered. So they planned to *drav* the *bawlo* – to poison his prize pig.

Now, there were several reasons why you might poison a pig, which was a serious business and not done often. Mostly it was done not to kill it or anything, but to make it poorly so that it could be bought cheap. Or sometimes it was done so that others could go along and fix it up and get in a farmer's good books. It could only be done by people who knew what they were doing, mind, as the weight of the pig was important when working out what to give it.

A couple of days after the deed was done, some of our men went along to the farm on some pretext or other. They was hoping that the landowner would complain to them how his pig was poorly. Then they would fix the pig up, and we would get right back in the landowner's good books and, as a result, get what was right out of him. So four of our men went off: Caleb Smith and his brother Absalom and two of Caleb's sons.

Maybe they was clumsy in the way they enquired after the pig's health. Anyroad, the landowner didn't beat about the bush. He marched them straight out to the sty. The pig was lying stone dead on its side. Whoever had given it the *drav* had overestimated just how big that sow was, and killed it.

When the landowner had shown them his dead pig, he took a whistle out of his pocket and blew on it. At that, a whole load of *gorjer* men ran out from a barn holding sticks. They beat our men black and blue, beat them into the ground. Caleb Smith came back with a lump on his head the size of a hen's egg and his brother Absalom had his jaw broken. One of the *gorjers* had jumped on his face when he was on the ground. He never spoke proper after that and his food had to be mushed up with a fork. His mouth never worked proper again.

Well, when the men got back from the beating, the women wept and howled, and begged them to leave that place, which they had always said was an evil place and they would now put the say out around our People just how evil it was so none of Us would ever come and dig the landowner's black earth again. But the men had their pride, of course, and did not want to leave without hurting the farmer back. Some were all for going and torching the farmer's barns but he would be expecting that, my Dadus said, and there would be nothing but another beating in it.

Then Caleb said, he had heard one of the men who beat on

them say how the pig was good for nothing and would have to be buried by the duck pond and they were lucky they weren't made to do it with their own bare hands. This set the men thinking. The least we could do, one of them said, was to have that pig. The *gorjers* wouldn't dare use it for anything, not with poison in it. But we knew precisely what it had had and we could still make use of it all right. The least we could do was dig up that pig and roast it fair when the wind would carry the smell of it across the fields to the landowner's house, and he would know we were feasting on his prize animal. We hadn't had any meat inside us for a good long while, that winter, so this revenge would be killing two birds with one stone, as they say. It was a right clever plan.

So, a night or two later, a group went over to the duck pond carrying spades. The pond was a little away from the farm itself and so they hoped would not be guarded, and it wasn't. They searched until they found some freshly turned earth. It was a large patch, a few feet away from the pond. My Dadus was in that group, and I heard him tell Dei when they got back later, that they was just raising their spades, when one of them said he saw the earth move a bit, rise and fall. They were doing the digging by moonlight, of course, so nobody could be sure of anything, but they stopped and had a discussion about whether the pig could still be alive in there. My Dadus said it was just the gases in the earth. But the fella who had seen the rise and fall said no, it wasn't a quick movement, like gas escaping, it was more like something breathing in there. Caleb Smith's eldest son what had been beaten was there with them, and he swore that there was no way the pig was still alive. He had seen it in its pen and it was dead as dead could be.

The more they stood there talking about it, the more they was getting a bit spooked. Then they heard a dog barking in the distance and wondered if maybe it was the landowner come to investigate – and that was a good enough excuse to leave it for the time being.

My Dadus was not in the next night's party on account of having stumbled on the way back and hurt his ankle. So Jabez Smith, Absalom's son, went in his place.

The next night it was black as black but windy so they reckoned that the clouds would clear from the moon by the time they got there. They crept to the same place and found . . . a big hole in the ground. They stood around it for a little while, shaking their heads in bafflement. That pig had been in the ground not the night before, they were sure of it. They had a bit of an argument about whether it was the same place but they were sure it was.

Then, one of them said, a cold feeling came over them all, all of them at once, a feeling of such overwhelming badness that they began to shiver. They all looked around in the dark – and then one of them saw it, a few feet away . . . It was white, just like it had been in life. It's eyes were glowing red. It was breathing through its nostrils and staring at them. It came towards them, just floating over the hole, and they turned and fled.

There was no more argument about whether we stayed in that place after that. The camp was packed up and ready to go before sunrise.

Looking back, now I am grow'd, I do not know if I fully believe this story. For maybe someone else had got there before them and dug up the pig – it was a valuable pig after all. Perhaps some *gorjer* neighbour who had helped the farmer bury it had decided to go back later and have it for himself. But the men swore they saw the ghost of the pig coming at them, after his revenge for having been poisoned.

Word got about, as it does, and after that, the Ghost Pig became the thing that mothers frightened their children with, across the whole of the Fens. I remember my own mother, when I got lost one day and didn't come back until after dark, taking me by the arm and leading me to the copse nearby. She was shaking with anger, she was that relieved I was back.

'Do you know what's in there?' she said, pointing into the still, dark trees, at the blackness in between. 'Do you know what walks round here?' I shook my head. *'The Ghost Pig!'* she exclaimed. 'And he *eats* children like you what get lost in the woods. Do you understand?'

Maybe it was just a story to make us behave, but my father believed it. He would go quiet when he talked about it.

Looking back now, I think I know what the Ghost Pig was – it wasn't the pig itself, not really. It was evil in the landowner and his friends. It was all the *gorjer* evil in all the *gorjer* world that got together and stamped on Absalom Smith's face when he was beaten and lying on the ground. That was what got the men so spooked. It was the bad things that are waiting for a person when all they are trying to do is a live a life – and it was the badness of having poisoned the pig in the first place. It was sort of like the realness of life that lies in wait for you and jumps out. That is why it was so frightening, for all of us. When you are a Traveller, you are never allowed to forget that whatever you have might be taken away from you at any minute. And all you have to do is one wrong thing – and I'm not saying we never did no wrong things – one wrong thing, and you get punished and punished far worser than the thing you did. That's what it's like being one of us. And the Ghost Pig is always out there, to remind you, in the dark or even in the daytime. Everybody has their own Ghost Pig, in my opinion. It follows you, even when you're not thinking about it. It never goes away.

I am usually good at forgetting. *Mi Deari Duvvel* forbid it should be otherwise. It was because I forgot-to-forget that Mehitable fell from the cart, that day, in the lane in the rain. I learned my lesson, after that. I reckon we all did. As soon as she was well again, I vowed I wasn't going to be tempting the *mullas*, the ghosts, no more, with the Travelling and the remembering and the wanting to live like I once had. We all of us get born into a stone cradle but some of us have the sense to climb out of it.

Mehitable pulled through. We went to Sutton. And I never forgot-to-forget again, not once.

# CHAPTER 13

I still had a few mixed feelings about going to the village, mind, for my only experience of houses had been a cottage in a graveyard and a box in a street in Cambridge which came to much the same thing, in my opinion. That was house-dwelling for you, I thought. We took the cart and bender tent and stopped at Mepal, then Elijah and Rose went on foot into Sutton to scout around for somewhere. I was left behind to keep an eye on the children – so we all said to each other – but in actual fact it was because I looked a bit too much like what I was. Rose and Lijah could pass for *gorjers* easy enough.

They came back with the news of having found not one but two little places, right on the outskirts of Sutton. Lijah had taken some dyke digging work for a month and even got a note from the old mush so's the landlord would let us off the down payment. The places were empty and needed a bit of work, but if we didn't mind that we could move in right away.

That's how easy it was to become a family of house-dwellers again.

My place was tiny. It had a little parlour with a kitchen alcove and a bedroom upstairs. After going up and down the stairs a few times, I worked out that if I used the settee for sleeping then I didn't need to go upstairs at all, which was a thing I'd never liked. I would be right next to the door. None of that sweating and trappedness like I had felt in my box room in Paradise Street. Suddenly, it seemed like not-such-a-bad little place. I would be close to the others but still able to come and go as I pleased and keep it as clean as I liked.

After Lijah and Rose had settled me in, they went next door with the children to sort out their place and I sat on the step – my step – with the door open. I looked up at the sky and felt as chuffed as a puppy with its first own bone. My little place – close enough to the others to keep an eye, like, but with my own door handles and cooking pots and feather duster. My own. I wasn't going to be odd-one-out no more – you need other people around you to make you that. From now on, it was going to be just me.

And there was something else which amazed me, 'til I got used to it. For the first time in my life, I had the lektiv. *Helectricity* was the proper word for it, Lijah told me. They'd had it Cambridge before we left there, but it had not come to Paradise Street, nor anywhere near. They put it in the theatres and people would go and see plays not to watch the actors on the stage but to sit and stare at the lights. As a consequence, I had always thought of it as a rich person's thing and could not believe I was going to have it in my own little home.

Lijah stood me in my sitting room and flicked the switch up and down, to show me how to use it. The light came through the wires, he said. After he'd gone, I did the same thing myself, on and off, for a good long while, until the old man over the road came across and said, was I trying to signal that I needed help?

Lijah got himself some steady work, just like he promised. He did the dyke work for a while, and then he went back to being a

pack-man. Being on the edge of a village was good for that. He
had a shed to keep his stuff in, and a few shops to buy extras, but
was near to the paths across the Fens and the outlying farms. The
walking everywhere was good for him, I reckon – and he was
good at chatting to the farmers' wives what were lonely and didn't
get to speak to many people. I think him being a bit older helped,
like, as he was a charming old-ish man now which is quite a different prospect to a charming young man. People weren't so wary
of him.

After a year or so, he got the wherewithal to go back to dealing
with the horses. We got ourselves another Kit. I'm not sure which
Kit it would've been by then. Kit the Fourth, probably. He wasn't as
nice as the First Kit, what had been my favourite, but he was
sweeter than the Third. Lijah would go out with Kit of an evening,
pulling the cart, and go and buy a horse off a fella. The deal would
take ten minutes, then they would shake hands on it and go and
spend the next three hours in the pub. After they had finished celebrating the deal, Lijah would take the horse he had just bought –
some old nag, ripe for doing up – and tie it to the back of the cart.
Then he would climb up into the cart, pull a blanket over himself
and say to Kit, 'Come on, Kit, take us home.'

Kit would plod home in the dark with Lijah sound asleep in
back of the cart. When Kit got to our cottages, he would stamp
about a bit. As I always slept with the door open and slept lightly,
I could easy hear Kit a-stamping and the jangle of the harness what
was hanging loose. So I would get up, release Kit from the shafts
and take him and the new horse to the little stables Lijah had at the
side of his place.

When the horses were settled, I would take a look under the
blanket to make sure that Lijah was actually in the cart, then leave
him to sleep it off and go back to bed.

Sometimes, as I turned, I would glance up at their cottage. Rose
never came down, either to check he was all right or to upbraid

him for being drunk. I think she had found a way of letting it not matter no more. They were paying their rent, and the children was fed.

They still had their ups and downs, did Rose and Lijah, but I suppose they must have been getting on a bit better as, to my surprise, I got two more grandchildren out of it. Fenella was born one springtime. Scarlet, the last of my grandchildren, popped out during an April storm which brought down the Elder tree in my back yard but led to an early hot spell.

Oh, we all loved those girls – especially Fenella. She was a fashion-plate, that child. Even when she was little. She could wear a hand-knitted cardy like it was a velvet gown. 'Mami . . .' she would say, sidling up to me when I was stitching a stocking or mending a tear in something. 'Mami, do you have any pearl buttons in your box?'

'You know right well I do, my acorn,' I would say, 'for you've been into it looking, haven't you?' She wouldn't've got away with that with her mother. Her mother would have gone crazed if Fenella had been in *her* sewing box, and well she knew it.

Funnily enough, I wouldn't have been too chuffed if any of the other girls had been into mine, but Fenella had a habit of charming things out of people. Curly hair she had – soft brown curls. The men were going to go doo-lally over her when she was older, everybody said. And they were right.

'It's just, I've lost a button . . .' she would say, looking down at her cardi, a cable-knit I'd done myself, with wooden buttons.

I would see the tail of thread hanging off and think, *lost* . . . Really?

I liked to tease that Little One a bit. 'Well, *biti mouse*, I suppose I could spare just one of my pearl buttons if you was good.'

Her face would be a picture of horror. 'But Mami, then they won't match!'

She was the only child in her village school with pearl buttons on a cable-knit cardi, I'm quite sure of that.

There was a special thing that Fenella and Scarlet both loved in the village, and that was Mayladyin'. We all had our own time of year, I suppose. In January, the boys had Plough Monday with the plough they carried round all decorated, and their lanterns. They got ale and cakes for their trouble. Even the old ladies like me had Goodnin' Day, for widows only, when we got given packets of tea or sugar. I wouldn't go round with the other widows as I thought it was undignified, but someone always left tea and sugar on my doorstep anyway. I wasn't too proud to take it in and drink it, I might say. Shortest day of the year, Goodnin' Day. One year, I thought about getting one of the children to write a note on a bit of paper, for me to stick on my door. 'It's nearly Christmas so blow the tea and sugar, how about a bit of brandy and some 'baccy for my pipe?' I never did it as I wasn't sure I could rely upon the villagers to see the humorous side.

The girls had Mayladyin', when they was allowed to dress up dolls and take them door to door, and get pennies for them.

Well, my Fenella, she was determined to have the prettiest doll in the village – dordy, yes, the preparations took weeks. A lace bonnet, she had to have, and little boots made of real leather cut from an old piece her dad had. Nearly ruined my fingers stitching them tiny boots. The evenings she spent round at my place, sorting it out. Scarlet was only just big enough to join in and luckily she was easily pleased with something that was a lot less effort. As long as it was pink, she didn't care.

One Saturday, I was at home. It was the first of May in a couple of days. There came the sound of clogs on my path and I thought, here comes Fenella, after something else for her May Lady. But very quickly I realised it wasn't Fenella's step. Fenella tripped along – skipped everywhere, that child – this step had a drag to it. It was Billy, as we called her. My Mehitable.

Billy was almost a young lady, then. She had stayed short and thin but had straightened out nicely, although she still wore a calliper and had something of a limp. She never had much to say for herself, but would often come round and sit with me, for no reason. She and her mother did not get on, and it seemed to be getting worse rather than better as she came into an age when she might be grow'd.

How bad things were between Rose and her daughter got more obvious when the other two girls came along, for the other two were so much more what daughters are meant to be.

'Mami,' she said, as she stepped through my open door, 'how are you today?'

'I'm all well and good, Billy,' I said, 'I'm just dandy. What brings you here? Aren't you supposed to be cooking food for that donkey?'

Lijah had bought a donkey the week before. It was a mangy old thing with holes in its pelt and half its teeth fall'd out. When I saw it, I asked Lijah if someone had paid him to take it. He said almost. He was going to fix it up and sell it but in the meantime it needed all its food cooking for it, as it couldn't eat a raw carrot or a turnip if its life depended on it.

Rose had gone berserk. 'Don't you think I've got enough to do?' she said.

So Billy got the job of cooking the donkey its food. She got all the jobs that no one else wanted, on account of how there were a lot of jobs she couldn't do with that leg of hers.

Billy's face darkened a little. 'I've got a pig's head and some sour bread boiling out back.'

'I was wondering what that stink was,' I said, as we moved toward the kitchen alcove bit and seated ourselves at the little table.

'Everyone else has gone out and left me to it. It'll need boiling more than an hour.'

'Don't you let it dry out or your mother will go something mental.'

'Don't I know it . . .'

'*Mehitable* . . .' She knew the warning tone in my voice. It doesn't do to let children speak ill of their parents, even when they're absolutely right.

She looked down at the tablecloth and plucked at it with one hand. There was something to be got-to-the-bottom-of here, I saw.

'If you're after getting away from the stink, then you've not gone very far, have you?'

'I've something to ask you, Mami.'

'Go on,' I said. I rose from my seat and took a step to the cupboard. I had some oaty biscuits in a tin and no grandchild of mine ever visited my house and went away without a little something in their stomach.

I put the tin on the table. 'Do you want some milk to go with?'

'No thanks, Mami.'

'Have you had your milk today?' Billy hated milk. You had to squeeze it down her.

'Mum made me, at breakfast.'

'Well quite right, too. Have you washed your hands lately?'

'Just before I came over.'

'So what is it you're after, *chai*?' I took an oaty biscuit myself. They have to be cooked in ovens, them biscuits, so I'd never had them as a child. I had a fierce liking for them, as a result and cooked them several times a week. I was mad about them.

Billy reached into her pocket and brought out a doll. It was a small thing but nicely turned out with a little skirt and bodice made of blue cotton. I recognised an old blouse of Rose's. Billy had snipped up some brown wool for hair and put it into long bunches and tied it with thread.

'I don't know what to do for shoes,' she said. 'Fenella's doing boots, so I can't do those. I'd like shiny black shoes but she's too small for anything stiff. Have you got a piece of anything that will do it?'

I took the doll and looked at it. A feeling of sadness came over me, like a cool wind blowing. I said quietly, 'Does your mother know about this?'

Her face darkened again. She took the doll back and held it in her lap. 'Well, Mami, what do *you* think . . .' she mumbled.

'*Mehitable . . .*'

She looked up sharply. 'She'll let me go if you say so. Oh please, Mami. Tell her it would be a good idea. I could keep an eye on Scarlet.'

I stared at her. I had a hollow feeling inside, a caving in, for all at once it had come to me how hard her life still was. Rose had never let Billy go Mayladyin', ever. She said it wasn't right for a child with a calliper to go dragging it around the village – it looked too much like begging. I'd agreed with her at the time and never thought more of it. And then Fenella comes along and she's such a pretty, sunny girl. And when she's big enough she rushes home from school one day all excited because she's going a Mayladyin' for the first time with her friends . . . and it never occurs to any of us to say no to Fenella. For Fenella is a proud, cheerful child, and Mayladyin' doesn't look like begging when she does it – no, it looks like a game that gets her a few pennies, that's all.

So off Fenella and Scarlet go, each year, and it never occurs to nobody that Billy might be sitting there and dying to go herself. Why did she never speak up before?

'Billy,' I said gently. 'Don't you think you're a bit old for all that? Mayladyin's for little girls. You're a young lady, you know. Why, I can't believe how fast you've grow'd.'

She looked at me, crestfallen. I hated to be the one to disappoint her but I knew if I didn't, then her mother would be a lot more blunt about it.

'Come on, now,' I said. 'What are you? Fourteen? Fifteen? Most girls your age were wed with babbies when I was young.'

'I'm thirteen, Mami.'

'Oh well, even so . . .' I pushed the biscuit tin towards her. 'Here, take another to have on the way home.'

She shook her head, then stood. She looked at the little doll, then let it drop on to my kitchen table. 'You have it, Mami. Maybe you can fix it up as a present for Scarlet some time. She hasn't seen it yet. You could make it look nice.'

I wanted to say, *it won't always be this bad, you know, Billy. Some day, you might have a real piece of luck and then you won't always feel like the nice things in life happen to other people.* I couldn't say that, of course, as I didn't know if it were true.

At the door, she turned. 'Mum wouldn't have let me anyway, would she?' she said, and the bitterness in her voice was as clear as church bells ringing.

I shook my head.

She went back to the pig's head that was stinking out the back yard.

Not long after that, Mehitable took my advice and started to become a young lady. That didn't improve relations with her mother any. Rose had a bit of difficulty in recognising that her first three were getting grown up, I reckon. Daniel left school and started his apprenticeship. Mehitable cut her hair short and made herself blouses on her mother's sewing machine – she was all for getting herself a position as a maid in a big house, if she could find anyone who would take her with that leg of hers. Bartholomew was still at school but played truant like the devil and took beer with his breakfast, just like his dad. You didn't need to look at the palm of his hand to see which way he was going. Barty-boy, my Barty-boy, what can I say of him? What he was like as a boy is all wiped out by what came later. Broke his mother's heart.

Fenella grew into a beauty. The boys would fight each other to carry her things for her. She was a fashion-plate.

Scarlet, tough as old boots. My baby.

I still liked my little place. I had got it just how I wanted. I didn't miss being on the road at all, although I never closed my front door unless it was really freezing. What I loved most was waking in the night and having that strange moment you have when you wake unexpectedly, the odd not-knowingness of where you are – or even who you are. Then it comes to you. *My name is Clementina Lee, widow, and I am living in a little house on the edge of a village called Sutton-in-the-Isle, west of Ely.* And I would think, *the strangeness of ending up here. During all the things that were happening to me in all the years previous. Here was waiting for me, all along.*

I would shift in my bed, turn my head and open my eyes, gazing through my open door from where I lay, at the whole expanse of *here* out there. The dark outside, the whole of the Fens stretching, lying flat and quiet . . . *This is what it must be like to be the King of Russia*, I sometimes thought, *as if the world was only made for you to inhabit it, and all the other people in it are different parts of you.* If it was a clear night, I could lie and watch the stars.

Sometimes I would just drift off back to sleep, all calm and quiet, thinking about the stars. And sometimes I would rise from my bed and pull on my boots and shawl and go outside. Some nights I would sit on my doorstep and smoke a pipe, but on others I would go for a little walk in the darkness, just a little wander around, not because I needed to particularly but because it was right nice to do it, maybe to pretend I was the King of Russia, or maybe for no reason at all.

It was on one of those nights, on one of my walks, that I had a strange encounter with my son. I had woken before dawn, as usual. It was pitch black outside – it must've been a cloudy night for it was completely starless and I could hardly see a thing. Nights like that were good. You felt the ground beneath your feet more better when it was all you had to go on.

I stood on my step for a minute, closed my eyes and breathed in deep, as I liked to do. Glory be to *Mi Duvvel*, I thought. The air feels good inside your lungs when it isn't shared with *gorjers*.

Having the air to myself. That was why I went out at night.

I turned up the lane, to do my usual circuit of the village. There was something right pleasant about going round the houses when all else was asleep. Sometimes there'd be a workman out and about and it always annoyed me terrible if I bumped into one of them – like they was interfering with me. I would never greet them, and I daresay word had got round the village that I was a queer old boot, which suited me just fine. It kept fools away and was good for business.

What I liked most was how even though the sky seemed pitch dark, the shapes of the trees would be even darker against it. It reminded me there were lots of different sorts of darkness in the world and that was a good thing. It meant that however much you knew, there was always something else beyond – and if there isn't anything beyond, then what would be the point?

Within a few paces, I would pass Lijah's cottage, and I always glanced that way, of course. That night, before I even neared it, I knew my Lijah was up and about. I could see the glow of a little flame. I spotted it as I came down my step. He was sitting on his doorstep, lighting his pipe.

The flame went out – if I'd walked by a minute later I wouldn't have known he was there.

The shape of him became him as I got close.

I didn't speak or anything. I just came and squatted down next to him, and wished I had my pipe with me too.

There was a long silence between us, while we both looked out at the dark.

'Thing is,' he said after a while. 'I haven't forgotten how she was.'

I said nothing.

'Might be a bit easier if I did, like.'

There was another long silence.

'Like when we went to the fair, just after we was wed. We walked around together, and I could see the other fellas looking at her, and then looking at me, for none of them had her on their arm, but I did.'

A wave of honesty came over me, and I wanted to cry out, but *it's never been right for you, Lijah. What did you have to go off and marry a gorjer girl for? When gorjers' merripen and Romani chals' merripen ven kitanee, kerk kosto merripen see, you should know that. Why didn't you stick with your own kind, for heaven's sake?*

*And you might not have your five fine grandchildren then, missus. What of that? Mrs Pure Adolphus Lee, Clementina Smith as was, Little Lemmy – let's wish the done undone, shall we? Let's wish you hadn't taken that journey in the mud – you wouldn't even have your Lijah then.*

Fortunately, I am quite good at ignoring the voices in my head when they talk inconvenient.

It didn't matter what the truth of it was, really, for I knew I could never say anything to him against his Rosie. He had fallen for her, good and proper, all those years ago back on the farm, and whatever his faults had been as a husband I was certain no other girl had turned his head since. She was his Rosie, pure and simple, and it wasn't my place to interfere. All I could do was keep my mouth shut.

'And there was one time when she was holding Dan and talking to him soft, when he was little, and he was holding on to her hair with his fists. She looked right fine that day.'

He would never have spoken like this in the daylight. It was like he was saying it to the darkness, like I wasn't there at all.

He tapped his pipe against the step. 'She don't like me, Dei. She used to, but she don't any more. Hasn't done for years.'

I suppose that was the moment I could have said something, but

I was that worried of saying the wrong thing that I didn't speak at all.

'This 'baccy's a bit damp,' he said. He had pushed it down with his finger and was trying to relight it. I rose from the step.

The warning signs were there, looking back.

I can remember, in East Cambridge, sitting of an evening, on one of the few evenings when Lijah chose to grace us with his presence. He would bring home news-sheets, sometimes, that he had lifted from somewhere, and he would give them to Rose and say, 'Go on, Rosie, read to us. Read to us about the S'ara desert.' I do believe he would have gone there himself to see what it was all about if he knew where it was.

And then there was that time me and him took little Scarlet out blackberry picking.

It was right warm that day. I can't remember what the others were up to but it was just the three of us. We were standing next to the hedgerow at the far end of the lane, just where it petered out into a fallow field. It was a hot day. I was gathering the berries from the top of the bush and Lijah was helping Scarlet collect them from the bottom branches, the ones she could reach.

Lijah had his favourite stick, the old, gnarled one that was worn dark and smooth. He was holding back the lower branches so that Scarlet could reach some of the blackberries inside the bush without pricking her fat little arms. He was being right good about it, as he would have done with any of the girls (not the boys, mind you) for he was pretending how he hadn't spotted the best clusters.

I was having to lean over them to pick mine, and was feeling a little cross on account of how it was taking a long time and I had jobs to do back home.

'Have a look in there, petal,' Lijah said to Scarlet. 'I can't see anything. I don't think there is anything in there.'

Scarlet bent and peered into the bush, then cried gleefully, 'Yes, there is, Dad! I can see them!'

'No!' he replied, in mock astonishment. 'There's no blackberries in there . . . never in a million years.'

Scarlet reached in and pulled out a few blackberries, already squashy in her hot little fist and not much use for anything but jam, they were that mashed. She held them up to me, with a look of triumph. 'Look what Dad and I have founded, Mami!'

She was that proud of herself. 'Well done, Scarlet. That's wonderful, that is,' I said. 'Now you put them in this tin here and I think we'd best be off home.'

On the way back they walked ahead a little, holding hands. I trailed behind with the half-full tin. The sun was beating down that day and I had on my dress that was a bit tight around the arms and on the itchy side.

I heard Scarlet say to Lijah, 'Dad, where did you get that stick from?'

'Ah,' he said, and I did not need to see his face to know the expression on it, 'well you might ask . . .'

Behind them, I rolled my eyes.

'This stick, this here stick? I got this stick in the S'ara Desert!'

Scarlet's voice was full of wonder. 'Did you really, Dad? When was that, Dad?'

'Lijah . . .' I muttered from behind, but he took no notice of me.

'Why, Little One, that was when I went off to war, before you was born. I was off a-fighting against the Boers what was trying to steal Africa from us . . .'

The signs were there. I should've known what was coming.

We had been living in the village for some years then and was well established, if you know what I mean. What I mean is, I don't think there was anyone who took against us, in particular, and I had got quite friendly with some of the other Old Folks. There were a few

Old Folks lived in our row as there was several little places like mine too small for anything but widows or widowers. At the far end of the row was Mrs Canning, quite a posh *rawnie* fallen on hard times. Her father had owned a jeweller's shop, she told me once. She didn't have any side to her, though, considering she was used to being quite high up in life. She was just a poor old *pivli rawnie* like the rest of us now.

She and me shared a smoke sometimes, sitting on her step if the weather was fine. She was much more up to date with what was going on in the world than me, was Edie Canning. She read the local paper, every week.

Sometimes I would say to her, 'So, what's up with the world, then?' and she would tell me how they were going to stop opening the library in Ely on Saturday afternoons and it was a disgrace as that was the only time the working men could get there and improve themselves. Last Thursday, Robert Cooter from Windmill Lane had chased his wife down the street with a rolling pin. Now there was a man who needed improving.

It was Edie Canning told me about the *Bell-jums*. They were a brave people, she said, but extremely small. She had met one, once. They wore tall hats to try and make themselves look bigger but not so's it would fool you. They ate nothing but bread and ham.

The Germans, they was different, mind. They were big fellas, and they ate twice as much as the Bell-jums and they had a hundred different sorts of cheeses. They were very cruel to their animals. When a horse got lame, they would beat it to death and then leave it to rot by the side of the road. Edie Canning's nephew had been to Germany and seen it happening with his own eyes.

I was shocked when she told me that. I thought the Germans probably had what was coming to them, if that's the sort of folk they were.

*

It seemed to me that all my life I had been able to not-think about the world. Lijah said to me once, 'Have you never wanted to go and see the sights of London, Dei?' and I said, 'What for? I've been to Thetford.' The Fens were world enough for me. They stretched as far as the eye could see, which is quite far enough to my way of thinking.

What I didn't realise was that if you don't go out and visit the world, it doesn't matter. Sooner or later, the world comes to visit you.

When the War started, a lot of the local lads rushed off, of course – the young ones, the ones who couldn't wait to get out of the village. But a fair few of the older men held back. The men who had children knew what leaving those children might mean. The high-ups knew it too. When they had killed off the first lot of volunteers, they brought in the Bachelor Bill, as it was called, and that used up the rest of the unmarried ones pretty sharpish, so it was only a matter of time before they started on the husbands.

I would like to tell you that it was then that my Lijah got forced into it, against his better judgement – but you'll have worked out by now that *better* and *judgement* were words that were not often joined together when Lijah was around.

No, Lijah went all of his own accord. He told me later that he volunteered because he thought that if he waited any longer then the army would fill up and they wouldn't let him in.

I was in their kitchen when he came back, that day. He hadn't told nobody what he was planning, of course.

Rose and I were standing by the range. She had just said, 'This coal we're using is brittle. I don't think it is Northamptonshire coal like the fella said.'

I was about to reply, when Lijah appeared at the back door. He stood there, framed in the light. In his hands, he was holding a piece of paper. He held it out for us to see, proudly, like it was a rabbit he'd just caught, or a bouquet of roses. I couldn't read what was written on the paper but I could see his mark at the bottom.

Rose took a step towards him.

'What is it?' I asked her, although I had a sinking feeling I could guess.

'Oh Elijah . . .' she said despairingly. 'Could you not have talked this through with your own wife first?'

Elijah frowned. 'They're paying a shilling a day,' he said. 'You get bread and kippers for breakfast when you're training. Square-bashing, they call it.'

'You don't like kippers,' I said.

Then, he glanced over his shoulder, and tossed his head. Side-stepping neatly, already the military man, he moved to make space in the doorway.

Something terrible happened. Into the space Lijah had left, stepped Daniel. And he was holding the same piece of paper as his father.

Rose gave a small cry, then clapped both hands to her mouth. I thought she might collapse and was ready for it. Instead, she just looked from one of them to the other, and her gaze burned.

Daniel realised straight up he should not do the proud bit and avoided her gaze. He glanced at his Dad, then down at the step. 'Mum, don't take on . . .' he said. I think it was the only time I ever heard him come close to arguing with her.

Lijah was looking deflated now. 'Oh don't make such a fuss, woman,' he growled at Rose, although she had not spoken another word. 'Everyone's at it. We thought you'd be proud of us.'

We? I knew the real source of Rose's anger. If Lijah wanted to go and get himself killed in Foreign Lands that was one thing – but he was taking her best son with him. Daniel was nineteen years old and had never been away from his mother. He was apprenticed to a sign-writer in Haddenham but still came home every night. He had turned down a chance to be a bricklayer in Whittlesey because it would have meant moving away from home.

'It won't be that bad,' muttered Lijah. 'Crikey the trouble we get in round here, it'll be a nice rest, won't it, Dan?' He nudged his son with his elbow.

He looked at me then, and grinned, expecting me to appreciate his levity. 'I think you had better go off somewhere for a bit, the both of you,' I said quietly.

Lijah glanced at me, a little surprised, for I hadn't taken him to task on anything he'd done for a while. Daniel turned immediately and went back down the path. After a moment, Lijah followed his son.

When they had gone, Rose sat on an upright chair and took her hanky from her pocket. She did not cry, though her face was twisted. 'Oh Clementina,' she said, 'what are we going to do?'

'I don't know,' I said and for once, I didn't.

# PART 4

## 1914–1929

# Rose

# CHAPTER 14

There was before the War, and there was after. It was like a door suddenly appeared in all our lives. You could go through it both ways, if you tried hard enough. If you really concentrated, you could think back to how it was before. The hardships you'd had seemed like adventures, looking back – rough, but liveable through. No one died, back then.

They did, of course. People died all the time. It just didn't feel like it, before.

Then there was after. After was a different land. So many men gone, just disappeared, and nobody supposed to scream that no, they weren't proud their best boy had vanished into thin air because they'd give up honour and all place in society to have him back, even if it was just a body to bury.

I went to church every Sunday when the War was on. I'd never been much of a churchgoer before, but during the War the whole village seemed to go. I suppose we all needed it in a way we hadn't before. Some of us might have gone for the right reasons, to pray for king and country and for the victory of our noble cause – but I reckon most people went for the same reason I did: to make their bargain with God. Send him back to me, just send him back, and I will do *this* or *this* or *this*. There wasn't a thing we wouldn't have offered.

Plenty of the people who went already knew their prayers would not be answered. I remember one Sunday, about a year before it ended. The church full, as usual. Clementina had come with me, and the girls. We were late, again as usual, and sat near the back.

The very front pew belonged to the Demoine family, who were the nearest we had to lords of the manor as they owned Middleton House a few miles out of the village. Sir James and Lady Demoine had been blessed with but one child, Charles, twenty-two years old when he was killed. He received the Military Cross post-humously, we later heard, after leading an attack on a German tank battalion.

This particular Sunday, Sir James and his wife were there, sat at the front as was their due, all alone in the family pew – childless now. They had had their son late and were getting on in years. It crossed my mind to wonder what would happen to the Demoine name and Middleton House when they passed on. Perhaps it would all end with them. It was not long after their boy had been killed, so I imagine there were quite a few people in church that day who were thinking the same as me. I wondered if the Demoines were aware of us staring at their backs and whether they were grateful for or hated our pity.

It was during the sermon. The vicar was saying something about Jesus' noble sacrifice on the cross. He hadn't even mentioned the War yet. Suddenly, in full view of everybody, Lady Demoine got to her feet. She raised her hand and pointed at the vicar and in a trembling voice, she shouted, 'Liar! Liar!' The words rang out, as clear as anything, echoing around the church, up to the rafters.

I was on the end of our pew, so could see her quite clearly. She was shaking from head to foot – I could see it in the arm that was pointing. I could not see her face but I could hear the hatred in her voice.

Nobody knew what to do. We all just sat there, even her husband who was gazing up at her. He couldn't have looked more shocked if the statue of the Virgin Mary in the alcove next to them had spoken.

Lady Demoine was breathing in great, heaving breaths. Her shoulders went up and down with the effort and the arm sank a little. Then she seemed to recover her strength.

'Liar! Liar!' she repeated, with an amazing amount of venom, still pointing at the vicar.

Her husband came to his senses at last, got to his feet and ushered his wife out of the pew. She made it to the end before she collapsed, weeping hysterically in great, howling cries. Her knees were gone and her husband had to hold her up and half drag her down the aisle. Not a soul moved to help him. They were the only people of quality in the whole church and it wouldn't have been seemly for anyone else to lay hands on her. There was nothing we could do except stare straight ahead.

Normally, if a person of such standing had made an exhibit of themselves in that way, it would have been the talk of the village for weeks, but none of us mentioned it as we filed out at the end of the service. I saw a couple of men shake their heads in bafflement but the women knew – they knew why the vicar's fine words had raged her so, and why she'd shouted *liar*. What woman hasn't wanted to do that at the whole world at least once in her life?

\*

We had been living in the village nearly fifteen years by then. Fifteen years. When you stay in one place, time goes more quickly, for some reason. Well, the days don't go quickly – they drag and drag – but the years? They fly past.

There comes a point when you stop trying to fill the holes in your life. What a great relief that is.

Our cottage was right on the edge of the village, with a big vegetable patch at the back that looked out over the Fens; just empty farmland, stretching away from us, like a great ocean. Every afternoon, you could watch the slant of the sun.

It was right for us – a decent roof over our heads but a little bit separate from the *gorjers* in the rest of the village. I had come to feel our differentness, as a family, and to be happy that we weren't slap bang in the middle of the village with everybody watching and judging us the whole time the way it had been when we lived in East Cambridge. We had been judged on Stourbridge Common, too, mind you. The judging never stops when you're neither one thing nor another – I had learned that by then. In East Cambridge my kids got picked on for being *gipsies* and on the road they got picked on for being *half 'n' halfs*. So from now on I wasn't making any allowances for anybody, any more. We was us, and anyone who didn't like it could *ife*.

The cottage was pretty small – especially once we had five children in it. Clementina had her own little place in a neighbouring row of one-up, one-downs. I think they had been almshouses, once. Her vegetable patch was on a slight rise, so she had a better view than us. We had a ditch at the back and a damp problem in the kitchen. Right opposite us was the Forage Works and when they opened the chaff cylinders a cloud of foul vapours would drift across the street. But in comparison with living cheek-by-jowl with Clementina, it was sheer heaven.

When Scarlet was old enough to go to school, I started taking in more sewing. I was fast and brought in a good little bit – and for the first time in my life I didn't have to go pleading to Elijah to keep food in the cupboards. Elijah was still drinking sometimes and the horse business went up and down but between the two of us, we managed. We was settled.

I'm not saying we were well off or anything, or that I didn't sometimes look at Elijah and curse the day he'd smiled up at me from the step of his *vardo*. Things always went a bit bad for us after each child was born, for some reason. He always wanted to disappear a bit then and of course that was the time I most objected to it.

We had a rum patch not long after Scarlet was born, I remember. She came out a wee bit early and needed a lot of feeding up. Elijah hadn't done a deal on a horse for a while and the hawking was not so good, so he'd taken on a bit of rod peeling. Tuppence ha'penny a bundle, he got. He hated piece work and always came home in a foul temper saying they were trying to cheat him somehow or other. Sometimes, when he'd been paid, he took what little he'd earned and went straight down The Toll House. They had regular dice games at The Toll House, and there wasn't a woman in Sutton unprepared to swallow those dice whole if she got the chance.

They always started the same, our arguments. He would come in looking all sheepish and boyish, and try to be affectionate – 'Ah, my Rosie . . .' That's how I knew for sure he was drunk. Then, when I pushed him off, or asked him where his earnings was, he would start off with a bit of humour. 'Oh, I've not *lost* the money, Rosie. I've just lent it to him 'til we play again!'

Ta-da!

I didn't respond to the humour any more than I did the affection. It was all as thin as the ice on a puddle.

'You're a drunken fool, Elijah Smith, and when your children want feeding tomorrow are you going to make jokes to them, then?'

We weren't exactly starving at that time, not like we'd been in Cambridge, but I liked to remind him we once had been and that it was his fault. That was when it would turn nasty.

'Is it any wonder I'm off down the pub when all I get here is . . .' On and on.

When you've been married more than a decade, then all arguments are the same arguments, really. The exact wording changes now and then, that's all.

It always ended the same way, with me going upstairs for the spare blanket and dumping it on the settee.

Scarlet woke me at dawn, that particular day, wanting a feed. When I'd sorted her out, I put her on my shoulder and took her downstairs. Elijah was out flat. I pulled the blanket off him and told him in no uncertain terms to take himself upstairs before the children got down. Then I set to, lighting the fires and getting breakfast ready.

They all pounded down: Daniel all excited like he was each morning. He was fourteen and would be finishing school soon and starting his apprenticeship. He couldn't wait. Mehitable – well, she was always surly of a morning. She wanted to finish school too but I wouldn't let her just yet. Fenella had only just started and I would need Mehitable to take her and look after her a bit. Bartholomew was eight and would be going to school for a while yet but I didn't trust him to keep an eye on his little sister for more than a minute.

There was the clamour and clatter of feeding them all and shouting at them to get their coats and shoes on, then they were gone.

Elijah didn't come down all morning. I went and did my shopping with Scarlet and came back and there was still no sign of him. Mid-afternoon, Scarlet was in her pram in the garden and I was shaking a mat out over the ditch at the back, when I looked up

and saw him at our bedroom window, staring down at me. I knew
that sullen stare. I knew what it meant, right enough.

I went straight to our little stable. Kit had his head bent in his
straw. He raised and shook it. 'Never you mind, Kit,' I said to
him, as I lifted his harness down from the wall.

Elijah was downstairs by the time I got back to the house. His
pack was all bundled up and he was pulling on his boots.

Do we really have to go through all this? I thought wearily.

'You're not going nowhere,' I said to him, arms folded. 'Not on
that horse, anyway.'

'I'll walk, then!' he spat at me, without looking up from where
he was tying his laces.

'Stagger, more like,' I spat back as I stepped past him into the
house.

'You'll be sorry,' he said, as he rose and hefted his pack on to his
back, 'when you get word I've found myself a nice little fancy
piece and am comfy settled down in the Garden of Eden! You'll be
sorry, then!'

That got my attention all right. But by the time I'd turned, he'd
strode off down the path.


When she first moved into her cottage, Clementina used a brick to
prop open her door. She said she couldn't sleep otherwise.
Recently, she had acquired a conch shell, a huge, gleaming thing it
was. Lijah must have got it for her somewhere, when he was out
hawking. I always think it's a bit strange how those things are
supposed to be natural. The pink bit inside looks all wrong. For
some reason, I had taken an instant dislike to this particular conch
shell and it always annoyed me.

As I stepped up her path that afternoon, I glanced down
at the conch shell, and felt cross, about everything in my life,
really – her included. After all these years I was used to her
peculiarities and sometimes we got along all right for months,

before something made me suddenly annoyed with her again.

She was sitting in her little kitchen, next to her table, on an upright chair. As I entered, she looked up without surprise.

'What do you want?' Only Clementina could make such a simple question sound so scornful.

I wasn't in the mood to beat about the bush.

'He's gone,' I said, and sat down on the other chair, even though she had not invited me to.

She drew on her little clay pipe and puffed out extravagantly. She knew I hated smoking and did not allow it in my own home.

'He's always going,' she said lightly.

'No,' I said firmly, bending forward to lean weight on my words. 'He's *gone*.'

She paused in the act of raising the pipe again and looked at me keenly. I knew she was working out how serious it was. She frowned slightly. There was a smoke-filled silence that hung in the air. I had to make her understand.

'He's gone,' I repeated, 'and he isn't coming back. I hid Kit's harness and he just put his boots on and said I could do what I liked, he'd *walk* to Cambridge if he had to.'

When I mentioned Cambridge, she knew how serious it was. If he got to East Cambridge, back to his old pals there and his old drinking habits, she knew that would be it. We'd never see him again.

Her gaze didn't leave my face for a second. 'What time did he go?'

'About an hour ago. Scarlet was screaming to be fed. She's asleep now. I had to put some potatoes on to boil before I came over. The others will be back soon.'

'What are you cooking with the potatoes?'

'Mrs Piggot gave me some goose fat and I've a bit of cured ham and an onion. Why?'

'Go and fry the onion. He won't be back before tea but you'd better save him some.'

I rose, mightily annoyed. Was that the best she could do? She put one finger in her mouth, then damped down the pipe with it, before laying it carefully on the table between us. Then she folded her hands in her lap. She looked down at them, composing herself, then looked back up at me, as if surprised I hadn't gone yet.

'Go on,' she said.

At the door, I turned.

She lifted her chin, jutting it in the direction of the path behind me. 'Go on,' she said softly. 'Go home to that babby and make the tea. I'll get him back.'

She looked down at her lap again, and closed her eyes.

I've never been a superstitious person, never. I'm not even that religious, although my mother was, and drilled it into me. Getting married in a church was more to do with wanting it to be proper in my head than doing it in the sight of God. The War was not yet upon us, at that time, and I hadn't been to church in years.

I believe there is a God, of course, and I've prayed often enough, in the bad times. But He and I don't really have a close relationship, on account of how I always feel I am complaining about my lot and asking Him what I've done to deserve Elijah. I think God probably has better things to do than concern Himself with me.

My mother believed in God, and tea-leaves, and in not walking under ladders, as if it was all one and the same.

I know what people say about Travelling folk, but I also know that Travelling folk have to make a living just like anybody else and it does them no harm whatsoever to let people believe they have special powers. I always thought there was something a bit funny about Clementina but she had never tried to show off, and I knew when she did fortunes in East Cambridge it was just to earn a bob. So I've no real reason to think she did anything special that day. I'm just saying what happened.

Elijah was home before nightfall, exhausted. There was a strange unease about him. He wouldn't at me look me properly. I thought his hangover had kicked in good and proper and sent him up to bed. I had saved him some tea, just like Clementina told me to, but he said he didn't want anything.

Once the children were asleep, I went in to him to check he was all right, expecting to find him lying spread-eagled on his back, fully clothed and snoring.

Instead, he had undressed himself and got into bed, but was sitting up leaning against the headboard, fully awake and staring straight ahead of him.

I had Scarlet on my shoulder. She was fretful that evening. She was still too little to sleep in the big bed with her sisters and was in a Moses basket Elijah had weaved which sat on top of the dresser in our room. I put her down into it, but she kicked her covers off and began to cry in that funny, sneezy little way she had.

'Can I look at her?' asked Elijah.

I turned to him, surprised. He had never taken much interest in any of the children when they were tiny. He liked them more when they could do things.

I lifted Scarlet out of the Moses basket and carried her over to him. He raised his legs so that I could lay her on them, with her head supported on his knees and her little swaddled feet pointing down. I sat on the edge of the bed so I could look at him looking at her.

Her woollen bonnet had fallen back as I laid her down. He stared at her, then said. 'What's wrong with the skin on her head. Why's it all flaky?'

'It's cradle-cap,' I said. 'None of the others had it so I don't know why she has. She'll grow out of it. Your mum has given me some oil to put on it at night.'

At the mention of his mother, he looked up sharply and said, 'When did she do that?'

'Last week.'

He looked down again at the baby. 'She's got a nose like yours, but eyes like mine,' he said thoughtfully.

*You've actually noticed something about your new baby*, I thought. I wanted to say it out loud but knew he would thrust her back at me if I did. I didn't want to break the spell.

A wave of tiredness came over me. I had been on my feet all day. It's always a mistake to sit down at the end of the day. You never want to get up.

'I've got to finish downstairs before I can come up,' I said. 'Do you want to keep her? I'll be done that much quicker.'

He didn't look up from his examination of his new daughter. 'Aye. All right.'

I didn't question him that night. I could tell it wasn't right. But in the morning when the children had all piled off to school, he didn't pull his boots on and leave the house as I expected him to, but sat in his armchair, sipping his tea. I went upstairs to feed Scarlet and change her, then took her out to the yard and put her in the pram, with the cat-net over her, so she could have a good bawl and get some fresh air in her lungs. Then I went back inside.

Elijah was still sitting in his armchair. I went over and took his empty mug from him, then, with this new quietness of his, felt bold enough to ask, 'What happened, Elijah?'

He didn't look at me, just stroked his chin. 'I was walking down the lane. I was in open country, just striding along like.' He paused. 'My feet went.'

'What do you mean?'

'What do you think I mean?' he snapped, a little of the
old Elijah returning. 'I mean what I say. My legs went. I fell
down.'

*I'm not surprised with what you'd drunk*, I thought to myself.

'I lay there, then started back. Took me hours. I couldn't walk
until I got . . .' He stopped there and tried a half-smile but it wasn't
at all convincing. Whatever it had been, it had frightened him
half to death.

I thought of him crawling back to Sutton on his hands and
knees. I confess the thought gave me no little pleasure.

He went out later, and I knew he'd gone to see his mother.

Like I said, I'm not a superstitious person by nature. But from
that time, I felt a bit more kindly towards Clementina. I don't
know whether she got Elijah back for us or not, but I knew for certain she had tried to, and I knew that she would do it again if
needs be. It was like when she'd helped deliver my two last
babies. I never doubted when she pulled those babies out, that she
was fighting to bring them out safe and sound.

Her conch shell still annoyed me, mind you. I still felt cross
every time I looked at it.

From then on, Elijah seemed a bit more happy in himself. After
that night when he had so nearly left us for good, then come back
and sat in bed and stared at his new baby girl – well, things
changed for Elijah after that, I think. It was like he had made his
mind up about something, in that bit of time he spent staring at
Scarlet. I think when he sat in bed and looked at her, he was realising that if he'd disppeared off to Cambridge like he was
intending, he might never have seen her again, might never have
even looked properly at her in his whole life. And even a man like
Elijah knew the wrongness of that. Something raw happened to
him, then. Scarlet was his kitten, after that, his little mouse, his

acorn. There wasn't a word for *little* or *precious* that he didn't lavish on that child.

He was soft on all the girls, even Mehitable. Bit tougher on the boys, mind. Overstepped the mark once or twice with them.

For a long time, I thought I was just no good with girls. Daniel was so easy, and Bartholomew was a little terror but of course he worshipped the ground his big brother walked on, so they were off together all the time. Mehitable was the one who clung to me, and the one I couldn't deal with. Other women said to me, a mother always loves the boys best, so I just thought, well, maybe that's it. Maybe I wasn't meant to have a daughter.

Then along came Fenella and Scarlet, and I didn't have any problem with them, and I loved them with a lightness I didn't know existed. I remember how I would plait Fenella's hair when she was little – she had such beautiful hair – it was a pleasure to dress it up. And I would sing to her while I did it, and think, I can't wait until this one's grown up so we can talk about things and I can lend her my best coat with the collar and show her how to do her powder and hitch a stocking without tearing it. All those things I had never shared with my own mother, and I was going to make up for that with Fenella. Peculiar, in a way – she was such a lovely little girl, and yet I couldn't wait for her to be a grown woman.

And it was then that things between me and Mehitable really went downhill, for I realised it wasn't that I couldn't love a daughter. I just couldn't love *her*.

If I'd been that bad a mother to her, then someone would've spoke to me about it, wouldn't they? Clementina or Elijah or even Dan – one of them would have said, *aren't you a bit hard on our Billy?*

There was one day: I think I was pregnant with Fenella at the time, so Mehitable must have been about seven or eight. She wasn't at school that day. She had had a stomach-ache in the morning. Well, of course, as soon as the boys had gone off, her stomach-ache seemed to get better right away, so I said to her, 'Don't think you're lounging around here all day while I work my fingers off,' and gave her a list of chores.

Elijah rose late – he'd had a few the night before. He ate breakfast quickly as he said he had to get all the way over to Horseley Fen and go and see a farmer about a pony. I was complaining to him about Mehitable pretending to be poorly, just to get off school, and how I was going to give her what for if she didn't help me that day. He went a bit quiet.

I left him to finish his mug of tea and took a load of laundry out to the line. I had washed it the previous afternoon but then rain had swept in across field and I hadn't been able to dry it. It had sat wet all night long and needed putting out as soon as possible.

It was a cold morning, still, with damp in the air but a glimmer of pale sun coming through and I thought, as I pegged my laundry out, that if the rain would just hold off 'til lunchtime I'd be all right.

I went back inside and cleared the breakfast things. Mehitable was clunking around upstairs.

I was just in the hallway, dusting in the cold light, when Elijah came through from the kitchen. He walked past me, opened the front door and put his pack down on the step. He walked past me again to get something from the back. While he was gone, Mehitable came down and limped over to the shoe-box under the stairs. She pulled out the brown lace-ups she had just inherited from Dan, sat down on the step and began to pull them on.

'Where do you think you're going?' I asked her. She hadn't even started her chores.

She looked up at me, in that half sly, half scared way she had, her small, dark eyes giving me a glance, then looked down again and concentrated on tying her laces. She muttered something.

I couldn't bear it when she muttered. It was a form of insolence, however much she may pretend it wasn't.

'Speak up, Billy, for heaven's sake.'

'I said, I'm going with Dad.'

'You're doing no such thing, my girl.' What did she think her father did each day? Went off on a little country walk for the fun of it? Lay in the long grass and looked at the sky? 'Your father has selling to do and you've to clean the upstairs before you think of going anywhere.'

'But . . .'

'I said you're not going.'

'She is.' Lijah strode back into the hallway, rubbing his hands on his trousers. I looked at him in astonishment, but he strode on past me to the front door, ruffled Mehitable's hair, then picked up his boots from where he'd left them ready and sat down on the step, next to her.

She smiled at him, and it cut me to pieces, that smile.

'What do you mean, she's going with you? She's work to do, and so have you.'

Lijah ignored me. He finished his laces, rose and hefted his pack on to his back. 'There's our lunch on that shelf, Billy,' he said to her. 'Do you think you can carry that?' He gestured to where I had put some bread and cheese and a bottle of beer into a tea-cloth and tied it all together.

'Yes, Dad,' she replied, and ran to get it.

'Lijah!' I said, as they turned to go. 'Mehitable has her chores and you need to set out at a fair pace, you can't just take a child with a leg like hers off gallivanting round the countryside.' He'd never taken one of the children across the Fens with him before, not even Dan, who could have kept up with him.

Mehitable had already limped off down the lane at an impressive pace. Lijah paused on the step and looked down at the ground. He spoke quietly, almost to himself. 'She's off school, isn't she? And I'm not leaving her, not with the mood you're in.' He pulled his hanky from his pocket, blew his nose and stuffed the hanky back in. 'She'll only get mistreated.'

He was gone.

I remember standing and staring at the open doorway, at the rectangle of white light they had left behind.

# CHAPTER 15

Then came the Great War. Daniel was eighteen years old when it broke out – on the threshold of everything.

As a man, I would say he was very similar to how he was as a boy. I never heard him raise his voice to argue with anyone, despite the fact that he was big enough to knock any man or woman flat, if he'd wanted. He had a large-featured face – took after my side of the family, right enough – big ears, he had, with very long ear-lobes, wide shoulders. I suppose he was everybody's idea of a strapping soldier lad. Elijah told me, when they went to sign up, the Recruiting Officer had looked up at Daniel and nodded with satisfaction. 'Aye, you'll do,' he said.

Elijah repeated that remark to me with a flourish, as if I'd be pleased and proud.

I would hazard a guess that it was a bit more difficult for Elijah to volunteer – he was nobody's idea of a strapping soldier lad, after all. No, he was everyone's idea of a small, wiry hawker, and a middle-aged one at that. He lied about his age, I suppose – and

I suppose by that stage they were starting to get not too particular.

A year after Elijah and Daniel went, Bartholomew joined up as well, as soon as he could pass for old enough. I had steeled myself for it. Once his dad and big brother were in, I knew it was only a matter of time before he joined up too. He and his father both had to lie to get in, one to make himself younger, the other older. It was only my Daniel who went to do his bit legitimate.

After it was over and the men came back – some of them, that is – it was common for the wives and mothers to talk, when they met in the street or at market, of how changed their menfolk were. Mrs Hinkin's husband had nightmares every night and tried to strangle her once, she told me. Mrs Mott's son twitched all the time.

Often I felt, having known the men before, that they came back not changed, but more so. It was like the war gave them licence to be what they had always been. The loud ones became louder, the quiet ones silent. Mrs Mott's son was always the nervy type – and Eli Hinkin had come close to murdering his wife on many an occasion, I was sure, long before the War got to him.

Alice Mott said to me, once, when we was stood in the queue at Bell's the baker's, 'Has your Elijah ever talked about what they did over there?'

I shook my head. 'He did tell me once about a charge they did to frighten the Hun. Scattered like geese, he said.'

Alice Mott was silent for a bit. We moved forward in the queue. 'My Benjamin can't abide dirt,' she said quietly. 'He won't go out and about in the fields, or even the garden sometimes. If it's raining, he stays indoors. I said to him, you've stood up to the guns of Germany my boy, you're not telling me you're frightened of a bit of water.'

My turn had come. 'Three cob loaves please, Mr Bell,' I said, and he turned to wrap them in paper. 'Was it muddy over there, then?' I asked Alice Mott.

'I think so,' she said, thoughtfully, 'from what he said.'

I don't think the men had any idea how dreadful it was for us who were left behind. I know they had a terrible time, some of them – you could see it in their faces – but in our own way we went through things as terrible, in our imaginings, I mean. There wasn't a minute of a single day when I didn't think to myself: what is happening to them, *right now*. I knew that if I ever got the news that one of them was gone, then I would cast my mind back to the day when it had happened, and I would run through that day, and I would think to myself, *as I shook out that pillowcase, was my Daniel running towards his death? As I collected the eggs, brushing straw from them as I laid them in the basket, was he lying on the ground, the life draining away from him?*

Not gas, I used to think, as I went about my daily business. Please let none of them be gassed. I could not bear the thought of one of them choking.

It was a week before Easter that I got the telegram. Bartholomew had joined up two months previous and just been sent to the front. Elijah and Daniel had been in the thick of things for a year. I was weeding the front garden and saw him cycle up the lane, bald Mr Carter with the squinty eye. He had his head down, as if to prevent the wind from buffeting him. I felt quite calm as I watched him dismount, lean his bike against our gatepost and, head still down, walk up our path. The minute he appeared, it seemed inevitable.

Which one is it? I thought to myself as I watched him approach. He hadn't looked up yet. He hadn't yet composed his face into the look that he must have acquired by then, as he handed the telegram over. It was clutched in his hand.

*I don't need to read it*, I thought. We all know the words of those telegrams off by heart by now. I just want to know, which one of them is it?

Mr Carter made his way steadily towards me, still not looking up.

I prayed and prayed that it would be Elijah.

I am not ashamed to admit that. I knew that if he had taken our sons off to war and got one of them killed, I would never, never forgive him. It would be finished between me and him, for ever. He might as well stay in France.

And then, another thought, as clear as water, *if my Daniel is dead, I do not want to go on living myself. He is the only thing in my life that has never been spoiled by anything. The only thing that is completely pure and good.*

At last, Mr Carter looked up. We were quite close by then, so he gave a small start at the sight of me standing there staring at him, waiting. I watched as he struggled to compose his face. He could not quite achieve the expression he wanted, and so settled for a meaningless grin. Without speaking, he extended the hand that was holding the telegram.

I stepped forward, over some withered tulip stems, and approached him. I think at this point we may have exchanged a few words.

I took the telegram and he handed me a small book and a pencil to sign for it. When he had retrieved them, he bid me good day and turned. He took care not to hurry back to his bike, for that would have been unseemly. He walked slowly down my path.

He righted his bicycle and mounted it, wobbling a little as he turned. Only in that action did he betray his haste, for the normal thing to do would have been to turn the bicycle before he mounted it. I watched Mr Carter cycle down the lane. He did not look back.

I stood in my front garden, holding the telegram, and I did not move. All at once, I felt as if I had all the time in the world. It was the middle of the day and the girls were out. Mehitable was at her cleaning job at Sampson's. Scarlet and Fenella had gone with Clementina to the Thursday market in Ely. I was quite alone and felt a strange sense of peace. It was as if everything that had happened in my life had been leading up to that moment. Once I had opened the telegram, then that would be it, the rest of my life would begin. So there was no hurry, then, not if I had the rest of my life.

I looked at the sky for a bit, then I walked back inside, closing the door gently behind me. I went into the kitchen, put the telegram on the table in front of me and sat down. *Which one of them is it?* I opened it, to find out.

My eyes passed over the *regret to inform you* and travelled quickly to the words I needed to see, the name.

Adolphus Daniel Smith. Missing presumed dead. It was my Dan.

I never managed to grow sundance in that front garden. We got given a nice big plant, by someone, but I stuck it in the wrong place. The problem was the beech tree, which stood by the gate. Not only did it keep the sun off, but the greedy roots sucked up all the water from the earth and the poor thing wilted from thirst, went quite green. That was why it wouldn't ever take. Later, when we moved to Peterborough, I grew a lovely sundance in the back garden there without any difficulty.

A week after Easter, we got another telegram. Adolphus Smith had been found in a field hospital, where he and some other casualties had been taken in error. When he came home on leave, he showed me where some shrapnel had grazed his chest and gone through a muscle on his upper arm. He had also broken a toe.

They should have been demobbed together, all three of them, but there was a bit of a problem with Bartholomew. He went Absent

Without Leave towards the end of it. Then, to get himself out of trouble, he joined up again under another name. So he ended up in a different regiment from his brother and his dad.

So Elijah and Daniel came back in January and it was near March before Bartholomew made it back, and then it was under his assumed name. John Hastings, he was calling himself, and Elijah said to me how I mustn't mention to anyone that he was back as the police might come for him.

It didn't stop the three of them all going down The Tollhouse to get *motto*, the first night he was back. They sang as they came back down the lane, their voices ringing in the black of night, and I lay in bed listening to them and thought, for once, that it was the sweetest chorus. Three male voices, belting out some not-too-polite army song, and they all belonged to me. They were all back.

Within a month, however, I started to hear different voices.

The first time it happened, we were sound asleep upstairs. Our bedroom looked out over the back so I was used to field noises like foxes or owls, but that night I was suddenly awoken by the most terrible howling sound. I sat up in bed. My first thought was that the dog had got free of his kennel and was caught in one of the rabbit snares. Elijah had a series of snares all set round the vegetable patch.

I was throwing my shawl round my shoulders when the sound came again – and this time, it froze my blood, for this time I recognised it as human.

Lijah had awoken too. He caught hold of my arm. 'Rosie . . .'

'What is it?'

'Rosie . . .'

I shook him free and went to our window, lifting the curtain gently aside with one finger.

Below our window, in the moonlight, I could see him. He was no more than a dark shape, moving restlessly to and fro, but there was enough light for me to make out that it was Bartholomew.

'What is he doing?' I said. Elijah had not left the bed.

'Leave him be,' he replied, flatly.

'What is he doing? He hasn't even got a coat on.' All I could make out was that Bartholomew was hunched over and swinging his arms back and forth, as if he was threshing. 'We should go down to him,' I said. 'He might hurt himself.'

'Leave him,' Elijah said, and his voice was rough and insistent. I glanced back at the bed and saw that Elijah had lain down again.

I stood by the window for a long time, watching my son below, not knowing what to do. If he had not been making that strange noise, then I would have gone down and guided him back into the house. But the noise frightened me. I knew that wherever Bartholomew was, it was not in the back garden at Sutton. Perhaps Elijah was right. The best thing was to leave him.

I watched the dark shape, its restless movements. It was one of my children, down there.

How little I know of you, or what has happened to you, I thought.

I assumed it would get better, but in fact it got worse, much worse. I began to realise that Bartholomew had not come back.

He drank all the time. He'd always been a drinker, like his dad, but when he came back from the war, it wasn't just in the evenings. It started from the minute he got up in morning, and it stopped only when he collapsed unconscious somewhere – in his bed, on the settee, sometimes in the yard. Elijah would not let me say a word to him, and even Daniel said I should let him be. He couldn't work or anything as officially he was still Absent Without Leave from the army and we were all trying to work out what was to be done about that.

One night, we were seated for an early supper. It was not often we were a group at table at that time, but Clementina had cooked a ham and brought it over. I had done the veg, and it was a strange old tea as it was like we were having Sunday lunch in the middle of the week.

It was more than a year since the war had finished. Lijah was hawking again. Daniel had gone back to his apprenticeship, which Slaker & Son had kept open for him. Mehitable had moved up to a big house outside Yaxley. She had started off as a live-in maid but was now full housekeeper. Scarlet was due to join her in a month, as a scullery girl. I didn't like the thought of Scarlet taking her first position so far away when she was still so young, but Mehitable said the lady of the house was the kindest person she'd ever known and was paying for her to get her leg looked at by a man brought all the way from London. Fenella was turning out to be a fine seamstress – I was right proud of what she could do. She had been offered a job in a cloak and gown workshop in Peterborough, and we were discussing it.

Daniel had just said, 'Mr Slaker has been talking of moving to Peterborough, Mum. I think it would be good, don't you think? I could keep an eye on Fenella, then.'

Fenella shot him a look, as if to say the last thing she needed was her big brother keeping an eye.

'You're fifteen years old,' I said to Fenella. 'You're not going.'

'Scarlet's going to Yaxley and she's younger than me.'

Scarlet stuck her tongue out at Fenella, triumphantly, and I picked up a spoon and gave her a sharp rap across the knuckles.

'That's different,' I said. 'It's live-in, and Billy will look after her. You'll have to find lodgings.'

'You could come to Yaxley with me instead!' Scarlet said brightly, and the withering look from Fenella said that she saw herself as something a bit better than a scullery girl.

*Good on you, girl,* I thought. Although I was objecting, I had in the back of my mind that I would probably let her go to Peterborough, if Daniel was going as well. There wasn't much in Sutton for a girl like Fenella – and certainly no young men fit for her when she was older. They were all gone now. I didn't want her spending the rest of her life in a village surrounded by empty fields. She deserved a chance at somewhere bigger and better.

Clementina was serving up – she could carve as good as any man. Elijah was at the head of the table, a bit morose as he often was when we got together. Bartholomew was seated at the far end and through the whole of this conversation, he was muttering to himself. I could see his lips moving restlessly as he stared straight ahead.

'Why don't we all move to Peterborough?' Clementina said, as she speared a fat pink slice of ham and stuck it on the top plate of the pile in front of her. I picked the plate up and handed it to Fenella, who passed it down to Bartholomew at the far end. She put it down in front of him.

'What do we want to do that for?' said Elijah, frowning.

'Well, why not?' Clementina said, doling out more ham, 'You've been saying for ages you've had enough of Sutton.'

'Oh, has he?' I murmured, but they took no notice of me. 'Well, I suppose it would be nice to be with Dan and Nelly,' I added.

Fenella's face lit up as she realised I was agreeing to her going.

'And it wouldn't be so far for the girls to come and visit,' added Clementina, meaning Scarlet and Mehitable.

At that point, Bartholomew raised an arm, lowered it swiftly, and then rushed it backwards across the table in a great sweeping motion. His plate with its slice of ham went flying across the room and smashed against the wall. Fenella, who was closest to him, let out a shriek of surprise and pushed herself back from the table as her own plate skidded off and landed on the floor. The pots of relish in front of them toppled and Bartholomew's mug of ale spewed its contents over the tablecloth.

We all froze. Bartholomew was on his feet and staring off into the middle distance. He gave a strange chortle, as if he found something amusing but couldn't quite catch his breath.

'Conducts sales of furniture and effects!' he shouted, before adding softly, 'and valuations of the same.'

I looked at Elijah, but he was looking down at the table.

'Conducts sales of live AND DEAD farming stock!' Bartholomew called out, then simpered, 'and valuations of the same.'

The rest of us stared at him.

'Conducts sales of houses, lands, reversionary interest and life policies!' Bartholomew stood up straight and proud, like a town mayor. He crouched down and brought his hands together, wiggling his fingers. He spoke in a squeaky little voice, like a mouse, 'and valuations of the same.'

'Elijah, do something,' I said, but Elijah did not move.

Bartholomew's voice took on a posh accent. 'Conducts sales of growing crops including grass.' He stood upright, lifted his finger up and clicked his heels together, then shouted, 'AND VALUATIONS OF THE SAME!'

There was a dead silence. We all waited to see what Bartholomew would do next. He looked around, then scratched his head. He looked down at the table and reached out a hand to pick up his mug of ale, then seemed surprised to see it on its side on the table. He turned, nonchalantly, stuck his hands in his pockets, bent his knees once, then strolled out of the room.

When he had gone, Fenella stretched out a hand and gently righted the two pots of relish. Daniel rose to his feet and retrieved Fenella's plate, then went and picked up the pieces of Bartholomew's broken one. They made small chinking sounds in the silence as he gathered them up.

In all this time, Elijah had not moved. Clementina and I were still standing.

'He's your *son* . . .' I said to Elijah, and I heard the tremble in my own voice and realised my eyes were brimming with tears.

Elijah did not respond.

'Elijah!' I said, more sharply, 'I said he's . . .' I could not finish.

Clementina put down the carving knife and spike and came round to my side of the table. She placed a hand gently on my arm. 'Go into the kitchen and get yourself a drink of water,' she said. 'I'll clear up a bit, and serve up.'

He disappeared the following spring, did Bartholomew. Fenella's cloak and gown job had fallen through and she was terrible disappointed, but that summer she got another offer, and I let her take it. Daniel had already moved to Peterborough with Slaker & Son. Scarlet joined Mehitable. So that was it. My children were gone, and the house that had always seemed too small was suddenly as cavernous as a grain store.

We stayed on in Sutton another two years. I suppose a small part of me was wondering if Bartholomew might come back. Elijah even went down to London for a few weeks and made enquiries about him – Bartholomew had talked of London, apparently. He said there were some rum old areas there now and a lot of fellas sleeping rough in the parks. When he told me that I got a bit upset. He didn't go into the details. We even wrote to some of the hospitals where they put the tommies who had gone wrong in the head, but there was no trace of Bartholomew under either of the names we had. Elijah was worried he'd do time in prison if we found him, on account of his desertion, but I didn't care. I just wanted to know where he was.

You get used to pain like that. It's like backache. You don't like it, but you forget what life was like without it.

We made our plans to move to Peterborough. Peterborough was the coming place, Elijah said. He went up there to visit and came back quite enthusiastic. It all looked big and new, he said. There were five different railway stations. There was a huge cathedral in the market square that made Ely marketplace look quite pokey. He started to talk about getting a market stall together, selling kitchen goods. Maybe if Scarlet and Mehitable got tired of domestic service, they could help him out.

I began to pack up our things and work out what we could take and what we should leave for the local auctioneer to sell off. Elijah brought the leaflet home so I could look at it. *Mr M. Beezley, Auctioneer and Land Agent*, it said at the top, *conducts sales of furniture and effects, and valuations of the same.*

# CHAPTER 16

I haven't hated Elijah, whatever he may think. If I have hated anything, it is the gap between what he is and what I wanted him to be.
When he and I first met, I thought he would make my whole life
right. But, of course, it wasn't his fault that my whole life was
wrong in the first place.

Maybe that is all love is; a need, a wanting. Maybe you never
love in the first place unless there is a hole in your life that needs
filling. You meet someone, and you put on to them the ability to fill
that hole, and you call it love – and when they only fill it a little bit,
or not at all, you are angry with them. Then they get confused.

Men have to speak in code. Why did my mother never mention
this to me? Maybe she meant to tell me when I was older, only she
never got the chance. Men can't say things outright. It's not in them.
Like Horace, on River Farm. Horace slapped me across the face and
drove me to run off with Elijah, and I am quite certain that when I
went, he thought me ungrateful. I am sure he believed that he cared
for me and was offering me the world, in his own fashion, and how

could I not realise his feelings for me? Horace had never known a minute's kindness in his whole life. All he had ever seen of men and women was the way that his father had treated his wives. It was probably Horace's idea of courtship, to bully and threaten. When I ran off, I am sure he was wounded and bewildered.

But there is right and wrong, that's what the men forget. They think that because they don't *mean* the bad things they do, then those bad things shouldn't hurt us. But a slap stings however it is meant.

A few days before our move to Peterborough, Clementina and I went to Ely market for the last time. Most of our furniture was sold – there was only the clothes to pack. Elijah had gone on ahead and was finding us a place to rent. He would come back for us with a cart, at the weekend.

We went to Ely market that day to sell rather than buy. Clementina had made a pile of things and put them in a crate: crockery and cooking pots we no longer wanted, and a few clothes. We would probably be in temporary lodgings when we first got to Peterborough, so there was no point in carting round a load of stuff. There was something satisfying about getting rid of things, even things which would have to be replaced once we found our new home.

We went early, so that Clementina could talk to the stall-holders as they were setting up. I was buying one or two things: eggs, as our laying hens had been sold the week before, and some green thread that I needed to finish off my last sewing job, the mending of a best suit for Mr Clifford, wheelwright.

I knew Clementina's tasks would take longer than mine, so I lingered at the thread stall, chatting to the Misses Oakley who ran it. They had some new gold lace in, in a beautiful filigree design, which they said had been made in London by the same firm that supplied blouses to the ladies-in-waiting of Queen Mary herself. I fingered it covetously, for I had been doing very ordinary jobs of late, and I thought of how it was high time one of my girls got engaged to be married so I could show them what I could do.

I had put down my basket – a large one Elijah had made for me. As I bent to pick it up, I winced. I had eaten porridge for breakfast and it always caused me digestive difficulties.

'Are you quite well there, Mrs Smith?' one of the Misses Oakley said to me, as she handed the green thread to me in a paper bag.

'Why, yes,' I said, surprised at the concern on her face. Odd she should say that, I thought, as only this morning, on the carrier-cart, a neighbour had told me I was losing weight and looking peaky with it. Well, if moving house makes me a little thinner then that's no bad thing, I thought. There's enough on me to spare a bit, after all. It was true, I had been off my food of late.

After I had bought the few other bits and bobs we needed, I still had time to spare, so I went round the back of the Corn Exchange. A fishmonger and his boy were skinning eels by the water-pump, throwing the skins against the cobbles to reveal the grey, jelly-flesh beneath. Just past them, another boy was leaning against the wall with one leg bent, playing a mouth organ. *Why Was I Born?* I think it was, but he was playing it so badly it was hard to tell.

Behind the Corn Exchange was a little tea shop. Come late morning, it got hectic as lots of folk would pile in there for tea and a bun after the shopping was done, but as it was still early I managed to get a seat in the window and enjoy the feeling that my errands were achieved. Clementina would be a little while yet, so I could take as long as I wanted. I watched the folk going past – all that hurrying – and listened to the boy with his tuneless mouth organ and felt the sweet ache of time going by. It's a symptom of getting on in years, I thought, allowing yourself to enjoy small moments of nothing in particular. My bun was fresh that morning and had candied peel inside but it was too big and I couldn't finish it.

I hefted my basket and left the tea shop. I thought I might as well take a wander down the High Street and back before I went up Bray Lane. I still had plenty of time. Although my basket was half empty, the size of it was awkward and as the pavement was busy, I kept having to lift it in front of me so folk could get past. I didn't want it bumped when I had eggs in it. A light rain began falling. My shoes were hurting as well. I had got no more than halfway down the street when I decided to turn back.

If I had done so one second sooner, I would not have seen him.

Just before I turned back, I looked ahead, up the street, and there he was. He was standing on the pavement, facing me, holding a fob and key and staring in my direction. He was wearing a new suit of dark grey wool. His shirt collar stood up stiff and white above the lapels, and he had a satin cravat at his throat, golden coloured like the lace I had been fingering. Very smart he looked, but aged, though.

As I approached, weaving through the people between us, he took his hat off and bowed to me. I saw that his hair was very thin on top, and what little of it remained was pure snow white.

'Hello, William,' I said.

He straightened and looked at me. 'Rose . . .' he said.

I didn't want to talk to him. I just wanted to stare, to take him in. He was both changed beyond all recognition and not changed – so smart, so much older, but still the same thin figure, the pale features. It was nearly thirty years since we had last set eyes upon one another.

I knew that if I did not speak, the situation would become awkward. 'William,' I said, 'what brings you to Ely?'

He gestured at the door before him. I saw, etched on the glass, *Childer & Watson, Chartered Accountants*. I opened my mouth in surprise. 'Why, William . . .'

At this, he gave a half-smile. 'Yes, it would appear I was never quite cut from the right cloth to be a farmer.'

Oh, I wanted to know everything. How had all this come about?

How had he got away from the farm and become an accountant, of all things? I would never have thought it of him in a million years. I wanted to sit him down in a coffee house and hold his hands and get him to tell me everything. What of Horace, and Henry? His father must be long dead by now . . . Had Horace ever managed to persuade anyone to marry him?

I had noticed the gold wedding ring on his finger. 'And you have a family?'

His half-smile became rigid. 'Yes. I married while I was still training. We had three sons. My youngest will be joining me in the office, soon. The eldest two were killed in France.'

'I am sorry to hear that, William.' Now I knew what had aged him, what had balded and whitened him and given him that strained look.

There was a brief silence, which I felt obliged to fill. 'I have five now, all grown up, of course.' What could I tell him about my children? That Daniel was doing well for himself and talking of setting up his own little business in Peterborough; that Mehitable and I no longer spoke to each other since she broke off her engagement with the chimney sweep and I told her she was getting on a bit and should have grabbed him while she got the chance; that Bartholomew had disappeared to London and broken my heart; that Fenella was the handsomest girl alive and everybody's favourite – and Scarlet, so much her own person, despite being the youngest – the strongest of them all, perhaps . . .

Instead I said, stupidly, 'My husband and my two boys served in France but they came back safe and sound, thank the Lord.' I suppose I wanted him to know that our family had done their bit too, but it came out all wrong. It sounded as though I was bragging that *mine* had survived.

'And how is Mr Smith?' The question sounded so absurdly formal, that I could not help giving a small laugh. How was Elijah? Same as ever – how else would he be?

William smiled back. We held each other's gazes and our stares were full, brimming.

He dropped his gaze and turned back to his door. 'My clerk will be waiting,' he murmured, unconvincingly.

'Of course,' I said, looking down and brushing at my skirt with my free hand, suddenly aware of what a smart, upstanding gentleman William was these days, and how I was no more than an ageing village housewife with a basket over her arm.

Before I let him go, though, there was something I wanted to ask him, and the years of not seeing each other made me bold. This was the last time I would ever come to Ely market, after all. I knew I would never see him again and gathered all my courage.

'William, I am sorry to ask you this . . .'

He looked back at me, his expression a little alarmed. He was frightened I was about to embarrass him.

I spoke hastily. 'You will think me foolish after all these years, but did you ever receive my letter telling you I was to be wed? It's just I've always wondered . . .'

'Yes, Rose, I did. I am sorry . . .' He looked down.

What was he sorry for? For not having had the courage to defy his father and come to the church to give me away? But he had paid for the church bells to be rung. That was enough for me, more than enough. Kind thoughts of William and his affection for me had cheered me many a time over the years, I realised. Even though his feelings for me had never come to anything, the thought that someone had regarded me softly at the most difficult time in my life had sustained me on many a black night. I wanted him to know how much his gesture had meant to me.

'William,' I said. 'When I came out of the church on my wedding day and heard the bells ringing, it was the happiest moment of my life. I still cherish the sound of those bells in my head.'

He looked up at me, his face closed and tense. I could not decipher his thoughts. 'I am glad to hear that, Rose,' he said.

'Now, if you will excuse me . . .' He bowed to me again, and lifted the key.

'Goodbye, William,' I said. 'Please give my regards to your wife. I wish you both well.'

'Goodbye, Rose.'

I walked back down the High Street, my head full of thoughts. It was only as I reached the market place again that it came to me. *Oh William*, I thought. *You loved me, didn't you? Loved me properly, I mean.* I thought back to the time on the farm – it seemed like such an age ago, and it was: another century, before the children, before the War that took so many of our children. Our generation has this great chasm in our lives, I thought, a chasm that has swallowed so much of what is dear to us. How can any of us clamber down and up its sides to get back to the past? But William had loved me. I was sure of that.

What if William had made his intentions clear to me at the time? Would I have loved him back? Married him, perhaps? Would I now be his wife, living in a smart town house somewhere in Ely, brushing fluff from the shoulders of my husband's smart new suit before he set off for work each morning? Then, after I had kissed him and waved him off from the doorstep, would I return inside and close the door, check that the maid was clearing the breakfast table, then go upstairs to my room and sit at my dresser, to spend my morning as I always did, staring at pictures of my two lost sons . . .?

You can't pick and choose, after all. If you want somebody else's life, you've got to take the whole of it. It isn't like plucking only the ripe cherries off a tree and leaving the ones you don't like the look of.

As I passed the market, I glanced around to see if I could spot Clementina, but if she was there, she was lost in the crowds. I decided to go on up Bray Lane and wait for her at our usual place. There were benches by the roadside where the carrier-carts pulled up and the rain had stopped. An omnibus service had started up on market days, but it was three times the cost of the carrier-cart and I couldn't abide the horrid smell of it.

It wouldn't have made any difference, I thought. Even if William had told me he loved me on the farm, I still would have run off with Elijah. At that time, I would have thought that marrying William would have tethered me to River Farm as surely as marrying Horace would have done.

The benches were all full when I got there and I had to stand, but pretty soon a carrier-cart going the other way rumbled into place and several women clambered up, so I was able to get a seat on the bench. A younger woman moved over for me as I sat down, and I thought how old I must seem to her.

There is no point in being wistful, I thought to myself. Yes, I would love to be married to William and live in a town house and have a maid – but would I swap my five healthy children for his dead two? He loved me, that's all that matters. I can hold on to that thought. He loved me, all those years ago, and he paid for the church bells to be rung as I came out into the sun.

My digestive system really was bothering me that day – it was the first day I began to think there was maybe something that needed sorting out. I'd better brew myself some mint leaves in hot water when I get home, I thought.

I suppose if it hadn't been for the move to Peterborough, I might have gone to the doctor sooner. As it was, it took us more than a year to settle – we had four different addresses in that time, due to Elijah taking a while to sort out a bit of regular income. Then there was the new house to establish – the new routine of just Elijah and me. Clementina had her own little place again. And there were the girls to be visited – and Fenella's engagement to her Tom. Fenella was married not three months when Mehitable upped and did it too, and gave me my first grandchild all within the space of a year.

So, what with one thing and another, I put up with the digestive problems for a good few years and got quite thin for the first time in my life, before I finally went along to Doctor Dodds and let him lie me down and press at my stomach with a frown upon his face. These things have a way of taking their course, so I doubt it would have made much difference if I'd gone before.

# CHAPTER 17

The world shrinks. That is what it is like, being ill. As getting out and about becomes more difficult, you lose the edges of the world, and then the things you are losing get nearer and nearer, closer to home. First you can no longer go on long journeys – then you can't go down the market square to Elijah's stall carrying his sandwiches wrapped in brown paper. Sooner or later, you can't even go to the end of your road for fresh bread to make the sandwiches with – Elijah has to do that himself. Then, getting out of bed gets more and more difficult so you lose the downstairs of the house – garden, hallway, kitchen, parlour – and then, when you are bedbound, you lose even your own bedroom, for you can see it from beneath your eider but it is like you are looking at it through a glass.

The glass is made of pain. Sometimes the pain thickens, becomes opaque. Then you can't see anything. At others, it is there, but almost see-through – you get so used to it you forget what it was like to see the world properly, not through the glass of pain.

People arrive, from the rest of the world. Mostly, they were just visitors from my own home, one of the family, but once in a while it was someone from a far-flung land, like the vicar from the local church. He didn't stay long. He was a young fella, embarrassed by old people and death and dying, I could tell. He went bright red when I asked him about the afterlife. I felt so sorry for him I pretended I was tired, so he had an excuse to leave.

It was not long after his visit that some odd things started to make their way into my room. Lijah struggled all the way up our narrow stairs with a old washstand, God knows why. He must have got it from one of the general stores he visited, or the marketplace. I heard him huffing and puffing and clunking up the staircase, as if he was trying to lug a camel. The door banged back, and in he came, all on his own, and without a word, started edging this thing across the carpet. It had a marble top, and shelves beneath, so it must have weighed a ton. When it was in place, flush against he wall, he went out and came back in with a cloth and some bleach and set to scrubbing the marble.

All he said was, 'The only thing that brings marble back to itself is a bit of bleach, you know. Bleach and elbow grease.'

I thought, *he should be wearing gloves for that job*, but it was one of those days when talking was bit tricky.

Other items of furniture followed, with a day or so interval in between; a mahogony chiffonier, a walnutwood whatnot with a plate glass back. The following week, engravings and chromos started going up on the wall. Lijah's hammering the nails was so loud it felt like he was knocking them into my forehead. A cane seat with a velvet cushion materialised next to the wardrobe one afternoon, while I was asleep. I believe the final item was a Brussels-pile bordered carpet, but I might have started to lose track by then. The room was so full I felt I was floating on a sea of furniture. My visitors could hardly get in the door.

*

The girls did most of the looking-after of me, the girls and Clementina. Daniel visited, of course, but neither he nor Elijah were comfortable sitting with me for too long. The girls always had things to do; move me over to slip a sheet from under me, or coax me to eat something. The men had no such function and without those things to do for me, they didn't really know what to do with themselves.

Elijah only sat down once. I think he thought I was asleep. I was, sort of, but woke with the weight of him sitting down on the edge of my bed, and the feel of his hand resting on mine.

I opened my eyes, and he moved his hand away.

'Shall I tell one of the girls to come up?' he said.

I nodded slowly. I was thirsty. 'Are they both here?' I asked. My voice was getting hoarse, whispery.

Fenella and Scarlet were taking it in turns to come round to look after me. Fenella had her own family now, and Scarlet was still working, but somehow they were managing it between them. There was always one of them there, however early I woke each morning, so I suppose they must have been sleeping on the sofa. Elijah was either in the spare room, or sometimes sleeping at Clementina's house which was just round the corner from ours.

'Aye,' he replied.

There was a pause.

'They're good girls,' I said quietly.

'They all are,' he said, quietly back.

Neither of us needed to say any more. Mehitable had not visited me since I became bed-ridden, not once. She sent a card. *Get Well Soon*. It had a line drawing of sweet peas on the front, filled in with coloured pencil. I had accepted that I was going to die without seeing Bartholomew again, he had been lost to us many years before, but Mehitable lived less than three miles away, over at Dogsthorpe.

'Ask Scarlet if I can have some fresh water,' I said to Elijah, and he nodded, then rose.

While he was gone, a strange thought came to me – and I don't know why I should have thought it then, after all those years. The pig. Toby, the Sapient Pig. It came to me how it was done. I had thought that Elijah must've somehow told the man my name, so that he could make the pig spell it. But he hadn't, of course, no more than he had paid for the church bells to be rung on the day we was wed. All Elijah had done was spoke my name, just before, and the woman next to us had heard and somehow signalled to the fella who had owned the pig.

Why did I want to believe, at the time, that it was him? What did it matter?

Then I began to think about Mehitable. I thought of all the times she and I had fallen out, when she was a child, and I thought of the sly look in her eyes and how close I had come to beating that child and how I had congratulated myself on not doing it. Considering what I had put up from Elijah, I thought how I had really done quite a good job – five children raised on nothing? I had worked my fingers to the bone for years and years.

I never hit that child – well, they all got a smack on the bottom when they were naughty, of course, and I used the spoon on their arms in the kitchen, once in a while. But I never, ever beat her properly, not like I got beaten by my stepfather. I pushed her around a bit a few times, but she was so wilful and difficult – I don't think anyone has the right to judge me unless they've had a child as wilful and difficult as she was.

A dark feeling that I cannot describe came over me.

I thought of the fantasies I used to have, as a child, of the kind of wedding I would have: the man who would be my husband; the home I would live in – somehow they never went away, not even when I married Elijah in front of his drinking pals, in a pawned hat.

Even when we crept like thieves down Paradise Street, sneaking off because we couldn't pay the rent, a part of me was still thinking how I would make the house all nice once I had all the things I coveted.

Being ill gives you plenty of time to think, so I thought some more. I thought about how strange it is that you can walk around knowing life is one way but still holding on to your belief that it is really, somehow, else. I suppose the trick is never to put the two pictures of your life together, never try to make them fit. It is not wise to think about how things really are, for there is always this yawning chasm between how our lives are and how we want them to be, a great, big black hole, big enough to fall into and disappear for ever.

All my life, I have congratulated myself on being a good person. And in comparison with some around me, mentioning no names but a certain son and his mother come to mind, I have been. But I saw, as I lay there thinking about Mehitable, that I have only been good in comparison to the bad that was done to me – my mother dying on me when I was young and my stepfather's unkindness to me, Elijah and his drinking. How wrong I had got it, all those years. That badness around me may have made me look good, in my own eyes, but it didn't mean I *was* good. It gave me excuses, that was all, when I passed on a little of the badness to others. When I was unkind to Mehitable, I was thinking in the back of my head, that my unkindness to her was as nothing compared to the big unkindness my mother did to me by dying on me.

All this time, I thought, I have walked around and thought of myself as a nice person, and I haven't been, at all.

Scarlet came up with a glass of water and my pills. She sat by my bed for a bit, in silence, then she said, 'Dad's gone round the corner to see Gran.'

I didn't reply. She looked at me. 'How was Dad?'

'Oh well, you know your Dad.'

She moved as if to leave, and without intending to, I found myself reaching out a hand and grasping her arm. She looked a little surprised and then sat down again, looking at me expectantly. Scarlet, such an uncomplicated child: broad, beaming face, solid and straightforward. I saw a lot of me in her, or how I would have liked to have been, if I'm honest.

She wasn't a child, of course, she was of age, that year. I had a feeling she might be married soon. Daniel had a friend he was thinking of going into business with. He had been to tea round at ours a little more than was necessary if he was nothing but a friend of Daniel's. I had seen looks between him and Scarlet.

She sat on the bed, just looking at me, saying nothing, just waiting. She always knew the right thing to do, that one.

'I wasn't a bad mother, was I?' I said to her, simply, looking intently at her face.

Her look of surprise was instant, and unforced. 'Oh no, of course you weren't, Mum, what a silly thing to say. The way you looked after us . . . You were the best mum in the world.'

I held on to her hand and squeezed it. 'Thank you, love.'

She frowned, glanced round all the stuff jammed into the room, looked back at me and said, 'What was Dad saying to you?'

'Nothing, oh nothing, I just, sometimes I wonder, you know. Sometimes I feel bad. When I think of how I was. I meant well, but sometimes it didn't always come out like that with you children. Always telling you off, and such, I feel bad about it.'

'Dad has no right to come in here making you feel bad.' Her face was agitated. She snapped at her father a lot, did that one, took his devotion to her quite for granted.

'Scarlet, I want to see Mehitable.' The sentence came out of nowhere. I was almost surprised to hear it myself – I hadn't been planning to say it.

Her indignation faltered. Her face closed. She hesitated.

I knew it was up to me to insist. Suddenly, I wondered if I had the energy for it. 'Scarlet, there's things Mehitable and I need to discuss. Before.'

'I won't have you talking like that.' The indignation was forced, this time.

'Please, will you speak to her for me. I know it's not an easy thing.'

She rose from her chair and began tucking the candlewick bedspread firmly underneath the mattress. 'I'll speak to her. I can't promise.'

'Thank you, love.'

I think Scarlet did more than speak to her – I think she insisted, for Mehitable came to me a few days later but so unwillingly it must have taken a prod with a red-hot poker to do it. The door to my room opened and in she came, sidling around the door but staying close to it, the way a cat does – ready to bolt at any moment.

She managed a thin smile. I tried to heave myself up, winced and fell back. She came over to help me, so we touched each other before we said so much as a word. As she lifted me and propped a pillow up behind my head, I felt what I always felt with her, that she was bracing herself for any closeness to me, in the same way she might brace herself against a cold wind in her face.

She smoothed my bedspread, then fetched the upright chair that was in the corner next to the wardrobe, the one the doctor used.

She placed the chair carefully at an angle, so she could sit facing me, then undid the top three buttons of her cardigan and pulled off her neckscarf. I daresay she found the room hot. I was keeping the windows closed as I felt cold so much of the time, even though the sun streamed through and in normal times I would have had every window in the house flung open on such warm days.

We did not speak, and the moment passed when we could have started off with a bit of small talk. *How's that boy of yours?* I could have said, or, *What's the news over in Dogsthorpe, then?* But the moment for that slid away from us, like a ball rolling downhill, and the silence became so long there was no pretending this would be a normal little chat.

I watched her in the upright chair. There she sat, my difficult grown-up daughter, fiddling with the scarf she had just removed, passing the fine fabric through a hole she had made with her thumb and forefinger. She reminded me of my mother, suddenly, with her sleek dark hair and her thin manner. Odd that she should be growing like my mother when I was never like her myself – that was a likeness that had skipped a generation entirely.

Mehitable – in her thirties now, older than my mother was when she died.

I let the silence go on too long, I suppose. I could feel her not wanting to be there, a feeling as solid as the oak wardrobe in the corner of the room. The not wanting grew with each passing second. I wondered if Scarlet had begged her to come. Maybe Scarlet and Fenella had done it together, like a pair of pincers.

'*Just go and see her, will you?*'

'*She's dying.*'

'*You'll be sorry later, if you don't.*'

I could imagine the whole scene.

It came to me that as I had summonsed her, it was up to me to speak first.

'Do you know why I wanted to see you?' I said, eventually, and saw her wince. She glanced away, then sighed.

'I've an idea,' she said eventually. Her voice was cold.

I thought back to when I used to smack her sometimes, when she was little, and how it wasn't that I wanted to hurt her, but the anger inside me used to build up, and she would just crouch down and take it and never even cry.

Pain began to blossom inside me, somewhere down in the pit of the stomach. I cursed that it came at that moment for I knew I wouldn't have long before I started to perspire. Soon after that, conversation would become impossible.

'I can't die until you say you've forgiven me.' There. It was out.

Her face was small and dark and set, and even then I could see what I had found so difficult in her as a child, that she would never reveal anything, that I could never work out what she was thinking.

She could have said, *for what*? Then I would have said, *for the fact that I wasn't very kind to you when you was little, when you was poorly*. Then we both would have understood that it was all right to talk not directly about things. Then the talk could have moved on quickly to being ordinary.

But instead, she said, 'Why d'you do it, Mum? Why were you like that with me all the time? You weren't with the others.' She was looking at me.

I had not expected this, this challenge from her. The pain began to radiate out, to travel up through my chest cavity and to my limbs. I would have to ask her to fetch one of the others, soon.

'I don't know,' I said, breathing hard. 'I do know that if you'd stood up to me, just once, I'd have stopped, but you just took it and took it, whatever I gave you. I never understood what you were about.'

'I was a child, Mum.'

'I know.'

My sight began to blur. The shape of her sitting in the chair wavered, became diagonal.

'I forgive you, Mum.' Her voice sounded distant.

I tried to arch my back slightly, as if I could lift myself away from the pain, but I knew it was no use.

'Do you really?' I could hear the wincing in my voice. I had to finish soon, 'or are you just saying that?'

'I do,' she said quickly. 'Mum, shall I get Scarlet or Fenella?' Her voice was high pitched with anxiety.

I nodded. The movement sent small rockets of pain up the back of my head. 'Get Scarlet.'

She left hurriedly. I closed my eyes and thought, I didn't even ask her about that boy of hers.

Scarlet came quickly, with the pills and a glass of tepid water. She sat by me and stroked my hand while the pills did their work, oh so slowly, and made the pain a dull, bearable ache, instead of a fire. Afterwards, she left and I dozed for a while.

Later, there was a light knock at the door. It opened, and Clementina came in. She was carrying a small tray with a china plate and a glass of milk. She set them both on the bedside table. On the plate was four pieces of bread cut into neat triangles and spread thickly with butter.

'I've brought you some supper,' she said.

My head felt as if it was stuffed with cotton wool. With Clementina's help, I managed to raise myself slightly. She plumped up the pillows behind me, then sat down on the upright chair and handed me the glass.

The milk was ice cold. It slipped right down. For the first time in a week, I drained it all. Clementina noted it as she took the glass from me.

She handed me the china plate. It was one of my favourites, a very old one from when Elijah and I were first married, with gilt edging, faded now, and yellow rosebuds. I looked down at it. The pieces of bread had been neatly arranged, overlapping each other.

'I haven't seen this plate in years,' I said, 'where d'you find it?'

'Billy made your supper,' Clementina replied. 'She found the plate at the back of the dresser.'

I lifted one of the pieces of bread and took a small bite, then put it back on the plate. Swallowing was very uncomfortable.

'Why didn't she bring it up herself?'

'She had to get back. You were asleep.'

There was a long silence between us. It came to me that Clementina, my mother-in-law, was the one member of my family I could rely on to tell me the truth.

'I've not got long, have I?' I asked her, looking her directly in the face.

She shook her head.

'What did Mehitable say when she came downstairs?'

For the first time ever, I saw hesitation in Clementina's eyes.

'Tell me,' I said quickly. 'Don't give me any guff. You, of all people . . .'

'She said you asked for her forgiveness and she gave it.'

'And?'

'Scarlet said did you mean it, and she said yes.'

'And what else?'

'Rose . . .' Clementina said. I thought how strange it was to hear her use my name, how we had known each other all these decades but hardly ever used each other's names.

I gathered all the little strength I had left. 'Clementina,' I said, 'I've never asked you anything my whole life, but I'm asking it now. I want you to tell me honestly what my daughter said when she got downstairs. What you've got to realise is that, however bad it was, if I don't know then I'll wonder and wonder and that is far worse and I think I've a right to know so I can get it straight in my head before I go.' It was the longest speech I had made for some weeks and it exhausted me. Towards the end of it, my voice was so hoarse she had to lean towards me to catch my words.

She stared at me, then said, 'Scarlet asked her did you mean it, and she said yes, then she said, I've forgiven her but don't go expecting me to put flowers on her grave every Sunday, I've forgiven her and that's it, I'm done with it.'

The pain returned anew, a long, slow wash of it, like the tide coming in. I closed my eyes and exhaled. When I opened them, Clementina was leaning forward to take the plate. 'She made you a nice supper,' she said quietly. 'She dug out that plate because she knew you liked it, and washed it too, and she went and opened a new bottle of milk from the larder so you'd get the cream of it cold.'

'Thank you,' I said.

After that, dying got a bit easier for a few days. The doctor visited every morning. Dan, Fenella and Scarlet popped in and out. Fenella liked to read to me from the paper and I didn't have the heart to tell her I wasn't interested as I knew it pleased her to be doing something for me. Whenever I got worried that she needed a break, I would say, 'I think I'll have a little sleep now.'

Fenella, always the beautiful one. She had taken to wearing her hair back off her face. It suited her but made her look older. I was worried how Tom and the girls would be managing without her but she never mentioned it.

I wasn't frightened in the times they left me alone. There is something wonderful about letting your mind wander around a bit, let it float free. Once you are released from spending all day, every day, worrying about what there is for supper and how you are going to keep the house clean – it's amazing how much time you have to think of other things. I found myself wondering, is this what it is like being a fine lady, a Lady Something, or a Dame or Baroness – or a Princess, even? Do they lie around, wondering what to think about? Of course, if you are such a person, then you do not even know that you have nothing to think about. You think thinking about nothing is being busy.

All sorts of odd things came in and out of my head. I remembered things I did not know were still inside me somewhere. I remembered how, in the bad days at Paradise Street, I had been so desperate for money that I had looked into Clementina's purse one day, when she was out walking Bartholomew up and down the road to get him to sleep. She had left her purse, a small velvet thing, with a drawstring, on the shelf by the door. I had gone to it and emptied it into my hands and had been disappointed to find nothing but a few farthings. Then I felt it, squeezed it in my hand, and realised there must be another pocket or a torn lining inside, as I could feel something hard.

I turned the purse inside out. There, it was, a secret little pocket, with a flap, stitched into the lining. I got quite excited at that point, for it came to me that Elijah's mother was just the sort of mad old lady who might have gold sovereigns hidden in a box under her bed. Maybe she's secretly wealthy, I thought. Her type often are. The coin I could feel was about the right size for a sovereign.

With a bit of fiddling, I managed to extract it, and then, of course, I was sorely disappointed. It was just a sixpence, one of the old sort, with the Queen's hair up in a bun and her looking like a younger woman – later, they made her look much older. Why on earth is she keeping an old sixpence buried secretively in her purse? I thought to myself. It was smaller than a sovereign, of course. I had let my imagination run away with me.

I had only just returned the coin to its secret pouch and replaced the purse on the shelf, when the door opened and in came Clementina, Bartholomew asleep on her shoulder.

I swear she guessed what I had been doing, for she gave me a look so poisonous that I turned and fled upstairs.

There were only a few occasions when Elijah and I were able to be alone together on River Farm, so it's not surprising they've stuck in my mind. There was one in particular . . . It was the only time we were able to be together for a few hours at a stretch. I can't remember the excuse I gave back on the farm, how I managed it.

May. Is there a better month? The sky is never brighter the whole year than it is in May. We had been lying on a bank of some sort, looking at the sky. There were woods behind us and nobody about. It was like we had the whole world to ourselves. I remember how we kissed, our carelessness. *Nobody knows where I am. Nobody can find me, lost in this man's kisses.* We did some talking as well, and some staring at the sky, and then a bit more kissing. I asked him how he learned to kiss so well and he got a bit funny with me, not liking to own up that he'd kissed a few other gorjer lasses, I bet, for that was one skill he certainly hadn't picked up among his own.

The grass around us was long and dry – the sun hot.

After a while, he jumped to his feet. He stood upright before me. I lifted a hand to shield my eyes from the sun, so I could look up at him.

'I'm tired of courting,' he declared. 'Let's box!'

I sat up. 'Box?'

'Aye, boxing. "Tis great sport and there's nothing better to watch than two fellas who know what they're about.' He was rolling up his sleeves. Then he reached out and pulled me up from the bank. He squared up to me. 'Come on, Rosie,' he nodded, 'you're a fair-sized lass. Let's see what you're made of.'

I thought he was mad, of course. But we circled for a while, and he made a few feigning jabs at me, with me shrieking 'Elijah!' in alarm, each time. Then, I do believe I managed to land one on him, for I was a good few inches taller. My fist glanced the side of his nose and he threw his face back in an exaggerated fashion. I stopped and dropped my hands, aghast I might have hurt him, and he took advantage of my dismay to throw himself upon me and push me backwards so I landed, winded and gasping, back on the bank.

I was panting. I could feel his weight upon me – a sweet weight, a weight that owned and claimed me, a weight that said, *I'll not release you for the world.*

He was silent for a while, still lying on me, using one hand to prop his face up, resting the elbow on the ground beside my head, and the other hand to stroke my hair back where I had gone a little sweaty at the temples.

'Why Elijah Smith,' I murmured, feeling him shift a little, 'I do believe you have told me an outright lie. You're not tired of courting at all.'

I lay on my deathbed and thought of this, and I forgave Elijah everything. I must tell him when he comes up, I thought, that I forgive him everything.

Later, there was a light tap at the door – and Clementina came in. She hovered at the door for a moment, and I could tell she was trying to work out whether I was asleep or not. Silly woman, I thought, of course I'm not asleep. After a moment, she came forward and rested two of her fingers gently against my neck. Then she stood up.

I opened my eyes. How had I seen her, before, if my eyes had been closed? My head is playing funny tricks with me, I thought.

Clementina was staring down at me. Her face was serious. Was something wrong?

'The children want to come up, to say their goodbyes,' she said quietly. 'Have you got enough puff for it?'

I nodded.

In they came, one by one: Dan, Fenella, Scarlet, in that order. Only Scarlet managed not to cry, and it was a great relief to me, for I felt as though I had not one ounce of strength left in me, and I could not bear one minute more of anybody else's grief. We held each other's hands in silence for a while, then talked a little, then we had a little more silence, and the silence was lovely.

'Shall I send Dad up?' she asked gently, after a while.

'No,' I said, 'I don't want your dad. I want your gran.'

She didn't seem surprised but then, all through her life, Scarlet rarely was.

When Clementina returned to me, it was as if she had aged

while she had been waiting downstairs. Slowly she came, clutching at the door handle with her bony fingers, leaning on her stick. She sat down on the upright chair and looked at me, with those piercing black eyes of hers, and suddenly, I would have given a wild laugh if I had been able, for I realised I now had licence to say whatever I liked to her, after all these years.

'Well, Mother,' I said, 'you said I'd sup sorrow until the day I died, and you were right.'

She nodded, and to my astonishment, I saw that her eyes were rimmed with tears.

'You're not going to let me down, are you, Mother?' I said, although my voice had suddenly become a strange whisper, hoarse but high. An odd calm had come over me.

Clementina looked at me, then sniffed loudly. 'What am I going to do?' she said, and her voice was practical as always.

'Oh, you'll manage . . .' I whispered, and a cloudiness descended upon me. My sight of her became misty, then was enveloped in white. *I am going where none of you can reach me*, I thought and I felt unfrightened and lucid and at peace.

# PART 5

1929–1949

# Clementina

# CHAPTER 18

We buried Rose in Eastfield Cemetery. It was a slow procession from the church – fitting it was, for it gave us all time to prepare ourselves for the bit that came next, the most awful bit, the putting of her in the ground. Lijah led the procession, with Dan next to him. The three girls walked behind, arms linked. I was walking behind them but could tell they were all crying. Fenella started them off – sobbing brokenly by the heave of her shoulders. Scarlet was shaking her head a little and breathing hard. Mehitable was motionless as she walked but I knew that tears would be streaming down her face, nonetheless. Mehitable. Who knew what was going on in her head? Scarlet and Fenella would recover in their own good time – but Mehitable had a double load of grief to deal with, mourning her mother and the mother she would have rather had.

I watched their backs as they walked and thought, how many different ways there are of crying, as many ways as there are unhappy people in the world.

And then we came to it: *ashes to ashes, dust to dust . . .* the swing and sway of the words, the waving of the vicar's arm, the blustering breeze and the sobbing of the three daughters. Rose's coffin was lowered. How dreadful, I thought, as it descended – how dreadful to be shut up in a box and put in a hole in the ground and have the earth cover you over, and to be stuck in there in the cold and dark, all alone, for all eternity. You can't burn people no more, Lijah told me. You can't get away with it. So we've all got to go in a hole in the ground, whether we like it or not.

Afterwards, we all stood around for a bit, as you do. The vicar spoke quietly to Lijah at one end of the grave then started moving around the company. Lijah was left alone, looking down into the hole where they had put his Rosie, forlorn as a boy. I was standing a little way off, watching him. I waited for one of his children to approach him and comfort him, but none of them did. They were all talking to each other, or the other mourners. After a moment or two, I went up to Lijah and put my hand on his arm.

'Come on, Lijah,' I said gently. 'It's time to go back to the house.'

He did not move. He was staring down at the grave.

'Come on, love,' I said.

He raised his head, and shook it slightly. 'Well,' he said, awkwardly, 'she's got a bit of peace now, I suppose.' He lifted the corners of his mouth in a grimace, shrugged and made a *humphing* sound. Then he scratched his ear, and stuck his hands in his pockets. I squeezed his arm.

As we turned to go, I saw that the girls were standing at the far end of the grave, all looking towards us. They turned and walked off down the path, after Dan.

The wake was in Rose and Lijah's house in Buckle Street. Once we got inside the door, the girls moved into action. Mehitable brewed up some large pots of tea – Mrs Loveridge had borrowed three enormous teapots from the Legion. Scarlet and Fenella set to with the sandwiches. Lijah and Dan and the other men went to the parlour for a smoke. The neighbours were all in, of course, and the women saw to the handing out of the sandwiches and cake and everyone talked quietly and bustled about as they do at these things. I did my best to help out and make a bit of conversation with folk but it's not really my strong point, idle chat. I was pleased when folk started to give their condolences and drift off. Dan stayed by the door to see them out. 'Are there many men left in the parlour?' I asked Scarlet as she came out balancing a pile of empty cups and saucers.

'Not many,' she said. 'With any luck we can all get off soon.' She bustled past me, into the kitchen. Oh we can, can we? I thought.

I felt a sudden need for a bit of air. Dan was still at the front door ushering folk out, so I went out the back. I went and stood in the middle of the garden and took a few long, deep breaths

Those terraces had long, thin gardens and low walls, so you could look right down over everybody else's garden. Washing was strung up, here and there. Pigeons were cooing in their coop at the end of number forty-two. It was an ordinary day; washing, pigeons, empty sky. I looked up at the sky and thought it had never seemed emptier.

I waited until I thought everyone but family would be gone before I went back inside. The clearer-uppers were still there. Mrs Lane and her daughter who was grown-up but retarded were washing plates and cups in the kitchen. Sally Loveridge was emptying ash trays into a tin can. I looked around for the girls but couldn't see them. I peered in at the parlour. Lijah was sat on a straight-backed chair with Mr Lane and his sons around him. They were still sipping tea. The air was white with cigarette smoke. They weren't saying much to each other, the men. I backed out and closed the door behind me.

I wondered what had happened to the children.

As I closed the parlour door, I heard footsteps on the stairs. They were all descending – Daniel first, with a few papers in his hand, then Mehitable, Scarlet and Fenella. Scarlet had some of Rose's old dresses over her arm.

Daniel glanced at me, and nodded, 'All right, Gran,' he said. 'Thanks for helping out this afternoon.' He went out of the front door.

It was only as Fenella, the last, was passing me, that it dawned on me they were all leaving. I caught her by the arm.

'Where are you lot off to?' I said, and I had a bit of difficulty keeping the sharpness from my tone.

Fenella looked a little embarrassed. She could never tell a lie, that one. 'Well, Gran, it's sort of wrapping up now, isn't it? You've got lots of help to clear up. Billy has to get back and we thought we'd walk her round. I hope you don't mind.'

Scarlet turned back. She came up close, so she could speak without being overheard. The door to the kitchen was stood wide open.

'Look, I'm sorry, Gran,' she said. 'But we just need to get off, okay? We'll see you and Dad tomorrow. We've done our bit for now. We stayed until everyone went.'

I stared at her. I lowered my voice as much as I could. 'What do you mean *stayed until everyone went?* What's your father supposed to do this evening, stare at the wallpaper?' I hissed, and I could feel my gaze blazing.

Scarlet lowered her voice still further. 'We've said goodbye to Dad, he's fine about it. He's got you, all right? He's got you. Now we need a bit of time to ourselves. She was *our mother*, all right?'

'There's still her things to be sorted.'

'That's what we were doing. Dan's got the paperwork. I've taken some dresses and Fenella will have the brooch. Billy don't want anything. The rest can just be disposed of now *please . . .*' I saw she was close to tears, 'just let us go, will you?'

She took Fenella by the arm and marched her towards the door. Fenella looked back and gave a weak smile. 'Bye then, Gran,' she said. They closed the door gently behind them.

Sally Loveridge came out of the kitchen. She had been waiting until our little exchange was over. She was holding a stack of clean plates. She gave me an ingratiating smile. 'Now,' she said, 'do you want me to stack these in the kitchen or take them through?' She indicated the parlour door with her head.

*Put them on yer 'ead and dance the fandango for all I care*, I thought. *Loving it, aren't you? Being so good and noble.*

'Kitchen'll be fine,' I said, then forced myself to add, 'thank you.' She went back inside.

Upstairs, in Rose and Lijah's bedroom, I manoeuvred my way around all the extra furniture and opened the wardrobe. Rose's house-coat was still there and a few old dresses, along with a couple of skirts and blouses. They had left the shoes – she always had very big feet, did Rose. I thought, there's probably some large woman out there who'd be glad of them but I'm blowed if I know her.

In the chest of drawers there was underthings and some fine stockings – they would all have to be disposed of in the proper manner. I laid out a clean sheet on their bed, and began piling everything else onto it. That night, when the house was empty but for me and Lijah, I could parcel it all up, then I would take it out to the garden.

No, I thought, not the garden. The neighbours. No, I will go and find a field, somewhere, and I will do what is right by Rose out in the open, without anyone watching, just her and me. I will set a match to all that is left of her, and say the right words in my head. She should be blessed on her way in the proper manner by someone, after all.

We do right by the dead in the hope that the living will one day do right by us.

A few weeks after we buried Rose, Lijah moved into my little house in Wellington Street, not far from the Corporation Depot. Well, there wasn't any point in him hanging around his and Rose's house, kicking his heels.

It's a strange thing, to be an old lady and have your son living with you when he is an old man too. You do not see the oldness in your own child. You look at him and see the boy who used to whimper in his sleep. And you can't help treating him like the boy who used to whimper in his sleep an' all – which doesn't go down so well sometimes when's he middle-aged and balding.

It was like we had returned to what we was before. Lijah had lived with me for the first twenty years of his life, on and off – and then there was a break in our arrangement when he went off and married and had five children – and then he came back to live with me for another twenty years. I do sometimes wonder if my life has been a bit peculiar.

It saddens me to relate this, but despite the fact that we had been a large family, once, it came pretty clear to me that now it was just me and Lijah. Scarlet and Fenella came round the day after Rose's wake, to help me brush the carpets what needed a good going over after a load of feet had been tramping on them. We cleaned the curtains too, tried to get the smoke out of them.

But as soon as their jobs were done, they made their excuses again and left. Billy came at the weekend and brought some steak and kidney with dumplings on top for us to heat up on Sunday. She didn't stay long either. Oh, they all did their bit, I'm not saying they didn't. But their bit was all they did. When I decided that Lijah should move back in with me, they all came and helped us pack stuff up and carried it round, and I had baked biscuits and cakes so we could all sit crammed round my little kitchen table for the rest of the afternoon and drink tea and eat 'til we were stuffed. And how long did they stay? Half an hour. There was a fruit cake didn't even get broken into.

Bright and cheery, they were with us. All full of helpfulness and not sharing anything. Lijah was too grief stricken to notice, but I noticed, all right.

One day, some weeks after Lijah had moved in with me, I decided to take the initiative and call by Daniel's sign-writing business. He was busy, which maybe accounts for how he was a little off with me. We were stood in his yard and he had just had a load of work in. One of the big breweries was opening up a string of pubs across the county, all with the same name. The idea was, Daniel explained, that wherever you went, you would be able to find a Crown & Anchor, and they would be all the same inside so you would get comfortable with them being all the same. And after a while, you wouldn't want to go nowhere different, as it being not-the-same would make you *un*comfortable. There was something about this that seemed not-right to me, although I'm not sure I can really put it into words.

So, he had a big job on that day. He had a row of signs constructed – must've been more than twenty of them, and three men going from one to the other. One was doing the background, another the anchor and another the crown. The lettering was done by Daniel himself as he wouldn't let nobody else near that.

We stood in his yard, and I said to him, 'Well, it's quite the little factory you've got here now I've come to find out what's up with you lot and why you're all being so off with me and your father.'

There was a pause. His voice went a bit careful. 'We all appreciate you looking after Dad,' he paused again. 'Don't think we don't.'

'So in other words, now he's moved in with me, you think that lets you off the hook.'

Daniel gave me a sideways glance. 'That's not the way it is, Gran. I don't think that's right fair, if you don't mind me saying so.'

'So why don't you come round more often?'

He took a deep breath. 'We was round only last weekend, Gran, and Scarlet dropped by after work on Wednesday, she told me.'

I couldn't find the words for it. It wasn't that they weren't coming to see us, it was that they were being dutiful and no more, and I wanted more.

'Gran, I don't want to be inhospitable or anything, but the lads are waiting for me to tell them what to do.'

*Ah yes, the big businessman now,* I thought bitterly. He hadn't even taken me into his office and offered me a cup of tea. I could have come up with a smart retort but I didn't have the heart for it, that day. I turned away.

As I walked off down the road, I could feel Daniel watching me go. I hoped his conscience was pricking him a bit. I even felt a little tearful and sorry for myself. I thought, *I didn't realise when we lost Rose we were losing the children as well. How has this happened?* I didn't turn around.

I bought myself a canary. Lijah had been promising me one ever since we'd moved up to Peterborough but there must have been a drastic canary shortage or something as he kept telling me he couldn't find the right one. 'I'm not fussed,' I kept saying to him. 'Anything yellow with a pair of wings will do.' In the end, I gave up on him and went out and got it myself from the market. Trouble was, I put it in the parlour and the chimney in there was not too efficient – not bad enough to pay for a sweep but blocked enough to make sure a bit of smoke and soot came in the room. Sooner or later, that yellow canary looked more like a blackbird. I couldn't let it out to hop around, even with the door closed. It would have made a right mess.

I liked talking to it, though. 'Good morning, *meero chiriclo,*' I'd say. '*Sar shin meero rawnie?*'

If he had been himself, Lijah would have made sarcastic remarks about my canary. But instead, he sat in the parlour in silence and watched me talk to it.

He hadn't done much since he'd moved in with me. Not even gone off down the pub. Sometimes he said, 'I'm off for a little walk now, Dei,' and I knew he was going to go and sit by Rose's grave. We didn't have much *lovah* at that time and it still only had a wooden cross on it. Before the funeral, Daniel had offered to pay for a piece of granite but Lijah got quite sharp with him and said nobody was paying for his wife's gravestone but himself. Still stubborn, even in his grief.

I never said it to him but that was the real reason I persuaded him to move in with me at Wellington Street, to save the rent on the Buckle Street house. I had a little money put by, but he would have to pull his socks up and get back to his market stall sooner or later.

He did, eventually, of course. Perhaps that is the most painful bit of losing someone, the bit when you realise that your life is going to carry on. It's painful, of course, because it makes you think that others will do that after you have gone, too, and none of us likes to think that, do we? The weeks turned into months, and Lijah went back to his market stall and his dealing and we saw the others from time to time but it was like we saw them through a fog. I put up with it and put up with it, thinking it would change but it didn't, it got worse, whatever *it* was, and in the end, I thought, I'm not prepared to just sit by while this family dissolves around me just because Lijah and me haven't got to the bottom of what's going on.

Scarlet. She was the answer to it. I knew that right enough. Scarlet had loved her mother fierce-like, in the way that youngest children do. I also knew she was the only one who would be honest with me if I tackled her head on. Mehitable and Fenella would have been scared of upsetting me, but not Scarlet, oh no. And she was the only one who didn't have a family of her own yet, so by rights she was the one who should have been looking after her father now he was a widower. So, it was her I decided to tackle.

Scarlet. She was a match for me any day.

I went round one Saturday afternoon. Scarlet was lodging with a Miss Cowley who worked in the same office as her. I waited at the end of Bishop's Road, sitting on a bench by the Recreation Ground, until I saw Miss Cowley go out. I wanted to talk to Scarlet in private.

I knocked on the door with the end of my walking stick. Scarlet opened it quickly, as if she had been passing when she heard me knock. It was two steps up to the door and being on the short side as I was, I was at something of a disadvantage as I looked up at her. She didn't seem at all surprised, standing there, and I felt as if I was suddenly seeing her for what she was, a large woman, broad of face, not pretty exactly but quite handsome, hair in careful waves – but for that hair, the image of her mother.

'Hello, Gran,' she said, moving back to allow me to step up.

'Scarlet,' I said, nodding to her.

She hovered for a moment while I put down my stick and unbuttoned my coat, which is a right fiddly job for me these days. Then she turned to the kitchen, to put the kettle on.

As soon as we was sat in the parlour with a cup of tea, I started. 'I've not come here to muck about,' I said, pushing my cup away from me. 'I've come here to find something out and find out straight.'

She had a dry sort of expression on her face. 'What might that be, Mami?' She was the only one of my grandchildren who still called me Mami, sometimes. It was her way of getting on my good side, I suppose, but it wasn't going to put me off, not that afternoon.

'Why are you lot being so off with me and your father? You come round and you can't wait to get out the door as soon as you've set foot inside it. It's breaking his heart.'

'Has he got a heart to break? That's news to me.' She took a sip of tea.

'Don't be insolent, my girl. Remember who you're talking to.'

At that, she had the grace to glance down, but still a bit muti-nous-like.

'He's got five children, he's entitled to be close to at least one of them.' It was a strange sort of logic, I suppose, but it made sense to me. 'And the man's been widowed this past year. Do you not think he could do with a bit of comforting from his own daughters?'

At that, her head shot up. 'Five children, well, yes, Gran, you're right. Let's take them one by one shall we? One: Daniel. Well I can't speak for Daniel, all I can say is I'm not sure whether he really feels like he's got a father seeing as he has had to be father to us all since he could nearly stand up. I saw Dad give him a back-hander that knocked him across the room once, when he was pissed, so we'll leave Daniel out of it, shall we?'

I was shocked she should use such language in front of me.

'Two: Billy. Well now, Billy was always closest to him out of all of us but she's having quite a hard time at home at the moment and could do without any extra bother. Three: Bartholomew. Oh no, there's no point in doing Bartholomew is there, as none of us have heard from him in years and why not? Because he's just like his father.'

'I can count, you know. You don't need to go on.' I hadn't expected this. This was horrible.

'Four: Fenella. Nellie's too good natured to hold grudges but she tends to agree with me on most things and she does on this, so there.'

She stopped. I saw a look of hesitation in her eyes. I couldn't help but let my voice be a bit dry sounding. 'Well, that leaves one we've not yet accounted for, don't it?'

She took a deep breath. 'Five. Five is me.' She looked me right in the eye. 'You were the only one with Mum when she died, Gran. What did you say to her?'

I thought that a mighty peculiar question. 'I told you. I said, whatever will we all do without you? And she smiled at me, and then she just went to sleep. I fetched you all straightaway, soon as I realised. Don't tell me you don't believe me, in the name of heaven, *mi biti chai*, what reason would I have to tell you else?' This was all getting far too deep for me.

'Why didn't she want Dad?'

'What do you mean?'

'When we all went up to see her that morning. I was last up. I said, do you want Dad, and she didn't. Why didn't she want to see her own husband?'

'How on earth should I know?'

At that, she looked defeated. She stopped, took another sip of tea, and sighed. Her broad shoulders sagged. 'I'll tell you why not. Because he only made things worse, that's why not. She was dying. She deserved a little peace, for once.'

She wasn't making a right lot of sense, I must say. 'Scarletina,' I said gently, my nickname for her. 'They were married a long time, your mum and dad, and I think maybe when you've been together that long maybe you're just not that important to each other any more. Maybe she'd said all she needed to say to him.'

Her eyes narrowed, and I sensed we were about to get to the marrow of things. 'Aye, and what had he said to her?'

I looked at her.

'He told her she'd been a rotten mother, that's what he did. He went in there and accused her of the worst thing he could think of, a week before she died, when he took in all those stupid bits of furniture that he'd insisted she should have when she couldn't even get up to use them. She was dying, and she should've been allowed to die in peace, and instead he went in and told her how useless she'd been with our Billy and Lord knows what else as well.'

I could not believe it. 'No, Scarlet, you must've got it wrong.'

She rose from her seat, her gaze firm. 'I've not got it wrong,

Gran, I've not at all. She pleaded with me, after he'd gone. You should have seen how agitated she was, desperate to see Billy. You were there that day when Billy went up, so you know all about it. After everything our father did when we were growing up. And when his wife was dying he went in there and accused her of all sorts and she died tormenting herself with everything she'd done wrong.'

I rose too. 'Don't you dare say that of your father. Your father loved you like anything! He thought the sun shone out of your plump backside when you was a baby! He doted on you!'

She crashed her fists against her forehead. 'You're not listening to me, Gran! *Listen* to me! I know he loved us, that doesn't mean he was any good at it, does it?'

I couldn't believe she could disrespect her own father so. 'So, you lot think you've had it hard, do you? You don't know what hunger is. You've know idea how little we had when he was growing up. Compared with the life he had, you lot lived like royalty. At least you had a roof over your heads . . . most of the time.'

She turned away from me, and spoke over her shoulder, her voice ringing with feeling. 'You're still not understanding me, Gran. I can forgive him not knowing any better. But I can't forgive him going into Mum when she was dying and taking away her peace of mind. Even if he didn't mean to do it, it was wicked. It was just as wicked for him not meaning it.'

I saw that I was wasting my time. Lijah's children would have to be reconciled to Lijah in their own good time. There was nothing more I could do.

It took me some time to raise myself from my chair. My knees had started to hurt bad when I got up and down.

Scarlet picked up my stick from where it rested against the table and handed it to me. Then she took my arm and helped me to the door. 'Do you want me to walk you back?' she asked.

'I'm not quite that far gone yet,' I said. 'Will be one day, mind.'

We made a slow journey to the hallway, and she lifted my coat and hat from the peg. I rested my stick against the wall, and put my things on. She wrapped my scarf once around my neck and then she tried to do my coat buttons for me, as if I was a child. I batted her fingers away. I still find it odd that I can't straighten my hands no more. I look at these strange, twisted things on the ends of my arms, like tree roots with their lines and lumps, and I think, are these really my hands?

Scarlet watched me while I fiddled with the buttons. I daresay it took a deal longer than it would have done if I had let her help.

'You and Mum didn't really like each other all that much, did you?' she said. She said it quite gently, just stating the fact, without any accusation.

I stopped what I was doing and looked at her. 'Your mum and I were close as close can be for thirty years,' I said. 'I don't know what to do now she's not here.'

She turned to open the front door.

As I stepped out into the bitter cold, I remembered a conversation I once had with Rose. We were mangling some laundry. It was February and freezing and we were out in the yard at Sutton. I was turning the handle and she was pulling the laundry out the other side – it was sheets, so it needed two of us. We always did the sheets together.

She was doing the bit I hated. I hated gathering heavy, wet cloth when it was cold. Your fingers would redden and freeze in a minute.

I sneezed.

Rose said, 'You've not got an ague there, have you?'

I shrugged.

'You want to watch it,' she said, as she pulled the sheet through. 'It was the Fen ague that killed my mother. It can carry you off in a trice.'

She had never raised the subject of her mother with me before. 'Was that when you was on the farm?' I asked her, lifting the next sheet from the tin tub.

'It was. It was the farm that killed her, for sure. We didn't have those sorts of agues in East Cambridge.'

All at once, I thought of my little Dei, broken on the tread-wheel in Huntington House of Correction. 'I lost my mother when I was young, too,' I said, as I pushed the edge of the sheet between the rollers 'til it caught. 'I'd just had Lijah.'

'What took her?' Rose asked. She had folded the sheet and was rubbing her hands together against the cold. The chill wind lifted her hair around her face as I looked at her. I wondered what she would think if I told her the whole story, about us being arrested and accused by the farmer and his *prosecutrix* and hard labour and cannon balls.

Well, what would any *gorjer* think if you told them a story of a *gipsy* that had died in prison?

'Same as yours,' I said, and took a deep breath as I pushed the mangle handle to its full height, always tricky for me as being on the small side it's hard for me to put my weight into it. 'An ague.'

'Well, like I said,' Rose said, as she grasped the emerging sheet from her side and began to pull, 'you want to watch it.'

Her sleeves were rolled up and the muscles on her forearms bulged as she pulled the sheet. She pursed her lips with the effort, frowning.

She was as strong as an ox, that girl. It never once occurred to me I might outlive her.

As I walked away from Scarlet's house I thought, if I could take Rose out of that box in Eastfield Cemetery and put myself in there instead, I'd do it in a trice. Lijah, Daniel, Mehitable, Fenella and Scarlet – all of them grieving away over Rose, all broken apart over it and unable to comfort each other. I loved them all, every sodding stubborn one of them, and would bring Rose back in a minute, if I could.

There are some people who are like threads in a knitted jumper – pull them out, and the whole garment starts to unravel, and you realise too late that you've pulled out the one bit of thread what was holding the whole thing together. Strange, when it looked like all the other bits of thread.

# CHAPTER 19

The odd thing about living as long as I have, is, you get so used to the idea of dying that it stops being real. You start to think you never will.

I've been expecting to die for decades. I thought I would when I was poorly, when we were stopped on Stourbridge Common. I had stomach-pains fit to bust after some young *grasni* from the next *vardo* gave me a stew with the wrong leaves in it. Kale is for cows, I told her – that's how come they eat it.

Then, when we were in Sutton, I had the *noomonia*, and that was a fair one for carrying off the old ladies like me. Then Rose died, and her being a generation down from me meant it felt all wrong. Surely it was my turn, not hers?

So I keep waiting, but it doesn't happen. And now I've got to the point where I can't get my head around dying at all. There've been too many false alarms.

*

I thought I had better try and take the subject seriously for a change. So, one evening, when Lijah and I were sat in the kitchen after supper, I tried to bring it up. It must have been a year or two after we lost Rose – or maybe it was longer than that.

It annoyed Lijah that I always wanted to sit in the kitchen of an evening. 'That's what we've got a sitting room for, Dei,' he would say, 'to sit in, you know.'

And I would say back, 'The parlour's for guests.'

And he would say, 'We never have any guests, Dei,'

And I would say, 'Well, whose fault is that?'

And that would be an end to it.

Anyroad, we were sat in the kitchen, both with mugs of tea in front of us, mine lovely and dark, and I thought it was time I took dying seriously.

'Lijah,' I said, 'I've decided it's time I took dying seriously.'

'Righto, Mum,' he said, and took a sip of tea.

I had a sudden urge to make him promise to burn me, with all my things, like we did in the old days on the road. That would give him what you might call a bit of a dilemma, as I don't reckon it's legal these days.

'I've thought about what I want, after,' I said.

'After what?'

'After I'm dead, you fool, what d'you think I'm on about?'

He would have rolled his eyes at the ceiling if he'd thought he could get away with it.

'I want to motor, so I do. I've never been in a motor car.'

'Haven't you?' He looked a bit surprised.

'Never in all my born puff.'

He scratched his head. 'Well I'm sure I can manage that, Dei.'

'I want a nice shiny black one, like all the posh folk have. And I want to motor nice and slow, all the way up Eastfield Avenue, so slow that folk have plenty of time to stop and stare and wonder who's in there.'

'All right, then,' he nodded.

'Apart from that, it's up to you,' I said, shrugging. 'It'll be your business when I'm gone, nobody else's. I'm not fussed about having crowds of people or one of those daft get-togethers where nobody says what they're thinking. Can't stand all that nonsense. You can put me in the hole with your own bare hands if you like.' Lijah frowned a little, as if he was trying to get his head around the idea of me actually dying, me not being here any more. 'But I do like the idea of a big shiny motor, so I do.'

There wasn't any one point when I realised things had got a bit better between us and the children. I just realised they had, bit by bit, as the years passed. But I'm not sure Lijah was ever close to them like he should have been. I don't know what you have to do to make that sort of thing happen between a mother or father and children what are grow'd. Maybe it's too late by then, too late for the sorting out of stuff. They do it in the moving pictures, I'm told. I've never been to the cinema myself but they say that on stage, when the piano plays, it's like lanternslides only the people can move about. They have writing at the bottom that says what the people are saying, and they are saying things like, 'You've never loved me, have you?' and the fella replies, 'No I haven't, but only because I lost my first fiancée in a tragic drowning accident.' After that, they come to an understanding.

People don't have those sorts of conversations where I come from. Leastways they didn't on the Fens, nor in East Cambridge, nor in Sutton – and especially not in the little brick houses of Peterborough. No, in all the places I've ever been, they come round for a cup of tea and they keep their private thoughts to themselves. They drink tea by the gallon, so they do, as enough of it might wash away the secret things what have got buried in the secret insides of themselves.

Except sometimes, in the dark. That's the time when you think about ghosts, and dead pigs and whether stories really happened the way you remember them or whether you are just a bit mad in the head and it would be better if someone shut you up so you won't do no harm to nobody.

We had a routine in the mornings, did Lijah and I. We were always up at first light. I would come down and light the fires and brew tea, then take my cup outside for a bit of a smoke in the fresh air. It was the only time the gas tower looked pretty, in the morning light. You couldn't see it from the back garden, so I liked to take my tea and my pipe out to the front step, even if I needed a shawl round my shoulders. A few folk would be about – people always greeted you right politely first thing in the morning on account of how the day hadn't been able to upset them yet. I would squat down on the step and chew on my pipe and sip my tea and as the dawn rose, the gas tower would glow – this huge orange cylinder, looming over the houses, like a big bucket of answers.

Lijah was usually up by the time I went back inside. Quite often, he'd have had his tea and a slice of bacon and onion roll and be getting himself ready for the outside world. He would sit in on a kitchen stool with his comb and his cap on the table in front of him. He was quite bald by then but for a small piece of hair that grew at the back of his head, which he had managed to grow as long as long could be, like a China-man. He oiled this, so he did, by dipping the comb in one of my saucers. Then he would wind the strand of hair round his head, until it stopped on his forehead, when he would fashion a kiss-curl out of the end of it. With his cap on top, it looked almost normal.

When we were Travellers, no decent mother would ever let her child fix his hair inside, nor use a saucer to do it. Sometimes, I watched him do this and wondered what we had come to.

'All right, Dei,' he said, when he had finished. He would rise up and pat his waistcoat pockets. 'It's off to the market for me.'

Mehitable and Scarlet had market stalls right next to each other, by then, selling woollens and hats and gloves. Fenella helped them out sometimes but she was a bit busy with her girls. Mehitable was renting her stall from a fella called Thompson and went down there every morning while her boy was at school. She didn't like Lijah going down the market when Thompson was around, on account of how Lijah might forget and start rokkering to her in Rummanus. That would be the end of it, then. She needed the bit of money on account of how the no-good she had married had upped and left her to raise her boy on her own. Always unlucky, Mehitable.

'Off to *dik* the big wide world, *amaro chavo*?' I would say to Lijah, as he set off.

'*Avali*, I am that, Dei,' he always replied.

I had a nasty moment, the other day. It was like I sort of woke up, and I was in the middle of the parlour. Thing was, I couldn't remember why I was there. And for a moment, I didn't even know where 'there' was. I looked around me for a bit. There was an empty birdcage hanging in one corner, from a standard lamp with the bulb and shade removed. There was a carriage clock on the mantel. Beneath me was carpet, in a swirly pattern. When I moved my toes inside my soft house-boots, I could see the knuckle of them bulge upwards, rising above the carpet like small sea-monsters. It was like these things were the pieces of a jigsaw puzzle that suddenly rearranged themselves into the right order and it came to me that I was in the parlour of my own little house.

For the life of me, I could not remember what I was doing in the middle of the parlour, or how I had got to be there.

Once, my father sent me to get him something from a market. And he gave me some pennies to buy myself a pie. I was stood in front of the pie stall and I must have looked like a poor, starving child or some such, as the stall-holder called out to me, 'Hey, come here, girlie.' I saw that in his hands he was holding a piece of brown paper, and there was a heap of broken pastry on it. I realised that he had been watching me while I was staring at his pies.

I had only been staring at them as I was wondering what sort of pie to choose but he must've thought I had no money for a pie. He was a giving me a broken one for free.

I took it, even though I was too embarrassed to thank him properly, and turned away and ate it, and it tasted every bit as good as a not-broken one, I must say. Having got it for nothing didn't spoil the flavour of it, neither.

As I'd got myself a free pie, I walked around the fair for a bit, wondering what to spend my pennies on.

I bought myself a little bird. The lady put it in a brown paper bag. I could feel its wings a-fluttering inside. It was a pretty feeling. On the way home, I stopped on a bridge and decided to take a peek at it, but when I opened the bag, the bird flew right away.

Just like my black canary.

I met a madman once, a real one. It was in a field. He came back with me to the camp and he frightened everybody but I liked him and fed him and gave him jobs to do. But as he was a real madman, we had to give him back. Some men came and got him. I wasn't there when they took him. Dei told me about it later. I think. No, I saw him. So I did.

There's going to be another war, apparently. It's the Germans again, still up to their old tricks. We didn't beat them good enough last time, so we've got to do it all over again. When Lijah told me about it, I got right agitated and made him promise not to go off, and he said, 'Dei, I'm in my sixties. They wouldn't have me in the army even to polish their boots.'

After a while I said, 'Was my grandson killed in the war?'

'No, Dei,' said Lijah. 'The boys came back safe and sound. We all did. We was lucky.'

'Well, where did he go, then?' I meant Bartholomew, my Barty-boy, the little terror.

Lijah knew who I meant, right enough. He sighed. 'Bartholomew was not right in the head after the war, and he went off to London and no one knows where he is, now.'

I frowned, just trying to get the pieces right in my head. 'And what about Daniel?'

'Daniel owns his own sign-writing business. He's done very nicely for himself. Got fellas working for him, now and a girl what's almost grow'd. We saw them Sunday.'

'Oh,' I said,' that's right.' Daniel's wife had served us lamb. She had put a little dish in front of me and shouted in my left ear, 'That's mint sauce, that is, Grandmother!' Snooty little cow.

This next war wasn't like the last one. In the last one, people just disappeared. Men marched off and some of them came back injured or not right in the head like Bartholomew – and some didn't come back at all. But it all happened somewhere else a long way away as I remember, not here.

This new war came here a bit more. They tried to set fire to the cathedral by the marketplace, did the Germans, although we put it out in time. Some people broke shop windows and said you shouldn't work at Werners.

It made things ugly, this war. If you didn't have curtains on your windows then you had to paint them with green paint and put up strips of sticky brown paper all over them to make your house so ugly the Germans couldn't be bothered to bomb it. Lijah said you couldn't get a horse for love nor money.

I get confused sometimes. Sometimes I wonder who I am telling my story to, for it is like I am telling a story over and over in my head. And sometimes it feels like I'm there, right back in it, and I lose myself, and then at other times it's just remembering, like any other old fool.

Sometimes, it's like there's someone listening. I found myself wondering the other day about who that someone might be, and I pictured a girl, who's waiting for me somewhere, and maybe she's someone else or maybe she's only me, the old me that used to exist and is still there underneath the layers of everything. Then, when I think this girl is me, I feel as though I am talking to her and warning her of who she's going to become, except she's not really listening, of course, as she's too flipping stubborn.

There are many things I don't believe in, but I do believe in ghosts. How could I not when I saw *Bafedo Bawlo*, the Ghost Pig, with my own very eyes? Sometimes I think I'm talking to a ghost but it is not the ghost of a dead person, oh no, as that would be an evil thing and it would drive me quite mad. No, it is like the ghost of someone not yet born. They are not evil. They are thin and pale and wispy, like made-up ghosts in the picture-books my grandchildren used to have – pretty little things, like dandelion fluff, not like real ghosts at all.

Lijah said to me once, when we were sitting together at the kitchen table after supper, smoking in silence, 'Dei, for what are you always muttering and talking to yourself these days? Are you going mad on me, or what?'

And I replied, 'I talk to myself, my son, as it's the only way I get a decent answer.'

Well, he might've been an Old Fella by then but he still needed slapping down once in a while.

It was when I went to buy tobacco that I saw it, the Ghost Pig, right here on a street in Peterborough, with my very own eyes.

I was on my way to Phipps', the newsagents. You could get the 'baccy at the stationers as well, but old Phipps liked me, for some reason. Probably my girlish charm. Anyhow, when he'd taken my ration card and weighed a quarter ounce for me, he always added a few scraps more, before he twisted the paper.

I had just paid for my quarter and tucked the paper into the special pocket in my handbag, when he said, all casual like, 'I see that new pub's opening on Friday, they've got a notice up. Have you seen it?'

'Another?'

'Aye, for all the lads been demobbed, I reckon. Those boys need a pint when they get home.'

'Another.'

I knew which one he meant. It was on the corner with Star Road. Yet another public house, as if Peterborough wasn't stuffed full of them already. Well, that will be nice and convenient for my Lijah, I thought to myself. He'll be able to roll home, if he wants.

'Your son won the competition, didn't he?' said Phipps. 'They all had to stand up and tell a story, and he won it.'

A boy had barged into the shop and asked for something, rudely, cutting into our conversation. I was a bit confused as I thought he'd asked for a red apple but Phipps was turning and opening a jar that had some sweets on sticks. The boy was looking anxious. He was probably on his way to school and shouldn't have been in Phipps' at all.

'A competition d'you say?' I said, cocking my head as though I hadn't heard him right, although in fact my hearing is perfect and always has been. It's useful to pretend it ain't, sometimes.

'Yes, the competition, to give it a name.' The schoolboy was hopping from one foot to another, holding out his copper to pay, but Phipps was making a point of ignoring him, to teach him some manners. 'They had a night in there last month. Did he not tell you? I suppose the idea was, get everybody interested. They had to stand up and tell a story and whoever told the best story that gave the landlord the idea for the name for the new public house gets to drink the first official pint on Friday, and then free for the rest of the night.'

Lijah hadn't mentioned any of this to me, but that was no surprise. He knew I wouldn't approve, and I didn't, but I must admit to feeling a little chuffed at the thought of my Lijah winning something. Well, that's a first, I thought.

The bell tinkled as I pushed open the door to leave the shop. I was still standing on the step, pulling on my gloves, when the schoolboy came barging out behind me, nearly knocking me off the step. *Chavos* these days have no idea about respect. If he hadn't been so quick, I'd have given him a clip round the ear.

I thought I'd take a wander up to Star Road and have a look at that new public house, even though my house was in the opposite direction. I wasn't in any particular hurry to get home, that morning.

So I walked up, taking it slowly as I have to do these days, and stood on the corner of Star Road and Wellington Street.

They'd done the place up nice, I'll say that for them – new window frames and a brand new door with a shiny brass handle. A man was up a ladder in front of the door. He was a-fixing the sign, which was covered in sackcloth and swinging lightly in the wind.

I stood looking up at him, and he glanced down.

'All ready, are you?' I asked, just by way of making conversation.

'Aye,' he said. 'It's creaking a bit. But it'll be all right. It's new.'

'So I hear.' I said. 'Are you the landlord?' I thought maybe he might tell me a bit about the competition Lijah had won. I was right interested in the idea of Lijah winning something.

'Nope,' he said, 'I'm just fixing it. The boss is pleased with it, though. Fella over at Walton did the painting. It's a *gipsy* legend, you know.'

I felt a certain tightening in my chest. 'What's that, then?'

The street was mostly empty but for a few children still late to get to school. The men were all off at work and it was a bit early for the women to be setting out to do their shopping. I was only out and about because I still got up early as ever and liked going to get my 'baccy while it was quiet.

The man up the ladder didn't reply. He just removed the sackcloth, to show me what he was fixing. He gave the sign a little push, to see if it would still creak.

The picture was of a snow-white pig with black patches and one black ear. It wasn't a normal pig, though, oh no. It was painted all fuzzy edged, and with light strokes so the background showed through a bit. It was staring out of the picture at me, and its eyes were glowing red. It was the Ghost Pig, sure enough. And it was living on the corner of my street.

I felt my chest tighten a little more, and my hand went to my throat. My blouse was buttoned up to my neck against the cold and I was overwhelmed with a desire to undo it. *Dadus, soskey were creminor kair'd? Chavi, that puvo-baulor might jib by halling lende . . .* The man looked down at me, his face creased in concern. There was a ringing in my ears. *Dadus, soskey were puvo-baulor kair'd? Chavi, that tute and mandi might jib by lelling lende.* My sight went a bit blurry. *Dadus, soskey were tu ta mandi kair'd? Chavi, that creminor might jib by halling mende.* The man looked back at his sign and gave it another little push with his finger. It swung silently, to and fro. I felt myself begin to swing as well, although whether it was up or down, I could not tell.

# CHAPTER 20

Thomas Freeman was a slightly built boy, light on his feet he looked. There was an easiness about him. It's hard to put it into words. He just had an air of knowing what he was about, what lay ahead of him in life. His father owned the bakery in Werrington, and probably his father before him. Thomas was the third child but the eldest son, so he'd take over in his turn. Maybe it was knowing his future was secure made him such a simple, cheerful sort of person. There was nothing to worry about for Thomas Freeman, oh no.

We first got talking one spring afternoon. I knew who he was, of course, as we had been stopped on Werrington Green long enough for us to work out who most of the *gorjers* were. I hadn't spoken to any of the village boys up 'til then, of course – such a thing would have been unthinkable back in them days. Some of them would throw mud at our *vardos* when they went past, but only if my Dadus or Redeemus Grey weren't around. I had first seen Thomas Freeman with that group, but he didn't throw any mud himself, just carried on walking, with his hands in his pockets. He didn't say anything to the other boys and he didn't look at me.

After they had gone past, I thought about the thin, light-haired boy who hadn't thrown mud. The other boys he was with looked a lot tougher than him, but there seemed something strong about him all the same, perhaps because he hadn't felt the need to join in. I wondered who he was, and what his name was, but knew there was no way of finding out as the heavens would have opened if I'd asked a question about a *gorjer* boy.

The next I saw him was a few days later, when I was walking down the lane that led to Walton. I was looking for nettles. Dei had said they were thick down that particular lane. Thomas Freeman was on his way back from somewhere, with a bundle tucked under his arm.

I saw the *gorjer* boy with the light hair walking towards me and I did what any girl in my position would have done. I crossed over the lane, as you would if you'd spotted a dog you didn't like the look of.

As we drew level, he stopped where he was and watched me pass, then called after me, 'There's no need to avoid me, miss. I don't bite, you know.'

I just kept my head down and quickened my pace. Course you bite, I thought dismissively. You all bite.

But as I kept walking, I thought how his voice had sounded friendly and regretful, not harsh like most boys' voices. He had sounded a little sad that I wouldn't acknowledge him. And the whole time I was picking nettles, bending low to grasp the bottom of their stems, I thought of the sadness and kindliness in his voice, and resolved that next time I came across him, as long as no one else was around, I would be bold and speak with him.

The opportunity did not come for some weeks, and I had almost forgotten about him by then. I was walking down the same lane, around the same time of day. Looking back on it, I wonder if I had not done that on purpose a few times, on the chance that he had been on a regular errand before and I might see him again.

I was not yet at the place where we had passed each other before. I was still quite close to the village. But it was a quiet, sunlit afternoon and no one was around, and as I neared a long wooden gate that led into a farmer's field, I saw that he was sitting on top of it, and I knew at once that he was waiting on the off-chance I might pass, and that for the last few weeks we had both been trying to bump into one another, and both been disappointed, until now.

I glanced behind me, to make sure no one else was around. I thought, *he'd be in as much trouble as me if we were seen together*. He was from an upright *gorjer* family, after all, with a good trade. The last thing they would want is for their prized eldest son to be seen talking to a *gipsy* girl.

I had never met any of his family, of course, but the thought of how unpleasant they would be to me if they got the chance was what made me bold enough to speak to him. I stopped in front of the gate and looked up at him.

'Good afternoon,' he said politely.

'It is indeed,' I said, loving my boldness, loving the newness of it.

'What is your name?' he asked. 'Mine's Thomas Freeman,' he added quickly, with the air of someone who was prepared to go first.

'I know,' I replied, even though I did not until that moment. 'You're the baker's lad.'

He looked surprised. 'How do you know that?'

*How do you think?* I laughed to myself. Could it be something to do with the way you ride round the village on your dad's bike after school, selling loaves from the front basket?

'My name is . . . Edith,' I said. Edith sounded good, I thought. Nice and proper.

'Edith,' he repeated.

We looked at each other for a bit, then he shuffled along the top bar of the gate, to allow me to climb up and sit on it to but not to be too close to him. I clambered up, and there we sat, like two birds, both of us glancing this way and that down the lane so that, from our vantage point, we could see if anyone approached.

'Where are you off to, then?' he asked after a bit.

'Just walking,' I said.

'I am on my way back from visiting my aunt and her family in Gunthorpe. She's a seamstress there, but she's not been well recently.'

'I am sorry to hear that,' I replied.

We were in a strange position, for it was clear that neither of us wanted to jump down from the gate and go off while neither of us could think of a decent reason for staying there either. I did not know what was happening between us, if anything – but I knew I was enjoying it, right enough. It made me feel like I wasn't a little girl, right at that minute, that I was myself, and that that self was somehow and importantly different from the girl I had been a few minutes before. It was a new, clean feeling, like being able to fly – not that I have ever been able to fly, of course.

'Have you got any brothers and sisters?' he said.

'No,' I said, 'I did when I was little but they all died.'

'Oh,' he said.

'What about you?' I asked.

'Oh loads of them,' he said. 'I've got two big sisters, Emily and Jane. I'm the eldest boy but I've got three younger brothers, Samuel, William and George, and then there are two little girls as well. There's always been loads of us. It's quite good like that when you've got a shop. Don't you get lonely on your own?'

It was a stupid question, so I didn't bother to answer it. We were quiet for a bit, then he said, 'I've never spoken to a *gipsy* before.'

There wasn't much I could say to that.

'Would you mind if I asked you a question?' he said politely.

I looked at him, the sun on his hair.

Without waiting for me to reply, he said, 'Is it true you all have your own secret language? I studied Latin at school but I never got the hang of it.'

'Well you can understand me, right enough,' I replied warily.

'I know,' he said, 'but I remember having a secret language with my brother when we were children, only we forgot it after a while, and I just wondered how you remember it, if you've never wrote it down.'

I confess this question flummoxed me a bit, so I said. 'I'll answer yours if you answer a question of mine after.'

'All right, Edith.'

'Well,' I said, 'the truth of the matter is, we can speak the same language as animals, you know, horses and dogs and foxes all understand each other, and so do we. We don't need to write it down, it's just in us, and that's the way it is. It isn't something we think about, you know, no more than you do, but we know ourselves to be greater than you for we understand you, but you will never understand us.'

The length of this speech surprised him, for he stared at me the whole while, impressed. 'So do you . . .'

'It's my turn now, I believe.'

'All right. Go on, then. Ask me anything.'

I tried to think of all the things I had ever wondered about the way *gorjers* live, all the things I had been curious about, but nothing came to mind, and out of nowhere, the words came, 'Would you like to kiss me, Thomas Freeman?'

The look on his face was one of such joy and astonishment that I could not stop myself grinning from ear to ear. He smiled and leaned towards me. I leaned forward too, and then gave him a sharp shove in the chest with one hand. He obliged me by tipping backwards, legs going right over, and landing on his side in the field.

I looked down at him over my shoulder and laughed. 'I didn't say you *could*, you know, I just asked if you wanted to!'

I jumped off my side of the gate and ran down the path, full of glee at my own wit, and happy as anything because I now knew for certain that a boy wanted to kiss me and I had never known that in my whole life before.

I had got no more than a few yards back towards the village when I looked ahead, then stopped dead on the path. Ahead of me, in the distance, was a dark, solid figure, right in the middle of the lane. He was some way off, but I knew from the size of him and the silhouette of his hat, that it was Redeemus Grey. He was standing stock still, so must have been staring along the path and seen me.

I glanced behind me and saw Thomas clambering over the gate. I looked back and realised that Redeemus Grey must be able to see him as well. What must it look like, me running down the lane, dishevelled and laughing, and a *gorjer* boy clambering the gate after me? My insides felt soft with fear, for I knew what a strict man Redeemus Grey was and how he'd be bound to tell my father what he'd seen and then I'd catch it. Mr Grey was terribly moral that way. He once took one of his own girls to the middle of the green and beat her with a stick in front of everybody because he'd caught her looking at a *gorjer* boy, never mind talking to one. There was no chance one of his girls would ever step out of line. They'd stay as pure as driven snow until he had them safely married off.

I gestured to Thomas, waving him back with my hand. His face creased in concern, and then he understood my gesture, turned and walked the other way. When I looked back toward the village, Redeemus Grey had also turned and gone – probably straight to tell my father.

Now I'm for it, I thought, and the thought quite wiped out my happiness at having pulled a trick on Thomas.

*

I walked back to the village as slowly as I had ever done, know-ing I had to go straight back to the green but wanting to delay the dread moment for as long as possible. As I came up Church Street, the vicar was leaving the churchyard, pulling the gate shut behind him. He glanced at me and I nodded politely, walking on.

But blow me if I hadn't gone more than a few paces when I realised he was hurrying after me and falling into step beside me. I kept my head down and walked quickly, for although he was a vicar, he was still a man and I thought, dordy, the reputation I'm going to get if I'm seen talking to two of them in one afternoon.

'Good afternoon, my child,' said the vicar, as we walked. 'Are you walking up to the green? Do you mind if I walk a few paces along with you?'

I kept my head down but nodded.

'Slow your pace a little, my child. I am not quite as young as you, remember.'

There was a little admonishment in his tone, so I unwillingly slowed my pace but still kept looking at the ground.

'I have seen you, of course, but do not know your name.'

'Emily, sir,' I said quietly.

'Emily,' he said. We walked a few paces in silence. Then he said, 'Forgive me for asking, Emily, but how old are you?'

'I do not know, sir,' I said.

'And have you had any schooling?' he asked next.

'No, sir,' I replied.

What was the point of this? We were approaching the green, so I stopped and faced him.

'Is there anything I can help you with, sir?' I asked boldly.

He looked down at me, a gaze of concern in his handsome face. He was a tall man with a shock of white hair and deep-set, brown eyes. He was concerned, yes, but also a little amused by me, I thought. I felt like a little rabbit before him. The feeling was not entirely unpleasurable. *Dordy, dordy, what is it with me this after-noon*, I thought, *am I giving off a scent or something?*

'Child, forgive me but I'll not keep you long. I just wanted to ask, are you happy with your degraded condition?'

I looked at him straight. Had *he* seen me talking with Thomas Freeman as well? 'What do you mean, sir?'

'I mean,' he lifted a hand towards the green, 'your road-side habits. Have you never wondered what it might be like to be a Christian girl, to live in a house and sleep in a bed and work and rest as the Lord intended?'

Oh, so that was it. Conversion. We had come across it many times before.

'I can't say as I have, sir.' Sometimes, it was worth encouraging them. You got presents if you baptised a baby, for instance. There were some Travelling families who did quite well going from parish to parish, finding God in each of them, and getting all ten of their children baptised every time.

'What if you were to take a position in a house, say, as a scullery maid? There are many advantages to such positions. Why, my own housekeeper is always saying she would well reward the right scullery girl if only she could find her.'

*Is it my soul you're after or my working skills?* I thought. At the time, it did not occur to me to think he might be after something else as well. I had met so few men, apart from our immediate group, that I had yet to learn that that is what they are all after, most of the time.

*Oh Dei and Dadus, why did you keep me so protected? Why did I not know what happened if you gave a man any sort of encouragement, and that sometimes it could happen whether you encouraged him or not?*

'Thank you, sir, but my mother is waiting for me.' I bobbed a little curtsey. I could think of no other way to be rid of him.

He leaned forward and laid a hand on my shoulder. 'Well, young lady, don't forget what I have said. Should you ever choose to live a different sort of life, then ways and means are open to you so to do.'

His hand was large, his grip firm. I knew nothing about men, but I knew this man felt he had the right to put his hand on my shoulder, and that I would be wise to keep my distance from him, however kindly he might seem.

I was troubled as I walked back to the camp, for my head was full of the encounters I had had that afternoon. I could not entirely distinguish between them: Thomas Freeman's smile and gentle voice, the vicar's hand upon my shoulder – the way my body felt warm and strange at night sometimes, a different body from the one I was used to. I wanted to be different, and was terrified of it. I could not name the feelings I had. But I felt as though I was on the verge of seeing the whole world in a new way, and although it was a frightening feeling, it was joyful as well.

My father was outside our *vardo*, whittling a stick. I looked at him warily as I approached. Redeemus Grey would surely have spoken to him straightaway. But Dadus looked at me and nodded in his normal, half-distracted manner, and I thought, maybe Redeemus Grey is not quite as hard a man as I have always thought him to be. Maybe he's decided to let me off – or maybe he just had other things on his mind.

That night, I lay on the grass between my Dei and Dadus – the weather was so fine, we were all sleeping outside, which was a thing that pleased me greatly at the time in my life when I was young, and safe. I loved stirring in the night, wakening a little, in that half-dreamy way. I loved lying on my back and looking up at the night sky, whether cloudy or star-lit, the whole of the eternity up there, opened up to me by the darkness, and me open to it too but safe between my parents. That night, I lay awake for ages with my arms flung above my head, as if to stretch out and show the all-of-me to the night sky, as if the very moon could swoop down and carry me high, high, high . . .

By the end of the week, a summer rain set in. It drizzled steadily through the next few days and the world went back to being damp and difficult, as it always does when it rains. The men and boys in our group started a good solid job on that Monday, up at Lowlands Farm. They were to build a new cow shed for the farmer, and clear some of his yards, and he wanted it done quickly so even the small boys were at it. Us girls were taking it in turns to go across the fields to the farm to take the men their victuals. They were out there from dawn 'til dusk, so it took several trips each day.

Come the Wednesday, it was my turn to do the to-ing and fro-ing, and what with helping with the preparation, that was most of my day occupied. Mid-morning, my mother prepared a basket of bread and cheese and sent me across the fields with it weighing heavily on my arm and my feet slipping on the wet grass. Before I left, she said that when I got back I was to put potatoes on the embers as she and Lena Grey were going out for eggs and she wanted the potatoes started.

A fine, warm drizzle fell as I crossed the fields. I was not really thinking about Thomas or the vicar that day. There is something about a change in weather that can make a week seem like a long time ago.

As I was approaching Lowlands Farm, I saw Redeemus Grey walking out of the yard. He saw me, and changed course to meet me on my way.

We met, and faced each other. There was a look on his face I didn't at all like, an angry look. I thought how he had spotted me talking with Thomas the previous week and wished that, if he was going to tell on me to my Dadus, he would do it quick and get it over with. Perhaps he was resenting me because he hadn't told yet, and would feel better when he had got me in trouble.

He held out one of his hands to take the basket. He was a large man, Redeemus Grey, with a huge round stomach and those fat lips that always look like they're inside out. 'That's for us, then.' He nodded at the basket.

I held it out reluctantly. I would have liked to have seen my Dadus and give it to him, not that there was any reason why I shouldn't give it to Redeemus Grey.

'I was on my way back to get something,' he said, 'Maybe I should give this to your father and walk back with you, eh?'

'I could fetch it for you, if you like,' I said hastily.

'All right, then,' he said, nodding. 'We need the trowel from my toolbox. Your father's got one but it's not as big as mine. We need mine.'

'I'll get it for you and be right back,' I said, and turned.

As I crossed the field, on the way back to the village, I congratulated myself on having avoided walking back with him, without ever asking myself why the thought of it made me so uncomfortable – or why, if he needed a trowel, he hadn't just sent one of the boys back to get it. Even if I had thought about it, I suppose I would have just assumed that he was disapproving of my friendship with Thomas Freeman and holding it against me. I don't think I would have put two and two together.

Between the fields and the village was a wide copse. The farmer used it for breeding game, I think. You didn't have to go through it to get back to Werrington, you could skirt round the edge. There was a narrow path between it and the hedgerow what bordered the field. It was as I passed down this path, skirting the corner of the copse that he stepped out, blocking my path.

He must have run like a hare to cut me off, as it would have taken him a few minutes longer to enter the copse at the top and cut through it to the edge of the field. He didn't have the basket with him, so must have stowed it somewhere.

I came to a halt, right in front of him. I felt sick and frightened inside of myself right away, even though I told myself it was just fat old Redeemus Grey and what was there to worry about, as he was nothing more than a man I didn't like much on account of his unpleasant appearance and manner with me.

There was a look on his face, a hateful look. I was beginning to realise I had seen that look on several occasions before.

Neither of us spoke for a while. I didn't speak because as long as we didn't say anything to each other then I could fool myself that there was nothing to worry about, that this was just one of those meaningless things that happens from time to time, instead of a disaster. I don't know why he remained silent. Enjoying himself, I suppose.

Eventually, I went to step round him. He moved to one side, blocking my path. I stopped, and tried the other way. I stopped again, took a deep breath, then turned on my heel to sprint back to the field, back to my father. That was a mistake, for it galvanised him into action, and later I was to wonder if maybe I could have talked my way out of it with promises. He caught me by the hair and pulled me backwards. The other hand came round my face to cover my mouth and pull me in close to him while he growled, 'You bite me and it'll be the worse for you.' I was trying to call out but could hardly make a sound and my heart was thumping loud in my ribcage as he dragged me into the copse, behind the bushes, and threw me down. He stood over me for a minute and I knew I had to talk fast. 'My mother'll be expecting me back, Mr Grey, she'll come looking for me in a minute, I'll be in trouble . . .' I got no further, for he was unbuttoning himself, and then he bent and pulled me into a sitting position. What he did then was a thing so awful I am ashamed to name it, for I did not even know it could be done. And while he did it, I began to choke and weep and he was talking to me saying, 'You'll not get the pleasure of them thin little boys that you'll get from me . . .'

and his voice was full of hatred, hatred spilling from him, salty like pig fat but thick as tar.

At first, when he made that strange sound, I though maybe he was dying and I'd be able to get away and he'd be found in the woods a few days later and nobody would ever know that it was me that killed him. He released my hair and stepped back a step or two, and that was when I turned on all fours and gagged into the wet leaves, spittle dropping down, my insides heaving.

I should have jumped up and run then – I could have got away if I'd run at that point. But I was so sick and frightened and shaking from head to foot, and I thought that was it. I even thought he might say sorry.

He was still standing over me and looking down at me. Maybe someone will come by, I thought. He'll have to move sharpish, then. Then I can hide in the bushes and sort myself out a bit before I go home. If I brushed the leaves off my skirts maybe I could make myself presentable. No one need know.

'I've seen you,' he said again, and his voice was just as vicious as before. 'I've seen you walking down the lane. Like it, do you? Walking past me like that, thinking all I can do is stare at it? Enjoyed yourself, have you, flaunting yourself to the *gorjer* boys 'cause you know they're too feeble to do anything about it? Didn't reckon on me, though, did you? I've heard you laughing, I've crept up on you when you've been behind the hedge, laughing to each other. I know what goes on in your filthy heads. My girls are just the same.' My head was swimming. What was he on about? His girls? He had been spying on us when we went to do our business, behind the hedge? Then I became more and more afraid, for I could tell that it wasn't over, that it had been going on for ages and I hadn't even known it. I didn't even like his girls. They were strange and sullen and I hardly even spoke to them if I could help it. And I thought of his wife and how quiet and bent she always seemed and how he had always been like just an ordinary man that we didn't like much and not this fat lump of hatred.

I glanced up at him. His breeches were still unfastened, and he was touching himself between his thumb and fingers. I looked away. I was sick with fear.

'Let's show you how it's really done then, shall we?' he said. And he knelt behind me and rested the flat of one thick, fat hand on my back to keep me bended. The other hand flung up my skirts, and then there was pain, just pain, and my face was in the dirt, and I was crying again and counting the seconds until it stopped and praying that no one came by to see me in such a low position, being done to as if I was nothing, and knowing I would always be nothing from now on because he was showing me how nothing I was.

When it was over, he lay on top of me. I was collapsed on the ground. His chest was over my face and I could hardly breath. There was a buckle or something sticking in my cheek. My other cheek was in the mud. He began to stroke my hair. 'So now you know, my little love,' he said, and his voice wasn't hateful any more. 'Now you know what all the fuss is about. You'll get to like it soon enough.' He rolled off me. I couldn't move. He did up his breeches, then stuck one of his hands in his pocket. 'Open your mouth,' he said.

All the fight had gone out of me then. I just remember thinking, please let him go away soon, then I can go back to the *vardo*. More than anything, I wanted to be in the *vardo* under a blanket like when I had the scarlet fever and Dei came and put wet rags on my forehead and sang to me.

'Here.'

I raised myself carefully on one elbow. My hair stuck to the mud on the ground and I had to free it with the other hand. He was holding a sixpence. He popped it onto my tongue, then closed my mouth by pushing at my chin. 'That's for keeping your mouth shut. You can buy yourself a bit of lace with that. I like lace on a girl.'

I gagged again and spat the coin into my hand. I sat looking at it on my palm.

He must have taken this for defiance, as he bent down and grabbed a handful of my hair and brought his face close to mine. His voice was low and filled with hate again. 'And if you speak a word of this out loud, I'll tell them all how you walked the length of Walton Lane with the baker's boy, laughing and talking with him, and went behind the hedge with him, and maybe I'll tell them how you sold yourself to me for the price of sixpence and they'll all know you for what you are then, won't they?'

Then he was gone.

I stood, unsteadily, and tried to brush some of the mud from my apron.

Going down to the stream was no good. I knew there wasn't enough water in the whole of the Great Ouse to wash away what had happened to me. And then I did something for which I have never forgiven myself. I put the coin in my apron pocket.

It might have all been different if my Dei had been at the *vardo* when I got back. Threats or no threats I could never have kept it from her if she had seen me in the state I was in. But she'd gone out for eggs. I was met on the green by Melinda Grey, Redeemus Grey's eldest, who took a long, hard look at me and pulled me into their *vardo*. Three of the young 'uns were in there and she tossed her head at them to go. 'What happened to her?' one of them said on the way out and Melinda snapped, 'She fell down in the spinney, now go and fix that fire unless you want a smack on the head.'

She tried to pull my things off me but my apron bow was too neat for her. I had to do it myself. When she saw the mud on my knees she stared for a moment before saying in a low, disgusted voice, 'Look at the state of you. Bundle it all up, for God's sake. You'll have to launder it straight off, all of it. I'll give you ours to mix in with it. It's your turn anyhow.' As I pulled my skirt down, I saw there was blood on the inside of it, and it was then I gave way. *He stabbed me*, I thought in terror. *I'll bleed to death.* I gave a low sob.

Melinda Grey took hold of my shoulders. 'Shut it, okay? Your Mam and mine will be back soon so you've got to pull yourself together.' She threw some of her sister's clothes at me. 'Put those on, then come down. If your Dei asks, say you came on early so I gave you some of my things to wear, helped you out.' She left the *vardo*.

I got dressed as quick as possible. I hated the idea that I was in *his vardo*, the place where he slept. My legs were still unsteady but I made it down the steps and Melinda was waiting with the tin bucket and a slab of grey soap. She handed them to me, then said, 'Wait here.'

While I waited, the three young 'uns sat in a row on the ground, staring at me. They know, I thought. Perhaps everyone will know when they look at me. I am different, now.

Melinda came back with a bundle of their underthings. Me and their two eldest girls and my cousin always took it in turns with the things the men and boys shouldn't see. 'Here,' she said. 'Orlanda has been on, so you'll have to scrub hers with a rock.'

There was something satisfied in her tone. I saw how it was, how now I would be washing underthings with a purpose and knowing it to be more than just another chore, like they'd been doing. I was one of them now.

'Go on,' Melinda said, 'and fix your hair while you're about it.'

It was only when I was down by the stream, on all fours, that I unfolded my dirty apron and found the sixpence. I looked at it. It was an old one, with the Queen a young woman with her hair up. I turned it over, staring at it, as if I'd never seen a sixpence before. On the other side was a coronet of leaves and the crown nestling atop of them, as if it was waiting there to be put on her head so's she would know she'd lost her youngness now and had to be Queen, whether she liked it or not.

I could have thrown the sixpence into the stream there and then I suppose, but there wasn't any point. It was far too late for that.

When a man doesn't want to leave you alone, there's nothing you can do about it. Too late, I realised that the only way out of my predicament would have been to have told Dei or Dadus straightaway, not have cleaned myself up. For once I had cleaned myself up, then I had been a party to the hiding of it, and then I was more afraid of being found out than I was afraid of Redeemus Grey. I wanted it to stop happening, but even more I wanted it to never have happened in the first place, and if my mother or father found out, then that would be impossible.

It was only a matter of time, and sure enough, that summer, I realised something was wrong. I started to feel peculiar. I got dugs, for a start, what I had never had before, being as flat as a pancake, like my Dei. And I felt exhausted all the time – not tired, normal tired, but completely done in, as if even walking to the end of the road was like crossing the whole of Cambridgeshire. I felt like that all day long. And then, as autumn came along, there was the unmistakeable swelling of my belly, low down, not soft like when you go to fat, but hard. I couldn't argue with that.

I was terrified. I didn't know what to say to Dei and Dadus. Luckily for me, my Dei was no fool. Nothing like that was going to get past her. She'd had her suspicions for a while before she took me up on it.

It was the only time she ever hit me. She said to me, 'Whose is it? Is it that baker's boy that you've been seen with?' I had not spoken to Thomas Freeman since what had happened with Redeemus Grey. I had avoided Walton Lane, and on the two occasions I had seen him in the village, I had run in the opposite direction.

I didn't know what to say to her, so I stayed mute. She took my silence for a yes, I suppose, and her small hand came swinging from nowhere and slapped me full across the face. It stung like anything, but I didn't move. I knew by then that I was going have to live with my mistakes.

She stared at me for a moment, then all at once, we both burst into tears. She took me in her arms and I sobbed like a baby and so did she, holding me so tight I thought she'd squeeze the life from me.

One of the best moments of my life was the moment we watched the others pull off Werrington Green. We had already moved into the cottage in the graveyard by then. We were not on speaking terms but happened to be walking along Church Road, all three of us, the morning they set off. They stayed stony faced, the lot of them, as they passed. Even my cousins who I had always got on well with. As their two *vardos* rattled by, I felt a huge weight lifting off and away from me at the thought that, with any luck, I would never set eyes on Redeemus Grey again.

The three of us stood in the street for a minute or two, then Dadus put his hand on my shoulder and said, 'Smiths should stick with other Smiths, I've always thought as much. When we want to move off, we'll go and join the Whittlesey lot.'

It was winter by then. Dei said, 'I thought I've told you to keep that shawl over your head. You've got to keep warm now, you know.'

One day, Dei said to me, 'If I go off to the marketstede tomorrow, I'll be gone all day. Can you manage?'

'Course I can, Dei,' I replied.

'Look after your Dadus, then.'

Dadus was out tending to the horse in the morning. I stayed in the cottage and did some knitting. He came back to get some water and talk about how it was time that horse had something more than chaff and mangold and he would have to go over to Gunthorpe the next day for linseed cake. Then he went out again.

As he left, I said, 'I'll do fried bread for tea when you get back, Dadus.' He nodded. He knew I always did it nice and crispy. We both liked it that way.

The trouble with the way I fry bread is, I like to shake it around a bit, and then you get fat spots all over the range. You have to give the range a good clean after I've been frying bread.

So the next thing I knew, I was outside in the cold and dark and the wind was howling fit to burst, as though there were ghosts in the trees a-shrieking for my child. It was the kind of evening that might have frightened me, under other circumstances, but I had something else on my mind.

I crawled a few yards, then the pain came again, and I had to stop and bend double. Behind our cottage was a large gravestone that had fallen over. I was heading for it. I don't know why. It was like the gravestone was a door floating down a wild river and I had to get to it or drown.

I made it to the gravestone. I grasped the sides. Beneath me would be the name of the person who was buried there, if I could read it. Above me, the wind was tossing the tops of the trees back and forth, back and forth – I could just see in the pitch dark, when I looked up. I think I was howling by then. There was no moon. The pain came again and I stopped thinking about anything else.

I was still on my knees, but as soon as I felt my baby slip from me, I rolled on one side quickly, to reach down for it and pull it up. I don't remember thinking I needed to do it – I don't recall saying to myself, *you must get that babby on your warm chest as soon as possible*. It was like my arms made their own decision, for there was a rawness about me, a hunger that dulled all pain. I scarcely noticed the strange slipperiness of this little thing what I was lifting to me.

The only light was the yellow glimmer from the cottage window, where we had tacked up an old blanket. The blanket had holes in it, and it was like there were small gold stars, gleaming but distant, shining down on me and my child. I could only just make out his face, screwed up and dark and furious – heavy browed, even then, annoyed at having been pushed into the world. *A baby . . . it's a baby . . .* I said to myself, over and over, as I held him. I could not have stopped myself from gazing at him for the world.

I huddled down on the rough gravestone, parted my blouse, and put him on me straightaway. He had not uttered a sound, but I knew he was all right as soon as his mouth fixed on me – the strangeness and discomfort of that tugging – and the feeling, too, that there was nothing more right than this. Whatever else might be wrong with the world was made right by just this.

I was still getting after-pains – my Dei explained later about how you had to get rid of all the stuff that came with him. *I hope she's back from market soon*, I thought, as I fed my newborn son. *There's no way I will be able to stand up until she comes to help me.* My legs were numb and shuddery. At that moment, I couldn't imagine ever walking again.

So I lay in the cold and dark and waited for my Dei. And I stroked Lijah's slimy little head and thought to myself. *This is it, now. It has happened. He is all I need, now, and all I will ever ask of him is one thing – that he outlives me.*

I saw then, how simple and straightforward the rest of my life would be. It would not matter what befell me and my baby. As long as he lived, that would be enough.

The storm died after a while and the wind dropped right down. The night became calm. When the carrier-cart eventually came up Church Street, I could hear the turning of its wheels. 'Dei!' I called out, long before she would have been able to hear me.

'*Dei!*'

I was surprised to hear how tiny my voice sounded, for I was as proud as a lion. I could not wait for her to come and discover me – us. '*Dei!*'

It would be a minute or two before she came. The cart would

have to pull up by the church. Then the driver would have to help her unload the things she had bought. Then she would have to pay him and open the cemetery gate and make her way down the path with her bundles. How sweet that little space of time was, when I could enjoy the thought of how much I was going to surprise her.

Even if Dei went into the cottage, the first thing she would say to Dadus would be, 'Where's our Lem?'

'You're going to meet my mother in a minute, *biti* boy,' I whispered to Lijah. The sweetness of that moment: the scattered handful of golden stars on the ragged blanket across our cottage window; the roughness of the gravestone beneath me; the small pains and the bitter cold; the knowledge that my Dei was coming; and the whispered bargain I was making with my son. *Live for ever, Lijah Smith. Tiny boy of mine, and mine alone. Never die.*

# EPILOGUE

## Peterborough – 1960

The colours of a wet spring day are green and grey. Mehitable Thompson thinks this as the hearse pulls into Eastfield Cemetery.

It is a mid-week morning, April. It has been raining for a month. The air is heavy with moisture and the ground pliant underfoot – easy work for the gravedigger. Mehitable thinks of earth as she steps down from the car and stands waiting as her father's coffin is pulled from the hearse; earth made heavy with rain, thick and dark, easy to break apart in great clods. She likes to plant her daffs on wet days like this one – but autumn has a different feel, of course.

Today, despite the drizzle and the cloudy skies, there is no doubting it is spring. The daffodils are dying off but a few tulip stems are splayed apart in bunches either side of the cemetery gates, their wide leaves whitening. It is damp but not that cold. None of them need their dark, heavy coats.

Scarlet steps down from the car behind Mehitable. She pauses to remove her woollen hat and smooth her hair back over her wide brow. She catches Mehitable watching her and smiles her broad, beautiful smile. Mehitable thinks, Scarlet, the baby of our family, in her fifties already. How old does that make me? That's the way it is with funerals. We all move up a step, one step closer to our turn. They'll start taking them out my pen pretty soon.

*My father, Elijah Smith, is dead*, Mehitable thinks to herself as they gather round the grave, *and the wet, dark earth is waiting*. He died in the spring.

The vicar says his piece. They gather round to bow their heads and drop handfuls of soil down onto Lijah's coffin. At a respectful distance, two young men wait to fill the rest of the hole after their departure. Nobody cries, although Dan's expression has an unnatural stiffness to it. Mehitable feels comforted by the rituals, glad of them. *Dad is where he should be. Maybe this time, for once, he will stay put.*

Her father has been living with them these last few years, ever since his own mother died – she sometimes feels he went from child to invalid in one fell swoop. It will be strange to have her house back, after all these years. They have got so used to Lijah's presence; his silences, his smell. At least I won't have to cook any more of those dreadful suet rolls, she thinks. He loved his suet, did her Dad.

His room won't take much clearing out. She has already looked: a few shirts, they can go to Barnados; a few bits of junk in the top drawer of the chest of drawers, one or two photos, his pipe, three handkerchiefs, two pairs of braces and a silk neckerchief. Under his bed were two pairs of shoes, a large stone from the garden and some yellowing newspapers.

She glances round the graveside group. Her husband stands slight apart, still shy even though he has known everyone for years. She sometimes feels he has never quite got over being her second husband. He has got to go to a meeting over at Ailsworth afterwards and she can feel his gentle impatience with proceedings. He catches her looking at him and smiles. She smiles back. Jim Thompson. Sometimes, she still cannot believe her luck. Jim winks.

She winks back. He was fond of Lijah, she knows, but, like her, is not inclined to be sentimental about his passing.

Her son Harry has come in his own car and he has brought Dan's wife Ida, their daughter Sally, and Sally's husband. Scarlet's two girls came in a car behind them, and they have brought poor Fenella's two with them. Tom, Fenella's widower, is poorly and couldn't make it. There are also a few of Lijah's old drinking pals from The Ghost Pig. It's a respectable turnout. They are all going back to Scarlet's house afterwards, although Mehitable suspects the drinking pals will melt away to toast Lijah's health in their own fashion.

Dan, herself and Scarlet; three children out of five. You should have the whole set at your funeral. But no one has heard of Bartholomew in decades and Fenella, poor old Nellie, lies beneath the earth a few yards away, eleven years dead. A car struck her as she crossed Cowgate one evening with her husband Tom. They never caught the driver.

No one should have to outlive a child, Mehitable thinks, no matter what they've done. Lijah lost a daughter within months of losing his mother – small wonder he got old soon after that.

Looking around the group, Mehitable feels warmly towards them all. For all their histories, they are all there, together, and there seems something fine about that. Everyone looks philosophical, rather than miserable. It is a *had-a-good-innings* sort of funeral, after all; a spring funeral, grey and green – hopeful.

After the internment, they stand around, talking quietly. Then, with no one in particular suggesting it is time to leave, they turn and walk down the path towards the cars. Scarlet comes up to Mehitable, reaches out and slips an arm through hers, drawing her in close. Then, as if a little embarrassed by the gesture, she says, 'Still cold, in't it? For April. I'm glad he went in the spring. I think he would have liked that. He liked things green and new.'

Mehitable sighs. Then she stops, slips her arm from Scarlet's and says without looking at her. 'I think I want to go and see Mum.'

Scarlet looks at her older sister. 'You sure?'

Mehitable shrugs. 'Well I don't think I'll be coming back here much so it's now or never.'

'Shall I come with you?'

'If you like.'

Dan is walking ahead with Ida and Sally. Scarlet calls after them. 'Dan, we're going to see Mum. We'll catch you up.'

Dan raises the flat of his hand in acknowledgement.

The two sisters turn and link arms again, more firmly this time, a mutual gesture. They stride briskly back down the path. Mehitable thinks, nice to have Scarlet to myself for a bit.

The path reaches a crossroad. They both stop and look around. It is a large cemetery. The graves stretch in all directions.

'I found Gran's conch shell in our garden shed last week,' Scarlet says. 'I didn't even know we'd got it. Do you remember that conch shell?'

'I remember the canary.'

'What happened to the canary?'

'It's this way, isn't it?' Mehitable points to the right.

Scarlet shakes her head, 'Don't think so. She'll be in the old bit.'

Mehitable frowns.

Scarlet adds, gently, 'We're talking over thirty years, Billy. It's a long time ago.'

*A long time ago*: the worlds held captured in that phrase. Mehitable closes her eyes briefly, clutching Scarlet's arm for support.

She can feel Scarlet's concerned gaze upon her. She opens her eyes and straightens herself.

'Come on, then,' she says.

They find it quickly: a large headstone, facing the path. They stand staring at it for some time. Mehitable looks up and sees that they are being watched by a pair of pigeons sitting on the branch of a nearby tree. The pigeons look down at her. One of them cocks its head on one side.

'Do you know something,' says Scarlet, in a well-blow-me kind of voice. 'I'd completely forgotten that Gran was in there with her.'

'Yes, well . . .' Mehitable says, a small laugh in her voice.

Their father had turned up on her doorstep one day, and when she had opened the door, he had looked up at her and said, 'I buried your Gran last week.' That was the first they knew about it. Scarlet had refused to talk to him for six months. *This time he's gone too far*, she'd said. She had a point.

Then came Fenella's death, the awfulness of it, and for a while after that, nothing else had mattered.

'Is it quite right, do you think?' Scarlet says. 'Them being in together. I mean, shouldn't Mum be in with Dad?'

'I don't know, really.'

'Well, either way, it's a bit late now,' Scarlet adds.

They stare at the gravestone. In its inscription, Clementina and Rose's positions are reversed. Rose is on top. *In Loving Memory* the curved lettering reads, then in impressive capitals, *ROSIE SMITH*.

Scarlet nudges Mehitable. 'Her name was Rose, not *Rosie*. Now that definitely isn't right. You should have your proper name on your gravestone, shouldn't you?'

'I don't know when he had the gravestone put up,' says Mehitable. Then she reads the rest of the inscription out loud. As she does, she is unable to keep her voice from sounding dry. '*A loving wife, a mother dear, a faithful friend lies resting here.*'

Scarlet ignores the sarcasm. 'That's nice,' she says firmly.

Underneath, in smaller letters, is inscribed, *also of CLEMENTINA LEE*.

'Well, Mum's on top of her at last,' murmurs Mehitable.

'I should think the two of them are pretty much mixed up together by now,' says Scarlet. 'Have we time to go and see Nellie?'

'We should catch up with Dan, really. Nellie's all right.' I want to feel more, thinks Mehitable. All these years, I've made such a big deal about not coming here; you'd think I'd feel something more than this.

She draws her coat tighter around her, even though she isn't cold. *It doesn't feel like anything to do with us*, she thinks, staring down at the grave. *It feels like it's more to do with Mum and Gran together. It doesn't matter whether we're here or not.*

Scarlet glances over her shoulder. Mehitable follows her gaze and sees that the others have nearly reached the gate.

*And there's Dad all on his own over there, and Fenella waiting for her Tom, and none of us above ground matter to them – I'm glad I don't believe in ghosts*, she thinks. *If our lot could climb out of these graves at night there would be some good old family rows going on in Eastfield Cemetery while the rest of them were trying to sleep.*

Scarlet says, 'I'll leave you here for a bit, shall I?'

Mehitable replies quickly, 'No, I'm coming,' but Scarlet has stepped away. Still, Mehitable cannot move.

A picture of herself comes into her head. She was walking home from school one day, alone. It was lunchtime and she should have been going back into her class. A girl two years older than herself had pushed her over in the playground. Daniel wasn't there that day or he would have dealt with it. She was alone, with the jeering, and she had got right up and walked out of school.

She remembered walking home, through Sutton, crying all the way, with mud on her dress, feeling nothing but a raw need to be at home.

*How old was I? Not small, surely, if it was Sutton. Old enough.*

She had walked back to the cottage, but when she got there, she had known how angry her mother would be and was too frightened to go inside. She had stopped crying by then and knew she would be in trouble for having walked out of school in the middle of the day. She didn't know what to do, so she sat on the front step and waited. She had left her cardigan behind at school and was cold. After a while, she began to shiver.

Eventually, her mother had opened the front door, on her way out on some errand. She had started at the sight of Mehitable, shivering and muddy, on the step. Then she had sighed, wearily, stared down at her and said, 'What do *you* want?'

Mehitable stares at her mother's grave. I never have to come here again, she thinks to herself. This is the last time I will dwell on it. She turns away.

As she and Scarlet walk briskly down the path, she thinks, funny how there is this huge wall between the living and the dead – and funny that I should think it funny. I could have stood at the side of Mum's grave and cursed her for all eternity, or wept and forgiven her everything, and none of it would have made any difference. She can't hear me, and the words just echo back. When you look at a grave it's about as significant as looking down into a puddle. All you see is yourself, peering back up.

Maybe, one day, someone will come and look at my grave, maybe somebody I don't even know, and all they will see is themselves peering back, but they won't know that. They will think it's me. She finds the idea heartening. I will be thought about. Someone will wonder what it felt like to be me. And that is how we live on, in other people's heads, in their thinking things about us, even if they get it wrong.

It's a nice thought, she thinks, that nobody can know us, that we are thought about but safe, secret. She pulls Scarlet in close and smiles at her. Scarlet smiles back. As they approach the gate, she sees that Dan, their brother, is waiting for them. He holds out his arms.

# Subverting Hatred

# FAITH MEETS FAITH

*An Orbis Series in Interreligious Dialogue*
Paul F. Knitter & William R. Burrows, General Editors
Editorial Advisors
John Berthrong
Diana Eck
Karl-Josef Kuschel
Lamin Sanneh
George E. Tinker
Felix Wilfred

In the contemporary world, the many religions and spiritualities stand in need of greater communication and cooperation. More than ever before, they must speak to, learn from, and work with each other in order to maintain their vital identities and to contribute to fashioning a better world.

The FAITH MEETS FAITH Series seeks to promote interreligious dialogue by providing an open forum for exchange among followers of different religious paths. While the Series wants to encourage creative and bold responses to questions arising from contemporary appreciations of religious plurality, it also recognizes the multiplicity of basic perspectives concerning the methods and content of interreligious dialogue.

Although rooted in a Christian theological perspective, the Series does not limit itself to endorsing any single school of thought or approach. By making available to both the scholarly community and the general public works that represent a variety of religious and methodological viewpoints, FAITH MEETS FAITH seeks to foster an encounter among followers of the religions of the world on matters of common concern.

FAITH MEETS FAITH SERIES

# Subverting Hatred

## The Challenge of Nonviolence in Religious Traditions

*Edited by*
*Daniel L. Smith-Christopher*

ORBIS BOOKS

**Maryknoll, New York 10545**

Published in Association with the
Boston Research Center for the 21st Century

The Boston Research Center for the 21st Century (BRC) is an international peace institute that envisions a worldwide network of global citizens developing cultures of peace through dialogue and understanding. The Center was founded in 1993 by Daisaku Ikeda, a peace activist and president of Soka Gakkai International (SGI), one of the most dynamic and diverse Buddhist organizations in the world. BRC programs include public forums, scholarly seminars, and peacemaking circles that are diverse and intergenerational, as well as the development of multi-author books for university courses. BRC books about education, comparative religion, and global ethics have been used in more than 400 college courses to date. The Center is located at 396 Harvard Street, Cambridge, MA 02138. Tel: 617-491-1090; Fax: 617-491-1169; Email: center@brc21.org; Website: www.brc21.org.

Founded in 1970, Orbis Books endeavors to publish works that enlighten the mind, nourish the spirit, and challenge the conscience. The publishing arm of the Maryknoll Fathers and Brothers, Orbis seeks to explore the global dimensions of the Christian faith and mission, to invite dialogue with diverse cultures and religious traditions, and to serve the cause of reconciliation and peace. The books published reflect the views of their authors and do not represent the official position of the Maryknoll Society. To learn more about Maryknoll and Orbis Books, please visit our website at www.maryknoll.org.

Library of Congress Cataloging-in-Publication Data

Subverting hatred : the challenge of nonviolence in religious traditions / edited by Daniel L. Smith-Christopher.
    p. cm. — (Faith meets faith series)
  Includes bibliographical references.
  ISBN-13: 978-1-57075-747-1
  1. Nonviolence—Religious aspects.   I. Smith-Christopher, Daniel L.
  BL65.V55S83 2007
  205'.697—dc22

                                                    2007007671

# Contents

# Foreword

In the summer of 2000, two families with young children were vacationing on the shore of Lake Tiberias on the border between Israel and Syria. Suddenly one of the children swimming in the lake seemed about to drown. One of the fathers noticed the swimmer's distress and plunged into the water, swam out, and helped the child reach the shallows and safety. The young father, however, died of exhaustion before he himself could reach the shore. The two families were strangers. The parents of the endangered child were Jewish; the family whose father lost his life was Muslim.

This true story is related in *Crossing the Divide: Dialogue among Civilizations*, published by the United Nations Group of Eminent Persons immediately after the terrorist attacks on the United States on September 11, 2001. The twentieth century was rife with war and violence. Everyone hoped that the twenty–first would be a century of peace. Then the 9/11 attacks seemed to dash those hopes. This act of violence shocked the world, ironically, just when the United Nations had designated 2001 the Year of Dialogue among Civilizations. The shadow of the attacks still darkens the world, as armed conflicts attributed to ethnic and religious differences continue to break out throughout the world.

In 1998, in the confusion accompanying the end of the Cold War, the Boston Research Center for the 21st Century first published this book, *Subverting Hatred: The Challenge of Nonviolence in Religious Traditions,* to address the urgent situation head on. In it, scholars representing eight major religious traditions pooled their wisdom to transcend their differences. By discussing religious peace philosophies, they made a profound attempt to overcome hatred and find a path to universal peace. Very well received among specialists, the book has been used as a textbook in more than 175 courses at American universities, including Harvard, Columbia, Stanford, Tufts, and the Yale Divinity School, since it was published. As the founder of the Boston Research Center for the 21st

Century, I am extremely happy that the book became a resource to help students—the leaders of coming generations—to learn wisdom about building peace while deepening their understanding of religions other than their own.

When differing groups, each convinced of its own rectitude, clash in hatred and violence it only leads to stalemate. All over the world, frequent conflicts aggravate animosity and resentment, thus tragically escalating violence. This ever ancient, ever new *aporia* (complex question) could be called human karma. Overcoming it requires a reexamination and recapitulation of the wisdom accumulated in cultures, ethnic groups, and traditional religions. Never before has this process been more strongly hoped for, or more urgently needed.

In the Foreword I wrote to the earlier edition of this book, I discussed traditional Buddhist pacifism, concentrating on the doctrine of nonviolence, or *ahimsa*. Buddhism teaches that inherent deep in human life are both the evil spirit, which breeds hatred, and the good spirit, which generates compassionate love and trust. From the evil spirit emerge violence (wrath), greed (uncontrollable desire), ignorance (fundamental egoism), and racial, cultural, ethnic, and religious discrimination and prejudice. Driving a wedge between human society and nature, the evil spirit is destructive energy and a major cause of indirect and cultural violence among individuals, religions, and races.

The good spirit, on the other hand, is rugged spiritual power toward nonviolence and the control of desire. It is altruism and the equality and union that altruism generates. Its uniting energy establishes ties among individuals, societies, ethnic groups, and all humanity and makes possible harmonious symbiosis with nonhuman nature.

Political and economic approaches to the confusion of our times do no more than treat symptoms and cannot affect essential solutions to the hatred swirling around in the minds of humanity. Though it may seem the long way around, the only course is to break the chain of hatred and violence in the human heart and cultivate the soft power of good oriented toward creative symbiosis. Then we must put that soft power to use in the building of peace.

I am convinced that developing and extending the good in human life constitutes religion's most important role in contemporary civilization. Interreligious dialogue is the way to learn from each other and to educe from each religious tradition's brilliant spirit the way to develop the good that should be pursued.

This book is a forum for interreligious dialogue in that it sheds light on the wisdom not just of Buddhism, but also of many other traditional religions from all parts of the world and offers diverse viewpoints on how to create a global society of peace and symbiosis.

Religions must no longer be rallying points for actions that bring harm and suffering to others. What we require most today is sustenance for a revival of the humanity inherent in all of us and exemplified in the tragic incident related at the opening of this Foreword. Religions should serve that purpose. And to this end, humanistic education that cultivates universal values and spirituality—the humanism that lies at the heart of all religions—is indispensable.

Education and religion are inseparable. Without education religion can become self-righteous. The reverse side of religion is humane education. And education reveals its true value only when backed up by profound spirituality and philosophy.

The urgent task we face is building solidarity among world citizens by using humanistic education to overcome differences and expand the circle of mutual understanding. Young people who bear the responsibility for a future of peaceful symbiosis and who are the key to subverting hatred must be the heart of our efforts. I hope that this book will help open the door on a new age free of hatred.

In closing, I should like to express my heartfelt gratitude to the authors, who unstintingly assisted in the project, and to everyone who worked tirelessly on this revised edition.

—Daisaku Ikeda
*Founder, Boston Research Center for the 21st Century*
*President, Soka Gakkai International*

# Preface

Why publish a tenth anniversary edition of *Subverting Hatred: The Challenge of Nonviolence in Religious Traditions?* Sadly, non-violence in the fullest sense of the term, as Gandhi used it, presents an even more urgent challenge than it did in 1998 when Orbis Books released the first edition. Since the attack on the World Trade Center of 2001 and the subsequent launch of the U.S.-led "war on terrorism," there has been heightened interest in learning about world religions in general and Islam in particular, especially among young people on college campuses. *Subverting Hatred*, originally developed by the Boston Research Center for the 21st Century (BRC) as a supplemental text for use in college courses, evidently fills a widening gap in the current literature. Since it was first published, it has been used in more than 175 courses at U.S. colleges and universities, with current interest in the book nearly doubling that of the earlier years.

We've heard from professors that they have found our book especially helpful in challenging a mindset against all religion that has, understandably, taken root among younger generations coming of age in the post-9/11 era. Many young people now equate the religious impulse itself with violence. The authors in this book speak from within their own faith traditions, and yet they take a clear-eyed view of how their traditions and texts have been used to justify violence and war. They present each tradition's peace teachings in detail and make a case for the centrality of these teachings to the mainstream tradition.

Given the timeliness of the contents, we wondered at first whether the book needed any revision at all. As its tenth anniversary approached, Masao Yokota, president of the BRC, persuaded us to undertake a thorough review of the book to determine how it could be made more useful. Patti Marxsen, the publications manager of the BRC, worked with Daniel Smith-Christopher, the inspired editor of the original volume, to explore necessary revisions. Finally, it was decided that the original chapters were still current and the original book needed only the addition of discussion questions to help highlight their contemporary relevance. But we wanted to add another chapter on Islam to speak directly to the recent situation within the United States. Augmenting Rabia Terri Harris's able treatment of the subject of nonviolence in Islam, we've included a personal perspective from a Muslim scholar, Amir Hussain, who has had firsthand experience in challenging recent media portrayals of Islam. We also decided a second indigenous perspective would be useful. The original volume offered only one, and yet indigenous traditions are numerous throughout the world and are making increasingly important contributions to contemporary peacemaking, as exemplified by the indigenous roots of the restorative justice movement. We were gratified, therefore, when a Māori contributor, The Reverend Don Tamihere, agreed to offer his perspective.

The most important step we could take in updating the book, we thought, was to ask Daniel Smith-Christopher, the person who had provided such outstanding intellectual leadership on the first volume, to write an extensive new introduction taking into account recent global developments. As always, eschewing the predictable, he composed an introduction that takes recent events into account and goes on to make an eloquent and persuasive case *against* the notion that "everything is different now." His new introduction restates in even stronger terms the original impulse behind the book.

As this latest edition goes to press, the title *Subverting Hatred* seems timelier than ever. Our original concept of "subverting hatred" was carefully chosen to imply a radical change of heart, an out-of-the-ordinary human transformation. Religions, at their best, foster such deep changes within human beings. For young people worried about the world situation, we hope this volume encourages you to see the possibilities for change that exist within the human heart, like stars glimmering in a darkened sky. May you be heartened by what you find in these pages, sensing perhaps *your* unique mission to create peace and happiness in a suffering world.

We are grateful to BRC founder Daisaku Ikeda and to Professor Donald Swearer for the timely revisions they have made in the Foreword and Epilogue respectively, and are appreciative, once again, to Amy Morgante, Kali Saposnik, and Helen Casey for their outstanding editorial work on the original volume and to

Patti Marxsen, Helen Casey (again!), and James McCrea for ably organizing and editing this anniversary edition. Finally, we have theologian Paul Knitter to thank for introducing us to Bill Burrows and his colleague, Susan Perry, at Orbis Books' Faith Meets Faith series, with whom we have been honored to collaborate on *Subverting Hatred* and its companion volume, *Subverting Greed.*

—**Virginia Benson**
*Executive Director*
*Boston Research Center for the 21st Century*

# Introduction

# "Everything is different now"

## Reflections on the Tenth Anniversary Edition of *Subverting Hatred*

*Daniel L. Smith-Christopher*

Within a day of the horrendous destruction on September 11, 2001, I was contacted by a local news reporter who had discovered my role as director of Peace Studies at Loyola Marymount University of Los Angeles. During the brief introductions at the beginning of the phone call, she learned that I was a Quaker.

"Quakers? You people are pacifists, right?" The moment I acknowledged this to be true, her pleasant tone evaporated, and her next question quickly followed: "Soooo, *now* what do you people have to say?"

I passed over the distasteful use of "you people," understanding that the expectation was clear and unequivocal: I should now renounce my commitment to nonviolence in the light of the horrible violence in New York, Washington, and Pennsylvania just the day before. I assured her that now was a time for mourning, not a time for violence or violent language and that, in any case, I would not be renouncing my commitment to nonviolence. Clearly disappointed, she persisted briefly: "But haven't things changed for you now?" When I was not drawn into an argument with this question, she quickly lost interest in the conversation. There would be no sound byte from an angry former pacifist after all.

The reporter's call was motivated by a sentiment that I have heard innumerable times since that fateful day: "Everything is different now." For those of us who live and work and pray within religious traditions, this point of view represents a particularly popular sentiment, and thus it seems an important place to begin an introduction to the tenth anniversary edition of *Subverting Hatred: The Challenge of Nonviolence in Religious Traditions*. In this edition, each contributor to this volume has written within his or her own tradition, just as in the first edition. Most of the chapters are unchanged since they were first published in 1998. Some new material is included. And yet the same principle holds: we each bring the perspective of our faith to expressions like "Everything is different now." As a Christian professor of religion for whom Christian Scripture guides life and work, my approach to this sentiment is colored by over two millennia of human experience.

Initially, of course, the paradox is immediately clear. How can one reflect on ancient religious wisdom and on writings that are over two thousand years old in order to shed light on the idea that "Everything is different now"? If this is true, then most religious wisdom would be, by definition, irrelevant because so much of it was written before 2001. Those of us working within faith traditions have an obvious bias against the notion that any new situations or issues would render religious wisdom "outdated." But the life of faith is about understanding change as well as continuity. Thus, understanding how ancient wisdom applies to contemporary realities is one of the consolations and the challenges of faith.

In the Western religious traditions of Judaism and Christianity, we are familiar with the fact that the Hebrew Scriptures express violent sentiments at times. Sadly, we are less familiar with the fact that these same scriptures often seriously question human propensities to violence, and, furthermore, regularly express deeply peaceful sentiments as well. In reply to the notion that "everything is different," I would like to suggest listening to the "blood of Jezreel." It may seem like a strange image at first; how does one "listen" to blood? The Judeo-Christian Scriptures, however, feature a striking image in Genesis 4, where history's first act of lethal violence is narrated: Cain murders his brother Abel and God tells Cain, "Your brother's blood is crying out to me from the ground" (Genesis 4:10).[1] To listen to blood is to hear cries of injustice and pain. A very late pre-Christian Jewish writing called 4 Esdras repeats this older sentiment about God "hearing" blood, and places it in the context of justice and injustice: "Innocent and righteous blood cries out to me, and the souls of the righteous cry out continually" (4 Esdras 15:8).

"Listening to blood" is thus a particularly striking way to speak of examining issues of violence and nonviolence. Why is it, then, that when we hear the modern sentiment that "everything has changed" in the context of international relations, it is usually accompanied by the same old, decidedly unchanged call to vengeance and still more violence. If we could "listen to blood" more carefully, we might see this spirit of vengeance more clearly. Furthermore, I want to suggest that "listening to blood" offers a way to seriously question what only appears to be "justice" or "righteousness" in the "new" situation of the twenty-first century. As strange as it seems, as we pay attention to these kinds of images and tune in to biblical "debates," we may hear a more peaceful perspective through a better understanding of this notion of "listening to blood."

## THE BLOOD OF JEZREEL

In the historical narrative in the Bible (the second book of Kings), there is described what can only be called a religious-inspired coup d'état that occurred roughly eight centuries before the time of Jesus. In the story, a prophet anoints a military leader by the name of Jehu to be the new king while the old king, Ahab, is still on the throne. Jehu seems to believe that part of the implication of his selection is God's displeasure at the behavior of the existing monarchs, King Ahab and his wife, Queen Jezebel. Jehu further appears to have determined that he is in a position to not only fulfill God's will, but to consolidate his rule at the same time by wiping out all the remaining descendents of the House of Ahab. The Bible states that he did so apparently with the tacit approval of God (at least there is no question of Jehu's "righteousness" when the deed is assigned to Jehu by a representative of the Prophet):

> So Jehu got up and went inside; the young man poured the oil on his head, saying to him, "Thus says the LORD the God of Israel: I anoint you king over the people of the LORD, over Israel. You shall strike down the house of your master Ahab, so that I may avenge on Jezebel the blood of my servants the

prophets, and the blood of all the servants of the LORD. For the whole house of Ahab shall perish; I will cut off from Ahab every male, bond or free, in Israel." (2 Kings 9:6–8)

It is, however, precisely this apparent approval of Jehu's violent actions that raises nagging questions about the opposite notion expressed in the prophetic book of Hosea. There, the prophet angrily states that God, in fact, was not at all pleased by Jehu's act of zealous bloodshed. Hosea furthermore suggests that the House of Jehu will face God's judgment as a result of this act: "And the LORD said to him . . . in a little while I will punish the house of Jehu for the blood of Jezreel, and I will put an end to the kingdom of the house of Israel" (Hosea 1:4).

Might one surmise that acts of zealous violence in the heat of political rage are precisely what is in question here? Should Jehu have raised serious questions about the instruction to wipe out all the male descendents of Ahab? The prophet Hosea strongly indicates that he should have reconsidered this level of violence! Has unjustly shed blood "spoken" in the name of God once again? In fact, the phrase used by the prophet Hosea, "the blood of Jezreel," refers to the location of Jehu's violent act, and understanding a bit more about that location helps to set the context for this apparent dialogue between two biblical texts.

In the Jezreel valley, a horrendous injustice had taken place in the years before Jehu led his revolt. Jezebel, the queen of the Northern Kingdom, had violated the older Mosaic laws of just distribution of resources by favoring the wealthy and the aristocratic elite. According to the biblical tradition, Jezebel and her royal husband Ahab both wanted a particular piece of land that belonged to a modest Hebrew man named Naboth. The land, the story goes, featured a beautiful vineyard. In their greed for this potentially profitable vineyard, Jezebel had the original tribal owner falsely accused of a capital crime and summarily executed so that she could confiscate his land and present it to her husband, King Ahab. There is no suggestion that Ahab was shocked or disappointed at his wife's behavior. Thus, Ahab and Jezebel stand forever as the biblical symbols of economic and political greed that imposes its will on the lives of common people. Here was the first occasion of the blood of Jezreel.

With this context, we understand that Jehu's revolt was inspired by a prophet filled with righteous anger against Ahab and Jezebel's policies of greed. The prophet Elisha finally put an end to a royal line by anointing a new king, Jehu. And Jehu, who apparently believed that it was his God-anointed duty to avenge the crimes of Jezebel and her corrupt husband Ahab, gathered the male descendents of Ahab in the valley of Jezreel and had the lot of them butchered. When Jehu was instructed by the prophet to destroy the House of Ahab (2 Kings 9: 7), and later when he murdered Joram in the name of Naboth (2 Kings 9:26), Jehu thought it was vengeance, blood-for-blood, not unjustified murder. Was Jehu the anointed avenger of Jezreel? Or was Jehu the butcher of Jezreel?

The prophet Hosea engages in an impressive act of "subverting hatred" by proclaiming that God will hold Jehu responsible for this bloody act of political violence. Evil is at its most powerful when it is disguised as righteousness. Jehu believed he was zealous for truth but Hosea states that Jehu was mistaken. In the prophet Hosea, we have a striking example of ancient self-criticism reflecting on an apparently righteous act. From this story, we learn that it is precisely in times of great anger that we are called upon to reflect on whether "everything" is really different, or whether our perceptions and proximity to violence play a role in the human propensity for violence. If we can untangle this confusion, then the morality of the ages is still in force, the ethics of the faithful are still the guiding light.

When the book, *Subverting Hatred* was first published in 1998, was it really such a "different time"? Has "everything" changed since then? Religious reflection is, by its very nature, an act of reflecting on the wisdom of ages past. Considering how the past might inform present faith and practice helps to resist any claim that moral and ethical notions can become outdated, at least in any profound sense. This is why religion has a vital role to play in our response to violence today.

## CLAIMS AND COMPARISONS

In the fall of 2001, I was the director of an international gathering on our campus on the subject of genocide. Among the books that I read in preparation for directing this conference was a book co-edited by Levon Chorbajian and George Shirinian. The linguistic features of these two last names will immediately clarify a deeper significance of their work; both are Armenian scholars and, thus, members of a culture only too familiar with the wrenching trauma of genocidal events in their history.[2] But it was the title of their book that has stayed with me and continued to haunt me. It was one of those moments when you quickly read the title of a book in passing, and then suddenly realize with some horror what it is you have just read. Their collection of essays is entitled *Studies in Comparative Genocide.* "Comparative"??

That a book could ever have been written with such a title immediately calls into question any claim that "Everything is different now." Different for whom? Can we be so narrow in our perspective, so self-centered, so ill-informed? This popular phrase, heard not only from the American media but just as prominently from American politicians, can be interpreted to imply that the times are "different" because now *we* are the ones who have suffered; *I* am the one who feels vulnerable. "Everything is different now" presents a questionable claim that some peoples ought to be, somehow, exempt from the innocent suffering of humanity throughout history. How can we understand ourselves more clearly? The faithful of all religious traditions are called upon to reflect on the truth that our suffering is a comparative suffering because there have been so many others. This clarification was part of the impact of the original edition of *Subverting Hatred.* With this new edition, we hope to affirm this important perspective.

## A CHRISTIAN PERSPECTIVE

The ancient Hebrews, like their modern descendents, knew great tragedy. Part of the power of the biblical texts is that they come from a people so deeply familiar with the ravages of ancient empires, of political and economic greed, of destruction. Most of the Old Testament, of course, comes from that time after 587 B.C.E., when Jerusalem was destroyed by the Babylonian Empire under Nebuchadnezzar II. I have observed elsewhere that a majority of Christians mistakenly think that the Hebrew Bible, referred to by Christians as the Old Testament, focuses most prominently on those few years of Hebrew political power under David and Solomon. But this period of "United Monarchy" ran only from 1020 to 922 B.C.E., before the kingdom of David and Solomon divided into two warring factions. The North eventually fell to Assyrian domination in 722 B.C.E. and the South (Judah) finally fell in 587 B.C.E. Thus, the period of the "United Monarchy" is but a passing moment for the Hebrews.

A good deal of the rest of the Hebrew Scriptures contains deep reflections on conflict and suffering, especially after the tragedy of the Babylonian destruction of Jerusalem. One can almost sense in many Old Testament books that some ancient writers believed that "Everything is different now" in the ashes of destruction in 587 B.C.E. Thus, such a narrow vision that "our" suffering makes "everything different" is not new at all. Some of the writers of the Bible engage in similar questions about how anyone else could possibly know what they knew, suffer what they suffered, and endure what they endured. The poems written immediately following Nebuchadnezzar's destruction of Jerusalem that make up the short book entitled Lamentations plaintively ask: "Is it nothing to you, all you who pass by? Look and see if there is any sorrow like my sorrow, which was brought upon me" (Lamentations 1:12).

Again, the poet asks if anything can be compared to the suffering of the Hebrews: "What can I say for you, to what compare you, O daughter Jerusalem? To what can I liken you, that I may comfort you, O virgin daughter Zion? For vast as the sea is your ruin; who can heal you?" (Lamentations 2:13).

It is often the case that our suffering suggests to us that we are unusual in our pain, that somehow we have paid a greater price than others. But already in the ancient writings of the Hebrew Bible, the prophets knew it was not quite so simple. The prophet Amos reminded his listeners that there were even comparisons to God's compassion and even God's involvement with the destinies of other nations. His voice offers this sobering insight: "Are you not like the Ethiopians to me, O people of Israel? says the LORD. Did I not bring Israel up from the land of Egypt, and the Philistines from Caphtor and the Arameans from Kir?" (Amos 9:7).

It is the vision of another prophet, Isaiah, that peace will be for all nations, for all peoples who stream to Zion and beat their swords into plows and their spears into orchard tools. All nations that are weary with suffering and warfare will come to know the need for a change—all nations, including the Hebrew people themselves:

> In days to come the mountain of the LORD's house shall be established as the highest of the mountains, and shall be raised above the hills; all the nations shall stream to it. Many peoples shall come and say, "Come, let us go up to the mountain of the LORD, to the house of the God of Jacob; that he may teach us his ways and that we may walk in his paths." For out of Zion shall go forth instruction, and the word of the LORD from Jerusalem. He shall judge between the nations, and shall arbitrate for many peoples; they shall beat their swords into plowshares, and their spears into pruning hooks; nation shall not lift up sword against nation, neither shall they learn war any more. (Isaiah 2:2–4)

Finally, when Jesus announces his mission of proclaiming release to the captives and sight to the blind in Luke 4, it is foreigners, the "others," he mentions as he cites the Old Testament examples of prophets who actually healed foreigners like Naaman the Syrian and the Sidonian woman. Here we see an example of God's concern for all people. Perhaps everything is not so different now.

In our moments of suffering, it is part of our God-given responsibility to know that we are not the only ones who suffer loss; we are not the only ones who are frightened or have been frightened. Perhaps a road that is far too little traveled is the road that leads to greater understanding of the fear and suffering of our fellow humans throughout the world. All people are God's people, and each life is the work of God's hand. The idea that we are special, that we are privileged, that we are unique too often invites the notion that we are above thoughts of sharing and identification with the suffering of others. Furthermore, persisting in our thinking that everything has changed suggests that old rules no longer apply, that old moral visions or ancient ethics of love and compassion are no longer valid. And yet, if anyone should question the privileging of "our own people" in this world—whoever those people might be—it ought to be those whose sacred writings demand that we humble ourselves before the creator of all peoples. So as a Christian and a professor of the Hebrew Bible, I feel compelled to ask, "For whom is everything suddenly different?" Human suffering is as great as it has always been. And the call to nonviolence is just as powerful and just as challenging today as it always has been. Evil is ever-present and evil, as we have seen, is rarely clearly recognized as evil by those involved. For the religious man and woman of the twenty-first century, evil is perhaps best expressed by Paul's New Testament sentiment that even "Satan can appear as an angel of light" (2 Cor. 11:14).

This image leads to one of the profound insights that comes from reflecting on the religious inspiration of violence in the modern world. Recalling Hosea's anger that Jehu did not question his orders to destroy the House of Ahab suggests to me, as a Christian, that I must learn to interrogate the light, not merely question the darkness. I must examine the treasured ideas I hold about what I think is right and righteous, not just search through the refuse of ideas that are clearly wrong, in order to begin to understand evil and violence in the world today. Other traditions may have other versions of this challenging insight. But from a Christian perspective, the danger of darkness concealed in light is clearly expressed in the Bible.

## THE ROLE OF RELIGION

In the years since September 11, 2001, as we have seen war and violence increase in the name of fighting terrorism, we often read that religion itself is the problem. In his book entitled *The End of Faith: Religion, Terror, and the Future of Reason*, the young philosopher Sam Harris declared in 2004 that religion is largely to blame for modern violence. Harris's thesis obviously struck a chord, as it was awarded the 2005 PEN Award for Nonfiction. Similarly, the very title of Jack Nelson-Pallmeyer's book published in 2005 asks the ultimate question we must face: *Is Religion Killing Us?*

In response, I can only remind the reader that part of the strength of the original assignment given to the writers of *Subverting Hatred* was the specific instruction to question our own traditions. Part of the honesty of dialogue that is so rare in modern religious discussions and debates is the ability to acknowledge the mistakes, problems, and difficulties of our own histories of religious practice so that we can then more effectively highlight the gifts of wisdom and insight that our traditions also offer to ourselves and to others. These gifts of wisdom then become prophetic criticisms of our own behavior, and not trophies to show off to others. After all, guidance must be allowed to speak first to the faithful within each tradition before it is humbly offered to those outside the tradition.

The use of righteousness to justify violence is a perversion of such gifts of wisdom. Perhaps, as we look more critically at our own traditions, we should remember to ask, Who pays the cost of our ideas of righteousness? Who suffers as a result of our good, our loyalty, our patriotism, our zeal? One of the most troubling aspects of the phrase "Everything is different now" is the implication that now we are somehow released from the guidance and wisdom of the ages. In place of this wisdom, we have too often opened our world to gut reactions of anger and frightened vengeance. It is the duty of the faithful adherent of religious nonviolence to reflect not only on that which may have changed, but also to stand firmly for that which has not changed. It is precisely because everything is not so different now that ancient wisdom and faith are still relevant in the modern world. Houses of worship can be places where we question the light and the dark, the apparently good as well as the obviously evil. If our politics, or our economics, or our very lives do not draw deeply from the wisdom of our various faith traditions in making peace, then we betray our faith traditions.

Within the pages of *Subverting Hatred* are several invitations to consider how faith not only guides those within our various traditions, but also how the insights and gifts of one spiritual tradition can enlighten and enrich those from other religious viewpoints. Sometimes these insights on peacemaking and spirituality can send us back to our own traditions with new eyes. As a Christian, I believe that deeply meaningful hours can be spent reflecting on the Four Noble Truths of the Buddha. Does not Jesus also speak of the impermanence of this life and the dangers of storing up treasures on earth rather than in heaven? Do not Tam Wai Lun's reflections on Chinese communities worshipping together raise interesting questions about the separation of Christians from each other? Finally, doesn't the profoundly insightful Islamic idea about the inward *jihad*—the struggle with evil within ourselves—remind Christians of Paul's warning us that we do not fight enemies of flesh and blood, but spirits of evil in the world? (Ephesians 6:12). Such insights are the gifts of listening to each other. Not only do we learn more about others, we learn more about ourselves. Surely this is one of the most hopeful results of listening to "the challenge of nonviolence in religious traditions"! Listening to one another presents special challenges at this time for Muslims and Christians, and so we are honored to have—in addition to the original chapter on Islam by Rabia Terri Harris—a new contribution from Dr. Amir Hussain who reflects on the challenges of living as a Muslim in North America since 9/11.

As the religious scholars who have come together to write *Subverting Hatred* demonstrate, faith is not a matter of a passing thought, a gut reaction, or an emotional appeal. Our reactions to crises must also involve quiet study, reflection, and questioning; that is who we are as human beings. In truth, people of faith ought to be the last ones taken in by the notion that "Everything is different now." We know better. Some things change. But there is something deeply embedded in centuries of religious wisdom that remains true, remains the same, and remains a guiding light for our lives, even in the twenty-first century.

## A CALL TO ACTION

The main purpose of *Subverting Hatred* is an invitation to reflect on religious traditions in the context of the current debates about violence and nonviolence, and to offer resources from within religious traditions that would support a nonviolent approach to pressing issues. Each tradition presented here offers its own understanding of how to respond to violence and how to nurture nonviolence. In these pages we encounter reflections on heroes of the faith like the "Muslim Gandhi," Badshah Khan, or the Buddhist activists Thich Nhat Hanh and Dr. B. R. Ambedkar. The invitation to reflect on the deep meaning of such examples of living faith is still the main benefit of a collection of writings such as this, but any call to reflection must acknowledge that eventually action ought to follow reflection. It is my conviction, furthermore, that in the twenty-first century our actions as adherents of nonviolence ought to reflect some new realities, even as they steadfastly resist the notion that "everything" has changed. And finally, we should take care that the challenges facing any move toward nonviolent actions in the twenty-first century include creative planning so that they are religiously inspired actions characterized as *invitational, creative, entrepreneurial, hybrid*, and *digital*. Let us consider each of these qualities as part of an action-oriented stance.

## INVITATIONAL

I believe that any actions planned, either as a result of reading *Subverting Hatred*, or a result of other forms of contemplation on nonviolence in a faith context, ought to be invitational. That is, actions should, by their nature, be inviting to others so that all can understand and even participate. Our use of religious symbols, stories, and rituals ought to be as transparently positive and peaceful as possible. But, at the same time, we need not cave in to modern anti-religious sentiments that would suggest that we abandon all use of our symbols, stories, or rituals as inappropriate. However, the symbols, stories, and rituals we choose ought to be typified by their inclusive, invitational, and open character rather than characterized by exclusiveness reserved for the devoted (thus implying proselytizing masked as peacemaking!). We should offer those gifts from within our traditions to invite participation in the common goals of peacemaking. Each of the traditions represented in this work offers luminous and sparkling gifts of peace. Dr. Shastri's Hindu reflections on vegetarianism, for example, certainly invite all of us to consider whether our religious ethics are properly expressed in our consumption habits.

## CREATIVE

Our actions should be creative and make use of the gifts of many people within each of our tradition's gifts of art and music and story, as well as careful and critical religious analysis and thought. Performance offered as a gift is by its very nature both creative and invitational. In the Christian tradition, historically, one might note the once inescapable presence of religious art in the form of cathedrals that called upon whole communities of skilled artists and craftsmen and often served as focal points for communal identity and faith. The joint temple festivals in Tam Wai Lun's reflections on the Confucian tradition are also suggestive of gift.

## ENTREPRENEURIAL

The reality of modern action is that it must often find ways to finance itself creatively and with some innovation. This is what I mean by peacemaking that is entrepreneurial. How can we harness the ever present reality of consumption toward the ends of peacemaking? The Fair Trade movement, where producers in developing countries are offered fair and just prices for their production is a wonderful start. How can our peacemaking and advocacy of nonviolence translate into the consumption of such "products of peace," and thus also generate the funds necessary for the work to continue?

## HYBRID

Peacemaking in the modern world must be "hybrid," that is expressed in terms that communicate the cross-cultural, multi-cultural, and trans-cultural realities of the modern world. To speak from our various traditions is not the same thing as being chained to traditional means or methods of expressing those traditions. Furthermore, with an open, hybrid approach we can borrow from one another as an expression of solidarity with one another. This is both an opportunity, but also a danger. It is one thing for Christians to be deeply impressed with the Four Noble Truths and then reflect back on their own teachings, but we must never crudely appropriate a tradition from outside our own faith without the full participation of those from whom this tradition is borrowed. Let us no longer, for example, borrow drums or rituals from Native-American spirituality without Native permission and participation in their use. Here is an appropriate place to reflect on our two indigenous contributions in this book from a Māori and Native-American perspective, both of which struggle with the oppression of stereotypes and the usurping of their sacred traditions by those with little or no appreciation of the peoples from whom they are taken.

## DIGITAL

Finally, our work must be digital. By this I merely invite us all to make full use of the potentially dramatic impact of communication technologies from the Internet to the use of simple video and audio devices to spread a message of peace. In the face of sophisticated use of these technologies by the purveyors of hatred, people of faith must become more adept in spreading their ideas, values, and insights. Like all of these practical thoughts, a more technological approach to faith will require cooperation and mutual instruction. But this is precisely the point—peacemaking is by definition a communal act, and faith, too, is communal.

Notice how Rabbi Milgrom's discussion of the ritual or worship context of passages can dramatically change how that passage is "heard." His call to "re-context" the violence in older traditions, and even some of the more violent passages of our various written traditions, is a fascinating call to "re-contextualize violence" using modern media of peace. In short, let us overwhelm violence by performing peace!

In closing, we Quakers have a saying that is often spoken when we hear or read a profound thought that strikes us as not only uncommonly wise, but potentially even inspired by God. We say that this brother or sister has "spoken to our condition." As each contributor in this volume shares his or her own faith tradition and its view of nonviolence, it continues to be our hope that this tenth-anniversary edition of *Subverting Hatred* will "speak to our condition." In a world where so much violence comes from our not carefully "listening to blood," we also hope that this book will demonstrate the continued relevance of faith traditions.

### REFERENCES

*New Revised Standard Version of the Bible*, 1989.

Chorbajian, Levon, and George Shirinian. *Studies in Comparative Genocide*. New York: Palgrave Macmillan, 1999.

Harris, Sam. *The End of Faith: Religion, Terror, and the Future of Reason*. New York: Norton, 2004.

Nelson-Pallmeyer, Jack. *Is Religion Killing Us?* New York: Continuum, 2005.

## NOTES

[1] All quotations from the Bible are from the *New Revised Standard Version*, 1989.

[2] Atrocities perpetrated by the Ottoman Empire against the Armenian people during the first quarter of the twentieth century are known as the Armenian Genocide. Over a half million people died between 1915 and 1923.

# 1

# Jainism and Nonviolence

## *Christopher Key Chapple*

The Jain religion, currently practiced by approximately four million persons in India and several hundred thousand scattered across the globe, emphasizes the observance of nonviolence as its central teaching. The themes and practices of the Jain religious tradition extend backward into the early phases of Indian history. Above all else, nonviolence, care for animals, care for monks and nuns, and worldly renunciation characterize this important faith.

### EARLY JAINISM

The earliest records of Indian religiosity can be found in the ruins and artifacts of the stone cities of the Indus Valley (*circa* 3500 B.C.E.). On various steatite seals, one finds depictions of animals being honored and adorned and meditating figures that indicate a proto-yoga tradition. It can be speculated that this proto-yoga tradition eventually gave rise to institutionalized monastic religious orders, including the Jainas, the Buddhists, the Ajivikas (who became extinct in the thirteenth century), and various sects of Yogis

Christopher Key Chapple is a professor of theological studies and director of Asian and Pacific studies at Loyola Marymount University in Los Angeles, where he also served as associate academic vice-president. He has authored or edited more than a dozen books on religion and ecology including *Reconciling Yogas* (SUNY Press, 2003), *Hinduism and Ecology* (Harvard Center for the Study of World Religions, 2000), and *Jainism and Ecology* (Harvard Center for the Study of World Religions, 2002).

*1*

and Sadhus. These traditions, which emphasize renunciation of the world, involve embarking on a quest for liberation from all societal norms through the embrace of anyone of a number of techniques for achieving spiritual ecstasy and liberation.

The *Rgveda*, the earliest of India's texts, describes the renouncers of India as follows:

> The longhaired one carries within himself fire
> and elixir and both heaven and earth.
> To look at him is like seeing heavenly
> brightness in its fullness.
> He is said to be light himself
> The ascetics, girdled with wind,
> are clad in brownish dust (naked).
> They follow the path of the wind
> when the gods have entered them.
> Wandering in the track of celestial nymphs and sylvan beast,
> the longhaired one has knowledge of all things,
> and with his ecstasy inspires all beings. (*Rgveda* 10.136)

The presence of the wandering, meditating ascetic has been part of India's landscape since the time of the Indus Valley Civilization. These proto yogis apparently held animals in high regard, as many images of meditators include groups of animals clustered around in seeming obeisance, and certainly without any fear of their human companion. Although we have no written source to confirm the attitudes toward animals in these portraitures, later texts of the Jain tradition attest to the primacy of a nonviolent ethic that looks benevolently on all beings.

By the time of historical Jainism (perhaps as early as 800 B.C.E.), *ahimsa*, or nonviolence, which includes not only abstention from physical harm to humans but also to animals, insects, and to a certain degree plants, becomes a hallmark of renouncer traditions. The earliest historical figure associated with this early tradition, Parsvanatha, taught a doctrine of harmlessness, or *ahimsa*, building on earlier practices. As a *Sramana*, or renouncer, he advocated the protection of various forms of life and perhaps advanced the systematized observance of religious vows that include nonviolence, truthfulness, not stealing, and nonpossession. According to the *Kalpa Sutra*, Parsvanatha lived 30 years as a householder, attained *kevala*, or liberation, 83 days after renouncing the world, and taught for 70 years as a Kevalin, an enlightened being, gathering 16,000 male monastic followers, 38,000 nuns, and thousands of lay disciples. He conducted his work in northeast India, primarily around the city of Varanasi, or Banaras. During his lifetime, thousands reportedly attained perfection. In his one hundredth year, he ascended Mount Sammeta and fasted for one month; finally "stretching out his hands, he died, freed from all pains" (Jacobi 1884, 275).

Although these stories of Parsvanatha are somewhat shrouded in hagiography and exact confirmation of his dates is difficult, several features indicated in these tales persist in contemporary Jainism: the predominance of women in religious orders, the keen adherence to vows of nonviolence, and the practice of fasting to death when the end is near.

The earliest textual material we have for the Jaina tradition is the first part of the *Acaranga Sutra*, recorded within several decades of the death of the twenty-fourth and last Tirthankara, Mahavira Vardhamana, also known as the Victor, the Jina, from which the word Jaina derives. This text dates from the fourth or fifth century B.C.E. (Dundas 1992, 20). Several passages attest to the Jaina commitment to nonviolence, providing the complete articulation of this cardinal principle of Sramanic religiosity in India:

All breathing, existing, living, sentient creatures should not be slain, nor treated with violence, nor abused, nor tormented, nor driven away.
This is the pure, unchangeable, eternal law. (I.4.1)

Injurious activities inspired by self-interest lead to evil and darkness. This is what is called bondage, delusion, death, and hell. To do harm to others is to do harm to oneself.
"You are the one whom you intend to kill!
You are the one you intend to tyrannize over!"
We corrupt ourselves as soon as we intend to corrupt others.
We kill ourselves as soon as we intend to kill others. (I.5.5)

With due consideration preaching the law of the mendicants, one should do no injury to one's self,
nor to anybody else,

nor to any of the four kinds of living beings.
A great sage, neither injuring nor injured,
becomes a shelter for all sorts of afflicted creatures,
even as an island, which is never covered with water.
(I.6.5.4)

Knowing and renouncing severally and singly
actions against living beings in the regions
above, below, and on the surface,
everywhere and in all ways—
the wise one neither gives pain to these bodies,
nor orders others to do so,
nor assents to their doing so.
We abhor those who give pain to these bodies
(of the earth, of water, of fire, of air, of plants, of insects,
of animals, of humans).
Knowing this, a wise person should not cause
any pain to any creatures. (I.7.1.5)

Each of these quotes attests to the centrality of avoidance of harm in the Jaina religion.

Stemming from this perception that harm to others injures oneself, the Jainas assiduously practiced vows to prevent such transgressions. By the time of Mahavira (540 to 468 or 599 to 527 B.C.E.) five vows guided the lives of all observant Jainas: nonviolence *(ahimsa)*, truthfulness *(satya)*, not stealing *(asteya)*, sexual restraint *(brahmacarya)*, and nonpossession *(aparigraha)*. These became universal among religious mendicants, appearing in slightly revised form in Buddhist monastic manuals and verbatim in Patanjali's *Yoga Sutras*.

## PHILOSOPHICAL JAINISM

During the next major phase of Jaina, which occurred in the second century of the common era, the scholar Umasvati articulated a philosophy of nonviolence that describes a universe brimming with souls *(jiva)* weighted by karmic material *(dravya)*, many of which hold the potential for freeing themselves from all karmic residue and attaining spiritual liberation. He laid the foundation for a theory of multiple karmic colors and a path of spiritual ascent through 14 stages, culminating in total freedom, or *kevala*. His theories of karma and rebirth provided both a physical and metaphysical underpinning to support the practice of nonviolence.

According to Umasvati's *Tattvartha Sutra*, countless beings *(jiva)* inhabit the universe, constantly changing and taking new shape due to the fettering presence of karma, described as sticky and colorful. The presence of karma impedes the soul on its quest for perfect solitude and liberation. By first accepting this view of reality and then carefully abiding by the five major vows (nonviolence, truthfulness, not stealing, sexual restraint, and nonpossession), the aspirant moves toward the ultimate goal of untrammeled spirituality. At the pinnacle of this achievement, all karmas disperse and the perfected one *(siddha)* dwells eternally in omniscient *(sarvajna)* solitude *(kevala)*.

This framework outlined by Umasvati grows to include the articulation of 148 distinct karmic configurations or *prakrtis*, to be overcome through a successive progression through 14 stages of spiritual ascent or *gunasthanas* (Tatia 1994, 279–285). Success in this process rests in the careful observance of *ahimsa*, through which one gradually dispels all karmas. Although no Jaina has achieved this state of ayogi *kevala* for several hundred years, thousands of Jaina monks and nuns in India practice a lifestyle that seeks to restrict and eliminate all obstructive karma through the observance of monastic vows.

To illustrate the nature of karma, a traditional story narrates how the personality types are associated with each of the primary five colors *(lesya)* of karma:

> A hungry person with the most negative black *lesya* karma uproots and kills an entire tree to obtain a few mangoes. The person of blue karma fells the tree by chopping the trunk, again merely to gain a handful of fruits. Fraught with gray karma, a third person spares the trunk but cues off the major limbs of the tree. The one with orangish-red karma carelessly and needlessly lops off several branches to reach the mangoes. The fifth, exhibiting white or virtuous karma, "merely picks up ripe fruit that has dropped to the foot of the tree." (J. Jaini 1916, 47)

This story inspires many Jains to work at developing daily practices that work at lightening the quality of one's karma. For instance, many Jains fast regularly, particularly toward the final third of their projected life span, in an attempt to guarantee a spiritually auspicious future birth.

## MEDIEVAL AND CONTEMPORARY JAINISM

In the third stage of Jainism, scholars such as Haribhadra in the eighth century and Hemacandra in the twelfth century, along with many others, have grappled with the issue of how best to articulate Jaina philosophy and practice, particularly in light of the broader Indian culture and society (see Cort 1998). During this time and up to the present, the Jainas have been quite effective in preaching the doctrine of nonviolence and convincing many Hindus and some Muslims to minimize the harm they cause, particularly to animals.

In the practice of nonviolence, Jainas refrain from all meat or meat-based foods. They avoid silk, which requires the slaughter of innumerable silk worms in its production. They participate in occupations that minimize harm to animals and humans, such as accounting, law, and certain forms of manufacturing. They actively seek to spare animals from slaughter or harm by buying animals from slaughterhouses for release and by maintaining extensive animal shelters.

Anthropologist Lawrence A. Babb describes nonviolence in the Jaina tradition as central to Jain identity. He also notes that this links Jainism to the asceticism practiced on a modified basis by the laypersons and in most advanced form by its monks and nuns: "It is clear that faithful adherence to Jainism's highest ethic, which is nonviolence, necessarily means a radical attenuation of interactions with the world and, in this sense, nonviolence and asceticism can be seen as two sides of the same coin" (Babb 1996, 9). He goes on to note that

> Ascetics drink only boiled water so as to avoid harming small forms of life that would otherwise be present. Their food must be carefully inspected to be sure that it is free of small creatures. They must avoid walking on ground where

there might be growing things, and they do not bathe so as not to harm minute forms of water-borne life. An ascetic carries a small broom *(ogha)* with which to brush aside small forms of life before sitting or lying. He or she also carries a mouth-cloth *(muhpatti)* with which to protect small forms of life in the air from one's hot breath. They may not use fire. They may not fan themselves lest harm come to airborne life. Although they are permitted to sing (and do so during rituals), they are not permitted to clap or count rhythms on their knees because of the potential lethality of their percussions. They may not use any artificial means of conveyance. (56)

However, it must be kept in mind that not all Jainas take up the rigorous vows reserved for monks and nuns. The 35 rules of conduct for the lay community stipulate that Jains must not enter into occupations that result in the "wholesale destruction of life" (Sangave 1997, 165). Specifically, Jains may not be "butchers, fishermen, brewers, wine-merchants, or gun-makers," nor may they take up jobs that involve "great use of fire, cutting of trees or plants, castrating bullocks, clearing of jungles by employment of fire, drying up lakes, rivers, etc." (165). Although Jains in the southern part of India are largely agriculturists and in years past many served as generals and warriors, they occupy a vast array of employment niches. Sangave has noted that they are "moneylenders, bankers, jewelers, cloth-merchants, grocers, and industrialists [and in] the legal, engineering, medical, and teaching professions" as well as in various departments of the Central and State Governments of India (166).

Jainism largely focuses on personal discipline. Its emphasis on strict observances of the nonviolence ethic has caused the tradition to draw criticism as "extremist" throughout Indian history; many of the early converts to Buddhism were drawn to preaching of moderation and the Middle Path. Because of its emphasis on interiority and a rigorous applied ethical code, and because of its alliances with power particularly in the southern Indian state of Karnataka during the medieval period, it might be asserted that the nonviolent ethic of the Jain tradition holds little in common with the Western tradition of peace movements.

Whereas most Jain monks and nuns in history have been in a sense cloistered from worldly involvement by their vows, a few exceptional Jain leaders have worked to influence the broader sphere through announcing their religious commitment and seeking to change the views of others. One example is Jincandrasuri II (1541–1613), the fourth and last of the Oadagurus, leaders of the Khartar Gacch (a subdivision of the Svetambara sect) who gained great fame for their religiosity. He traveled to Lahore in 1591 where he greatly influenced the Mughal emperor Akbar the Great. Jincandrasuri convinced Akbar to stop an infanticide planned after one of Akbar's sons fathered a daughter under inauspicious astrological influences; a Jaina ceremony was held to mitigate the situation. As noted by Babb, who has written extensively on the Dadaguru tradition,

> Because of Jinabhadrasuri's influence Akbar protected Jain places of pilgrimage and gave orders that the ceremonies and observances of Jains were not to be hindered. He also forbade the slaughter of animals for a period of one week per year. (Babb 1996, 124)

In addition to these recorded historical instances, several miracles attributed to Jinabhadrasuri continue to inspire Khartar Svetamabra Jains in north India.

A contemporary activist leader of Jainism, Acarya Tulsi (1914–1997) similarly challenges the notion that monks utterly disengage from worldly life. Acarya Tulsi was appointed head of the Svetambara Therapanthi sect in 1936 at the young age of 22. For 58 years he served as its preceptor and leader and took up the task of promulgating the Jain principle of nonviolence to a wide audience and brought Jainism into dialogue with some of the broader contemporary issues of environmental degradation and nuclear escalation. He relinquished the office of Acarya to Yuvacharya Mahapragya in 1994. Deeply concerned about the prolongation of the Second World War, he wrote a plea for peace in June 1945 in which he articulated nine rules or universal basic principles that provide an outline of how to apply nonviolent principles. When Mahatma Gandhi received a published version of the following list, he lamented that it had not been published sooner.

1.  The principle of nonviolence should be widely propagated throughout the world. Strong dislike and hatred for violence should be aroused in the hearts of mankind. *"Life is as dear to others as to one's own self, and not death."* This lesson should be widely taught and made the very breath of everyone. That will be sowing the seeds of peace.
2.  Anger, pride, deceitfulness and discontent are the root causes of all unrest. All dispute and discord in this world owe their origin to these four causes. Every effort should be made to minimize these in every human being.
3.  Outlook of education should be changed. Material gain or worldly ascendancy should never be the theme of education, rather stress should be laid on the development of inner self. Efforts should be made to achieve this end by every State and by International Cooperation.
4.  The basis of all future governments should be justice, equity and good conduct and they should not be for exploitation or for selfish interests.
5.  The scientific discoveries for material gains should be discontinued. At least they should never be used for the purposes of war.
6.  More and more propaganda should be undertaken to preach real universal fraternity instead of national solidarity. Every endeavor should be made to minimize economic and political rivalry. Nationalization which encourages young people to clash with other states should never be preached.
7.  The habit of hoarding more than is necessary should be curtailed. Mutual rivalry, jealousy and the temptation to usurp power from others should be reduced. There should be no attempt to usurp or encroach on others' land or property as this is the cause of all armed conflicts.
8.  No kind of unjust and oppressive steps should be taken by any person, nation or state against the weak, the depressed or the colored or other particular castes or communities. Principles of justice, impartiality and humanity should be more and more developed and practiced by every person, nation and state.
9.  No principle or religion should be propagated by use of ordinary force or armed force or undue influence, etc.

> Every thing is more easily understood by the right type
> of education and honest preaching than by use of force.
> For preaching any idea or faith, no kind of force or
> undue advantage should be taken and along with this
> all legitimate steps should be taken to protect religious
> truth. Religious freedom should be granted to every indi-
> vidual. (Kumar 1997, 42)

These principles continue to ring true more than 50 years after
they were written; conflicts throughout the world today, including those in South Asia, can be interpreted as violations of one or
more of these basic rules.

On March 2, 1949, Acarya Tulsi initiated a campaign of self-
correction that garnered attention throughout India. He issued a
list of vows to be followed by all in order to promote nonviolence
and peace. In light of the social problems made evident in the years
surrounding the Second World War and in the context of an India
newly liberated by the activism of Mahatma Gandhi, Vinobha
Bhave, and others, these vows helped provide a code of conduct
for universal application:

1. I will not willfully kill any innocent creature.
2. I will not attack anybody.
3. I will not take part in violent agitations or in any
   destructive activities.
4. I will believe in human unity.
5. I will practice religious toleration.
6. I will observe rectitude in business and general
   behavior.
7. I will set limits to the practice of acquisition.
8. I will not resort to unethical practices in elections.
9. I will not encourage socially evil customs.
10. I will lead a life free from addictions.
11. I will always be alert to the problem of keeping the
    environment pollution-free. (Kumar 1997, 71)

As he walked through India on several occasions, and as he
prepared his own monks, nuns, and lay disciples to promulgate
Jain teachings, Acharya Tulsi worked for the social uplift of India.
He campaigned against the ostracism of widows, child marriages,

and ostentatious funeral practices. He sought to heal the rift between North and South India in the 1960s. He sent many disciples to the Punjab during the 1970s and 1980s to help quell the rampant terrorism during the height of the Hindu-Sikh rift. During the stock market scandals of 1994, he worked to heal difficulties within the Indian Parliament (Kumar 1997, 33–36). He also lent support to various environmental initiatives, including the 1995 Ladnun Declaration for a Nonviolent World and Ecological Harmony through Spiritual Transformation. Recognized by Mahatma Gandhi, Jawarlal Nehru, and Indira Gandhi, as well as such Indian Presidents as Sarvepalli Radhakrishnan, V. V. Giri, Fakruddin Ali Ahmed, and Gyani Zail Singh, Acarya Tulsi provided a model of how commitment to nonviolence and a life of asceticism can have a positive effect on the world.

## CONCLUSION

Jain nonviolence, while not necessarily opposed to social uplift, focuses most directly on one's own spirituality, emphasizing that the avoidance of harm propels one away from karmic negativity toward increasing states of purification. I do not want to suggest that we dismiss the Jain vision as eccentric, extreme, or irrelevant. Rather, I would like to suggest that the virtue theory of the Jainas might help us with the perpetual challenge of how to integrate a vision of harmony and peace with the realities of a world fraught with suffering.

One of the most appealing aspects of India's renouncer traditions (Jainism, Yoga, and Buddhism) can be found in their emphasis on karma theory and voluntarism. According to these systems, the world through which we move depends, in large part, upon our own interpretations and projections. Due to our own personal choices, we set our own course, whether by force of habit or through a process of careful reflection and self-determination. Karmic theory suggests that by probing into the causes of our behavior, change can be effected.

The changeful choice advocated by each of these traditions requires a framing of life within the constraints of the ethical principle of nonviolence. Violent activities, stemming from an objectification of others and a consequent desire to control others, must be stemmed and substituted with nonviolent behavior. This requires a willingness to enter into a commitment to adopt new modalities of thought and action.

From a Jaina perspective, in order for nonviolence to be integrated into one's personal and interpersonal life and into work environments, one needs to investigate ways in which to foster virtuous conduct, cooperation, and communication. In the process, one might need also to look at the broader world situation and be willing to take risks. These risks might entail an evaluation of leisure activities. Do I cause harm to myself or others in the interests I pursue? One might also need to evaluate the quantity of goods one consumes and how much garbage results. Furthermore, one might need to reflect on the effect food has on one's body, and the effect of food production on the wider environment.

As we enter into the twenty-first century, violence will continue to confront us. Some violence will occur in our communities throughout our nation, and between nations worldwide. Violence will assault us remotely through television or other forms of media. Violence will simmer within us at times of unexpected stress and at times when our boundaries feel threatened and we feel the need to confirm our position. Other forms of violence will erupt when the structures of propriety and society clash with the realities of difference: difference in culture, in economic status, and between competing groups and within groups. By cultivating a commitment to not harm others and a commitment to work at helping others, the Jains have effectively advanced the cause of peace and nonviolence through the application of nonviolent vows.

Jain nonviolence invites the people of the earth to live sparingly and compassionately. Jainism began with brave naked ascetics in India and developed over several centuries into a sophisticated philosophy and way of life. In the *Acaranga Sutra*, Mahavira advises his nuns and monks to "change their minds" about things; rather than seeing big trees as "fit for palaces, gates, houses, benches . . . boats, buckets, stools, trays, ploughs, machines, wheels, seats, beds, cars, and sheds," they should speak of the trees as "noble, high and round, with many branches, beautiful and magnificent" (II.4.2.11–12). So also, with a different view, with a different eye, if educated in a nonviolent perspective, people might likewise change the way they see the world and construe the world and others.

## STUDY QUESTIONS

1. What are the five vows that guided the lives of the first Jains?
2. Comment on the age and significance of the spiritual traditions of "renunciation" in the spiritual practices of ancient India.
3. How has Jain belief influenced professional vocation and employment decisions of historic and modern Jains?
4. Identify and discuss the enduring significance of Acarya Tulsi. How might his "list of vows" alter the world we live in today, if it were adhered to by large groups of people?

## BIBLIOGRAPHY

*Anuvibha Reporter*, vol. 3, no. 1 (October–December 1997).

Babb, Lawrence A. *Absent Lord: Ascetics and Kings in a Jain Ritual Culture*. Berkeley: University of California Press, 1996.

Chapple, Christopher Key. *Nonviolence to Animals, Earth, and Self in Asian Traditions*. Albany: State University of New York Press, 1993.

Cort, John E., ed. *Open Boundaries: Jain Communities and Cultures in Indian History*. Albany: State University of New York Press, 1998.

Dundas, Paul. *The Jains*. London: Routledge, 1992.

Griffith, Ralph T. H., trans. *The Hymns of the Rgveda*. Delhi: Motilal Banarsidass, 1973.

Jacobi, Hermann, trans. *Jaina Sutras: The Acaranga Sutra*. Oxford: Clarendon Press, 1884.

Jaini, Jagmanderlal. *The Outlines of Jainism*. Cambridge: Cambridge University Press, 1916.

Jaini, Padmanabh S. *The Jaina Path of Purification*. Berkeley: University of California Press, 1979.

Kumar, Muni Prashant, and Muni Lok Prakash 'Lokesh.' In *Anuvibha Reporter* 3, no. 1 (October–December 1997).

Sangave, Vilas A. *Jain Religion and Community*. 2nd ed. Long Beach: Long Beach Publications, 1997.

Tatia, Narhmal, trans. *That Which Is: The Tattvartha Sutra of Umasvati*. San Francisco: Harper Collins, 1994.

Tobias, Michael. *Life Force: The World of Jainism*. Berkeley: Asian Humanities Press, 1991.

# 2

# The Peace Wheel

## Nonviolent Activism in the Buddhist Tradition

*Christopher S. Queen*

The Buddhist tradition is often praised for its peace teachings and the exceptional record of nonviolence in Buddhist societies over 2,500 years. While these praises are justified, it is important to recognize that Buddhism's contribution lies not primarily in its commitment to peace *per se*—most world religions are committed to "peace" in some fashion—but in the unique perspectives and techniques Buddhists have developed for achieving peace within and between individuals and groups. One should also note at the outset that violence has not been unknown in Buddhist societies. Wars have been fought to preserve Buddhist teachings and institutions, and Buddhist meditation and monastic discipline have been adapted to train armies to defend national interests and to conquer neighboring peoples.

Nevertheless, the Buddhist tradition offers rich resources for peacemaking and the cultivation of nonviolence. Among these are

Christopher S. Queen is lecturer in religious studies and dean of students for continuing education in the Faculty of Arts and Sciences at Harvard University. He is board president of the Barre Center for Buddhist Studies and co-founder of the Dharma Chakra Mission, a social service organization in Bodh Gaya, India. His books include *American Buddhism: Methods and Findings in Recent Scholarship* (Curzon, 1999), *Engaged Buddhism in the West* (Wisdom Publications, 2000), and *Action Dharma: New Studies in Engaged Buddhism* with Charles Prebish and Damien Keown (RoutledgeCurzon, 2003). He is working on a book on B. R. Ambedkar and the conversion of India's untouchables to Buddhism.

its founding manifesto, the Four Noble Truths (Pali *ariya sacca*),[1] offering relief from the causes of human suffering; its cardinal moral precept, to refrain from harming living beings *(ahimsa)*; the practices of lovingkindness, compassion, sympathetic joy, and equanimity *(brahmaviharas)*; the doctrines of selflessness *(anatta)*, interdependence *(paticcasamuppada)*, and non-dualism *(sunyata)*; the paradigm of enlightened beings *(bodhisattvas)* who employ skillful devices *(upaya)* to liberate others from suffering; and the image of the great "wheel-turners" *(cakravartin)* and moral leaders *(dhammaraja)* who conquer hearts and minds—not enemies and territories—by their exceptional wisdom and kindness.

These teachings have found ardent champions in every culture touched by the Buddhist *dharma* (Pali *dhamma*, "teaching," "truth," "path"), principally those of India and Sri Lanka, Southeast Asia, China, Tibet, Korea, and Japan. In the modern world, nonviolent struggles for human rights and social justice have found Buddhist supporters in Asia and the West, spawning a new "engaged" style of Buddhist activism. Perhaps most notably, the Nobel Peace Prize has twice been conferred on Buddhist leaders during the past decades for their tireless efforts to liberate their compatriots from totalitarian regimes: His Holiness the Dalai Lama of Tibet in 1989 and Aung San Suu Kyi of Burma in 1991.

In this chapter we shall see how the Buddha and Asoka, Buddhism's greatest king, transformed the ancient Indian tradition of sacred warfare (symbolized by the chariot wheel) into a tradition of sacred peacemaking (symbolized by the "truth wheel" or *dharmacakra*). In the following sections, we shall examine the central teachings of Buddhist nonviolent peacemaking; historical challenges to the Peace Wheel tradition; the rise of socially engaged Buddhism; and two twentieth-century practitioners of Buddhist nonviolent activism.

## TWO CHARIOTS IN ANCIENT INDIA

In the legend of the Buddha's life, a sage predicts that the young prince, Siddhartha Gautama, will become a "wheel-turner" *(cakravartin)* in the Vedic tradition of Aryan princes. The symbolism of the *cakra* ("wheel") recalled, for the prince's contemporaries in the Himalayan foothills of Northeast India in the sixth century B.C.E., the sun-disk of the sky-god Vishnu and the chariot wheels of a universal conqueror or "wheel-turner." Indra, lord of the gods, was said to conquer the universe with his war chariot. "With the unassailable chariot-wheel, O Indra, thou has overthrown the 60,099 warriors of the Sushravas" (*Rigveda* I.53.9). Known as the "chariot-fighter," Inda mirrored on high the conquest of the Indian subcontinent by Indo-European charioteers at the dawn of the Iron Age.[2]

In the *Sutta Nipata*, one of the earliest collections of Buddhist verse, Sela, a Brahmin well-versed in Vedic hymns, on meeting the Buddha for the first time and noting that he has the 32 physical characteristics of a *cakravartin*, exclaims,

> You deserve to be a king, an emperor, the lord of chariots,
> whose conquests reach to the limits of the four seas,
>     Lord of Jambu Grove [India].
> Warriors and wealthy kings are devoted to you;
> O Gorama, exercise your royal power as a king of kings, a chief of men!
>
> The Buddha replied: I am a king, O Sela, supreme king of the Teaching of Truth;
> [But] I turn the wheel by peaceful means—this wheel is irresistible.[3]

The Buddha declares himself a *Dhammaraja*, or King of Truth, rather than a Lord of War. And, he implies, in a contest between a Lord of War and a Prince of Peace, the latter will be victorious.[4]

Whether the composition of these verses preceded or followed the tradition's designation of the Buddha's first sermon as "Turning of the Wheel of the Law" *(dharma-chakra-pravartana)*, the notion that the Buddha transformed an ancient symbol of military conquest into a metaphor of nonviolence—a Peace Wheel, for the purposes of our discussion—was well established by the appearance of the first Buddhist art and architecture in the third century B.C.E.

The most famous image in Indian art, found today on Indian currency, is the lion capital of a polished sandstone pillar that the Buddhist king Asoka Maurya (ruled 270–232 B.C.E.) erected at one of the northern borders of his vast realm.[5] As prominent as the pillar's four lions, broadcasting the king's "lion's roar" *(simhanada)* to the four directions of the empire, was the many-spoked

Peace Wheel that appears below each lion to identify Asoka's policy of *Dharma-Vijaya*, "conquest by righteousness."[6] Following years of bloody campaigns throughout India, Asoka suffered deep remorse for the loss of life he caused. Becoming a Buddhist convert, he proclaimed a new era in one of his many Rock Edicts,

> For many hundreds of years in the past, slaughter of animals, cruelty to living creatures, discourtesy to relatives, and disrespect for priests and ascetics have been increasing. But now . . . the sound of war drums has become the call to Dharma, summoning the people to exhibitions of the chariots of the gods, elephants, fireworks, and other divine displays. [Now the] inculcation of Dharma has increased, abstention from killing animals and from cruelty to living beings, kindliness in human and family relations, respect for priests and ascetics, and obedience to mother and father and elders.[7]

In the Buddhist Asoka's India, the state's vast stockpile of war chariots is saved, with fireworks and elephants, for patriotic holiday parades in an era of prosperity and peace.

For centuries the radical shift in social values wrought by Buddha and Asoka—from violence to reconciliation—was symbolized in stone art and architecture, from the low-relief sculptures representing the Buddha himself as a Peace Wheel, revered by followers at *stupa* sites (giant reliquary mounds) at Sanchi and Bharhut (*circa* 100 B.C.E.), to the well-known Preaching Buddha (Gupta period, *circa* 475 C.E.), in which the sitting Buddha demonstrates the wheel-turning hand gesture *(dharma chakra pravartana mudra)*, while the Peace Wheel is venerated by the Lord's disciples below. The presence of two deer identifies the scene as the Deer Park at Sarnath, site of the first sermon.[8]

In 1948, following India's independence from colonial rule, the ancient chariot wheel, now symbolizing the rule of law in a peaceful society, was placed on the national flag of India.

## TURNING THE WHEEL OF PEACE: CORE TEACHINGS

"A study of early Buddhist literature reveals the fact that the concept of peace appears as the pivotal point in the Buddhist system of social ethics," wrote O. H. Wijesekera, an eminent Sri Lankan scholar.[9] The Pali word for "peace," *santi* (Skt. *shantz*), ordinarily refers to what we would call "inner peace" and what in Buddhist psychology is called *nibbana* (Skt. *nirvana*), the complete absence of craving, agitation, suffering, and aggression. While the notions of peace and nonviolence in Western cultures are generally identified with inter-group relations, Wijesekera observes, "in Buddhism and other Indian religions, the primary emphasis is on the *individual* aspect of peace, and its social consequences are held to follow only from the center of the individual's own psychology."[10]

When the Buddha turned the Dharma Wheel after his enlightenment under the Bodhi tree, he expounded the Four Noble Truths: that all life is unsettled by feelings of dissatisfaction and pain *(dukkha)*; that the arising *(samudaya)* of this disease is caused by ignorance of life's impermanence and a constant craving for comfort and security; that it is possible to achieve the extinction *(nirodha)* of these mental factors and to find the peace of nirvana; and that the Eightfold Path *(magga)* to this goal includes right (efficacious) views, aspirations, actions, speech, livelihood, effort, mindfulness, and concentration.[11]

Taken alone, the Four Noble Truths address the emotional needs of individuals—for inner peace, freedom from suffering, and a true understanding of existence. But the means to this goal, particularly the "steps" of right action, speech, and livelihood on the Eightfold Path, point directly to the social dimension of relationships in community. For laypeople, the great majority of Buddhists, *right action* entails the pledge to observe the Five Precepts *(panca sila)*: abstention from taking life, from taking what is not given, from sexual misconduct, from false speech, and from the use of intoxicants. Here the quest for inner peace begins with the solemn vow of *ahimsa*, i.e., to protect all sentient beings from harm and injury. As we saw in the case of Asoka, this includes animals as well as humans, and, significantly for the early Buddhist community of monks *(bhikkhu sangha)*, the abstention from killing animals in the ritual sacrifices of the Vedic religion. Indeed, the only religious "sacrifice" that the Buddha recommended to the Brahmin Kutadanta was the practice of the ethical Precepts themselves.[12]

In the ancient world no less than today, the practice of non-injury to others involved a complex calculus of intention and result. For example, not only was meat a dietary staple in most Buddhist countries, but the need for self-defense, law enforcement, national defense, and even agriculture (as the Jain followers of Mahavira, Buddha's contemporary, were quick to point out) inevitably involved some harm to living beings. One element in the Buddhist approach was to practice the Middle Way of moderation, avoiding professions involving killing (hunting, butchering, military service), i.e., practicing "right livelihood," on the one hand, and the Jain extreme of protecting insects by wearing a mask and sweeping the ground ahead when walking, on the other. Another element in the Buddhist approach to non-harming was to stress the *intention* or state of mind of the actor: monks could accept meat in their begging bowls as long as animals were not hunted or slaughtered expressly to feed them; similarly, a layperson might unintentionally harm another, say, in a household accident, without incurring the bad karma associated with premeditated assault or homicide.[13]

The most significant contributions of early Buddhism to the practice of nonviolence, I would suggest, are its techniques to counter the three evil roots *(hetu)* of action—hatred, greed, and delusion *(dosa, lobha, moha)*, the seeds of violence itself.[14] Here we learn that each of these reactions has its antidote: lovingkindness *(metta)* to counter hatred, generosity *(dana)* to counter greed, and wisdom *(panna)* to counter delusion. While it may be argued that greed and delusion are equal partners with hatred in the instigation of violence, it is irrational anger and hatred toward other individuals and groups that most often fuels the flare-up of violence and mayhem.

Accordingly, it is *lovingkindness meditation (metta bhavana)*, cultivating goodwill toward oneself and others, that may be called the root practice in Buddhist nonviolence.[15] As the first exercise in a series of trainings called the "Divine Abodes" *(brahma vihara)*, lovingkindness is complemented by the practices of compassion *(karuna,* sympathy for those in pain), joy *(mudita,* appreciating the good fortune of others), and equanimity *(upekkha,* maintaining impartiality in times of gain and loss). To meditate on loving kindness, the practitioner begins by directing loving attention to his or her own state of being, repeating the formula in Pali or in one's own language:

| | |
|---|---|
| *Aham avero homi* | May I be free from enmity |
| *Abbyapajjho homi* | May I be free from ill will |
| *Anigho homi* | May I be free from distress |
| *Sukhi attanam pariharami* | May I keep myself happy |

In a fashion similar to Christians' endeavor to love others as one-self, the Buddhist then extends the wish for freedom from enmity, ill will, and distress, and for happiness step-by-step to others—a beloved teacher or parent, a dear friend, a neutral or unknown person, and finally to a repellent or hostile person. "As one does this, one's mind becomes malleable in each case before passing on to the next."[16] Similar meditative training is recommended for the cultivation of compassion, joy, and equanimity.

The Buddhist approach to nonviolence, then, is grounded in a systematic "attitude adjustment" in which negative, reactive states such as hatred, greed, and delusion are transformed into positive social orientations through meditative self-training. But this reorientation to inner and outer peace entails other steps on the Eightfold Path: *right views* that establish a conceptual frame-work for meditative and ethical practice, *right aspiration* and *right effort* that motivate and sustain the practice; *right mind-fulness*, by which the new attitudes are applied to situations and relationships in moment-to-moment living; and *right concentra-tion*, by which the practitioner moves from merely "performing peace," as it were, to what the Vietnamese Zen Master Thich Nhat Hanh calls "being peace"—involuntarily exemplifying the enlightened mind of *nirvana*.[17]

While it is not possible here to treat all of the teachings of the Peace Wheel tradition, let us turn briefly to the conceptual world of Buddhist morality and then to the Bodhisattva's Path of univer-sal liberation.

## BUDDHIST PEACEWORK IN THEORY AND PRACTICE

The teachings of *karma*, moral causation, and *samsara*, the cycles of rebirth that encompass humans, animals, deities, and the damned, have formed the symbolic universe of many Asian cul-tures through the ages. In the Buddhist version, the human realm is superior even to the divine in that only a man or woman may cultivate the moral qualities that lead to Buddhahood and the final release from cyclic existence. Because moral causation is deeply individual—each person reaps his or her own rewards and pun-ishments—and because the penalties for unwholesome reactions such as anger and violence are extreme—rebirth as a tormented being in one of the hell realms—the incentives to ethical behavior have always been great in Buddhist societies. But rather than cutting individuals off from one another, the notion of a circle of life connects all beings. Every being was once your own mother and thus deserving of respect, many believe, and the dangers posed by tormented beings offer opportunities for merit-making:

> Malicious spirits were not to be appeased with sacrifice but rather tamed through the power and goodwill of the holy individual. The theme of the human sage using superior mental powers to convert ogres came to typify in later centuries the way in which Buddhism interacted with the spirit cults it encountered in every land to which it spread. As for the benign spirits, the early texts treat their foibles with a gentle humor entirely devoid of awe.[18]

Needless to say, these habits of respect and goodwill could be anticipated at the purely human level as well, as Buddhist missionaries carried the Dharma throughout Asia.

But here is a paradox in the Buddhist view of liberation, for ultimately there are no "selves" to be respected, saved, reborn, or perfected in Buddhahood. Indeed, the teaching of *no-self* or *self-lessness* (Pali *anatta*, Skt. *anatman*) lies at the heart of Buddhist psychology and ethics. As a corollary of the teaching that all phenomenal existence is impermanent *(anicca)*, the doctrine of "no-self" affirms the conditioned, composite, and unstable nature of personality and explains why any effort to grasp or hold onto a permanent identity leads to disappointment, frustration, or even violence. Acceptance of this teaching, on the other hand, denies nourishment to the evil roots of action: How can one hate other "non-selfs"? How can one approach them with greed and grasping? How can one suffer in delusion when the truth of human nature is realized?[19] The result of this way of thinking is a more fluid and open-ended approach to others and to situations, suggesting multiple solutions to human problems and a reduction of the likelihood of conflict.

Another teaching that has supported the ethics of nonviolence in Asian Buddhism is that of dependent origination (Pali *paticcasamuppada*), the interdependence of all actions and beings in the cycle of rebirth, and thus the profound interconnectedness of the moral universe. While this psycho-cosmic conception—called the central insight of the Buddha's enlightenment—is related to the notions of selflessness and rebirth, it was developed in later Buddhist philosophy in the teaching of emptiness (Skt. *sunyata*), the deep interactivity and non-dualism of existence, in which each entity or person derives his, her, or its qualities from relationships and not a fixed essence, identity, or "own-being." Indra's Net, the metaphor of a web of jewels in which the facets of each reflect all of the others in the net, is another way of expressing the interdependence of all beings. The ethical implications of these doctrines have been obvious to Buddhists through the ages: realization of the impermanence and interdependence of selves in society and nature entails the deepest respect for all. To tear the fabric of this sacred relativity through violence entails dire consequences.[20]

As the Dharma ripened in India and was carried to neighboring cultures of Central, East, and Southeast Asia, new peace teachings evolved. Perhaps the most dramatic feature of the reform movement that came to be called the *Mahayana* (the great or universal vehicle) was the heroic activism of the bodhisattvas. The term bodhisattva (a being, *sattva*, destined for enlightenment, *bodhi*) had always meant a future buddha. In the popular *Jataka Tales* of Shakyamuni Buddha's previous lives (357 as a human, 66 as a god, and 123 as an animal), the bodhisattva often sacrificed his or her life so that others might live. But in Mahayana teaching, where the possibility of limitless buddhas arose with the belief that *everyone has the potential to become a buddha*, myriad bodhisattvas appeared—disguised as the clever layman next door, for example *(Vimalakirtinirdesa Sutra)*, as a kind of Superman or guardian angel who swoops down to save people from fires and floods (as in the *Prajnaparamita* or Perfection of Wisdom literature), as one who uses artful devices *(upaya kausalya)* to bring deluded or resistant people to the Buddhist path (as in the *Saddharmapundarika* or *Lotus Sutra*), or as one who protects mothers, children, and helpless members of society (as does the gentle *Kuan Yin* or *Kannon* of China and Japan).

These Buddhist saints, saviors, or "messiahs" (as one scholar has called them) have one thing in common: each has made a vow to postpone his or her own *nirvana* and remain in *samsara* long enough to save all beings from harm and bring them to enlightenment. Such an ideal, which combines the zeal of the barnstorming evangelist with the resourcefulness and patience of the social worker, may rightly be taken as a paradigm for the Buddhist peace-maker activists of today.[21]

Finally, the feature that places Mahayana Buddhism most squarely in the Peace Wheel tradition of Buddha and Asoka is its universalism (the *maha* in Mahayana), its promise of liberation to all people, but particularly to persons considered less qualified by society at large. As a harbinger of human rights thinking today, the *Lotus Sutra* presents the cases of Devadatta, the Buddha's evil cousin, and the Dragon King's precocious daughter, both of whom are revealed to be worthy of the highest spiritual attainment. In the case of Devadatta, who had been condemned to the hell realms for trying to kill the Buddha and stirring up discord among the monks, the Buddha predicts full redemption and Buddhahood. The Dragon Girl, barely turned eight, demonstrates her profound mastery of the Dharma and her own perfect Buddhahood before a cosmic assembly of enlightened beings and disciples. Just as the Buddha admitted untouchables, women, and a serial killer to his religious order, and just as Asoka extended his vast welfare system to the poor, the sick and elderly, criminals, animals, and forests, so the bodhisattva ideal of Mahayana Buddhism was extended across boundaries of gender, ordination, and social class.[22] Commenting on the universalism of the *Lotus Sutra*, Burton Watson concludes, "We learn that even the most depraved of persons can hope for salvation . . . in a realm transcending all petty distinctions of sex or species, instant or eon."[23]

## CHALLENGES TO BUDDHIST NONVIOLENCE

As a practical ideology of nonviolence and universal humanism, Buddhism has made inestimable contributions to the diverse cultures of Asia. In Sri Lanka and Southeast Asia where *Theravada* ("elder-teaching") Buddhism took root, the daily appearance of monks on begging rounds served to exemplify the ideals of kindness and equanimity throughout the lay population. In the Tibetan cultural area, where as many as one-third of the able-bodied men entered monastic vocations, the quiet life of contemplation and service was revered as the acme of human achievement. In China, Korea, and Japan, Buddhism brought with it the moral cosmology of karma and rebirth and a pantheon of heavenly buddhas and bodhisattvas committed to the liberation of suffering humanity. At the popular level in all of these societies, the Buddhist teachings of non-injury, compassion, generosity, and selflessness have leavened the natural human tendencies of tribalism, territoriality, avarice, and violence.

But Buddhism became more than a source of popular piety and morality in its peregrination through Asia. The Peace Wheel tradition we have sketched became a mainstay of royal ideology—a powerful and pervasive civil religion, according to Donald K. Swearer. Following the paradigmatic reign of Asoka Maurya,

> Royal patronage of the Buddhist monastic order was reciprocated by institutional loyalty and the construction of religious cosmologies and mythologies that valorized the king as propagator of the Buddha's religion *(sasana)* and as the key to the peaceful harmony and well-being of the universe.[24]

Buddhist kings in ancient Ceylon, Thailand, Burma, and Cambodia, for example, were expected to embody the "ten royal virtues" *(dasarajadhamma)* of generosity, moral virtue, self-sacrifice, kindness, self-control, non-anger, nonviolence, patience, and righteousness. But they were also expected to keep social order and to regulate the claims of competing parties in the struggle for existence.

In the creation story of the *Aggañña Suttanta*, warring parties elect history's first king when social chaos breaks out over land and food. Such a king must be handsome, capable, and entitled to collect taxes to support the throne; but equally important, he must be one who is "wrathful when indignation is right, who should censure that which should be censured and should banish him who deserves to be banished." In a word, the Buddhist king must be prepared to use force to bring discipline and order to society.[25]

Here we encounter the paradox of the Peace Wheel in Buddhist history and the source of periodic challenges to the tradition of nonviolent social change. For with the evolution of a Buddhist civil religion, with its vesting of temporal power in the person of the *Dhammaraja* ("righteous ruler") and ultimately of the nation-state, a new bifurcation of powers came to be called *the two wheels of dhamma*. As S. J. Tambiah observes:

> [Buddhism is] a totality that includes the relation between *bhikkhu* and king (who encompasses and includes the

householders), between the Buddha and Cakkavatti (Chakravartin) as the two wheels of the dhamma, between the sangha and the policy and society in which it is located, between this-worldly and other-worldly pursuits. It is this totality that also makes Buddhism a world religion and not merely the pursuit of a few virtuosi.[26]

The Buddha and Asoka had transformed the ancient symbolism of the war-chariot wheel into an emblem of peace that had both religious and socio-political dimensions. For the Buddha this move involved his renunciation of the throne to become a spiritual teacher; for Asoka it involved the renunciation of military violence as the primary instrument of social control. But with the emergence of the Buddhist state as a dominant force in Asian history, the tradition of nonviolent sovereignty was, on notorious occasions, ignored or forgotten. Let us consider three examples.

In the *Mahavamsa* or Great Chronicle of Sri Lanka, King Dutthagamani (ruled 101–77 B.C.E.) experienced deep remorse after his bloody defeat of the Hindu Tamils. But unlike the parallel story of his Indian predecessor Asoka, Dutthagamani fought not only to unify his island kingdom, but also to defend the Buddhist way of life. His enemies were not only armed aliens with ties to the mainland, *they were Hindus, the worshipers of alien gods.* And unlike Asoka, the Sinhalese king was comforted by eight Buddhist monks who assured him that, in spite of the thousands slain in the battle, "only one and a half humans perished"—one who had pledged allegiance to the Buddha, the Dharma, and the Sangha (the "three refuges" of Buddhism), and another who had vowed to follow the Buddhist precepts. All the other Hindu Tamils were "unbelievers and men of evil life"—subhuman and deserving of death.[27] One sees in this example the way in which ancient religious hostilities overwhelm the peace teachings of each tradition in the conflict (note that Hinduism shares the Buddhist reverence for life, *ahimsa*); and religious, no less than political, leaders fuel the fires of bigotry and hatred. Surely Jewish, Christian, and Muslim militants in the Middle East, and Protestants and Catholics of Ireland, hold no monopoly on religious intolerance and holy war.

Similar examples of the compromise of the Peace Wheel tradition may be drawn from the history of Buddhist kingdoms in Southeast Asia, as Trevor Ling has done in *Buddhism, Imperialism, and War* (1979). According to Ling, "Buddhism in Southeast Asia has been successfully employed to reinforce the policies and interests of national rulers, often in their competition with one another for resources or prestige." The author chronicles the history of military violence within and between the Buddhist states of Thailand and Burma, as well as the efforts of civil and clerical officials to formulate the notion of Buddhist "holy warfare." A dramatic example is the speech delivered by the Thai Buddhist Patriarch (highest-ranking monk) on the occasion of the coronation of King Rama VI in the year 1910. The patriarch praised the new king as one ready to sacrifice his life for religion and country, thus setting the highest example of righteousness for all citizens. He said that the new king would bring prosperity to the Buddhist sangha and the kingdom of Thailand by directing the affairs of state with efficiency. Finally, he praised the king for steps he had already taken to prepare for war in times of peace: strengthening the army and navy, founding the Corps of Wild Tigers (an elite tactical force), and starting "the Boy Scout Movement to foster in boys the warrior spirit." In the printed version of his sermon, the patriarch disputed the view that the Buddha ruled out "all wars and people whose business it was to wage war." Rather, the Buddha had condemned only "militarism . . . an intolerant and unreasoning hatred, vengeance and savagery which causes men to kill from sheer blood-lust."[28]

A third example of the subversion of the Peace Wheel tradition may be found in the near-universal support by Buddhist institutions and leaders for Japan's military excursions in the Sino-Japanese war of 1894–95 and the Russo-Japanese War of 1904–05; for the rise of militantly nationalistic "imperial-way Buddhism" *(kodo Bukkyo)* during the years 1913–1930; and particularly during the Pacific War against Japan's East Asian neighbors and the United States in World War II. In a sobering study, *Zen at War* (1997), Brian A. Victoria shows how the major Japanese Buddhist lineages lined up to demonstrate lock-step patriotism in the decades following the ascendancy of Emperor Meiji in 1868. In decreeing that "all absurd usages of the old regime shall be abolished and all measures conducted in conformity with the righteous way of heaven and earth," the young emperor had sought to disestablish a moribund and corrupt Buddhism in favor of the traditional state cult of Shinto. But by the first decade of the twentieth century, after Japan's bloody victories over China and Russia, Buddhist clergy and intellectuals had already aligned their spiritual tradition with the medieval "way of the warrior" *(bushido)* and with the prowess of the Japanese war machine. Here is the best-known Buddhist missionary to the West, D. T. Suzuki, in his first English-language publication on Zen Buddhism, for the *Journal of the Pali Text Society:*

> The calmness and even joyfulness of heart at the moment of death which is conspicuously observable in the Japanese, the intrepidity which is generally shown by the Japanese soldiers in the face of an overwhelming enemy; and the fairness of play to an opponent, so strongly taught by Bushido —all these come from the spirit of the Zen training, and not from any such blind, fatalistic conception as is sometimes thought to be a trait peculiar to Orientals.[29]

By war's end, Zen temples were sponsoring meditation training camps for the armed forces, raising money for the purchase of new aircraft (e.g., *Soto I* and *Soto II*), and recruiting middle school boys to fly *kamikaze* ("divine wind") missions for the love of the emperor and in service to the Buddha. Alluding to a famous metaphor in Zen training, Victoria concludes that for these boys, in search of adventure and sacrifice, "Truly may it be said that their lives were now 'as light as goose feathers.'"[30]

## THE DAWN OF ENGAGED BUDDHISM

Over time, the symbol of the turning wheel in Buddhism came to mean not only the exposition of the Buddha's enlightenment in skillful teachings and trainings, and the pacification of human hearts and societies by virtuous teachers and rulers, but also the rise of new schools of thought (e.g., the *Madhyamika* and *Yogacara*) and complexes of belief and practice (*Mahayana* and *Vttjrayana*).[31] While the acknowledgment of its own impermanence, implicit in the wheel symbol, is, paradoxically, a perennial characteristic of the Buddhist tradition, it may also be credited for the openness and energy with which Buddhists have adapted to new cultural and political realities.[32]

The global emergence of socially and politically engaged Buddhism over the past century may be regarded as the latest turning of the Peace Wheel, and credited to the vigorous encounter of Buddhist values with those of the West.[33] The term *engaged Buddhism* was coined during the 1960s by the Vietnamese Thien (Zen) master, Thich Nhat Hanh, to describe the activism of a small group of monks and laity who opposed the violence committed by both sides in the American Indo-China War.[34] But unlike the ultra-nationalist Buddhists we have described in the preceding discussion, Thich Nhat Hanh and the Unified Buddhist Church did not side with any of the combatants in the struggle. Rather, their allegiance was to nonviolence and peace itself. They attempted to "call the attention of the world to the suffering endured by the Vietnamese" by placing their own bodies in the midst of the conflict. This took the forms of walking between the battle lines in an effort to stop the bullets, for example, and of immolating themselves in gasoline fires on the streets of Saigon, as broadcast in the famous wirephoto of the Venerable Thich Quang Duc in 1963.[35]

By the 1990s engaged Buddhism was associated with a vast array of activities both within and outside of the international peace movement: in the struggle of the Tibetan people for self-determination and survival after 40 years of the Chinese occupation; the struggle of the Burmese and Cambodian peoples for human rights and democratic institutions; the rural development programs of the Sarvodaya Sramadana movement in Sri Lanka and the Asian Cultural Forum for Development in Thailand; the struggles for human rights of India's *Dalit* ("oppressed") or ex-untouchable populations, many of whom are converts to Buddhism; and the peaceful activism of three organizations inspired by the Nichiren tradition of Japanese Buddhism: the Rissho Kosei-kai, the Nippansan Myohoji, and the Soka Gakkai.

Engaged Buddhist leaders such as Tibet's Dalai Lama and Aung San Suu Kyi (leader of the Burmese opposition) have been awarded the Nobel Peace Prize for their struggles, while many others, such as Thich Nhat Hanh, Dr. A. T. Ariyaratna of Sri Lanka, Sulak Sivaraksa of Thailand, and Nikkyo Nawano and Daisaku Ikeda of Japan, have received international recognition for their tireless campaigns for social and political change.

In the West, engaged Buddhism has taken such forms as the Buddhist Peace Fellowship in Berkeley, California, founded in 1979; the urban social service programs of Soto Master Bernard Glassman and the Zen Peacemaker Order in Yonkers, New York; and the wilderness retreat and AIDS hospice programs sponsored by Dr. Joan Halifax and the Upaya Foundation in Santa Fe, New Mexico. Environmental and anti-nuclear activism, prison education and meditation programs, and lobbying initiatives on behalf of human rights and economic justice campaigns at home and abroad are only a few of the activities of Buddhist activists in North America, the United Kingdom, countries of the European Union, South Arica, and Australia.[36]

Engaged Buddhists have brought new beliefs and practices to the Peace Wheel tradition. Unlike followers of dharma in the past, who accepted the traditional Buddhist *theodicy*—the belief that suffering is caused by the ignorance and cravings of the sufferers themselves, and that one may overcome suffering and achieve *nirvana* only through individual effort—many engaged Buddhists have come to believe that much suffering in the world, particularly of the kind related to poverty, injustice, and war, is caused by the ignorance, cravings, and cruelty of persons other than the sufferer. Further, most contemporary Buddhists do not practice nonviolence, generosity, lovingkindness, and selflessness *in order to transcend this world* (i.e., to avoid rebirth in the future) or to help others to transcend the world. They practice out of the sense that their *deep relatedness* to others—as fellow beings on a planet or within an ecosystem, for example—obligates them to try to relieve that suffering, and that the net effect of such efforts will be a better world for all beings, human, animal, and vegetable. Finally, most engaged Buddhists believe in the efficacy of *collective practice* of the dharma, that is, in confronting the institutional abuses of negligent or oppressive governments and multinational corporations by such collective means as peace marches, rallies, demonstrations, boycotts, letter writing campaigns, "base communities" for social action, and nongovernmental organizations that publicize human suffering and work to overcome it.[37]

The inner-worldly (as opposed to other-worldly) orientation of engaged Buddhism is also reflected in the *egalitarian values* and non-hierarchical structure of its social organizations, which generally feature lay leadership and the equal participation and leadership of women. The *pragmatism* or activist bias of engaged Buddhism is accompanied by a de-emphasis on doctrinal ortho-doxy that takes many forms: the *non-attachment to views* that Thich Nhat Hanh has called "the most important teaching of Buddhism" and placed at the head of the 14 precepts of his Order of Interbeing; and the *agnosticism* that Stephen Batchelor recommends for practitioners in *Buddhism without Beliefs*.[38] In both instances, there is a recognition that much of the violence in society and history has been sustained by a die-hard insistence on religious dogma, political ideology, and legal jurisdiction.

## TWO EXEMPLARS OF ENGAGED BUDDHISM

As a way of bringing the new Buddhism into sharper focus and of tracing its continuity with the ancient Peace Wheel tradition of nonviolent activism—let us look briefly at two of its most cele-brated practitioners, B. R. Ambedkar (1891–1956), the Indian civil rights leader and Buddhist convert, and Daisaku Ikeda (b. 1928), the Japanese leader of an international lay Buddhist organization.

Bhimrao Ramji Ambedkar, the eighth of 14 children born to a Mahar family in one of the historically "untouchable" communi-ties of Maharashtra in central India, was tutored by his father, a schoolmaster with the rank of major in the British Colonial Army.[39] Ambedkar's path to political and spiritual leadership was paved with an extraordinary education—capped by doctoral degrees from Columbia University and the London School of Economics, and a law degree from Grays Inn in London and a meteoric career. Ambedkar pursued teaching and law school administration in Bombay, newspaper publishing, legal defense work for the grow-ing civil rights movement on behalf of low-caste and untouchable citizens, service as representative to the Round Table talks in London that laid the groundwork for Indian independence, and leadership roles as cabinet minister and draftsman of the consti-tution for independent India in 1947. While raised as a Hindu, Ambedkar became deeply disillusioned over the seemingly unbreak-able bond between Hinduism and caste discrimination. In 1935 he shocked India by declaring that he would seek a new religion that offered liberty, equality, and fraternity to the lowest members of society, and that he would "educate, agitate, and organize" until this spiritual revolution was complete.[40]

On October 14, 1956, during the twenty-five hundredth anniversary year of the Buddha's enlightenment, on the date traditionally associated with King Asoka's conversion, and in the central Indian city of Nagpur, associated with the preservation of the Buddhist Dharma, Dr. Ambedkar, his wife, and nearly one-half million untouchables embraced Buddhism. Six weeks later, Ambedkar died at the age of 65, and six months later his final work, the highly original *The Buddha and His Dhamma*, was published.[41]

In the writings and speeches of his final years, B. R. Ambedkar offered his followers a bold, engaged Buddhism directed to the relief of every kind of suffering—material, social, political, and spiritual. Even when advocating "agitation" for human rights, however, Ambedkar's Buddhism was unfailingly nonviolent, founded on his deep trust in the powers of moral suasion, collective protest, and constitutional law. Ambedkar's legacy—and his debt to the Peace Wheel tradition—may be seen today in the continuing struggle of the Dalit communities in India and abroad to find dignity and social justice, and in the revival of Buddhist practice in the land of its birth.

Daisaku Ikeda was born in Tokyo in 1928, the fifth of eight children in a family of seaweed farmers. As a teenager he lived through the devastation of World War II, which claimed the life of his eldest brother. In the years of poverty, ill-health, and social dislocation following the war, Ikeda sought the guidance of Josei Toda (1900–58), the second president of the Soka Gakkai, "Value Creation Society," a lay Buddhist organization whose activities are based on the Buddhist teachings of the thirteenth-century reformer, Nichiren. Toda and the society's founder, Tsunesaburo Makiguchi (1871–1944), had been imprisoned in 1943 for refusing to support the war effort, an ordeal that contributed to Makiguchi's death. During the 1950s, Ikeda assisted Toda in building Soka Gakkai through vigorous recruitment of members throughout Japan. In 1960, Ikeda succeeded his mentor as president, and in 1975 he launched Soka Gakkai International (SGI) in recognition of the increasingly global character of the organization. Today SGI boasts more than 10 million members in Japan and some 1.3 million members in 190 other countries and territories worldwide.[42]

As SGI president, Daisaku Ikeda has channeled his tireless energies toward the support and reform of the United Nations as the world's premier peacemaking body; toward dialogues on peace and human rights with world leaders and thinkers, such as Nelson Mandela, Mikhail Gorbachev, Rosa Parks, Arnold Toynbee, and Linus Pauling; and toward educational and cultural projects such as the founding of the Soka Schools and Soka Universities (Japan and the United States), the Min-On Concert Association, and Tokyo Fuji Art Museum. In these activities, Ikeda has attempted to direct the wealth of Buddhist insight and practice to the relief of human suffering at the individual and collective levels:

> Global society today faces myriad interlocking crises. These include the issues of war, environmental degradation, the North-South development gap, divisions among people based on differences of ethnicity, religion or language. The list is long and familiar, and the road to solutions may seem all too distant and daunting.
>
> It is my view, however, that the root of all of these problems is our collective failure to make the human being, human happiness, the consistent focus and goal in all fields of endeavor. The human being is the point to which we must return and from which we must depart anew. What is required is a human transformation—a human revolution.[43]

## CONCLUSION

In this chapter we have explored some of the teachings and practices of the Peace Wheel tradition that date back to Gautama Buddha and Asoka Maurya. We have seen that, from the time of its earliest records, the Buddhist dharma has been directed to the achievement of inner peace and world peace through nonviolent means. Like other religious traditions, the successive turnings of the Peace Wheel in the Theravada, Mahayana, and contemporary engaged Buddhist movements have been rooted in the possibility of a life free of hatred, greed, and delusion. But, perhaps unlike other spiritual traditions, Buddhist nonviolent activism has been grounded in a practical curriculum of skillful actions appropriate for taming and transforming the mind, serving others in society, and affecting compassionate social change through collective action.

In facing history's report on the discord and warfare within Buddhist societies, we acknowledge that the Peace Chariot is only as reliable as its drivers and mechanics. On the other hand, Buddhists may take heart in the knowledge that their cherished vehicle of nonviolent peacemaking is still running, carrying new passengers, and bringing relief and joy to those who suffer.

## STUDY QUESTIONS

1. Briefly discuss the "Four Noble Truths" and suggest how they may be related to peacemaking techniques.

2. Explain the symbolism of the "wheel" and the meaning of becoming a "wheel turner." How do these symbols relate to the Buddha's transformation?

3. How did the Mahayana idea of a "bodhisattva" develop Buddhist activism in the world?

4. What does Queen mean when he suggests that Buddhist peacemaking is rooted in a "systematic attitude adjustment"?

5. Briefly discuss three examples of how the peaceful nature of Buddhism can become controversial when Buddhism becomes a "national" religion.

## SUGGESTED READINGS

Himmalawa Saddhatissa. *Buddhist Ethics*. Boston: Wisdom Publications, 1997. A reliable introduction to basic teachings and practices in Theravada Buddhism.

Kenneth Kraft, ed. *Inner Peace, World Peace: Essays on Buddhism and Nonviolence*. Albany: State University of New York Press, 1992. A lively overview of the application of Buddhist teachings to a range of contemporary issues.

Christopher S. Queen and Sallie B. King, eds. *Engaged Buddhism: Buddhist Liberation Movements in Asia*. Albany: State University of New York Press, 1996. In-depth analysis of the rise and shape of the new Buddhism.

Thich Nhat Hanh. *Love in Action: Writings on Nonviolent Social Change*. Berkeley, CA: Parallax Press, 1993. Two decades of writings by an exemplar of engaged Buddhism.

Johan Galtung and Daisaku Ikeda. *Choose Peace*. London: Pluto Press, 1995. Dialogues between an activist and a scholar on the relationship between spirituality and history.

## NOTES

[1] Buddhist words will be provided in Sanskrit or Pali, depending on context or familiarity to English readers. Sanskrit *dharma* will be preferred

over Pali *dhamma* in most cases because of its familiarity. Likewise, the Sanskrit version of Buddha's name, *Siddhartha Gautama*, is more familiar than the Pali *Siddhattha Gotama*. Diacritical marks have been omitted.

2  O. H. DeA. Wijesekera, "The Symbolism of the Wheel in the Cakravartin Concept," in *Buddhist and Vedic Studies* (Delhi: Motilal Banarsidass, 1994), 267–73.

3  Sutta Nipata III. 7 .5–7. See *The Sutta-Nipata*, trans. H. Saddhatissa (London: Curzon Press, 1985), 65.

4  The transformation of the war chariot to a peace chariot in ancient Buddhism makes an interesting counterpoint to the events in the Hindu poem *Bhagavad Gita* (an episode in the Indian national war epic *Mahabharata*). Here the protagonist, young general Arjuna, attempts to prevent a war from his place in the lead chariot, only to be reminded by his charioteer, the divine Lord Krishna, that his caste duty is to fight. See *The Bhagavad Gita: Krishna's Counsel in Time of War*, trans. Barbara Stoler Miller (Toronto: Bantam Books, 1986). The contrast between the two traditions is heightened by the fact that the historical Buddha and the legendary Arjuna are of the same caste, the *kshatriya* or military/administrative caste.

5  For a thorough discussion of the relationship between Buddhist social ethics and the state, represented by the image of "the two wheels," see Gananath Obeyesekere, Frank Reynolds, and Bardwell Smith, eds., *The Two Wheels of Dhamma: Essays on the Theravada Tradition in India and Ceylon* (Chambersburg, PA.: American Academy of Religion, 1972).

6  See Robert E. Fisher, *Buddhist Art and Architecture* (London: Thames and Hudson, 1993), 20.

7  From Rock Edict IV, in N. A. Nikam and Richard McKeon, eds. and trans., *The Edicts of Asoka* (Chicago: University of Chicago Press/Midway, 1978), 31.

8  Fisher, *Buddhist Art and Architecture*, 20–55. The ancient Buddhist ritual of circumambulation *(pradaksina)* of the *mandala-* or wheel-shaped Buddhist *stupa* while reciting, chanting, or singing the words of the liturgy may be regarded as a ritualized "turning of the wheel of the Dharma" accessible to both ordained and lay practitioners. See Sukumar Durr, *The Buddha and Five After-Centuries* (London: Luzac, 1957), 163–78; and Govinda, *The Psycho-Cosmic Symbolism of the Buddhist Stupa* (Emeryville, CA.: Dharma Publishing, 1976).

9  O. H. DeA. Wijesekera, "The Concept of Peace as the Central Notion of Buddhist Social Psychology," in *Buddhist and Vedic Studies* (Delhi: Motilal Banarsidass, 1994), 94.

10  Ibid.

11  For a modern interpretation of the Four Noble Truths, see Walpola Rahula, *What the Buddha Taught* (New York: Grove Press, 1959), 16–50.

[12] See discussion in Hammalawa Saddhatissa, *Buddhist Ethics* (Boston: Wisdom Publications, 1997), 60.

[13] Ibid., 60ff.

[14] These mental factors are perhaps more tellingly called *asavas*, emotional "secretions."

[15] See Sharon Salzberg, *Lovingkindness: The Revolutionary Art of Happiness* (Boston: Shambhala Publications, 1997).

[16] Ibid., 62–64.

[17] See Thich Nhat Hanh, *Being Peace* (Berkeley: Parallax Press, 1987).

[18] Richard H. Robinson and Willard L. Johnson, *The Buddhist Religion: A Historical Introduction*, 4th ed. (Belmont, CA: Wadsworth, 1997), 22–23.

[19] For a profound discussion of this teaching in the Pali literature, see Steven Collins, *Selfless Persons: Imagery and Thought in Theravada Buddhism* (Cambridge: Cambridge University Press, 1982).

[20] See Joanna Macy, *Mutual Causality in Buddhism and General Systems Theory* (Albany: State University of New York Press, 1991); Frederick J. Streng, *Emptiness: A Study in Religious Meaning* (Nashville: Abingdon Press, 1967); Francis H. Cook, *Hua-yen Buddhism: The Jewel Net of India* (University Park: The Pennsylvania State University Press, 1977).

[21] See Har Dayal, *The Bodhisattva Doctrine in Buddhist Sanskrit Literature* (London: Kegan, Paul, Trench, Trubner, 1932); Leslie S. Kawamura, ed., *The Bodhisattva Doctrine in Buddhism* (Waterloo, Canada: Canadian Corporation for Studies in Religion, 1981); Donald S. Lopez Jr. and Steven C. Rockefeller, ed., *The Christ and the Bodhisattva* (Albany: State University of New York Press, 1987).

[22] On Asoka's welfare policies, see Robert A. F. Thurman's succinct discussion in "Edicts of Asoka," in *The Path of Compassion*, ed. Fred Eppsteiner, 111–19 (see note 37 below).

[23] Burton Watson, trans., *The Lotus Sutra* (New York: Columbia University Press, 1993), xviii–xix. The episodes concerning Devadatta and the Dragon Girl occur in chapter 12, 182–89. This tendency in Mahayana thought was eventually expressed in the teachings of "universal Buddha-Nature" *(Tathagatagarbha)* and "original enlightenment" (Japanese *hongaku shiso*) in such schools as the Indian Yogacara, Chinese T'ien T'ai (Japanese Tendai), and the meditation or Ch'an/Zen schools of East Asia. Some scholars have recently debated whether this direction in Buddhist thought was compatible with the spirit of the ancient Dharma, and whether it may support a social ethic based on human rights and nonviolence. See Jamie Hubbard and Paul L. Swanson, eds., *Pruning the Bodhi Tree: The Storm over Critical Buddhism* (Honolulu: University of Hawaii Press, 1997).

[24] Donald K. Swearer, *The Buddhist World of Southeast Asia* (Albany: State University of New York Press, 1995), 64.

[25] For the significance of the Agganna Sutta in Buddhist civil religion, see S. J. Tambiah, *World Conqueror and World Renouncer: A Study of Buddhism and Polity in Thailand against a Historical Background* (Cambridge: Cambridge University Press, 1976), 9–18. In this connection it is useful to compare the circumstances surrounding the debate over the anointment of Israel's first king in the biblical narratives of Samuel.

[26] Ibid., 15–16.

[27] *Mahavamsa* 25:101–11, cited by S. J. Tambiah, *Buddhism Betrayed: Religion, Politics, and Violence in Sri Lanka* (Chicago: University of Chicago Press, 1992), 1.

[28] Trevor Ling, *Buddhism, Imperialism, and War* (London: George Allen & Unwin, 1979), 136ff.

[29] Quoted by Brian Victoria, *Zen at War* (New York: Weartherhill, 1997), 105.

[30] Ibid., 129.

[31] Robinson and Johnson, *The Buddhist Religion*, 33.

[32] I once asked a Burmese meditation master if the teaching of impermanence was not itself a "permanent truth" about reality. He smiled, fluttered his fan, and called on another student.

[33] For a discussion of the scope and history of engaged Buddhism, see Christopher S. Queen, "Introduction: Sources and Shapes of Engaged Buddhism," in *Engaged Buddhism: Buddhist Liberation Movements in Asia*, ed. Christopher S. Queen and Sallie B. King (Albany: State University of New York Press, 1996).

[34] "In the 1930s, the Buddhist scholars [in Vietnam] had already discussed the engagement of Buddhism in modern society and called it *Nhan Gian Phat Giao*, or engaged Buddhism," wrote Thich Nhat Hanh in *Vietnam: Lotus in a Sea of Fire* (New York: Hill and Wang, 1967), 42.

[35] See Thich Nhat Hanh, *Vietnam: Lotus in a Sea of Fire*, and *Love in Action: Writings on Nonviolent Social Change* (Berkeley: Parallax Press, 1993); Sallie B. King, "Thich Nhat Hanh and the Unified Buddhist Church: Nondualism in Action," in Queen and King, *Engaged Buddhism*, 321–64.

[36] See Christopher S. Queen, ed., *Engaged Buddhism in the West* (Boston: Wisdom Publications, 2000).

[37] For examples of the burgeoning literature on engaged Buddhism in many of these areas, see Fred Eppsteiner, ed., *The Path of Compassion: Writing on Socially Engaged Buddhism* (Berkeley: Parallax Press, 1988); Kenneth Kraft, ed., *Inner Peace, World Peace: Essays on Buddhism and Nonviolence* (Albany: State University of New York Press, 1992); Joanna Macy, *World as Lover, World as Self* (Berkeley: Parallax Press, 1991); Allan Hunt Badiner, ed., *Dharma Gaia: A Harvest of Essays in Buddhism and Ecology* (Berkeley: Parallax Press, 1990). Parallax Press is the premier publisher of the writings of Thich Nhat Hanh and other engaged

Buddhist authors, while the quarterly *Turning Wheel: Journal of the Buddhist Peace Fellowship* (published in Berkeley since 1979) is the leading periodical of engaged Buddhism in North America.

[38] For a discussion of the theme of "Buddhist self-negation" among Buddhist actions, see Sallie B. King's concluding chapter in Queen and King, *Engaged Buddhism*, 422–30; for Stephen Batchelor's Buddhist agnosticism, see *Buddhism without Belief* (New York: Riverhead Books, 1997).

[39] See Sangharakshira, *Ambedkar and Buddhism* (Glasgow: Windhorse Publications, 1986) for a readable introduction; Dhananjay Keer, *Dr. Ambedkar: Life and Mission*, 3rd ed. (Bombay: Popular Prakashan, 1971) for a full biography; Christopher S. Queen, "Dr. Ambedkar and the Hermeneutics of Buddhism Liberation," in Queen and King, *Engaged Buddhism*, for a discussion of the Indian leader's place in Buddhist thought.

[40] Tellingly, both of Ambedkar's slogans were taken from human rights struggles he had studied in the West: the French Revolution *(liberté, egalité, fraternité)* and the American labor movement ("Educate, Agitate, Organize").

[41] Ambedkar's collected works, *Dr. Babasaheb Ambedkar: Writings and Speeches*, edited by Vasanr Moon, are available in 15 volumes from the Education Department of the Government of Maharashtra, Bombay, 1987–1995.

[42] For a discussion of Soka Gakkai's history and contribution to the rise of engaged Buddhism, see Daniel A. Metraux, "The Soka Gakkai: Buddhism and the Creation of a Harmonious and Peaceful Sociery," in Queen and King, *Engaged Buddhism*, 365–400. Biographical details taken from "Daisaku Ikeda: A Profile," a pamphlet available from Soka Gakkai International, n.d.

[43] Daisaku Ikeda, "Thoughts on Education of Global Citizenship," delivered at Teachers College, Columbia University, June 13, 1996 (Tokyo: Soka Gakkai, 1996), 24–25. See also Ikeda's book-length dialogues with authorities on world peace: Aurelio Peccie (founder of the Club of Rome) and Daisaku Ikeda, *Before It Is Too Late* (Tokyo: Kodansha International, 1984); Johan Galtung (founder of the International Peace Research Institute and professor of peace studies at the University of Hawaii) and Daisaku Ikeda, *Choose Peace* (London: Pluto Press, 1995).

# 3

# Subverting Hatred

## Peace and Nonviolence in Confucianism and Daoism

*Tam Wai Lun*

Both the Confucian and Daoist traditions began in the period of Warring States (403–221 B.C.E.). As a response to the hostile and chaotic situation of the warring period, both traditions condemned offensive war and discouraged the use of arms in the ordering of a state. Ironically, China was eventually unified under the Qin dynasty (221–206 B.C.E.) by warfare. Wars on the borders have remained a major concern throughout Chinese history.

This paper will argue that the ideal of peace and nonviolence taught in the Confucian and Daoist traditions was realized at a regional level in traditional Chinese society. Peacemaking was carried our by Chinese people at the grassroots level—people who read few or no written texts.

People at the grassroots level are related to the two elite traditions in two ways. Confucian values basically provide the frame-

Tam Wai Lun is professor in the Department of Cultural and Religious Studies and executive member of the Centre for the Study of Humanistic Buddhism and the Centre for Catholic Studies at the Chinese University of Hong Kong. He has published ethnographic descriptions of local religion in Southeast China in John Lagerwey's 30-volume Traditional Hakka Society Series (International Hakka Studies Association, École Française d'Extrême Orient, and Overseas Chinese Archives, 1996–2006).

work of their kinship system, and their local religion is loosely connected with religious Daoism. Here we touch upon the complicated problem of the two terms, Confucianism and Daoism, which we must clarify before proceeding any further.

There has been a long tradition among scholars of trying to understand Chinese religion from the point of view of three teachings: Confucianism, Daoism, and Buddhism. Of the three, Buddhism is imported from India while Confucianism and Daoism are indigenous Chinese religions. Recent research, however, has shown that the threefold division for understanding Chinese religion is inadequate, as it represents mostly the ideas of well-educated elites (Lopez 1996, 3ff.). Another way of studying Chinese religion is to focus on those aspects of religious life that most Chinese people, especially the common people and the uneducated, share. Such aspects of Chinese religion are often described by a separate category: Chinese popular religion. This approach also reflects a recent trend in research in social science and humanities that is characterized by a general move away from studies of the elite (Teiser 1996, 25). It also involves an understanding of religion as not only a system of beliefs but also a system of rituals and practices.

## THE ELITE AND THE FOLK CULTURE

Studying Chinese religion from the bottom up does not necessarily exclude the elite class. Most scholars believe in a two-way exchange between the cultures of the two tiers: the lower class and the elite (Redfield 1959, 86–87). Elements from the culture of the lower classes are often adopted by the elite, while the elite culture at times shapes the culture of the lower class. Common elements, therefore, can be found in both levels of culture. One example is found in the kinship system in China. Confucian ethics, an elite culture, informs the Chinese family system both on the elite and popular levels. Confucian ethics is expressed in the form of lineage regulations and rules written in all lineage registers. These are passed on orally to the illiterate family members. Chinese on the folk level is, therefore, shaped by the Confucian teaching through their lineage and kinship system. Similarly, Daoism and, to a certain extent, Buddhism also informs religious life at the popular level. Not only the pantheon but also the forms of rituals from the elite religious systems are adopted by local ritual masters, also known as local Daoists.

The terms Confucianism and Daoism cover a broad range of phenomena (Teiser 1996, 5–6). Confucianism refers to the Five Classics that Confucius (551–479 B.C.E.) is believed to have edited, which were made the foundation of the official system of education and scholarship in 136 B.C.E. Confucianism also denotes a state-sponsored cult with complex rituals, a cult responsible for temples built throughout the Han empire in honor of Confucius. Finally, Confucianism includes a conceptual scheme synthesizing Confucius's ideas and various cosmologies popular long after him. Scholar Dong Zhongshi (ca. 179–104 B.C.E.) was instrumental in this synthesis.

As for the word Daoism, scholars usually divide it into two forms: philosophical Daoism and religious Daoism (Creel 1970, 11, 24). There are two texts associated with the former: 1) the *Daodejing* (a classic on the Way and Its Power), attributed to Laozi who lived during the sixth century B.C.E., and 2) the *Zhuangzi*, named for its author Zhuangzi (ca. 370–301 B.C.E.). Daoism also refers to religious movements that began to develop in the late second century C.E. Examples of some of these movements are the Celestial Master *(Tianshi Dao)* in the second century, the Great Purity *(Taiqing)* in the fourth century, the Highest Clarity *(Shanqing)* in the second half of the fourth century, Numinous Treasure *(Lingbao)* in the fifth century, and the Supreme Unity *(Tayi)* and complete Perfection *(Quanzhen)* in the twelfth century. Obviously, it is not possible to discuss all aspects covered by the two terms, Confucianism and Daoism, in one short essay. This paper will therefore seek to examine the themes of peace and nonviolence in Confucian and Daoist tradition as practiced on the folk level.

About 70 percent of the Chinese population still lives in villages despite recent widespread urbanization of the country (Lagerwey 1996, 2). An investigation of village life is, therefore, indispensable to any understanding of China, especially traditional China.

As we have pointed out, the elite culture and the folk culture are not unrelated. We will start our investigation from the elite level, although our focus will be on the popular level. As for the elite level, we will limit ourselves to the Confucian classic, *Analects*, and the Daoist classic, *Daodejing*. We will also include a brief discussion of Mozi (470–391 B.C.E.), a critic of Confucian ideas, who produced the earliest systematic essay in Chinese history arguing against warfare. These are the most important documents from the ancient Chinese written traditions that support the position of nonviolence.

Our discussion will first examine the themes of peace and non-violence in the two classics. Second, we will investigate to what extent and in what ways the ideals of peace and nonviolence taught in the classics have penetrated to and are still carried out at the grassroots level in China. Again, we could not cover the whole of China in a short essay such as this. We, therefore, will concentrate on a 1996 fieldwork study entitled "The Structure and Dynamics of Chinese Rural Society in South China," conducted by John Lagerwey and other Chinese scholars. The project is an ongoing ethnographic study that covers three provinces in the South, namely, Fujian (south), Jiangxi (south), and Guangdong (north and east). Based on some of the findings of Lagerwey's project, we are seeking by personal interviews of old people to investigate how the Chinese in villages of South China manage to bring peace and avoid violence in their daily life, an ideal advocated in both the Confucian *Analects* and the Daoist *Daodejing*.

When the Duke of Wei consulted Confucius about military formation, Confucius replied that he had never studied the matter of commanding troops (*Analects* 15:1). In reality, Confucius had discussed with his disciples whom he would take with him when he led the armed forces. This shows that he indeed was knowledgeable in military affairs, but he was not willing to give advice on military matters.

In his discussion with his disciples about the minister Guanzhong, Confucius praised him for repeatedly helping Duke Huan to unite the feudal lords without the use of force (*Analects* 14:16). Confucius described Guanzhong as a man of benevolence—the supreme virtue in Confucius's teaching, although Guanzhong fell short of benevolence by serving Duke Huan, who had his brother, Prince Jiu, killed. Apparently, according to Confucius, bringing peace among the states compensates for Guanzhong's serving an immoral king. We can see how Confucius emphasizes peacemaking.

When he discussed government with Zigong, Confucius commented that among the three necessary qualifications for good government (food, arms, and trust by the people), if one had to give up one of these three, one should give up arms (*Analects* 12:7). Not only does Confucius put a low priority on the use of military force, but also on the use of other forms of force in law enforcement like capital punishment (*Analects* 12:9). On the matter of the proper ordering of the state, Confucius teaches a return to virtue. He supports government by personal virtue. A virtuous ruler, according to Confucius, could lead his people by example and the model of his own goodness. Commenting on Confucius's ideas, Mencius observes,

> Confucius rejected those who enriched rulers not given to the practice of benevolent government. How much more would he reject those who do their best to wage war on their behalf. In wars to gain land, the dead fill the plain; in wars to gain cities, the dead fill the cities. . . . Hence those skilled in war should suffer the most severe punishments. (*Mencius*, Book IV; Part A, 14)

Mencius is right in claiming that Confucius discourages the use of arms in government, but we must add that Confucius did not reject war without qualification. When he heard that Chenheng killed his lord, Duke Jian of Qi, Confucius went in person to request Duke Ai of Lu to send an army to punish Chen (*Analects* 14:21). Confucius condemned the sending of untrained common people to war (*Analects* 13:30), but when they were properly trained for seven years, they should be ready to "take up arms" (*Analects* 13:29). Therefore, Confucius did not deny totally the role of arms in government. He taught that one should repay an injury with justice but repay a good turn with a good turn (*Analects* 14:34). The use of arms cannot be totally avoided, but according to *Analects*, fasting, war, and sickness were the things over which Confucius exercised care. As the orthodox Confucian tradition advocates benevolent government, it rejects the way of a despot, or the way of force, in favor of the idea of a "kingly way" or the way of moral power (Chan 1963, 50). The idea of benevolent government in the Confucian tradition discourages the use of force and puts the Confucian tradition close to our modern idea of peace and nonviolence.

In the Daoist classic *Daodejing*, we find even stronger statements rejecting the use of force in government. In the *Daodejing*, Laozi states:

> One who assists the ruler of men by means of the
>   way does not intimidate the empire by a show of
>   arms. . . .
> Where troops have encamped
> There will brambles grow;
> In the wake of a mighty army
> Bad harvests follow without fail. (*Daodejing* 30:69)

The way of Daoism teaches simplicity, spontaneity, tranquility, weakness, and non-action *(wuwei)*, which means taking no action that is contrary to nature and letting nature takes its own course (Chan 1963, 136). Such a teaching naturally denies the use of force and violence. In chapter 31, Laozi continues:

> It is because arms are instruments of ill omens and there are things that detest them that one who has the way does not abide by their use. . . . When one is compelled to use them, it is best to do so without relish. There is no glory in victory, and to glorify it despite this is to exult in the killing of men. One who exults in the killing of men will never have his way in the empire. (*Daodejing* 31:72)

Therefore, according to the *Daodejing*, the use of force and arms is a curse to the country. Although *Daodejing* does not totally rule out the use of force, Laozi claims that war is found only in the empire when the concepts of Daoism do not prevail (*Daodejing* 41).

The first systematic argument against warfare in China is advanced by Mozi who lived in the period of Warring States. Mozi is noted for his teachings of universal love for all humans. To begin with, Mozi was a student of Confucianism. Dissatisfied with Confucius's complicated teachings on decorum, Mozi became a critic of the Confucian tradition. His essay "Against Offensive Warfare" is the first of its kind in Chinese history. In order to complete his self-assigned mission of "promoting what is beneficial to the world and to eliminate what is harmful" (Mo Tzu 1963, 39), Mozi and his followers worked actively in bringing peace and non-aggression among the states. He and his followers even risked their lives in assisting in the defense of a besieged state (Lowe 1992, 18).

Mozi's essay, "Against Offensive Warfare," consists of three parts: 1) Mozi first demonstrates by logical argument the unrighteousness of war. 2) He then details the wastefulness and economic unprofitability of wars of conquest. 3) Finally, Mozi points out that war benefits neither Heaven, nor spirits, nor human beings.

In demonstrating the unrighteousness of war, Mozi argues that the unrighteousness of an act is in proportion to the harm caused to others. Stealing horses and cattle is, therefore, worse than stealing chickens and pigs, which is, in turn, worse than stealing peaches and plums. The murder of one hundred men is worse than the murder of 10 and, in turn, the murder of 10 is worse than the murder of one. Mozi laments that people can readily recognize small acts of unrighteousness but fail to perceive great unrighteousness like war (Mo Tzu 1963, 50).

In pointing at war as unproductive and destructive, Mozi observed that in war the productivity of the state will be diminished and there will be a great loss in human resources and materials. According to Mozi's calculation, an army is composed of at least hundreds of nobles, thousands of commoners, and tens of thousands of laborers. A war takes months or years, during which production comes to a standstill. Only one-fifth of the equipment needed for war, such as chariots, horses, and tents, can be recovered after use. To subdue a small walled city of three to seven square miles involves the death of literally hundreds of thousands of people (Mo Tzu 1963, 54–55). A successful invasion gains only a small amount of land. Mozi concludes that for a successful invasion, gains *are less than losses* since one gains what is in surplus, land, but loses what is insufficient, human resources.

Although there were four states during the period of Warring States that succeeded in expanding their territories through offensive warfare, Mozi reminds us that there were ten thousand other small states involved in wars which became extinct. This proves that offensive war is an unsuccessful strategy in ordering a state. War is likened to a drug that proves beneficial only to some and is, therefore, not effective (Mo Tzu 1963, 59). It is, however, interesting to note that an eloquent statesman like Mozi, who argued rigorously against warfare, still supported a just war against tyrant rulers. When the sage kings engaged in war, it was not offensive but "punishment" and they merely acted as Heaven's human instruments (Mo Tzu 1963, 56). This pragmatic position is universal in Chinese ancient writings.

As we can see, Mozi and both the Confucian *Analects* and the Daoist *Daodejing* support the idea of peace and nonviolence. Both traditions, based on pragmatic motives, are against warfare. War causes death and damage. Moreover, it is counterproductive and there is more lost than gained. Both traditions also reject war on the basis of their vision of government. For Confucians, it is a benevolent government that uses less force, and the Daoist favors the course of nature which uses no force. It is, therefore, clear that in the textual tradition of China there are ample supports for the pursuit of nonviolence and peacemaking.

To what extent and in what way these ideals are shared and carried out in Chinese villages of the South is our next concern. In our discussion of Chinese villages, we have chosen ethnographic reports from three representative locations. They are Heyuan of the Fujian province, Zhongyuan of the Jiangxi province, and Pingshi from the Guangdong province.

## HEYUAN IN THE FUJIAN PROVINCE

Heyuan is the name of the river that runs through two counties in Fujian Province. Along the river, there are 13 villages comprised of some 10 major lineages. According to their lineage registers, the residents of the 13 villages came to the area between the period of the end of the Song (1279 C.E.) and the beginning of the Ming (1369 C.E.) dynasties. The 10 lineages can be loosely described as the Hakka people or the Guest People, meaning that they were immigrants from the North and spoke a related Hakka dialect. There is evidence to show that the original inhabitants of the area are *She* people, now a minority race in China. Challenge to the life of the Guest People comes from two fronts. One is from competition among the Guest People of different lineages for scarce resources. The other is from competition with the aboriginal people. As the fieldworker Yang Yanjie observes, compared with other areas, Heyuan has fewer conflicts and less violence between lineages and villages (Yang 1996, 271). A major factor accounting for peaceful relations between lineages in the Heyuan area is the rotating worship of their local god, Marquis Hehu.

There are at least two different versions with regard to the origin of the local god Marquis Hehu. According to the local gazette, Marquis Hehu was a local official who gave alms to the people during a famine. Upon his death, people built a temple in his memory. The oral tradition, however, presents Hehu as the spirit of a frog or a turtle who once helped the emperor of the Tang dynasty, Li Shimin (R. 627–650 C.E.), to cross a river when his enemy pursued him. When Li became the emperor, Hehu was granted the title of Marquis. No matter what his origin, Hehu is very popular in the area. People call him grandpa *(gongtai)*. Although there is a permanent temple for Marquis Hehu that is situated in the middle of the Heyuan area, the major ritual associated with the god consists of rotating worship. This means that the statue of the god is circulated among the 13 villages in Heyuan for worshipping.

The rotating worship of the god starts with the celebration of his birthday, on the 2nd of February of the lunar calendar. The birthday of the god is an occasion for the people of the 13 villages to gather together in the temple of the god. A one-day, elaborate offering or *jiao* ritual is organized by the 13 villages. A *jiao* ritual is a Daoist ritual consisting of lavish sacrifices to local gods and spirits, adapted and performed by local Daoists (Lagerwey 1987, 20–21). A committee formed by representatives of the 13 villages oversees all the details of the event.

The order of circulation varies in the course of time but the principle remains the same. The statue of the god is taken, in turn, to stay in one village for one year. Therefore, after the joint celebration of the god's birthday, the village whose turn it is to receive the god will take the statue of the god back to their village. Before they take the god back home, the god will first be taken on a big parade to the market of the village, then on to neighboring villages. Yang reports that the people joining the parade sometimes form a line as long as two to three kilometers (Yang 1996, 257). After the parade, the god will be brought back to the lineage hall of the hosting village. Depending on whether the village is multi-lineage, the god will take turns staying in different lineage halls in the village. During the stay of the god, the responsibility for worshipping is divided among the branches of each lineage. Within each branch, every family will be assigned one to two days, depending on the size of the family, and will be held responsible for the worshipping of the god. The responsibility includes hiring a team of musicians to play music in the lineage hall and offering pork and chicken, the best food in a Chinese village, to the god. Above all, the family has to be a host to a dinner of 10 to 20 tables, inviting guests from the village.

During his one-year stay in the village, the god will be visited by other villages on two occasions. Because of its large area geographically, Heyuan is divided into upper and lower sections. When the god stays in one of the five villages situated in the upper parts, all five villages come to visit the god with lanterns on the fifteenth of the first lunar month, that is, the Yuanxiao festival. The same applies to the eight villages in the lower Heyuan. Visiting of the god coincides with the celebration of the Yuanxiao festival. On the fifteenth day of August, the village that will receive the god in the next year has to come to visit the god.

On the first day of February, one day before the birthday of the god, the one-year stay of the god in the village ends. The god will be sent back to the temple. Thirteen villages will come together again for the performing of another elaborate *jiao* ritual. An important joint meeting of the representatives from the 13 villages will be held to discuss any matters arising from the rotating worship. Then, on the second of February, comes the celebration of the god's birthday, which also marks the beginning of another cycle of rotating worship. The god will be taken to stay for a year in another  village.

The key to peace in Heyuan is the human tie created through the worship of their local god, Marquis Hehu. As we have seen, the rotating worship of their local god requires complex organization. It involves all levels of cooperation and collaboration. The celebration of the god's birthday is a joint function of the 13 villages. An organizing committee has to be formed by representatives from the 13 villages. While the god is taking turns staying in each of the 13 villages, neighboring villages have to organize visits to the god. During the stay of the god in each village, every family takes turns organizing a banquet for the god and for their fellow villagers. It is through the rotating worship that the 13 villages are brought together to strengthen the ties both within each village and among the 13 villages. We will see below that the role of local religion in maintaining the peace of the region is prominent in South China.

## ZHONGFANG OF THE JIANGXI PROVINCE

In a valley 10 kilometers east of the Yudu county seat in the Gannan region of Jiangxi Province, there is a group of 15 villages known as *wuchang* (house area). During the time of the Republic of China (1912–1949), this region was called Zhongfang. Each village is uni-lineage and there are altogether eight different lineages. The Zeng lineage occupies seven out of the 15 villages while the Li lineage occupies two. Six other lineages occupy one village each.

According to the fieldwork report by Ziyu (Ziyu 1997, 106), the two dominant lineages, Zeng and Li, have a history of conflicts. Ziyu describes a recent conflict between the two lineages. One Zeng family member built a flat yard for his drying of grains near the border of two villages inhabited by Zeng and Li. The Li protested on the basis of geomantic influence, and a fight was about to break out. This was resolved as a result of reconciliation efforts by a member of the Li family. It is worth noticing that conflicts do not lead to armed fights or bloodshed according to the report. An explanation again may be found in the local religion of the area.

The 15 villages worship three popular local gods known together as the three grandpas: Zhang, Gao, and Lai gong. Zhang and Lai gong were dressed as civil officials while Gao gong was a military official. Both Gao and Lai gong died martyrs in the cause of justice. When Gao was a military official, the prince oppressed his people. Gao fought against the prince with his army but was killed by the prince. Legend has it that Gao eventually became a god.

Lai gong was a civil official killed by a boatman who extorted money from him on his trip crossing a river. Lai was killed because he refused to yield to the wicked boatman. Comparatively speaking, there are many more stories circulated about the Zhang gong than Gao and Lai gong. He was a Daoist trained in Mt. Qi. He engaged in a contest of magic with another local Daoist, Hanyi gong. Zhang deeply moved the old mother of Mt. Qi, a divine instructress, by drinking up the water used to wash her wounded leg. She eventually taught Zhang to become an immortal. Despite his becoming an immortal, Zhang likes to turn himself into a big-headed fun-loving god who goes out to play with twelve-year-old children, thereby preventing them from doing their adult-defined duties. Zhang is best described as an "unruly god" (Shahar and Weller 1996).

The three grandpas have a temple, and their worship centers on their temple festival which is in May and lasts for half a month. The

15 villages take turns receiving the gods in sedan chairs into their lineage hall where they stay for one night. The date on which the gods arrive is so important that the traditional Dragon Boat festival (Duanwu) is celebrated at the same time. This means that the festival of each village is different, and it changes each year as the order in which the village receives the gods is determined by rotation.

The most exciting part of the temple festival of the three grandpas is the ritual that takes place just before the gods are passed on to the neighbors. It is called *lian pusa* (refining the gods or practicing with the gods) and is also known as *zaying* (to set up the base camp) (Ziyu 1997, 109). Five flags with different colors are set up in four directions. The sedan chairs on which the gods are seated are carried by youths zigzagging through the flags. The youths wear no clothes on the upper part of their bodies in order to show off their muscles. They only carry one handle of the sedan chair to allow maximum shaking of the chairs. Running ahead of them is another youth carrying a flag. Should he not run fast enough, the youths carrying the sedan chairs will crash into him with their chairs. The running is accompanied by loud shouting, which shows the strength and power of the gods and the people carrying them. It is important to recognize this ritual in the context of the many conflicts between the villages, especially between the two biggest lineages, Zeng and Li. The noise and muscular demonstration of the ritual can then be understood as the channeling and symbolizing of the conflicts and clashes between neighboring lineages.

The conflict and tension arises from scarce resources among the 15 villages in Zhongfang of Yudu. Although conflict seems to be inevitable, armed conflict and bloodshed are avoided. The eight lineages, although competing for scarce resources, manage to live peacefully together. Again, the key for peace is to be found in the rotating worship of a local god. Unlike Heyuan, the god in Zhongfang of Yudu is circulated and stays in each village only for one day. The half-month event of the god's temple festival is an occasion for the 15 villages to come together to coordinate the circulation of the god's statue. As we have pointed out, the ritual involved in passing the god's statue from one village to another expresses conflicts between villages symbolically, in a non-harmful way. The ritual, therefore, functions as a safety valve for the 15 villages.

## THE PINGSHI OF GUANGDONG PROVINCE

The Pingshi township is situated on the border between two provinces, Hunan and Guangdong, and it acts as a trans-shipment center for the two provinces. While people in Hunan supply pigs for Guangzhou, the capital of Guangdong, they rely on Guangzhou for the import of salt. Before the building of a railway in 1933, goods were shipped back and forth between Guangzhou and Pingshi by using the Wu River. According to residents still living in Pingshi (Tam 1998), in the past, there were more than a hundred ships docked along the river in Pingshi every day. Because of the intense commercial activities, a commercial street one-and-a-half kilometers long with more than two hundred shops was developed along the Wu River in Pingshi. Most owners of the shops lived on the second floor of the shops, forming a community of about a thousand people. Surrounding the commercial street were 80 villages with 42 lineages. According to one old person living on the street, there used to be a lineage hall on the street that housed the tablets of ancestors of the 42 lineages. Apparently there was joint ancestor worship, details of which are forgotten. Of the 42, there were 10 dominating lineages. Representatives of the 10 lineages would meet in the street at an interval of between two to five years to resolve any conflicts arising between the lineages. Despite the complex mixture of lineages in the street, there were never any armed fights, conflicts, or bloodshed among lineages living in the area.

Just as there is a mixture of lineages from different provinces in Pingshi, there is also a complicated mixture of temples in the area. Unfortunately, not a single one survived the Cultural Revolution (1966–1976). There had been a temple for one of the most popular gods in Guangdong—Guandi. There was also a temple for the famous Mazu goddess in Fujian. There were altogether some 20 temples in the area. On the commercial street itself, there were six major temples. In addition, there were three chambers of commerce: one for Jiangxi, one for Hunan, and one for Guangdong provinces. All of the chambers of commerce had statues of their local gods and they functioned partly as temples. Among the six temples in the street, the temple for the General god was the most popular. According to the legend, the General god was a general in the Eastern Han dynasty (24–220 C.E.) who was sent to the South to fight the Barbarian. He died in the war, and the people built a temple to commemorate him.

Pingshi has become a famous tourist spot for boat-drifting in China, owing to the strong current of the Wu River. While people today seek excitement by drifting down the stream, people in the past risked their lives in transporting goods on the river to and from Guangzhou and Pingshi. At the start of every trip, all boatmen would go to worship in the temple of the General who protected them from accidents on the river.

The climax of worship for the General god remained its temple festival. It was held in conjunction with eight other major temples in the area. Every temple had its own temple festivals but all of them would join in the celebration of other temple festivals. Therefore, the eight temples took turns in hosting a temple festival. Four of the eight temples were in the commercial street: the temple for the General (Jiangjun), the temple of the three worlds (Sanjie) with Guandi as the main deity, the temple for officials of the altar (Tangong), and the temple for the returning dragon (Huilong) with Mazu as the main deity. The other four temples were in the neighboring villages: Liantang, Guitang, Tangkou, and Shuinui wan. The names of gods in these temples have mostly been forgotten as these temples failed to survive the Cultural Revolution in the sixties. The celebrations of the temple festivals were quite uniform. A parade would first be organized by representatives from major lineages in Pingshi, which visited all the eight temples. During the procession, the god who was celebrating a birthday led the line while the other seven gods followed behind. Then, there was an elaborate *jiao* ritual consisting of sacrifices and deliverance of the souls of those who had a violent death or who died without offspring.

The case of Pingshi once again has shown the role of local religion in lineage alliance, which contributes substantially to peace in the region. Pingshi's economy is different from other traditional Chinese villages in that commerce has replaced the traditional economy of agriculture. It is a community of multi-lineages with different places of origin. Yet, the mechanism for resolving potential conflicts among lineages remains the same as in other areas. Although they do not share a single local god, residents of Pingshi organize joint religious functions, thereby bringing together people of different faiths. Joint ancestor worship not only strengthens the ties among the 42 lineages but also creates an occasion to discuss problems and resolve conflicts between lineages. Joint temple festivals also help to bring people together and strengthen their ties.

## CONCLUSION

We have studied three different locations in South China where there are, due to scarce resources, either existing or potential conflicts and tensions among lineages living in the area. Armed conflicts and bloodshed are, however, avoided because of the existence of an informal mechanism that prevents and channels conflicts. This mechanism is provided by the temple festivals of the local religions. A temple festival basically celebrates the birthday of a god. It is an elaborate event that calls for cooperation from different lineages in the region. An organizing committee provides an occasion for discussion of interests, settling of differences, and resolution of disputes.

A large-scale parade is the climax of every temple festival. The parade allows each lineage to organize its own troupe, be it for a lion dance, dragon dance, or other performance. The parade is often a demonstration of the strength of a lineage. The strength of a lineage is shown by the extravagance of its performance and the number of male youths participating in the parade. Field observation tells us that the noisy and powerful procession in the temple festival also functions as a safety valve for a non-harmful symbolic expression of conflicts and clashes among lineages.

Another salient element of the temple festival is its communal character. Not only will representatives of lineages come together for the occasion but also every single member of the community will come. All participate in the festival and enjoy the carnival spirit of the event that obviously helps to ease tension and subvert hatred arising from competition for scarce resources in daily life. The coming together of the whole community generates a community spirit which is heightened by the entertainment provided by the festival, including theatrical productions which are a must in every single temple festival.

The elite Confucian and Daoist traditions support the position of nonviolence, and the people at the grassroots level realize the ideal of nonviolence through their practice of local religions. Faith in their local gods has helped the Chinese people to work together with their competitors for scarce resources. Their faith challenges them to act fairly and to share equally the responsibility to serve the gods. In serving their gods, the Chinese people strive to enlarge their brotherhood and sisterhood beyond family lineage. Religion also provides a basis for creative cooperation and coexistence of lineages in a region.

Temple festivals become the key for regional peace in China as they help to express and channel inter-lineage conflicts and tensions in symbolic but non-harmful ways. Temple festivals also call for creative and democratic cooperation among neighboring lineages which is realized in the form of rotating worship. It is local temple festivals which help to maintain regional peace and prevent destructive bloodshed and armed conflicts among lineages. In this connection, temple festivals could be developed as "social capital" (Bourdieu 1986, 248) which produces profit in the form of regional stability and tourist attraction.

Lineage alliance and regional identity based on local religion can be resources for reconciliation and peacemaking as well as potential weapons for inter-communal conflict (Lamley 1990). Armed conflicts and bloodshed among lineages are not well documented in China. They are, therefore, difficult to study. In the history of Taiwan, armed conflict between Cantonese and Hakka people based on regional, cultural, and religious differences is a well-known occurrence (Ino 1965, 929–57). Some have claimed that, since the Qing dynasty (1644–1912 C.E.), on average, there has been an armed battle every eight years (Committee of Historical Documents in Taiwan Province 1979, 42 [Taiwan sheng]).

The dual function of lineage alliance as the root of nonviolence and yet as a fuel for conflict calls for further studies and research. This dual function can be a resource for reconciliation and peacemaking as well as a potential weapon for inter-communal conflict (Lamley 1990).

## STUDY QUESTIONS

1. Why does Tam Wai Lun suggest that an understanding of Chinese religious life requires a "bottom up" approach to the study of Chinese religion?

2. How did Confucius's observations of actual leaders during his time praise values such as peace?

3. What is the name of Mozi's famous essay, and what are the three major parts of his arguments against warfare?

4. Briefly outline the three examples of local village practices that Tam Wai Lun uses to illustrate Chinese peacemaking, and summarize what is common among them.

5. Can you speculate how Tam Wai Lun's examples may suggest models for other cultural contexts, using other means of cooperation and exchange between groups?

## ANNOTATED BIBLIOGRAPHY

Bourdieu, Pierre. "The Forms of Capital." In *Handbook of Theory and Research for the Sociology of Education*, ed. John G. Richardson, trans. Richard Nice, 241–258. New York: Greenwood Press, 1986.

Chan, Wing-tsit. *A Sourcebook in Chinese Philosophy*. Princeton: Princeton University Press, 1963.

Confucius. *The Analects*. Trans. D. C. Lau. New York: Penguin Books, 1970.

Creel, Herrlee G. *What Is Taoism? And Other Studies in Chinese Cultural History*. Chicago: University of Chicago Press, 1970.

Ino, Kanori. *Taiwan Bunkashi* (Cultural Monograph of Taiwan). Tokyo: Tokoshoin, 1965. Ino's book contains one chapter that deals with regional armed conflict in Taiwan. It enables us to see the dual function of lineage and regional alliance in Chinese society, namely as both resource for reconciliation and cause of violent conflict.

Lagerwey, John. Preface to *Meizhou diqu de miaohui yu zongzu* (Temple Festivals and Lineage in Meizhou), ed. Fang Xuejia. Hong Kong: International Hakka Studies Association, Overseas Chinese Archives, and École Française d'Extrême-Orient, 1996. This series, which will have 10 volumes, contains one of the most updated ethnographic reports on traditional rural society in South China. The series is a product of Lagerwey's project on the structure and dynamics of Chinese rural society. The project studies Chinese society through traditional religious festivals and it provides ample primary sources for research in peace and nonviolence in Chinese society. Although all essays are written in Chinese, Lagerwey has provided the readers with a helpful summary in English in the beginning of each volume. Essays written in English to review volume one to five of the series are planned for publication in a conference volume, *Ethnography in China Today: A Critical Assessment of Methods and Results*, ed. Professor Daniel Overmyer.

———. *Taoist Ritual in Chinese Society and History*. New York: MacMillan Publishing, 1987.

Lamley, Harry J. "Lineage Feuding in Southern Fujian and Eastern Guangdong under Qing Rule." In *Violence in China: Essays in Culture,* ed. Jonathan N. Lipman and Stevan Harrell. Albany: State University of New York Press, 1990.

Lopez, Donald S., Jr., ed. *Religions of China in Practice.* Princeton: Princeton University Press, 1996.

Lowe, Scott. *Mo Tzu's Religious Blueprint for a Chinese Utopia: The Will and the Way.* Lewiston/Queenston/Lampeter: The Edwin Mellen Press, 1992. Lowe's book is a helpful study on Mozi, who put forward the first systematic argument against offensive warfare in Chinese history. Lowe's book contains a summary of Mozi's argument and critical discussion on other studies on Mozi.

*Mencius.* Trans. D. C. Lau. New York: Penguin Books, 1970.

Redfield, Robert. *Peasant Society and Culture: An Anthropological Approach to Civilization.* Chicago & London: University of Chicago Press, 1956.

Shahar, Meir and Robert P. Weller, eds. *Unruly Gods: Divinity and Society in China.* Honolulu: University of Hawai'i Press, 1996.

Taiwan sheng wenxian weiyuan hui (Committee of Historical Documents in Taiwan Province). *Taiwan shi* (History of Taiwan). Taipei: Zhongwen tushu guan, 1979.

Tam, Wai Lun. "Yuebei diqu Lao pingshi zhen laojie di shequ jiegou yu zongjiao wenhua" (The Social Structure, Commerce and Religious Culture of the Old Street in the Lao Pingshi Township in Northern Guangdong). Paper presented at the Second International Conference on Hakkaology, Institute of Ethnology, Academia sinica, Taipei, November 6, 1998. This paper as well as the section on Pingshi of the present chapter is based on the author's fieldwork studies conducted in Pingshi during the months of July and December 1997.

Teiser, Stephen F. "The Spirits of Chinese Religion." In *Religion of China in Practice,* ed. Donald Lopez, 3–37. Princeton: Princeton University Press, 1996.

Tzu, Lao. *Tao Te Ching.* Trans. D. C. Lau. New York: Penguin Books, 1963.

Tzu, Mo. *Basic Writings.* Trans. Burton Watson. New York: Columbia University Press, 1963.

Yang, Yanjie, *Minxi kejia zonzu shehui yanjiu* (Field Studies of Hakka Lineage Society in Minxi). Hong Kong: International Hakka Studies Association, Overseas Chinese Archives, and École Française d'Extrême-Orient, 1996. Yang's book is the only book in the series written by one author. It contains precious information and analysis of Hakka lineage and society in Minxi. Yang's study on the rotating worship—a sociological pattern in the Hakka countryside—represents a pioneering study on the subject.

Ziyu (Li Yaohua). *Zhongfang sangong yingshen jishi* (Welcoming the Sangong of Zhongfang). In *Gannan diqu di miaohui yu zongzu* (Temple Festivals and Lineages in Gannan), ed. Luo Yong and John Lagerwey, 94–110. Hong Kong: International Hakka Studies Association, Overseas Chinese Archives, and École Française d'Extrême-Orient, 1997. This volume of the series collects ethnographic essays in Gannan of Jiangxi Province. It contains wonderful reports of important temple festivals in different counties and villages. It is another important primary source for the study of how religious practice of temple festivals in China increases communication and cooperation, and thus reduces violence and conflicts. A review essay on this volume written by the present author appears in the conference volume, *Ethnography in China Today: A Critical Assessment of Methods and Results*, ed. Daniel Overmyer.

# 4

# *Ahimsa* and the Unity of All Things

## A Hindu View of Nonviolence

### Sunanda Y. Shastri and Yajneshwar S. Shastri

In order to speak of issues of war and peace in Hindu thought,
it is imperative that one survey the classic literature on the subject
of *ahimsa*, which has developed over thousands of years on the
Indian subcontinent. In Hindu traditions, nonviolence is termed
*ahimsa*. *Ahimsa*, however, is not equivalent to pacifism, conscientious objection to war, or civil disobedience as understood in Western
circles. It is a philosophical, religious, and ethical concept with a

Sunanda Shastri holds a doctorate from Gujarat University, Ahmedabad, India, in
Sanskrit and is senior assistant professor in the Department of Sanskrit in the School
of Languages at Gujarat University. She is fluent in six languages: Sanskrit, English,
Hindi, Marathi, Kannada, and Gujarati. She is author of more than forty articles
and six books, including *Naradasmruti: A Historical, Social, Political, and Legal
Study, Sanskrit for Beginners*, and *Teachings of Upanishads*. She has been a visit-
ing scholar at Loyola Marymount University three times, teaching Sanskrit and
Upanishads.

Yajneshwar S. Shastri is director of the University School of Psychology, Education,
and Philosophy and professor and head of the Department of Philosophy at Gujarat
University, Ahmedabad, India. An internationally known scholar of Indology specializing in Indian philosophy and comparative religions, he is fluent in Sanskrit,
English, Hindi, Kannada, Marathi, and Gujarati, and has been visiting professor
at Cleveland State and Loyola Marymount Universities. The author of numerous
articles and books, including *Foundations of Hinduism, Traverses on the Less
Trodden Path of Indian Philosophy and Religions,* and *Harmony among the
Religions of India*, he is president of the Global Peace Foundation based in Gujarat.

number of important connotations. *Ahimsa* is not used in a purely negative sense but is used as a positive antidote to violence.

*Ahimsa* is the negation of violence *(himsa)*. One can see the wide range of *ahimsa* by noting the meanings of *himsa:*

Treating one's self as different from others
Failing to realize the fundamental unity of all beings
Torturing or destroying one's own body by ignorance
Causing pain to others
Troubling others physically, mentally, or vocally
Hurting or injuring others by speech, mind, and body
Killing or separating the life force from the body of others
Destroying, knowingly or unknowingly, the properties and
    wealth of others
Exhibiting hatred towards others
Intimidating, beating, tying up, destroying and taking the
    livelihood of others
Stealing the property or belongings of others
Injuring other harmless beings for the sake of one's own
    pleasure
Hurting innocent beings by using harsh words
Oppressing or harassing people by levying undue taxes
Cutting down the various (especially medicinal) trees and
    plants
Acting against the wishes of parents and teachers
Abusing of students (by a teacher)
Exploiting and taking unfair advantage of others, wrong think-
    ing, and wrong action (*Rgveda* I.114.7; II.12.10, II.33.15;
    VII.104.7, 12, 16, 19; *Ishavasya Upanishad* 3; *Manu-
    smruti,* I.29; IV.162; V.45; VII.285, 288, 293, 297, 310;
    XI.63; *Mahabharata Shantiparva,* 71.15; *Anushasana-
    parva,* XIII.113.8; 115.19; *Shabdakaipadruma, A Sanskrit
    Dictionary on* Ahimsa, n.d.)

The essence of all these various meanings of violence is that violence causes pain or suffering in one way or another. *Ahimsa* is an antidote to all these kinds of violence. But there is far more to *ahimsa* than merely non-hurting or non-killing. It includes giving up concepts of "otherness," "separateness," "selfishness," and "self-centeredness" and identifying oneself with all other beings.

*Ahimsa* is a positive doctrine of love, friendship, and equality among all living beings of the universe. This has as its basis the acceptance of the ultimate goodness of mankind. It renounces hatred and cultivates compassion based on a sense of oneness of all and feelings of kinship with all life forms. Therefore, according to Hindu tradition, *ahimsa* is to be understood as a mental attitude we cultivate toward others.

Sometimes, however, we may have to appear to be cruel and injurious even though our heart is full of love and kindness. Shakespeare beautifully expresses this in *Hamlet* when he says, "I am cruel only to be kind." Mothers sometimes may scold or beat their children, but their intention is not to hurt their children. It is to improve the children's behavior and make them good citizens. A surgeon may appear cruel and bloody while performing operations but his action cannot be called *himsa*. So, the concept of *ahimsa*, in Hindu traditions, includes two ethical ideals: one is the pursuit of the good of humanity *(lokahita)* and the other is devotion to the good of all living beings and the environment *(sarvabhutahita)*.

## SPECIFIC TEXTS AND TRADITIONS THAT SUPPORT THE POSITION OF NONVIOLENCE

The Four Vedas are the foundational scriptures of the Hindu culture. The earliest Veda is the *Rgveda* (*circa* 3000 B.C.E.) and it is believed to be the earliest poetic and religious document of the human race. The *Rgveda* uses the term *himsa* in the sense of physical injury and killing, and *ahimsa* in the sense of physical non-injury. Forgiveness is asked for committing violence towards others. It is also mentioned in the *Rgveda* that non-injury is beneficial in establishing friendship and cultivating a sense of oneness. The *Rgveda* also states that "man must protect other men from all sides." The spirit of nonviolence is seen in the immortal passages of *Rgveda* such as:

> Come together, talk together,
> Let our minds be in harmony.
> Common be our prayer,
> Common be our end,
> Common be our purpose,
> Common be our deliberations,

Common be our desires,
United be our hearts,
United be our intentions,
Perfect be the union among us. (*Rgveda* X.191.2–4)

In these passages, the unity of mankind is emphasized in order to maintain peace and harmony in the universe and society.
The *Yajurveda* declares that:

May all beings look at me
With friendly eye.
May I look at all
With friendly eye.
May all look at one another
With friendly eye. (*Yajurveda* XXXVI.18)

*Yajurveda* prohibits killing of animals and birds by stating: "No person should kill animals and birds helpful to all; rather, by serving them one should attain happiness" (*Yajurveda* XIII.47).

In *Samaveda*, it is said that: "We slay no victims, we worship entirely by the repetition of the sacred verses" (*Samaveda* I.II. IX.2).

The *Atharvaveda* says:

Lord by your grace I keep
goodwill towards all,
known and unknown
human beings. (*Atharvaveda* XVII.1–7)

These Vedic statements clearly imply that to maintain peace, harmony, and friendship, we should give up hatred, violence, and a sense of separateness.

The Vedic philosophy provides a theoretical basis for performing nonviolence by reflecting a vibrant, encompassing worldview which looks upon all objects in the universe, living and so-called non-living, as being rooted in and pervaded by one divine power, *Sat*. (*Sat* literally means absolute or ultimate reality.) In this universe everything is interconnected, interrelated, and interdependent. All things are a manifestation of that one supreme power or spirit, the great forces—the earth, the sky, the wind, fire, oceans, as well as various orders of life including human beings, plants, trees, animals. All are bound to each other within the great rhythms of nature. There is an organic unity in the whole universe. This idea is beautifully described in one of the hymns of the *Rgveda* (X.90.1–4).

According to *Upanishadic* literature *(Vedanta)*, everything in the universe is rooted in pure-consciousness and pervaded by pure-consciousness. The *Vedanta* declares the spiritual unity of all existence in categorical terms by stating that "In this cosmos, whatever exists—living and non-living—all that is, is pervaded by one divine 'consciousness'" (*Ishavasya Upanishad* 1). This all-pervasive nature of Brahman or ultimate reality is beautifully described in several *Upanishads*. The *Mundaka-Upanishad*, for example, states:

Indeed, this Brahman (pure-consciousness)
is the Immortal Being.
In front is Brahman, behind is Brahman.
It is to the right and to the left.
It spreads forth above and below,
Indeed, Brahman is the effulgent universe.
    (*Mundaka Upanishad* II.II.12)

The *Aitereya Upanishad* declares, "The Reality behind all these things of the universe is the Brahman, which is pure-consciousness. All things are established in consciousness, work through consciousness, and their foundation is consciousness" (III.V.3). "All that is, is Brahman," says *Chandogya Upanishad* (III.XIV.1). The *Taittiriya Upanishad* clearly states that "There is an all-pervading higher reality—Brahman, out of which we are born and to which we will ultimately return" (III.1.6). The *Svetasvatara Upanishad* also establishes the close relationship between the divinity—Brahman—and the external universe, identifying natural phenomena with the Brahman, from which all the worlds sprang (IV.II.3–4).

One could continue with dozens, if not hundreds, more texts along these lines, but the general point is clear, namely, that the sense of duality or separateness is the root cause of hatred and violence. Therefore, the *Ishavasya Upanishad* advises us to see one's own self in everything and everything in one's own self; then we will not hate anyone. In loving others we are loving ourselves, and when hurting others we are hurting ourselves, because we all carry the same divinity. Once this unity of all is realized, it is thought that there will be no sorrow, no grief, and no delusion, and peace will prevail in the heart of every being. The essence of the Vedantic notion then is that the Brahman, the pure-consciousness, is inseparable from its manifestations. To hurt or violate any creature or object in nature is to hurt or violate Brahman itself. This notion of fundamental sameness is the basis for nonviolent action towards all. Killer and killed: both are divine from the perspective of this classic.

The term *ahimsa* is also used in a moral sense in several texts of the Hindu tradition. The first reference to *ahimsa* in a moral sense is found in *Kapisthalakathasamhita*, which is a pre-*Upanishadic* reference. Here, there is a reference to the non-killing of animals in sacrifice (XXXI. 11). The *Chandogya Upanishad* uses the word *ahimsa* in the list of religious virtues, such as truthfulness, nonviolence, austerity, straightforwardness, and charity (111.17.4). *Ahimsa* should be practiced by one who desires to attain the world of Brahman and not to "return again" (VII. 14.1). In later *Upanishads* the practice of *ahimsa* is glorified. "Seeing an all-pervading self in everything is the highest form of *ahimsa*," says *Jabaladarshana Upanishad* (I.8). "It is the practice of *ahimsa* which takes one to the state of immortality," states *Naradaparivrajakopanishad* (III.45). The *Shandilya Upanishad* defines *ahimsa* as "not to cause pain to any living beings at any time either mental, vocal, or physical" and says that it is one of the ten moral restraints, strictly to be followed by yogis (I.1).

Nonviolence is glorified in the later texts of the classical literature of the Hindu tradition. These texts might have been influenced by the ascetic and yogic traditions. In the *Ramayana* of Valmiki, one of the great epics of the Hindus, it is mentioned that the descendants of Rama (the race of the Ikshvaku) are the lovers of *ahimsa* (V.31.4). The *Mahabharata*, another great Hindu epic composed by Vyasa, contains an extensive discussion of the importance of *ahimsa* and also provides a concise philosophical definition of *ahimsa* from the Hindu perspective. It says, "Action which is against one's own desires should also not be done to others. One should never do that to another which one regards as injurious to one's own self. Therefore, one should treat all others as one's own self" (XIII.113–8.115–19). One who does not injure or does not take away the lives of living beings is not bound by karma

(*Shantiparva* 277). It is important to note that the "golden rule," namely, that "One should never do that to another which one considers undesirable for oneself," was formulated in *Mahabharata* long before the rabbinic and Christian era.

According to the *Mahabharata*, the practice of *ahimsa* is a duty which is complete with respect to its reward (*Shantiparva* 272, 20). The merit of a man practicing *ahimsa* is said to be inexhaustible and enables one to become free from all sins (XIII.116.41; *Shantiparva* 35.37). An action which is done with violence kills faith and, faith being destroyed, it ruins the man. The merit of other penances is destroyed if one practices *himsa* (*Shantiparva* 192.17, 246.6). Thus, *ahimsa* is the highest form of religion, virtue, and duty *(ahimsa paramodharmah)*.

The *Anushasanaparva* of the *Mahabharata* beautifully describes the merit and importance of *ahimsa* in several verses. In these passages, *ahimsa* is exalted as the best of all actions, giving birth to righteousness and serving as the best possible means of purification. The following few selected passages indicate the significance of nonviolence within a Hindu context:

Those right-souled persons who desire beauty, faultlessness of limbs, long life, understanding, mental and physical strength, and memory should abstain from acts of violence. (XIII.115.8)

*Ahimsa* is the path of righteousness. It is the highest purification. It is also the highest truth from which all *dharmas* (virtues) proceed. (XIII.125.25)

*Ahimsa* is the highest *dharma* (virtue, duty). *Ahimsa* is the best austerity. *Ahimsa* is the greatest gift. *Ahimsa* is the highest self-control. *Ahimsa* is the highest sacrifice. *Ahimsa* is the highest power. *Ahimsa* is the highest friend. *Ahimsa* is the highest truth. *Ahimsa* is the highest teaching. (XIII. 116.37–41)

Here again, as we have noted in other texts, it is stated that *ahimsa* really means seeing or treating others as one's own self, giving up a sense of separateness:

That person who indeed *sees* being as
like his own self, who has cast aside the stick,
and whose anger is conquered, prospers happily
in the life to come. (XIII.114.6)

Even the gods are bewildered at the path
of the one who seeks the abode of no abode,
who sees all beings with the being of oneself
as that of all beings. (XIII.114.7)

From not holding to the other
as opposite from oneself
there is the essence of *dharma*. (XIII.114.8)

The *Bhagavadgita*, the famous philosophical text of the Hindus
(which is part of the *Mahabharata*), does in certain circumstances
support war and violence to remove injustice and evil forces from
society, and to purify society. Philosophically, however, the text
repeats the themes previously noted by asking spiritual aspirants
to look on all as analogous with one's own self (VI.32) and that
one should commit no violence, thinking that the lord or divinity
is in everything (XI.34, IV.27).

*Bhagavadgita* mentions *ahimsa* as one of the divine qualities,
which is to be cultivated and practiced by one and all (XVI.2,
XVII.14). Sri Shankaracharya, the greatest exponent of Advaita
philosophy (non-dualism), when commenting on the *Bhagavadgita*,
said that a yogi should be nonviolent towards others and should
identify the self of all beings with his own. Also, he should do only
to others that which is desirable and pleasant to his own self, but
should refrain from doing that to others which is undesirable and
unpleasant for himself (VI.32).

Yogasurra of Patanjali mentions *ahimsa* as the basis of ethical
practices, a universal principle which is to be practiced by one and
all irrespective of religion, race, creed, and sex. It is said that if
*ahimsa* is practiced and mastered, total enmity disappears from
one's mind and heart, and others also give up hatred in the proximity of one practicing *ahimsa* (II.35). One must practice *ahimsa*
in its broadest sense—unrestricted by caste, place, time, and circumstances. *Ahimsa* here is required as the foremost virtue by

aspiring yogis. Yogic *ahimsa* here means absence of oppression towards all beings, in all respects, and for all times (Vyasa on *Yogasutra* II.30–32).

Ancient Hindu law and sociological texts also uphold the practice of *ahimsa*. The Laws of *Manu (Manusmruti)*, which influenced and shaped Hindu society for a long period, include *ahimsa* as one of the characteristics of *dharma*—a duty, the path of righteousness and cardinal virtue, which is to be followed by all (X.63). It must be practiced for the welfare of all human beings (II.158). *Manu* further states that violence disturbs one's mind and results in ill-health whereas nonviolence brings sound health (XI.52). The Laws of *Manu* prohibit meat-eating for higher classes (Brahmins—intellectuals, thinkers, and priests) and encourage other classes of people not to eat meat. The laws of *Manu* state that the merit of not eating meat by killing or causing the killing of animals is equal to the merit of hundreds of horse sacrifices (V.53). According to *Manu*, "Immortality is the highest fruit of *ahimsa*" (VI.60). Several other ancient Hindu law texts, such as *Bodhayanadharmasutra, Yajnavalkyasmruti,* and others, glorify the merit of practicing *ahimsa*. According to these texts, *ahimsa* is a kind of internal purification (*Bodhayana* III.1–23) and by its practice one accumulates good karmic consequences (*Yajnavalkyasmruti* I.8, I.122).

It is interesting to note that though these ancient legal texts glorify the practice of nonviolence, they consider that killing animals in sacrifice does not qualify as violence. The laws of *Manu* add that the killing of animals prescribed in the sacrifice should be construed to mean *ahimsa* because the laws have Vedic sanction, and moral duties spring from the Vedas. Vedic *himsa* is morally equal to *ahimsa* in the sense that both produce the same good result. Animal sacrifice brings good for all (V.41, 44; VI.12). Commentators and other lawmakers justified *Manu* and allowed the eating of meat obtained through ritual sacrifice.

## NONVIOLENCE AND VEGETARIANISM IN HINDU THOUGHT

The case of animal sacrifice actually serves to illustrate Hindu debates and principles related to the conception of violence and nonviolence. It is a common misconception that the entire ancient Hindu tradition supported animal sacrifice and meat-eating as part of the sacrificial process. The Vedic or Hindu tradition as a whole never supported animal killings in sacrifice. Animal sacrifice was vehemently opposed by *Upanishadic* sages, philosophers, social thinkers, intellectuals, and literary persons from ancient times. A few ritualists, however, the followers of the path of ritualism known as *mimamsakas* or *karmakandins*, supported and practiced this animal sacrifice in the name of attaining heaven. When this ritualistic class became very powerful, they influenced the ancient Hindu lawmakers to accept killing animals in sacrifice and, ironically, to declare it as equal to nonviolence.

These bloody animal sacrifices did not fail to arouse criticism and protest. Even ancient *Samaveda* opposed this cruel act (I.II.IX.2). *Upanishadic* sages criticized not only animal-killing in sacrifice but questioned the merit or efficacy of performing sacrifice itself. In more than one place the *Upanishad* decries the value of sacrifice. *Upanishadic* seers treated all beings as essentially equal and considered the ritual as ineffective and meaningless. They felt it was far better to see the self *(atman)* in all beings than to perform even a hundred sacrifices. Performing any animal sacrifice is based on ignorance of the nature of self, and the "right knowledge" can dispel this ignorance. Right knowledge was considered the root of *ahimsa*.

Followers of the Sankhya system of philosophy opposed the *mimamsakas'* animal sacrifice in the name of religion; they called it a sinful act, an impure act, which was based on *himsa*. They insisted it was irrational and baseless to say that animal sacrifice is not violence (*Sankhya Karika* I.2, 6.84; commentaries by Vachaspti Mishra and Vijnanabhikshu).

Even some commentators of *dharmashastras* (law texts) criticized animal sacrifice (Govindananda on Brahatmanu). In *Mahabharata* we find opposition to animal sacrifice: "Man loses merit earned from other penances by resorting to sacrificial killing. Men who are engaged in killing animals deserve to go to hell" (*Anushasanaparva*, XIII.69; *Shantiparva* 272.18). Opposition to animal sacrifice is found also in *purana* (mythology) literature, such as *Bhagavata* (I.9.52. V.26.25) and *Matsyapurana* (142.13). In the vast Hindu mythological literature (*puranas* consisting of 400,000 verses), the practice of *ahimsa* is praised. Ancient and very popular Puranic texts, such as *Agni, Bhagavata, Vishnu, Matsya, Kurma, Vayu,* and *Varaha,* are also full of the praise of *ahimsa*.

Although in the early period of Vedic civilization meat-eating was not strictly prohibited and vegetarianism was not strictly followed, by the time of the *Upanishadic* (classical), the killing of animals and birds for one's own pleasure and food was considered a great sin, and the practice of vegetarianism became the hallmark of the upper class. People like Brahmins and monks were prohibited from eating non-vegetarian food and liquor (*Manu* II.177). This strict vegetarianism is practiced today by the Brahmins of Hindu society. People of other classes were not prohibited from eating meat, but they were encouraged and advised not to eat meat by the glorification of the merit of non-killing of animals and birds and of not eating meat (*Manu* V.53). The *Mahabharata* criticizes meat-eating in the strongest terms: "The meat of other animals is like the flesh of one's own son. That foolish person, stupefied by folly, who eats meat is regarded as the vilest of human beings" (XIII.114.11). Such statements from the scriptures made a deep impact on the minds of the common people. Greater status was accorded to those who were able to follow a strict vegetarian diet. Even today, those who are allowed to eat non-vegetarian food in Hindu society do not eat meat daily. Occasionally they eat meat, but on certain days of the Hindu calendar they do not eat meat.

## VEGETARIANISM AND ECOLOGICAL BALANCE

The practice of nonviolence in the form of vegetarianism is closely connected with the preservation of ecological balance. The *Yajurveda* lays down the rule that "no person should kill animals and birds helpful to all; rather, by serving them one should attain happiness" (XIII.47).

To preserve animal life, Hindu culture and religion associated different animals and birds with various gods and goddesses so that human beings would not kill them. It was also ordained in the Hindu tradition that one should not take food without also offering food to birds and animals, which is technically known as *Vaishvadevayajna*. *Vaishvadevayajna* is one of the daily observances that must be observed by all householders. This is still practiced by many adherents of Hindu tradition. Similarly, several plants, trees, and herbs are considered worthy of worship, and flowering and fruit-bearing trees are looked upon with great reverence and love and often considered equal to hundreds of children. Plants and flowers are associated with various gods and goddesses, so human beings may not cut and destroy them for the sake of quick money. Ancient Hindu law texts have prescribed several expiations and punishment for cutting trees.

In short, *ahimsa* in Hindu thought is so wide-ranging in its application that one can legitimately argue that the Earth is considered a Mother and a living presence. Hindus pray to Mother Earth in order to ask forgiveness for touching her with their feet, a prayer offered daily in the morning by every devout Hindu.

## KARMA AND REBIRTH

The practice of nonviolence in Hindu tradition is also in some way linked to the doctrine of karma and rebirth. According to this doctrine, every being reaps the fruits of his or her own deeds, whether good or bad, right or wrong. We reap what we sow. Bad deeds result in unpleasant consequences and good deeds in pleasant consequences. The result of all actions may not appear in this life so, to reap the fruits of past deeds, one has to take birth again. Each individual has to reap the fruits of his or her own actions. An individual's good and bad deeds decide his or her rebirth in a lower or higher category of life form. So, acts of nonviolence are considered as morally good deeds which bring happiness and cause birth in a higher category of life form. Acts of violence are morally bad and cause birth in a lower-category of life form.

The practice of nonviolence extends even to small life-forms— an idea that is deeply rooted in Hindu practice even today. For example, Hindu men and women generally do not use ant-killers; instead, they sprinkle turmeric powder to disperse ants or they gather them up to put them outside.

## EXCEPTIONS TO THE PRACTICE OF NONVIOLENCE

The Hindu tradition accepts four stages of life: the stage of studenthood, the stage of householder, the retirement stage, and the stage of renunciation (monkhood). Applications of *ahimsa* to these stages also differ. *Ahimsa* is sometimes described as a common duty, sometimes as a specific duty. In the stage of studenthood, retirement, and monkhood, *ahimsa* must be practiced vigorously. In monkhood, it should be practiced absolutely, whereas, in the stage of a householder's life, a householder is exempted from following the absolute form of *ahimsa* because he has to compromise in order to fulfill his own specific duties. A householder cannot totally neglect his family, social responsibilities, and material well-being. It is impossible for a householder to practice *ahimsa* in any extreme degree so it has to be practiced in moderation in accordance with common sense and one's own family and social responsibilities. The principal object is to maintain social order and the well-being of the people.

## RELATIONS WITH THE WORLD

Hinduism is neither a dogma, nor a cult, nor a mere religion in a narrow sense. It is a culture, a way of life. It deals with all aspects of human existence. It does not repudiate the world and negate social values. Human life is considered a long journey towards perfection and, in this journey, natural desires and inclinations of man to possess and enjoy the good things of life cannot be overlooked. But everything must be in accordance with a moral and social order. Certain exceptions are mentioned with respect to practicing nonviolence. When an enemy attacks and kills hundreds of innocent beings or molests women, if one does nothing but stand back as a witness, this is not *ahimsa*; it is cowardice and weakness. One's duty is to fight and kill an enemy in such circumstances. If a beast enters into a cattleshed, one's duty is to kill the beast; otherwise, valuable cows will be killed. Fishermen may inflict injury on fish. This is required for their livelihood. A butcher's livelihood is based on killing some animals. So, their actions cannot be considered total violence. A warrior may kill his enemies on the battlefield because it is his duty to defend the country and to protect the people. The practice of *ahimsa* is not applicable in dealing with wicked people. So, the Hindu conception of *ahimsa* is universal, but its application is practical. Hindu nonviolence historically includes morally justifiable violence.

## THE RELATION OF PEACE AND NONVIOLENCE
## WITHIN THE HINDU TRADITION

In the Hindu tradition, the term *shanti* is used for peace. The word *peace* is understood in two senses: One is spiritual peace and the other is peace in society and nature. The attainment of spiritual peace is considered the highest goal of human existence. This spiritual peace can be achieved through giving up a sense of separateness and plurality and identifying one's own self with all other beings in the universe (*Ishavasya Upanishad* 6–7). Eternal peace belongs to those who see unity or oneness behind all modifications of the universe (*Kathopanishad* V.13). The concept of duality is considered the root cause of violent action. The Hindu tradition hopes and aspires toward peace for all beings. The Vedas declare, "May there be peace in plants, trees, earth, directions, fire, water, wind, air, sky, heaven, animals, and human beings" *(Yajurveda)*. The idea of peace in Hindu tradition is clearly evident from the daily prayers of devout Hindus which state, "May everyone be happy, may everyone be free from diseases, may everyone see good fortune, and may no one be unhappy" (Y. S. Shastri 1994, 72).

It is important to note that to establish peace in society, ancient Hindu lawmakers pointed out in several places *(Manusmruti, Naradasmruti)* that social peace can be established with the help of strict laws and punishments. If everyone were virtuous, good, honest, and nonviolent, there would be no need for any laws as such; however, since this is not so, society needs laws and punishments to bring peace into society.

## THE ROLE OF WAR, PEACE, AND NONVIOLENCE IN HINDU TRADITION

The Hindu tradition has always held a balanced view about nonviolence and war. It always adopted rational and practical ways to maintain the social order, peace, and the well-being of all the people. Its final aim was to achieve spiritual peace, but it never neglected material well-being and social harmony. Whenever there was a rise of evil forces in society, Hindus first tried to establish peace through applying peaceful means, but when this attempt failed, they took the path of war to purify society. War against evil forces and violence against anti-social elements such as criminals is not considered nonviolence but a duty. Soldiers on the battlefield who kill their enemies do not engage in *himsa*, but are carrying out a professional duty—a duty toward one's own country, culture, and society—and this duty is considered an act of heroism. One must not allow evil forces to conquer society. Man must not be a mute witness to evils and injustice.

In Vedic literature, war against wicked persons, evil forces, and untruth is praised as an act of purification (*Rgveda* VIII.104.1, 7, 12, 13, 19). The victory of truthfulness is glorified. The *Bhagavadgita* considers war as one of the solutions to purify society. In present-day Hindu society, there is a feeling, especially among the younger generation, that Indians have had enough talk of nonviolence. We have preached nonviolence in India for thousands of years. But in the modern world, perhaps we must rise to the call of Lord Krishna in the *Bhagavadgita* to be strong, powerful, and prepared for war, if the occasion demands. In this age of competition and wickedness, nonviolence seems to carry no weight. This is why 90 percent of the Indian population supported the nuclear tests conducted in the 1990s.

In spite of glorifying the practice of nonviolence by Hindu texts and tradition for thousands of years, there is still violence towards the weaker elements of society—women, the lower classes, and animals. This was true in ancient times but has continued in intensified forms to the present day. Women have continued to suffer great violence. In a world where there is a great desire for luxuries and where there is rampant consumerism, there are increased pressures on women to provide ever greater dowries. This practice has led to excessive violence against women. In addition, poor people are harassed, deprived of rights, and often treated as "untouchables"—a great blot on the otherwise glorious civilization of the Hindus.

In the name of industrialization and modernization, forests and hundreds of wild animals have been destroyed and water has been polluted with industrial wastes and chemicals, killing many living beings. The pressures of consumerism and self-centeredness have led to riots and increased hatred across community lines.

## A YEARNING FOR PEACE

Every tradition in the world talks about peace. This talk of love for peace has been going on for thousands of years but, in spite of it, human history tells us that in every tradition there have been wars. War is not advisable, but preparation for war is going on everywhere. The whole world wants peace, yet the whole world prepares for war.

The *Ramayana* and the *Mahabharata*, the two great epics of the Hindus, depict the story of war and its terrible consequences and the importance of peace. In *Ramayana*, war was conducted as a struggle between good and evil, truth and untruth. Rama, the hero of the epic, represents righteousness, truthfulness, honesty, dutifulness, compassion, self-control, faithfulness, humility, courage, generosity, and non-anger. Ravana, the villain of the great epic, though highly learned, represents passion, vanity, egocentricism, arrogance, vainglory, anger, and ambition. His life is governed by passion and sex. The consequence of that war was the destruction of many lives and, ultimately, the destruction of the race of Ravana. Peace was established not through peaceful means but by violence and war.

In the *Mahabharata*, a horrendous 18-day war is described. In this large-scale war, kings of the entire Indian subcontinent were involved. Hundreds of thousands of heroes, kings, soldiers, great masters in archery and weapons, elephants, and horses were killed in 18 days. The war was fought between two cousins but it was also a war between good and evil forces. Lord Krishna tried to prevent the war through a peace treaty. He tried to tell Kauravas about the tragic consequences of war. But his efforts were in vain. War was inevitable. Even Arjuna, the war hero of the *Mahabharata* (one of the Pandavas), was horrified by the thought of war. On the battlefield, he was reluctant to fight. He implored Lord Krishna to stop the war. At that juncture, Lord Krishna advised him to perform his duty as a warrior, either to win the fight against evil forces in society or to die in the attempt. He convinced Arjuna that there cannot be ultimate peace without war. The result of this war was that it devoured a large portion of the population, left untold miseries for widows and children, and created millions of orphans.

The wars of the two great epics point out that peace cannot necessarily be established by peaceful means and thus suggest to many Hindus that sometimes war is necessary.

## HINDU HEROES WHO EXEMPLIFY
## THE NONVIOLENT TRADITION

Despite this allowance for "justified war," thousands of wise men and women saints, sages, religious leaders, and poets have preached and followed the path of nonviolence. Hindu scriptures are full of their stories. The lives of Sri Chaitanya Mahaprabhu and Mahatma Gandhi are the best examples of the practice of non-violence in the recent Hindu past.

Chaitanya Mahaprabhu (1486–1534) lived according to the principle of *ahimsa*. His way of propagating nonviolence was chanting the glory of the Lord. In his lifetime, he converted many cruel people who later became compassionate beings. The story is told that once Chaitanya Mahaprabhu heard that hundreds of cows and bulls were killed every year to feed the Muslim ruler of his area. He was saddened about the slaughter of innocent animals so he went to the court and met the Muslim ruler to explain the significance of nonviolence. He said that cows give us milk so they are like our mother. He said that bulls help to plow fields to produce food grains so they are like our father. Killing these cows and bulls to eat meat is like killing our mother and father and eating their meat. The Muslim ruler was convinced by Mahaprabhu's argument and ordered no more killing of cows and bulls and became an ardent practitioner of nonviolence. Mahaprabhu also converted many criminals and dangerous bandits of his time into great devotees of the Lord. They became compassionate beings. His way of nonviolence attracted thousands of followers.

In modern times, Mahatma Gandhi has been the greatest advocate of the principle of nonviolence. His nonviolent methods made him the leader of the freedom movement in India. He has influenced and inspired many great world leaders. He used nonviolence as a weapon to overthrow British rule, social injustice, and the fight against exploitation. According to Gandhi, equanimity towards all living beings is *ahimsa*—and in this we recognize his debt to classic Hindu thought and to ascetic traditions. He expounded a comprehensive philosophy of nonviolence. He tried to apply nonviolence in *every* walk of life: domestic, institutional, economic, and political. He was unique in extending nonviolence to the domain of economics, thus introducing moral values as a regulating factor in international commerce (Tahtinen 1976, 118, 123).

According to Gandhi, even criminals, whose crimes are a disease in need of a cure, must be treated with nonviolent methods and regarded as our brothers. Prisons should be used as institutions of reform and not as places of punishment (Tahtinen 124). For Gandhi, *ahimsa* meant a transformation of the heart that would result in the freedom of his country and the creation of a casteless society. Gandhi wrote:

Violence is not of the very essence of human nature. One thing we can learn from history is that if war cannot be abolished, there is absolutely no hope for the future of the human race, as sooner or later society is bound to annihilate itself. The reason is quite clear: The advancement of scientific technology and the life-destroying power of the nations are increasing. If war is not soon avoided or abolished, a conflict will arise in which entire nations and races will be completely blotted out of existence and even vast continents will be reduced to impotency and dissolution. One thing is clear, therefore; war must be abolished at all costs, if civilization is to survive. Then the madness of violence must be recognized, its causes removed, and its implements destroyed. But how can it be done? It can be done by one means only: the manifestation of a better spirit. It is a change of character and conduct through a change of ideas, reason, and good will—these are the only agencies in a civilized age for effecting such changes. (Gandhi 1948–49)

## CONCLUSION

Human conflicts continue to arise. Animals are sacrificed in the name of science and economy. Trees and plants are destroyed in the name of progress. Land is poisoned by using various pesticides, chemicals, and fertilizers, thus endangering the entire food chain. Great rivers and oceans are polluted by chemical wastes. Nuclear tests are killing hundreds of water animals and other lifeforms. At this juncture, the need for a comprehensive sense of nonviolence has become more pressing than ever before.

The Hindu concept of the spiritual unity of all existence—the Vedantic notion that all things share a fundamental sameness—may work as a basis for establishing a new world peace and may contribute to the long elusive goal of unity among all humanity.

### STUDY QUESTIONS

1. What is "Vedic literature" and how does it speak of peace?
2. In what ways is vegetarianism related to Hindu understandings of *ahimsa?*

3. How does *ahimsa* apply to the "four stages of life"?

4. In what ways have modern Hindus attempted to balance the demands of modern life with the religious value of *ahimsa*?

5. In what ways do Sunanda and Yajneshwar Shastri express concern about this process of matching ancient values to modern life?

## BIBLIOGRAPHY

**Works in English**

Bose, N. K. *My Days with Gandhi*. Calcutta: Nishana, 1953.

———. *Selections from Gandhi*. Ahmedabad: Navajivan Publishing House, 1948.

Chapple, Christopher Key. *Nonviolence to Animals, Earth, and Self in Asian Traditions*. Albany: State University of New York, 1993.

Gandhi, M. K. *Nonviolence in Peace and War*. Vols. 1 and 2. Ahmedabad: Navajivan Publishing House, 1948–1949.

Koshelya, Walli. *The Conception of Ahimsa in Indian Thought*. Varanasi: Bharatamanisha, 1974.

Shastri, Y. S. *A Collection of Prayers*. Ahmedabad: Yogeshwar Parkashan, 1994.

Tahtinen, Unto. *Ahimsa: Nonviolence in Indian Tradition*. London: Ryder, 1976.

**Works in Sanskrit**

*Agnipurana*. Ed. Khemaraj. Bombay: Shrikishan Dass, n.d.

*Astadasasmrtayah*. Bombay: Gujarat Printing Press, 1981.

*Atharvaveda*. Trans. M. Bloomfield. Oxford: Oxford University Press, 1897.

*Bhagavadgita*. Trans. J. Goyandaka. Gorakhpur: Gita Press, 1969.

*Isadidasopanishad*. Delhi: Motilal Baharasi Dass, 1964.

*Ishavllsya Upanishad*. Trans. Swami Chinmayananda. Bombay: Central Chinmaya Mission Trust, 1992.

*Mahabharata*. Shantiparva and Anusasanaparva. Poona: Bhandarkar Oriental Research Institute, 1932.

*Manusmrti*. Ed. Pandya Pranajivan Harihar. Bombay: Gujarat Printing Press, 1886.

*Ramayana*. Ed. J. Goyandaka. Gorakhpur: Gita Press, 1943.

*Rgveda*. Trans. R. T. H. Griffith. Delhi: Motilal Banarass Dass, 1973.

# 5

# Indigenous Traditions of Peace

## An Interview with Lawrence Hart, Cheyenne Peace Chief

## Daniel L. Smith-Christopher

In discussions of the religious basis for peace and nonviolence, it is rarely the case that indigenous religious traditions within national borders are mentioned, yet many of these religious traditions have a great wealth of traditional teaching about peace, which often includes rituals, practices, and teachings that honor peace and values of nonviolence.

These important traditions among indigenous peoples around the world can be cited totally apart from the influences of missionizing traditions such as Islam and Christianity. Many indigenous traditions taught the values of nonviolence and peacemaking for centuries before the arrival of Islamic or Christian missionaries. In some of these societies, for example, violence is virtually unknown (Montagu 1978), while in other societies, the value of

Daniel L. Smith-Christopher, a life-long Quaker, is professor of Theological Studies (Old Testament) and director of Peace Studies at Loyola Marymount University in Los Angeles where he has taught since 1989. He has published numerous articles and books on biblical analysis and peace studies, most recently *Jonah, Jesus, and Other Good Coyotes: Speaking Peace to Power in the Bible* (Abingdon Press, 2007) and *The Old Testament: Our Call to Faith and Justice* (Ave Maria Press, 2004). He is working on a commentary on the prophet Micah. Before beginning his teaching career, he was a volunteer peace worker in Israel/Palestine from 1986–1988, and he maintains an active interest in peace issues, especially in the Middle East.

nonviolence and/or peace is honored and considered an ideal goal even in the midst of societies that also practice violence (Bohannan 1967; Mead 1937; Augsburger 1992). In other cases, some of the indigenous religious traditions have combined with Christianity or Islam to form a unique, culturally nuanced expression of that larger world tradition. An obvious frontier in peace research would not only be the traditions of peacemaking in various indigenous societies, but the relationship of those traditions to the arrival of Christianity, Islam, and other transnational religious traditions (Hefner 1993).

In contemporary indigenous societies around the world, the persistence of peacemaking traditions gives voice to the *religious hope* of "subverting hatred." In some small and localized groups, perceptions of holiness and religious values have led many people to stand against the practice of warfare within their traditions. In some cases, these values have led members of these indigenous traditions to carry their values of peacemaking into dialogue with wider societies. One thinks, for example, of the Southwestern American Hopi nation, many of whom declared status as conscientious objectors during American conflicts on the basis of the nonviolent ethos of Hopi tradition (a story that has yet to be fully explored, incidentally). Note, as an example of combined indigenous/Christian traditions, the Mexican group known as "Los Abejos" (The "Bees"). They have engaged in a consciously chosen nonviolent campaign in Chiapas against Mexican military excesses. Further, in Australia it is often noted that violent confrontation against Western settlers in Australia by the Aboriginal Australians is generally absent. Ironically, this lack of violence is dismissed as the result of weakness or explained as some kind of realization by Aboriginals that Western settlement is inevitable. What we need instead is a studied appreciation of many Aboriginal Australian cultures that have sophisticated ethics against interpersonal violence and/or long established ritual forms of conflict resolution that are preferred to confrontational violence.

What follows is one important example of an indigenous tradition of peacemaking. It might well serve as an invitation to additional studies of indigenous traditions.

Lawrence Hart is one of the four "Principal Chiefs" (that is, one of four chosen from forty Chiefs of the Nation) of the Southern Cheyenne. He is also the executive director of the Cheyenne

Cultural Center in his hometown of Clinton, Oklahoma, in the United States. Lawrence Hart has been actively involved in cultural, economic, and religious rights issues far beyond the confines of his own Cheyenne nation and currently also serves on the Review Committee of the Native American Graves Protection and Repatriation Act, a national advisory body. This interview was conducted for *Subverting Hatred* in the summer of 1998.

## INTERVIEW

*Can you please describe your culture's ideas about peace? Do you have specific ceremonies that are dedicated to making peace between enemies? Can you describe them?*

**Hart:** We have a council of forty-four peace chiefs that was instituted by Sweet Medicine, our culture's hero. There are two legends about the council. The first is about a woman who had a vision or dream (some say it was influenced by her visiting another tribe) and in that vision she suggested that the Cheyenne organize a council of chiefs. There would be ten men chosen from four societies, and from within that forty, four would be selected as the principal chiefs. Then the four that were chosen as principal chiefs would be replaced with additional men from the societies so the total would be forty-four.

The other legend is that Sweet Medicine instituted this council. Even if he did not, he gave a lot of instructions about how the chiefs were to live their lives and how they were to be peace chiefs. Sweet Medicine told them that they were essentially to be peacemakers. They were not to engage in any quarrels within the tribe regardless of whether their families or children were involved. They were not to engage themselves in any force or violence, even if their son was killed right in front of their teepee. *You are to do nothing but take your pipe and smoke.* There are many other such instructions, but that is the primary one.

There are other aspects to this commitment—such as, if you see your wife of children harmed by anyone, you do not take revenge. Being a chief actually is a way of life. A chief already has generally proven himself in terms of courage or valor when he is selected from within the four societies. Currently, these four societies are the Elk Soldiers, Bow Strings, Dog Soldiers, and Kit Fox.

When men are selected from within these societies, they must make a complete break, a complete reversal of who they are. Once they were warriors, but, when they are selected, they become peace chiefs. They are inducted through a ceremony with many rituals. They no longer use force or violence. The families of the chiefs are held almost to that same standard. It's wise that before someone becomes a chief they clear it with the family as well as extended family. Some refuse this opportunity to be a chief.

There are other aspects to this commitment, too. For example, the chief's home becomes a kind of sanctuary, even in contemporary times. Tribal members can go to the chief's home and be safe. No one should be bothered there. Finally, one of the more traditional ways of practicing nonviolence is for the chiefs to meet together in making peace—to ultimately have the ritual of smoking a pipe together with the adversary.

*Do you have any sacred traditions, stories, or artifacts that your culture values that somehow speak of traditions of peace?*

**Hart:** The main symbol, of course, is the pipe that is carried by the chiefs, especially the four principal chiefs. Sweet Medicine also gave to the Cheyenne four sacred arrows: two are for the enemy, two are for food. So that means, even though we have peace traditions, we also have warrior societies who protect the tribe.

*Have there been debates among your people about the use of violence in gaining equal rights and justice? How do you feel about these debates? How do you think people in your cultural and religious tradition(s) would feel, for example, about Gandhian methods of nonviolent activism? Do you have similar traditions or ideals in your religious tradition?*

**Hart:** When I work for human rights, I would not use force or violence. I believe that nonviolence is generally the stance that the chiefs would take. The Cheyenne would understand that this kind of activism was conducted by some of our peace chiefs in the 1860s when there was a lot of violence on the high plains. In one instance, the chiefs recommended that they sit down and discuss peace with Colorado territorial Governor Evans and his militia. These talks took place at Camp Weld near Denver in September of 1864. The

Cheyenne chiefs were very serious about the peace overtures they were making, but as soon as they left, according to the records, Colonel John M. Chivington and Governor Evans began to plot against the Cheyenne. Their attack occurred two months later, on November 29, at Sand Creek where many of these same peace chiefs were camped. There ensued what is known as the Sand Creek Massacre.

What we really don't do is engage ourselves in any kind of activity for human rights as chiefs directly, in the sense of being activists. We certainly work for justice issues, but not traditionally as "activists." Although, for myself, I appreciate Gandhi and Martin Luther King Jr., we do not actively engage ourselves in nonviolent activities.

*Do you think your nonviolent beliefs are shared by most of the people in your tradition or are you in a minority among your own people?*

**Hart:** I think we're certainly not in the majority. Nonviolent members are in the minority, but at the same time, I think we're appreciated, especially by those who know this tradition. You should know that in our history, sometimes the peace chiefs have had to stand against our own warriors who believed that war was the best action to take in given circumstances. It is frequently expected —and often did happen—that the chiefs would oppose their own warriors.

*Do the teachings about peace in your tradition actually suggest practical steps in making peace? Do you think these teachings have wider political significance?*

**Hart:** Oh yes. The chiefs mediate disputes. The chiefs don't take sides. I think these ideas have the potential for wider application, but it's sometimes very difficult. One of the things that we see today, especially in activities that involve the total community like powwows or special dances, is that there is a lot of patriotism exhibited in many ways. Veterans are highly honored among the Cheyenne. Many people say that's an irony for me as a peace chief. Furthermore, we Cheyenne have our own flag song and many people say, "It's our national anthem." We have alongside this a tradition of being peacemakers. I myself am very conscious of this kind of patriotism that is exhibited especially with other tribes. These tribes highly influence our own, and sometimes they have no such strong peace tradition like our own.

One way in which our young men, and now young women, gain recognition and status is to go into the military and make some kind of achievement. When they do, they are recognized and honored. At the same time, in many of our other more traditional dances held around the local communities, the very first dance is always for the chiefs, that is, the peacemakers. So we have many ironies that occur within our culture.

Generally, a chief also is a servant of the people, not a leader as much as a servant. Not only is he a peacemaker, but he is also expected to help people in ways that he can, and in this kind of servant stance, chiefs are generally recognized last. For example, they are the last to be served at a meal when there is a community gathering (and such gatherings always involve a large meal). Everyone is fed first and the chiefs are fed last. And if they get nothing to eat, that's okay, then the children and especially the elders have been fed first. Then usually right after the meal there will be a dance. And in that dance, chiefs are given recognition. Then, the chiefs are recognized first. It's basically the only time they're recognized first. They are given that kind of esteem, that kind of recognition by the community for who they are.

*Please choose two "heroes" or "heroines "from your tradition— one recent (perhaps still living) and one in history. These two persons should be people who, in your mind, best represent your culture's striving for peace. Please tell us about them and what you think their most important message of peace is for us.*

**Hart:** I have many role models. My favorite is White Antelope. He was a chief who was prominent in the 1850s to 1860s and was killed at Sand Creek. He was one of the chiefs who went to the council at Camp Weld with territorial Governor Evans. On the morning of the attack, he had apparently risen early and had gone out from his village just a bit. When he saw the troops on the horizon he thought that they knew that the Cheyenne were at peace, especially consequent to the peace council at Camp Weld. Even when the charge was sounded for the troops to attack the village, he thought it was a mistake and ran forward toward them and tried to stop them. When he saw that it was a deliberate attack and not a mistake, he stopped and stood there and began to sing his death song. And he continued to stand there, totally unarmed, and sang until he was shot down. I have many such role models, but that's my favorite.

My own grandfather was John Peak Hart, and he was a more contemporary peacemaker. He made peace with the Mountain Ute in Colorado. At one time a century ago, the Mountain Utes were our enemies. It was John Peak Hart, as he was known by the Mountain Utes, who created a friendship with them. In that sense he was active in making peace with a tribe that had been our traditional enemies. I was just a small child, in pre-school years, when I would go with him each summer when he traveled to Colorado. Many times today, when I'm in the Four Corners area, whether it's with the Mountain Utes or Navajo, when I say I'm a grandson of John Peak Hart, they tell me he is well remembered by them.

I need to mention a woman because I have an appreciation for many of the women in our tradition. There is one. I knew her by her Cheyenne name. In English her first name was Pamela and her last name was "Stands-in-Sight," so Pamela Stands-in-Sight. She's been gone probably fifteen years now, but I got to know her and she was a really beautiful person. She was the daughter of a chief who became the wife of a chief, the mother of a chief, and then the grandmother and great-grandmother of a chief. And that's unusual. I don't think that's mentioned anywhere among our people.

*What do you think are the greatest gifts that your culture can offer the rest of the world? Is there a specific wisdom about peace that you think the rest of the world would benefit from?*

**Hart:** I think to live the kind of life a Cheyenne chief lives is one such contribution we could offer. In fact, there is an expression in our language, I'll say it in Cheyenne, *"E-ve-hon-e-wo-stane-hev."* Translated, it means that person is "living the life of a chief." It's a high compliment and generally would be given to one who is a peacemaker. I think that if people in the world could have lives like that—to emulate the Cheyenne chiefs—then that would be a great contribution.

*Remember that this book is also for students and scholars who are interested in studying the issues of peace and religion more carefully. In your opinion, what are the most important issues related to your religious and cultural tradition that are in need of further study? What are the most important un-studied issues with regard to nonviolence and peacemaking?*

**Hart:** I think generally when people hear the word "Indian" they begin to immediately conceive of typical stereotypes, including the one perpetuated by Hollywood and television in its early days. Indians were, and sometimes still are, portrayed as war-like and cruel, and often they were the villains. I think people need to "unlearn" that stereotype. And they can do it by engaging in studies of the peace traditions within different tribal groups. The Cheyenne aren't the only nation who have important peacemaking traditions—there are others, but I think more needs to be published about them. The Navajo, for example, have peacemakers, and the Iroquois nations had a peace tradition.

I'm not sure, though, that one could really get at the heart of our traditions without actually experiencing them. You know, you can study and you can read and hear our traditions, but somehow I think you have to just simply live it in order to gain a full understanding of it. This is because, along with the traditions, there is a high degree of spirituality associated with everything we do as chiefs. There are many rituals that we use whenever we gather together that are enriching. When we talk about some of these rituals, they sound mundane. But it's just indescribable what happens when we perform them. Traditionally, we gather in a teepee. We never gather anywhere else when the chiefs get together. One of the first things we do is use just a plain bucket of water with a dipper. The bucket might be three-quarters full of water and, in a special ritual, that water is blessed by one of the chiefs who has the authority to do that. I don't have that authority myself, but there are others who do. Then the water is passed from one person to another around the circle and each takes a dipper of water and drinks it until everyone is served that water. Everyone has participated in that ritual of taking water.

When we gather together like that, we have generally gathered from different communities where we live, or different jobs we might have. We've come with a certain amount of "baggage" and there may be some things that are preoccupying our minds, but when we go through this ritual, even as simple as it is, it tends to unite us so that we can think—ultimately think with one mind, one heart. Now the Iroquois have their own rituals. They verbally say "Let us combine our hearts and minds together" after a series of statements, but in our case we take this water and it has the same effect, it combines our heart and mind, and when we talk about a major issue everyone has a right to talk. No one is interrupted, and we talk around the circle until we are finished talking about that issue. We can either move on or continue to talk about that issue.

There are other such rituals that have a very high degree of spirituality. What I want to say is that you can read about it, you can almost visualize what I've just described, but then, you really need to experience it. What I want to say is, as good as literature is, as good as books are, there is a limitation. One can grasp a good understanding of our tradition, one can be influenced by it, by experiencing this kind of life.

### SUGGESTED READINGS

**Hart:** One of the books that I appreciate very much is *The Peace Chiefs of the Cheyenne* by Stan Hoig (Norman: University of Oklahoma Press, 1980). He has another important book on the Sand Creek Massacre (*The Sand Creek Massacre*, Norman: University of Oklahoma Press, 1961) that gives a good perspective of what happened there. He's a good author, a contemporary author. There are good studies by Peter J. Powell, especially his two-volume series called *Sweet Medicine* (Norman: University of Oklahoma Press, 1969), and another two-volume set entitled *People of the Sacred Mountain* (San Francisco: Harper and Row, 1979). This series is about our sacred mountain, which is Bear Butte in South Dakota. Another author whom I really appreciate is Donald J. Berthrong, whose most recent book is entitled *The Cheyenne and the Arapaho Ordeal* (Norman: University of Oklahoma Press, 1976).

I don't think one should overlook George Bird Grinnell's books, such as *The Fighting Cheyenne* (Norman: University of Oklahoma Press, 1976) and *The Cheyenne: Indian New Heaven* (New Haven: Yale University Press, 1923). Those are good books. There's still another one by Karl N. Llewellyn and F. Adamson Hoebel called

*The Cheyenne Way* (Norman: University of Oklahoma Press, 1941). Llewellyn and Hoebel's book is a very scholarly work published in 1941 and it has to do with Cheyenne jurisprudence. It has many accounts of the Cheyenne as peacemakers.

## STUDY QUESTIONS

1. What are some examples of indigenous rituals of peacemaking?
2. Who is Sweet Medicine and what are the "four arrows"?
3. Explain the basic outlines of Cheyenne society, according to Hart, and how this reflects the four arrows of Sweet Medicine.
4. Briefly explain the significance of White Antelope and the work of John Peak Hart as examples of Cheyenne peacemaking.
5. What is the meaning of "living the life of a chief" and why does Hart relate this to the work of peacemaking?

## BIBLIOGRAPHY

Augsburger, David W. *Conflict Mediation across Cultures: Pathways and Patterns*. Louisville: Westminster/John Knox Press, 1992.

Bohannan, P., ed. *Law and Warfare*. Garden City: Natural History Press, 1967.

Hefner, R. W., ed. *Conversion to Christianity: Historical and Anthropological Perspectives on a Great Transfirmation*. Berkeley and Los Angeles: University of California Press, 1993.

Mead, Margaret, ed. *Cooperation and Competition among Primitive Peoples*. Boston: Beacon Press, 1937.

Montagu, A., ed. *Learning Non-Aggression*. Oxford: Oxford University Press, 1978.

# 6

# The Struggle for Peace

## Subverting Hatred in a Māori Context

*Donald S. Tamihere*

May peace be widespread;
May the ocean glisten like the precious greenstone;
And may sunlight dance across your pathways.[1]

The Māori of Aotearoa-New Zealand[2] possess rich and vibrant peace traditions. From the passive resistance of Parihaka in the face of British colonial aggression (Scott 1975; Elsmore 1989, 213–32) to the inspired pragmatism of Ruataupare's egalitarian renewal[3] (*Te Ao Hou* 1968, 8), the legacy of peace that exists within Māori tradition is worthy of aspiration. And yet, as a people, Māori have yet to fully realize their own peace traditions. Māori social indicators rival the worst in the world for health, domestic violence, youth suicide, crime, and incarceration. As a minority people in their own land, Māori continue to suffer injustice at the

The Reverend Donald S. Tamihere is a Māori Anglican priest and biblical scholar specializing in Old Testament Studies and Māori cultural exegesis. Reverend Tamihere has a keen interest in the intersection between Māori and biblical concepts of peace and how they are applied to the life of church and community. In addition to his work as priest-in-charge of an urban Māori congregation, he is an executive member of the Christian Conference of Asia's Forum for Theological Education and the founding director of the Anglican Center for Youth Ministry Studies.

hands of the state, and are fighting for the survival of their traditions, language, and culture. As one Māori commentator has put it, "We struggle without end" (Walker 1990, 24).

But it is against the backdrop of struggle that Māori traditions of peace were born. The desire to find a new and better way is one common to all humanity, and Māori are no exception. Notions of peace, and the concepts that undergird those ideals, shine within Māori cultural thought like beacons. Sometimes distant and elusive, often unachievable, they are continually there to remind and to guide.

This chapter is presented as a commentary on Māori traditions of peace and nonviolence, and their potential for the subversion of hatred in the modern Māori context and elsewhere. The scope of this chapter prevents an exhaustive treatment of the subject here. However, it is hoped that this small glimpse might inspire readers to seek further and learn something of themselves by peering into a Māori world.

Before we explore Māori peace traditions, it will be helpful to first look at their broader cultural underpinnings. These include the fundamental concepts of Māori cultural thought, Māori social structure, Māori worldview, and the experience of British colonization begun in the early 1800s, the context within which one of the most prominent Māori traditions of peace was born. This chapter will conclude with a look at some of the challenges that contemporary Māori face and consider the question of whether Māori are equipped to subvert the forms of hatred that they experience.

## THE MĀORI WAY

*Tikanga Māori*, or the "Māori way,"[4] is a term that refers in general to the body of knowledge, values, beliefs, and practices held in common by Māori (Mead 2003, 1–10). This includes not only the traditional customs and norms that are unique to Māoridom, but also the living and evolving expressions of culture and identity that exist within contemporary Māori society. While tribal variations exist, the understanding and practice of *tikanga* Māori by the Māori community remains fairly consistent. This is because *tikanga* Māori is premised on principles and ideals that are commonly subscribed to within Māori society (Mead 2003,

25–35; Orbell 1995, 186–88). The most fundamental of these principles and ideals are:

- *Manaakitanga*—the privilege and obligation of offering hospitality, nurture, care, and provision. From the word *manaaki*, which also means blessing.
- *Whanaungatanga*—the nurture and maintenance of friendship and kinship ties. Derived from the word *whanau*, which can also mean family or birth, depending on context.
- *Wairuatanga*—the belief that the spiritual world permeates and is integral to every aspect of physical existence. The word *wairua*, usually translated as spirit, means literally "two waters."
- *Kotahitanga*—the holding of unity and consensus as the ideal. From the word *kotahi*, meaning one.
- *Rangatiratanga*—the inalienable right of Māori to be self-determining. From the word *rangatira*, usually translated as chief, leader, and elder. The literal meaning of *rangatiratanga* is weaving people together.
- *Mana*—the inherent power and potential of individuals and communities. As a concept, *mana* also refers to prestige and esteem that is both active (gained or earned) and passive (projected or conferred).
- *Utu*—the obligation of response and reciprocity. *Utu* has both positive and negative connotations, depending on the action or deed being responded to. As a word, *utu* can also be translated as equivalence, cost, fair return, and revenge.
- *Tapu*—the sanctity and inviolability of a given object, place, or being. *Tapu* is perhaps the most important component of *tikanga Māori*. Where *tapu* exists, there is an obligation to behave in a manner that is appropriate and that does not violate that *tapu*. As a word, *tapu* can also be translated as restricted, forbidden, and holy.
- *Noa*—balance and restoration. *Noa* is most often understood in conjunction with *tapu* as balancing or opposing forces. *Noa* can be translated also as freely approachable, common, or profane.

Durie notes that these principles tend not to be followed strictly as a list of rules. Instead they exist as "conceptual regulators" (Durie 1994, 3–5) that are referenced or alluded to in custom, ritual, and practice. This extends to accepted ritual protocols *(kawa)* and communal knowledge *(matauranga Māori)*, which form the basis for social validation of personal and public *tikanga*. Within Māori peace traditions, concepts such as *tapu, noa*, and *mana* are absolutely pivotal.

## MĀORI SOCIAL STRUCTURE AND WORLDVIEW

Traditionally, Māori society has been based in the interrelationship between *whānau* (immediate and extended family), *hapū* (subtribe or groupings of *whānau*), and *iwi* (tribe or groupings of *hapū*). *Hapū* and *iwi* in particular formed the primary political alliances of Māori society, and as such were the base from which "national" identity was claimed and expressed. It is not uncommon for *hapū* and *iwi* to differ from each other in dialect, custom, and worldview.

A traditional Māori view of the world is holistic and incorporative of the human interdependency with flora, fauna, earth, sea, and sky.[5] This interdependency is not seen as merely physical, but rather as incorporating the totality of the living being.[6] Generally speaking, no relational separation is made between the spheres of thought and emotion, spirit, and physical existence. Rather, these spheres are deemed to affect, influence, and permeate each other to such an extent that the boundaries between them blur or, more correctly, do not exist.

The incorporative nature of traditional Māori worldviews has manifested itself in very practical and pragmatic ways. During the first few decades of the early 1800s, when Māori first came in contact with British colonial settlers, called Pākeha in Māori,[7] this was very evident: "For the first few years they tended to regard Pākeha as a curiosity and to observe the strangers' different customs without being touched by them. The Māori took what aspects of the introduced culture suited them, and disregarded the rest as inappropriate and unnecessary to their way of life" (Elsmore 1989, 3).[8] This taking onboard of what "suited them" extended also to the faith introduced by settler missionaries. Far from merely being syncretic, Māori embraced new and correlative concepts of life and spirit in a way many Pākeha, so used to mono-culture and mono-thinking, could not comprehend. Māori continue, in many forms, to hold differing ideas of faith and culture in tension. This is in part because of colonization and the dual reality of living as a Māori in a non-Māori world, but also because of the latent potential such tensions offered for growth and greater understanding. Many Māori traditions of peace evolved out of a melding of Māori cultural concepts with Christian understandings introduced by settler missionaries (Davidson 1997, 45–48).

## COLONIZATION AND THE TREATY OF WAITANGI

No introduction to Māori worldview would be complete without outlining what has been singularly the most defining factor within Māori society in the last two hundred years: Pākeha (British) colonization (Kawharu 1989, 319–21).

Prior to 1840, contact with Pākeha was mainly with whalers, sealers, and missionaries who came to Aotearoa via colonies in Australia. Settlers during this period developed strong relationships with Māori. This was partially a pragmatic choice, as Māori were by far the majority with an estimated population of 250,000 compared to fewer than 2000 Pākeha who were domiciled in the country (Orange 1987, 12–24).

Following increasing expansionist interest from France, Spain, and the United States, British settlers looked to enshrine in legislative form their "right" to live in Aotearoa. This culminated in the signing in 1840 of the Treaty of Waitangi, an agreement between Queen Victoria's British Government and the Māori chiefs of Aotearoa, whose signed declaration of independence in 1835 had already been recognized by the British parliament (Davidson 1997, 20–26).

The Treaty expressly guaranteed Māori undisturbed possession of their lands and "all the rights and privileges of British citizens" (Te Puni Kokiri 2001a, 10) in return for allowing British subjects to settle under Victorian governance. Consequently, there was a massive increase in the number of British migrants coming to Aotearoa, a practice that was expedited by colonial companies in England selling settlement rights while actively promulgating dubious land seizures in Aotearoa. Tensions and skirmishes escalated into full-scale war, and by the mid 1860s the full might of the British military was being deployed against Māori "rebels" (Davidson 1997, 20–26).

When the so-called Land Wars ended in the 1870s, Māori resistance, though ingenious and gallant, was eventually overwhelmed with devastating effect by the British military machine that had conquered vast areas of the known world. The settler government began confiscating huge tracts of land as "punishment" for Māori rebellion, often taking prime land unconnected to any alleged rebels, and eventually reduced Māori owned land from 66,400,000 acres in 1840, to less than 3,000,000 today (Walker 1990, 18–40).[9]

The loss of economic base caused by land confiscations, and the subsequent subsistence living that it caused, brought about a massive decrease in the Māori population. This was exacerbated by introduced diseases like influenza that ravaged the population, reducing it to less than 40,000 by the year 1900 (Walker 1990, 80). Settler commentators, noticing the sharp trend, postulated that the Māori race would be extinct within decades, with some decreeing that everything should be done to "help smooth the pillow of a dying race"(*Te Ao Hou* 1967, 60). Despite such predictions, the Māori population began slowly to increase after the turn of the century. During both World War I (1914–1918) and World War II (1940–1945), Māori fought alongside their Pākeha neighbors "for King and for Country" in the hope that equality of citizenship might be gained once more. Despite losing, by some estimates, up to 75 percent of their male population during those wars, Māori were not accorded what they had hoped, and remained second-class citizens in their own land (Gardiner 1992, 1–18).

By the 1960s, there were growing calls for Māori assimilation into English culture to be accelerated "for their own good." Māori children were forbidden to speak their own language at school, with dissenting children being beaten soundly for their efforts. A curriculum of "Home Economics" and "Manual Training" was instituted to nurture Māori as a cooking and laboring race (Hunn 1961, 14–16; Simon and Smith 2001). Despite the negative attentions of successive governments, Māori culture experienced a renaissance in the 1970s and '80s that brought about a resurgence in Māori language and customs some feared would be lost. The establishment of the Waitangi Tribunal in 1975, charged with adjudicating historic land grievances and transgressions of the Treaty of Waitangi since 1840, was a watershed for Māori. Though unpopular with mainstream New Zealand, the Tribunal slowly began addressing treaty breaches and facilitating settlement with Māori tribes wrongfully alienated from their lands (Te Puni Kokiri 2001a, 14–16). Though these settlements generally represent a pitiful attempt at redress (some equating to only a few cents on the dollar repaid for assets confiscated), they have in many cases provided Māori tribes with an economic base that has radically improved their ability to be self-determining and to procure advancement for their members.

Throughout the history of colonization and the Treaty, Māori have never contested the fact that they agreed to partnership with Pākeha, and that Pākeha should be accorded their full right under the Treaty. Notable too is the complete lack of vindictiveness to date shown by Māori claimants to the Waitangi Tribunal. A prominent Pākeha commentator on the Treaty, Pat Sneddon, reflected recently on the grace he had seen demonstrated by Māori claimants. In particular, he notes the actions of Ngati Whatua tribe who had had their land forcibly confiscated by the New Zealand Government as recently as the mid-twentieth century after the Waitangi Tribunal had awarded them restored ownership of part of their lands:

> The first thing Ngati Whatua did was to give a huge chunk of Bastion Point back to Aucklanders. That's right, they gave it back to you and me for our unimpeded use. I refer to the most expensive land with the best views in all of Auckland. The land where Michael Joseph Savage rests. Ngati Whatua agreed to manage this jointly with the Auckland City Council for the benefit of all the people of Tamaki Makaurau. What therefore is it that enables a people who sought for 150 years to get some form of justice that recognised their cultural destitution, to react in their moment of triumph with such generosity to those who had dispossessed them? What underpins such an act of munificence? To put it simply; the recovery of the *hapu rangatiratanga*. (Sneddon 2004, 3)

Such acts illustrate Māori capacity to adhere to their own values, regardless of the circumstance. Values such as *manaakitanga, aroha, hohou rongo,* and *rangatiratanga* are evidenced by Ngati Whatua's benevolence despite more than a century of hurt. As it is said, "If we can secure peace in our own land, it will spread to others."[10]

## MĀORI TRADITIONS OF PEACE

Of all the values espoused within Māori wisdom tradition, peace is the most commonly expressed. This is both from a pragmatic standpoint ("It is better to be dead than alive without peace"),[11] and from a metaphorical one ("Forgiveness forged by a woman is like a greenstone door; a lasting peace").[12] The concept of peace takes many forms within Māori wisdom tradition, of which the following are only a few.

### RONGO: GOD OF PEACE

The Māori language has several words for peace, of which *rongo* is one.[13] Amongst the pantheon of traditional Māori gods, Rongo is known as the god of peace. Rongo is also the god of cultivated foods, and particularly the *kūmara*,[14] whose need for intense cultivation could only be successfully maintained in times of peace. Hence the *kūmara* is also associated with peace, and was incorporated in cooked form within traditional rituals of *hohou rongo*— the restoration of the balance between *tapu* and *noa*. Within Māori wisdom tradition, Rongo is generally represented in opposition, or in counterbalance, to other gods representing war, conflict, and death. Most common was Tūmatauenga (or "Tū"), who was god of warfare, industry, and invention, and brother to Rongo (Hiroa 1958, 454–65). The saying "The heaped fish of Tū; The heaped fish of Rongo" (Best 1896, 7) is a reference to those who have died in battle,[15] and a dark reminder that war and peace will always contend with one another. The saying "One dedicated to war can never achieve peace" implies that the goal of peace requires a certain pathway (Stowell 1913, 138).[16] Another saying, "The harvest of Tū; The harvest of Rongo" (Williams 1908, 6),[17] compares the piled heaps (gardens and crops) of food that are produced under Rongo (in times of peace) to the piled bodies produced under Tū (in times of war).

A less gruesome saying is "Tū without; Rongo within" (Metge 1976, 231),[18] which refers to the traditional sacred meeting place called the *marae* where Tū is said to reign outside the house and where debate and oratory contests occur while Rongo reigns within where host and guest can dwell and sleep in safety. The saying also implies that conflict belongs outside, and peace within.

Besides Tū, Rongo is also often paired with Haumia-tiketike (Haumia), another of his brothers and the god of wild and uncultivated foods. Haumia, however, is not presented as an antithesis to, but rather as another aspect of what Rongo represents. The saying "Rongo and Haumia are hidden" (Best 1977, 73)[19] refers to the "hiddeness" of the *kūmara* and the *aruhe*, which both grow below ground. This saying also refers to the difficulty often inherent in securing a lasting peace. The saying "Eat the abundance of Rongo and Haumia" (Best 1975, 50),[20] is further encouragement to consume oneself with the search for peace.

## HOHOU RONGO

Where the state of peace achieved after a cessation of hostilities was called *rongo*, the process of negotiating peace was called *hohou rongo* (Mead 2003, 167). *Hohou rongo* means literally to "bind peace," thus suggesting stability and permanence as the primary goal. Traditionally, the "binding" of peace was demonstrated symbolically through the exchange of prized possessions, through arranged marriages (thus uniting formerly antagonistic parties), and/or through the nominating of dominant land features as permanent reminders of the peace agreement. A mountain, for instance, could be set aside as an enduring symbol of the new peace accord, and as a reminder to future generations that as long as the mountain stands, peace must be honored (Mead 2003, 169).

The term *hohou rongo* also refers to the seeking of forgiveness for wrongs done and to the process of reconciliation. Peace was achieved through the perpetrator being made accountable to victim and community alike by confessing and taking ownership of his or her wrong, while at the same time providing for the victim and community to determine the terms of any punishment, restoration *(utu)*, and peace.

It is partly from this aspect of *hohou rongo* that some of the modern framework for restorative justice has been developed. Restorative justice was first introduced within the New Zealand judicial system in 1989 as an alternative to the standard retributive justice frameworks that were being employed. Incorporating *hohou rongo, whanaungatanga, kotahitanga,* and *rangatiratanga*, legislation was introduced to establish Family Group Conferences (FGCs) to deal with young offenders. These conferences provided a forum for young offenders to take responsibility for their actions, to be held accountable to their own family and the victim's family, and for victims and their families to determine reparation and ways in which the offender might be "set back on track" (Bowen 2002, 8). Though neither a panacea nor able "to supplant completely conventional criminal court processes" (Schmid 2001, 4), the restorative justice system initiated for young offenders in Aotearoa-New Zealand has been highly successful and effective. This is due to the ability of the framework to account for cultural diversity and community involvement, the needs of the victim, and the rehabilitation and restoration of the offender.

## TATAU POUNAMU

One of the more beautiful metaphors for peace contained within Māori wisdom tradition is that of the *tatau pounamu,* or the greenstone door.[21] The phrase *tatau pounamu* was used to symbolize peace and cessation of hostilities. The durable quality of *pounamu* also symbolized the stability expected from peace agreements. The saying "Let our peace be like the greenstone door, unbreakable for all eternity" (Reed and Brougham 1987, 83),[22] captures this. Another saying, "Do not break the frame that supports the greenstone door, lest you stray from the precepts of your ancestors" (Best 1903, 20–21),[23] suggests that while the *tatau pounamu* itself may endure, the *rākau* (wood or props) used to support it might fail. This is illustrated further by the saying "The peace undermined by the seahorse,"[24] which is a reference to the seahorse whose head and shoulders are still (peaceful), but whose tail is frantic and constantly moving. Thus the image of the *tatau pounamu* represents the paradoxical nature of peace: its enduring strength and its inherent fragility.

### Subverting Colonial Hatred: The Story of Parihaka

I am the fruition of righteousness;
A balm from within the sacred feather;
My sacred feather is an assurance to the world.[25]

When speaking of peace and nonviolence within Māori tradition, no story is more widely honored than that of Parihaka, a village in the Taranaki region of the North Island of Aotearoa-New Zealand. Founded during the so-called "Māori Wars" of the 1860s—when British colonial forces moved *en masse* to illegally and punitively confiscate Māori land for settlement and expansion—Parihaka became a bastion for literally thousands of local Māori displaced from their ancestral homes (Scott 1975, 22ff.). By 1870, Parihaka had become one of the largest Māori settlements in the country, and was a social and economic force to be reckoned with.

Led by two *rangatira*[26] prophets, Te Whiti-o-Rongomai and Tohu Kakahi, the people of Parihaka committed themselves to passive resistance in the face of increasing British colonial aggression.[27] This was no light matter, as resistance in any form meant potential harm, injury, or even death. That the residents were so galvanized in their commitment to nonviolence is testament to the inspiration and moral courage provided by Te Whiti and Tohu.

Te Whiti and Tohu based their teachings on a combination of ancient Māori and Christian missionary teachings—a fact that befuddled many colonists, who viewed Māori spirituality as pagan and incompatible with "civilized" religion—and promoted the extension of peaceful relationship, forgiveness, and hospitality, even to colonial aggressors. Te Whiti, in particular, became known for his seamless merging of Māori and Christian belief: "Te Whiti was said to be deeply learned in all the old legends and incantations of his people . . . to the aged, by a single couplet from some old charmed rhyme, he can create anew the vigour of their race . . . to the young men he can utter, with electrifying energy burning words from the Book of Books which was taught them by missionaries" (Elsmore 1989, 215).

Māori living beyond the environs of Parihaka were employing whatever means they could to keep their land. Initially, many local tribes quietly succumbed to the colonial government's threats of confiscation. This, it seems, in the hope that British settlement would be only a temporary affliction. Other tribes chose to meet aggression with aggression, and engaged in bloody and brutal battles up and down the Taranaki coast. What was very clear was that the colonial government was stubbornly committed to its policy of "creeping confiscation" through extensive surveying and reallocation of Māori land, and was becoming tired of passive resistance: "If Te Whiti takes up arms it will take a very short time to deal with Te Whiti. He is much more troublesome to us as a prophet than he ever would be if he took down his firelock and used it on settlers" (Scott 1975, 69).

Aided by their followers, Tohu and Te Whiti engaged in a campaign of strategic nonviolent resistance that included the quiet dismantling of surveyors' equipment huts, the removing of survey pegs, and erecting fences and plowing land with deliberate disregard for surveyor's boundaries. Groups from Parihaka engaged in long marches around the original borders of their lands, reasserting both to local settlers and government forces their ownership and intent to remain. This strategy—several decades before the emergence of a young Mahatma Ghandi, and a generation before the births of Martin Luther King Jr. and Nelson Mandela—was so successful, that the colonial government was galvanized to end the Parihaka struggle once and for all.

On November 5, 1881, a force of armed government soldiers, settler militia, and other volunteers, together numbering some 1,500 men, descended on Parihaka. Though prepared to fight and kill, the colonial force met no resistance. Te Whiti and Tohu, who had known about the impending arrival of the colonists, had instructed their people to remain passive, and even to go so far as to provide their adversaries with food, drink, and blankets if needed. As Scott notes, this action was not what the colonial force had been expecting:

> There was a line of children across the entrance to the big village, a kind of singing class directed by an old man with a stick. The children sat there unmoving, droning away, and even when a mounted officer galloped up and pulled his horse up so short that the dirt from its forefeet spattered the children, they still went on chanting perfectly oblivious, apparently, to the Pakeha, and the old man calmly continued his monotonous drone.
>
> I was the first to enter the Māori town with my company. I found my only obstacle was the youthful feminine element. There were skipping parties of girls on the road. When I came to the first set of girls I asked them to move, but they took no notice. (1975, 113–14)

Despite the stoic refusal shown by Parihaka's children, the constabulary persisted with its intent to seize Te Whiti and Tohu. With no resistance or complaint, Te Whiti and Tohu were eventually arrested along with some 1,600 of their followers, and removed from Parihaka. Most were taken to the South Island and imprisoned under a special act of Parliament (the Native Prisoners' Trials Act) that allowed them to be incarcerated indefinitely without trial. Many of the prisoners died under harsh and terrible conditions. The few people who were not arrested (due only to a lack of transport) were driven out, made destitute by the loss of land and economy.

What remained of the Parihaka settlement was slowly and systematically destroyed—buildings, fences, even crops were crushed and burned. An undisclosed number of the colonial force, perhaps deranged by the blood-letting that they had expected but did not receive, took to slaughtering livestock, and in some accounts, raping women who remained in Parihaka.

To the last, Te Whiti and Tohu, their followers both young and old, remained steadfast in their belief in peaceful, nonviolent resistance to the unwarranted aggression of the colonists. Though both Te Whiti and Tohu returned to Parihaka after their release from prison, their hope for the return of their lands and a full restoration of their settlement was never fulfilled. To this day, the lands confiscated by the colonial government remain alienated from the original Māori owners. The words of Te Whiti-o-Rongomai as he was led away captive by armed constabulary spoke for his people: "We look for peace and we find war. Be steadfast, keep to peaceful works; be not dismayed, have no fear" (Scott 1975, 117).

## SUBVERTING HATRED: THE TWENTY-FIRST-CENTURY CHALLENGE FOR MĀORI

As a society, Māori in the twenty-first century face a number of daunting challenges. Statistics show that Māori within Aotearoa-New Zealand struggle against many social and economic barriers. For example, more Māori are likely to be poor—earning an average of $14,800 each compared to the national average of $40,000. More likely to be sick—exhibiting the highest statistical ratio in the country of heart disease, type 2 diabetes, asthma, and cancers caused by smoking. More likely to be unemployed—with 56 percent of Māori adults unemployed compared to the national average of just under 6 percent. More likely to be uneducated—only 5 percent of Māori have a tertiary qualification, of which a Diploma in Primary School Teaching is the most common. More likely to be incarcerated—with Māori constituting 50 percent of the total prison population. And, sadly, more likely to commit suicide—especially Māori females between the ages of 15 and 19 (Te Puni Kokiri 2000, 8–52; 2001b).[28] Such statistics may or may not demonstrate the kind of hatred that contemporary Māori face. Indeed, rather than these statistics, descriptors like war and violence would perhaps be more readily understood. But the fact is that hatred is not always so blatant or obvious as it is in the guise of war. Hatred also assumes other, more persistent forms.

One example is the continued injustice that Māori face from the state. Since the signing of the Treaty of Waitangi in 1840, successive governments have implemented over one hundred pieces of legislation that directly violate the terms of the Treaty (Walker 1990, 4–22). This includes legislation specifically designed to alienate Māori-owned land. As recently as November 2004, the Seabed and Foreshore Act was enacted to remove Māori claim to ancestral title over the seabed and foreshore, and vest ownership exclusively with the government (Stavenhagen 2006, 12). Māori were not only stripped of the legal possession that they had enjoyed unbroken for generations, but were now no longer able to pursue the economic benefit of the untapped oil and gas reserves that their seabed and foreshore contained.

This development was considered so serious by the United Nations Commission on Human Rights that it dispatched a special rapporteur to investigate the effect of this new legislation on Māori and the state of Māori society as a whole. After an extensive investigation that included consultation with twelve different government agencies, various members of Parliament, and numerous Māori tribal groups throughout the country, the special rapporteur concluded that the New Zealand Government had breached not only its own Bill of Human Rights, but also the United Nations' Human and Indigenous Rights provisions. The special rapporteur also noted the persistent negative portrayal of Māori by New Zealand media (Stavenhagen 2006, 17) and evidence of historical and institutional discrimination against Māori (Stavenhagen 2006, 14).

Demographic statistics such as those mentioned above are symptoms of broad systemic failures, and "arguably represent the underlying institutional and structural discrimination that Māori have long suffered" (Stavenhagen 2006, 15). From a Māori stand-point this presents, I would contend, a kind of three-way threat to Māori. The first and most obvious threat is the hatred that is vis-ited upon Māori from external parties like the state and those that perpetuate institutional discrimination and oppression. The sec-ond threat is the potential for the inculcation of bitterness and hate amongst Māori toward their antagonists. While such bitterness is arguably justifiable, the story of Parihaka incarnates reasons from within *tikanga Māori* itself as to why Māori should aspire to make peace with their antagonists. The third and perhaps most insidi-ous threat is the potential for Māori, because of their social con-text, to visit hatred upon themselves. Certainly those within Māoridom who are guilty of violent crime and abuse can be accused of this. So too those who make up part of the demographic of Māori drug and alcohol abuse, suicide, and preventable disease. This self-hatred, for that is what it is, deserves to be subverted as much as any external form of hatred does.

The question should be asked then, Are Māori equipped to sub-vert the hatred that they face? I would answer yes. *Tikanga Māori*, in terms of its conceptual framework, its body of knowledge, and its collective experience, provides Māoridom with the tools to pur-sue and attain peace. But while injustice remains, the concepts of peace present within Māori tradition—and the fulfillment of human potential that they imply—are at once like "the whirlwinds of *Tawhirimātea*": present, strong, compelling, and yet impossible to hold.[29] The story of Parihaka illustrates this further, as an historic lesson in patience, nobility, tactics, and perseverance, that ultimately ended without the fruition of hoped-for peace and restoration.

In closing, another saying from Māori oral tradition is rele-vant: Let peace and justice be joined.[30] Peace cannot exist without justice. Justice must be pursued, but not at the expense of peace. As unfair as it seems, *tikanga Māori* places the burden of restora-tion and forgiveness upon Māori themselves. The concept of *rongo* asks Māori to walk the higher path. The concept of *hohou rongo* asks Māori to build bridges and maintain an open door. The con-cept of *tatau pounamu* asks Māori to build peace that is sustain-able. These requests may not be welcome or attainable, but they are there. What remains then is that Māori must decide as indi-viduals and as a people whether they are prepared to adhere to their own *tikanga* and subvert hatred in all its forms, the exact same decision that faces all humankind.

## STUDY QUESTIONS

1. How does Tamihere suggest that Māori conversion to Christianity is itself an indication of a Māori philosophy of "pluralism"?

2. Tamihere begins his essay with a review of traditional Māori philosophy and spirituality. How does this relate to the proverb "Water captured in a gourd ceases to be the river it once was"?

3. What is the significance of the Treaty of Waitangi? Why was the Waitangi Tribunal called in 1975 and what does it try to accomplish in modern New Zealand?

4. What are the two aspects of peace in the phrase "the greenstone door"?

5. In what way did Te Whiti anticipate Gandhi's methods of passive resistance at Parihaka?

6. Using the example of the Māori of New Zealand, or Native Americans, discuss why "peace" as a practical value may be especially difficult for such minorities living in the world today.

## BIBLIOGRAPHY

Best, Elsdon. *In Ancient Māoriland*. Rotorua, NZ: F. F. Watt, 1896.

———. *Maori Marriage Customs.*Tuhoe Tribe. TNZI 1903, 36:14–67

———. *Māori Religion and Mythology*. Wellington, NZ: Museum of New Zealand, Dominion Museum, Bulletin 10, 1924.

———. *The Pa Maori*. Wellington, NZ: Government Printer, Dominion Museum Bulletin 6, 1975.

———. *Forest Lore of the Maori*. Wellington, NZ: Government Printer, Dominion Museum Bulletin 14, 1977.

Bowen, Helen. *Recent Restorative Justice Developments in New Zealand/Aotearoa*. Auckland, NZ: Restorative Justice Trust, 2002.

Davidson, Allan. K. *Christianity in Aotearoa*. Wellington, NZ: New Zealand Education for Ministry, 1997.

Durie, Eddie. *Custom Law, Working Paper*. Wellington, NZ: Waitangi Tribunal, 1994.

Elsmore, Bronwyn. *Mana from Heaven: A Century of Maori Prophets in New Zealand*. Auckland, NZ: Reed Publishing, 1989.

Gardiner, Wira. *Te Mura o te Ahi: The Story of the Māori Battalion*. Auckland, NZ: Reed, 1992.

Hiroa, Te Rangi. *The Coming of the Māori*. Wellington, NZ: Whitcombe and Tombs Ltd, 1958.

Hunn, Jack K. "Report on the Department of Maori Affairs, 24 August 1960." In *Appendices to the Journal of the House of Representatives*, G-10: Wellington, NZ: Government Printer, 1961: 14–16.

Kawharu, I. Hugh, ed. *Waitangi: Maori & Pakeha Perspectives of the Treaty of Waitangi*. Auckland, NZ: Oxford University Press, 1989.

Mead, Hirini M. *Tikanga Māori: Living by Māori Values*. Wellington, NZ: Huia Publishers, 2003.

Metge, Joan. *Māori Literature Booklet*. Wellington, NZ: Victoria University, 1976.

McKenzie, Donald F. *Oral Culture, Literacy & Print in Early New Zealand: The Treaty of Waitangi*. Wellington, NZ: Victoria University Press, 1985.

Orange, Claudia. *The Treaty of Waitangi*. Auckland, NZ: Bridget Williams Books, 1987.

Orbell, Margaret. *Māori Myth and Legend*. Christchurch, NZ: Canterbury University Press, 1995.

Reed, A. W., and Aileen Brougham. *The Reed Book of Maori Proverbs*. Auckland, NZ: Reed, 1987; rev ed. 2004.

Schmid, Donald J. *Restorative Justice in New Zealand: A Model for U.S. Criminal Justice*. Wellington: Ian Axford Trust, 2001.

Scott, Dick. *Ask That Mountain: The Story of Parihake*. Auckland, NZ: Reed, 1975.

Simon, Judith and Linda Tuhiwai Smith, eds. *A Civilising Mission? Perceptions and Representations of the New Zealand Native Schools System*. Auckland, NZ: Auckland University Press, 2001.

Sneddon, Pat. Speech at St Columba's Church, Auckland, NZ, May 7, 2004.

Stavenhagen, Rudolfo. *Report of the Special Rapporteur on the situation of human rights and fundamental freedoms of indigenous people, Rodolfo Stavenhagen: Mission to New Zealand*. New York: United Nations Economic and Social Council, 2006.

Stowell, Henry M. *Māori-English Tutor and Vade Mecum*. Christchurch, NZ: Whitcombe and Tombs, 1913.

*Te Ao Hou*. Wellington, NZ: Department of Māori Affairs, No. 59, 1967.

*Te Ao Hou*. Wellington, NZ: Department of Māori Affairs, No. 65, 1968.

Te Puni Kokri (Ministry of Māori Development). *Progress Towards Closing Social and Economic Gaps Between Maori and Non-Maori*. Wellington: Government Print, 2000.

Te Puni Kokiri (Ministry of Māori Development). *He Tirohanga ō Kawa ki te Tiriti o Waitangi*. Wellington: Government Print, 2001a.

Te Puni Kokiri (Ministry of Māori Development). *Te Māori i Nga Rohe: Māori Regional Diversity*. Wellington: Government Print, 2001b.

Walker, Ranginui. *Ka whawhai tonu matou: Struggle without End*. Auckland, NZ: Penguin Books, 1990.

Williams, H. W. *He Whakatauki, He Titotito, He Pēpeha*. Gisborne, NZ: Te Rau Kahikatea, 1908.

## NOTES

¹ It is traditional within Māori culture to begin any form of oratory or prose by quoting a proverb, poem, or other saying, as a means of "setting the scene." The saying I have used here is translated from the traditional Māori blessing: *Kia hora te marino; Kia whakapapa pounamu te moana; Kia tere te kārohirohi.* While the exact tribal origins of this blessing are unclear, the blessing is a ubiquitous one throughout Maoridom. The word *pounamu* (translated as greenstone in the text) refers to the highly prized nephrite jade indigenous to Aotearoa-New Zealand and traditionally used by Māori as material for intricate jewelery, ornaments, and weapons. *Pounamu*, due to its value, was also used for gifts on significant occasions. *Pounamu* is distinctive from jade found in other countries due to its darker green hues and deep luster.

Note well that some of the sayings used within this article exist primarily within Māori oral tradition, and not necessarily within a written corpus per se. As such they cannot be referenced according to Western academic norms. Oral tradition is the foremost repository of Māori wisdom and experience. It is a living tradition whose integrity is checked and balanced within a Māori society that continuously references and validates that tradition within its own formal and informal settings. Though tangible expressions exist, such as *whakairo* (intricate carving), *ta moko* (tatoo), and *kowhaiwhai* (painted symbols), to name a few, it is the spokenness of Māori culture, through *whakatauki* (proverbs and wisdom traditions), *mōteatea* (rhythmic chant), *tauparapara* (prose), *waiata* (song), and *haka* (a synthesis of chant and movement often simplistically referred to as a "war-dance") that are its highest expressions. Regarding Māori oral tradition, McKenzie says, "In practice, the oral mode rules. By compelling those who speak eloquently to substitute a mode in which they are less fluent, literacy can function insidiously as a culturally regressive force. Such at least is how many Māori experience it . . . there are few Māori writers and very few who write in Māori, but the tradition of oral composition and exposition continues, it is the only tradition with 'literary' structures or styles, and the 'sound' of the text is usually all there is to be read. Even within university departments of Māori studies, the book is suspect. Manuscripts and printed texts in libraries, publications by Pākeha on Māoridom, are seldom consulted; oral etiquette, debate, and transfer of knowledge on the *marae* are what matter. Such conditions encourage the spontaneous, orally improvised, dramatic recreation of shared stories for themes and an evolutionary concept of texts; the fixed text, catching in print an arbitrary moment in the continuum of social exchange, demands a different sense of history and its own literal re-play" (McKenzie 1985, 19).

² Aotearoa is a modern Māori name for New Zealand, as opposed to the older names *Te-Ika-a-Maui* (North Island) and *Te Wāhi* (te Wai) *Pounamu* (South Island). These islands later became know as New Zealand when they were "discovered" by the Dutch explorer Abel Tasman in 1642, some seven centuries after the first arrival of ancient Māori.

³ A Ngāti Porou chieftaness, ascendant c.1830, developed the philosophy of *tangata* rite (meaning literally "All people are equal") as part of a radical repositioning of her people and her own *rangatiratanga* (leadership). Under *tangata* rite, people who were formerly slaves or of ignoble birth were given equal status with Ruataupare's own descendants, and her tribe became known as *Te Whanau a Ruataupare*—The family of Ruataupare. See *Te Ao Hou* (1968, 8).

⁴ The word *tikanga* is derived from the word *tika* (meaning right, true, and correct), and depending on context can also be translated as custom, manner, ethic, lore, protocol, and cultural norm.

⁵ One particular traditional Māori *tauparapara* illustrates this by saying: "Woven above; woven below; woven within; woven without; woven to the heavens; woven to the earth; woven to our ancestral home; woven to all living things; woven with cords that can never be broken; woven into our seeking; woven into enlightenment." The original Māori reads: *Tuia ki runga; tuia ki raro; tuia ki roto; tuia ki waho; tuia ki te rangi; tuia ki te whenua; tuia ki Hawaiki te hono-i-wairua; tuia ki te mauri o te Ao; tuia ki te here e kore e taea te momotu; ki te Wheiao, ki te Ao Marama.* Generally speaking, *tauparapara* are forms of prose, poetry, or ritual chants that are employed by orators at the beginning of a formal speech or address. *Tauparapara* often recount myths, legends, historical events, and *whakapapa* (genealogy), and utilize a number of oratorical and rhetorical devices, including rhyme, meter, doublet, and alliteration. They serve to "set the scene" for the orator's delivery.

⁶ Namely *tīnana* (body and physicality), *hinengaro* (mind and emotion), and *wairua* (spirit and spirituality).

⁷ The word *Pākeha* refers to the pale skin of European people, akin to the *Kehakeha*, which is a form of white linen flax.

⁸ This attitude was later encouraged in young Māori by Sir Apirana Ngata (1874–1950), the first Māori member of Parliament and the first Māori law graduate, who composed the now ubiquitous exhortation: "Grow, oh young one, to the fullness of your days / Let Pākeha knowledge aid the industry of your hands / Let the treasures of your Māori ancestors fill your heart and adorn your intellect / And let God guide your spirit, for He is the Creator of all things." In Māori the saying reads: *E tipu, e rea, mo nga ra o tau ao / Ko to ringa ki nga rakau a te Pakeha, hei ara mo to tinana / Ko to ngakau ki nga taonga a o tipuna Māori, hei tikitiki mo to mahuna / A, ko to wairua ki te Atua, nana nei nga mea katoa.*

⁹ Land loss estimates do not include foreshore and seabed confiscations.

¹⁰ The original Māori reads: *Ka hohouia te rongo ki tēnei pā, e whakaaiohia i tētahi pā.* The word *pā* refers to land, or region, and also to the fortified villages early Māori lived in.

¹¹ In Māori this saying reads: *Pai atu te mate i te oranga okikore.* The word *okikore*, meaning literally to have no rest, here refers to peace.

¹² This saying in Māori reads: *He hohourongo wahine, he tatau Pounamu.* The reference to a peace "forged by a woman" alludes to the constructive and less confrontational manner Māori women generally have when compared to Māori men. Some Māori men might beg to differ.

¹³ There are various other words and metaphors such as *marie, rangimarie, aio, marino*, and so on.

¹⁴ Sweet potato. This traditional pre-Pākeha staple was relished for its sweet taste. The species of *kūmara* grown in Aotearoa originates from ancient South America, suggesting a link between the peoples of those lands.

¹⁵ The word *ika* here conjures the image of war-dead lying stricken like helpless fish. The saying in Māori reads: *Te ika a Tū; Te ika a Rongo.*

¹⁶ The saying in Māori reads: *He tangata tō Tū; He tangata ano tō Rongo.* This can be translated literally as "One kind of man for war; another kind for peace."

¹⁷ The saying in Māori reads: *E pūkai tō Tū; E pūkai tō Rongo* meaning literally "The food-heaps of Tū; the food-heaps of Rongo."

¹⁸ The Māori reads: *Tū ā waho; Rongo ā roto.*

¹⁹ The saying in Māori reads: *Ko Rongo, Ko Haumia he mea huna.*

²⁰ The Māori reads: *Kainga te tahua a Rongo rāua ko Haumia.*

²¹ *Pounamu* is a form of nephrite precious stone, native to Aotearoa-New Zealand, and treasured by both ancient and modern Māori alike. *Pounamu* represents the highest value, and is often exchanged as gift or as honor.

²² The Māori reads: *Me tatau Pounamu, kia kore ai e pakaru, ake, ake.*

²³ The saying in Māori reads: *Kei whati ngā rākau o te tatau pounamu i muri nei, kei pōhēhē koutou ki ngā ara kōrero tūpuna.*

²⁴ The saying in Māori reads: *Te āio i kauia e te kiore.* The word *kiore* also means rodent.

²⁵ This saying in Māori reads: *He puāwai āu nō runga i te tikanga; He rau rengarenga nō roto i te raukura; Ko tāku raukura rā he manawanui ki te Ao.* It is a saying widely attributed within Māoridom to Te Whiti-o-Rongomai, but oddly not quoted by authors like Dick Scott. The sacred feather referred to is the white feather worn by Parihaka people as a sign of passive resistance. The feather symbolises both the *tautoko* (blessing) of Māori *wairua* (spiritual energy), and the presence of the Holy Spirit. Parihaka descendants still wear the feather to this day.

[26] *Rangatira*—chiefly; of noble descent: "Te Whiti-o-Rongomai and Tohu Kakahi, were both well-connected members of the area. Te Whiti was Ati Awa with Taranaki connections; Tohu was of the Ngati Ruanui people and also had links with the Taranaki tribe. The two men were related being brothers-in-law" (Elsmore 2004, 211).

[27] See Scott (1975, 11–25) for accounts of armed raids and confiscations carried out by colonial forces.

[28] Statistics from *New Zealand Census 2001*; 2006 results were not available at the time of writing.

[29] In Māori this saying reads: *Ngā parōrō a Tawhirimātea*. Tawhirimatea is a deity or departmental god associated with winds, clouds, and weather.

[30] In Māori this saying reads: *Kia tūhono te aio me te tika*.

# 7

# Nonviolence in Islam

## The Alternative Community Tradition

*Rabia Terri Harris*

> How should you not fight for the cause of God and of the
> feeble among men and of women and the children who are
> crying: Our Lord! Bring us forth from out of this town of
> which the people are oppressors! Oh, give us from Your
> presence some protecting friend! Oh, give us from Your
> presence some defender!
>
> Qur'an, Surah Baqarah

> You have not been seen save as a mercy to the worlds.
>
> Qur'an, Surah Anbiya'

Islam is rarely associated with nonviolence in the public mind. The
fear that medieval Christendom felt at the swift and broad expansion of Oar ai-Islam, the "House of Islam"—with its formidable

Rabia Terri Harris is founder and coordinator of the Muslim Peace Fellowship, an
influential forum for progressive Islamic thought. In this role she writes and speaks
widely on a variety of social and spiritual issues. Harris, who embraced Islam in
1978, is a practicing chaplain and a contributing editor and columnist at *Fellowship*
magazine, a bimonthly publication of the Fellowship of Reconciliation, an organization devoted to interfaith issues and international peace and justice. A scholar
of Islamic studies and translator of medieval Arabic mystical texts, Harris is a
senior member of the Jerrahi Order, a three hundred-year-old Muslim religious
society headquartered in Istanbul.

and vigorous competing culture—is echoed in the fear that modern Westerners often feel at the appearance of Muslims in contemporary conflicts. This negative mindset also dominates the news: the enemy is depicted as clutching a Damascene dagger between his teeth. Seldom acknowledged is another face of Islam, the face turned away from Europe—for the Islamic religion spread throughout Southeast Asia and Africa by way of merchants and teachers, without any military involvement at all.

Islam makes no distinction between "church" and "state." There is scarcely any such entity as an Islamic church, and an Islamic state has always been a controversial institution. This means that Islam makes no distinction between the affairs of this world and those of the next, seeing them as a seamless unity—a reflection of the unity of God. One of the objectives of Muslim life is to make this unity a real experience for human beings. And one of the major obstacles to the human experience of a unity of faith and life is the presence of injustice.

> Say: My lord has commanded justice.
> (Qur'an, Surah A'raf, 29)

The establishment of justice, the Prophet taught us, requires ceaseless activity. The name for this activity is "jihad." The work of nonviolence is the ultimate root of jihad.

## THE PROPHET'S JIHAD

The word "jihad" does not mean holy war. Jihad means struggle, or effort. On the basis of a famous hadith of the Holy Prophet,[1] it is traditionally divided into *al-jihad al-akbar*, the Greater Struggle—the inward effort of confronting our lower nature—and *al-jihad al-asghar*, the Lesser Struggle—the outward effort of confronting social injustice. This lesser struggle is not all of one kind, but of many. It includes teaching, and the active pursuit of a culture of peace, as well as resistance to oppression.[2] Where jihad does refer to resistance to oppression, it is also not all of one kind, but embraces both armed and unarmed forms of struggle.

The Holy Prophet engaged in both forms of struggle. This fact is of key significance, for the practice of the Prophet—the Sunnah—stands immediately next to the Qur'anic revelation as a definitive guide for Muslims in every dimension of life. The Qur'an recommended the Prophet to us as "a beautiful example" (Surah Ahzab, 21), and ordered him to say to his community: "If you love God, follow me. God will love you and forgive your sins" (Surah Al-I 'Imran, 31). In consequence, as Schimmel writes, "In war and peace, at home and in the world, in the religious sphere as in every phase of working and acting, the Prophet is the ideal model of moral perfection. Whatever he did remains exemplary for his followers" (Schimmel 1985, 54).

If the Prophet engaged in armed struggle, therefore, it is clearly permissible and approved by God that Muslims should engage in armed struggle. But the question remains: Under what circumstances?

There is no license in Islam for any war (indeed, for any human enterprise) that falls outside the bounds of the divine commandments and Prophetic practice. Yet there may be fundamental disagreements about how the necessary analogies between these principles and current situations are to be drawn:

> Differences in the interpretation of the Prophet's sociopolitical activities can easily arise. The material at our disposal is many-sided and often contradictory, and the very history of early Islam poses numerous problems for the faithful as to how to implement the Prophet's ideals. Herein lies one reason for the difficulties that modern nations face when they attempt to create a truly "Islamic" state based on the teachings of the Koran and the Prophetic sunna. (Schimmel 1985, 54)

As we shall see, it is not only modern nations that have faced these difficulties. Such difficulties have formed a painful problem for the Muslim community from the very beginning. The same "beautiful example" that inspired the great heroes of nonviolence in Islamic history was also appealed to for justification by the fiercest opponents of these advocates of nonviolence.

To understand the problems of interpreting the Islamic tradition and applying this tradition to contemporary political issues (as well as critiquing some of these), we must consider how Muslims view the course of the life of our Prophet and also reexamine what we know of the role of the "lesser struggle" against social injustice in it.

## THE LIFE OF THE PROPHET

The life of the Prophet of Islam is an extraordinary story and needs an extended format to do it any justice. The subject has inspired hundreds of volumes of narrative, documentation, and commentary. We can sketch only the briefest and most inadequate of outlines here.

The prophetic career of Muhammad, the Messenger of Allah (peace and blessings be upon him),[3] fell roughly into two parts, each with its own great theme. His first task was to persist with unwavering endurance in the face of an increasingly bitter communal repression. This drama unfolded in the Prophet's home city of Mecca, where he began at the age of forty to receive revelations and to call people to the way of God. At this time he drew to himself a growing handful of staunch and committed souls. Soon that handful was strong enough to threaten the Meccan elite with a vision of their own economic demise by means of a social and spiritual revolution. This elite group did its utmost to prevent such an outcome. The early Muslims resisted the ensuing assaults with legendary courage.[4]

After twelve years of nonviolent resistance, the tide of events turned. A new challenge, and the demands of a new kind of patience, opened a second stage in the Prophet's career. The citizens of Yathrib, an oasis town rife with tribal bloodshed that was situated two hundred miles to the north of Mecca, were impressed by Muhammad's (s) probity and invited him to relocate as a disinterested arbiter among them. The Muslim community quietly shifted from Mecca to what came to be known as Medina and 622 C.E. became Year One of the Islamic calendar.

With the relocation, the persecution of a local minority became an open war between contending towns—towns with radically different social systems. This state of affairs continued for eight perilous years, yet the Muslim community continued to grow. In 630 C.E. the Muslims gained the victory when they captured the city of Mecca *without* bloodshed.[5] The entire city adopted the religion of its peaceful conqueror. All tribal claims to vengeance among Muslims—old or new—were formally abolished. This did not, however, mean an end to all the fighting. The Prophet hoped to extend *Pax Islamica* throughout the Arabian peninsula and as far beyond as God willed. When the Muslims won—and they continued to win—they offered to Christians and Jews a religiously protected status and to different groups of pagan Bedouin a number of different choices from simple truce to adoption by the community. (The Bedouin eventually universally converted, at least in name.) War inside the community was forbidden for all (Hourani 1991, 19).

Three years after the conversion of Mecca to Islam, the Messenger who had brought about this social miracle left this world. But the ripples of his message continued to spread. People came into Islam by choice and not by force. Contrary to lingering medieval propaganda, conversion by force is and always has been rigorously prohibited by Islam. People made the decision to convert not only because of the positive impression they received of the carriers of the message, but also probably because they saw Islam as the wave of the future.

Yet the curious relationship between the Way of Peace (for that is what "Islam" means)[6] and the military exploits of its promoters remained ambiguous and troubling. Within a scant few decades after the Prophet's passing, that ambiguity built to its first terrible crisis. The crisis continues to recur.

## THREE LOST CAUSES

In the year 680 C.E., just forty-eight years after the Holy Prophet had gone to meet his Lord—leaving his community to face the temptations of victory without him—a small band of men, women, and children walked into the deserts of Iraq. They were not armed for war. Their leader, al-Husayn ibn `Ali (r), had received a letter from the people of the city of Kufa. The letter implored him to come to the people's aid against the powerful new rulers of the young Islamic state, rulers whom they perceived to be unjust. Al-Husayn (r) was a grandson of the Prophet and an heir to his revered grandfather's courage, charisma, moral stature, and sense of responsibility. He gathered his family and friends about him and they all came together to answer the Kufans' call.

It appears, however, that the Kufans panicked. Before al-Husayn's party was anywhere near their city, the Kufans fled to the side of their enemies, the officers of the reigning government, raising an alarm against the ally whom they had themselves summoned. The band of seventy-two peaceful members of the family of the Prophet found itself surrounded by more than a thousand heavily armed soldiers of the nervous Islamic state. For three days under the desert sun the soldiers prevented all access to food and water for al-Husayn's party. And then, according to tradition, when the tiny group of state enemies was "sufficiently weakened," the soldiers slaughtered them all, down to the last infant child (see Schimmel 1986). The incident became notorious as the Massacre at Karbala.

Al-Husayn (r) is known in Islamic tradition as the Prince of Martyrs. There is every indication that he, like the other members of his party, understood exactly what the dangers were and what his fate was likely to be. That did not stop him. He was motivated by something that Gandhi has taught the twentieth century to call *satyagraha*—"soul force." In those days it was known under its more universal name of faith. And the best work of faith, as the Prophet had said, is "to speak a word of truth to an unjust ruler" (*Sunan Abu Dawud* 4330).

The Prince of Martyrs died willingly in pursuit of the best work of faith. While the prospect of his death had not stopped him from proceeding, it stopped Islamic history in its tracks. The Massacre at Karbala horrified the Muslim world, religiously delegitimized the early state's authority, made irrevocable the great sectarian schism of Sunni and Shi'i Islam, and sowed a seed of conscientious opposition to power deep into the fertile ground of the Muslim spiritual tradition.

In the short run, however, the massacre consolidated the control of the ruling 'Umayyad forces. God did not grant worldly victory to the party of al-Husayn.

In the year 922 C.E., another man named Husayn—the profound mystic and widely loved spiritual teacher al-Husayn ibn Mansur al-Hallaj (r)—prepared himself to die. He had been held in the dungeons of the Baghdad government for a decade on charges that combined treason and blasphemy. Yet the vizier had only just found the means to maneuver the highest judge in the land into issuing a death sentence for this particular prisoner.

The 'Abbasid government that held al-Hallaj had come to power, some 173 years earlier, on a wave of popular discontent with the corruption of its predecessor. The earlier 'Umayyad dynasty had been overthrown, in part, through the bitter memory of its role in the martyrdom of al-Husayn ibn 'Ali. The following regime was no less corrupt and bloody—but it was much cannier about public relations. The Sunni `Abbasids had worked hard to be seen as the champions of Islam, and they were so seen. Except, that is, by the Shi'i politicians of the minority opposition, who claimed that their alternative ideas of government, should they gain the very same state power, would infallibly do a better job.

The Sunni rulers rationalized that troubles were divine punishment for people's sins, while the Shi'i argued that troubles were a divine punishment for bad theology. When social and economic hardships and the cry of injustice continued, "God's will" was conveniently invoked by all.

Al-Hallaj upset this nice political calculus. He came out of the world of the Sufis, mystics, and ascetics who viewed themselves as conservators of the "heart-transmission" of the Holy Prophet. The Sufi community of his time was delicately situated and subject to official persecution. The community attempted to preserve itself through the use of obscure, nonconfrontational language and the maintenance of a very low profile. Hallaj scandalized his fellow Sufis by speaking directly to the public at large of the truths of spiritual experience. This not only put them all at risk, it threatened to shake the foundations of society, for if every individual is authorized to seek (and perhaps find) the holy and to appeal directly to divine justice—if "God's will" is with the people—then what justification remains for the existence of any coercive state?

Hallaj, often called Mansur, "The Victorious" (Schimmel's translation, lit. "The Helped"), after his father, had no fear of the worst power of the state. He had long spoken of death as an ecstatic union with his divine Beloved. On 26 March 922 C.E. his hands and feet were cut off, he was hanged on the gallows, and then decapitated; his body was burned and its ashes cast into the Tigris. The story goes that he went to his place of execution in chains, but dancing (Massignon 1975; Schimmel 1975, 62–77).

Another terrible martyrdom. Once again, the soul of the community trembled with the resonance of the call to prayer—a resonance that could never be extinguished. Not only have Muslim poets in the great literary languages praised al-Hallaj for more than a millennium as the embodiment of true spiritual love, but in addition:

> Hallaj's name has found its way into the remotest corners
> of the Islamic world. It can be discovered in the folklore of

East Bengal and the Malayan archipelago; it has been used by some Sufi fraternities in their celebrations, and a Tunisian order has an entire litany in honor of the martyr-mystic. Mansur's suffering through "gallows and rope" has become a symbol for the modern progressive writers in India and Pakistan who underwent imprisonment and torture for their ideals like "the victorious" of old. (Schimmel 1975, 77)

But the social movement that "The Victorious" might have sparked, and that the `Abbasid power structure so feared, never caught fire. There was no revolution.

What is victory? In the year 1983 C.E., the great Pathan leader and man of God `Abdul-Ghaffar Khan (r)—known to his people as Badshah Khan, the king of khans, and to those few Westerners who follow South Asian affairs as "the Frontier Gandhi"—resigned himself once again to imprisonment. The nervous government of the young Islamic state of Pakistan, now led by the dictatorial General Zia, could not tolerate that Khan (or indeed any voice of opposition) should be heard in the land. Yet the Movement for Return to Democracy, a coalition of all civilian parties, was nonetheless attempting a widespread nonviolent resistance to his rule.

Khan understood prison well. After all, he had spent the equivalent of one out of every three days of his life there. And in prison he had found his enlightenment:

> As a young boy, I had had violent tendencies; the hot blood of the Pathans was in my veins. But in jail I had nothing to do except read the Qur'an. I read about the Prophet Muhammad in Mecca, about his patience, his suffering, his dedication. I had read it all before, as a child, but now I read it in the light of what I was hearing all around me about Gandhiji's struggle against the British Raj. (Easwaran 1984)

His whole being was devoted to the unarmed struggle against oppression. It was in the first half of the twentieth century that Khan called his notoriously vengeance-prone Pathan countrymen, the inhabitants of the geopolitically crucial northern "gateway to India," to join Gandhi's nonviolent war against British domination:

> I am going to give you such a weapon that the police and the army will not be able to stand against it. It is the weapon

of the Prophet, but you are not aware of it. That weapon is patience and righteousness. No power on earth can stand against it. When you go back to your villages, tell your brethren that there is an army of God, and its weapon is patience. Ask your brethren to join the army of God. Endure all hardships. If you exercise patience, victory will be yours. (Easwaran 1984)

To the astonishment of both the Indians and the English, the fiery, honor-obsessed Pathans heeded the summons of their Badshah, who had already won their loyalty through twenty-one years of ceaseless village-to-village travel in the service of popular awakening and education. They loved him. What is more, his call to a glorious battle in which absolute courage disdained all lesser arms appealed to their sense of reckless grandeur. Pathan men (and some women) were raised for a violent death. And what death could be more splendid than this?

Badshah Khan indeed raised his army of Khudai Khidmatgars, "Servants of God," and trained them with military discipline. His red-shirted nonviolent Muslim soldiers eventually numbered more than a hundred thousand. A great many of them died as martyrs to nonviolence, just as they had anticipated. They were instrumental in winning Indian independence.

But Khan, alone of all the prominent Muslim leaders of his time, had opposed the subsequent partition of India. In July 1947, when the creation of Pakistan became a virtual certainty and a general referendum was announced, he instructed the members of his army not to vote against Frontier inclusion in the new entity: they were instead to abstain. Pathan country consequently became a Pakistani province. And three weeks after Gandhi was assassinated (January 30, 1948), Badshah Khan pledged his sorrowful allegiance to the new separatist state.

His promise of loyalty did not save him. In March he was elected head of the Pakistan People's Party. In June he was imprisoned and the army of Khudai Khidmatgars was brutally suppressed. The Pathans had freed themselves from British domination but, in another bitter irony, they fell under the domination of their brothers in Islam.

It is unclear, as yet, how far Badshah Khan's greatness will shine from his beloved Frontier country. Perhaps his name will come to illuminate the hearts of Muslims as widely as his predecessors' have done. Peculiarly, he is still unknown, for the machinery of state disinformation was turned full-blast against him: many ordinary Pakistanis and Afghans, for instance, believe that he was merely a nationalist agitator and subversive, and that he died a Hindu. But Hallaj, too, was condemned as a magician, a political manipulator, and a deceiver, and the party of al-Husayn was roundly condemned from official pulpits for many years after he was killed. Still, no disinformation has succeeded in concealing the magnificence of their faith. Their fearless integrity has outlived all desperate efforts to manipulate his story.

In and out of Pakistani jails for the four decades after Independence, as he had been in and out of British jails for the preceding three, Badshah Khan never gave up his work. He tirelessly preached the betterment of the Pathan people and Hindu-Muslim unity. But the Movement for Return to Democracy was crushed, and Badshah Muslim proponents of nonviolence, therefore, are faced with a dilemma. Muslims know that unarmed resistance to oppression draws the eternal blessing of Allah, reflects His mercy, and manifests a sublime and noble soul. History has not shown us, however, that nonviolence is always a reliable tool for the removal of oppression. The question is, is armed resistance such a tool? Our contemporary experience has not shown that it is. Yet, on the basis of the paradigmatic experience of the Prophet, we are inclined to believe that it must be.

## ISLAMIC JUST WAR THEORY

Much of the Qur'an speaks of struggle—the struggle of the inevitable victory of the true over the false, the right over the wrong. Islam, based upon that revelation, is expected to be the religion of winners. Where is our victory now? Somewhere in those few short years between the passing of the Prophet and the murder of al-Husayn (r), the line that divides jihad for human liberation, on the one hand, and conquest for imperial consolidation, on the other hand, began to be hard to see. The Messenger had urged the Muslims to fight for the cause of God. Later leaders could do the same thing, but without necessarily having the same cause in mind. For the original community, God was close, because His Prophet was in their midst. Then, God seemed to become distant, and revealed words began to be turned to ideological ends.

The new Islamic empires needed new territories for economic reasons. If conquest could be religiously justified, consciences could be eased. Like America "saving the world for democracy," the Muslims had a mission for the betterment of mankind. And indeed, Muslim governments were generally no worse and frequently markedly better than the forms of government they superseded. (Far too little attention has been given, for instance, to the routine achievement of multi-religious tolerance within Islamically inspired realms.) But just as in the American case, a gap developed between the ideals of the statesmen-soldiers and their policies, and between their policies and their practice—a gap it was more comforting to deny.

Most Muslim scholars between the post-Prophetic period and the dawn of the modern era considered the topic of warfare from a legal perspective and assumed that open conflict between realms ruled by Muslims and those ruled by others was simply inevitable. And as the Prophet had won all his contests, the Muslims would assuredly win theirs. Opinion diverged over whether these contests could be provoked, or only accepted. Theoretical arguments centered on such technicalities as whether it was religiously permissible to enter into a treaty with non-Muslims with a term longer than ten years—that is, the length of the Prophet's longest agreement (AbuSulayman 1993).

But despite the constant citation of holy precedent, most of the medieval Muslim theories of war may be read as a rationalization of imperial "facts on the ground." And for some centuries—from the eighth century C.E. into the eighteenth, with a brief break for the Mongol invasion—the "facts on the ground" remained essentially the same. Muslim societies flourished; Muslim armies went from strength to strength. Establishment Muslim theorists in all fields found less and less need for engaging in fresh thinking. As the old American adage says: "If it ain't broke, don't fix it."

With the emergence of the modern era, the insularity of all civilizations collapsed, and all the rules changed. Time-honored rationales that had made culturally dominant victors comfortable in Islamic governments and palaces no longer worked. It was a vastly disorienting shock for Dar al-Islam. In the wake of all the uproar of new defeats, colonization, persecution, and social fragmentation, Muslims have only begun to work out a coherent new position in the world. Nothing seems useful, and nobody is happy. Islamist intellectual A. A. AbuSulayman writes tartly:

> If there exists any one word to describe the crisis of Muslim thought in the field of external affairs today, that word is "irrelevance." The aggressive attitude involved in the classical approach to jihad as militancy is clearly irrelevant today to a people who are weak and backward intellectually, politically, and technologically. (AbuSulayman 1993, 97)

AbuSulayman, together with many contemporary Muslims, is suspicious and impatient in the face of belated and apologetic reevaluations of Islam as "Peace Above All," for such talk was the resort of those defeated and colonized generations who had to beg for respect and promise to be good:

> The "liberal" approach, which emphasizes thinking in terms of peace, tolerance, and defensiveness, has also proved irrelevant in a world facing ever-increasing struggles for political, social, and economic liberation. For Muslims, whose energies are needed almost exclusively in the struggle against the conditions, both internal and external, that contribute to their human misery, this approach has proved to be no longer tolerable or useful. (AbuSulayman, 1993, 97–98)

For many contemporary Islamic just war theorists, there is an essential analogy to be drawn between the suffering Muslim peoples of today and the beleaguered and vulnerable community around the Prophet. These theorists attempt, therefore, to re-analyze the Prophet's successful jihad to find those key political and strategic insights which will once again liberate the oppressed. They hope thus to restore to Islamic nations that life of dignity and meaning which is encapsulated in the phrase "the sovereignty of God."[7]

Unfortunately, this central historical and textual analogy generally fails. Parts of its failure are acknowledged. Everyone recognizes, for instance, that the current community lacks much of a resemblance to the community of the Prophet. Bur, rather than considering why an inappropriate analogy remains so devilishly attractive as a political formula in the modern era, these theorists undertake strenuous efforts to *make* it fit. Among activists, this may mean pressuring present-day Muslims to more closely approximate the image of those Muslims who were liberated long ago—thus producing real oppression for the sake of an imagined liberation. Or it may mean redefining "the enemy" to signify something the Prophet never would have allowed. The Prophet, for example, instructed his fighting men that they must never kill old men, women, children, or anybody who merely uttered the phrase, "There is no god but God," or "I give myself up to God"—no matter what the provocation (e.g., Mishkat al Masibih 838).

Turning to God for the sake of sovereignty and power is different from turning to God for the sake of God. Do religiously inspired political activists genuinely seek liberation and godliness, as the Prophet did, or do they only seek a release from humiliation and a return to empire? Perhaps they themselves are not sure.

The departure of some modern Islamists from the narrow legal formulations of classical theory represents, in itself, a major (and still contested) intellectual revolution. But it is a revolution that has not yet gone far enough. Many Islamists are still attempting to force the similarity of historical contexts and situations, rather than to derive fundamental principles. Consequently, their theories often have wholly neglected the important area of motive. Yet the Prophet gave great importance to motive. He warned us that all acts have the value of their intentions: God, from whom victory is sought, reads the thoughts of the heart. We tell ourselves we seek justice and the Way of God. That claim will be evaluated in the Scales of God—scales whose calibration is fine. Abu Hurayrah reported that the Prophet said:

> The first man (whose case) will be decided on the Day of Judgment will be a man who died as a martyr. He will be brought forward, God will make him recount His blessings upon him, and he will recount them. Then God will ask, "And what did you do (for Me)?" He will say, "I fought for You until I died as a martyr." God will say, "You have told a lie. You fought so that you might be called a brave warrior. And you have been so called." Judgment will be pressed against him, and he will be dragged face downward into Hell. (Sahih Muslim 4688)

Whether aspiring champions of religion are motivated by private ego or by that collective manifestation of ego known as empire, the results are likely to be the same.

In their reanalysis, the Islamists have concentrated wholly on the Prophet's tactics, while ignoring his priorities. For him, the social struggle was only the lesser jihad: the critical struggle was within. No matter what techniques he used, *he could not have established justice if he himself had not been just.* As modern Muslim spiritual master M. R. Bawa Muhaiyadeen wrote of this realization:

> Be in the state of God's peacefulness and try to give peace to the world. Be in the state of God's unity and then try to establish unity in the world. When you exist in the state of God's actions and conduct and then speak with Him, that power will speak with you. (Muhaiyaddeen 1987, 39)

As long as the lesser jihad remains severed from the greater, there can be no true understanding of power. The Prophet has clearly taught us that power is not what the ego takes it to be, and that winning is not necessarily a visible satisfaction. Power and victory are with God alone, and God is neither a banner nor an abstraction. Without a wider understanding of power among Muslims that parallels the Prophetic understanding, oppressor will merely succeed oppressor, and the secret of the Prophet's victory will remain a secret.

## NONVIOLENCE: RETURN OF THE REPRESSED

> Let there be no compulsion in religion: truth stands out clear from error. Whoever rejects evil and has faith in God has grasped the most trustworthy hand-hold, which never breaks. (Surah Baqarah, 256)

The Prophet's change in tactics between Mecca and Medina may receive several interpretations. The classical approach is based on the notion of abrogation: that later decisions make former decisions obsolete. Thus, unarmed struggle has been superseded by armed struggle, which is now obligatory upon the faithful (within a variety of legally disputed limits), until Islam is acknowledged everywhere (AbuSulayman 1993, 116–18). Some modern Islamists modify this view to make it situational. In situations of weakness, unarmed struggle is to be preferred. In situations of strength—and given the existence of oppression, not otherwise—armed struggle is to be preferred. The assumption remains that armed struggle is superior, but must wait, for practical reasons, upon the accumulation of sufficient military power (Peters 1996; Hashmi 1996). This view corresponds to what Gandhi termed "the nonviolence of the weak."

The third view is that power only accumulates to people through the unarmed struggle and continues to reside there. Armed struggle is only a branch, which dies if torn from its root—for it is only unarmed struggle that teaches reliance on God. The assumption here is that power, in its essence, is non-coercive. It is only dissipated, never generated, through coercion. From this perspective, power is not a magic trophy to be fought for, but an infinite spiritual resource that infuses into those who abandon their own objectives for the objectives of their Creator. This is its definition in the Qur'an.

> Have you not seen the one who disputed with Abraham concerning his Lord, because Allah had given him worldly dominance? So Abraham said, "My Lord is the one who causes life and death." He said, "I cause life and death." Abraham said, "Allah makes the sun rise in the east. Make it rise in the west!" The one without faith was speechless. Allah does not guide tyrannical people. (Surah Baqarah, 258)

> For whoever fears Allah, Allah will provide a way out (of difficulty), and sustain him from (sources) he does not anticipate. Whoever trusts in Allah, Allah is sufficient to him. Allah is the Accomplisher of His purpose, and has established a destiny for everything. (Surah Talaq, 2–3)

> What army shall help you apart from the Beneficent? Those without faith are only deluded. (Surah Mulk, 20)

The Qur'anic definition of power becomes obscured when worldly dominance is ascendant. It comes to the fore when dominance is rejected. The Prophet steadily shunned all trappings of kingship and insisted that he and his followers commit themselves to servanthood. Thus his most serious troubles began in Medina, when worldly dominance began to appear as a possibility for the Muslims. Abu Hurayrah reported that the Prophet said: "You people will be keen to have the authority of ruling, which will be a thing of regret for you on the Day of Resurrection. What an excellent wet nurse it is, and how bad for weaning!" (Bukhari 9:262).

Abu Hurayrah also reported that the Prophet said: "Those among the people who are the best at this business (ruling) are those who hate it most" (Bukhari 4:699).

## WHAT THE SUFIS CAN TEACH US

And thus it is that the Qur'anic definition of power is best preserved among those Muslims who have been most consistent in avoiding the pursuit of worldly dominance: the Sufis. The Sufis are mystics and ascetics. But what are mystics and ascetics? The Sufi enterprise is many-stranded. Like every other lengthy human undertaking, Sufism has had its historical ups and downs, its eras of special concentration upon this theme or that. And among the artifacts of its history are the impressions held by many that Sufism and the rest of Islam are only distantly related; that Sufi interests are wholly interior and neglect the "real world" of human interactions; that Sufi writing is a thicket of impenetrable esoteric arcana and of precious little relevance to the conduct of life. In some circumstances, these impressions are accurate. In others, they are not. In still others, they have been deliberately created. (Hallaj tore that veil, and paid for it with his life. Most Sufis have been more prudent.)

For many Muslims today, Sufism symbolizes the withdrawal from political engagement that led to the collapse of the Muslim empire. To such people, it represents an embarrassment to be suppressed. But by dismissing the Sufi tradition, Muslims lose all access to a vast treasury of insights persistently collected since the Prophetic era, insights which form a vital and necessary complement to the rest of Islamic thought. Only through a particular kind of ignorance could AbuSulayman have written that in classical Islam, "Social sciences, such as political science, psychology, sociology, and social psychology, were absent" (AbuSulayman, 87). These are sciences in which the Sufis specialize. They are simply unnamed and, therefore, go unrecognized by outsiders. It is true that they do not take the form of other Islamic sciences or of

Western sciences either: they can't. Islamic social sciences must deal with a conceptually different kind of politics: the politics of what the Qur'an calls power, to which the state is irrelevant, and in which the Greater Jihad comes first. The `Abbasid empire found this "politics of the greater Jihad" dangerous. Today's Muslims may yet find it indispensable.

Muslim proponents of nonviolence can challenge the world peace community to reconsider its fundamental goal. Is the universal core of nonviolence the quietism which is appropriate to some spiritual traditions, or is it to struggle for justice in a just fashion with the goal that our current opponents might gladly become our future allies?

> The good and the evil are not equal. Repel (evil) with that which is better: then the one between whom and you was enmity shall become like an intimate friend. (Surah Ha Mim, 34)

Muslims in our turn must consider closely whether such a jihad, given the monstrous brutality of modern war, can now be religiously licit or divinely acceptable if it is anything but unarmed. Bawa Muhaiyadeen writes: "It is compassion that conquers. It is unity that conquers. It is Allah's good qualities, behavior, and actions that conquer others. It is this state that is called Islam. The sword doesn't conquer; love is sharper than the sword. Love is an exalted, gentle sword" (Muhaiyadeen, 34).

This is old territory in spiritual terms, but an intellectual frontier. Everything is waiting to be done. It is time to put together the pieces, to see the alternative Islamic community tradition as rich with important messages for all of us. It is time for Muslims to reclaim the principle of *no-compulsion*, which the rest of the world calls nonviolence, as our own and to share it with our global community.

## STUDY QUESTIONS

1. Explain the meaning of *jihad*, taking the concepts of the "greater" and "lesser" *jihads* into consideration.

2. Briefly outline the conquest of Mecca and why Harris considers this a critical episode for later thinking on Islamic attitudes to war and peace.

3. What was the impact of the massacre at Karbala?

4. In what ways can it be argued that state/national power have compromised some of the peaceful teachings of Islam?

5. What, in Harris's views, are some of the critical modern challenges facing Islam in the modern world?

## SUGGESTED READINGS

AbuSulayman, `AbdulHamid A. *Towards an Islamic Theory of International Relations: New Directions for Methodology and Thought*. Herndon, Virginia: International Institute of Islamic Thought, 1993.

Dukrrani, Tehmina. *Edhi: A Mirror to the Blind*. Islamabad, Pakistan: National Bureau of Publications, 1996. Abdul-Sattar Edhi, the great contemporary champion of nonviolence in Pakistan, is wholly committed to the service of the poor. His nature is startlingly fierce and provides an edifying contrast in style to the gentle Badshah Khan.

Easwaran, Eknath. *A Man to Match His Mountains: Badshah Khan, Nonviolent Soldier of Islam*. Petaluma, CA.: Nilgiri Press, 1984. The only biography of this modern martyr available in the West, it suffers from the biases of its author who, while sympathetic, is more an admirer of Gandhi than a keen observer of Islamic nonviolence. A biography of Badshah Khan that would be genuinely useful to Muslims remains to be written. Easwaran's book should be read in conjunction with Dukrrani.

Esack, Farid. *Qur'an, Liberation, and Pluralism*. Oxford: Oneworld Press, 1997. Esack, an important organizer of resistance to South African apartheid, currently serves as one of that country's Commissioners of Gender Equality. He is also the first Islamic liberation theologian. This book is a groundbreaking example of essential new hermeneutics.

Hashmi, Soh ail H. "Interpreting the Islamic Ethics of War and Peace." In *The Ethics of War and Peace*, ed. T. Nardin. Princeton: Princeton University Press, 1996.

Hourani, Albert. *A History of the Arab Peoples*. Cambridge: The Belknap Press of Harvard University, 1991.

Lings, Martin. *Muhammad: His Life According to the Earliest Sources*. Rochester, Vermont.: Inner Traditions International, 1983. Any adequate inquiry into any aspect of Islam must be based upon a familiarity with the character and calling of its Prophet. This version of his biography is packed with traditionally transmitted historical details, while successfully conveying a taste of the tremendous impact of his personality and faith.

Massignon, Louis. *The Passion of al-Hallaj, Mystic and Martyr of Islam*. 4 vols. Princeton: Princeton University Press, 1975.

Muhaiyadeen, M. R. Bawa. *Islam and World Peace: Explanations of a Sufi*. Philadelphia: The Fellowship Press, 1987. This long meditation on the topic by a modern Sri Lankan Sufi master contains a wealth of unique insights, as well as key traditional stories and teachings on the achievement of peace.

Peters, Rudolph. *Jihad in Classical and Modern Islam: A Reader.* Princeton: Markus Wiener Publishers, 1996.

Robson, James, trans. *Mishkat al-Masabih.* Sh. Muhammad Ashraf, Lahore, 1975.

Satha-Ananad, Chaiwat (Qader Muheiddeen). *The Nonviolent Crescent: Two Essays on Islamic Nonviolence.* Alkmaar, Holland: International Fellowship of Reconciliation, 1996. Qader Muheiddeen of Thailand is one of the few contemporary Muslim scholars devoting himself to the development of nonviolence theory. This monograph contains, along with a case study of a nonviolent Muslim action in Thailand, his influential essay arguing that the indiscriminate nature of modern warfare renders it automatically religiously illicit, or *haram.*

Schimmel, Annemarie. "Karbala and the Imam Husayn in Persian and Indo-Muslim Literature." *Al-Serat* XII (1986).

———. *And Muhammad Is His Messenger.* Chapel Hill: University of North Carolina Press, 1985.

———. *Mystical Dimensions of Islam.* Chapel Hill: University of North Carolina Press, 1975.

The curious reader is also referred to *As-Salamu `Alaykum*, the newsletter of the Muslim Peace Fellowship (Box 271, Nyack, New York 10960).

## NOTES

[1] Hadith, generally translated as "tradition," is more literally "report," or "news." The hadith literature contains a vast body of accounts of the Prophet's sayings and actions, the majority of which are accompanied by a careful listing of the series of reporters through whom each account was conveyed. Medieval Muslims developed painstaking sciences for weighing the authenticity of such reports: modern Muslims are hesitating on the brink of expanding their predecessors' efforts. The hadiths are second only to the Qur'an as an authoritative source of Islamic teaching. This chapter cites two of the most highly regarded traditional collections, *Sahih Bukhari* and *Sahih Muslim*, but it makes reference to two others, *Mishkat al-Masabih* and *Sunan Abu Dawud.*

[2] A number of hadiths indicate the fluidity of the concept of jihad. For instance, the Prophet's wife `A'ishah (r), when she asked the Prophet whether women should not fight, was told that the best jihad is a properly performed Pilgrimage (Bukhari 4:43). Concerning the Qur'anic verse, "Urge the faithful to strive. If there are twenty steadfast among you, they shall overcome

two hundred" (Surah Anfal, 65), an early commentator, said, "I see that this verse applies to the commanding of good and the forbidding of evil" (Bukhari 6:175). The Prophet stated, "The one who looks after a widow or a poor person is like a warrior in Allah's cause" (Bukhari 7:265).

3 It is Islamic custom not to mention the names of the prophets, their companions, or holy people who have passed away without a benediction. The traditional benediction for the name of the Prophet is, in Arabic, *salla Allahu `alayhi wa sallam*: "May God bless him and grant him peace." We shall abbreviate it hereafter by (s). The traditional benediction for Companions of the Prophet is *radiya Allahu `anhu*: "May God be pleased with him (or her)." We have abbreviated it by (r).

4 For instance, there is the celebrated story of Bilal (r), a black slave from Abyssinia, whose master staked him out in the midday sun with a huge rock on his chest, vowing that he would stay that way until he renounced the teaching of the Prophet and worshipped the local gods. Bilal endured, repeating "One, One." One of the wealthiest Muslims was able to negotiate his ransom. He was bought and freed and subsequently became the first Caller to Prayer in Islam (Lings, *Muhammad*, 79).

5 The events of the capture of Mecca make a case study in the tactics of nonviolence. Two years previously the Muslims had marched toward Mecca in large numbers—but unarmed, for Pilgrimage. The Meccans had felt that they could not fight unarmed pilgrims without inflicting serious damage on their own politically crucial prestige. They also felt that it would be equally disastrous if the Muslims successfully entered their town. They met the Pilgrimage party well outside the sacred precincts, for negotiations. The Prophet, instead of continuing the march, and in circumstances of great tension, made a truce with the Meccans, permitting them to specify conditions unfavorable to the Muslims. His people were dismayed, but he assured them that the treaty constituted a victory.

For two years people of Mecca and Medina talked freely, with the result that the Muslim community doubled in size, and the Muslims were able to consolidate their position in other directions. Then a Meccan ally tribe broke the truce, and the Prophet again marched on the city, this time in arms. However, there was now almost no resistance. Stating that he intended to treat his former enemies as Joseph had treated his brothers, he granted a general amnesty (Lings, 245–56, 297–303).

6 Literally, Islam means surrender or submission (to the divine will), but both of those words are so semantically loaded in English as to be almost incapable of communicating the real impact of the term. The word derives from the same root as the word for peace—*salam*—and essentially conveys reconciliation with God. Muslims greet each other with greetings of peace; Muslim five-times-daily prayers are regularly concluded with the remembrance, "Our God, Thou art Peace; Peace is from Thee."

7   Radical Islamist ideologies agree that the work confronting activists is the restoration of divine order. They differ considerably in their understanding of the relation between the divine order and human nature, but tend to give minimal attention to the deep issues surrounding either term.

# 8

# Life as a Muslim Scholar of Islam in Post-9/11 America

*Amir Hussain*

The lyrics of a song called "Pacing the Cage," by Canadian singer-songwriter Bruce Cockburn have been running through my mind for some time:

Sometimes the best map will not guide you
You can't see what's round the bend
Sometimes the road leads through dark places
Sometimes the darkness is your friend
Today these eyes scan bleached-out land
For the coming of the outbound stage
Pacing the cage
Pacing the cage.[1]

Those words have been oddly appropriate for the lives of Muslims in America ever since the terrorist attacks of September 11, 2001. But there are other songs that figure into my experience of that fateful day.

Amir Hussain is associate professor in the Department of Theological Studies at Loyola Marymount University, Los Angeles, where he teaches world religions. He specializes in the study of Islam, focusing on contemporary North American Muslim societies. Born in Pakistan, Hussain immigrated to Canada with his family when he was four. His most recent publication is an introduction to Islam for North Americans entitled *Oil and Water, Two Faiths: One God* (Wood Lake Books, 2006), and he is currently working on a textbook entitled *Muslims: Islam in the 21st Century*.

On the evening of Monday, September 10, 2001, I led the second session for my course entitled Death and Dying in the World's Religions. For that particular class, I had asked students to answer the following question: "What object, film, song, piece of music, art or writing helps you to understand death?" My own contribution to the discussion was Lou Reed's, "Magic and Loss," a song occasioned by the death of two of his closest friends. The song ends with the line: "There's a bit of magic in everything and then some loss to even things out."

The next day, I was awakened by a telephone call from a friend in the early morning, insisting that I turn on the television. I did and, like everyone else in America, I watched the horrors of 9/11 on my TV screen. My first thoughts were for my friends in New York City, including an editor who lives a few blocks away from the World Trade Center. It took me most of that terrible day to confirm that my friends were still alive. During that day I was contacted by our provost, who put together a small committee to deal with the issues arising at my university from these events. We cancelled classes that afternoon and decided to hold a memorial on our campus that Friday, September 14. Suddenly, we were living in the "post-9/11 era," a period that I will describe here from the vantage point of a professor of Islam and a Muslim born in Pakistan who has spent almost all of his life in North America.

Those of us who teach Islam suddenly saw a tremendous increase in the number of messages on the list-serve for the Study of Islam section of the American Academy of Religion (AAR). The usual few messages per day were replaced by fifty to seventy-five for the rest of that September in 2001. We were all called upon to make numerous presentations to various groups who wanted to learn more about Islam because, it seemed, the desire to understand Islam was palpable, even though it came with a sense of confusion and bewilderment. My colleagues and I felt a new responsibility beyond our universities, and our efforts at "teaching" Islam continued unabated for months as the world situation worsened and the War on Terror began to look like a war against Islam. Among other things, I was one of a group of Muslim scholars who contributed to a book entitled *Progressive Muslims* (Safi 2003). This was our attempt to answer the question, "Where are the voices of moderate or progressive Muslims?" Now more than ever, we feel it is crucial for us to provide our voices that might be silenced in our countries of origin, or would have been silent here in North America in past decades.

A year after 9/11, I found an essay by novelist Mark Slouka to best express the impact of what had happened to Americans in the wake of this horrible attack:

> . . . I believe, to put it plainly, that last year's attack was so traumatic to us because it simultaneously exposed and challenged the myth of our own uniqueness. A myth most visible, perhaps, in our age-old denial of death.
>
> Consider it. Here in the New Canaan, in the land of perpetual beginnings and second chances, where identity could be sloughed and sloughed again and history was someone else's problem, death had never been welcome. Death was a foreigner—radical, disturbing, smelling of musty books and brimstone. We wanted no part of him.
>
> And now death had come calling. That troubled brother, so long forgotten, so successfully erased, was standing on our porch in his steel-toed boots, grinning. He'd made it across the ocean, passed like a ghost through the gates of our chosen community. We had denied him his due and his graveyards, watered down his deeds, buried him with things. Yet here he was. He reminded us of something unpleasant. Egypt, perhaps.
>
> This was not just a terrorist attack. This was an act of metaphysical trespass. Someone had some explaining to do. . . . (Slouka 2002, 36)

But who would do the explaining? Elected officials? Media personalities? Ordinary Muslims going about their daily lives? Or professors of religion like me? In many ways, the burden of "explaining" seemed to fall to Muslims in North America. But first it was necessary to understand something about Muslim Americans. Let us begin there. It is important to remember that many Muslims in North America are a marginalized post-colonial people; that is, immigrants who carry a history weighted with the legacies of empires. Mohammed Arkoun, a leading Western scholar of Islam, describes the intersection of colonialism and human rights with respect to Muslims:

The colonial adventure ended badly. It is difficult to speak to a Muslim audience today about the Western origin of human rights without provoking indignant protests. We must not lose sight of the wars of liberation and the ongoing, postcolonial battle against Western "imperialism" if we want to understand the psychological and ideological climate in which an Islamic discourse on human rights has developed in the past ten or fifteen years. (Arkoun 1994, 109)

History is not often found in the headlines, and, as Arkoun suggests, Muslims are often misunderstood as a people opposed to human rights. Furthermore, to be a Muslim in the United States often means a life of double marginalization due to the colors of our skin and our status as members of a religious minority. After all, the majority of North American Muslims are "brown" (at least 25 percent African American, 35 percent South Asian, and 33 percent Middle Eastern) and, therefore, automatically affected by the racism that is present. As members of a religious minority, we are further marginalized in a nation that is primarily Christian. And of course many other factors contribute to Muslim identity in North America. There are questions of religious affiliation within Islamic belief. Is one a Sunni or a Shi'i? Is one a member of the Ahmadiyya, a Muslim group that is proscribed in Pakistan? Or is one a member of the various Sufi orders that are found in North America? Is one a member of the working class, or does one have a higher socio-economic status? Can one pass as "white," or does one's ethnicity prohibit this?

As North Americans, many Muslims have learned and adopted popular North American notions of equality and justice. As Muslims, many North Americans have similar notions, rooted for example in the Qur'anic verse about God being with the "oppressed on the earth" (28:5). As North American Muslims, we may therefore be doubly shocked or scandalized when the secular North American environment does not live up to its universalist values, or its promise of equality. Muslims, like other Americans, struggle with inequities and have a deep desire for social justice.

There are also a great many questions of representation involved in understanding the socio-political position of Muslims in America. Who "represents" Muslim interests in North America? One group, or many? A wide variety of groups claims to speak for North

American Muslims, but some of them are in competition with each other, each one claiming to be "the" authentic voice of Muslims. In Canada, for example, there is a struggle between the Canadian Islamic Congress and the Muslim Canadian Congress. In November 2004, the Progressive Muslim Union of North America was launched to the acclaim of many Muslims, and the concern of many others. Those of us who attempt to "explain" or "teach" Islam have to talk about these issues of identity and representation. If nothing else, we must convey the reality that the Muslim world in North America is not one-dimensional. We also need to dispel neat dichotomies of good and evil that often enter into perceptions of Islam. We need to focus on the facts, beginning with a clear picture of how life in America changed for Muslims in the wake of 9/11.

## POST-9/11 LIFE IN AMERICA

On September 15, 2001, Balbir Singh Sodhi, a Sikh gas station owner from Mesa, Arizona, was murdered. He was the first fatality of the hate crimes following the terrorist attacks on 9/11. This violent death represented the extreme end of the discrimination that many North American Muslims (or those who, like Sodhi, unfortunately "look the part") experience—albeit more subtly—in day-to-day life. This perception of a double standard increased following the attacks on September 11, 2001. The Council on American-Islamic Relations (CAIR) released its seventh annual report on the status of Muslim civil rights in the United States on April 30, 2002, some seven months after the attacks (CAIR 2002). The report detailed the 1,516 complaints that CAIR received, a three-fold increase from the previous year. Some 2,250 people were affected by these complaints. What was most troubling for CAIR was that the majority of the complaints involved various levels of government: "Of all the institutional settings tracked by this report, the largest number of complaints involved profiling incidents at airports or those at the hands of government agencies, especially the INS, FBI, and local law enforcement authorities" (CAIR 2002, 11).

Clearly, Muslims in America were disturbed by this sudden attack on their civil rights that seemed to be exacerbated by the Patriot Act and increased security at airports. While the signing into law of the Patriot Act on October 26, 2001 and the passenger profiling at the nation's airports did not target American

Muslims only, many North American Muslims were concerned by these two developments. Like many Muslims, I have had my own experiences with such ethnic targeting, when I was fingerprinted and photographed coming back to the U.S. from a trip to Canada (see Hussain 2005).

But of even greater concern were the estimated 1,200 Muslims who were detained, the 5,000 Muslim foreign nationals who were "voluntarily" interviewed, and the three Muslim charities (Holy Land Foundation for Relief and Development, Global Relief Foundation, and Benevolence International Foundation) that were closed by the federal government. For many American Muslims, the problem was not simply that of social discrimination, but the perception that they were being targeted by their own government. This was particularly galling for the American Muslims who had voted for George W. Bush in the 2000 presidential election precisely because he had spoken out against the "secret evidence" that was often used against Muslims. For many American Muslims there was a sense that basic human rights were reserved, somehow, for other Americans, and that while they considered themselves American, they were not considered as such by their own government.

Two particular cases have captured a great deal of attention and serve as pointed examples of the discrimination experienced by Muslims in the years following 9/11, even though the U.S. government has claimed to want to enter into dialogue with "progressive" or "moderate" Muslims. In one case, Professor Tariq Ramadan, a scholar of religion born and raised in Switzerland (of Egyptian heritage), had just accepted a tenured position to teach at Notre Dame in 2004 when his visa was revoked by the U.S. State Department, apparently based on a broad reading of the U.S. Patriot Act. Many people spoke out against this action, including two major relevant academic groups (I am a member of both), the Middle East Studies Association and the American Academy of Religion. These two associations wrote a joint letter protesting the decision to revoke his work visa. In that letter, we stated, "Denying qualified scholars entry into the United States because of their political beliefs strikes at the core of academic freedom." The American Association of University Professors also took up the cause. His request was denied again in 2006 and he spoke a second time at AAR by videoconference. He is currently at Oxford University.

A second case is more bizarre and, in truth, more complicated. In September 2004, Yusuf Islam—the musician formerly known as Cat Stevens—was also denied entry into the United States. Again, as with Dr. Ramadan, no official reason was given, only unsubstantiated allegations that he might have been associated with terrorist activities or funded terrorist causes. In my mind, the best analysis of the situation was given by Jon Stewart on his comedy show *The Daily Show with Jon Stewart:* "In the War on Terror, we finally got the guy who wrote 'Peace Train.'"

Yusuf Islam is one of the best-known and most respected Muslims in the United Kingdom. As a Western pop star who converted to Islam, he is the perfect person to illustrate the intertwining of Muslims and the West. Among his many charitable accomplishments were the building of an Islamic school, and support for Bosnian orphans whose parents were murdered by Serbian Christians. In the month after 9/11, he wrote the following words in an editorial that was widely circulated: "Today, I am aghast at the horror of recent events and feel it a duty to speak out. Not only did terrorists hijack planes and destroy life, they also hijacked the beautiful religion of Islam and split the brother-and-sisterhood of mankind, many of whom are still sorrowfully ignorant and unaware of each other. The targeting of unsuspecting civilians going about their daily work was energised by nothing but blind irreligious hatred" (Stevens 2001). Islam donated the royalties from his box set to charity, with a portion going to the World Trade Center Fund. Of his own background, he wrote that: "I belonged to that idealistic movement that grew up in the Sixties and Seventies with undiminished dreams and hopes for a more peaceful world. There are multitudes of people around the world who don't want more war and destruction. And I, as a Muslim, am still one of those" (Stevens 2001). To bar him entry to the United States with no reason given seems to suggest that our government is really not interested in any sort of meaningful dialogue with representatives of the world's Muslims.

Students on college campuses have also encountered discrimination. I taught at California State University, Northridge from 1997 to 2005, and moved to Loyola Marymount University in 2005. In both places, there has been difficulty for many of our exchange students in border crossings and obtaining U.S. visas. This has also been a problem for Muslim and non-Muslim faculty members. There has also been great concern about the monitoring of Middle East Studies. In October 2003, Bill HR 3077 ("to amend Title VI of the Higher Education Act of 1965 to enhance international education programs") was passed by the U.S. House of Representatives but not heard by the Senate. It was reintroduced as Bill HR 509, and includes a similar provision to the earlier bill for the creation of an "International Higher Education Advisory Board" to monitor academic work on Middle East Studies. As of this writing, the bill was still being considered.[2]

Clearly, there is heightened suspicion, if not a double standard, at play regarding civil liberties. Many American Muslims also see a double standard when it comes to "contentious dialogue" and Islam. Alan Dershowitz, a professor at Harvard University and perhaps the most famous lawyer in America, has publicly spoken in favor of the use of torture to extract information from suspected terrorists. Nathan Lewin, a prominent Washington attorney, has called for the execution of the family members of suicide bombers. American Muslims are left to wonder, if prominent American lawyers can call for the use of torture and the execution of innocent civilians—and remain respected partners in the civil conversation—isn't there an obvious double standard for Muslims? In the years since 9/11, this question has been on the minds of American Muslims as incidents like those mentioned above have become all too commonplace.

## TEACHING AFTER 9/11

In recent years, there has been a great deal written about scholars as public intellectuals. I prefer a different concept, the scholar as citizen. Although I teach in a private university, I have an obligation to the state and its citizens. This is confirmed by the mission of the university, which comes from its Jesuit heritage and values, "the service of faith and the promotion of justice." For me, it is important to reach different audiences. I reach some in my classes and others with the scholarly writing that I have done. But I reach a far greater number of people with my editorial pieces in newspapers, or my work with various local and national media. My students do not know me from my scholarly writing, but they recognize me from television on the History Channel, or on the local news, or on talk shows such as *The Tavis Smiley Show* or *Politically Incorrect with Bill Maher*.

I mention this because I think it signals a shift for some of us as academics. Most of us work in universities where peer-reviewed journal articles and scholarly monographs are considered of ultimate importance. I have been fortunate to have those, and I recognize the value of scholarship, one of the hallmarks of the university. However, the other hallmark is teaching, and so I understand the need to get our work "out there," to people who do not have the ability to take our classes or read our scholarly prose. And I am well aware of the numbers involved: I am sure that no more than fifty people have read any of my scholarly pieces, but a million or so have read my work in the *Los Angeles Times,* and several million have seen me on network television. I get far more e-mail about television appearances than I have ever received about a scholarly article. In the case of Islam and Muslim communities, it is all the more important to get my work out to the widest possible audience. I also realize that it has become important to teach "media literacy" alongside of religion.

After the events of 9/11, many of us made curriculum changes. I used to start with a standard historical introduction to the Prophet Muhammad and the Qur'an. I now have students start by reading a book that describes how the news media construct reality (Postman and Powers 1992). Most of my students get their information about Islam and Muslim lives from television, so I think it is important to begin with how the television news works. I also use a videotape of Bill Moyers interviewing Jon Stewart and talking about *The Daily Show with Jon Stewart.* My students are admirers of Stewart's work, and agree with me that the satirical news that he presents is better informed than the "real" news. I have also had colleagues from local television stations come to my class to talk about ratings, and how important they are to the local news.

Having discussed media constructions of Muslim lives, I sometimes then move to something of a case study to demonstrate how, in the American media, Palestinians—whether they are Muslim, Christian, or secular—are constructed as Muslims. I next ask students to read a graphic novel (comic book) that describes something of the realities of Palestinian experience (Sacco 2002) and contrast that presentation with the ways in which Palestinians are perceived in America. There is a great advantage to using a comic book in class (aside from the reactions of students who are either delighted or appalled to have a comic book on the reading list).

Some students still think that a photograph is objective, that it "tells the truth." They do not consider how it is composed. It is much easier to show this with drawings, where it is obvious that one person has made the drawing from their perspective, and someone else might do it very differently. Eventually, we do get to the Qur'an. And when we do, my students have a much clearer sense of the cultural barriers to studying it objectively.

Teaching and learning also occur among scholars. The study of Islam section of the American Academy of Religion used to be a small group of scholars who mostly talked only with one another. Post 9/11, it became a much larger group, and we are now asked to reach out and talk to all sorts of people outside our group. One of us, Carl Ernst, has written about his own recent experiences: "[I]t still amazes me that intelligent people can believe that all Muslims are violent or that all Muslim women are oppressed, when they would never dream of uttering slurs stereotyping much smaller groups such as Jews or blacks. The strength of these negative images of Muslims is remarkable, even though they are not based on personal experience or actual study, but they receive daily reinforcement from the news media and popular culture" (Ernst 2003, xvii). Ernst goes on to point out that in workshops on key issues in Islamic studies in 1992 and then a decade later, it was determined that "the real issue is to humanize Muslims in the eyes of non-Muslims" (Ernst 2003, xvii).

Of course, this concern to "humanize" Muslims does not mean that we should take a defensive or apologetic attitude toward the very serious problems that exist within Muslim communities. We need to discuss issues such as gender discrimination, religious arrogance and intolerance, violence, and so on. However, we need to make clear that when these problems are viewed as the only reality of Islam, the richness and beauty that exists as well are hidden from awareness. Teaching Islam today means teaching the fullness of the tradition with cultural sensitivity and a critical mind.

## WHERE WE GO FROM HERE

In trying to understand recent events, I am reminded of the relationship between narrative and history. The Latin and Greek roots, respectively, of both words have to do with the telling of stories. While the knowledge of established historical facts may disappear quickly, the narratives that are constructed from that history develop great force and help to shape our lives.

As a personal example, in 2004, I watched with great interest the state funeral of former President Ronald Reagan, who was the first U.S. president during my adult life. Furthermore, the Reagan Presidential Library is some fifteen miles from my house; so many of the events were very close to home. I remember certain incidents about his presidency, like his handling of the air traffic controllers strike; the policy that stated "ketchup is a vegetable" in school lunches; the social implications of the closing of mental institutions when he was California's governor; and the Iran-Contra scandal, in which profits from the sale of weapons to Iran were used to fund a guerrilla group in Nicaragua. Reagan also helped to arm the Afghanis in their war against the Soviet invasion, and spoke of the *mujahideen*, an Arabic word meaning "those who struggle" in holy wars, as "freedom fighters." For me, these controversial issues and policies constitute the Ronald Reagan of history.

But in watching the funeral, I was amazed to hear pundits talking about him as "the greatest president of the twentieth century." That was the Reagan of narrative, the one that some people remember, not the Reagan of history. In this narrative, he was given credit for single-handedly ending the Cold War. His state funeral was replete with military honours—a twenty-one-gun salute, horse and caisson, military pallbearers—even though he did not serve in World War II. There was no talk of events from his presidency, especially with regard to Iran and Afghanistan, coming back to haunt the modern world, even though scholars like Mahmood Mamdani have written convincingly about how Reagan and the Cold Warriors of his administration helped to arm and train the *mujahideen* in what was the largest covert operation in the history of the CIA.

In constructing their narratives of both American Muslims and the modern Muslim world, pundits often have no regard for history. What matters to them is the narrative that is constructed, and not the historical truths about things. So we look at events in contemporary Afghanistan or Iran with no thought to our histories in those parts of the world, as if the American government had no part to play in events there. All that seems to matter is the story that we want tell: Iran is evil (even though the American president helped to arm that country after Americans were held hostage there), Afghanistan is worse (even though four months before the horrors of 9/11, the Bush administration gave the Taliban $43 million for their help in the War on Drugs).

## ISLAM IN THE WEST

In 2001, the United Nations adopted the metaphor of "dialogue of civilizations" for worldwide discussions during that year. This vision was in stark contrast to the idea promulgated by Harvard University political scientist Samuel P. Huntington of a "clash of civilizations" (Huntington 1993 and 1996). In addition to these metaphors of "clash" and "dialogue," there are also concepts of "Islam" and "the West" that seem to present both aspects of culture and religion as mutually incompatible. For several reasons, I prefer the phrase "Islam in the West."

First, "Islam in the West" acknowledges the reality of Muslims living in the West. Islam is the second largest religion in Canada, Britain, and France, and may well be the second largest religion in the United States. One of the most famous men in the world is an American Muslim, Muhammad Ali. In 2006, the most outstanding player in the world's most popular sporting event, the FIFA World Cup, was a French Muslim of Algerian descent, Zinedine Zidane. Islam itself is, of course, a "Western" religion, sharing deep roots with Judaism and Christianity.

Second, the phrase "Islam in the West" recognizes the entwined heritage of Islam and the West. The West, as we know it, would not be what it is without the contribution of Muslims (as well as the contributions of many other peoples, to be sure). Consequently, the danger of presenting Islam as "Islam and the West" (whether it be within a clash or a dialogue) is the generalization, implication, and subsequent obfuscation of what is actually a complicated, multicultural social and historical dynamic. Like the history/narrative split mentioned above, this kind of thinking denies a certain truth. It denies the truth of the interconnectedness of our religious histories. It is this truth that was articulated brilliantly by my mentor, the late Professor Wilfred Cantwell Smith: "Those who believe in the unity of humankind, and those who believe in the unity of God, should be prepared therefore to discover a unity of humankind's religious history" (Smith 1981, 4).

If we pursue truth, with the idea of "Islam in the West" in mind, it's not hard to find a host of ways in which Islam has influenced Western life and thought. But here, a few examples will suffice. One aspect of Muslim contributions to the construction of the West is in literature. María Rosa Menocal published a groundbreaking book in 1987, *The Arabic Role in Medieval Literary History*. In that book, she talked about a derivation for the English word "troubadour" (in Provençal *"trobar"*) from the Arabic word *taraba*, meaning "to sing": *"Taraba* meant 'to sing' and sing poetry; *tarab* meant 'song,' and in the spoken Arabic of the Iberian peninsula it would have come to be pronounced *trob*; the formation of the Romance verb through addition of the *-ar* suffix would have been standard" (Menocal 1987, xi). In other words, the tradition of troubadours, playing guitar and singing love poetry, which is a hallmark of mediaeval European society, has deep roots in the Islamic world.

Another example of "Islam in the West" relates to popular music. We have already mentioned Yusuf Islam, who returned to recording pop music in 2006. In the contemporary world, one of the best modern troubadours is Richard Thompson, himself a British convert to Islam who now lives in the United States.[3] It may challenge our assumptions of Muslim life when we consider that one of the best guitar players in the world is a Muslim. Of spirituality in music, Richard has said in an interview on his web page: "Music is spiritual stuff, and even musicians who clearly worship money, or fame, or ego, cannot help but express a better part of themselves sometimes when performing, so great is the gift of music, and so connected to our higher selves. What we believe informs everything we do, and music is no exception."

Still another example of cross-cultural fertilization is science and philosophy. The "Greek heritage" of philosophy was preserved by Muslim scholars, most notably the medieval philosophers Ibn Rushd (Latinized as Averroes) and Ibn Sina (Avicenna). The Western philosophical tradition would not be what it is were it not for their works that were widely read by medieval European philosophers. In fact, to this day in seminaries in Iran, the works of Aristotle are read and commented upon. And of course we all should be aware of the Muslim contributions to science and mathematics, not the least of which is our numbering system (Arabic numerals as opposed to Roman) and basic terms such as "algebra" or "algorithm."

## CONCLUSION

I work in secular North America as a Muslim scholar of Islam teaching in a Catholic university. It is here where Muslims are trying to live out the poetry of their ordinary lives in all of the splendid diversity that those lives are lived. It is here, we hope, that we can be seen as full participants in our societies and not as threats to the common good. Again, this does not mean that we are naïve or silent about the problems in our communities. The quest for truth must turn inward as well as outward and help us avoid seeing ourselves as innocent victims. Similarly, we as Muslims should not shift the blame for our internal problems to outsiders. We need to deal with the social and ideological problems such as hunger, abuse, and discrimination. We need to address the alarming conservatism among some Muslims, whose ahistorical and non-contextual readings of Islam allow for misogyny and violence against Muslims and non-Muslims. As scholars we can provide different alternatives, different narratives to give meaning to our lives and allow us all to be fully human.

As a Canadian, I have made a conscious and voluntary choice to live in the United States. As with many immigrants, I love the ideal of America as expressed in the Constitution and the Bill of Rights, and consider America to be a wonderful place to live. When asked what I miss most about Canada, my standard answer is that with the American gaze currently fixed firmly inward, I miss the world. As such, I often feel somewhat of an exile. As a Muslim academic in post-9/11 America, it is that metaphor of exile that has helped me to best comprehend things. With his usual brilliance, the late Professor Edward Said wrote this about the condition of exile: "Most people are principally aware of one culture, one setting, one home; exiles are aware of at least two, and this plurality of vision gives rise to an awareness of simultaneous dimensions, an awareness that—to borrow a phrase from music—is *contrapuntal*" (Said 2002, 186). Perhaps this is the best descriptor for those of us who teach Islam in America post 9/11, especially those of us who are Muslim. We live contrapuntal lives that weave in and out of various dimensions, ever aware of discrimination and difference, ever aware of narrative and history, and ever aware of the hard work that needs to be done for the possibilities of understanding and peace.

## STUDY QUESTIONS

1. What are some of the difficulties experienced by Muslims living in America today?

2. How does Hussain deal with the social injustices of Muslim life in his essay, for example, the role of women?

3. In what ways is the Patriot Act that was passed after the terrorist attacks of 9/11 particularly problematic for Muslims?

## BIBLIOGRAPHY

Arkoun, Mohammed. *Rethinking Islam: Common Questions, Uncommon Answers*. Translated by Robert D. Lee. Boulder: Westview Press, 1994.

CAIR. *Stereotypes and Civil Liberties: The Status of Muslim Civil Rights in the United States, 2002*. Available online at http://www.cair-net.org/civilrights2002.

Cockburn, Bruce. "Pacing the Cage." From the music cd *The Charity of Night*. Rykodisc, 1996.

Ernst, Carl W. *Following Muhammad: Rethinking Islam in the Contemporary World*. Chapel Hill: University of North Carolina Press, 2003.

Huntington, Samuel. *The Clash of Civilizations and the Remaking of the World Order*. New York: Simon & Schuster, 1996.

——. "The Clash of Civilizations." *Foreign Affairs* 72, no. 3 (1993): 22–49.

Hussain, Amir. *Oil and Water: Two Faiths, One God*. Kelowna, British Columbia: Wood Lake Books, 2006.

——. "Reflections on Exile." *Amerasia Journal* 30, no. 3 (2005): 17–23.

——. "Misunderstandings and Hurt: How Canadians Joined World-Wide Muslim Reactions to Salman Rushdie's *The Satanic Verses*." *Journal of the American Academy of Religion* 70, no. 1 (2002): 1–32.

Mamdani, Mahmood. *Good Muslim, Bad Muslim: America, the Cold War, and the Roots of Terror*. New York: Pantheon Books, 2004.

Menocal, María Rosa. 1987 [reprinted 2004]. *The Arabic Role in Medieval Literary History: A Forgotten Heritage*. Philadelphia: University of Pennsylvania Press, 1987; reprinted 2004.

Postman, Neil and Steve Powers. *How to Watch TV News*. New York: Penguin, 1992.

Sacco, Joe. *Palestine*. Seattle: Fantagraphic Books, 2002.

Said, Edward W. "Reflections on Exile." In Edward W. Said, *Reflections on Exile and Other Essays*, 173–186. Cambridge: Harvard University Press, 2002.

Safi, Omid, ed. *Progressive Muslims: On Gender, Justice, and Pluralism*. Oxford: Oneworld, 2003.

Slouka, Mark. "A Year Later: Notes on America's Intimations of Mortality." *Harper's Magazine*, September 2002, 34–43.

Smith, Wilfred Cantwell. *Towards a World Theology: Faith and the Comparative History of Religion*. Philadelphia: Westminster, 1981.

Stevens, Cat (Yusuf Islam). "They have hijacked my religion." *The Independent*, October 26, 2001.

## NOTES

This chapter is dedicated to the blessed memory of three of my teachers, all of whom were wonderful exemplars of Christian lives: Victor Hahn, who in the fourth grade taught me the value of learning; and Willard Oxtoby and Wilfred Cantwell Smith who encouraged that value in the university. I am indebted to Michel Desjardins, Tazim Kassam, Patti Marxsen, Pat Nichelson, Bruce M. Sullivan, and Philip Tite for their help in various incarnations of this chapter.

[1] "Pacing the Cage," written by Bruce Cockburn © 1997 Golden Mountain Music Corp. (SOCAN). Used by permission.

[2] Information on HR 509 is available on the Internet at <http://thomas.loc.gov/cgi-bin/bdquery/z?d109:h.r.00509:>.

[3] For more information, see his web page: <http://www.richardthompson-music.com>.

# 9

# "Let your love for me vanquish your hatred for him"

## Nonviolence and Modern Judaism

*Jeremy Milgrom*

### INTRODUCTION

For too long has my soul shared space with hatred of peace
I am peace,[1] but when I speak, they opt for war.

Psalm 120:6–7

One of the greatest sorrows of my spiritual life has been the realization that one can easily make a case, based on Jewish sources,
for perpetuating violence. As a former Israeli soldier currently
active in the Israeli human rights community, I have seen violence
promoted and inflicted from both sides. As a Conservative rabbi
trained to participate in the creation of a Jewish public space, I
have been burdened with the understanding that the pursuit of the

Jeremy Milgrom is an American-born rabbi who has lived in Israel since 1968 and
has helped establish, lead, and promote many Israeli peace initiatives including
Peace Now, Yesh G'vul, and Rabbis for Human Rights. As pastor and teacher, he
unifies his commitment to pacifism, global anti-war activism, anti-religious dialogue, human rights, combating anti-Semitism, and advocacy for the Bedouin in
the pursuit of a just peace (a one-state solution with the right of return for
Palestinian refugees) in the Middle East. He lectures frequently in Israel, Europe,
and the United States.

Zionist dream over the last one hundred and twenty years has been inseparable from violence, thus giving violence widespread local and international Jewish legitimization.

This chapter will attempt to stake out the claim for Jewish nonviolence as part of the struggle that I, as an heir to a nineteenth-century Jewish universalist optimism, never thought needed to be fought; it is my prayer that the turn of the millennium heal the spiritual devastation of the twentieth century, most notably (in this context) the return of violence to Jewish consciousness and practice.

## JUDAISM AND NATIONALISM

Modern Jewish nationalism, whose roots are ancient, has both engendered and been influenced by European nationalism, and shares its material achievements and moral failures. It is based on a particularism, that is, a narrowed perspective derived from the foundational Israelite covenant in the Bible whose scope was cosmic and intent benign. The interaction between Jews, the biological successors to those Israelites, and the world has been the story of both fruitful reciprocity and a calamitous incompatibility. The ideological descriptions, prescriptions, and visions of this relationship to the world are both negative and positive. We find them in the Bible (written during the first millennium B.C.E.), rabbinic literature of the following millennium, and the subsequent Jewish medieval and modern literature. The story of violence in Judaism that is contained in all these works must be appreciated in order to clear the deck and make room for a fruitful discussion of the nonviolent alternative.

Finally, we cannot proceed further without positing the complex duality of things Jewish. The term "Jewish" has ethnic connotations relating to the Jewish people, as well as spiritual connotations relating to the Jewish religion. Jewish religious teachings will, therefore, be constantly resonating with the situational reality and needs of Jews. Furthermore, the extent to which Judaism can be seen as a global, and not tribal, religion will be determined not only by the weight of Jewish sensitivity to other religions and cultures but also by the ability and desire of non-Jews to appropriate Israel's story as its own.

## THE PLACE OF THE BIBLE IN JEWISH CULTURE:
## THE PEOPLE AND THE BOOK

Mohammed's seventh-century definition of Jews (and Christians) as *ahel al-kitab* (People of the Book) attests to the age-old centrality of the TaNaK (the Hebrew Bible, the "Old Testament" from a Christian perspective) to Judaism. However, the first book that a traditional Jew encounters in daily practice is not the Bible but the prayer book, and the determining texts in religious jurisprudence are, again, not the Bible but the Talmud and medieval law codes. Therefore, while the Bible has played a pivotal role in establishing and developing not only Jewish values and attitudes but also those of the entire Western world, in order to appraise the Bible's real impact on Jews today, it would be useful to outline its place in a variety of contemporary Jewish cultures.

For a considerable percentage of the Jewish people, particularly those living in Israel (where Jewish communal life is less likely to be organized around a synagogue than it was during the Diaspora), the Bible is not experienced in a ritual setting but is rather a national literature, a cultural treasure acquired in school, whose relevance is reinforced through constant political indoctrination.[2] Thus, national pastimes, such as hiking and archaeology, are dressed with verses from the Bible containing ancient place names that have been newly restored, providing an alternative system of symbols and rituals that bypass certain features of traditional Jewish religiosity but end up with a similar nationalist orientation with its sacred spaces—a unique form of "civil religion." This appropriation of biblical verse and terminology is a critical aspect of the modern Israeli reality, but since this essay is meant to explore the *religious* sides of Jewish culture, we shift our attention to the presence of the Bible in Jewish ritual.

In the central communal event of the week, three to five chapters of the Torah (the five books of Moses) are liturgically read and studied. This annual liturgical cycle allows the synagogue-going Jewish community to re-experience the Genesis narratives, the enslavement in and exodus from Egypt, and the forty years of wandering in the desert as well as to re-encounter the chapters of civil and ritual law that provide the raw material for the exposition *(midrash)* of Jewish law *(halachah)*. One might argue that the process creates an internalization of the outlook of the biblical historiographer.

Other sections of the Bible are used with differing frequency. Some psalms are incorporated into the statutory daily, weekly, or holiday prayer cycle. A wider selection of psalms finds its way into private devotional use. Some chapters of the prophetic and historical books are attached to the weekly Torah readings as *haftarot*, and other chapters are read on particular holidays. Independent reading of the Bible on its own is relatively rare and, since most of the Bible does not make its way into liturgical use, large sections, aside from the Torah, are a lost resource to most religious Jews, including those who are well-versed in rabbinic texts.

## FROM VIOLENCE TO NONVIOLENCE: READING VIOLENCE IN AND OUT OF JEWISH TEXTS

The regular worshipper in weekly services in which the Torah is read does not encounter a carefully screened, morally acceptable, and pre-selected Sunday School text but rather the full biblical narrative, which at times reads like an X-rated story permeated with the entire range of lamentable human failings. More jarring still are the prescriptive passages, particularly in the Book of Deuteronomy, demanding the physical eradication of idolaters (whether an individual idolater, or a family, a clan, a city, a nation, or a cluster of nations of idolaters) and the decimation of Israel's political enemies (Deut. 7:1–2; 13:2–19; 20:16–17). These commandments of violence posit the existence of a God whose attributes include those of a terrifying, partisan warrior (Ex. 15:3; Deut. 34:29).[3]

Yet, as a pulpit rabbi, I have hardly ever witnessed the revulsion of sensitive congregants because of an encounter with these texts or their subsequent distancing from anything to do with religion. I believe people who leave (or never entered into) synagogue life do so for other reasons. In fact, the atmosphere that pervades every synagogue I have ever attended, or heard of, during the reading of even the most violent of these passages is (thank God) never one of agitation or incitement. It is, instead, something close to the meditative, contemplative, peaceful core of religion. There is obviously something between or beyond the lines of those texts that allows the worshipper to defuse and transcend the unbridled call for violence previously noted.

The prevailing fashion in liberal circles to decry the grave danger in the ritual use of these texts indicates a basic ignorance of the actual dynamic of synagogue life. There is nothing easier than finding scriptural quotations on any subject: All that is required is an ability to read a concordance coupled with a particular bias. The question is: How accurately can any set of verses reflect the beliefs of a culture? At best, culling quotations from old sources can tell us something about an early stage of that culture's development. As difficult as it may be in today's politically polarized world, we will have to drop our prejudices and make an honest effort to enter into the spiritual environment of the devotees of this culture to find out what the quotations in mind really meant— and mean—to the devotees.

For most worshippers, entering the synagogue is a means of escape from the outside world and a search for refuge in a Jewish space. The verbal content of that which is chanted may be of relatively small importance to the worshipper who primarily experiences community. Frequently, when the verbal content is not translated into the vernacular, its actual meaning is partially or totally inaccessible (not a completely undesirable situation, considering some of these texts). In many cases, the normative meaning of a violent commandment or memory has been moderated, spiritualized, allegorized, or deactivated by Jewish tradition. The following fall into this category: divinely inspired wars *(milkhamot mitzvah)* against Canaanites; the war against Amalek; and even animal sacrifice. Receiving the text through this filter, the worshipper is basically deaf to its literal meaning *(pshat)*. For attentive and demanding listeners, however, the plain text exists and is incorporated into their lives in sophisticated, albeit ambiguous, ways.

## STUDYING IS THE HIGHEST RELIGIOUS PRIORITY

For more than two thousand years, well back into the time of the Second Temple, the focal and dominant Jewish (religious) activity has been *talmud torah*, Torah-related study. Religious leaders have no hierarchical status but are judged on the basis of their proficiency in the texts. The position of authority is the rabbi (teacher) and the highest accolade is *talmid khachamim*, a student of the sages (plural, *talmidey kkhachamim*).[4]

The subject matter of *talmud torah* began as the application of *torah shebichtav*, the literal Torah, to everyday life. But with the emergence of *torah shehbehalpeh*, derived Torah (the rabbinic law codes of late antiquity and the Middle Ages and their interpretation) the focus of *talmud torah* was shifted away from the five books of Moses to the massive secondary literature. Surprisingly, this huge corpus is not considered to be esoteric or off-limits to all but specialists. About one-third of Israel's Jewish teenagers, those enrolled in religious high schools, spend upwards of five classroom hours a week on these texts, while students of the elite Yeshiva high schools devote much more time to *torah shehbehalpeh* than to secular subjects.[5]

Since political power (and its accompanying need for organized violence) was only a remote possibility during most of the period that *torah shehbehalpeh* was developed, there was no demand to expound or expand on those sections of Torah dealing with violence, and they fell into relative neglect. The energy of the scholars went into more pragmatic concerns, such as the dietary laws and the observance of the Sabbath. While messianic stirrings[6] were not unusual during almost two thousand years of exile (that is, from even before the end of the Jewish political entity in 70 C.E. to the founding of the modern State of Israel in 1948), certain discussions, such as the kind of armaments that would come into use in the battle of Armageddon, were never seen as necessary. In fact, even though the laws having to do with animal sacrifices continued to be studied,[7] it was not so much so that the Temple ritual could be reinstituted, but rather this study served as a kind of psychological denial of the destruction of the Temple (the second Temple having been destroyed in 70 C.E.). Similarly, even though Jews continued to study the laws of capital punishment long after the Sanhedrin had lost authority to execute, there was no attempt to update the technology involved.

Volumes of traditional commentary have been written on a single halachically (legal) or midrashically (exhortatory) interesting chapter of the Torah. This amount of material written on subjects considered to be of serious interest to Jewish life dwarfs the material available for *all* the "troublesome passages" that are the concern of this article. Indeed, the texts that we thought might incite are actually greeted with a certain inattentiveness when they are read in the synagogue.

Yet, the potential for life-threatening applications of violent texts still exists, as does the fear that even if scholars of hatred might be sequestered in halls of study, their teachings could leak to a troubled public and find fertile ground.[8] Zionism is the most significant development in twentieth-century Judaism. The willingness of Zionists "to get one's hands dirty" carries with it, at the very least, the chance that biblical texts of violence will be reactivated. There is clearly a need for developing a methodology of reading these texts that will counter this danger. What follows is one such attempt to wrestle with the story of violence without apologetics or denial and yet to emerge with a nonviolent Torah.[9]

## FROM CREATION TO DESTRUCTION: A SYMPATHETIC READING OF TEXTS ON VIOLENCE IN THE BIBLE

### GENESIS

Before focusing on its main topic, which is the historic interaction between God and Israel, the Bible attempts to provide a theological history of the human race and the world at large. The dream world in which the human story begins (in both its versions, the first and second chapters of Genesis) is hierarchical yet harmonious: God commands and blesses; man is given a mate; in giving woman her name, man dominates her; humans rule and give names to the animals, but do not kill them (Gen. 1:29–30). All are vegetarian.

This hierarchy of man over woman over animals is portentous because it anticipates the first chain reaction of disobedience: the eating of forbidden fruit, whose consequence is a sharpened hierarchy in which domination and hostility are more the rule than the exception (Gen. 3:14–19). Violence enters through the back door: after the banishment from Eden, God posts the Cherubs with "a flashing rotating sword," the first weapon, to keep Adam from re-entering Eden (3:24). God also moves away from primordial intimacy with other creatures as well: having clothed Adam and

Eve with animal skins (3:21), God now accepts Abel's animal sacrifice (4:4).

The violence of antediluvian society (Gen. 6:13), precipitated by the murder of Abel and the brutality of Lamech (5), escalated to a deterioration of a higher order. Notice how Lamech testifies to his victimhood (4:23) and uses it as a basis for the privileged degree of revenge that he claims—eleven times that of Cain.[10] Lamech, like the serpent in the Fall, echoes God's words, but is actually using them to his own advantage.

The Bible asserts both a human predisposition towards violence and a divine determination to purge the world of violence (Gen. 6:5; 8:21). Alas, God's solution, the flood, is a wholesale destruction of (human) sinners and (plant and animal) innocents in an attempt to wipe out sin (Talmud Bavli, Berachot 10, on Ps. 104:35).[11] The reestablishment of God's covenant with the human race and with the world (9) is a lesson in both repentance and disarmament. God regrets the flood and puts the rainbow in the sky as a promise never again to unleash such devastation.

Sadly, a comparison of the divine order prescribed in Genesis chapters one and nine shows that victory over violence has not yet arrived. Following the institutionalization of animal sacrifice, the dietary laws are revised to allow for the slaughter and eating of animals; violence against humans, by animals as well as by fellow humans, is anticipated and, in the case of murder, capital punishment is sanctioned as well. Far from the harmony and optimism prescribed in the creation story, the postdiluvian world is admittedly imperfect. Jewish tradition sees its role as working towards the repair of the world, *tikkun olam*.

Organized, glorified human violence will not appear again in the Bible until the time of Abraham, the Bible's first war hero (Gen. 14), who is, not coincidentally, also the Nation Builder par excellence (12:2). On this, compare the hassidic tradition attributed to the Rabbi of Apt:

> When God promised to make of Abraham "a great nation," the Evil Urge whispered to him: "'A great nation'—that means power, that means possessions!" But Abraham only laughed at him. "I understand better than you," he said. "'A great nation' means a people that sanctifies the name of God."[12]

This implicit critique of Jewish nationalism has its roots, of course, in the Prophet Samuel's response to the popular demand for the institution of a monarchy (1 Sam. 8).

While this episode of sanitized warfare[13] in Genesis is uncharacteristic of the Patriarchs who looked after their own interests in more subtle ways, there runs a strain of family discord throughout the book of Genesis. The rivalry between brothers (sometimes reflecting the rivalry between wives) reaches its violent peak with the staged murder of Joseph by his brothers (Gen. 37), and the rest of Genesis is an attempt to find a happy end to that cycle of hatred. God acquiesces to Abraham's problematic behavior towards his first-born, Ishmael, and first initiates and then cancels the divine command that Abraham immolate his second son, Isaac, at the last moment (22). This model of parenting does not continue in the narrative to the very next generations, but will leave its mark in Israeli law and later Jewish history: fathers will invoke the binding of Isaac when they slaughter their children to "save" them from forced conversion by the Crusaders.

Yisrael Yuval analyzes the literary records of medieval martyrdom and shows how fathers slaughtered their children, intending it as an offering based on the texts retelling Abraham's offering of Isaac. These fathers were surely aware of the tradition that claimed that Abraham actually did slaughter his son and that Isaac was resurrected, so that in seeing themselves as Abrahams, called by God to sacrifice their sons, they were also imploring God to intervene and resurrect their children. Yuval's article, and particularly his decision to demythologize the horror of medieval martyrdom, aroused such strong reactions that the Historical Society of Israel, who published his article, devoted a double issue of their journal to the controversy he aroused (Yuval 1993).

While this survey focuses on reading problematic texts of violence, three cases of nonviolent conflict resolution indicate that a basically optimistic attitude toward subverting hatred predominates in the patriarchal narratives: the division of land between Abraham and Lot (Gen.13); Isaac's successful battle for water (26); and the reconciliation between Jacob and Esau (33). Left to their own devices,[14] the Patriarchs know how to do the right thing and how to distance themselves from violence (e.g., the repeated condemnation by Jacob of the massacre of the Shechemites done by Simeon and Levi) (34:30; 49:5–7).

ANALYSIS

This retelling of the Genesis narrative aims to show the biblical author's desire to color the violence of the tale in a tragic light. Not only is the violence undesirable, it is a tragic development from conditions and patterns of behavior that overpower the protagonists. The most tragic figure in Genesis, and throughout the Bible, is God (attributed to the preeminent Talmudist Saul Lieberman; cf. Muffs 1992, 4, 160). God, far from being an omnipotent Aristotelian unmoved mover, is a model of frailty and regret. The nuanced reading of the text shows us that God seems to have had no choice but to build domination into creation. But we, who see how this ostensibly harmless domination leads to hierarchy and disobedience and finally violence, can take measures to establish the conditions of partnership necessary for a nonviolent society. The biblical God is an emotional God with whom we can commiserate when desperate, extreme measures are taken (the flood) and whom we can celebrate when God learns to control his awesome divine power (the rainbow).

## EXODUS TO DEUTERONOMY

While God seems to stay in the wings during the patriarchal saga,[15] particularly in the Joseph story, the Exodus story is one of full-scale divine intervention. The violence of the Ten Plagues has a double purpose: to humble haughty Pharaoh (Ex. 5:2) and to bring him and others—the Egyptians, the Israelites, the entire cosmos (9:16)—to acknowledge God. (The operation is a success but the subject dies and, in the process, Pharaoh becomes a more sympathetic character while the supposedly humble Moses inherits the mantle of pride. (Cf. 7:5; 11:3.)

Incidentally, this portrayal of Moses is not the first, or last, case where the Israelite main character is shown in a less favorable light than his pagan protagonist (e.g., Abraham and Pharaoh in Gen. 12, Abraham and Abimelech in Gen. 20, Isaac and Abimelech in Gen. 26, Jacob's sons and the Shechemites in Gen. 34, and Jonah and the sailors in Jon. 1). This portrayal cannot be accidental, considering the Bible's bias against paganism, and is another example of the usefulness of nuanced reading to reveal the internal textual potential for fighting prejudice within the text.

In Exodus, the use of force is more than instrumental: it is of the essence—reality itself is terrifying and humans must realize their total dependence on an omnipotent God whose ways are unknowable.[16] It has been argued, for example, that the drowning of the Egyptians in the Red Sea (whose suffering, incidentally, is mourned at every celebration of the Passover Seder) is not directly necessary for saving Israel physically but rather to strengthen the faith of the Israelites (Ex. 14:31) and thereby ultimately ensure their survival. Elements of this line of reasoning that attempts to deflect the emphasis and meaning away from using the episode as a defense for violence begin already in the Hellenistic period in the work known as Wisdom of Solomon. God's victory over Egypt is meant to terrify the enemies next in line, the Canaanite nations, so that they flee the incoming Israelites or are decimated.[17] According to the most extreme passage (Deut. 20:16–17), the Israelite army cannot accept the surrender of the indigenous nations; they, like the idolatrous Israelite city (13), fall under a total ban, *kherem*, and *must* be put to death.

## ANALYSIS

This latter passage condemning the idolatrous city indicates both the scope and the rationale for this ban and gives us a sword with which we will attempt to cut the Gordian knot of divine or divinely-inspired violence:

> You shall put its inhabitants to the sword, all of them, including their cattle. The booty you should collect outside and burn the city and its booty as a complete offering to God; it shall remain a mound of ruins, never to be rebuilt. Let nothing out of all that comes under the ban be found in your possession, so that God may turn from his anger and show you compassion and be compassionate to you and increase you as he swore to your forefathers, provided that you obey God and keep all God's commandments which I give you this day, doing only what is right in the eyes of the Lord your God. (Deut. 13:16–19)

Typical of the Deuteronomic author is the appeal to Israel's desire for self-preservation, which Israel can achieve only through its maintenance of the covenant with God. Most striking about this passage, however, is the juxtaposition of cruelty and compassion: humans are required to reach unbelievable levels of cruelty in order to receive divine compassion.[18] On the one hand, we find the instrumentality of the Other, that is, the non-Israelites, which we saw in the case of the Exodus, but here the immolation of the idolater is not so much to enhance God's reputation, nor is it a deterrent to Israel's enemies. Rather, the sacrifice seems necessary simply to satisfy God.

Could we possibly get any further from the fundamental biblical postulate basic to religious humanism that, created in God's image, there is a divine spark in every human being that makes the preservation of all human life the highest priority? On the positive side, we find here not only the divine promise of compassion for God's faithful, in harmony with the rest of the divine commandments, but the granting to humans of a power to manipulate God's emotional state that takes God from anger to compassion, a power with cosmic ramifications (an idea that, though marginal in the Bible, is greatly expanded in the mystical tradition of the Kabbala). Rabbinic tradition (Babylonian Talmud Yebamot 79a) sees in the divine promise, "so that God will show you compassion," in the passage cited above the granting to humans of the implicitly divine capacity for compassion ("As God is considered to be merciful, so too, should you be merciful") (Sifre Deut. Ekev. 49). To the rabbis, compassion is part and parcel of the religious life.

While rabbis understood God's capacity for mercy to be limitless and worthy in principle of human emulation, *imitatio dei*, the rabbis sought to limit the human application of compassion, saying, "One who is kind to the cruel will, in the end, be cruel to the kind" (Kohelet Raba 7:16). But this occasion was not one of those times, and the rabbis indicate that this commandment would never be applied (Tosefta, Sanhedrin 14.1; Bavli, Sanhedrin 71a). And finally, God's dependence on human beings, that is also shown in this passage, gives us a foot in the door in moral decision-making, one which the rabbis exercise in their modification of the application of the *kherem* against the indigenous nations of Canaan.[19]

Modern biblical scholarship holds that the historiography of the Deuteronomist author reflects the anxiety, anger, and sadness experienced as the fortunes of the Judean kingdom tumbled towards destruction and exile in the sixth century B.C.E. (see Greenberg 1972, 349). The Israelites didn't enter the land with the cry for *kherem* on their lips; rather, they left it with a pathetic hindsight, a retrospective formula for salvation, something like, "If only we had removed these pagan nations, there would have been no one to lead us to temptation, to worship their idols for which we are now being punished." Only this frustration over a failed opportunity can explain the amazing proximity we find in Deuteronomy of God's love for us with the hardness we must show the dangerous Other.[20]

COMMENT

Clearly, texts with violence do not necessarily preach violence and violent texts do not necessarily produce violent acts or people. Certainly, they may cause us to squirm with embarrassment[21] for the fact that extremist positions (e.g., those of the Deuteronomist) became canonized, bur those extremist texts don't have the force to overcome the powerful counter-tendency within the tradition towards peace, which leads us into the peace passages.

## SOME STATEMENTS ON PEACE IN JUDAISM

Major rabbinic texts from late antiquity eloquently declare: "*Gadol Hashalom*"[22]—peace is the highest of values. To establish the precise direction the concept of peace will take in Judaism, it is helpful to study the context in which the word "peace" appears in the Hebrew Bible (translations from the New English Bible):[23]

I will grant peace to the land,
and you shall lie down to sleep with no one to terrorize you.
(Lev. 26:6)

Shall not peace and truth be in my life. (2 Kings 20:19)

Righteousness shall yield peace
and its fruit be quietness and confidence forever. (Isa. 32:17)

Love and fidelity have come together,
justice and peace join hands. (Ps. 85: 11)

My (God's) peace is love and mercy. (Jer. 16:5)

As Schwarzschild writes:

> An adequate though informal definition of *shalom* as used
> in biblical, rabbinic and subsequent literatures is approxi-
> mated when people say that the peace they seek is not
> merely the absence of war, or even of private violence, but
> the presence and continual growth of all creative human
> powers. The many variants of the etymological root of
> *shalom* in Hebrew usage make it clear that the basic idea
> can perhaps best be rendered in English by such terms as
> wholeness, integrity, etc. . . . Within that ethical totality
> called peace or wholeness all other human virtues and val-
> ues are therefore subsumed. In such texts, to which many
> others could be added, truth, justice, righteousness, and
> grace are all collapsed into one value, and other moral val-
> ues could easily be conjoined . . . peace is the word that des-
> ignates the achievement of all human values in concert . . .
> when any significant one of them is left out not only will
> peace fail to be achieved, but also the others may, for lack
> of balance, easily come into conflict with one another.
> (Schwarzschild 1994, 17–18)

While individuals in the Bible use the word for peace, *shalom*, to
apply to their personal state of affairs, it would seem more appropriate to apply the category of *shalom* to a collective people. The
following passages could be expounded to teach that the individual cannot break away from the public to seek a private peace:

> [Contrary to the surrounding] I will do my thing and peace
> will dwell upon me. (Deut. 29:18)

> I am peace, but when I speak, they opt for war. (Ps. 120:6–7)

Be of the disciples of Aaron, loving peace, pursuing peace, loving one's fellow men and bringing them close to the Torah. (*Mishnah* Avot 1:12)

Thus, peace functions inclusively. The only way to ensure peace is to share it.

## NONVIOLENCE IN JEWISH TEXTS

On the interpersonal level, while the Hebrew Bible doesn't explicitly demand or expect a totally nonviolent lifestyle (Leibowitz 1982, 174), it commands the love of one's neighbor and sees love as the proper response to situations of conflict that breed hatred and vengeance: "Do not hate your brother in your heart; reprove him, and be sinless. Do not take revenge or harbor a grudge, rather love your neighbor as yourself; I am YHWH" (Lev. 19:17–18).

Relating to this passage, the medieval French exegete, Yosef Bechor Shor,[24] asks: How does God expect one who has been wronged to the point of wanting to take revenge to love one's neighbor? One thus sees the wisdom in the way Hillel of the first century paraphrased this: "That which is hateful unto you, do not do to your comrade" as the central principle of Judaic verse (Bavli Shabbat 31a). Bechor Shor finds the answer in the last, overlooked phrase of the passage: "I am YHWH: Let your love for Me overcome your hatred for him, and keep you from taking revenge; in this way love vanquishes hatred, and peace will come between you." This is the way of the Torah, "whose ways are pleasant, and all of whose paths are peace" (Prov. 3:17).

The Bible's desire to limit vengeance is concretized in the institution of Cities of Refuge. These places were created to protect the accidental murderer from being hunted down by avenging relatives. Capital punishment, so prevalent in the Bible's penal system, is virtually eliminated in the first major post-biblical code of Jewish law, the *Mishnah* (second century C.E.). The rabbis who compiled the *Mishnah* insisted on unrealistically severe laws of evidence in capital cases, indicating that they were not willing to allow human courts to take human life and risk irreversible miscarriages of justice. The result of their judicial caution is remarkably in line with the suggestion that among the Ten Commandments, *lo tirtzakh*, prohibits manslaughter as well as murder.

It is instructive to examine an illustrative case of rabbinic discussion in order to see how the scriptural, and then rabbinic, tradition is taken up and made a part of the ongoing life of the Jewish faith. For example, the popular notion that Judaism commands the preemptive killing of an attacker intent on homicide *("haba l'horgecha, hashkem l'horgo")* disregards the fact that, far from being dogmatic or prescriptive, the quotation under discussion is but a midrashic resolution of an unintelligible verse from a biblical narrative. In the biblical narrative, David does *not* kill Saul, even though Saul has made his lethal intentions known for some time and acted upon them (1 Sam. 24:9). The Masoretic reading, *"v'amar l'harogcha vatakhos alecha,"* seems corrupt, and the rabbis determine that David is referring to a teaching from *torah shebehalpeh ("v'amra Torah. . .")* that would have justified his killing Saul. This quote is borrowed from its original context (Talmud Bavli Brachot 62b) and then applied *("l'halacha")* in case law for justifiable homicide, in the extreme case of the thief intruding into a home in the dark (Talmud Bavli, Sanhedrin 72a–b, on Ex. 22:1).

The rabbis explain the Torah's exempting of the killer from punishment by constructing the following chain of cause and effect: The thief has assumed that the homeowner is prepared to attack him and is therefore willing, in self-defense, to strike the homeowner preemptively. This, in turn, justifies the homeowner's anticipatory strike (probably with a household implement, and not a weapon). The biblical passage stipulates that the homicide is not justified "if the sun has risen upon him"; one can assume that this is because the homeowner can now see he is not in mortal danger and has no longer a need for a preemptive strike. However one develops the implications of this passage for the rare personal encounter, the tragic spiral of fear described here is, in my opinion, too narrow a ledge for justifying the stockpiling of lethal weapons by individuals, and certainly is not applicable to situations of international conflict.

## REJECTION OF MILITARISM

Judaism's long-standing rejection of militarism predominates in Jewish texts of every age. The Book of Deuteronomy warns Israel against taking pride in its military successes and imagining them to be independently achieved; it sees these attitudes as the height of human pride and folly and dangerously close to idolatry: "Take care lest you forget YHWH your God . . . lest you eat well, build good houses and dwell in them, prosper . . . and say to yourself: it is through my might and prowess that I have all this" (Deut. 8:11–18). In fact, it would be a mistake for Israel to imagine that it was morally virtuous enough to merit its material inheritance; it is rather that others were worse than they, and also that God needed to fulfill the promise made to the Patriarchs (Deut. 9:5).

This anti-militarist attitude is reflected in the downplaying of the role of the Hasmoneans in the Tana'itic explanations of the origins of Hanukkah. The prophetic reading *(haftarah)* chosen by the rabbis for the Sabbath that falls during Hanukkah includes the famous verse from Zechariah: Not by force or by might, but with My spirit, says the Lord (Zech. 4:6), which is at the core of the nineteenth-century universalist, pre-Zionist understanding of Hanukkah.[25] Similarly, we find statements against Bar Kochva whose unsuccessful revolt against the Romans in 132–135 C.E. brought even more devastation to the Jews of Palestine than the Great Revolt of 70 C.E., in which the Second Temple and Jerusalem were destroyed.[26] Until recent years, the military profession was so antithetical to the heart and experience of the Jew that the Passover Haggadah found in a Jewish home was likely to portray the wicked son as a soldier. (By contrast, a Haggadah published by the Israeli Ministry of Defense Publishing House, *circa* 1970, shows glossy pictures of the devastation of the Egyptian army in Sinai during the 1967 war as a modern update of the ten plagues of antiquity.)

## ISAIAH 2 AS THE IDEAL

One can hardly begin to outline the expressions of the ideal of peace, and the age of peace, any better than by citing the book named for the late eighth-century prophet, Isaiah of Jerusalem, which reads:

At the end of days, the mount of the house of YHWH will be established at the top of the mountains, raised above hills, and all peoples will stream to it. Many nations will begin to say, "Let us go up to the mount of YHWH, to the house of the God of Jacob, so that he teach us his ways, and we will follow his paths, for teaching will go out of Zion, YHWH's word from Jerusalem. He will adjudicate among the peoples, and discipline many nations; they will break down their swords into shovels, their spears into pruning hooks: nations will not raise swords against each other, not train for war any more. (Isa. 2:2–4)

More important, however, are the texts that indicate a clear perception of the importance of such sentiments in Jewish life. Notable in the following series of comments are the teachings of R. Yohanan Ben Zakkai, who was famous for enlisting Roman support for the establishment of the rabbinic seat at Yavne and thereby exercising a nonviolent alternative to the disastrous Great Revolt initiated by Jewish zealots (whose suppression led to the destruction of the Second Temple and the destruction of Jerusalem):

One is not allowed to carry neither a sword nor a bow, nor a shield nor a club nor a spear [on the Sabbath], and if one is carried, an expiatory sacrifice must be brought. Rabbi Eliezer says, [it is allowed because] they are considered as ornament. The sages respond, [they cannot be considered as ornaments because] they are loathsome, as it is written, "They shall grind their swords into plowshares, and their spears into pruning hooks; nation shall not lift up sword against nation, neither shall they learn war any more (Isa. 2:4)." (*Mishnah* Shabbat 6:4)

In Exodus, we find the admonition: "If you build an altar to me (God) do not use hewn stones, for your sword will have been raised on it, thereby defiling it" (Ex. 20:22). In this connection, Rabbi Simon ben Eleazar used to say, "The altar is made to prolong the years of man and iron is made to shorten the years of man; it is not right for that which shortens life to be lifted up against that which prolongs life."

Rabbi Yohanan ben Zakkai says of this passage from Deuteronomy,

Behold it says, "Thou shall build . . . of whole stones." They are to be stones that establish peace. Now, by using the method of *kalvakhomer*, you reason: If, in the case of the stones for the altar, which do not see nor hear nor speak, yet, because they serve to establish peace between Israel and their Father in heaven, the Holy One, blessed be He: "Thou shalt lift no iron tool upon them, how much more so should he who establishes peace between human beings, between husband and wife, between city and city, between nation and nation, between family and family, between government and government be protected so that no harm come to him." (Deut. 27:6)

How does one draw practical guidance from such reflection? Note that justice and peace, according to Isaiah 2, are integrally connected. The order of these two elements is critical: first, justice is established, and only afterwards does peace become a reality. The aggrieved party is not expected to give up his claim and be pacified; on the contrary, he has the right and the obligation to demand justice. Peace without justice is surrender, which, when achieved under the guise of peace, is built on the flimsy foundations of falsehood; it only plants the seeds of future oppression. Attempts at reconciliation initiated before injustice is redressed can theoretically still lead to nonviolent conflict resolution, but they force the disadvantaged party to rely on the goodwill of the oppressor to yield not to pressure but rather through persuasion— an assumption that goes against the very experience of oppression.

## OF ISAIAH'S VISION OF JERUSALEM—THEN AND NOW

For contemporary Judaism, the question is inevitably asked: In what way can this passage be applied to the Israeli-Palestinian conflict? The following rabbinic statement is found in the *Mishnah* (third century C.E.): The world is based on three elements: justice, truth, and peace (Avot 1). This is a paraphrase of Isaiah's doctrine. The statement is important for us because it transfers the realm of responsibility from the eschatological and the divine to the present and the human. Justice, truth, and peace are interconnected and mutually dependent; they must be aspired to, and can be approached, if not attained, through the ongoing human commitment to and search for God's word.

Justice is a simple concept that is well understood instinctively. It is the assurance of equitable treatment. In situations of dispute, attaining justice depends on distilling the truth in front of an objective judge who has the confidence of both parties and whose judgment results in the restoration of peace. However, what works for individuals or groups within a society with an implied or explicit social contract may be hard to apply internationally. It is very hard for different countries to agree on and give authority to an outside power. Thus, the absence of a judge who is perceived to have the inherent right to judge is a major impediment to the resolution of international conflict. Second, established governments tend not to recognize the legitimacy of "popular committees" or other unincorporated nongovernmental organizations. The very notion of the equality of the disputants cannot be taken for granted. And finally, the idea of the natural rights of a nation, which correspond to that of individuals, must be investigated.

While it may be relatively simple for individuals or communities to establish, through religious principles or on humanist grounds, the inviolability of life, liberty, and the pursuit of happiness for individual human beings, it will be harder to do so for nations; there may not be a basis for evaluating competing myths of nationhood or for establishing group rights to which other groups must yield. But giving up on the establishment of international justice means acknowledging that the world is a jungle where only the fittest survive.

The most tragic abdication of religion and reason by Zionists regarding their obligation towards justice in the Israeli-Palestinian conflict is in the general legitimization given to the usurpation of the land of the Palestinian refugees. Palestinians' claim to their ancestral land is not political or geo-political, as is the right of national self-determination, which can only be realized within the limitations of political structures. The right of individuals to their homes is primary and undeniable and no amount of apologetics or global shuffling can eradicate it. The demand for the restitution of the refugees to their land is seen by virtually all Israeli Jews as tantamount to the dismantling of the state of Israel and the disintegration of Israeli Jewish society. Yet, the lack of progress towards the resolution of this issue not only dooms Israelis and Palestinians to perpetual violent struggle but it also negates the basis of, and perhaps even de-legitimizes, the very existence of the state of Israel.

## A JEWISH GIFT

Judaism has a tool that must be activated for this situation: *takanat hashavim*, the ordinance for a compassionate justice in the restoration of misappropriated property: In the past, in order to encourage a thief to return stolen property, the strict rules of restoration required one who had misappropriated a wooden beam (and already used it to build a roof) to dismantle whatever the stolen beam had been used for and to restore the very same beam. In later times, rabbis have allowed for the beam's value to be paid. In our case, we could use this principle to foster a gradual restoration of Arab homes—built by Palestinians before 1948 and involuntarily surrendered when the refugees were expelled or fled in fear—to the descendants of the original owners. Jewish homes or neighborhoods built on expropriated or "abandoned" Palestinian land could be maintained so long as equivalent plots of land be given to the heirs instead. Thus, *takanat hashavim*, applied assiduously but compassionately, would work towards the restoration of Palestinian roots without visiting trauma on Jews. Jews could thus be brought to recognize the higher good involved in their making room for the fulfillment of the dreams of other "lovers of Zion."

Isaiah's vision posits the involvement of YHWH as adjudicator in national disputes and the willingness of the nations to accept YHWH's decision as a result of the universal acceptance of YHWH as God. In the context of modern international, interreligious confict resolution, there clearly has to be found an agency of similar authority. In the absence of unanimously accepted, supernatural revelation, the best we can aspire to is a pooling of the collective wisdom of humanity—a synthesis of the divine as revealed to all societies throughout history. The practical translation of this vision is an inspired United Nations dedicated to human and environmental survival through the agency of the constituent member nations.

The reciprocal relationship between inner peace and interpersonal peace requires us, as it does all religious leaders, to recognize the religious imperative to contribute to peacemaking. This involves strengthening trust between individuals and congregations through fostering dialogue and positive human encounters. This, in turn, will foster the understanding that establishing the truth is a dialogical and dialectical process:[27] One side and one text cannot possibly contain all the truth but each human encounter can move us closer to the truth. We are dependent on each other for arriving at the truth which our sources contain. We are, in fact, each other's most indispensable resource.

## STUDY QUESTIONS

1. What are the important literary sources of Jewish thought other than the Bible?

2. Why does Milgrom suggest that reading violent texts from the Bible in the context of worship significantly changes the impact of these texts?

3. What is the central point Milgrom is making about the *amount* and *extent* of rabbinic commentary on violent texts of the Bible?

4. What are the three cases of nonviolent conflict resolution noted by Milgrom in the book of Genesis?

5. What example of Jewish tradition does Milgrom offer as an example of the biblical resources available for modern peacemaking in Israel/Palestine?

## BIBLIOGRAPHY

Bleich, J. David. *Contemporary Halakhic Problems.* Vol. 1. New York: Ktav Publishing House and Yeshiva University Press, 1977.

Friedman, Maurice. "Hasidism and the Love of Enemies." In *The Challenge of Shalom: The Jewish Tradition of Peace and Justice*, ed. Murray Polner and Naomi Goodman, 40–48. Philadelphia: New Society Publishers, 1994.

Greenberg, Moshe. "Herem." In *Encyclopedia Judaica*, vol. 8, 344–350. Jerusalem: Keter Publishing House, 1972.

Harkabi, Yehoshafat. *The Bar Kokhba Syndrome: Risk and Realism in International Politics.* Chappaqua, NY: Rossel Books, 1983.

Leibowitz, Yeshayahu. "War and Heroism in Israel, Past and Present." In *Faith, History and Values* (Hebrew). Jerusalem: Akademon Press, 1982.

Muffs, Yochanan. *Love and Joy: Law, Language and Religion in Ancient Israel.* New York: The Jewish Theological Seminary of America, 1992.

Polner, Murray and Naomi Goodman, ed. *The Challenge of Shalom: The Jewish Tradition of Peace and Justice.* Philadelphia: New Society Publishers, 1994.

Schwartz, Richard. *Judaism and Global Survival.* New York: Vantage, 1984.

Schwarzschild, Steven S. *"Shalom."* In *The Challenge of Shalom: The Jewish Tradition of Peace and Justice*, ed. Murray Polner and Naomi Goodman, 16–25. Philadelphia: New Society Publishers, 1994.

Wald, M. *Jewish Teaching on Peace.* New York: Bloch, 1944.

Yuval, Yisrael. "Vengeance and Damnation, Blood and Defamation: From Jewish Martyrdom to Blood Libel Accusations." In *Zion* 58, no. 1 (1993).

## NOTES

[1] A literal translation from the Hebrew, which is highly irregular. This leaves it up to the reader/worshipper to decide whether the author is actually saying "I am peace," or perhaps "I am at peace," "I am with peace," or "I am for peace."

[2] With the roots of Israel's intellectual and political elite being basically Marxist, it may not be surprising for its culture to have Bolshevik characteristics.

[3] "Happy are you, people of Israel, peerless, redeemed by God, your protecting shield, *for whom the sword is your pride* [or *who is the sword of your pride*]." The syntax is ambiguous: does the phrase modify God, like the phrase before it, or is it elliptic, modifying Israel? In Deuteronomy, which constantly attributes all of Israel's military successes to God (Deut. 8:11–18), the latter is more likely. Medieval Jewish commentators Saadia Gaon and Sforno favored this interpretation.

[4] The singular is popularly thought to take a variant form, *talmid khacham*, meaning either "a student of a sage," which suggests that wisdom and authority can be derived from a single personality, or "a wise student," which gives the student a higher standing than allowed by tradition. I thank Professor Shmuel Safrai of Hebrew University for this information.

[5] An ironic, yet indicative, result of this supreme emphasis on *torah shebbehalpeh* is that in a Yeshiva high school "secular subjects" include Bible classes.

[6] Including those surrounding Jesus (the Jew) of Nazareth.

[7] David J. Bleich, *Contemporary Halakhic Problems*, vol. 1 (New York: Ktav Publishing House and Yeshiva University Press, 1977), 244–69. Bleich points out that so many technical issues remain unclear that one cannot speak of a halachic preparedness for a non-supernatural reinstitution of the sacrificial cult.

[8] See the arguments and imagery of the eulogy, *"Baruch Hagever,"* written in memory of IDF Captain Baruch Goldstein, M.D., who massacred twenty-nine worshipping Muslims in the Ibrahimiye Mosque/Cave of Machpelah on Purim, 1994.

9   Calling this reading "Torah" is not a public relations ploy designed to achieve the imprimatur of tradition. Instead, it expresses the conviction that God's living word is true to the extent that it allows for a multiplicity of interpretations. Recent interpretations emerging seem to contradict or to surpass earlier understandings.

10   This passage surely resonates in the famous response of Jesus to Peter, that he must forgive seventy times seven (Matt. 18:22).

11   In this passage, Rabbi Meir prays for the death of troublesome highwaymen and Bruria responds with: "Is such a prayer permitted? It is written: 'Let sins cease,' not sinners. Further, look at the end of the verse: 'And let wicked people be no more.' Since sins will cease, there will be no more wicked people. Rather, pray that they should repent."

12   See Maurice Friedman, "Hasidism and the Love of Enemies," in *The Challenge of Shalom: The Jewish Tradition of Peace and Justice* (Philadelphia: New Society Publishers, 1964), 45–46.

13   We don't hear of casualties in this and many other battle descriptions in the Bible. The Israelites actually report that all their men survived the victorious war against the Midianites (Num. 31:49), which in today's Israeli newspeak would be formulated as "all our forces returned *b'shalom*."

14   On the relatively rare occasions that the Patriarchs invoke God in their relationships with others, it is not to claim privilege but rather to indicate a state of blessedness and to justify their own self-denial and generosity (14:22–24; 33:10–11; 39:9; 41:51–52; 42:18; 43:29; but cf. 45:9 when Joseph almost regresses to power-hungriness). The model of their reliance on God is Genesis 15:6, "And because he [Abraham] put his trust in the Lord, He reckoned it to his merit" (new JPS translation).

15   Compared to chapters 1–11 of Genesis, and the rest of the Torah, in this part of the book of Genesis, God maintains a private presence. God is active in fulfilling the promise of continuity, intervening to protect the wives (Sara 12:17 and 20:3–7, 17–18; Hagar, 16 and 21) and relatives (Lot and his family, 18–19); helping the Patriarchs find wives (24, and implicitly, by giving Jacob extraordinary strength, in 29) and solving infertility and difficult pregnancies (18, 21, 25, and 30), and by bringing Joseph to Egypt, masterminding the survival of the family, and through them, a multitude of people (45:5; 50:20). It seems as if the god we need for our families and for global survival is a much more gentle god than the one that our national existence requires.

16   This is one of many insights I gained from Yisrael Knol's seminar on Jewish Theology given at the *Shalom* Hartman Institute, 1995.

17   The wars against Sihon and Og, in the Transjordan, are reported twice: in Num. 21, a complete military victory is recorded; in Deut. 2:31–3:7, the institution of an almost total *kherem*—the cattle are spared

and taken as booty—is added. Perhaps the Deuteronomist regards the Transjordan as a part of the Promised Land.

18 Similarly, Pinchas is awarded a "covenant of peace" right after driving his spear through the Israelite and Moabite idolaters (Num. 25:1–15).

19 See Yerushalmi Shevi'it 6:1, in which Joshua is seen to have followed the more flexible laws of Deut. 20:10–15 in apparently disregarding verses 16–18.

20 One frequently sees a rapid shift in the emotions of the Deuteronomist author wherever the stakes are high or highly charged memories are recalled; for instance, in Deut. 23:4–7, in the passage forbidding the absorption of the Ammonite or Moabite into the Israelite people, we find a relatively long description of their inhospitality in the desert and Moab's attempt to have Israel cursed by Balaam. This description flows into a theocentric description of Israel's release from that predicament and then into a sudden transition from the recalling of God's love for Israel to a ferocious commandment to maintain eternal hostility towards them.

21 For those who venerate the text, this apprehension is much worse than embarrassment; it is *khilul hashem*, desecration of God's name, and brings with it deep soul-searching and acts of penitence. Thus, the raising of consciousness of the problematic nature of text is the first step toward energizing a religious peace camp.

22 *Gadol Hashalom*—"Great is Peace," a phrase that appears in a number of places in rabbinic literature, is best known as the refrain in an extensive section in *Midrash Raba* (and parallel collections) on the Priestly Blessing (Num. 6:22–27), which ends with "may God grant you peace." While the rhetorical intention of *gadol* (great) is actually the superlative ("the *greatest* [value] is peace"), one must remember that the rabbis make ultimate claims for the supremacy of various commandments (e.g., observing the Sabbath and studying the Torah).

23 For a fuller collection of scriptural quotations on peace, see Wald 1944; Schwartz 1984 cites additional anthologies of classical Jewish statements on peace.

24 This relatively obscure source was brought to the attention of the students of his Schechter Institute Rabbinical School seminar by Professor Moshe Greenberg.

25 Compare the original medieval text of "Maoz Tzur" to the nineteenth-century adaptation by Leopold Stein, rendered in English by Jastrow and Gottheil and known as "Rock of Ages." We bring here the first and last verses of the original, skipping the four middle historical verses retelling the stories of Exodus, Exile, and Restoration, the downfall of Haman, and the victory of the Maccabees:

Fortress, rock of my salvation
It is proper to praise you

My temple will be established
And there we will offer a thanksgiving offering
When You prepare a slaughter
Of the blaspheming enemy
I will complete the dedication of the altar
With the singing of a psalm

Expose your holy arm
And hasten the end, salvation
Avenge the blood of your servants
From the wicked nation
The hour is late
There is no end to the bad days
Reject the red one,
In the shadow of Zalmon
Raise up seven shepherds

The nineteenth-century version reads:

Rock of Ages let our song
Praise Thy saving power;
Thou amidst the raging foes
Wast our shelt'ring tower.
Furious they assailed us
But Thine arm availed us
And Thy word
Broke Their sword
When our own strength failed us

Kindling new the holy lamps
Priests approved in suffering
Purified the nation's shrine
Brought to God their offering.
And His courts surrounding
Hear in joy abounding
Happy throngs
Singing songs
With a mighty sounding.

Children of the martyr race
Whether free or fettered
Wake the echoes of the songs
Where ye may be scattered.

Yours the message cheering
That the time is nearing
Which will see
All men free
Tyrants disappearing.

The original calls for apocalyptic violence and revenge, ending in an eschatological restoration of sacrificial ritual in the only place it is allowed, the Temple Mount. This original version is particularistic and resonates with anti-Christian polemic. The nineteenth-century version, by contrast, is inclusive ("all men free") and universally non-territorial ("where ye may be scattered"), relegating the priestly ritual to the past (middle verse). It, too, is eschatologically pulsating but redefines the Jewish mission as the fight against tyranny.

26  For recent thoughts along these same lines by a modern Israeli military leader, see Harkabi 1983.

27  See the works of Martin Buber. See also the prayer for peace by Rabbi Nahman of Bratzlav (nineteenth century): "There should be no hatred, jealousy, rivalry, triumphalism or pettiness between people, only love and a great peace, that everyone should experience love from one another, and be sure that each wants good to befall the other, and to love them and for them to succeed, so that all could come together and speak with each other and explain the truth to one another."

# 10

# Political Atheism and Radical Faith

## The Challenge of Christian Nonviolence in the Third Millennium

*Daniel L. Smith-Christopher*

> You have heard that it was said, "You shall love your neighbor and hate your enemy." But I say to you, Love your enemies and pray for those who persecute you.
>
> Jesus of Nazareth, Matthew 5:43–44

> Live in harmony with one another; do not be haughty, but associate with the lowly; do not claim to be wiser than you are. Do not repay anyone evil for evil, but take thought for what is noble in the sight of all. If it is possible, so far as it depends on you, live peaceably with all.
>
> Paul of Tarsus, Romans 12:16–18

> Do not be astonished, brothers and sisters, that the world hates you.                                1 John 3:13

This essay is a reflection on the apparently strange juxtaposition of the three New Testament passages listed above. How could the seeking of peace result in the hatred and the animosity of wider society? The answer, I would argue, cuts to the heart of the modern issue of Christian nonviolence in the late twentieth century and may well force Christians to face the full implication of what nonviolence actually means as a religious value—namely, a direct challenge to the concept of nationalism.

The title of this essay is taken from an aspect of early Christian relations with Roman imperial society in the first three hundred years of Christianity. Because the early Christians refused to honor or participate in the state religion, Christians were frequently, and ironically, accused of "atheism." They did not "believe in" (as we would say today) the national gods of Rome. They certainly refused to deify and worship the emperor. This act of political defiance is what I refer to as "political atheism." I believe it is an appropriately provocative way to speak of radical Christian commitment to nonviolence.

The important partner with political atheism is "radical faith"— a Christian radical faithfulness to Jesus that interrogates and challenges all forms of nationalism, patriotism, and cults of violence that are so much a part of modern warfare and its preparations. Retired Professor Colonel Harry G. Summers has written that "the passions of the people . . . are the engines of war." If this is so, then Christian nonviolence, which is a radical faith, must renew the call to political atheism in the twenty-first century just as it called Christians to political atheism in the first centuries of the Christian movement.

The dominant Christian position in relation to warfare is the doctrine of the "just war." Although it does not have the status of official doctrine in the Roman Catholic Church, just war is certainly the predominant tradition. In some mainstream Protestant traditions, the just war doctrine most certainly does have confessional status. I contend that radical Christian commitment to nonviolence at the end of the twentieth century does not, in fact, struggle against a calm or reasoned proposition of the just war doctrine. In the modern world, to apply the just war doctrine simply requires too much information for Christians to be able to determine if a particular war is just or not. Tom Engelhardt, in his recent analysis of the culture of war (he refers to it as "The Culture of Victory") in the United States, suggests that already in the 1950s:

> the world could be fathomed only by adepts. . . . Electronic "eyes" and "ears" picked up the enemy worldwide, but their products could be interpreted only by "cryptanalysts, traffic analysts, photographic interpreters, and telemetry, radar,

and signal analysts . . . who produced material for, at best, a few thousand people with high enough security clearances to see the finished intelligence product. . . . Least equipped for the new struggle was the public. (Engelhardt 1995, 116)

In such circumstances where we have little available, reliable information, how are we to go about ethical decision-making? Does not the just war doctrine become, in the absence of real information in the era of hyper-managed media coverage, merely a form of rallying the masses rather than encouraging true debate? When so much information is "top secret," we are asked merely to "have faith" in our leaders. The religious connotation is suggestive. Christian nonviolence confronts this virtual *religious zeal* for violence expressed in notions like: "father/mother-land," "national homeland," or expressed in carefully (and often literally) orchestrated calls to "stand to the last man," "defend our way of life," "never back down." In short, modern warfare is fueled more by emotionalism and patriotic jingoism than careful ethical consideration. Modern Christians radically committed to the nonviolence of Jesus face the mentality of the crusade (see Yoder 1984).

## WARFARE AS RELIGION

War, as the ancients knew at least as well as the U.S. State Department, is a religion whose gods are demanding. The most successful of the empires of the ancient Near East and later, in the West, were scrupulous in their certainty that their gods of war were well-pleased, well-fed, and well-known. The unprecedented age of peace during the reign of Augustus (31 B.C.E.–14 C.E.) was commemorated in Rome with an altar to peace, *built on the field of Mars, the god of war* (Wengst 1987, 7–19). We are beginning to understand the widespread significance of the ancient Roman emperor cult as the essential amalgam of religion, power, and the state:

The spirit of empire ran deep and wide. The remarkable cohesion of Roman society itself at the center of the empire can only be explained by the way in which the revival of Roman religion and traditional morality was substituted for what were previously political processes . . . in a reconfiguration of Roman power relations. . . . Thus, as Greeks went about their lives, they were constantly reminded of the importance of the emperor, whose presence pervaded public space. (Horsley 1997, 13, 21)

Roman society was threatened by the stubborn opposition from early Christians whose bold rejection of such activities as the emperor cult and its violence earned them the accusation of atheism. Their refusal to honor the state gods, which were of the essence of Roman identity, brought active persecution as well (Womersley 1988, 99–133; Vogt 1965, 82–83). Religion and power are always a tempting mix. Yet, centuries later, it is still true that if one challenges the gods of war—whether they are national, ethnic, or religious—in the name of Christianity, this is tantamount to standing against the tide of Western civilization and its *own* gods.

In short, to assert a faith that embraces the nonviolence of Jesus is to proclaim oneself an atheist in relation to the preferred gods of nationalism and patriotism. This assertion of faith becomes all the more difficult when such war jingoism incorporates the language of the Bible and Christian faith. Thus, the challenge of modern nonviolence in the Christian tradition is to proclaim radical faith *and* political atheism, a proclamation that has repercussions for both the church and the state.

## ROME OR THE KINGDOM OF GOD: "YOU CANNOT SERVE GOD AND MAMMON"

Recently, there has been some debate about the nonviolence of the earliest Christians, with some scholars suggesting that Christians refused Roman military service because of its religious requirements as much as, or perhaps more than, any aversion to killing (see Hunter 1992). In fact, many of the early Christian martyrs who refused military service did so precisely because participation in military service amounted to participation in a rival religion—a religion that mandated violent activities. Marcellus, circa 298 C.E., was martyred soon after proclaiming his clear perception of the connection of violence with nationalist religious zeal:

I am a soldier of Jesus Christ, the eternal king. From now I cease to serve your emperors and I despise the worship of your gods of wood and stone. . . . It is not fitting that a

Christian, who fights for Christ his Lord, should be a soldier according to the brutalities of this world. (Hornus 1960, 133–35)

Such witnesses are not unusual in the early centuries of Christianity. By the fourth and fifth centuries C.E. nonviolence in Christianity had come to be considered both a minority position and a heresy. To this day, it remains in an adversarial position to the majority of traditions in Christianity. Indeed, although there are many divisive issues of practice and belief which modern Christians have decided are no longer worthy of acrimonious debate, there is yet no peace on the issue of peace. This is due, in no small measure, to the fact that few issues other than the debate on war and its widespread "Christian" support reveal Christians in a more shameful display of self-interested sophistry—a tradition dating at least to Augustine and perpetuated by Aquinas (see Marrin 1971, 52–73).

Christian nonviolence is the refusal to be moved by flag and state. It is also the refusal to participate in the liturgies of destruction and in the hymnic glorification of violence as national epic and identity (see Engelhardt 1995). In short, Christian nonviolence is political atheism in the name of radical faith in Jesus, who commands his followers to love even the enemy. Indeed, as Klassen points out, the love of enemies is the strongest assertion by Jesus. Christian compassion is to know no national or ethnic or political boundaries (Klassen 1984, 84–92). Jesus was aware that his message would divide old loyalties and create new ones. Jesus said that his word would be like a "sword" that would divide even family loyalties. The passage concludes with Jesus's teaching that "one's foes will be members of one's own household" (Matt. 10:34–36). This is an image borrowed from the "verbal swords" of the Hebrew Prophets (Isa. 49:2; Jer. 25:16; cf. Job 5:15). Such expectations of new social formulations match precisely the call to love enemies.

## JESUS AS NONVIOLENT RABBI

It is often argued, even by those who advocate the nonviolence of Jesus, that nonviolence was a new teaching. But the gospel teachings of Jesus of Nazareth with respect to violence are consistent with other Hebrew/Jewish developments, such as quietism and a nonviolent ethos among the early teachers of Pharasaic Judaism (see Kimmelman 1968; Genot-Bismuth 1981). Nonviolence is most certainly reflected in the teachings of R. Yochanon Ben Zakkai—nearly a contemporary of Jesus—whose peaceful teachings included his rejection of the ill-fated war against Rome in 67–70 C.E.; his own bias in favor of the widely noted Pharasaic loathing of capital punishment; his favorable comments on military exemptions in Deuteronomy 20; and his famous meditation on peacemakers as "stones of God's altar." Peacemakers are, metaphorically, like the literal stones used to build altars (Deut. 27:6). Peacemakers should have no contact with iron (and by implication, then, with weapons) (Neusner 1962; Neusner 1970; in this volume, Milgrom).

Notably, however, the pacifist teachings of Jesus are nowhere explicit in the context of making ethical decisions with regard to participating in warfare *per se*. The question, "Shall we fight in the military?" was a non-question for Jews of Palestine, a territory occupied by Rome. The question for a Jew of first-century Palestine with respect to lethal violence was a question about the tactics of resistance to the occupying powers. In virtually all cases, Jesus's teachings about "loving enemies" and "praying for those who persecute you" applied to relations with the occupying power. Marcus Borg, arguably one of the most important contemporary scholars of the historical Jesus, has written:

> Jesus said, in deliberate contrast to the limitation of love to one's compatriot, "Love your enemies." . . . What would this have meant in teachings directed to Israel in the late twenties of the first century? It had an inescapable and identifiable political implication: the non-Jewish enemy was, above all, Rome. To say "Love your enemies" would have meant, "Love the Romans; do not join the resistance movement," whatever other implications it might have had. (Borg 1998, 136–46)

In short, Jesus's teaching was intended to overturn the so-called patriotism that would call for killing the enemy. The most significant location of Jesus's ethical teachings in relation to violence is in the body of teachings that the Gospel of Matthew calls "The Sermon on the Mount." There, beginning already in one of the famous blessings, Jesus honors peacemakers: "Blessed are the peacemakers, for they will be called the children of God" (Matt. 5:9).

Later in the discourse, Jesus elaborates on this peacemaking, and especially how his teaching differs from the expected traditions of behavior:

> You have heard it said, "An eye for an eye and a tooth for a tooth." But I say to you, Do not resist an evildoer. But if anyone strikes you on the right cheek, turn the other also. You have heard it said, "You shall love your neighbor and hate your enemy." But I say to you, Love your enemies and pray for those who persecute you. (Matt. 5:38–48)

Even when a disciple took up a sword to defend Jesus himself, Jesus commanded that he put the sword away, for: "all who take up the sword will perish by the sword" (Matt. 26:52).

What is certainly clear is that Jesus's teaching on violence was understood by early Christians as speaking directly to the issue of participation in lethal violence, even in the cause of national defense. For the first three centuries of Christianity, the normative interpretation of the teachings of Jesus by Christians was that obedience to Christ precluded participation in the military. But more must be said. What is clear in the teachings of Jesus is how his advocacy of peacefulness is tied to his view of the nature of the community he founded. Christian nonviolence was not a general ethical maxim. It was a rule for the community of disciples and followers, directing them in the way they were to live in the midst of those who lived quite differently: "Jesus called to them and said, 'You know that among the Gentiles those whom they recognize as their rulers lord it over them, and their great ones are tyrants over them. But it is not so among you, but whoever wishes to become great among you must be your servant'" (Mark 10:42–43).

Although there is nothing in the gospel portraits of Jesus that contradicts the pacifism of Jesus, there are occasionally noted objections (see Yoder 1994; Anderson 1994). One such classic objection is the phrase, "Think not that I come to bring peace, I have come to bring a sword." But this phrase, as has already been noted, appears in the context of how Christian faith may divide former loyalties—even within the family. Jesus resolves this apparent contradiction with a teaching totally consistent with loving enemies: "one's foes become a part of one's household" (Matt 10:36).

The famous cleansing of the Temple episode, where Jesus over-turns the tables of the moneylenders (noted in all four gospels), is often cited as inconsistent with a peace-loving Jesus. None of the accounts of this episode implied that Jesus actually engaged in bod-ily harm to those gathered in the Temple complex. But such action as Jesus exhibited is just as readily an illustration for the form of nonviolence that Jesus does advocate—active, resistant, and inter-ested in public, prophetic demonstration. This is in the tradition of prophets like Jeremiah and Isaiah (both of whom are explicitly invoked by Jesus in his famed "house of prayer/den of robbers" image drawn from Jeremiah 7:11 and Isaiah 56:7). In short, the Temple episode is only inconsistent with a weak passivity—one that is too often set up by Christian advocates of a nonviolent Jesus (see Hiller 1966, 27–49).

## THE "OLD TESTAMENT": TOWARD A HEBRAIC NONVIOLENCE

On a widespread popular level, what Christians refer to as the "Old Testament" is often *functionally* ignored in Christian faith and practice. Yet, there have always been voices within the Christian tradition that call for a serious Christian theology of the Old Testament (Ollenburger 1992, 1991; Brueggemann 1997). However, for the vast majority of contemporary Christians, in both Catholic and Protestant traditions, the Old Testament remains largely a source of Sunday School stories for children. It is also the source for the occasional conservative diatribe against sins appar-ently thought to be insufficiently condemned in the New Testament (such as homosexuality) and a source for the occasional prophecy about Jesus. In such contexts, the Hebrew Bible is used to defend nationalist patriotism and military bravado when it serves the pur-poses of Christians. It is discarded as if it doesn't apply to "us Christians" when it is not useful—for example, when attempting to blunt the nonviolence of Jesus.

When we focus on the issue of violence in the Hebrew Scrip-tures, we find an emphasis on the fate of the ancient Israelite state—on the conquest of the land of Canaan by the Hebrews (Joshua) and the wars of conquest engaged in by the kings of Israel and Judah (Judges and 2 Kings). But this is not the whole of Hebrew history. The Hebrew Bible also deals with the concept of

a violent *God*, a concept apparently opposed to the perception of
the peaceful Jesus of the New Testament.

Scholars deal with the contradictory portrayals of God in the
two Testaments in the following ways: (a) they minimize the relationship between the Testaments by relegating the Hebrew Bible
to mere background; or (b) they argue for a kind of progressive
understanding of the nature of God from primitive to sophisticated
(they imply that violence is primitive and peacefulness is sophisticated); or (c) they maintain that certain practices pertain to certain ages. Options (a) and (b) minimize the Jewish identity of Jesus
and remove the teachings of Jesus from their continuity with the
Prophetic tradition of social justice, the Wisdom traditions, and
the Apocalyptic traditions; and run serious risks of fueling anti-
Semitism. Furthermore, apart from the gospels, major sections of
the New Testament become unintelligible when cut off from their
roots in the Hebrew tradition. Option (c), a *that was then, this is
now* theology, seems a hopelessly circular argument that requires
a set of criteria from outside the tradition.

## LISTENING TO DEFEATS AS WELL AS VICTORIES

An alternative approach to explaining away the troubling parts
of the Hebrew Bible would begin by insisting that we not only listen to the victories of Joshua, David, and so on, but also the
defeats, and especially the defeat and exile of both Jewish states.
In the context of defeat, the biblical historians pass judgment on
the earlier military bravado and condemn virtually every king of
Israel and Judah, with the sole exception of Josiah, who is not
praised for warfare but rather religious reform. It is important to
note that the Hebrew Scriptures were at least edited, if not all written, *after* the failure of the monarchy. Given Israel's history of state
formation and monarchy, it would have been surprising if ancient
Israel did *not* provide the examples it does of lyrical self-glorious
celebration of violence and power. Such bravado in the ancient
Near East reaches barbaric, even grisly proportions, for example,
in Neo-Assyrian inscriptions. These inscriptions arguably reached
the pinnacle of excess for using sheer military terror in both practice and propaganda in ancient Near Eastern civilization. A Neo-
Assyrian document records an official's response to a local village
revolt as follows: "I built a pillar over against the city-gate and I

flayed all the chief men who revolted, and I covered the pillar with their skins" (noted in Saggs 1963).

It is also important to note that ancient warfare was always and everywhere a religious act. In their inscriptions and monuments, the Neo-Assyrians, the Egyptians, the Babylonians, the Persians, and the Greeks all maintain that war was often won by the participation not only of their own gods, but also that of the gods of their defeated enemies (Cogan 1974, 6; cf. Kang 1989).

It is undeniable that there are similar barbaric moments in Hebrew history. For example, there is the practice of the "ban"—the killing of all persons after the conquest of a village. One should also note the presence of poetic bloodlust in the final verses of Psalm 137. However, when warfare was recorded in Hebrew tradition, there was, paradoxically, often also a conscious attempt to minimize military celebration and self-glorious relishing of victory.

With respect to the conception and role of God, it is common to find in the Hebrew Bible that God is almost exclusively the agent of warfare by means of a miracle. On many occasions, human involvement is virtually excluded or minimized (Ex. 14–15; Judg. 7). The late Jewish work, the Wisdom of Solomon, actually tries to argue the justice of God's violence. In this book, the enemies of Israel had a choice to leave peaceably or respond to less threatening violence before lethal violence would be resorted to (Wisd. of Sol. 19:13–17).

Interestingly, Millard Lind's thesis is that the early pre-monarchical Hebrew ideology of warfare was actually anti-military, precisely because wars were conducted by "miracle." In fact, wars were often "fought" by God alone. Lind argues that this early ideology of wars fought by God, or miraculous Yahweh Wars, was displaced by the development of the monarchy, which brought with it more of the typical ancient Near Eastern militarism and its religious accoutrements (Lind 1980). As Mendenhall has stated it:

> The glorification of Yahweh as the "divine warrior" who led his people to victory over the kings in the old poetry of the Federation period . . . [gave] . . . way to the glorification of a professional warrior for his superior ability to commit murder. The old "heroic" mentality that regarded military successes as a major theme of epic chant returns with a vengeance very soon after the reversion to Bronze Age pagan

political organization in Israel. Yahweh was not nearly so reliable a source of "security" as an effective military general. The theme that rose to such horrendous atrocities during the Assyrian Empire dominates also most of the history of Ancient Israel and Judah. (Mendenhall 1975, 158).

But perhaps this theological shift may have emerged *after* the development of monarchy, and was thus a reflection of its excesses and mistakes (see 1 Sam. 8).

Similarly, in his classic analysis, Max Weber suggests that the "pacifistic patriarchal legends" and the later "pacifistic prophets" (whose message was of destruction by God alone) had their origins in proletarian protests of the monarchy's professionalization of the military (Weber 1967, 100–3).

What is clear is that the Hebrew Bible is notoriously underwhelming as a "national epic literature." It seems bent on disallowing human pride in military accomplishment. With its constant moralistic reminders of mistakes, sins, and failures, the Hebrew Bible is interested in the human need for God, not power. Even David, the most potentially epic figure in the entire historical narratives, is remembered as much for his failures and abuses of power as for his successes. In the later historical revisions in the books of Chronicles, he is condemned as a man with "blood on his hands" (1 Chron. 28:3, cf. Hosea 1:4, where Jehu is condemned for a political assassination that appears to be commanded in 2 Kings 9:7).

## THE HEBREW PEACE TRADITION

I would argue that the Hebrew peace tradition developed late and was a result of Israel becoming stateless. This fall of the monarchy began in 597 B.C.E. and was violently completed in 587 B.C.E., when a number of the Hebrew intellectual and political leaders were exiled to the Neo-Babylonian heartland (what is today southern Iraq). Though often minimized in ancient Israelite religious development, I posit that this exile was a central turning point in biblical theology. This is because it engendered the rise of competing strategies of survival for the future of Israel (see Smith-Christopher 1989). These strategies developed out of diverse responses to two questions: "What does it *now* mean to be the people of God?" and "How do we live in exile?"

With respect to the first question, we can cite here the debates between those who advocated violence and those who advocated nonviolence. On the one hand, there were those who wanted the violent and vengeful destruction of the enemies of God (Ps. 137; Jer. 50, 51); on the other hand, there were those who spoke of the people's new role as a "light to the nations," where Jerusalem would become a world center of learning that required world demilitarization and peaceful conversion of weapons to farming tools (Isa. 2).

In response to the second question, how to live in exile, Jeremiah's famous Letter to the Exiles (29) gives advice. He echoes the Deuteronomic exemptions from military service: build houses, marry off your offspring, and plant gardens (see Deut. 20). By recommending those activities that exempt a Jew from fighting, it can be argued that the emphasis here was placed on nonviolent resistance. Further justification for this interpretation is provided by Jeremiah's conclusion to his letter: "Seek the peace of the city where you live—for in its peace you will find your peace."

Is Jeremiah's advice to be understood as applying to the short- or the long-term? Before his untimely death in 1997, John Howard Yoder had speculated that Jeremiah 29 was not so much an interim ethic as the basis for an "exilic ethic" and possibly an exilic ecclesiology of the Christian church (Yoder, personal correspondence and unpublished manuscripts).

## NONVIOLENCE AND UNIVERSAL MISSION

The prophet we know only as "Second Isaiah" (that is, chapters 40–55) formulated a doctrine of redemptive suffering for the exiled Israelite peoples which would then be the basis for a *universal renewal of humanity*. This was a renewal not limited only to the restoration of the Israelite peoples themselves, but which also sought to redefine their relationship to their former enemies (Isa. 2; 19:24–25; 49:6). Included in this developing Hebraic theology of nonviolence and universal mission are the following: the stories of Jonah (a *midrash* based on Isa. 49:6); the little book of Ruth's redefinition of "foreigners" (Ruth, a foreigner, gained acceptance and succeeded whereas Hagar, another foreign woman, had been rejected [Gen. 16, 21]); and the book of Daniel, particularly in its renunciation of violent resistance in chapter 11 (see Smith-Christopher 1989).

There are important hints that this view of renewal may also be related to the honoring of the "quiet/peaceful one" in Wisdom traditions (see Prov. 11:30; 14:29; 16:32; 17:9; 20:3; 24:15–18; 25:21–22), which is itself related to the Egyptian ideal of the non-violent wise one (Schupak 1993). The Hebrew image of the patient wise one is also honored in the nonviolence and non-vengeful image of the intertestamental portraits of Joseph and Taxo (see Harrelson 1977; Licht 1961; Collins 1977).

The loss of statehood led some late Hebrew writers to reject state violence—especially a renewed call to Hebrew state violence—and to advocate an embrace of exile as a "calling" rather than a punishment (Jer. 29; Isa. 49:6). Finally, the powerful story of Jonah moves in an entirely new direction. It radically redefines the nature of being the people of God, a people of mission with a message of reconciliation (see Isa. 2 wherein this reconciliation will lead to the destruction of all weapons). The conclusion, then, is that there is not one singular and consistent answer in the Hebrew Scriptures to the problem of war and relations to the enemy. In fact, there are conflicting interpretations of the tradition of violence, even within the canon of the Hebrew texts. Jesus, then, can be identified as standing faithfully in one, but not all, of these differing post-exilic, Hebraic traditions.

Jesus did not create the Hebrew tradition of nonviolence. He stands in this peace tradition with other early rabbinic teachers (cf. R. Yochanon Ben Zakkai in Neusner 1962, 1970). However, Jesus clearly radicalizes Hebrew nonviolence and clarifies its central importance for the character of his movement. If the nonviolence of Jesus, then, was not only consistent with other rabbinic ethical teachings of the time (whether the majority or not), but also clearly intended to establish the basis for an alternative community in the world, how did the followers respond?

## CHRISTIAN NONVIOLENCE AND THE EARLY CHURCH

The Apostle Paul continued the peace teaching of Jesus, but Paul couched his ethical expectations of the Christian life in even stronger contrast to imperial Roman polity. The Christian fellow-ship, in Paul's view, was an alternative fellowship that was, at the same time, an open challenge to the claims of Rome. As Dieter Georgi has suggested: "Paul sees the congregation as a pluralistic model society" (Georgi 1997, 156). Richard Horsley, in a sum-mary statement, noted how many loaded terms Paul chose from Roman political language. Paul gave them a radically Christian alternative reading: "Insofar as Paul deliberately used language closely associated with the imperial religion, he was presenting his gospel ["good news"] as a direct competitor of the gospel ["good news"] of Caesar" (Horsley 1997, 140). Paul wrote his own peace theology in texts such as Romans 12:9–21, often echoing the teach-ings of Jesus: "Bless those who persecute you, bless and do not curse them . . . live in harmony with one another. . . . If it is pos-sible, so far as it depends on you, live peaceably with all."

From Paul onward, the normative position in the first three centuries of Christianity was to affirm the nonviolence of Jesus (Hornus 1960; Hunter 1992). With the example of Hippolytus (d. 236 C.E.), the apostolic tradition and the Canons clearly reveal this Christian attitude by the early third century:

> The soldier who is of inferior rank shall not kill anyone. If ordered to, he shall not carry out the order. . . . The believer who wishes to become a soldier shall be dismissed because they have despised God.

> Canon 13: Of the magistrate and the soldier: Let them not kill anyone even if they receive the order to do so.

> Canon 14: Let a Christian not become a soldier: A Christian must not become a soldier. . . . Let him not take on himself the son of blood. (Hornus 1960, 163)

It is clear that the political implications of this nonviolence were not missed by early Christian writers. Note in the pseudopigraphic "Epistle of Diognetus" the striking ambivalence about matters of state and national pride:

> They dwell in their own countries, but only as sojourners; they bear their share in all things as citizens, and they endure

all hardships as strangers. Every foreign country is a fatherland to them, and every fatherland is foreign. . . . They find
themselves in the flesh, and yet they live not after the flesh.
Their existence is on earth, but their citizenship is in heaven.

This nonviolent legacy, however, did not last.

Since Ambrose and Augustine, the majority of Christian scholars of Christian ethics have not denied that the gospel teachings are
pacifist. Rather, they have turned to arguments about "responsible" Christian ethics of peace and war; that is, they focus on just
war. According to the just war view, Christians must consider ethical arguments to determine whether a particular conflict is just or
not and to determine whether, as Christians, they can participate
in the conflict. A just war, according to these Christian ethicists,
must be waged only by a legitimate authority and only for a just
cause. Further, war must be the last resort; non-combatants must
not be injured; and weapons used must be able to discriminate. The
goal must be peace rather than gain. The literature on the just war
tradition is vast, as befitting the difficulties of the intellectual
alchemy that is necessary to transform the nonviolence of Jesus into
a call to arms (cf. Ramsey 1968, 1978, 1988; Yoder 1984).

While there are many variations on the notion of a just war,
the ethics of the just war have virtually nothing to do with Jesus.
This notion would not have been recognized in the first three centuries of Christianity. No one supposes that Jesus meant to speak
of just wars, and it is clear that St. Augustine was forced to draw
heavily on Greek and Roman sources in creating the earliest definitive version of the idea (see Markus 1983). The normative pacifism of the early church has yet to be overturned as a canon of
historical scholarship.

## ONWARD CHRISTIAN SOLDIERS

What John Howard Yoder has called "The Constantinian Shift"
changed everything. By 311, the famous Edict of Milan made Christianity, among other faiths, openly legal. By 420, "official Christianity" was beginning to officially persecute heresies. By 436, the
radical transformation of official Christianity was complete, for
by then, *only Christians* could serve in the Roman legions. The
church was then armed with the power of the Roman legions, and

nonviolence came to be viewed as a heresy and an occasional prophetic voice. In the West, prophetic voices have rarely been the subject of serious study. However, in medieval sources, these voices are occasionally heard in protest against the Christian preparation for the Crusades. The role of the peace witness in the centuries from Constantine to the beginnings of the Crusades is an area of research that ought to be further investigated. This would include research into the notion of violence among the Byzantine writings of the Eastern Christian tradition.

Christian nonviolence since Constantine, while not exactly an unbroken chain, is certainly traceable in a long series of episodes. These are typically associated with circumstances of marginality and/or a zeal for a return to the pristine teachings of the earliest church and its simple gospel. The Crusades provided a major test of Christian nonviolence in the early years of the second millennium. In fact, it is not widely known that Christian advocates of nonviolence actually opposed the Crusades. For example, Pietro Valdes founded the Waldensians, a northern Italian movement that was pacifist in its origins in the twelfth and thirteenth centuries (see Biller 1983; Haines 1981; Cameron 1984). There were also other opponents of crusading. In his groundbreaking study, Throop wrote that

> Force having failed miserably in efforts to recover the Holy Land, thoughtful and pious men . . . began to insist that the crusades were misguided efforts. Men of this type, as capable of self sacrifice and martyrdom as the early crusaders, felt that the recovery of the Holy Land could only come through the use of Christ's own methods: the preaching of the gospel. This pacifist missionary ideal, revived during the early thirteenth century, was deeply antagonistic to the militant crusading ideal of the twelfth century, the ideal which Gregory endeavored so valiantly to resuscitate. Out of the extraordinary religious ferment of the fifteenth century there had grown a perception of the disparity between apostolic poverty and ecclesiastical wealth, between the peace preached by Christ and the holy war urged by his vicar. (Throop 1940, 288; cf. Siberry 1985; Kedar 1984)

The pacifist Cistercian Abbott Isaac of Letoile, in his condemnation of warfare and crusading, thundered against the formation of the military "Orders" of monks, calling them a *monstrum novum*, a "new monstrosity." Walter Mapp, an Englishman, became a convert to the Christian pacifist cause and also an outspoken critic of the Crusades on the basis that Christ told his disciples to put away their swords. Finally, Peter of Chelcice, who stood on the left wing of the Czech reform movement, provided one of the clearest expressions of pre-Reformation Christian nonviolence when he wrote: "If St. Peter himself should suddenly appear from Heaven in order to begin to advocate the sword and to gather together an army in order to defend the truth and to establish God's order by worldly might, even then I would not believe him" (Brock 1972, 37–38).

It is significant that Christian nonviolence, particularly during the Crusades, continued to be advocated in the face of the zealous calls for war that used the language of Christianity. In other words, Christian nonviolence continued to be viewed as a form of political atheism. This is also clearly illustrated in examples taken from the histories of the three main "Peace Churches"—those Christian movements for whom nonviolence is a matter of explicit doctrine of faith—the Mennonites, the Church of the Brethren, and the Quakers.

## POLITICAL ATHEISM AND THE PEACE CHURCH TRADITION OF CHRISTIAN NONVIOLENCE: MENNONITES, BRETHREN, AND QUAKERS

Among the three Peace Churches are the theological descendants of the Anabaptist movement (Mennonites, Amish, and Hutterites). The Anabaptists were part of the "Radical Reformation." They were so named because they were to the left of the more famous reformers, Luther, Calvin, and Zwingli. The word "Anabaptist" (literally "re-baptizer") derives from early and insistent advocacy of the rite of adult, or "believer's baptism" (that is, baptism as a willed act to accompany a free choice to become a Christian). Rejection of violence was among the earliest doctrinal characteristics of this movement. While infant baptism was considered a symbol of citizenship in a nation-state, re-baptism was interpreted as an act of political atheism. Thus, in re-baptism, there is the powerful symbolism of rejecting the kingdom of this world for an alternative kingdom of Christ. This made the re-baptizers essentially exiles. The Anabaptists themselves consistently spoke in charged political terms about higher loyalties.

With respect to these higher loyalties, in 1527 the attempt was made to lend some kind of formal cohesion to the rapidly growing peasants' religious movement. The result was the Schleitheim Confession. The confession clearly stated a position with respect to war and Christian nonviolence: "Thereby shall fall away from us the diabolical weapons of violence, such as sword, armor and the like, and all of their use to protect friends or against enemies, by virtue of the word of Christ 'you shall not resist evil'" (Yoder 1977, Article IV).

The Church of the Brethren (often known by their nickname, the "Dunkers" or "Dunker Brethren," a reference to their practice of a believer's baptism by immersion three times in a trinitarian formula), cannot really be considered separately from Anabaptism. The Brethren movement began around 1708 with a group in Schwarzenau that was thoroughly acquainted with Anabaptist ideas. The group was also influenced by the renewal movements surrounding German Pietism (increased Bible study, better preaching, emphasis on personal faith, etc.).

Notable among the records of early persecution of the Church of the Brethren are the recorded conversations of John Naas of Nordheim. After Nass refused induction, the King of Prussia asked him:

> "Why will you not enlist with me?" "Because," replied Naas, "I have already, long ago, enlisted into one of the noblest and best of enrollments, and I would not, and indeed could not, become a traitor to Him. My captain is the great Prince Immanuel, our Lord Jesus Christ. I have espoused his cause and therefore cannot, and will not, forsake him." (Bowman 1941, 54)

Note, once again, the issue of split political as well as theological loyalties in conversation with the state.

Finally, Quakerism grew out of the turbulent, violent events precipitated by the Puritan uprising in England, which culminated in the English Civil War from 1642 to 1645. The Puritan uprising was a reformist movement in the tradition of John Calvin, driven by evangelical zeal and fueled by political anger. A spectrum of ideologies contributed to the Puritan movement that filled the ranks of Cromwell's "New Model Army." Radical Puritans read Daniel and Revelation. They were confident that the Jerusalem described within these texts was not, in fact, the Jerusalem located in the Middle East but was a metaphor for England herself.

The founder of the Quaker sect, George Fox, was the son of a Puritan and the focal point for the convergence of a number of early Quaker leaders. Fox was certainly orthodox in his Christian faith. He laid heavy stress, however, on the implication and modern meaning of the spiritual presence of Jesus Christ—the "inward light" whom Fox referred to as "our present teacher." Certainly, there was a fluidity to early Quaker belief on violence. Not all the earliest Quakers were pacifists; George Fox himself was offered an officer's rank in Cromwell's army. Fox's response to this offer has become a classic statement in Quaker tradition:

> I told them I lived in the virtue of that life and power that took away the occasion of all wars: and I knew from whence all wars did rise, from the lust, according to James. And still they courted me to accept their offer . . . but I told them I was come into the covenant of peace, which was before all wars and strifes was; and they said they offered it in love and kindness to me, because of my virtue, and suchlike, and I told them that if that were their love and kindness, I trampled it under my feet. (Brock 1972, 259)

Fox's statement is a classic case of political atheism. Fox rejected the mainstrain definitions of Christian faithfulness, loyalty, and action with respect to warfare and opts for an alternative belief and practice. His revolutionary zeal went away from a war with "carnal weapons" and in the direction of a "Lamb's War," a profound early Quaker image derived from Revelation. The concept of the Lamb's War may best be described as a nonviolent, spiritual "jihad." One early Quaker's witness, when he refused to accept the so-called faith of statecraft and warfare, is instructive:

> Before the first summons came I received a summons from the Prince of Peace to march under His banner, which is love, who came not to destroy men's lives but to save them. And being enlistees under this banner I dare not desert my

colors to march under the banner of the kings of this earth.
(Brock 1972, 291)

It is appropriate to ask here, Does the Quaker belief system
call into question not only direct participation in warfare but also
reaping the benefits of warfare? John Woolman, whose *Journals*
remain a classic of early American literature, dealt with this question by refusing to wear dyed clothing because most commercial
cloth was dyed by slaves. In 1774, Woolman asked Quakers to
consider whether the "seeds of war" could be found in the very
clothes that they wore (Woolman 1971, 255). More recently,
Leonard Friedrich, a German Quaker, was arrested by the Nazis
and sent to Buchenwald in 1942 for his *"pacifistische juden-
freundliche"* opinions (the official Nazi SS papers are still in the
possession of Friedrich's descendants).

## CONCLUDING OBSERVATIONS

The challenge of Christian nonviolence, as we have seen, is not
new. Throughout the history of Christianity, we find a persistent
criticism of violence and numerous examples of people who actually lived according to their nonviolent beliefs.

Reinhold Niebuhr, the great Christian ethicist of the twentieth
century, believed that it was good to have a few pacifists around,
the way it is good to have a few saints around. But Niebuhr seriously miscalculated. Pacifists are not otherworldly saints nor are
they agreeably quiet museum exhibits of ethical curiosities. Rather,
they are heretics. They are atheists who stand against the religion
of military gods. As we have demonstrated, it is their willingness
to live and die for their beliefs that makes their persistent faith in
nonviolence so dangerous to those in power.

It is, after all, one thing to say we will beat our swords into
plowshares. Many Christians join hands and say these words about
peace with tearful emotion. But when someone actually takes ham-
mer to blade, whether figuratively, by refusing military induction,
or literally, as in the case of Father Daniel Berrigan and his friends
who broke into arms plants and smashed missile parts with ham-
mers (see Stringfellow and Towne 1971), the crowds turn ugly and
frantically try to crush the heresy of political atheism.

It seems hardly necessary to underscore the fact that political atheism does not mean disengagement from the world. In his famous prayer, Jesus recognized that his teaching would lead people to "not belong to the world" (John 17:14); however, he does not ask that his followers be taken out of the world (John 17:15). Jesus advocated care for the sick, the prisoner, the hungry, and the oppressed (Matt. 25:31–46). It is perfectly clear from his admonitions that Christian nonviolence must always be an engaged nonviolence. An alternative interpretation is that Christian nonviolence is a *missionary* nonviolence—which sends its adherents into a violent world to be agents of change and examples of an alternative view of reality.

Christianity, which began as a Hebraic movement, retains ethical expectations that are decidedly "this-worldly" (see Epistle of James). The building of alternative institutions—schools, hospitals, various care facilities—are obvious expressions of Christian radical faith and have always been a part of nonviolent Christian faithfulness in the world (see Gish 1974; Brown 1971; Yoder 1977, 1994; Wink 1984–1992; Borg 1998).

Yet, Christian advocates of nonviolence maintain their skepticism for all purely political solutions to social problems. Jacques Ellul, for example, wrote of the dangers of the "political illusion" (see Ellul 1967) and the Brethren scholar Vernard Eller suggested the language of a Christian "anarchism" (see Eller 1987). Advocates of engaged Christian nonviolence have always struggled with the level of militancy that their passion for justice can engender. Do we resist corruption and set up alternative societies by free choice (Amish) or remain engaged in wider society, always risking compromise? How forceful can that engagement be, yet remain faithful to both nonviolence and liberty of conscience? What happens when our political allies come to power and we find ourselves now confronting their "new" or "liberated" violence that is just as deadly?

The compelling call of Jesus to a new reality is a call which, as we have shown, is fundamentally radical. This radical faith refuses the call to worldly battles because Christians are already engaged in a different battle:

> For our struggle is not against enemies of blood and flesh,
> but against the rulers, against the authorities, against the
> cosmic powers of this present darkness, against the spiritual

forces of evil in the heavenly places. Therefore, take up the whole armor of God, so that you may be able to withstand on that evil day, and having done everything to stand firm. Stand therefore, and fasten the belt of truth around your waist, and put on the breastplate of righteousness. As shoes for your feet put on whatever will make you ready to proclaim the gospel of peace. With all of these, take the shield of faith, with which you will be able to quench the flaming arrows of the evil one. Take the helmet of salvation, and the sword of the spirit, which is the word of God. (Eph. 6: 12–17)

Political atheism can only be sustained in the presence of radical faith. For Christians to take the wine and bread of solidarity with Christ is to break ranks with the gods of nationalism—it is to renew the call to what the early Quakers christened as "the Lamb's War": "but the people who are loyal to their God shall stand firm and take action: The wise among the people shall give understanding to many" (Dan. 11:32b–33a).

## STUDY QUESTIONS

1. What historical circumstance of early Christianity does Smith-Christopher allude to with his concept of "political atheism"?

2. In what way can the nonviolence teachings of Jesus be considered a method of resisting Roman domination?

3. What is the meaning of the "Constantinian Shift"? Shift from *what*?

4. How do the issues of the Constantinian Shift parallel the concerns of other writers in this volume who raise issues about the mixing of religious values and national power?

5. How does Christian nonviolence encourage a suspicion of all human political systems?

## BIBLIOGRAPHY

Anderson, Paul. "Jesus and Peace." In *The Church's Peace Witness*, ed. Miller and Gingerich, 104–130. Grand Rapids: Eerdmans, 1994.

Biller, Peter. "Waldensian Abhorrence of Killing, pre. c. 1400." In *Studies in Church History* 20 (1983): 129–46.

Borg, Marcus. *Conflict, Holiness, and Politics in the Teachings of Jesus.* 2d ed. Harrisburg, Penn.: Trinity Press International, 1998.

POSTAGE WILL BE PAID BY ADDRESSEE

# BUSINESS REPLY MAIL

FIRST CLASS MAIL     PERMIT NO. 10241     CAMBRIDGE, MA

## Boston Research CTR 21st Century

396 HARVARD ST
CAMBRIDGE, MASSACHUSETTS 02138-9508

# $3 STUDENT REBATE

*The Boston Research Center is always interested in feedback about course use of our books. Please provide your mailing address so we can send your rebate promptly. No personal information will be shared or added to any mailing list.*

What is the title of the book that you bought? _____

In what course is it being used? _____ Semester? _____

Who is teaching the course? _____

At what college/university is the course being taught? _____

Your name: _____

Your Address: _____

_____ City: _____ State: _____ Zip: _____

*Thank you for your purchase!*

For further information, check us out at www.brc21.org

Bowman, Rufus. *The Church of the Brethren and War, 1708–1941.* New York: Garland, 1941.

Brock, Peter. *The Political and Social Doctrines of the Unity of Czech Brethren.* The Hague: Mouton, 1957.

———. *Pacifism in Europe to 1914.* Princeton: Princeton University Press, 1972.

Brown, Dale. *The Christian Revolutionary.* Grand Rapids: Eerdmans, 1971.

Brueggemann, Walter. *Theology of the Old Testament: Testimony, Dispute, Advocacy.* Minneapolis: Fortress Press, 1997.

Cahill, Lisa Sowle. *Love Your Enemies: Discipleship, Pacifism, and Just War Theory.* Minneapolis: Fortress Press, 1994.

Cameron, Euan. *The Reformation of the Heretics: The Waldenses of the Alps 1480–1580.* Oxford: Oxford University Press, 1984.

Collins, John J. *The Apocalyptic Vision of the Book of Daniel.* Missoula, Mont.: Scholars Press, 1977.

Cook, Michael. "Jesus and the Pharisees—The Problem as It Stands Today." In *Journal of Ecumenical Studies* 15 (1978): 441–60.

Cogan, Morton. *Imperialism and Religion.* Missoula: Scholar's Press, 1974.

Eller, Vernard. *King Jesus Manual of Arms for the Armless: War and Peace from Genesis to Revelation.* Nashville: Abingdon, 1973.

———. *Christian Anarchy.* Grand Rapids: Eerdmans, 1987.

Ellul, Jacques. *The Political Illusion.* New York: Knopf, 1967.

Engelhardt, Tom. *The End of Victory Culture.* Amherst: University of Massachusetts Press, 1995.

Finkel, Asher. *The Pharisees and the Teacher of Nazareth.* Leiden: E. J. Brill, 1964.

Finkelstein, Louis. *The Pharisees: The Sociological Background of Their Faith.* Philadelphia: The Jewish Publication Society of America, 1940.

Genot-Bismuth, Jacqueline. "Pacifisme Phariseien et Sublimation de l'Idée de Guerre aux Origines du Rabbinisme." In *ETR* 1 (1981): 783–89.

Georgi, Dieter. "God Turned Upside Down." In *Paul and Empire: Religion and Power in Roman Imperial Society,* ed. Richard Horsley, 148–157. Harrisburg, Penn.: Trinity Press International, 1997.

Gish, Art. *The New Left and Christian Radicalism.* Grand Rapids: Eerdmans, 1974.

Haines, Keith. "Attitudes and Impediments to Pacifism in Medieval Europe." In *Journal of Medieval History* 7 (1981): 369–89.

Harrelson, W. "Patient Love in the Testament of Joseph." In *Perspectives in Religious Studies* 4 (1977): 4–13.

Hiller, Kurt. "Linkspazifismus." In *Ratioaktiv, Reden 1914–1964,* 27–49. Limes Verlag, 1966.

Hornus, Jean Michael. *It Is Not Lawful for Me to Fight*. Scottdale, Penn: Herald Press, 1960.

Horsley, Richard, ed. *Paul and Empire: Religion and Power in Roman Imperial Society*. Harrisburg, Penn.: Trinity Press International, 1997.

Hunter, David. "A Decade of Research on Early Christians and Military Service." In *Religious Studies Review* 18, no. 2 (1992): 87–94.

Kang, Sa-Moon. *Divine War in the Old Testament and in the Ancient Near East*. New York: W. de Gruyter, 1989.

Kedar, Benjamin. *Crusade and Mission*. Princeton: Princeton University Press, 1984.

Kimmelman, Reuven. "Non-Violence in the Talmud." In *Judaism* 17, no. 3 (1968): 316–34.

Klassen, William. *Love Your Enemies: The Way to Peace, Overtures to Biblical Theology*. Philadelphia: Fortress Press, 1984.

Licht, J. "Taxo, or the Apocalyptic Doctrine of Vengeance." In *Journal of Jewish Studies* 12 (1961): 95–103.

Lind, Millard. *Yahweh Is a Warrior*. Scottdale, Penn: Herald Press, 1980.

Markus, R.A. "Saint Augustine's Views on the 'Just War.'" In *The Church and War, Papers from the Ecclesiastical History Society*, 1–14. Oxford: Blackwell, 1983.

Marrin, Albert, ed. *War and the Christian Conscience*. Chicago: Henry Regnery, 1971.

*Mekhilta of R. Ishmael*, trans. J. Lauterbach. 3 vols. Philadelphia: Jewish Publication Society of America, 1933–35.

Mendenhall, George. "The Monarchy." *Interpretation* 29 (1975): 155–70.

Neusner, Jacob. *From Politics to Piety: The Emergence of Pharasaic Judaism*. Englewood Cliffs: Prentice-Hall, 1972.

———. *A Life of R. Yochanon Ben Zakkai*. Leiden: E. J. Brill, 1962.

———. *The Development of a Legend: Studies in the Traditions Concerning R. Yochanon Ben Zakkai*. Leiden: E. J. Brill, 1970.

Ollenburger, Ben. "From Timeless Ideas to the Essence of Religion: Method in Old Testament Theology before 1930." In *The Flowering of Old Testament Theology*, ed. Ollenburger, Martin, and Hasel, 3–19. Winona Lake: Eisenbrauns, 1992.

———. Introduction to *Holy War in Ancient Israel*, by Gerhard Von Rad., ed. Marva J. Dawn. Grand Rapids: Eerdmans, 1991.

Pawlikowski, John. *What Are They Saying about Jewish-Christian Relations?* New York: Paulist Press, 1980.

———. *Christ in the Light of Jewish Christian Dialogue*. New York: Paulist Press, 1982.

Piper, John. *Love Your Enemies*. Cambridge: Cambridge University Press, 1980.

Polner, M. and N. Goodman. *The Challenge of Shalom*. Philadelphia: New Society Publishers, 1994.

Polner, M. and J. O'Grady. *Disarmed and Dangerous: The Radical Lives and Times of Daniel and Philip Berrigan.* New York: Basic Books, 1997.

Punshon, John. *Portrait in Gray: A Short History of the Quakers.* London: Quaker Home Service, 1984.

Ramsey, Paul. *The Just War: Force and Political Responsibility.* New York: Scribner, 1968.

————. *Speak Up for Just War or Pacifism: A Critique of the United Methodist Bishops' Pastoral Letter "In Defense of Creation."* University Park: Pennsylvania State University Press, 1988.

Ramsey, Paul and R. A. McCormick, ed. *Doing Evil to Achieve Good: Moral Choice in Conflict Situations.* Chicago: Loyola University Press, 1978.

Saggs, H. W. F. "Assyrian Warfare in the Sargonid Period." *Iraq* 25 (1963): 149–62.

Schwarzschild, Steven. "Shalom." In *The Challenge of Shalom*, ed. M. Polner and N. Goodman, 16–25. Philadelphia: New Society Publishers, 1994.

Shoeps, H. J. *Theologie und Geschichte des Judenchristentums.* Tuebingen: Mohr, 1949.

Shupak, Nili. *Where Can Wisdom Be Found? The Sage's Language in the Bible and in Ancient Egyptian Literature.* Fribourg, Switzerland: University Press/Goettingen: Vandenhoeck and Ruprecht, 1993.

Siberry, Elizabeth. *Criticism of Crusading: 1095–1274.* Oxford: Oxford University Press, 1985.

Smith-Christopher, Daniel. "The Book of Daniel." In *The New Interpreter's Bible*, vol. 12. Nashville: Abingdon Press, 1996.

————. "Between Ezra and Isaiah: Exclusion, Transformation and Inclusion of the 'Foreigner' in Post-Exilic Biblical Theology." In *Ethnicity and the Bible*, ed. Mark Brett, 117–142. Leiden: E. J. Brill, 1996.

————. *The Religion of the Landless: The Social Context of the Babylonian Exile.* Bloomington, Ind.: Meyer-Stone, 1989.

Stringfellow, William and A. Towne. *Suspect Tenderness: The Ethics of the Berrigan Witness.* New York: Holt, Rinehart and Winston, 1971.

Summers, Harry G. "What Is War?" In *Harper's Magazine* (May 1984): 75–78.

Throop, Palmer. *Criticism of the Crusades.* Amsterdam: N. V. Swet and Zeitlinger, 1940.

Vermes, Geza. *Jesus the Jew.* 2d ed. London: SCM, 1983.

Vogt. *The Decline of Rome.* London: Weidenfeld and Nicolson, 1965.

Weber, Max. *Ancient Judaism.* Trans. Gerth and Mertindale. Glencoe: Free Press, 1967.

Wengst, Klaus. *Pax Romana and the Peace of Jesus Christ*. Philadelphia: Fortress Press, 1987.

Wink, Walter. *The Powers*. 3 vols. Philadelphia: Fortress Press, 1984–1992.

Womersley, David. *The Transformation of The Decline and Fall of the Roman Empire*. Cambridge: Cambridge University Press, 1988.

Woolman, John. "A Plea for the Poor." In *The Journal and Major Essays*, ed. Phillips Moulton. New York: Oxford University Press, 1971.

Yoder, John Howard. *The Politics of Jesus*. 2d ed. Grand Rapids: Eerdmans, 1994.

———. *The Christian Witness to the State*. Newton: Faith and Life Press, 1977.

———. *When War Is Unjust*. Minneapolis: Augsburg, 1984.

———, trans. *The Schleitheim Confession*. Scottdale: Penn. Herald Press, 1977.

———. "The Constantinian Sources of Western Social Ethics." In *The Priestly Kingdom: Social Ethics as Gospel*, 125–147. Notre Dame: University of Notre Dame Press, 1984.

Zerubavel, Yael. *Recovered Roots: Collective Memory and the Making of Israeli National Tradition*. Chicago: University of Chicago Press, 1995.

# Epilogue

# Reflections on Nonviolence and Religion

*Donald K. Swearer*

Since 9/11, the invasion of Iraq, and the war on terror, global realities have been overpowered by hatred, violence, and the fear of violence. Too often, religion has been excoriated as the major culprit in this maelstrom of anger, hatred, and violence—Sunni vs. Sh'ia in Iraq, Tamil Hindu vs. Sinhala Buddhist in Sri Lanka, Protestant vs. Roman Catholic in Northern Ireland, fundamentalist vs. liberal Protestant Christian in the United States and so on. As Smith-Christopher suggests in his introduction, religion becomes a convenient scapegoat for the secular critic who conveniently ignores the ideals of peace and nonviolence valorized in the world's religions, or who knowingly or unknowingly downplays the many political, economic, and sociological factors contributing to situations of hatred and violence. As the newly added essays by Don Tamihere on the Māori community in New Zealand and Amir Hussain on Muslims in post-9/11 America demonstrate, it was the politics of colonialism and of terrorism respectively that were

Donald K. Swearer joined the faculty of the Harvard Divinity School as distinguished visiting professor of Buddhist Studies and director of the Center for the Study of World Religions after retiring from Swarthmore College in 2004. His recent publications include *Becoming the Buddha: The Ritual of Image Consecrations in Thailand* (Princeton University Press, 2004), *Sacred Mountains of Northern Thailand and Their Legends* with Sommai Premchit and Phaithoon Dokbuakaew (Silkworm Books, 2005), and *Religion and Nationalism in Iraq: A Comparative Perspective*, co-edited with David Little (2006).

overriding forces, even though race and religion contributed to violence against the "other."

*Subverting Hatred* seeks to redress the imbalance of such forces by demonstrating two coexisting but seemingly paradoxical truths: 1) the world's religions have not consistently embodied the principles of peace and nonviolence; and 2) the world's religions have made significant contributions to the ideals of peace and nonviolence. As the essay on Islam frames this paradox, "The same 'beautiful example' [Muhammad] that inspired the great heroes of nonviolence in Islamic history was also appealed to for justification by the fiercest opponents of these advocates of nonviolence." Rabbi Jeremy Milgrom faces a similar paradox as he wrestles with the story of violence in the Hebrew scriptures and arrives at the conclusion that a nonviolent Torah exists. Each of the essays in this book acknowledges the problematic relationship religion has to peace and nonviolence in distinctive ways, and then vigorously pursues the positive contributions made by religion to "subvert hatred." Given the thoughtful self-observation this volume represents, it is worth asking: "In what ways have the religious traditions represented here contributed to the ideals of peace and nonviolence and, furthermore, can they continue to do so?" I shall examine this essential question in terms of four interconnected themes: worldview and practice; symbols and stories; weakness and strength; inner peace, world peace, and justice.

## WORLDVIEW AND PRACTICE

Each religious tradition embodies a worldview and a way of life that flows from that worldview. For example, Christians affirm that because "God is love," they should love their neighbors as themselves. To be sure, Christians debate both the meaning of neighbor and of love, but the principle of "love thy neighbor" grounded in a belief in a loving God is at the very core of Christian ethics and, indeed, of Christian identity. Similarly, as Christopher Queen points out, Buddhist worldview concepts of not-self, dependent origination, and emptiness undergird the Buddhist ethical value of compassion; and, for Sunanda and Yajneshwar Shastri, the Hindu view of the ultimate oneness underlying the multiplicity of the visible universe is expressed ethically in a nonviolent lifestyle of harmony and mutuality. From this perspective, violence contravenes the very nature of reality; it destroys both inner peace and the peace of the world.

To the debate regarding strategies for promoting world peace, all of the world's religions insist that actions should reflect one's view of the nature of the world. The Buddhist insistence that one's way or path in the world begins with "right view" admirably illustrates this. Even though insistence on right view has, at times, led to doctrinal chauvinism and exclusive claims to truth, the authors of this volume contend that religious worldviews have promoted and continue to promote peace and nonviolence. As the Buddhist Eightfold Path illustrates, understanding the world not in dualistic terms but as the matrix of mutual interdependence entails both not-killing and compassionate regard for the other, be it human, animal, or the earth itself. Similarly in the Māori case, the concept of the interwoven nature of all things and all aspects of human life grounds the ethical values of compassion, hospitality, kinship, reciprocity, and peace.

My father's frequent admonition to me as a child was, "Do as I say, not as I do." This contradiction is of the same kind as the challenge to the underlying assumption that believing in a loving God leads to loving behavior, or that Daoist naturalism promotes caring behavior toward the environment, or that the Buddhist image of the Jeweled Net of Indra promotes mutual understanding and harmony between majorities and minorities. While religious worldviews may indeed be compatible with the ideals of peace and nonviolence, the question remains, "How does one translate what the text *says* into what one actually *does?*" Taking the dilemma of living and upholding a religious tradition a step further, "How does worldview affect behavior?"

The essay on Confucianism and Daoism suggests an answer to this question, namely, that how we live in the world is as much or more a consequence of the communities that form our identities and our participation in communal activities, especially rituals, as it is a shared worldview. The point is a simple one and contradicts my father's comment regarding words and deeds. Much of the time we find ourselves more influenced by the examples and actions of those around us than by what they merely say or, if you will, what the text teaches. As was in fact true in my father's case, actions and words (or texts) should be mutually reinforcing. Tam Wai Lun points out that Mozi and both the Confucian *Analects* and Daoist

*Daodejing* support the ideals of peace and nonviolence, but that among the thirteen villages in Fujian Province along the Heyuan River, a major factor in maintaining peaceful relations is not the teachings of texts but the shared worship of their local *jiao* or god, Marquis Hehu. In another example we see that among the eight lineages in the Zhongfang region of Jiangxi Province, a two-week temple festival honoring their local deity provides a crucial venue for resolving conflicts that arise from competition for scarce resources.

Such perspectives help us to question whether the communities in which we live foster the values of harmony, compassion, and nonviolence, or, instead, promote the opposite—machismo competition, strident self-assertion, and violence. Recent studies of American cultural and social attitudes by Robert Putnam and others reveal a disturbing decline in community participation from Parent Teacher Associations (PTA) to Boy and Girl Scout organizations, a pervasive "bowling alone" cultural mentality. Paradoxically, these studies also point to a yearning for a sense of community belonging, family values, and a less violent society. Each of the essays in this volume insists that true nonviolence does not end with the United Nations' Universal Declaration of Human Rights or a militarily enforced peace in Bosnia and Rwanda—important as statements and programs like these are—but in the building of communities of mutual regard. And it is important to realize that these must be built not simply according to a pragmatic calculus, but with a profound sense of the necessary connection between human flourishing and the very nature of the universe we inhabit.

## SYMBOLS AND STORIES

Symbols and stories are at the very heart of religious communities. Symbols, such as the cross for Christianity, the dynamic interaction of *yin* and *yang* in the Chinese tradition, or the Hindu mantra *(Om)* convey a multiplicity of meanings that both encompass their traditions and point beyond them. Symbols, by their very nature, are dynamic and multivalent. The Christian cross symbolizes the seemingly contradictory meanings of the atoning power of self-sacrificial love, the *imperium* of the Holy Roman Empire, and the righteous militancy of the Crusades, to name a few. Likewise, the metaphors and narratives that ground a religious community's sense of identity likewise contain multiple meanings. For example, the image of the Buddha seated in meditation under the Tree of Enlightenment may be read as the culminating episode in a story of ascetic withdrawal from worldly concerns, but for contemporary Buddhist environmentalists, it represents the imperative to conserve forests in the face of the wholesale degradation of the natural environment. The essays in this volume demonstrate the continuing relevance of religious symbols, master metaphors, and stories to the ongoing work of religiously grounded peace activists.

Christopher Queen's reconfiguration of the Wheel of the Law as the Wheel of Peace employs a symbol at the core of the Buddhist tradition to serve the ideals of peace and nonviolence. In early Indian Buddhism a dual meaning was ascribed to the symbol of the wheel: the power of the Buddha's teaching *(dharma)* and the sovereign power of the king. Queen proposes that the Buddha's first teaching, "Turning the Wheel of the Law," transforms the ancient Indian symbol of military conquest associated with the high gods Vishnu and Indra into a metaphor of nonviolence, and that early Indian Buddhist texts draw a picture of the Buddha as a Prince of Peace specifically in opposition to a Lord of War. The same "radical shift in social values" described by Queen holds true for King Asoka, the greatest Buddhist monarch in the history of Indian Buddhism, whose rule by righteousness called for abstention from killing animals and cruelty to living beings and the positive extension of loving kindness to all sentient beings.

In an even more striking reconfiguration of meaning, Rabia Terri Harris renders the term "Islam" not in its more conventional sense of submission or surrender to the divine will but through its etymological link to *salam* (peace). She then proposes a new definition—Way of Peace or reconciliation. Furthermore, while Harris recognizes the imperialistic significance of *jihad*, often translated as "holy war," she points out that in the Qur'an the term means struggle or effort, especially regarding the establishment of justice, and that the work of nonviolence is the ultimate root of *jihad*. The qualities of struggle and justice central to *jihad* challenge quietistic nonviolence even as they challenge mainstream Muslim attitudes toward power from the alternative perspective of the Sufi Islamic community as represented, for example, by the late Guru Bawa Muhaiyaddeen: "It is compassion that conquers. It is unity that conquers. . . . The sword doesn't conquer; love is sharper than the sword."

The authors of this volume share with their readers stories of figures who personify the ideals of nonviolence, human dignity, peace, reconciliation, and justice. Some appeal to the founders of traditions such as Muhammed, the Buddha, Mahavira, and Confucius; others recall classical figures in their histories like White Antelope, Al-Hallaj, Chaitanya, Jinacandras, and Rabbi Yochanon Ben Zakkai. But equally, if not more, compelling are modern exemplars who represent by their very contemporaneity a relevance to our times. For example, the figure of Mahatma Gandhi looms large among contemporary exemplars of the nonviolent struggle for human dignity, civil rights, and social justice as does one of his most prominent heirs, Martin Luther King, Jr. Many readers will be introduced for the first time to perhaps lesser known but other notable figures and their work such as Gandhi's Pathan Muslim contemporary, 'Abdul-Ghaffar; B. R. Ambedkar's work among the Dalit untouchable community of India; Acarya Tulsi's nine principles of nonviolence; the Cheyenne Chief, Lawrence Hart; and, Te Whiti-o-Rongomai and Tohu Kakahi, Māori exemplars of nonviolence in the face of British colonial aggression. These exemplary lives are instructive, but more important, they demonstrate the ideals of peace, justice, and nonviolence not simply as universal principles but as realistic options for how to live in the world.

## STRENGTH IN WEAKNESS

The paradox of strength in weakness lies at the very core of the power of nonviolence. Gandhi, referred to by the news commentators of his day as a "little brown man in a loin cloth," brought the might of the British colonial empire to its knees. The Gandhian legacy of strength in weakness, furthermore, inspired movements of nonviolent social change throughout the world from Vietnam to the United States. The struggle for civil rights of the 1960s in the United States embodied not only commitment to the constitutional value of universal, guaranteed individual rights, but also the Christian ideals of self-sacrificial love and forgiveness. The Gandhian paradox of strength in nonviolence became the paradox of *agapic* love that brought down the principalities and powers of segregation.

Throughout history the strongest advocates of peace and nonviolence have often spoken from the periphery of political and economic power. For Daniel Smith-Christopher, the very marginality of the peace churches within the Christian tradition—Mennonites, Brethren, Quakers—represents their power. The "just war" position of the Christian mainstream may contribute to the policy debates, but must inevitably compromise with the power of practical politics called *realpolitik*. With "The Constantinian Shift" in the fourth century, nonviolence essentially became a Christian heresy, despite its legitimacy during the preceding three centuries when the church stood at the political margins. The Christian peace churches adhere to a higher vision of "subverting hatred" beyond the promises of military solutions, political guarantees, and legal warrants. When George Fox, the early Quaker leader, was offered an officer's rank in Cromwell's army he responded, "I told them I lived in the virtue of that life and power that took away the occasion of all wars." The uncompromising stance of the peace churches on nonviolence upholds a standard that exposes the limits of a more pragmatic, realistic peace witness. Paradoxically, the radical demand of the peace churches at the margins both judges the limits of the just war position and, at the same time, empowers the peace testimony of the mainstream Christian churches.

The paradox of strength in weakness is found in other religious traditions too, but perhaps nowhere so dramatically as among the Jains, for whom, as detailed by Chapple, not only nonviolence but also nonpossession lies at the core of their religious identity. Jains, as Chapple demonstrates, have exerted an influence far beyond their numbers, an influence that stems, in part, from their radical adherence to the value of nonviolence. In another chapter, we learn how Daoism's classic text, the *Daodejing*, highlights the truth of strength through weakness and action through nonaction. It celebrates the emptiness of valleys rather than the majestic power of mountains and the natural flow of the universe rather than assertive dominance over it. When asked to become part of the political mainstream, the Daoist philosopher Zhuangzi replied that he would prefer being a turtle dragging its tail in the mud. In conventional terms, weakness and marginality imply insignificance or ineffectiveness and yet both Jains and Daoists have made major contributions to the discourse of peace and nonviolence in India and China.

Among engaged Buddhist leaders, the Dalai Lama, Thich Nhat Hanh, Daisaku Ikeda, Maha Ghosananda, and Sulak Sivaraksa stand out as spokespersons for the nonviolent resolution of conflict, world peace, human rights, and social justice. Despite his international visibility, the Dalai Lama lives in exile from his homeland. His power resides in his moral witness rather than temporal strength—a position he utilizes to speak tirelessly on themes of compassion and love of enemies and for peace and justice. In his 1989 Nobel Peace Prize acceptance speech, he outlined a Five Point Peace Plan as a framework for a negotiated settlement with the People's Republic of China that calls for the transformation of Tibet into a Zone of Nonviolence (ahimsa), for China to end its policy of ethnic cleansing, for respect for the fundamental human rights and democratic freedoms of Tibetans, and for the restoration and protection of Tibet's natural environment. The Dalai Lama's vision for peace and justice for Tibet has yet to be realized but His Holiness continues his nonviolent struggle in the hope that eventually his moral vision will bear political fruit.

## INNER PEACE, WORLD PEACE, AND JUSTICE

Peace and nonviolence connote an ethos ordinarily associated with society or the state; however, as suggested by the full title of this volume, *Subverting Hatred: The Challenge of Nonviolence in Religious Traditions*, religions have taken an especially strong interest in promoting individual lives of non-hatred, nonviolence, love, and compassion. Whether at the level of the individual or society, the religious witness to the values of peace and nonviolence recognizes both a problematic to be overcome or negated, and a goal or way of living in the world to be achieved. For example, the *hadith* acknowledges the most difficult struggle *(jihad)* for the Muslim to be the inward effort of confronting our base nature and sees the equally important but lesser struggle as the outward effort of confronting social injustice. The social consequences of following the Buddhist Eightfold Path—right views, aspirations, actions, speech, livelihood, effort, mindfulness, and concentration—depend on the individual's success in negating hatred, greed, and ignorance. *Santi*, the Hindu term for peace, has a dual meaning: spiritual peace and peace in society and nature. Although spiritual peace is considered to be the highest achievement, it entails overcoming a sense of separateness and identifying with all beings in the universe. In this way *Santi* requires both inner peace and world peace. In various ways, all religious traditions link the transformation of social and political violence to the transformation of inner violence. Put in a more general term, religious traditions consistently affirm the teaching, "A good tree bears good fruit."

Engaged Buddhism as represented, in particular, by the Vietnamese monk Thich Nhat Hanh challenges the conventional separation between the individual and the world. It condemns the violent Other that excludes our own connectedness to the world "out there." In his powerful poem, "Please Call Me By My True Names," written after he had heard the news of the rape and murder of a 12-year-old Vietnamese girl by Thai pirates who raided a refugee boat in the Gulf of Siam, Nhat Hanh writes:

I am the 12-year old girl, refugee on a small boat,
who throws herself into the ocean after being raped by a
        sea pirate,
and I am the pirate, my heart not yet capable of seeing and
        loving.

Please call me by my true names,
so I can hear all my cries and my laughs at once,
so I can see that my joy and pain are one.

Please call me by my true names, so I can wake up,
and so that the door of my heart can be left open,
the door of compassion.

Jainism offers a striking example of the connection between nonviolence as an individual achievement involving a highly disciplined, simple, even ascetic lifestyle and nonviolence in society based on the premise that harm to others injures oneself. All observant Jains affirm the principle of nonviolence *(ahimsa)* although with different lifestyle consequences for monks and laity. Lay persons avoid occupations that harm animals and humans, are vegetarians, and avoid wearing material such as silk because it involves the slaughter of silk worms. Jain monks and nuns follow a more rigorous regime, drinking only boiled water, not walking or sitting where there might be living things, and wearing a mouth mask to prevent breathing in small organisms. While Jain monks tend to lead a cloistered life, some like Acarya Tulsi are social activists working for the cause of peace and nonviolence. Tulsi worked tirelessly in India for the uplift of widows and children and the

206    *Donald K. Swearer*

alleviation of tensions between Hindus and Sikhs in the Punjab. Furthermore, his "list of vows" acclaimed by Gandhi to promote peace and nonviolence has a general relevance beyond India.

World peace also requires justice, a theme deeply rooted in "the religions of the Book" (Judaism, Christianity, Islam), although not absent from the other religious traditions represented in this volume. Acarya Tulsi's principles of nonviolence are one example. They include a strong appeal to the theme of justice: "No kind of unjust and oppressive steps should be taken by any person, nation or state against the weak, the depressed, or the colored, or other particular castes or communities. Principles of justice, impartiality and humanity should be more and more developed and practiced by every person, nation, and state."

Since the time of the early church fathers, the mainstream Christian position on war and nonviolence has been the just war option, not the antithetical position taken by the peace churches (Mennonites, Brethren, Quakers). Just-war theory justifies violence to achieve peace under certain conditions (for example, waged only by a legitimate authority for a just cause, as a course of last resort, protection of non-combatants, using no weapons of mass destruction, with the goal of peace rather than self-aggrandizement). Smith-Christopher challenges the just-war option on the grounds that the complexity of modern warfare undermines the possibility of determining whether or not a war is just.

Most Muslim scholars from the post-Prophetic period to the early modern period, considering conflict inevitable, fashioned a just-war view based on the historical precedent of Muhammed's life and the Qur'an. Legalistic arguments centering on technicalities did not question the basic concept of the just war. Not unlike the position Smith-Christopher holds regarding Christianity, Rabia Terri Harris sees medieval Muslim theories of war not as an attempt to struggle with the question of justice and nonviolence but as rationalizations of imperial "facts on the ground." She finds both an aggressively militant attitude toward *jihad* and a liberal assertion of peace, tolerance and defensiveness to be inadequate. Harris proposes a more spiritual alternative that places greater emphasis on *jihad* as inner struggle: "Be in the state of God's peacefulness and try to give peace to the world. . . . When you exist in the state of God's actions and conduct and then speak with Him, that power will speak with you" (Guru Bawa Muhaiyaddeen).

The conflict between the state of Israel and the Palestinians offers a particularly difficult challenge to contemporary Jewish advocates of the pursuit of peace by nonviolent means. Jeremy Milgrom does not shy away from this challenge. Taking the prophet Isaiah as his text, he argues that peace and justice are integrally connected, but that peace depends on justice and not the other way around: "Peace without justice is surrender." Transforming Isaiah's eschatological context to contemporary Israel with the help of Mishnah Avot, or record of the oral law, Milgrom proposes that a just solution to this conflict might be adjudicated by applying the principle of *takanat hashavim* (ordinance of compassionate justice in the restoration of misappropriated property) as a basis to restore property built by Palestinians involuntarily surrendered before 1948 and as a formula for allowing Jews to retain abandoned Arab property. Milgrom acknowledges that such a legal solution has less chance of success when the participants lack a shared religious belief in God's ultimate authority, but hopes that an "inspired United Nations dedicated to human and environmental survival" might serve as a functional equivalent. Even if such a legal agreement were to be worked out, however, one wonders whether such a justice could be the basis of true *shalom* (peace)— an ethical totality that subsumes all human virtues and values, truth, justice, righteousness, and grace—especially in the light of escalating political conflict in the Middle East.

The primacy given to justice by Jeremy Milgrom in the Israel/Palestine context is tragically reinforced by Don Tamihere's account of the systematic destruction of the Māori settlement of Parihaka in New Zealand by the British in the 1880s. In this case the commitment to passive resistance and nonviolence by the settlement's two inspiring leaders, Te Whiti-o-Rongomai and Tohu Kakahi, grounded in the Māori worldview of interconnectedness, proved ineffectual against British injustice and could not withstand the brutal confiscation of Māori land and property. Amir Hussain's moving narrative by a Muslim academic in post-9/11 America is another example of injustice; and like other essays in *Subverting Hatred*, Hussain posits the need to ground justice in the knowledge of our shared humanity. In particular, he encourages an awareness that our distinctive histories are interconnected, a view to which his mentor Wilfred Cantwell Smith bore witness: "Those who believe in the unity of humankind, and those who believe in the unity of God, should be prepared therefore to discover a unity of humankind's religious history."

*Subverting Hatred* demonstrates that religious traditions should not be seen, as Daniel Smith-Christopher observed in his Introduction to the first edition, as merely annoying distractions in contemporary peace and conflict studies. Nor should we understand religious witness to peace and nonviolence, as the book's editor contends in this edition, as human experiences that have been changed by 9/11. Religious traditions—their worldviews, symbols, stories, and rituals—and their culturally embedded histories and contemporary narratives provide a critical resource for peace and conflict studies and for the practical working out of peacemaking issues.

The essays in this volume begin to explore the variety of ways in which religions have both legitimized violence and sanctified nonviolence, justified war and, at the same time, valorized peace. These essays also demonstrate that while conflict and reconciliation are issues of war and peace belonging to nation-states and treaties and laws, they are ultimately human matters. As Daisaku Ikeda affirms, the final solution to war, violence, and conflict requires a transformation of the vision of what it means to be truly human. In the best sense, religious traditions offer such a worldview and practice.

## Other Titles in the Faith Meets Faith Series

*John Paul II and Interreligious Dialogue*, Byron L. Sherwin and Harold Kasimow, Editors

*Transforming Christianity and the World*, John B. Cobb, Jr.

*The Divine Deli*, John H. Berthrong

*Experiencing Scripture in World Religions*, Harold Coward, Editor

*The Meeting of Religions and the Trinity*, Gavin D'Costa

*Subverting Hatred: The Challenge of Nonviolence in Religious Traditions*, Daniel L. Smith-Christopher, Editor

*Subverting Greed: Religious Perspectives on the Global Economy*, Paul F. Knitter and Chandra Muzaffar, Editors

*Christianity and Buddhism: A Multi-Cultural History of Their Dialogue*, Whalen Lai and Michael von Brück

*Islam, Christianity, and the West: A Troubled History*, Rollin Armour, Sr.

*Many Mansions? Multiple Religious Belonging*, Catherine Cornille, Editor

*No God But God: A Path to Muslim-Christian Dialogue on the Nature of God*, A. Christian van Gorder

*Understanding Other Religious Worlds: A Guide for Interreligious Education*, Judith Berling

*Buddhists and Christians: Toward Solidarity through Comparative Theology*, James L. Fredericks

*Christophany: The Fullness of Man*, Raimon Panikkar

*Experiencing Buddhism: Ways of Wisdom and Compassion*, Ruben L. F. Habito

*Gandhi's Hope: Learning from Others as a Way to Peace*, Jay B. McDaniel

*Still Believing: Muslim, Christian, and Jewish Women Affirm Their Faith*, Victoria Erickson and Susan A Farrell, Editors

*The Concept of God in Global Dialogue*, Werner G. Jeanrond and Aasulv Lande, Editors

*The Myth of Religious Superiority: A Multifaith Exploration*, Paul F. Knitter, Editor

*A Muslim View of Christianity: Essays on Dialogue* by Mahmond Ayoub, Irfan A. Omar, Editor

*Of Related Interest*

Paul F. Knitter & Chandra Muzaffar, editors
## *Subverting Greed*
*Religious Perspectives on the Global Economy*
ISBN 1-57075-446-2

Scholars from seven traditions (African Igbo, Hindu, Buddhist,
Confucianist, Jewish, Christian, and Muslim)
offer views on globalization.

"This is a valuable book for anyone interested in the problems of
world poverty, economics or the attempts of the world's religions
to come to grips with a rapidly growing crisis."
—*Catholic Library World*

"Every now and again a book appears which
illuminates brilliantly the most pressing concerns of the
contemporary era and has the potential to reach a large audience.
. . . The editors have succeeded in bringing together a most
insightful group of thinkers from entirely different traditions
to encourage them to think about the problem of what 'global
capitalism' is doing to all of us."
—*World Affairs*

"A must read whether one agrees or disagrees with its conclusions."
—*Multicultural Review*

Please support your local bookstore or call 1-800-258-5838.
For a free catalog, please write us at
Orbis Books, Box 308
Maryknoll, NY 10545-0308
or visit our website at www.orbisbooks.com

Thank you for reading *Subverting Hatred*. We hope you profited from it.